HARRY TURTLEDOVE

SETTLING ACCOUNTS: IN AT THE DEATH

BALLANTINE BOOKS

NEW YORK

2008 Del Rey Books Trade Paperback Edition

Copyright © 2007 by Harry Turtledove

Excerpt from *The Man with the Iron Heart*
copyright © 2008 by Harry Turtledove

All rights reserved.

Published in the United States by Del Rey Books,
an imprint of The Random House Publishing Group,
a division of Random House, Inc., New York.

DEL REY is a registered trademark and the Del Rey colophon
is a trademark of Random House, Inc.

Originally published in hardcover in the United States by Del Rey Books,
an imprint of The Random House Publishing Group,
a division of Random House, Inc., in 2007.

This book contains an excerpt from the forthcoming book *The Man with the Iron Heart* by Harry Turtledove. This excerpt has been set for this edition only and does not reflect the final content of the forthcoming edition.

LIBRARY OF CONGRESS CATALOGING-IN-PUBLICATION DATA

Turtledove, Harry.
Settling accounts. In at the death / Harry Turtledove.
p. cm.
ISBN 978-0-345-49248-7
1. United States—History—20th century—Fiction.   2. United States—History—
Civil War, 1861–1865—Fiction.   3. Confederate States of America—History—
Fiction.   I. Title.   II. Title: In at the death.
PS3570.U76S477 2007
813'.54—dc22   2007007439

Printed in the United States of America

www.delreybooks.com

9 8 7 6 5 4 3 2 1

Settling Accounts:
In at the Death

Praise for
Harry Turtledove and the Settling Accounts saga

[*In at the Death*] pulls out all the stops in a panoramic display of historical speculation. Turtledove sets the standard for alternate history and once more proves his worth. —*Library Journal*

In at the Death forms an excellent coda to this massive series of eleven novels." —SF Site.com

"First-time readers can jump in and enjoy Turtledove's richly rearranged cultural and political landscape." —*The Kansas City Star*

"Turtledove never tires of exploring the paths not taken, bringing to his storytelling a prodigious knowledge of his subject and a profound understanding of human sensibilities and motivations."
—*Library Journal*

"War takes the center stage in this jarring, action-packed alternative history thriller. . . . A variety of perspectives and gruesomely detailed battle scenes make [*The Grapple*] not only entertaining but hauntingly realistic as well." —Cinescape

"Historian Harry Turtledove, an alternate history standard bearer, has brought us through the timeline with full plausibility and story-telling skills that make for engrossing reading. . . . There are no cardboard figures here. Anyone who likes the intellectual mind play of alternate history is likely already onto the work of Harry Turtledove. Readers new to the genre will find much more of this to like. . . . Only thing better than a good writer is a good *prolific* writer, and Harry Turtledove is indeed." —Sci Fi Dimensions

"[*The Grapple*] is a fascinating and enthralling work that will grab and keep reader interest. . . . The best in the series to date."
—SFRevu

"Compelling . . . [*The Grapple*] proves that the third time is a charm." —*Publishers Weekly*

"Turtledove is a master of 'alternate history.' "
—*Wisconsin State Journal*

BOOKS BY HARRY TURTLEDOVE
Every Inch a King

The Guns of the South

THE WORLDWAR SAGA
Worldwar: In the Balance
Worldwar: Tilting the Balance
Worldwar: Upsetting the Balance
Worldwar: Striking the Balance

COLONIZATION
Colonization: Second Contact
Colonization: Down to Earth
Colonization: Aftershocks

Homeward Bound

THE VIDESSOS CYCLE
The Misplaced Legion
An Emperor for the Legion
The Legion of Videssos
Swords of the Legion

THE TALE OF KRISPOS
Krispos Rising
Krispos of Videssos
Krispos the Emperor

THE TIME OF TROUBLES SERIES
The Stolen Throne
Hammer and Anvil
The Thousand Cities
Videssos Besieged
Noninterference
Kaleidoscope
A World of Difference
Earthgrip
Departures

How Few Remain

THE GREAT WAR
The Great War: American Front
The Great War: Walk in Hell
The Great War: Breakthroughs

AMERICAN EMPIRE
American Empire: Blood and Iron
American Empire: The Center Cannot Hold
American Empire: The Victorious Opposition

SETTLING ACCOUNTS
Settling Accounts: Return Engagement
Settling Accounts: Drive to the East
Settling Accounts: The Grapple
Settling Accounts: In at the Death

Settling Accounts: In at the Death

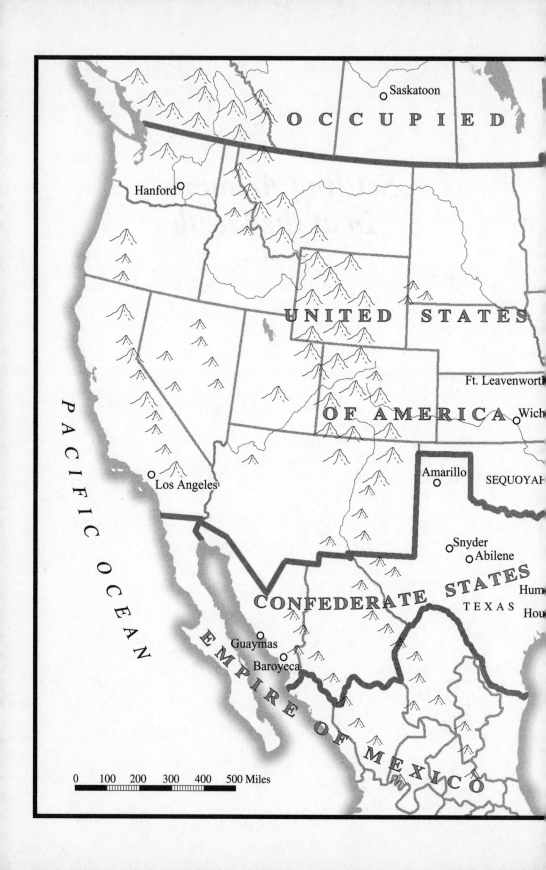

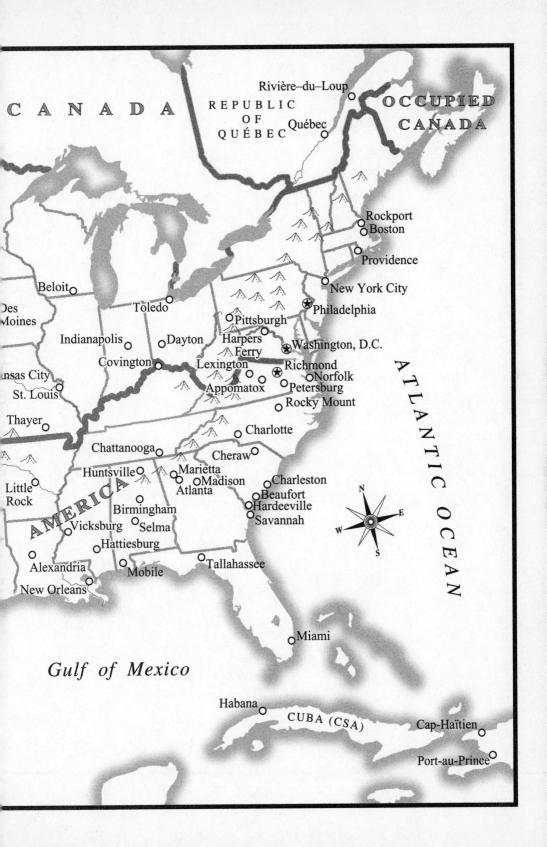

I

Brigadier General Clarence Potter crouched in a muddy trench north of Atlanta. Overhead, U.S. bombers flew through what looked like flak thick enough to walk on. Potter saw smoke coming from a couple of enemy airplanes, but the airplanes went on about the business of pounding the hub of the Confederate States of America flat.

Most of the bombs fell behind Potter, in the heart of Atlanta. As usual, the United States were going after the railroad yards and the factories that made the capital of Georgia so vital to the CSA. As far as Potter could tell, the latest bombardments were overkill. By now, Atlanta's importance was gone with the wind.

The locals, those who hadn't refugeed out or been blown sky high, seemed stunned at what had happened to their city. Disasters, to them, were for other places. New Orleans had suffered the indignity of capture in the War of Secession. Louisville had been lost in that war, wrecked in the Second Mexican War, lost again in the Great War, and spent an embarrassing generation as a U.S. city afterwards. Richmond had been battered in the Great War, and was taking it on the chin even harder now. But Atlanta? Atlanta just kept rolling along.

Except it didn't. Not any more.

Bombs were falling closer now, working their way north. Potter had seen that happen before. The lead airplanes in a formation would put their bombs about where they belonged—or where the bombardiers thought they belonged, anyhow. Bombardiers farther back would use those early explosions as targets. But, being human, the bomber crews

didn't want to hang around any longer than they had to, so they released their bombs a little sooner than they might have. Work that all
the way back through a bomber stream, and . . .

"And I'm liable to get killed by mistake," Potter muttered. He was
in his early sixties, in good hard shape for his age, with iron-gray hair
and cold gray eyes behind steel-rimmed spectacles. His specialty was
intelligence work, but he commanded a division these days—the Confederacy was running low on capable, or even incapable, line officers.
His cynical cast of mind either suited him for the spymaster's role or
came from too many years spent in it. Even he didn't know which any
more.

"General Potter!" a soldier yelled. "You anywhere around, General
Potter?" No doubt for his own ears alone, he added, "Where the fuck
you at, General Potter?"

"Here I am!" Potter shouted back. Not a bit abashed, the runner
dove into the trench with him. "Why are you looking for me?" Potter
asked crisply.

"*You're* General Potter? *Our* General Potter?" The young soldier
didn't seem convinced despite Potter's dirty butternut uniform and the
wreathed stars on either side of his collar.

"Afraid I am, son." Potter knew why the runner was dubious, too.
"Back before the Great War, I went to college up at Yale. I learned to
talk like a damnyankee to fit in, and it stuck. Now quit dicking around.
What's up?"

"Sir, General Patton's on the telephone, and he needs to talk to you
bad," the kid replied.

"Oh, joy." Potter had no trouble containing his enthusiasm. No
matter what George Patton imagined he needed, Potter knew *he* didn't
need to talk to Patton. But Patton commanded an army, not just a division. He headed all the forces trying to keep the USA away from Atlanta. Potter knew damn well he had to render unto Caesar—not that
Patton thought Julius Caesar, or anyone else, his equal. "All right. Field
telephone still at the same old stand?"

"Uh, yes, sir."

"Then you stay here. No point getting both of us blasted just because General Patton's got the galloping fantods."

"Thank you, sir." The runner gaped at him.

Potter hardly noticed. He scrambled out of the trench, getting more
tomato-soup mud on his uniform. Fall 1943 had been wet. *A good*

thing, too, he thought. *Without the rain and the mud, the damnyankees'd probably be at the Atlantic, not Atlanta.* He knew he exaggerated. He also knew he didn't exaggerate by as much as he wished he did.

He scuttled over the cratered landscape like a pair of ragged claws. *Who was the crazy Englishman who wrote that poem?* He couldn't come up with the name. Bombs whistled down from above. None did more than rattle his nerves.

The field telephone was only a couple of hundred yards from where he'd sheltered when bombs started falling. The soldier with the ungainly apparatus and batteries on his back huddled in a foxhole. Barring a direct hit, that was fine. Potter wished he hadn't thought of the qualifier. The operator held out the handpiece to him.

"Thanks," Potter said, and then yelled, "Potter here!" Field-telephone connections were generally bad, and bombs going off in the background definitely didn't help.

"Hello, Potter. This is Patton!" The army commander also shouted. No one was likely to mistake his rasping voice for anybody else's, even over a field telephone. Potter supposed the same was true of his own. That turned out not to be quite true, for Patton went on, "If the damnyankees capture a telephone, they can put on one of their men claiming to be you and talk me out of everything I know."

"Heh," Potter said dutifully. He was sick of being suspected and twitted because of the way he talked. "What do you need, sir? The runner said it was urgent."

"He's right," Patton answered. "I'm going to send the corps that your division is half of against the U.S. forces between Marietta and Lawrenceville. You'll go in by way of Chamblee and Doraville, and cut off the Yankees east of there. Once we drive them out of Lawrenceville or destroy them in place there, we reopen communications from Atlanta to the northeast."

"Sir, do you really think a one-corps attack will shift the U.S. forces in that area?" Potter tried to ignore the sinking feeling in the pit of his stomach. Patton's answer to every military problem was to attack. He'd won great triumphs in Ohio and Pennsylvania in 1941 and 1942, but not the one in Pittsburgh that might have knocked the USA out of the war. And his counterattacks against U.S. forces in Kentucky and Tennessee and Georgia this year had cost the Confederate States far more men and matériel than they were worth.

"We need to reopen that route now, General," Patton replied. "Even if that weren't obvious to anyone with a map, I have orders from the President."

What Jake Featherston wanted, Jake Featherston got. The only thing the President of the CSA wanted that he hadn't got was the one he'd needed most: a short, victorious war. Even getting a war the country could survive didn't look easy any more.

Speaking carefully, Potter said, "Sir, the Yankees already have more force in place than we can throw at them. If you try to knock a brick wall down with your head, you hurt your head worse than the wall."

"It's not so bad as that, Potter," General Patton insisted. "They offer us their flank. We can go through them like a ripsaw through balsa wood."

Potter admired him for not saying *like a hot knife through butter*. Patton had his own way of speaking, as he had his own way of doing things. For better and for worse, he was his own man. Right now, in Potter's view, it was for worse.

"If that's their flank, it's not soft, sir," Potter said. "And they have lots of artillery covering the approach. As soon as we start moving, we'll get plastered." Two bombs burst close enough to rattle him. "Hell, we're getting plastered now."

"We've had this argument before, farther north," Patton said heavily.

"Yes, sir. I have to say the results up there justified me, too," Potter said.

"I don't agree. And I don't have time for your nonsense, either, not now. As I say, my orders come from the President, and leave me no room for discretion," Patton said. "You will attack, or I will relieve you and put in someone else who will."

Do I have the courage of my convictions? Potter wondered. To his relief, he discovered he did. "You'd better relieve me, then, sir," he said. "I'm sorry for the men you'll throw away, but I won't be a party to it."

"You son of a bitch," Patton said. "You yellow son of a bitch."

"Fuck you . . . sir," Potter said. "Sorry, but you won't get to pin the blame for your mistakes—and the President's mistakes—on me."

"Brigadier General Russell will go forward to take your division," Patton said. "Don't wait for him. You *are* relieved, effective immediately. Come back here to central headquarters at once—at once, do you hear me? We'll see which shelf the War Department decides to put you on after that."

"On my way, sir," Potter answered, and hung up before Patton could say anything else. He shouted for a driver.

His yells attracted a captain on his staff before they got him a motorcar. "What's the commotion about, sir?" the officer asked.

"I've been relieved," Potter said bluntly. The captain's jaw dropped. Potter went on, "Brigadier General Russell will take over for me. He's going to send you northeast to try to cut off the damnyankees in Lawrenceville. I don't think you can do that, but give it your best shot. When I told General Patton I didn't think you could, he pulled the plug on me. Orders from the President are that you've got to try. I wish you luck." He meant that. This wasn't the first time he'd got caught between loving his country and looking down his nose at the man who ran it.

He had time for a handshake before a command car showed up. The driver didn't seem happy at being out and about with bombs falling. Potter wasn't happy, either. What could you do?

They made it. They took longer than they would have without all the air raids—but, again, what could you do? Atlanta had taken a nasty beating. One little diner had a jaunty message painted on the plywood that did duty for a front window: OPEN FOR BUSINESS WHILE EVERYTHING AROUND US GOES TO HELL.

"What did you do—walk?" Patton growled when Potter strode into headquarters, which were in an ugly building on Block Place, just west of the cratered remains of the railroad yard.

"Might have been faster if I did," Potter answered.

Patton muttered. Potter wasn't contrite enough to suit him. Most men, seeing their military career going up in smoke, would have flabbled more. "I spoke with the President," Patton said.

"Oh, boy," Potter said.

Patton muttered some more. Potter wasn't impressed enough to suit him, either. Of course, Potter had had more to say to—and about—Jake Featherston than Patton ever did. "There's an airplane waiting for you at the airport," Patton ground out. "You're ordered back to Richmond."

"So the damnyankees can shoot me down on the way?" Potter said. "Why didn't Featherston order me executed here?"

"I wondered if he would," Patton retorted. "Maybe he wants to do it personally. Any which way, get moving. You'll find out what he has in mind when you get there—if you do. I hope you sweat all the way. Now get out."

"Always a pleasure," Potter said, and flipped Patton a salute in lieu of the bird.

Atlanta's airport was at Hapeville, nine miles south of town. The airplane was a three-engined transport: an Alligator, so called because of its corrugated aluminum skin. U.S. transports were bigger and faster, but Alligators got the job done. The Confederate States had had to rebuild their military from scratch in the 1930s. Not everything got fully modernized: too much to do too fast. Most of the time, slow, obsolescent transports didn't matter too much.

If, however, a U.S. fighter got on your tail . . .

Cussing Patton under his breath, Potter *did* sweat till the Alligator, which also carried several other officers and a nondescript civilian who might have been a spy, got well away from Atlanta. The airplane wasn't out of the woods yet; he knew that. U.S. aircraft from Kentucky and Tennessee raided western North Carolina and Virginia. But his odds had improved.

He started sweating again when they neared Richmond, which vied with Paris as the most heavily bombed city in the world. They got down just before sunset. Two hard-faced men in Freedom Party Guard camouflage uniforms waited for Potter. "Come with us," one of them growled as soon as he got off. Having no choice, he did, and wondered if he was going for his last ride.

Without much modesty, false or otherwise, Lieutenant Michael Pound reckoned himself the best platoon commander for barrels in the U.S. Army. He also would have bet he was the *oldest* platoon commander for barrels in the Army. He'd been learning armored warfare ever since most of his counterparts were born.

Right now, things were pretty simple. The Confederates were pushing north and east out of their defenses in front of Atlanta. If they broke through, they would cut off and probably cut up a lot of good men.

Michael Pound didn't think they had a chance in church of breaking through. He stood up in the cupola of his green-gray barrel to get a better look around than the periscopes could give him. His shoulders barely fit through the opening; he was built like a brick. He needed—and hated—reading glasses these days, but he still saw fine at a distance.

His barrel sat under the pines near the edge of a wood. The crew had draped branches over the glacis plate to help hide the big, bulky machine. The other four in the platoon sat not far away, in the best cover their ingenious commanders could find. Soggy fields of red mud—which looked unnatural to someone from close to the Canadian border like Pound—lay to the south. If the Confederates wanted to try coming this way, they couldn't very well fool anybody.

Which didn't mean they couldn't get fooled. From behind, Pound could see trenches and foxholes and machine-gun nests. From in front, most of those would be camouflaged. He could see the signs marking the borders of minefields, too. The enemy wouldn't spot them till too late . . . unless the sappers who'd laid the mines wanted them seen, to channel C.S. attacks.

More U.S. infantry waited among the trees with the barrels—and Pound's platoon was far from the only armor on hand. If the bastards in butternut figured this was an exposed flank, they'd get rapped on the knuckles in a hurry.

And they did. They must have. Artillery started screaming down on the fields and on the pine woods. Michael Pound ducked into the turret and clanged the hatch shut. He felt sorry for the poor bloody foot soldiers. They'd get bloodier in short order. Air bursts were very bad news for troops caught under trees. Shells fused to burst as soon as they touched branches showered sharp fragments on the ground below.

No sooner had that thought crossed his mind than fragments clattered off the barrel. They sounded like hail on a tin roof, which only proved you couldn't go by sound.

"Lord help the infantry," said Sergeant Mel Scullard, the gunner. He managed to put up with having a longtime gunner set over him—at least, he hadn't tried to brain Pound with a wrench while the platoon commander slept.

"I was thinking the same thing," Pound replied. "It does even out some, though. Nobody fires antibarrel rockets or armor-piercing rounds at them."

"Goddamn stovepipe rockets," Scullard said. "If I caught a Confederate with one of those things, I'd shove the launcher up his ass and then light off a round. And that, by God, would be that."

"My, my. How the boys in the striped pants who put together the Geneva Convention would love you," Pound said.

The gunner's opinion of the Geneva Convention and its framers was blasphemous, scatological, and almost hot enough to ignite the ammunition stowed in the turret. Laughing, Pound wagged a forefinger at him. Scullard used a different finger a different way.

Pound peered through the periscopes set into the cupola. Had he been standing up, he could have used field glasses for a better view. Another rattle of sharp steel against the barrel's armored skin reminded him there were times to be bold and times to be smart, and this sure as hell looked like a time to be smart.

And he could see enough, if not quite everything he wanted. "They're coming, all right," he said. "Infantry first—probably probing to find out where the mines are and whether we've got any weak spots. And when they find some, that's where the barrels will try and get through."

"Let the goddamn barrels come," Scullard said. "They'll regret it."

In the first year and a half of the war, U.S. forces were sorry more often than not when they came up against C.S. barrels. Confederate machines had bigger guns, stronger engines, and thicker, better-sloped armor. But the newest U.S. models finally got it right. Their 3½-inch guns outclassed anything the enemy used, and their powerplants and protection also outdid the opposition. With problems elsewhere, the Confederates were slow to upgrade their barrels.

Some of the machines advancing now weren't barrels at all, but squat, ugly assault guns. Pound, a purist, looked down his nose at them. But throw enough of them into the fight and something would probably give. Quantity had a quality of its own.

"What's the range to those bastards?" he asked.

Scullard checked the rangefinder. "More than a mile and a half, sir. Even a hit at that range isn't a sure kill—they've got thick glacis plates."

"Take a shot at the lead machine anyway," Pound said. "If you do kill it way the hell out there, the rest of them will know right away they've got a tough row to hoe."

"I'll do it, sir," the gunner answered. Then he spoke to the loader: "Armor-piercing!"

"I thought you'd never ask," Joe Mouradian said, and handed him a long, heavy cartridge with the nose painted black.

Scullard traversed the turret a little to the left. He peered through the rangefinder again, raised the gun, peered once more, muttered, and brought the cannon up a hair farther. Pound wouldn't have hesitated so much. He had uncommon confidence in himself. He wasn't always right, but he was always sure. He was sure he ought to keep quiet now. Scullard's style was different from his, but the gunner usually hit what he aimed at.

If he didn't hit here, Pound intended to say not a word. It *was* long range, even for a gun that fired on a fast, flat trajectory like the 3½-incher.

Boom! Inside the turret, the noise wasn't too bad. Right outside, it would have seemed like the end of the world. Michael Pound looked through the periscopes, hoping he could see the shot fall if it missed.

But it didn't. The lead Confederate assault gun suddenly stopped. Greasy black smoke spurted from it. A hatch in the side opened. Somebody bailed out. More smoke belched from the hatch.

"Good shot! *Good* shot!" Pound thumped Scullard on the back. "Now kill the next one. The others will think twice about coming on after that."

"I'll try, sir," the gunner said, and then, "AP again, Mouradian!"

"Right." The loader slammed another round into the breech.

Scullard traversed the turret to the right. He fired again, then swore. That was a miss. Pound swore, too; he saw no puff of dust to mark where the shot came down. The wet weather complicated lives all kinds of ways.

Scullard tried again. This time, the shot went home. The assault gun slewed sideways and stopped, a track knocked off its wheels. The enemy could probably fix it, but that would take a while. In the meantime, it was out of the fight, a sitting duck. Odds were somebody would blast it before it got fixed.

Other U.S. barrels opened up. More C.S. assault guns and barrels got hit. Others stopped to return fire. Having expended three rounds from this spot, Pound figured it was time to move. They would have a good idea where he was, the same as if he'd lit three cigarettes on a match. He ordered the barrel back and to the left to a secondary firing position he'd marked out ahead of time.

Nobody ever said the Confederates lacked guts. They pressed the attack hard. Pound could see only his little part of it, like any soldier at the front. Thanks to the mines and the machine guns and the barrels and the fighter-bombers that swooped down on the enemy, the men in butternut never made it across the open ground and into the pine woods. They tried three different times, which only meant they paid a higher price for failure than if they'd left well enough alone after the first time.

When they sullenly pulled back late that afternoon, Pound said, "We ought to go after them. We might be able to walk right into Atlanta."

"Easy to walk *into* Atlanta, sir," Scullard said. "If we do, though, how many of us'll walk out again?"

Pound grunted. Having seen what the fighting in Pittsburgh was like, he didn't want to wind up on the other end of that. But watching the enemy get away went against all his instincts.

Then rockets started screaming down on the open ground in front of the woods and on the trees as well. Blast made even the heavy barrel shudder on its tracks. The Confederates were doing everything they could to discourage pursuit. He feared the foot soldiers were catching it hard.

Even so . . . "They won't take Lawrenceville away from us like that," he said.

"No, sir," Scullard agreed. "We'll likely try a flanking move from there, I bet. If we can make them leave Atlanta without us going in and taking it away from them, that sounds goddamn good to me."

"To me, too," Pound said. "The cheaper, the better."

The order to move forward came early the next morning. The axis of the advance was southeast: not straight towards Atlanta, but deeper into central Georgia. That warmed the cockles of Michael Pound's heart. It also told him that General Morrell, whom he'd known for many years, still had what it took. Morrell was all but inviting the Confederates in Atlanta to strike at his flank again. If they did, he would give them lumps.

They didn't. Watching their first counterattack fail must have taught them something. Pound didn't—wouldn't—believe they'd lost too many men and too much equipment for another try. They'd counterattacked again and again, all the way down from the Ohio River—usually before they should have. And it had cost them a lot more than standing on the defensive and making U.S. forces come to them would have done. Maybe they were finally wising up.

But if they were, it was liable to be too late. If they didn't come out of Atlanta, men and barrels in green-gray would curl around and cut them off from the east and south as well as from the north. And what would stop Irving Morrell's armor from slashing across the rest of

Georgia to Savannah and the Atlantic and cutting the Confederacy in half?

Nothing Second Lieutenant Pound could see.

Here and there, the Confederates still fought hard. The Freedom Party Guard units, in their mottled uniforms, had the best gear the CSA could give them and a vicious determination to use it. They took few prisoners, and mostly didn't let themselves get captured. And their fanatical resistance got them . . .

Not very much. Jake Featherston didn't have enough Guard outfits to go around. He didn't come close. In between the towns they defended and the strongpoints they manned lay . . . again, not very much. Most Confederate soldiers, like most soldiers most places, weren't so enthusiastic about dying for their country. Militias of beardless boys and old men mixed bolt-action Tredegars from the last war with hunting rifles and shotguns. Some of them were brave. It hardly mattered. They didn't have what they needed to fight a real army.

Mel Scullard machine-gunned a kid who was running up to the barrel with a Featherston Fizz. The youngster fell. The burning gasoline from the bottle made his last minutes on earth even worse than they would have been otherwise.

With cold eyes, the gunner watched him die. "You want to play against the first team, sonny, you better bring your best game," he said.

"That's about the size of it," Pound agreed. "And most of *their* first team is in Atlanta, and it's doing them less and less good the longer it sits there. In the meantime, by God, we'll just clean up their scrubs."

Cassius began to think he might live through the war. Black guerrillas who took up arms against the CSA and the Freedom Party always hoped to live, of course. But hoping and believing were two different things. Sooner or later, he'd figured, Gracchus' band would run out of luck. Then he'd either die on the spot or go to a camp the way his mother and father and sister had. Quick or slow, it would be over.

Now . . . Maybe, just maybe, it wouldn't. He'd already watched U.S. fighter-bombers stoop on a truck convoy the Negroes stalled with a land mine planted in a pothole. What followed wasn't pretty, which didn't mean he didn't like it. Oh, no—it meant nothing of the sort.

And the rumble and growl of artillery in the northwest wasn't distant or on the edge of hearing any more. Now it grew into an unending roar, louder by the day and as impossible to ignore as a toothache. Whenever the guerrillas camped for the night, the same phrase was on their lips: "Damnyankees comin' soon."

They wanted the U.S. soldiers to get there soon. They would likely die if the U.S. soldiers didn't. They called them damnyankees anyhow. There as in so many other things, they imitated Confederate whites. They found yellow women prettier than brown ones and much prettier than black ones. They liked straight hair better than kinky, sharp noses better than flat. In all of that, they were typical of the Confederacy's Negroes.

The main way they weren't typical was that they were still alive.

Not far away, trucks rattled through the darkness, bringing C.S. troops forward to try to stem the U.S. tide. The guerrillas let most convoys go. They couldn't afford to get into many real fights with real soldiers. Gracchus had enough trouble scraping up new recruits as things were. Except for the scattered, harried rebel bands, not many Negroes were left in the Georgia countryside.

"Suppose the damnyankees come," Cassius said, spooning up beans from a ration a Mexican soldier would never open now. "Suppose they come, an' suppose they kill the Confederate sojers an' the ofays who put on white shirts and yell, 'Freedom!' all the goddamn time."

Gracchus was gnawing on a drumstick from a chicken liberated from a white man's coop. "Then we wins," he said, swallowing. "Then we starts puttin' our lives back the way they was 'fo' all this shit happen."

In a way, that sounded wonderful. In another way . . . "How? How we do dat, boss?" Cassius asked. "All the Yankee sojers in the world ain't gonna give me my ma an' pa an' sister back again. They ain't gonna bring back all the niggers the ofays done killed. We is like ghosts of the folks what used to be here but ain't no more."

Gracchus scowled as he threw the leg bone aside. "We ain't ghosts," he said. "The ones who got killed, they's ghosts. I bet this whole country have more hants'n you kin shake a stick at, this war finally done."

Cassius didn't exactly believe in hants. He didn't exactly not believe in them, either. He'd never seen one, but so many people were sure they had, he had trouble thinking they were all crazy or lying. He did say, "Hants ain't slowed down the ofays none."

"Might be even worse without 'em," another Negro said.

"How?" Cassius asked, and nobody seemed to want to answer that.

He didn't want to take the argument with Gracchus any further. He didn't want the guerrilla chieftain to think he was after that spot himself. As far as Cassius was concerned, Gracchus was welcome to it.

But, even if he kept quiet, he still thought he was right. Blacks in the CSA had had a vibrant life of their own, much of it lived right under the white majority's noses. With so many Negroes dead, how would the survivors ever start that again? How could they even live alongside the whites who hadn't tried to stop Freedom Party goons from stuffing them into trains for one-way journeys to camps, who'd often cheered to see them disappear? What could they be but a sad reminder of something that had once been alive but was no more? And if that wasn't a ghost, what was it?

The next morning, a scout came back in high excitement. "The Mexicans, they's pullin' out!" he said.

"They ain't goin' up to the front to fight?" Gracchus asked. "You sure?"

"Sure as I's standin' here," the scout replied. "They's marchin' south."

"They ain't here to fight the damnyankees," Cassius said. "They is here to keep us in line."

Francisco José's men were less enthusiastic about going after Negroes than white Confederates were. But their being here let the Confederacy put more men in the field against the United States. They did inhibit the rebel bands . . . some.

"If they's buggin' out fo' true, they must reckon the Confederate Army can't hold the Yankees back no mo'." Gracchus' voice rose with excitement. "Do Jesus, I hope they's right!"

The black guerrillas got another surprise the next day. A Confederate captain approached a scout with a flag of truce. The scout blindfolded him and brought him into camp. No one offered to take the blindfold off once he got there, either.

That didn't seem to faze him. "I have a proposition for you people," he said.

"Go on. Say your say. Tell your lies," Gracchus answered.

"No lies. What I ask is very simple: leave us alone while we fight the USA," the C.S. officer said. "You stay quiet, we won't come after

you. We'll even give you rations so you don't have to plunder the countryside."

"Put rat poison in 'em first, I reckon," Gracchus said.

"If you agree, I will come back as a hostage and food taster," the
captain said. "Don't jog our elbow. That's all we want. You tell us no,
you'll get the stick instead of the carrot. I promise you that."

"Shoulda started leavin' us alone a hell of a long time ago," Cassius said.

Shrugging, the soldier said, "Maybe you're right, maybe you're
wrong. Too late to worry about it now, though. It's water under the
bridge."

"Easy fo' you to say, ofay." Some of Gracchus' rage and hatred
came out. "You ain't got no dead kinfolks."

"Hell I don't," the captain said, and Cassius realized he hated them
at least as much as they hated him. "Damnyankee bombs blew up my
mother and father and sister. Another sister'll limp forever on account
of 'em. And you're helping the USA. Far as I'm concerned, we ought to
feed you rat poison, and better than you deserve. But I don't give those
orders. I just follow them."

"You got nerve." Gracchus spoke now with a certain reluctant admiration.

"I told you—I've got orders," the Confederate said. "So what'll it
be? Will you back off and let us fight the United States, or do we come
in here and clean out all of you raggedy-ass coons?"

Gracchus didn't answer right away. He wasn't an officer with a
chain of command behind him and the automatic authority to bind and
to loose. He couldn't order his fighters to obey a truce if they didn't
want to. Cassius knew *he* didn't. He spoke to the captain: "You coulda
done that, reckon you would've a long time ago."

"You don't get it, boy," the white said, and never knew how close
he came to dying on the spot. He continued, "Before, you were just a
rear-area nuisance. But if you think we'll let you fuck with us when the
front's so close, you better think again."

Maybe he had a point of sorts. But even if he did . . . "What happens when the Yankees push you outa here?" Cassius ground out. "You
reckon we ain't got us a lot o' bills to pay? You reckon we ain't gonna
pay 'em soon as we git the chance?"

That got home. The C.S. captain bit his lip. "All the more reason
for us to get rid of you now," he said.

"You kin try." Gracchus seemed to have made up his mind. "Yeah, you kin try, but I don't reckon you kin do it. When the war started, you coulda got what you wanted from us easy. All you had to do was leave us alone. Well, you didn't do nothin' like that. You know what you done. Like my friend here say"—he named no names—"we owes you too much to set it down. We takes you back to your own folks now. Ain't got nothin' left to say to each other no more."

As the scout led the blindfolded officer away, Cassius found himself nodding. Gracchus had nailed that, probably better than he knew. All across the Confederate States of America, whites and Negroes had nothing left to say to each other.

"Reckon we better get outa here," Gracchus said after the white man in butternut was gone. "They ain't gonna wait around. Soon as he tell 'em we say no, they gonna pound the shit outa where they thinks we's at."

He proved a good prophet. Artillery started falling not far from their camp inside of half an hour. A couple of Asskickers buzzed around overhead, looking for targets they could hit. The Negroes stayed in the woods till nightfall.

"You reckon they come after us from the same direction as that captain?" Cassius asked Gracchus.

"Mos' likely," the guerrilla leader answered.

"Maybe we oughta rig us an ambush, then," Cassius said. "That'll learn 'em they can't run us like we was coons an' they was hounds."

"We *is* coons," Gracchus said with a grim chuckle. He clapped Cassius on the back. "But yeah, you got somethin' there. We see what we kin do."

Next morning, right at dawn, close to a company of Confederate soldiers approached the woods where the guerrillas sheltered. Cassius and a couple of other Negroes fired at them, then showed themselves as they scurried away. That was dangerous. A fusillade of bullets chased them. But nobody got hit.

Shouting and pointing, the Confederates pounded after the fleeing blacks. Down deep, the ofays still thought Negroes were stupid and cowardly. They wouldn't have pursued U.S. soldiers with so little caution.

The machine gun opened up from the flank and cut them down like wheat before the scythe. The Confederates were brave. Some of them tried to charge the gun and take it out with grenades. They couldn't work in close enough to throw them. The white soldiers broke off and retreated. They did it as well as anyone could, leaving not a wounded man behind.

"We done it!" Cassius whooped. "We fuckin' done it!"

Gracchus was less exuberant. "We done it this time," he said. "Ofays ain't gonna make the same mistake twice. Next time, they don't reckon it's easy."

That struck Cassius as much too likely. Gracchus moved his band away from the ambush site as fast as he could. Artillery and bombs from above started falling there a few minutes later—probably as soon as the beaten Confederate soldiers could send back word of where they ran into trouble.

Armored cars and halftracks began patrolling the roads around the guerrilla band. The Negroes got one with a mine, but the vehicles trapped them and hemmed them in, making movement deadly dangerous. Before long, they started getting hungry. The rations the Confederate captain had promised in exchange for quiet seemed better to Cassius every time his belly growled.

"Reckon we kin hold 'em off when they come again?" he asked Gracchus.

"Hope so," the guerrilla leader answered, which was a long way from yes.

Cassius made sure his rifle was clean. He didn't want it jamming when he needed it most. How much good it would do him against a swarm of Confederates supported by armor . . . he tried not to think about.

Then one night the northwestern sky filled with flashes. Man-made thunder stunned his ears. The C.S. attack the guerrillas were dreading didn't come. The Confederates needed everything they had to hold back the U.S. forces hitting them.

And everything they had wasn't enough. Soldiers and vehicles in butternut poured back past and through the guerrillas' little territory. They weren't interested in fighting the blacks; they just wanted to get away. Wounded men and battered trucks and halftracks floundered here and there. The Negroes scrounged whatever they could.

And then Cassius spotted an advancing barrel painted not butternut but green-gray. It had a decal of an eagle in front of crossed swords on each side of the turret. He burst into unashamed tears of joy. The damnyankees were here at last!

After capturing Camp Determination and the vast mass graves where its victims lay, Major General Abner Dowling had trouble figuring out what the U.S. Eleventh Army should do next. He'd handed the United States a huge propaganda victory. No one could deny any more that the Confederates were killing off their Negroes as fast as they could.

Some of the locals were horrified when he rubbed their noses in what their country was up to. The mayor of Snyder, Texas, and a few of its other leading citizens killed themselves after forced tours of the graves.

But others remained chillingly indifferent or, worse, convinced the Negroes had it coming. *Only coons* and *goddamn troublemakers* were phrases Dowling never wanted to hear again.

He scratched at his graying mustache as he studied a map of west Texas tacked on the wall of what had been the mayor's office. Snyder, under military occupation, was doing without a mayor for now. "What do you think, Major?" he asked his adjutant. "Where do we go from here?"

Major Angelo Toricelli was young and handsome and slim, none of which desirable adjectives fit his superior. "Amarillo's too far north," he said judiciously. "We don't have the men to hold the front from here to there."

Dowling eyed the map. If that wasn't the understatement of the year, it came in no worse than second runner-up. "Abilene, then," he said. It was the next town of any size, and it didn't lie that far east of Snyder.

"I suppose so." If Major Toricelli was eager to go after Abilene, he hid it very well. Dowling knew why, too. Even if the Eleventh Army captured Abilene . . . Well, so what? Taking it wouldn't bring the USA much closer to victory or do anything more than annoy the Confederates.

With a sigh, Dowling said, "We've pretty much shot our bolt, haven't we?"

"Unless they're going to reinforce us, yes, sir," his adjutant answered.

"Ha! Don't hold your breath," Dowling said. Hanging on to the men Eleventh Army had was hard enough.

"Maybe you'll get a new command, sir," Major Toricelli said hopefully.

"Sure. Maybe they'll send me to Baja California." Dowling's voice overflowed with false heartiness.

His adjutant winced. The USA had tried to take Baja California away from the Empire of Mexico during the last war, tried and failed. This time around, the United States seemed to have succeeded. And, having taken Baja California away from Mexico, what did the USA have? Baja California, and that was all: miles and miles and miles of the driest, most godforsaken terrain in the world.

Holding Baja California mattered for only one reason. It let the United States sit over the Confederates in Sonora. U.S. ships could block the outlet to the Gulf of California. U.S. airplanes in Baja California could easily strike the C.S. port at Guaymas. Of course, Confederate aircraft in Sonora could hit back at the warships and the air bases. They could, and they did. The luckless brigadier general in charge of that operation was welcome to it, as far as Abner Dowling was concerned.

"With what you've done here, you ought to get a command closer to the *Schwerpunkt*," Major Toricelli said.

"How about Sequoyah?" Dowling asked innocently.

That *was* closer to the center of things than west Texas, which didn't mean Toricelli didn't wince again anyhow. Sequoyah was a bloody mess, and probably would go on being one for years. Thanks to a large influx of settlers from the USA, it had voted not to rejoin the Confederacy in Al Smith's ill-advised plebiscite. But the Indian tribes in the east, who'd prospered under Confederate rule, hated the U.S. occupation. And most of the oil there lay under Indian-held land.

The oil fields had gone back and forth several times in this war. Whoever was retreating blew up what he could to deny the oil to the enemy. When the United States held the oil fields, Confederate raiders and their Indian stooges sabotaged whatever wasn't blown up. That led to U.S. reprisals, which led to bushwhacking, which led to hell in a handbasket.

"About the only thing we could do to make Sequoyah work would be to kill all the redskins in it." Dowling sighed. "And if we do that, how are we any better than the goddamn Confederates?"

"Those Indians really are fighting us," Toricelli said.

"Sure." Dowling's chins wobbled as he nodded. "But if you listen to Confederate wireless, you hear all the stories about the terrible wicked black guerrillas. Some of that's got to be bullshit, sure. But not all of it, because we both know the War Department helps the guerrillas when it can."

Major Toricelli looked unhappy, but he nodded. One of the reasons Dowling liked him was that he would look facts in the face, even when they were unpleasant.

As if on cue, a soldier from the signals unit stuck his head into the office and said, "Sir, we just got a message that needs decoding."

"I'll take care of it," Toricelli said, and hurried away. Dowling wondered what was going on. Eleventh Army wasn't important enough to receive a lot of encrypted transmissions. The Confederates were welcome to read most of the usual messages it did get.

"Well?" Dowling asked when his adjutant came back forty-five minutes later.

"Well, sir, we're ordered to step up air attacks against Abilene." Toricelli had the look of a man who'd gone hunting in the mountains and brought home a ridiculous mouse.

"We can do that," Dowling allowed. He even understood why the order was coded—no point to letting the Confederates haul in more antiaircraft guns to shoot down U.S. bombers. But, after what he and Toricelli were talking about, the order felt anticlimactic, to say the least.

Colonel Terry DeFrancis was one of the youngest officers of his rank in the Army. He was also one of the better ones; his fighters had established U.S. dominance in the air over west Texas. "Pound the crap out of Abilene?" he said when Dowling told him about the new order. "Sure. We can do that, sir. I'll step up the recon right away, so we know what we're up against."

"Step up the recon over other targets, too," Dowling said. "No use advertising what we're up to."

"Will do, sir," DeFrancis promised. "You're sneaky, you know that?"

"Well, I try." Dowling paused to light a cigarette. No two ways about it—Raleighs and Dukes beat the hell out of anything the USA made. And Confederate cigars . . . Reluctantly, Dowling brought his mind back to the business at hand. "That's one thing I had to pick up on my own. General Custer never much went in for being sneaky."

"What was it like serving under him?" Colonel DeFrancis asked.

"It wasn't dull, I'll tell you that. He always knew what he wanted to do, and he went ahead and did it." Dowling nodded. That was true, every word of it. It was also the sanitized, denatured version of his long association with the man who was, by his own modest admission, the greatest general in the history of the world. Dowling suspected he'd kept Custer from getting sacked several times. He also suspected he'd kept himself from getting court-martialed at least as often. But Terry didn't need to hear about that.

"Was he as much of an old Tartar as everybody says?" DeFrancis had already heard something, then.

"Well . . . yes." Dowling couldn't say no without making himself into a bigger liar than he wanted to be.

"But he won the war, pretty much. He got the job done. Morrell was under his orders when he used that armored thrust to roll up the Confederates and take Nashville."

"That's true." Dowling gave a reminiscent shiver. Custer and Morrell had gone against War Department orders to mass their barrels. Dowling himself had lied like Ananias, writing reports that denied they were doing any such thing. Had Philadelphia found out he was lying, or had the attack failed . . . The aftermath wouldn't have been pretty.

And it wasn't a sure thing, not ahead of time. A lot of Custer's straight-ahead charges at the enemy failed, and failed gruesomely. Dowling knew how nervous he was before the barrels crossed the Cumberland. If Custer had any doubts, he never showed them.

"You know, Colonel, he really is the hero of the last war. In an odd way, he's the hero of the whole first part of this century," Dowling said. "He knew what he wanted to do, and he found a way to make it work."

"We just have to go and do the same thing, then," DeFrancis said. "I expect we can." He saluted and hurried off.

Abner Dowling stubbed out his cigarette. He didn't have George Armstrong Custer's relentless drive, or even Terry DeFrancis'. He was a sane man in a business where the crazy and the obsessed often prospered. He hoped his ability to see all sides of a problem gave him an edge over commanders with tunnel vision. He hoped so, but he was a long way from sure it did.

Major Toricelli stuck his head into the office. "Sir, there's a local who wants to see you. His name is Jeffries, Falstaff Jeffries. He runs the big grocery on the edge of town."

"Has he been searched?" Dowling didn't want to talk to a people bomb, or even a fellow with a pistol in his pocket. But his adjutant nodded. So did Dowling. "All right. Send him in. You know what's eating him?"

"No, sir. But I expect he'll tell you."

Falstaff Jeffries didn't live up to his name. He was short and skinny and somber, nothing like Shakespeare's magnificent clown. He did have the virtue of coming straight to the point: "Where am I going to get more food, General?"

"Where were you getting it?" Dowling asked.

"From farther east. That's where everything comes from out here," Jeffries answered. "Except now I'm on the wrong side of the line. Folks're gonna start getting hungry pretty damn quick unless somebody does something about it."

"I don't think anyone will starve," Dowling said. "Plenty of rations, if it comes to that."

The storekeeper looked at him as if he'd just ordered no presents at Christmastime. "Rations." Jeffries made it into a swear word. "How in blazes am I supposed to run a business if you go around handing out free rations?"

"A minute ago, you were talking about people going hungry," Dowling reminded him. "Now you're flabbling about where your money's coming from. That's a different story, and it's not one I care much about."

"That's on account of you don't have to worry about feeding your family." Falstaff Jeffries eyed Dowling's expanse of belly. "You don't worry about feeding at all, do you?"

"I told you—nobody'll starve," Dowling said tightly. "Not you, not your family, and not me, either."

"But my store'll go under!" Jeffries wailed.

"There's a war on, in case you didn't notice," Dowling said. "You're alive, you're in one piece, your family's all right. Count your blessings."

Jeffries muttered something under his breath. Dowling wouldn't have sworn it was "Damnyankee," but he thought so. The grocer rose. "Well, I can see I won't get any help here."

"If you think I'll open our lines so your supplies can get through, you're even crazier than I give you credit for, and that's not easy," Dowling said.

Jeffries took a deep breath, then seemed to remember where he was and to whom he was talking. He left without another word, which was no doubt wise of him. Abner Dowling hadn't acted like a military tyrant in the west Texas territory Eleventh Army had conquered, but the temptation was always there. And, if he felt like it, so was the power.

Lieutenant-Colonel Jerry Dover was not a happy man. The Confederate supply officer had had to pull back again and again, and he'd had to wreck or burn too much that he couldn't take with him. His dealings with the higher-ups from whom he got his supplies, always touchy, approached the vitriolic now.

"What do you mean, you can't get me any more antibarrel rounds?" he shouted into a field telephone. Coming out of the restaurant business in Augusta, he was much too used to dealing with suppliers who welshed at the worst possible time. "What are the guns supposed to shoot at the Yankees? Aspirins? I got plenty of those."

"I can't give you what I don't have," replied the officer at the other end of the line. "Not as much getting into Atlanta as there ought to be these days."

Dover laughed a nasty, sarcastic laugh. "Well, when the U.S. soldiers come marching in, buddy, you'll know why. Have fun in prison camp."

"This is nothing to joke about, goddammit!" the other officer said indignantly.

"Who's joking?" Dover said. "Only reason they haven't gone in yet is, they don't want to have to fight us house to house. But if you don't get out pretty damn quick, they'll surround the place—and then you won't get out."

"General Patton says that won't happen," the other officer told him, as if Patton had a crystal ball and could see the future.

"Yeah, well, when a guy wants to lay a girl, he'll say he'll only stick it in halfway. You know what that's worth," Dover said. "You want to keep the Yankees away from your door, get me those shells."

"I don't have any I can release."

"Aha!" Jerry Dover pounced. "A minute ago you didn't have any at all. Cough up some of what you're holding out on me, or you'll be sorry—will you ever."

"If I do that, they'll put my tit in a wringer," the officer in Atlanta whined.

"If you don't, you'll get your ass shot off," Dover said. "*And* I'll tell all the front-line soldiers you're holding out on me. You can find out if our guys or the Yankees get you first. Doesn't that sound like fun?"

"You wouldn't!" The other officer sounded horrified.

"Damn right I would. I was in the trenches myself the last time around. I know how much real soldiers hate it when the quartermasters don't give 'em what they need to fight the war."

"I'll report your threats to General Patton's staff!"

"Yeah? And so?" Dover said cheerfully. "If they put me in the line, maybe I'm a little worse off than I am here, but not fuckin' much. If they throw me in the stockade or send me home, I'm safer than you are. Why don't you just send me the ammo instead? Don't you reckon it's easier all the way around?"

Instead of answering, the supply officer in Atlanta hung up on him. But Dover got the antibarrel ammunition. As far as he was concerned, nothing else really mattered. If the other man had to tell his superiors some lies about where it went, well, that was his problem, not Dover's.

Even with that shipment, the Confederates east of Atlanta kept getting driven back. Too many U.S. soldiers, too many green-gray barrels, too many airplanes with the eagle and crossed swords. If something didn't change in a hurry . . . *If something doesn't change in a hurry, we've got another losing war on our hands*, Dover thought.

He'd never been one who screamed, "Freedom!" at the top of his lungs and got a bulge in his pants whenever Jake Featherston started ranting. He'd voted Whig at every election where he could without putting himself in danger. But he had some idea what losing a second war to the USA would do to his country. He didn't want to see that happen—who in his right mind did? Following Featherston was bad. Not following him right now, Jerry Dover figured, would be worse.

He stepped away from the field telephone, shaking his head, not liking the tenor of his thoughts. How could anybody in the Confederacy have thoughts he liked right now? You had to be smoking cigarettes the Quartermaster Department didn't issue to believe things were going well.

Or you had to read the official C.S. Army newspaper. A quartermaster sergeant named Pete handed Dover a copy of the latest issue. It was fresh from the press; he could still smell the ink, and it smudged his fingers as he flipped through *The Armored Bear*.

If you looked at what the reporters there said, everything was wonderful. Enemy troops were about to get blasted out of Georgia. *A shattering defeat that will pave the way for the liberation of Tennessee and Kentucky*, the paper called it. *The Armored Bear* didn't say how or when it would happen, though. Soldiers who weren't in Georgia might buy that. Jerry Dover would believe it when he saw it.

The Armored Bear spent half a column laughing at the idea that the damnyankees could threaten Birmingham. *This industrial center continues to turn out arms for victory*, some uniformed reporter wrote. A year earlier, the idea of U.S. soldiers anywhere near Birmingham really would have been laughable. C.S. troops were battering their way into Pittsburgh. They went in, yes, but they didn't come out. Now the story sounded more as if the writer were whistling his way past the graveyard. Had the Yankees wanted to turn on Birmingham, it would have fallen. Dover was sure of that. They thought Atlanta was more important, and they had the sense not to try to do two things at the same time when they could make sure of one.

Photos of night-fighter pilots with gaudy new medals on their chests adorned the front page. The story under the photos bragged of air victories over Richmond, Atlanta, Birmingham, Vicksburg, and Little Rock. That was all very well, but why were U.S. bombers over all those towns?

And another story bragged of long-range rockets hitting Washington, Philadelphia, Pittsburgh (not a word about the great battle there the year before), and Nashville (not a word that Nashville was a Confederate city, either).

There is no defense against these weapons of vengeance. Traveling thousands of miles an hour, they strike powerful blows against the Yankee aggressors, the paper said. *Soon improved models will reach New York, Boston, Indianapolis, and other U.S. centers that imagine themselves to be safe. Confederate science in the cause of freedom is irresistible.*

Jerry Dover thoughtfully read that story over again. Unlike some of the others, it told no obvious lies. He hoped it was true. If the Confederates could pound the crap out of U.S. targets without wasting precious pilots and bombers, they might make the enemy say uncle. It struck him as the best chance they had, anyway.

On an inside page was a story about a football game between guards and U.S. POWs down at Andersonville, south of Atlanta. A photo showed guards and prisoners in football togs. Dover thought the piece was a failure. So what if the guards won? If they were healthy enough to play football, why the hell weren't they healthy enough to fight?

Maybe that wasn't fair. And maybe the guards had pull that kept them away from the slings and arrows of outrageous fortune. Dover knew which way he'd bet.

The story almost pissed him off enough to make him crumple up the paper and throw it away. Almost, but not quite. One thing in chronically short supply was toilet paper. Wiping his butt with the football-playing guards struck him as the best revenge he could get.

Later, he asked if Pete had seen the story about the Andersonville football game. The noncom looked disgusted. "Oh, hell, yes," he answered. "Closest those bastards ever get to real Yankees, ain't it?"

"Looks that way to me," Dover said. "I wondered if you saw things the same."

"Usually some pretty good stuff in *The Armored Bear*," Pete said. "Shitheads who turn it out fucked up this time, though."

Maybe he imagined soldiers—sergeants like himself, say—sitting around a table deciding what to put into the Army newspaper. Dover would have bet things didn't work like that. The writers likely got their orders from somebody in the Department of Communications, maybe in a soldier's uniform but probably in a Party one. Everything in the paper was professionally smooth. Everything made the war and the news look as good as they could, or a little better than that. No amateur production could have been so effective . . . most of the time.

But when the truth stared you in the face, what a paper said stopped mattering so much. "Reckon we can stop the damnyankees?" Pete asked. "If we don't, seems like we're in a whole peck o' trouble."

"Looks that way to me, too," Dover answered. "If they take Atlanta . . . Well, that's pretty bad."

We should have stopped them in front of Chattanooga, he thought glumly. *Now that they're through the gap and into Georgia, they can go where they please.* The paratroop drop that seized Lookout Mountain and Missionary Ridge from the Confederates and made them evacuate

Chattanooga was a smart, gutsy operation. Dover admired it while wishing his side hadn't been on the receiving end.

When night fell, he slept in a tent with a foxhole right next to it. U.S. bombers came over at night even more often than in the daytime. The heavy drone of engines overhead sent him diving into the hole even before the alarm sounded. Bombs burst with heavy thuds that reminded him of earthquakes. He'd never been in any earthquakes, but he was sure they had to be like this.

Antiaircraft guns thundered and lightninged, filling the air with the sharp stink of smokeless powder. Dover listened hopefully for the concussive thud of stricken bombers smashing into the ground, but in that he was disappointed. Fewer bombs fell close by than he expected from the number of airplanes overhead, which didn't disappoint him a bit.

Then something fluttered down from the sky like an oversized snowflake and landed on top of his head. He grabbed the sheet of cheap pulp paper. The flash of the guns showed him a large U.S. flag, printed in full color, with text below that he couldn't make out in the darkness and without his reading glasses.

"More propaganda," he murmured with a sigh of relief. If the damnyankees wanted to drop their lies instead of high explosives, he didn't mind a bit. Had that been a bomb falling on his head . . .

He stuck the sheet into a trouser pocket and forgot he had it till the next morning. Only when it crinkled as he moved did he remember and take it out for a look.

Confederate soldiers, your cause is lost! it shouted, and went on from there. It urged him to save his life by coming through the lines holding up the picture of the Stars and Stripes. Maybe U.S. soldiers wouldn't shoot him if he did that, but it struck him as a damn good recipe for getting shot by his own side.

If his own side's propaganda was bad, the enemy's was worse. *Look at the disaster Jake Featherston has led you into. Don't you want true freedom for your country?* it said. All Jerry Dover wanted— all most Confederates wanted—was to see the Yankees go away and leave his country alone. They didn't seem to understand that. If the sheets falling from the sky meant anything, they thought they were liberators.

"My ass," Jerry Dover said, as if he had a U.S. propaganda writer in the tent with him. The United States had invaded the Confederate States four times in the past eighty years. If they thought they'd be welcomed with anything but bayonets, they were even bigger fools than Dover gave them credit for—not easy but not, he supposed, impossible.

And if the Confederates wanted to change their government, they could take care of it on their own. All the bodyguards in the world wouldn't keep Jake Featherston alive for long if enough people decided he needed killing. No Yankees had to help.

Dover started to chuck the propaganda sheet, then changed his mind. "My ass," he said one more time, now happily, and put it back in his pocket. As with the story in *The Armored Bear*, he could treat it as it deserved.

November in the North Atlantic wasn't so bad as January or February, but it was bad enough. The *Josephus Daniels* rode out one big swell after another. On the destroyer escort's bridge, Sam Carsten felt as if he were on God's seesaw. Up and down, up and down, up and down forever.

"You still have that hydrophone contact?" he shouted down the speaking tube to Vince Bevacqua.

"Yes, sir, sure do," the chief petty officer answered. "Coming in as clear as you can expect with waves like this."

"All right, then. Let's give the submersible two ashcans," Sam said. "That'll bring it to the surface where we can deal with it."

He shouted the order over the PA system. The launcher crew at the *Josephus Daniels*' bow sent the depth charges flying into the ocean one at a time, well ahead of the ship. They were set to detonate not far below the surface. Sam felt the explosions through the soles of his feet.

Something rude came out of the speaking tube. "Had my earphones on when the first one burst," Bevacqua said. "That'll clean your sinuses from the inside out." He paused, then went on, "The sub's making noises like it's blowing water out of its dive chambers. Ought to be coming to the surface."

"We'll be ready for anything," Carsten promised.

And the destroyer escort was. Both four-inchers bore on the submarine when it surfaced. So did several of the the ship's twin 40mm antiaircraft guns and her .50-caliber machine guns. A swell washed over the sub's bow—and almost washed over the conning tower, too. This weather was tough to take in the *Josephus Daniels*. It had to be ten times worse in a submersible.

Sailors ran up a flag on the sub: the white, black, and red jack of the Imperial German Navy. Sam breathed a sigh of relief. "This is the one we're supposed to meet, all right," he said.

"So it would seem, sir," Lieutenant Myron Zwilling agreed. Sam wished he had more use for the exec. Zwilling was brave enough and more than willing enough, but he had all the warmth and character of an old, sour-smelling rag. Men obeyed him because he wore two stripes on his sleeve, not because he made them want to.

The submersible's signal lamp started flashing Morse. "We—have—your—package," Sam read slowly. "He knows English, then. Good."

He handled the destroyer escort's blinker himself. WILL APPROACH FOR PICKUP, he sent back.

COME AHEAD. BE CAREFUL IN THESE SEAS, the sub signaled.

Sam wished Pat Kelly were still aboard. But his old exec had a ship of his own, a newer, faster ship than the *Josephus Daniels*. He was probably showing his whole crew what a demon shiphandler he was. Sam wasn't, and never would be. Neither was Zwilling. Since he wasn't, Sam kept the conn himself.

As he steered closer to the submersible, he ordered Bevacqua to keep paying close attention to any echoes that came back from his hydrophone pings. The CPO laughed mirthlessly. "Oh, I'm on it, Skipper. Don't you worry about that," he said. "It's my neck, too, after all."

"Good," Sam said. "Long as you remember."

German subs weren't the only ones prowling the North Atlantic. Plenty of U.S. boats were out here, too. More to the point, so were British, French, and Confederate submarines. The odds against any one of them being in the neighborhood were long, but so were the odds against filling an inside straight, and lucky optimists did that every day.

In both the Great War and this one, U.S. admirals and their German counterparts dreamt of sweeping the British and French fleets from the North Atlantic and joining hands in the middle. It hadn't happened then, and it wouldn't happen this time around, either. The enemy kept the two allies apart, except for sneaky meetings like this one.

NEAR ENOUGH, the submersible's captain signaled. But Sam steered closer, anticipating the next swell with a small motion of the wheel. The sub's skipper waved to him then, seeing that he knew what he was doing. He lifted one hand from the wheel to wave back. THROW A LINE, came the flashes from the ugly, deadly, rust-streaked boat.

IS THE PACKAGE WATERPROOF? Sam asked.

JA, the submersible skipper answered. Sam knew more German than that; his folks had spoken it on the farm where he grew up. He ordered a line thrown. A German sailor in a greasy pea jacket and dungarees ran along the sub's wet hull to retrieve it. Sam wouldn't have cared to do that, not with the boat pitching the way it was. But the man grabbed the line, carried it back to the conning tower, and climbed the iron ladder, nimble as a Barbary ape.

The German skipper tied the package, whatever it was, to the end of the line. Then he waved to the *Josephus Daniels*. The sailor who'd cast the line drew it back hand over hand. When he took the package off it, he waved up to Sam Carsten on the bridge.

After waving back, Sam got on the blinker again: WE HAVE IT. THANKS AND GOOD LUCK.

LIKEWISE FOR YOU, the German answered. He lifted his battered cap in salute. Then he and the other men on the conning tower disappeared into the dark, smelly depths of the submersible. The boat slid below the surface and was gone.

A moment later, the sailor brought the package—which was indeed wrapped in oilskins and sheet rubber, and impressively sealed—up to the bridge. "Here you go, sir," he said, handing it to Sam and saluting.

"Thanks, Enos," Carsten answered. The sailor hurried away.

"Now into the safe?" the exec asked.

"That's what my orders are," Sam agreed.

"Wonder why the brass are making such a fuss about it," said Thad Walters, the Y-ranging officer.

"Beats me," Sam answered with a grin. "They pay me *not* to ask questions like that, so I'm going to lock this baby up right now. Mr. Zwilling, come to my cabin with me so you can witness that I've done it. Mr. Walters, you have the conn." Having a witness was in the orders, too. He'd never had anything on board before that came with such tight security requirements.

"Aye aye, sir." The exec's voice stayed formal, but he sounded more pleased than otherwise. Red tape was meat and drink to him. He would have done better manning a desk ashore and counting turbine vanes than as second-in-command on a warship, but the Navy couldn't fit all its pegs into the perfect holes. You did the best you could in the slot they gave you—and, if you happened to be the skipper, you did the best you could with the men set under you. If they weren't all the ones you would have chosen yourself . . . Well, there was a war on.

Sam's cabin wasn't far from the bridge. It wasn't much wider than his own wingspan, but it gave him a tiny island of privacy when he needed one. Along with his bed—which he didn't get to use enough—he had a steel desk and a steel chair and the safe.

He shielded it with his body as he spun the combination so the exec couldn't see it: more orders. The metal door swung open. "I am putting the package in the safe," he intoned, and did just that. "The seals are unbroken."

"Sir, I have observed you doing so," Myron Zwilling said, like a man giving responses to a preacher in church. "And I confirm that the seals are unbroken."

"All right, then. I'm closing up." Sam did, and spun the lock once more to keep it from showing the last number.

"Now we go back to Boston?" the exec said.

"Just as fast as our little legs will carry us," Sam replied. Zwilling gave him a look of faint distaste. Sam sighed silently; if the exec was born with a sense of whimsy, he'd had it surgically removed as a kid. And the *Josephus Daniels'* legs were indeed little. She couldn't make better than about twenty-four knots, far slower than a real destroyer. The only reason that occurred to Carsten for picking her for this mission was that she was one of the most anonymous ships in the Navy. The enemy wouldn't pay much attention to her. If he didn't command her, he wouldn't pay much attention to her himself. As they left the cabin, Sam added, "I am locking the door behind me."

"Yes, sir," Zwilling said. "You're also supposed to post two armed guards outside until you remove—whatever it is—from the safe."

"Go get two men. Serve them out with submachine guns from the arms locker and bring them back here. I'll stand guard in the meantime," Sam said. "If Jake Featherston's hiding under the paint somewhere, I'll do my goddamnedest to hold him off till you get back with the reinforcements."

"Er—yes, sir." The exec seemed relieved to get away.

This time, Sam sighed out loud. Pat would have sassed him right back instead of taking everything so seriously. Well, what could you do?

Before long, the armed guards took their places in front of the door to the captain's quarters. Sam went back to the bridge. "I have the conn," he announced as he took the wheel from Walters. "I am changing course to 255. We are on our way back to Boston." He rang the engine room. "All ahead full."

"All ahead full. Aye aye, sir." The response came back through a speaking tube. The black gang would wring every knot they could from the *Josephus Daniels*. The only trouble was, she didn't have many knots to wring.

Every mile Sam put between himself and the spot where he'd met the U-boat eased his mind. That it also meant he was one mile closer to his own country did nothing to make him unhappy, either. He wanted nothing more than to get . . . whatever it was out of his safe and off his ship. He didn't like having men with automatic weapons outside his door at all hours of the day and night. Were it up to him, he would have been much more casual about the mysterious package. But it wasn't, so he followed orders.

He also followed orders in maintaining wireless silence till he got within sight of Cape Ann, northeast of Boston. A couple of patrolling U.S. seaplanes had already spotted him by then and, he supposed, sent their own wireless signals, but nobody—especially not his exec— would be able to say he hadn't done everything the brass told him to do.

Two Coast Guard cutters steamed out from Rockport and escorted the *Josephus Daniels* across Massachusetts Bay as if she had royalty on board. Sam didn't think the Germans could have dehydrated the Kaiser and stuffed him into that flat package, but you never could tell.

When a pilot came aboard to steer the destroyer escort through the minefields outside of Boston harbor, Sam greeted him with, "The powers that be won't like it if you pick the wrong time to sneeze."

The pilot had flaming red hair, ears that stuck out like jug handles, and an engagingly homely grin. "My wife won't like it, either, sir," he answered, "and that counts a hell of a lot more with me."

"Sounds like the right attitude," Sam allowed. Myron Zwilling clucked like a fretful mother hen. Yes, he worshipped at Authority's shrine.

They got through the invisible barricade and tied up in the Boston Navy Yard. As soon as they did, a swarm of Marines and high-ranking officers descended on them. One of the captains nodded when he saw the guards outside Sam's door. "As per instructions," he said.

"Yes, sir," Sam said, and when was that ever the wrong answer?

Everybody waited impatiently till he opened the safe and took out the package. He wondered what would happen if he pretended to forget the combination. Odds were the newcomers had somebody who could jigger the lock faster than he could open it with the numbers.

"Here you go, sir." He handed the package to a vice admiral. "Any chance I'll ever know what this is all about?"

"No," the man said at once. But then he unbent a little: "Not officially, anyhow. If you can add two and two, you may get a hint one day."

Even that little was more than Carsten expected. "All right, sir," he said.

"Officially, of course, none of this ever happened," the vice admiral went on. "We aren't here at all."

"How am I supposed to log that, sir? 'Possessed by ghosts—summoned exorcist'?" Sam said. The vice admiral laughed. So did Sam, who was kidding on the square.

Camp Humble wasn't perfect, but it came as close as Jefferson Pinkard could make it. The commandant probably had more experience with camps designed to get rid of people than anybody else in the business. One thing he'd learned was not to call it that or even think of it like that. *Reducing population* was a phrase with far fewer unpleasant associations.

That mattered. It mattered a surprising amount. Guards who brooded about the things they did had a way of eating their guns or otherwise doing themselves in. If you gave it a name that seemed innocuous, they didn't need to brood so much.

Back at Camp Dependable, outside of Alexandria, Louisiana, guards had actually taken Negroes out into the swamps and shot them. That was hard on the men—not as hard as it was on the Negroes, but hard enough. Things got better when Jeff thought of asphyxiating trucks. Then the guards didn't have to pull the trigger themselves. They didn't have to deal with blood spraying everywhere and with screams and with men who weren't quite dead. All they had to do was take out bodies and get rid of them. That was a hell of a lot easier.

And the poison-gas chambers he'd started at Camp Determination in west Texas were better yet. They got rid of more blacks faster than the trucks did, and saved on fuel besides. The prairie out by Snyder offered plenty of room for mass graves as big as anybody could want. Everything at Camp Determination would have been, if not perfect, at least pretty damn good, if not for the . . .

"Damnyankees," Pinkard muttered. "God fry the stinking damnyankees in their own grease." Who would have figured the U.S. Army would push into west Texas? One of the reasons for building Camp Determination way out there was that it was the ass end of nowhere. The enemy hadn't seemed likely to bother a camp there.

But the Freedom Party underestimated how much propaganda the USA could get out of the camps. And earlier this year the United States had attacked everywhere they could, all at once: not seriously, but hard enough to keep the CSA from reinforcing the defenders in Kentucky and Tennessee, where the real action was. And it worked. Kentucky and Tennessee were lost, and Georgia was in trouble.

And Camp Determination was lost, too. The United States had bombed the rail lines coming into the camp so it couldn't reduce population the way it was supposed to. And they'd also bombed the crap out of Snyder; Jeff thanked God his own family came through all right. The Confederate defenders finally had to pull back, so now the Yankees had all the atrocity photos they wanted.

And Jefferson Pinkard had Camp Humble. Humble, Texas, just north of Houston, lay far enough east that the United States wouldn't overrun it unless the Confederacy really went down the drain. The USA had a much harder time bombing the rail lines that came through here, too. So Negroes came in, they got into trucks that took them nowhere except to death, or they went into bathhouses that pumped out cyanide instead of hot water. After that, they went up in smoke. Literally.

Pinkard scowled. The crematorium wasn't up to snuff. The outfit that built it had sold the CSA a bill of goods. The smoke that billowed from the tall stacks stank of burnt meat. It left greasy soot wherever it touched. Sometimes bits of real flesh went up the stacks and came down a surprising distance away. You couldn't very well keep Camp Humble's purpose a secret with a thing like that stinking up the air for miles around.

Somebody knocked on the door to Jeff's office. "It's open," he called. "Come on in." A guard with a worried look obeyed. Guards who came into the commandant's office almost always wore a worried look; they wouldn't have been there if they didn't have something to worry about. "Well?" Jeff asked.

"Sir, we got us a nigger says he knows you," the guard said.

"And you waste my time with that shit?" Pinkard said scornfully. "Christ on a crutch, McIlhenny, it happens once a trainload. Either these coons know me or they're asshole buddies with the President, one. Like anybody'd be dumb enough to believe 'em."

"Sir, this here nigger's named Vespasian," McIlhenny said. "Says you and him and another coon named, uh, Agrippa used to work together at the Sloss Works in Birmingham. Reckon he's about your age, anyways."

"Well, fuck me," Jeff said in surprise.

"He's telling the truth?" the gray-uniformed guard asked.

"I reckon maybe he is," Jeff said. "The last war, they started using niggers more in factory jobs when white men got conscripted. I did work with those two, hell with me if I didn't."

"We didn't send him on right away," McIlhenny said. "Wanted to find out what you had in mind first. You want, we can get rid of him. Or if you want to see him, we can do that, too."

"Vespasian." Jefferson Pinkard's voice was far away. He hadn't thought about Vespasian in years. Sometimes the years he'd put in at the steel mill seemed to have happened to someone else, or in a different lifetime. But he said, "Yeah, I'll talk to him. He wasn't a bad nigger—not uppity or anything. And he worked pretty hard."

"We were gonna put him in a truck," the guard said. If they had, Vespasian wouldn't be seeing anybody this side of the Pearly Gates. He looked apprehensive. Asphyxiating somebody the commandant really knew wouldn't do wonders for your career.

"Well, I'm glad you didn't." Pinkard heaved his bulk out of the chair behind his desk. A lot of fat padded the hard muscles he'd got working in the foundry. He grabbed a submachine gun off a wall bracket and made sure the drum magazine that fed it was full. If Vespasian had some sort of revenge in mind, he wouldn't go on a truck after all. Instead, he'd get ventilated on the spot. "Take me to him. He in the holding area?"

"Sure is, sir," the guard answered. Camp Humble had one, to give the guards the chance to deal with prisoners who were dangerous or just unusual.

"You searched him?" Jeff took nothing for granted. Some of the people who worked for him were dumb as rocks.

But the guard nodded. "Sure did, sir. Up the ass and everything." He made a face. "He ain't got nothin'."

"All right, then," Jeff said. It sounded as if the men in gray were on the ball this time.

When they got to the holding area, he found two more guards aiming assault rifles at Vespasian. One of them blinked. "Be damned," he said. "This mangy old coon wasn't blowing smoke, then?"

Vespasian wasn't exactly mangy, but he was only a shadow of the burly buck who'd worked alongside Jefferson Pinkard half a lifetime earlier. He was gray-haired and scrawny, and looked like a man who'd been through hell. If his train ride from Birmingham to Camp Humble was like most, he had. A powerful stench clung to him. He hadn't washed in a long time, and hadn't always made it to a toilet or a slop bucket, either.

He nodded to Jeff not as one equal to another, but as a man who knew another man, anyhow. "Really is you, Mistuh Pinkard," he said, his voice desert-dry and rough. "Been a hell of a long time, ain't it?"

"Sure as hell has," Jeff answered. He turned to the guards. "Get him some water. Reckon he can use it."

"Do Jesus! You right about that," Vespasian croaked. When the water came—in a pail, not a glass—he drank and drank. How long had he gone without? Days, plainly. And when he said, "That was mighty fine," he sounded much more like his old self.

"What ever happened to that no-account cousin of yours or whatever the hell he was?" Jeff asked. "You know the one I mean—the guy they threw in jail. What the hell was his name?"

"You mean Leonidas?" Vespasian said, and Jeff nodded. The black man went on, "They let him out after the las' war was over—decided he weren't no danger to the country or nobody else. He kept his nose clean afterwards. Got married, had a couple chillun. Died o' TB a little befo' the new war start."

"How about that?" Jeff said. "I plumb lost touch with Birmingham lately." He hesitated, then waved the guards away. "I'll be all right, dammit," he told them. "I got a gun, and he ain't dumb enough to give me no trouble." They didn't like it, but the man who made the rules could break them, too. When the guards were out of earshot, Jeff asked Vespasian, "Ever hear what happened to that gal I used to be married to?"

"Yes, suh." Vespasian nodded. "She went downhill pretty bad. Got to drinkin' an' carryin' on with men. Ain't heard nothin' 'bout her in a while, though. Dunno if she's alive or dead."

"Huh." Jeff's grunt was more self-satisfied than anything else. Run around on him, would Emily? Whatever she got after he cut her loose served her right, as far as he was concerned. "Bitch," he muttered under his breath. "Probably had a goddamn taxi meter between her legs."

Vespasian either didn't catch that or had the sense to pretend he didn't. He lifted the pail to his mouth again. Pinkard tensed. If he threw it . . . But he set it down and wiped his mouth on his filthy sleeve. "Ask you somethin' now, suh?"

"Go ahead," Jeff told him.

"What you do with me, now that I'm here?"

"You give people trouble?"

"Now, Mistuh Pinkard, you know I ain't like that," Vespasian said reproachfully.

"I sure do." Jeff nodded. "I told McIlhenny the same thing when he said you were asking for me. So you just stay in the barracks and do like the guards tell you, and everything'll be fine."

"Sure weren't fine comin' here." Vespasian didn't sound as if he believed a word of it. He was nobody's fool, evidently. Jeff knew what kind of lies he was telling. He didn't have anything against Vespasian as a man, but he didn't have the kind of affection for him that would have made him want to keep his former coworker around in defiance of the rules. The rules said the Confederacy needed to get rid of blacks. They caused the country more trouble than they were worth. From everything Jefferson Pinkard had seen, that was the gospel truth. And it was just Vespasian's hard luck that he'd finally wound up at Camp Humble.

So Jeff shrugged and spread his hands and went right on lying. "I am sorry about that, honest to God. Wish it could've been better. But there's a war on." That was the handy-dandy excuse for anything these days.

"Ain't no reason to leave a man in his own filth. Ain't no reason to have people die on the way to this here place," Vespasian said. "What's gonna happen to us all now that we's here?" Fear and apprehension roughened his voice.

"You got to remember, this is nothin' but a transit camp," Jeff said—one more lie piled on all the others. "You'll get some food, you'll get cleaned up, and we'll send you on the way again." And so they would, on a journey from which Vespasian wouldn't come back. "Then you'll sit out the war somewhere else. Once we're done licking the damnyankees, I reckon you'll go on back to Birmingham. We'll sort all that shit out then."

"I got to wait till we lick the USA, reckon I'll be at that other camp forever," Vespasian said.

The gibe held much more truth than Jeff wished it did. It also played on his own fears. He tried not to show that, but he did call the guards back. "Take him off to the barracks that's scheduled for the bathhouse next," he told them. "Once he gets cleaned up, we'll go from there."

"Yes, sir," the guards chorused. One of them nudged Vespasian. "Come on. You heard the boss. Get moving."

Away Vespasian went. Did he know Jeff had just ordered him liquidated? Pretty soon, he'd go up the crematorium stack, one more smudge of soot in a system that didn't work as well as advertised. Jeff might have found a lesson there had he been looking for one. Since he wasn't, he didn't worry about it. He had a job to do, and he aimed to keep at it till it was done.

Congresswoman Flora Blackford was sick to death of war. She didn't know of anyone in the USA who wasn't. But she also didn't know of anyone except a few fools and lunatics who wanted to make peace with the Confederate States and Jake Featherston. There'd been more doubt and disagreement during the Great War. Had the European powers patched up a peace then, odds were the USA and CSA would have done the same. Now . . . The one thing Featherston had done was unify the United States—against him. No arguments about workers' solidarity now, not even from the hardcore wing of the Socialist Party. Getting rid of the enemy came first.

Her secretary stuck her head into Flora's inner office. "The Assistant Secretary of War is on the line, Congresswoman," she said.

"Thank you, Bertha. Put him through," Flora said.

She picked up the telephone on her desk even before the first ring finished. "Hello, Flora," Franklin Roosevelt boomed. "How are you this lovely morning?"

Flora looked out the masking-taped window. It was pouring rain, and the weatherman said there was a chance of sleet tonight. Winter hadn't got to Philadelphia, but you could see it coming. Roosevelt's office down in the bowels of the War Department was only a few blocks from hers. "Have you been down there so long you've forgotten it's not July any more?" she asked.

He chuckled merrily. "Well, you can see when you come over."

Telephone lines coming out of the War Department and the Congressional office building were supposed to be the most secure in the USA. Saying too much over them wasn't a good idea anyhow. Roosevelt had something interesting, though. Flora was sure of that. "On my way," she told him, and hung up.

Had the weather been halfway decent, she would have walked. As things were, she flagged a cab. Even the short ride showed her a couple of hits from the new Confederate rockets. They were aiming at the center of government, but weren't especially accurate; they fell all over Philadelphia. No warning was possible. The only thing you could do to stay safe was to be somewhere else when they came down.

"Ain't they terrible? Ain't they wicked?" said the cab driver, a middle-aged woman. "How come we don't got nothin' like that?"

"I expect we're working on them." Flora wasn't exactly giving away military secrets by admitting that.

"We shoulda done it first," the cabby said. "Blow them Confederate bastards to kingdom come without our boys gettin' hurt."

"That would be good." Flora thought of her own son. Joshua was in basic training now. Pretty soon, if the war didn't end first, they'd give him a rifle and turn him loose on the enemy. The enemy, unfortunately, had rifles—among other things—too.

Flora paid the driver, opened the cab's door, opened her umbrella, and splashed up the broad stairs to the entrance to the War Department. She didn't get *very* wet, but she didn't exactly stay dry, either. At the entrance, soldiers examined her ID with remorseless care before letting her in. She didn't get very far in even then, not at first. A hard-faced woman frisked her in a sandbagged revetment that could blunt the force of a people bomb. Only then did a private with peach fuzz escort her down, down, down to Franklin Roosevelt's office.

"You look like something the cat dragged in," the Assistant Secretary of War exclaimed. "Can I fix you a drink? Purely medicinal, of course."

"Of course," Flora said, deadpan. "Thanks. I'd love one."

The medicinal alcohol turned out to be some fine scotch. "Confiscated from a British freighter," Roosevelt explained. "I arranged for a friend of mine in the Navy Department to get some good Tennessee sipping whiskey, and this is how he scratched my back."

"Nice to have friends," Flora said. "I like scotch better, too."

"I still owe him a little something, or maybe not such a little something," Roosevelt said. "The Navy's been nice to us lately."

"Has it?" Flora said. When Roosevelt nodded, she went on, "Does that have something to do with why you called me over?"

He beamed at her. "I knew you were smart. It sure does. A few days ago, one of our destroyer escorts met the U-517 somewhere in the North Atlantic. The Navy and the Germans worked out just where. It doesn't matter anyhow, except that they *did* meet. The skipper of the submersible passed a package to the skipper of the *Josephus Daniels*—that's the destroyer escort. Our ship brought the package in to Boston, and now we've got it."

"What is it?" Flora asked. "Something to do with uranium, unless I'm crazy."

"Right the first time," Franklin Roosevelt agreed. "We finally managed to talk the Kaiser into letting us know just how far along the Germans are."

"And?"

"And they're ahead of us. Well, no surprise—most of the top nuclear physicists come from Germany or Austria-Hungary, and Bohr from Denmark is working for them, too," Roosevelt said. "But this will speed us up. I don't know all the details yet. Our people are still trying to figure out what the details are, if you know what I mean. It's good news, though."

"Sounds like it," Flora said. "Have we got any good news about these Confederate rockets?"

"Not much." Roosevelt's jaunty smile slipped. When it did, she could see how worn and weary he was. He looked like a man busy working himself to death. She couldn't even say anything, because he was far from the only one doing the same thing. He paused to light a cigarette and suck in smoke through the holder he liked to use. "About all we can do is bomb their launchers, and they've made them portable, so the damn things—excuse me—aren't easy to find."

"And in the meantime we sit here and take it," Flora said. "Can we bomb the factories where they make the rockets?"

"When we find 'em, we'll bomb 'em," Roosevelt promised. "I wish the Confederates would paint *Rocket Factory* on the roof in big letters. It sure would make reconnaissance a lot easier. We do keep plugging away."

"I'm so glad," Flora murmured, which made Roosevelt laugh.

"What about the town where they're working on uranium? Are we still giving it the once-over?"

"Every chance we get," he replied. "They've got antiaircraft fire like you wouldn't believe all around Lexington—oops. Pretend you didn't hear that."

"Pretend I didn't hear what?" Flora said, and Franklin Roosevelt laughed again.

"Yeah, the flak is thick enough to land on, the pilots say," he continued, "and they put night fighters in the air, too. They've quit pretending it's not important. They know we know it is, and they're doing their best to keep us away."

"I take it their best isn't good enough?"

The Assistant Secretary of War shook his strong-jawed head. "Not even close. We're punishing them—that's the only word for it. I happen to know their boss researcher went to Richmond not long ago to squall like a branded calf. I wish I would have found out sooner. I might have tried to arrange to put him out of action for good."

"You have people in Richmond who can arrange that?" Flora asked with faint, or maybe not so faint, distaste. The Confederates made a policy of rubbing out U.S. officers they found dangerous. Turnabout was fair play, but even so . . . "War is a filthy business."

"It sure is. And the only thing worse than a war is a lost war. Two of those a lifetime ago almost ruined the country forever," Roosevelt said. "So, yes, there are people who would have tried to make sure Professor So-and-So never stood up in front of a blackboard again. No guarantees, of course, but we would have had a go at it."

"Would killing him make that much difference to the Confederate war effort?"

"No way to be sure, but we think so. He gets almost anything he wants when it comes to money and equipment. They know how important a uranium bomb is for them. If they get it first, they can still lick us. If they don't, we'll knock them flat and then we'll start kicking them."

"*Alevai,*" Flora said. Roosevelt looked quizzical; no reason he should know Yiddish. She explained: "It means something like *hopefully* or *God willing.*"

"He'd better be willing. If He's not, He's as sleepy as Elijah said Baal was," Roosevelt said. "They *need* licking, dammit. That Camp Determination turned out to be even worse than you said. I hadn't imagined it could, but there you are. What General Dowling found would gag a maggot. It really would."

Flora resisted the impulse to shout, *I told you so!* She had, over and over again, but it was too late to do anything about that now. Instead, she said, "It's not the only camp they're running. They've got plenty more, from east Texas to Alabama. If we can wreck the rail lines going into them, we slow the slaughter, anyhow."

"We're doing some of that," Roosevelt said. "It's not our top priority, I admit. Beating the enemy in the field is. But we're doing what we can." He clicked his tongue between his teeth. "With all the effort the Confederate States are putting into the camps, I think Featherston would just as soon kill off his Negroes as beat us. If that's not insane, it's certainly strange."

"Depends on how you look at things," Flora replied. "Even if they lose, the Negroes will still be gone for good. And the Freedom Party thinks it *is* good."

"If they lose, the Freedom Party is gone for good. I don't think they've figured that out yet," Roosevelt said grimly. "If they lose, chances are the Confederate States of America are gone for good, too. I'm sure those goons haven't figured that out yet."

"What do we do with them?" Flora asked. "Can we occupy everything from the border of Alaska all the way to the Rio Grande?"

"Can we *not*?" Roosevelt returned, and she had no good answer for him.

"What we got from the Germans really will help us build our bomb?" she said. He was bound to be right about one thing: winning came first.

"The physicists say it will. They're right more often than they're wrong, seems like. They'd better be, anyhow," Roosevelt said. "I just pray some British or French sub hasn't carried papers like that to the Confederacy."

"*Oy!*" That dismayed Flora into Yiddish again. "That would be terrible!"

"It sure would," Roosevelt said. "And the Confederates have something to trade for it, too. I bet the English and the French would just love to shoot rockets way into Germany."

"*Oy!*" Flora repeated. "What can we do about it?"

"Sink all the submersibles we can, and hope we get the one that's packed full of secret plans," Roosevelt answered. "And yes, I know—

what are the odds? But we can't very well tell the enemy not to help their allies. That would make them more likely to do it, not less."

"I'm afraid you're right," Flora said after thinking it over. She sighed. "When we broke into Georgia, I thought the war was as good as won. But it'll come right down to the wire, won't it?"

"Maybe not. Maybe we'll just knock them flat," the Assistant Secretary of War said. "But they've got some rabbits they could pull out of the hat. We'll do everything we can to steal the hat or burn it, but if they hang on to it . . . Last time around, we could see we'd win months before we finally did. Not so easy to be sure now. That's not for public consumption, of course. Officially, everything's just fine."

"Officially, everything's always fine. Officially, everything was fine when the Confederates were driving on Lake Erie to cut us in half," Flora said.

"Can't go around saying things are bad and we're losing. People might believe us."

"Why? They don't believe us when we tell them everything's just fine. By now, they must figure we lie to them all the time." Flora listened to herself with something approaching horror. Had she really turned so cynical? She feared she had.

The British ambassador is here to see you, Mr. President," Jake Featherston's secretary announced.

"Thanks, Lulu. Send him in," the President of the CSA said.

Lord Halifax was tall and thin, with a long bald head and a pinched mouth and jaw. He reminded Jake of a walking thermometer, bulb uppermost. No matter what he looked like, though, no denying he was one sharp bird. "Mr. President," he murmured in an accent almost a caricature of an upper-class Englishman's.

"Good to see you, Your Excellency." Featherston held out his hand. Halifax shook it. His grip wasn't the dead fish you would expect. The President waved him to a chair. "Have a seat. Glad you came through the last raid all right."

"Our embassy has an excellent shelter. Indeed, these days the shelter *is* the embassy, more or less," Halifax said. "The chaps who stay on, I'm afraid, draw hazardous-duty pay."

You can't stop the United States from bombing the crap out of your capital. That was what he meant, even if he was too much the diplomat to come out and say it. "Yeah, well, I hear the Germans and Austrians up in Philadelphia get bonuses, too," Jake said. *They may be hurting us, but we're still in it.* In meetings like this, words were smoke screens, concealing what lay behind them.

"Indeed," Halifax said, which might have meant *It could be* or, just as easily, *My ass.*

"I'm hoping your country can do more to keep the Canadians fired up against the United States," Jake said.

"Believe me, Mr. President, we're doing everything we can, this being in our interest as well," Lord Halifax replied. "The naval situation in the Atlantic remaining complex, however, we cannot do as much as we would wish. And events on the Continent naturally influence other commitments of scarce resources."

Jake had no trouble translating that into plain English. The Germans were pushing England and France back. The limeys didn't have so much to spare for adventures on this side of the Atlantic as they'd had when things were going better closer to home.

"What the damnyankees aren't using up there, they're shooting at us," Featherston said. "If we go under, they aim everything at you. How long do you think you'll last if they do?" They had a generation earlier, and the United Kingdom didn't last long. Chances were it wouldn't now, either.

And Lord Halifax couldn't shoot that one back at him. The USA could go after Britain in a big way if the CSA went under—could and would. But if Britain went down, Germany wouldn't care about the Confederacy. The Confederate States were no threat to the Kaiser, not till they got a uranium bomb. When they did, the whole goddamn world needed to watch out.

"I said we were doing everything we could, Mr President, and I assure you I meant it most sincerely," the British ambassador said. "We appreciate the CSA's importance to the overall strategic picture, believe you me we do. Our task would become much more difficult if the United States was prosecuting the Atlantic war with all their energy and resources."

You are *tying the damnyankees down for us.* Again, Halifax's words were pretty straightforward. He had to figure Jake could see that much for himself. And Jake could.

He leaned forward across his desk toward the limey. "Fair enough," he said, his rasping voice and harsh, half-educated accent contrasting sharply with Halifax's soft, elegant tones. "Now we come down to it. If you need us in the war, if you need us to lick the USA for you, why the hell won't you tell us what all you know about uranium bombs? We've got our own project going—you can bet your bottom dollar on that. But if you give us a hand, it helps you and us both. Sooner we start blowing the damnyankees sky-high, the happier everybody'll be. Except them, I mean."

Halifax's bony face never showed much; he would have made a dangerous poker player. But his eyebrows rose a fraction now. Maybe he hadn't expected Jake to be so direct. If he hadn't, he didn't know the President of the Confederate States as well as he thought he did.

"Uranium is an extremely delicate subject," he said at last.

"Tell me about it!" Featherston exclaimed. "Even so, you think the United States aren't working on a bomb of their own? Suppose they get it before we do. They'll blast Richmond off the map, and New Orleans, and Atlanta—"

"Assuming Atlanta hasn't fallen by then," Halifax said.

Fuck you, Charlie. Featherston almost said it, and diplomacy be damned. At the last instant, he bit his tongue. What he did say was, "Yeah, well, suppose they knock us out of the war. Then what? How long before London goes up in smoke? About as long as it takes to get a bomb across the ocean."

Lord Halifax looked physically ill. "The United States aren't our only worry on that score," he choked out.

"I know. Damn Germans started this whole mess. Somebody should've strangled that Einstein bastard when he was a baby." Jake scowled. "Too late to get all hot and bothered about it now. Look, I don't even know how far along you guys are. Maybe we're ahead of you."

The British ambassador winced, ever so slightly. *Ah, that got him,* Jake thought with an internal grin. The mere idea that backward half-colonials across the sea could get ahead of the high and mighty lords of creation on their own foggy island had to rankle.

To make sure it did, Jake added, "After all, we're a long ways ahead of you when it comes to rockets. Ask the Yankees if you don't believe me."

Halifax winced again, more obviously this time. Jake Featherston's internal grin got wider. "Quite," Halifax muttered: a one-word admission of pain.

"Reckon we can work a swap?" Jake asked. "We'll tell you what we know. We're not afraid of our allies. If you want to shoot rockets at the Germans, more power to you. Blow 'em to hell and gone. I won't shed a tear, and you can bet your . . . backside on that."

"An interesting proposal," the ambassador said. "I am not authorized to agree to it, but I shall put it to the Prime Minister. If he deems it feasible, we can proceed from there."

"How long will that take?"

"My dear sir!" Lord Halifax spread his hands. "That's in Winston's court, I'm afraid, not mine. I will say he is not a man in the habit of brooking delay."

Featherston wondered if they really did speak the same language. He thought he understood what the British ambassador meant, but he wasn't sure. Hoping he did, he answered, "He'd better not wait around. You're in trouble, and so are we. The more we can help each other, the better our chances, right?"

"One could hardly disagree," Halifax said.

"Fair enough." But Jake wasn't smiling. He was scowling. "Thing you've got to remember is, this cuts both ways. You want what we know about rockets—any fool can see you do. You want to get, but you don't want to give. And I'm here to tell you, your Lordship, sir, that ain't gonna fly."

Lord Halifax *was* a diplomat. If Featherston's bluntness offended him, he didn't let on. "I assure you, Mr. President, I intend to make your views plain to the Prime Minister. What happens after that is up to him."

Jake knew perfectly well he would have the hide of any Confederate ambassador who exceeded his authority. In fairness, he couldn't blame Winston Churchill for feeling the same way. But his definition of fairness was simple. If he got what he wanted, that was fair. Anything less, and the other side was holding out on him.

Most of the time, he admired Churchill. Like him, the Prime Minister had spent much too long as a voice crying in the wilderness. In a way, Churchill had a tougher job than he did. Britain needed to worry about fighting both the USA and the German Empire.

But Britain hadn't been invaded the last time around. She hadn't been disarmed and had to start over. All she'd lost was Ireland—and the way the Irish felt about their longtime overlords meant she might be better off without it. With Ireland gone, the British didn't have to

worry about keeping the lid on a country where a third of the population hated the guts of the other two-thirds. Ireland was under British
control now, to keep the USA from using it as a forward base, but military occupation had a whole different set of rules. The limeys weren't
as tough on the micks as the Freedom Party was on Confederate Negroes, but they didn't take any crap, either.

"Tell him not to wait around, that's all," Jake said. "For his sake
and ours."

"Winston is a great many things, but not a ditherer. He may from
time to time find himself mistaken. He hardly ever finds himself un-
sure," Halifax said. "I do not know what his answer will be. I am confident you will have it in short order."

"Good. Anything else?" Jake was no ditherer, either.

"The United States are making a good deal of propaganda capital
from that camp they captured in Texas," Lord Halifax said. "Did you
have to be quite so open in your destruction of the colored populace?"

"You know what, Your Excellency? I don't give a shit how much
the damnyankees squawk about that." Jake wasn't being truthful, but
he didn't care. He had to make the limey understand. "What we do inside our own country is nobody's business but ours. We've had a nigger
problem for hundreds of years—even before we broke away from England. Now I'm finally doing something about it, and I really don't care
who doesn't like that. We're going to come out of this war nigger-free,
or as close to nigger-free as I can make us."

"Your solution is . . . heroic," Halifax said.

Jake liked that better than the British ambassador probably intended. He felt like a hero for reducing the CSA's colored population.
"I keep my campaign promises, by God," he said.

"No one has ever doubted your determination." Lord Halifax got
to his feet. "If you will excuse me . . ." He left the President's office.

When Lulu looked in after Halifax was gone, Jake Featherston
asked, "Who's next?"

"Mr. Goldman, sir."

"Send him in, send him in."

Saul Goldman had grown bald and pudgy in the twenty-odd years
Jake had known him. That had nothing to do with anything. The little
Jew still made a damned effective Director of Communications. Because he did, he could speak his mind to the President, or come closer
than most of the glad-handing yes-men who surrounded Featherston.

"I don't know how I can present any more losses in Georgia," he said now. "People will know I'm whistling in the dark no matter what I say."

"Then don't say anything," Jake answered. "Just say the Yankees are spewing out a pack of lies—and they are—and let it go at that."

Goldman cocked his head to one side, considering. "It could work . . . for a while. But if Atlanta falls, sir, it's a propaganda disaster."

"If Atlanta falls, it's a fucking military disaster, and the hell with propaganda," Featherston said. "I don't think that'll happen any time soon." He hoped *he* wasn't whistling in the dark. The news from Georgia was bad, and getting worse despite the fall rains.

"You know more about that than I do. I'm not a general, and I don't pretend to be," Goldman said.

"Don't know why the hell not," Jake told him. "Seems like every damn fool in the country wants to tell me how to run the war. Why should you be any different?" He held up a hand. "I know why—you aren't a damn fool."

"I try not to be, anyhow," Goldman said.

"You do pretty well. Half of being smart is knowing what you're not smart at," Jake said. "Plenty of folks reckon that 'cause they know something, they know everything. And that ain't the way it works."

"I never said it was," Goldman answered primly.

"Yeah, I know," Jake said. "You make one."

As far as Irving Morrell knew, he was unique among U.S. generals, with the possible exception of a few big brains high up in the General Staff. His colleagues thought about winning battles. After they won one, if they did, they worried about the next one.

Morrell was different. He thought about smashing the Confederate States of America flat. To him, that was the goal. Battles were nothing in themselves. They were just the means he needed to reach that end.

Back when the CSA still had soldiers in Ohio, he'd drawn a slashing line on the map, one that ran from Kentucky through Tennessee and Georgia to the Atlantic. That was where he was going now. He aimed to cut the Confederacy in half. Once he did, he figured the Confederate States would do what anything cut in half did.

They would die.

The question uppermost in his mind now was simple: could he go on to the ocean without bothering to capture Atlanta first? Would the enemy die fast enough afterwards to make the risk worthwhile?

He pondered a map. The chart was tacked to the wall of what had been a dentist's office in Monroe, Georgia, more than fifty miles east of Atlanta. He would have used the mayor's office, but a direct hit from a 105 left it draftier than he liked.

Monroe had had a couple of big cotton-processing plants, both of them now rubble. It had had a couple of fine houses that dated back to the days before the War of Secession, both of them now burnt. War had never come to this part of the CSA before. It was here now, and it made itself at home.

Reluctantly, Morrell decided Atlanta would have to fall before he stormed east again. It gave the enemy too good a base for launching a counteroffensive against his flank if he ignored it. Too many roads and railroads ran through the place. He couldn't be sure enough his air power would keep them all out of commission to ignore it. Taking chances was one thing. Taking stupid chances was something else again.

He didn't want to charge right into the city. He aimed to envelop it instead. That way, the Confederates couldn't do unto him as the USA did unto them in Pittsburgh. An attacking army that took a city block by block put its own dick in the meat grinder and turned the crank.

No help would come to Atlanta from the north or the east, and the bulk of the CSA's strength lay in those directions. The Confederate States were like a snail. They had a hard shell that protected them from the United States. Once you broke through, though, you found they were soft and squishy underneath. How much could they bring in from Florida or Alabama? Not nearly enough—or Morrell didn't think so, anyhow.

Back when he first proposed his slash, the General Staff estimated it would take two years, not one. When Chattanooga fell, he'd hoped to prove them wrong. He might yet, but racing ahead for the sake of speed wasn't smart.

"Then don't do it," he muttered, and headed out of the office. On the floor lay the dentist's diploma from Tulane University, the glass in the frame shattered. Morrell wondered whether the man was still practicing in Monroe or had put on a butternut uniform and gone up toward the front.

Two black men carrying rifles stalked along the street. They wore armbands with USA on them. White civilians fell over themselves getting out of their way. They waved and nodded to Morrell: not quite salutes, but close enough. He nodded back. The Negro guerrillas made him nervous, too. But they scared white Confederates to death, which was good, and they knew more about what was going on here than U.S. troops did, which was even better.

Sometimes they shot first, without bothering to ask questions later. Morrell was sure they'd killed a few people who didn't deserve killing. But how many Negroes who didn't deserve killing were dead all across the CSA? A little extra revenge might be too bad, but Morrell didn't intend to lose any sleep about it.

Except for guerrillas, not many Negroes were left in and around Monroe, or anywhere U.S. armies had reached. White people seemed to suffer from a kind of collective amnesia. More often than not, they denied there'd ever been many blacks close by. In Kentucky, they said the Negroes mostly lived in Tennessee. In Tennessee, they said the Negroes mostly lived in Georgia. Here in Georgia, they pointed two ways at once: towards Alabama and South Carolina. Was that selective blindness, a guilty conscience, or both? Morrell would have bet on both.

"Young man!" A Confederate dowager swept down on him. "I need to speak to you, young man!"

Morrell almost looked over his shoulder to see whom she meant. He'd passed fifty a couple of years before, and his weather-beaten features didn't seem young even to himself. But her gray hair and the turkeylike wattles under her chin said she was some distance ahead of him. "What can I do for you, ma'am?" he asked, as politely as he could.

"Young man, I know you come from the United States, and so are ignorant of a good deal of proper behavior, but I must tell you that colored people are not permitted to go armed in this country," she said.

He looked at her. He did his best to look through her. "They are now."

"By whose authority?" she demanded.

"Mine." He tapped the stars on his shoulder strap.

"You should be ashamed of yourself, in that case," she said.

Of itself, his hand dropped to the .45 he wore on his belt. "Lady, I think you better get lost before I blow your stupid head off," he said. "You people did your best to murder every Negro you could catch, and you have the gall to talk to me about shame . . . There's not a word low enough for you."

"The nerve!" The matron flounced off. Reality hadn't set in for her. He wondered if it ever would, or could.

Over in Texas, General Dowling had taken local big shots through the Confederate death camp and into the mass graveyard so they could see with their own eyes what their country had done. Some of them had the decency to kill themselves afterwards. Others just went on the way they had before.

Morrell wished he had one of those camps to show the locals. Then they wouldn't be able to shrug and pretend there'd never been that many Negroes in this part of the CSA. But he feared the matron wouldn't be much impressed afterwards. She was one of those people for whom nothing seemed real if it didn't happen to her.

Somebody'd painted YANKS OUT! on a wall. Morrell grabbed the first soldier he saw. "Get some paint and grab a couple of these assholes and have 'em clean this shit up," he told the man in green-gray. "If they give you a hard time, do whatever you have to do to get 'em to pay attention."

"Yes, *sir*!" the soldier said, and went off to take care of it with a grin on his face.

Artillery rumbled, off to the northeast. Morrell cocked his head to one side, listening, gauging. Those were Confederate guns. The enemy was still trying to blunt the U.S. attack and drive Morrell's forces back. He didn't think Featherston's men could do it. Before long, counterbattery fire or air strikes would make those C.S. gun bunnies sorry they'd ever been born, and even sorrier they'd tried messing with the U.S. Army.

From what Morrell had seen, the only thing Confederate civilians were sorry about was that their army hadn't done a better job of keeping the damnyankees away. Somehow, that left him imperfectly sympathetic.

"General!" Another woman called to him. This one was young and blond and pretty, pretty enough to remind him how long he'd been away from Agnes. She also looked mad enough to spit nails.

"Yes?" He'd give her the benefit of the doubt as long as he could.

"Those niggers of yours!" she snapped.

"What about 'em?" Morrell didn't want them getting out of hand and raping all the women they could catch. He could understand why they'd want to. He could sympathize, too. But he wasn't running a mob. He was running an army, or trying to.

"They *looked* at me. They *leered* at me, the grinning apes," the blond woman said. "You ought to string them up and horsewhip them."

Morrell needed a moment to realize she was dead serious. When he did, he almost wished the Negroes had dragged her into an alley and done their worst. "That's not how things'll work from here on out, so you'd better get used to it," he said. "Nobody gets whipped for looking. Heck, I'm looking right now. You're worth looking at, no offense."

"Well, of course." As pretty women often did, she took her good looks for granted. "But I don't mind it from you—too much. You're a Yankee, but you're not a nigger."

"If they touch you and you don't like it, you can complain. If anybody touches you and you don't like it, you can complain," Morrell said. "But they can look as much as they want."

"You mean you won't do anything about it?" The blond woman sounded as if she couldn't believe her ears. She looked disgusted, almost nauseated.

"That's what I said," Morrell told her.

"You damnyankees really *are* animals, then." She pursed her lips, perhaps getting ready to spit at him.

"If you do anything stupid," he said, "you'll find out just what kind of animal I am. You won't like it—I promise."

He didn't shout and bluster. That had never been his style. He didn't need to. He sounded like a man who meant exactly what he said, and for a good reason: he was. The local woman stopped looking like somebody saving up spit. She did look a little deflated. Then she gathered herself, flung, "Nigger-lover!" in his face instead of saliva, and stalked off. Fury gave her a fine hip action. Morrell admired it. He was sure the Negro auxiliaries had, too.

Up till now, he hadn't had much use for Negroes. Few whites in the USA did. Had he seen a couple of black men staring at a white woman's butt on a street corner in, say, Indianapolis, that might have offended him. In Monroe, Georgia? No. In fact, he smiled. The enemies of his enemies were his friends, all right.

After dark, Confederate bombers came over Monroe and dropped explosives on the U.S. soldiers in and around the town—and on their own people. A thin layer of low clouds hung above Monroe, so the Confederates might as well have been bombing blind. They couldn't come over by day, not unless they wanted to get slaughtered. In their shoes, Morrell supposed he would have preferred bombing blind to not bombing at all, too.

He had a few minutes' warning from Y-ranging gear that spotted the approaching bombers and sounded the alarm before they started unloading. U.S. night fighters were also starting to carry Y-ranging sets. So far, those sets were neither very strong nor very easy to use, but they were already making night operations more expensive for the CSA. Pretty soon, electronics might make nighttime raids as risky as daylight ones.

Crouching in a trench with bombs crashing down around him, Morrell could see a day where neither side on a battlefield would be able to hide anything from the other. How would you fight a war then? You could be so strong you'd beat your enemy even if he did see what you had in mind. You could, yes, but it wouldn't be easy, or economical.

Or you could make him think all your fancy preparations meant one thing and then go and do something else instead. Morrell nodded to himself. If he had his druthers, he would play it that way. If the enemy kept staring at the cape, he wouldn't see the sword till too late. You saved your own men and matériel that way . . . if you could bring it off.

The all-clear warbled. Morrell got out of the trench and went back to his cot. He didn't know how much damage the Confederates had done. Probably some—probably not a lot. Without a doubt, they'd screwed a lot of U.S. soldiers out of a night's sleep. That counted, too, though no civilians who hadn't got up groggy after an air raid would think so. Morrell yawned. His eyes closed. Air raid or not, the Confederates didn't screw him out of more than forty-five minutes.

Jonathan Moss had been on the run ever since a tornado let him break out of the Andersonville POW camp. Joining Spartacus' band of Negro guerrillas had kept the Confederates from getting him (it had also kept the guerrillas from shooting him and Nick Cantarella). But joining them also ensured that he stayed on the run.

U.S. forces weren't far away now. The rumble of artillery and the thud of bursting bombs came from the north by day and night. Running off to the troops from his own side would have been easy as pie . . . if not for God only knew how many divisions' worth of Jake Featherston's finest between him and them.

"We gots to sit tight," Spartacus told his men—again and again, a sure sign they didn't want to listen to him. "We gots to. Pretty soon, the Yankees, they comes to us. Then we is free men fo' true. We is free at las'."

Moss and Cantarella caught each other's eye. Moss doubted it would be so simple. By the New York infantry officer's raised eyebrow, so did he.

And, however much they wished they weren't, they turned out to be right. For a long time, the countryside a hundred miles south of Atlanta had been a military backwater: peanut farms and cotton fields, patrolled—when they were patrolled—by halfhearted Mexican soldiers and by militiamen whose stamina and skill didn't match their zeal. Good guerrilla country, in other words.

No more. With the U.S. irruption into northern Georgia, with the threat to Atlanta, southern Georgia suddenly turned into a military zone. Encampments and supply dumps sprouted like toadstools after a rain. Truck convoys and trains brought supplies and soldiers up toward the front.

All that gave Spartacus' band and the other black guerrillas still operating chances they'd never had before. If they mined a road and delayed a column of trucks, if they sprayed machine-gun bullets at a tent city in the middle of the night, they really hurt the Confederate war effort. From everything Jonathan Moss gathered from the news and rumors he picked up, the Confederate States couldn't afford even fleabites on their backside. They already had too much trouble right in front of them.

The enemy seemed to feel the same way. When Spartacus' guerrillas did strike, the men in butternut went after them with a ferocity they hadn't seen before. If Spartacus hadn't been fighting in country he knew better than the enemy did, the Confederates would have wiped out his band in short order. As things were, his men scrambled from woods to swamp, half a jump ahead of their pursuers.

Moss developed a new appreciation for possum and squirrel and turtle. The Negroes called one kind of long-necked terrapin, chicken turtles, presumably because of how they tasted. Moss couldn't see the resemblance. He didn't spend much time bitching, though; any meat in his belly was better than none.

Looking down at what was left of himself one weary evening, he said, "Back before the war, I had a potbelly. One of these days, I'd like to get another one."

"Some of the shit we eat makes Army rations look good," Nick Cantarella agreed. "Don't know that I could say anything worse about it."

Amusement glinted in Spartacus' eyes as he looked from one white man to the other. "I's mighty sorry to inconvenience you gents— *mighty* sorry," he said. "If 'n you knows where we kin git us some ribs and beefsteaks, sing out."

"Steak! Jesus!" Cantarella started to laugh. "I even stopped thinking about steak. What the hell's the point?"

"How about Confederate rations?" Spartacus asked, the mockery gone from his voice.

Hearing the change in tone, Moss grew alert. "What do you have in mind, boss?" he asked.

Spartacus smiled; he liked hearing the white men in his band acknowledge that he outranked them. "They got that new depot over by Americus," he said.

"Think we can hit it?" Cantarella asked.

"Hope so, anyways," Spartacus answered. "I got me a pretty good notion where they keeps the ration tins, too. See, here's what I got in mind . . ."

He sketched on the muddy ground with a stick. He wouldn't have done so much explaining for the other Negroes, but he thought of the escaped U.S. soldiers as military professionals, and valued their opinion. With Nick Cantarella, that was justified. Moss knew it was a lot less so for him.

He listened to Spartacus and tried to look wise. Cantarella, sure as hell, had a couple of suggestions that made the guerrilla leader nod in admiration. "Yeah, we do dat," Spartacus said. "We sure 'nough do dat. Featherston's fuckers, dey don't know which way dey should oughta run."

"That's the idea," Cantarella said. "If they go in a bunch of wrong directions, the right one gets easier for us."

The guerrillas struck at night. They stayed under cover while the sun was in the sky. Doing anything else would have asked to get slaughtered. A Negro threw a grenade into the depot from the north, while another black banged away with a Tredegar—trying to stir up the anthill.

They did it, too. Whistles shrilled. Men shouted. Soldiers boiled out after the Negroes. Moss hoped the guerrillas had splendid hidey-holes or quick legs.

As soon as the Confederates were well and truly stirred, the guerrillas' machine gun opened up from the west. Nick Cantarella had finally persuaded the gunner to fire short bursts and not squeeze off a belt of ammo at a time. It made the weapon much more effective and much more accurate.

Somebody inside the supply dump yelled, "Let's *get* those coons, goddammit! They come around here, they give us the chance to wreck 'em. We better not waste it." Shouted orders followed. The officer—he plainly was one—knew what he was doing, and how to get his men to do what he wanted.

A scream said at least one machine-gun bullet struck home. The Confederates fired back. They also started moving against the machine gun. A few black riflemen posted near the guerrillas' heavy weapon discouraged that. They were more mobile than the machine-gun crew, and gave the C.S. attackers some unpleasant surprises.

But the big surprise the guerrillas had in mind came from the far side of the supply depot. As soon as the Confederates were well engaged to the west, Spartacus whistled to the rest of the band and said, "Let's go!"

As it always did when he went into action, Jonathan Moss' heart pounded. He clutched his Tredegar and loped forward. Cutters snipped through the strands of barbed wire around the depot. The supply dump was new and in a rear area. The Confederates hadn't had the time or energy to protect it the way they would have closer to the front.

"No shootin' here, remember—not unless you got to," Spartacus called quietly. "In an' out fast as you can, like you was screwin' with her pappy asleep right beside you." From the way some of the Negroes chuckled, they'd done things like that.

Most of them carried rifles or pistols or submachine guns. Three or four, though, pushed wheelbarrows instead. Moss couldn't imagine a homelier weapon of war. But a man with a wheelbarrow could move much more food than someone who had to carry a crate in his arms or on his back.

"What the hell?" a Confederate called—the Negroes weren't quiet enough to escape all notice.

"We're on patrol here," Moss said, doing his best to imitate a Southern accent. "Why the devil aren't you chasing those damn niggers?"

"Uh—on my way, sir."

Moss heard rapidly retreating footsteps. He knew he'd better not laugh out loud. In his own ears, he hadn't sounded much like a Confederate at all. But he had sounded like a white man, and the soldier never dreamt he'd run into a damnyankee here. To him, anybody who sounded like a white had to be on his side, and anybody who sounded like an authoritative white had to be entitled to order him around.

"How d'you like being a Confederate officer?" Nick Cantarella whispered.

"Fine, except the bastards don't pay me," Moss whispered back.

"Hell they don't," Spartacus said. "We's at the payoff now. In there, boys—grab an' git!"

The Negroes rushed into the tent that sheltered crates of rations from the elements. Soft thumps announced that several of those crates were going into the wheelbarrows. The guerrillas emerged, their grins the most visible thing about them.

Then a shot rang out. "Jesus God, we got chicken thieves!" a Confederate screamed.

One of the chicken thieves shot him an instant later. "Scram!" Spartacus said—surely the most succinct order Moss had ever heard. It was also just right for the circumstances.

Firing as they went, the guerrillas withdrew from the depot. Men with rifles and submachine guns covered the wheelbarrows' retreat. When a bullet struck home with a wet slapping sound, a hauler dropped. Nick Cantarella grabbed the wheelbarrow handles and got it moving again.

They made it out of the supply dump and back into the woods. Moss' greatest worry was that the Confederates would pursue hard, but they didn't. "Shit, they already did more than I figured they would," Cantarella said. "They're rear-echelon troops, clerks and stevedores in uniform. If they wanted to mix it up, they'd be at the front."

"I guess," Moss said. "I'm not complaining, believe me."

Cantarella gave him the ghost of a grin. "Didn't think you were. That was smart, what you did there to keep the one asshole off our ass."

"Thanks." Praise from the other Army officer always made Moss feel good. It made him feel like a real soldier, not a pilot stuck in the middle of a ground war he didn't understand—which he was.

Once the guerrillas got clear of the depot, Spartacus abandoned the wheelbarrows. His men grumbled, but he held firm. "Gotta do it," he said. "Otherwise, them wheels show the butternut bastards every place we been. Trail's a lot harder to get rid of than footprints."

Moss and Cantarella took their turns playing pack mule along with everybody else. White skin gave them no special privileges here. If they'd tried to claim any, they wouldn't have lasted long. Moss wondered whether Confederates caught in like circumstances would have been smart enough to figure that out. After some of the things he'd seen in Georgia, he wouldn't have bet on it.

His back grumbled at lugging—toting, they said down here—a heavy crate. He was the oldest man in the guerrilla band. Spartacus, who'd been a Confederate noncom in the Great War, was within a couple of years of him, but Spartacus was the CO. Nobody expected him to fetch and carry.

After what seemed like forever, the Negroes and the U.S. soldiers they'd taken in got back to the swampy hideout from which they'd started. And then . . . to the victors went the spoils. "Let's eat!" Spartacus said, and they did.

C.S. military rations were nothing to write home about. In truces to pick up wounded men, Confederate soldiers traded tobacco and coffee to their U.S. counterparts for canned goods made in the USA. And U.S. rations, as Moss knew too well, wouldn't put the Waldorf out of business any time soon.

But greasy hash and salty stew filled the belly. Moss' had rubbed up against his backbone too often lately. He was amazed at how many tins of meat he could bolt down before he even started getting full.

"Man, I feel like I swallowed a medicine ball," Nick Cantarella said after a while.

"Yeah, me, too," Moss said. "I like it."

He lit a cigarette, the way he might have after a fine meal in a fancy restaurant. He'd had plenty to eat, and nobody was shooting at him right this minute. How could life get any better?

Cincinnatus Driver wanted to strut through the streets of Ellijay, Georgia. Strutting wasn't in the cards when you walked with a cane and a limp, but he felt like it anyway. How could a black man from the USA *not* want to strut in a little town his country had taken away from the Confederacy?

Here I am! he felt like shouting. *What are you ofay bastards gonna do about it?* And the whites of Ellijay couldn't do one damn thing, not unless they wanted the U.S. Army to land on them with both feet.

The hamlet seemed pleasant enough, with a grassy town square centered on a rock fountain. Groves of apple and peach trees grew nearby; Cincinnatus had heard the trout and bass fishing in the nearby stream was first-rate. Ellijay probably made a nice place to live . . . for whites.

Whenever the locals saw Cincinnatus, though, the way they acted gave him the chills. They stared at him as if he were a rare animal in a zoo—a passenger pigeon come back to life, say. They hadn't thought any Negroes were left in these parts, and didn't bother hiding their surprise.

"What're you *doin'* here?" a gray-haired man in bib overalls asked around an enormous chaw.

"Drivin' a truck for the United States of America," Cincinnatus answered proudly. "Helping the Army blow all this Confederate white trash to hell and gone."

He thought the Georgian would swallow the cud of tobacco. "You can't talk that way! You ought to be strung up, you know that?"

Along with his cane, Cincinnatus carried a submachine gun some Confederate soldier would never need again. He gestured with it. "You try, Uncle, an' it's the last dumb thing you ever do."

"Uncle? *Uncle?*" That pissed the white man off as much as Cincinnatus hoped it would. It was what Confederate whites called Negroes too old to get called *boy.* Throwing it in the local's face felt wonderful. "You can't speak to me that way! I'll talk to your officer, by God, and he'll teach you respect."

Cincinnatus laughed in his face. "You're the enemy, Uncle, and we done beat you. We don't need to waste respect on the likes of you."

Muttering under his breath, the local stomped off. Cincinnatus hoped he did complain to an Army officer. That would serve him right—wouldn't it just? Cincinnatus tried to imagine what the officer would tell him. He couldn't, not in detail, but it would boil down to, *Tough shit, buddy. Now fuck off and leave me alone.* He was sure of that.

Technically, Cincinnatus wasn't even in the Army. The U.S. Navy accepted Negroes, but the Army didn't—though he'd heard talk that that might change. If it did, it would matter to his son, but not to him. He was both overage and not in any kind of shape to pass a physical.

But he could still drive a truck. A lot of drivers were overage civilians, many of them with not quite disabling wounds from the Great War. They freed up younger, fitter men to go to the front and fight. And, when Confederate bushwhackers hit them, they showed they still knew what to do with weapons in their hands, too.

When Cincinnatus first volunteered to drive after getting back to U.S. territory, he'd carried a .45. He patted the ugly, functional submachine gun with almost the affection he might have shown his wife. Elizabeth had got him out of some tough spots, and so had the captured Confederate piece. And it didn't talk back.

U.S. 105s north of Ellijay thundered to life. Somebody—a spotter in a light airplane, maybe—must have seen Confederates up to something. With luck, the guns would disrupt whatever it was. Before long, Confederate artillery would probably open up, too, and maim or kill a few U.S. soldiers. Always plenty of fresh meat on both sides in war.

U.S. forces might push farther east from Ellijay, but they were unlikely to go farther north soon. They held this part of Georgia mostly to keep the enemy from bringing reinforcements down towards Atlanta. They didn't want any more of it—they were shield, not sword.

The drivers guarded their own trucks. Several men who weren't on sentry duty sat around a liberated card table playing poker. Soldiers probably would have sat on the ground, but it wasn't comfortable for geezers with old wounds and assorted other aches and pains. Green U.S. bills and brown C.S. banknotes went into the pot. They had good-natured arguments—and some not so good-natured—about what Confederate money was worth. Right now, in the drivers' highly unofficial rate of exchange, one green dollar bought about $2.75 in brown paper.

"Call," Hal Williamson said. A moment later, Cincinnatus' friend swore as his three sevens lost to a nine-high straight.

"Come to papa." The other driver raked in the pot.

Williamson got to his feet. "Well, that's about as much money as I can afford to lose till Uncle Sam gives me some more," he said.

One of the kibitzers sat down in the folding chair he'd vacated and pulled out a fat bankroll of green and brown. "I'm not here to lose money," he announced. "I'm gonna win me some more."

"Emil's here. We can start now," another poker player said. The guy with the roll flipped him off. The other man turned to Cincinnatus. "How about you, buddy? Got any jack that's burning a hole in your pocket?"

"Nope," Cincinnatus said. "Don't play often enough to get good at it. Don't like playin' enough to get good at it. So why should I throw my money down the toilet?"

"On account of I got grandkids who need shoes?" suggested the man sitting at the card table. "We need suckers in this here game— besides Emil, I mean."

"You'll see who's a sucker," Emil said. "You'll be sorry when you do, too."

"If you're no good at somethin', why do it?" Cincinnatus said.

"Well, there's always fucking," the other driver replied, which got a laugh.

"Maybe *you* ain't no good at that," Cincinnatus said, which got a bigger one. "Me, though, I know what I'm doin' there."

"That's telling him," Williamson said.

Cincinnatus' answering grin was crooked. Even his buddies seemed surprised when he held his own in banter or didn't turn cowardly when he got shot at or generally acted like a man instead of the way they thought a nigger would act. It might have been funny if it weren't so sad. These were U.S. citizens, men from a country where Negroes mostly had the same legal rights as anybody else, and they thought—or at least felt down deep somewhere—he ought to be a stupid buffoon.

What about white people in the Confederate States? His mouth tightened, the grin disappearing altogether. He knew the answer to that, knew it much too well. They thought Negroes were so far below ordinary human beings that they got rid of them without a qualm. And what would the local in overalls say about that? He'd probably say the Confederacy's Negroes had it coming.

"Fuck him, too," Cincinnatus muttered.

"Who? Dolf there?" Williamson nodded toward the poker player who'd gone back and forth with Cincinnatus. "What'd he do to you?"

"No, not Dolf. This peckerhead redneck I was talkin' with in town," Cincinnatus answered, not even noticing he was tarring the Confederate with the same kind of brush whites in the CSA used against blacks. "He reckoned I was uppity. If I was really uppity, I would've plugged the son of a bitch."

"Probably no great loss," Williamson said. "We're gonna have to kill a lot of these Confederate assholes to scare the rest into leaving us alone." Again, Confederate whites might have talked about Negroes the same way.

The next morning, soldiers loaded crates of 105mm shells into the back of Cincinnatus' truck. The convoy of which he was a part rattled north to replenish the guns that had been firing at the Confederates the day before. The artillery position was only a few miles away. Even so, a halftrack and three armored cars came along with the trucks. No one inside Ellijay seemed eager to take on the assembled might of the U.S. Army, but things were different out in the countryside. It seethed with rebellion.

Two bushwhackers fired from the undergrowth that grew too close to the side of the road before the convoy got halfway to where it was going. One bullet shattered a truck's windshield. Another flattened a tire. The armored cars sprayed the bushes with machine-gun fire. Cincinnatus hadn't seen any muzzle flashes. He would have bet the soldiers in the armored cars hadn't, either.

One of those cars stayed behind to help the truck driver with the flat change his tire—and to shield him from more bullets while he worked. Cincinnatus hoped the driver would be all right. He had to keep going himself. He wished a barrel with a flail were preceding the convoy. That way, it would probably blow up any land mines before they blew up people. As things were . . .

As things were, they didn't run into—or over—any. Cincinnatus figured the convoy was lucky. He also figured it had no guarantee of being lucky again on the way back. Who could guess what holdouts or stubborn civilians were doing while nobody in a green-gray uniform could see them?

Gun bunnies unloaded the crates. "We'll give 'em hell," one of them promised. Cincinnatus nodded, but the artillerymen couldn't do anything about the enemies likeliest to hurt him.

He wished he could stay by the gun pits. Bushwhackers didn't come around here. But then, as he was driving back towards Ellijay, he heard thunder behind him. A glance in the rear-view mirror told him the artillerymen were catching it. Wherever you went, whatever you did, the war would reach out and grab you and bite you.

Snipers fired a few shots at the trucks on the way back to the depot.

When they got there, one of the drivers said, "You guys are gonna have to help me out of the cab. They got me in the knee."

"Jesus, Gordie, how come you ain't screamin' your head off?" another driver asked. "How the hell'd you make it back?"

Gordie started laughing to beat the band. "On account of I lost that leg in 1915," he answered. "Fuckers ruined the joint in my artificial one, but that's about it."

"How'd you work the clutch without your knee joint?" Cincinnatus asked.

"Grabbed the leg with my hand and mashed down on the sucker," Gordie said. "Wasn't pretty. Don't figure I did my gear train any good. But who gives a damn? I made it back. 'Course, the leg's just a piece of junk without that joint. Better find me a wheelchair or some crutches— I ain't goin' anywhere without 'em."

Cincinnatus had a lot of parts that didn't work as well as they should have. He wasn't out-and-out missing any, though, and he never would have imagined that losing a leg could prove lucky for anybody. If they'd already got you there once, they couldn't do it again.

The supply dump stocked both wheelchairs and crutches. That didn't surprise Cincinnatus, although it saddened him. Maimed men were a by-product of war. The powers that be understood as much.

Gordie's leg went out for repairs. Technicians who dealt with such things were also necessary. When it came back, the amputee was full of praise. "Feels like I just got new spark plugs on my Ford," he said. "Joint's smoother and easier to work than it ever was before, I think. Quieter, too." He still walked with a rolling gait like a drunken sailor's, but so did anybody who'd lost a leg above the knee. The roll locked the joint till the next step. Cincinnatus also thought the artificial leg was quieter now than it had been.

Except for harassing fire as he drove his routes, everything seemed pretty quiet. He'd drifted into a backwater of the war. Part of him wanted to be doing more. The rest—the larger portion—thought that part was out of its tree.

III

George Enos, Jr., liked being back on the East Coast. When the *Josephus Daniels* came in to the Boston Navy Yard for refit or resupply—or even to deliver a package—he had a chance for liberty, a chance to see his wife and kids. Unlike a lot of sailors, he preferred getting it at home to laying down money in some sleazy whorehouse and lying down with a girl who was probably more interested in the current crossword puzzle than in him.

That didn't stop him from lying down with a whore every once in a while. It did leave him feeling guilty whenever he did. That, in turn, meant he drank more on liberty than he would have otherwise. He couldn't get drunk enough to stop feeling guilty, which didn't keep him from trying.

When he came into Boston, he didn't have to worry about it. He could go to bed with Connie with a clear conscience. And, being away so much, he felt like a newlywed whenever he did. Most of his married buddies weren't lucky enough to have caught a warm, willing, pretty redhead, either.

"I wish you didn't have to leave," she said, clinging to him with arms and legs the night before he was due back aboard his ship. When she kissed him, he tasted tears on her lipstick.

"Wish I didn't have to go, too," he answered. "But it'd be the Shore Patrol and then the brig if I tried to duck out. They'd bust me down to seaman third, too. You fight the Navy, you're fighting out of your weight."

"I know," she said. "But—" She didn't go on, or need to. *But* covered bombs and torpedoes and mines and everything else that could mean this was the last liberty George ever got. She clung to him tighter than ever.

He found himself rising to the occasion once more, which told how long it had been since his last liberty. In his thirties, he didn't do that as automatically as he had once upon a time. "Hey, babe," he said. "Hey."

"Ohh," Connie said when he went into her—more a sigh than a word. He wasn't sure he could come again so soon after the last time, but he did, a moment after she gasped and quivered beneath him. But then she started crying all over again. "I don't want you to go!"

"I don't want to, either. But I've got to." He stroked her hair and kissed her in the hollow of her shoulder, all of which made things worse instead of better.

Finally, after she cried herself out, she reached for a tissue and blew her nose. "Good thing the lights are out," she said. "I must look like hell."

"You always look good to me," he said, and that started her crying again.

He wasn't very far from blubbering himself, but he didn't. He did fall asleep a few minutes later. Connie couldn't tease him about that, because she'd already started to breathe deeply and slowly herself.

She fed him an enormous plate of bacon and eggs the next morning. The way the boys stared at it said how unusual it was. They ate oatmeal as they got ready for school. Connie ate oatmeal, too, and drank coffee that smelled like burnt roots. "Rationing that bad?" George asked.

"Well, it's not good—that's for sure," his wife answered. "Better for us than for a lot of folks. I know people at T Wharf, so I can get fish for us. We're tired of it, but it's better than going without."

"Sure." George remembered his mother talking about doing the same thing during the last war. All over the country, no doubt, people were doing what they could to get along.

What George could do was shoulder his duffel bag, kiss Connie and the kids good-bye, and head for the closest subway station. When he came up again, he was on the other side of the Charles, half a block from the Boston Navy Yard.

He and the duffel got searched before the guards let him in. "All right—you're not a people bomb," one of the men said.

"Has that happened here?" George asked.

"Not here at the Yard, no, but it sure as hell did in New York City. Twice," the guard answered.

"Jesus!" George said. "Nobody's safe anywhere any more. I'd rather put to sea. At least out there I know who's on my side and who isn't." With a nod, the guard waved him on.

Armorers were bringing crates of ammunition aboard the *Josephus Daniels*. They were eloquently obscene, creatively profane. George had heard that before among men with especially dangerous trades. It gave them a safety valve they couldn't find any other way. He paused not just to give them room but also to admire their invectives. He'd thought he'd heard everything, but they showed him he was wrong.

He was almost sorry when they finished and walked down the pier. "Permission to come aboard?" he called as he set foot on the destroyer escort's gangplank.

"Granted," answered Thad Walters, who had officer-on-deck duty. After the formal response, he unbent enough to ask, "Liberty good?"

"Yes, sir," George said. "Kids are growing like weeds. Connie pisses and moans about the rationing, but she's sure keeping them fed." He turned to salute the flag at the stern.

"Well, that's good." The grin on the OOD's face said he knew George and Connie didn't spend all their time talking about rations. He was younger than George himself. Chances were he didn't spend all his time thinking about Y-ranging gear, either. He went on, "Well, stow your gear below and get used to the ship again. You'd better—we put to sea tomorrow morning, early and"—he looked at the cloudy sky— "not too bright."

"Aye aye, sir." After his own apartment, the accommodations be-lowdecks were a rude reminder that he was back in the Navy's clutches. Everything was cramped and smelly. Instead of a bed to share with his wife, he had a hammock in a compartment full of snoring, farting sailors. If he tried to roll over, he'd fall out.

Some kid was bragging about how many times he'd done it in a whorehouse. Only a couple of guys were even half listening to him, and they mainly seemed interested in telling him what a liar he was. George thought the same thing. Anybody who boasted about what a great lover he was had to be lying, even if he didn't always know it.

Chow was another disappointment: some kind of hash and lumpy mashed potatoes. Connie would have been ashamed to put slop like that on the table no matter how bad rationing got. The coffee was better than hers, though. The Navy and the Army got most of the real bean that came into the USA; civilians had to make do with ersatz.

Maybe because he'd gone without real coffee for a couple of days and it hit him harder when he drank it again, maybe because his own mattress had spoiled him, he had a hell of a time going to sleep that night. He knew he'd stagger around like a zombie in the morning, but he lay there in the hammock staring up at the steel ceiling not nearly far enough above his head.

A pilot had brought the *Josephus Daniels* in through the minefields shielding Boston harbor from enemy submersibles. Another one took her out again. A small patrol boat followed the destroyer escort to pick up the pilot and bring him back. George stayed at his 40mm mounts till well after the pilot was gone. The powers that be had installed the guns to shoot at airplanes, but they could also do dreadful things to subs forced to the surface.

"We have ourselves a new assignment." Sam Carsten's voice blared from the loudspeakers. George still thought it was bizarre that he'd met the man now his skipper when he was a kid in Boston. Carsten went on, "We're heading for Bermuda, and then for the central Atlantic. We're going to try to find convoys bringing food up from Argentina and Brazil to England and France. And when we do, we'll sink 'em or capture 'em."

Excitement tingled through George. This was the work his father had done in the last war. It was what finally made Britain decide she'd had enough. And it was the work that cost his father his life.

"Some of you poor devils are polliwogs," the skipper boomed. "When we get to the Equator, King Neptune and the shellbacks aboard will take care of that."

George laughed. He'd been initiated into the shellbacks when he crossed the Equator for the first time. He could hardly wait to give the new fish a taste of what he'd got.

And he had another reason for wanting to get down by the Equator. The North Atlantic was kicking up its heels. He had a strong stomach, and he'd known worse seas than this in a fishing boat that made the *Josephus Daniels* seem as sedate as a fleet carrier. That meant he kept down what he ate. It didn't mean he enjoyed himself. And using the heads was rugged, because a lot of guys were desperate and weren't neat. Some of them didn't make it to the heads. The skipper had clean-ing parties out all the time. They almost kept up with the sour stink. Almost, here as in so many places, was a word nobody really wanted to hear.

The ship approached Bermuda from the northeast. That made for more time at sea, but lessened the chance of meeting C.S. bombers or seaplanes on the way in.

"No liberty here," Carsten announced as they tied up in the har-bor. "Sorry, guys. We don't have time. On the way back to the USA, I'll give you the best blowout I can, and that's a promise."

By the way the old-timers on the destroyer escort nodded, the skip-per kept promises like that. George wasn't surprised. Keeping them seemed in character for Carsten. Being a mustang, he knew what rat-ings liked better than most officers with Annapolis rings did. And one of the things they liked was officers who delivered on their promises.

Because of the threat from the Confederate mainland, the crew spent the night at battle stations, four hours on, four off. A handful of bombers did come over. Bermuda had Y-ranging gear far more power-ful than the set the *Josephus Daniels* carried; sirens started shrieking before the destroyer escort picked up the bombers.

And even after the ship did, the gunners were firing by earsight, hoping to get lucky or to nail a bomber caught by the blazing search-lights ashore. Yellow and red tracers crisscrossed the night sky.

U.S. night fighters were up over Bermuda, too. George wondered if they had their own Y-ranging sets. If they did, it didn't seem to do them much good. He heard the harsh crump of bombs—none very close—but saw no bombers going down.

Even after the all-clear sounded, ships and land-based guns kept throwing shells around. George was glad he had a helmet on. Shrapnel clattered down from the sky like sharp-edged hail. It could kill the people who'd fired it even if it didn't do a damn thing to its intended targets.

"Boy, I enjoyed that," he said when the other gun crew relieved him and his comrades.

"You be able to sleep?" his opposite number asked.

"Fuck, yes. I don't care if the Confederates come back and the noise starts up all over again. I'll sleep."

And, some time in the wee small hours, the Confederates *did* come back. They couldn't take Bermuda away from the USA, but they could make sure the United States didn't enjoy holding it. George opened his eyes when the shooting started again, then closed them and began to snore louder than ever.

The *Josephus Daniels* sailed the next morning, her tanks topped off and ammunition replenished. The Atlantic was a changed beast; as the destroyer escort steamed south, the ocean went from tiger to kitten. The sun shone warm and bright. The air turned sweet and mild. George was reminded of the weather in the Sandwich Islands. It didn't get any better than that.

British submersibles. French submersibles. Confederate submersibles. Misguided U.S. submersibles. Confederate seaplanes. Maybe even bombers and torpedo-carriers from a prowling British carrier. This part of the Atlantic was like the Sandwich Islands in more ways than the weather: it was also full of danger. Standing by the breech of the twin 40mm, George hoped he wouldn't follow in his father's last footsteps, as he'd already followed in so many.

Dr. Leonard O'Doull watched Sergeant Vince Donofrio chatting up a well-fed blond Georgia farm girl with a mixture of amusement and exasperation. The senior medic seemed to try his luck with everything female from fourteen to fifty. This one—her name was Billie Jean—fell toward the lower end of the range, but not so low that she didn't have everything a woman needed. She also had an inch-long cut on her left index finger, which was what brought her to the U.S. aid station in the first place.

Donofrio had given her a shot of novocaine and put a couple of stitches in the cut. In O'Doull's professional opinion, it needed nothing but a bandage, but Donofrio had motivation beyond the purely professional.

"I never reckoned Yankees could be so kind and helpful," Billie Jean said, which showed the sergeant had made some progress, anyhow.

"I'm a medic. We help everybody on both sides." Donofrio turned to O'Doull for support. "Ain't that right, Doc?"

"That's our job." O'Doull could hardly deny it—it was true. He said it himself, somewhere between once a day and once a week. Here, though, he wished he weren't agreeing with the horny sergeant. He'd never sewn up a pretty girl's wound in the hope of getting into her pants.

Then he shook his head and started to laugh. When he sutured a cut on Lucien Galtier's leg up in Quebec, that put him in the good graces of the man who became his father-in-law. It didn't hurt him with Nicole, either. Still, he wasn't inclined to look at Vince Donofrio and Billie Jean Whoozis and intone, *Bless you, my children.*

As if Vince cared. "Can I walk you home, sweetie?" he asked.

Billie Jean frowned. O'Doull gave her points for that. "I don't know," she said. "Some of the guys here, they don't like it if they see a girl walkin' with a Yankee." At least she didn't say *damnyankee.*

"Like I said, I'm a medic," Donofrio said. "I don't give trouble, and I don't want trouble." He had a .45 on his hip, just in case. So did O'Doull.

He also had the gift of gab, even though his boss was the Irishman. He talked Billie Jean into letting him tag along. And he talked O'Doull into letting him go, which was harder. "You be back in an hour, you hear me?" O'Doull growled. "And I don't mean an hour and one minute, either. I don't see you here in an hour's time, I send a search party out after you, and you won't like it when they find you."

"I promise, Doc." The senior medic crossed his heart. Billie Jean laughed.

Ten minutes later, corpsmen brought a soldier with a hand wound into the aid station. He'd passed out, or he would have come in under his own power. One look at the injury told O'Doull the hand would have to go. He hated to do it, but he didn't see any way to save the mangled remnants. He wished Vince were there to pass gas, but he could act as his own anesthetist.

"What happened to the guy, Eddie?" he asked as he put the ether cone over the wounded man's mouth and nose. "Do you know? This is about as ugly a hand wound as I've ever seen."

"I thought the same thing, Doc," the corpsman answered. "He was by a boulder when we found him, and the boulder had blood all over it. I'm guessing, but I'd say a big old chunk of shell casing mashed his hand against the rock."

O'Doull nodded. "Sounds reasonable. But he'll have to make do with a hook from here on out. I hope he wasn't left-handed, that's all."

"Didn't even think of that." Eddie looked and sounded surprised.

The amputation went as well as an operation like that could. The cutting was over in a hurry; patching things up, as usual, took longer. At last, O'Doull said, "Well, that's about all I can do. Poor bastard won't like it when he wakes up."

"Any other doc would've done the same thing—only not as well, chances are," Eddie said. They'd worked together a long time.

"Thanks," O'Doull said wearily. "I'd like a drink, but I think I'll settle for a cigarette." He stepped outside the aid tent to light up. He'd smoked the Raleigh almost down to the butt when he happened to look at his watch. An hour and five minutes had passed since Vince Donofrio decided to walk Billie Jean home, and he wasn't back. O'Doull swore in disgust. He didn't care if Vince had got lucky. The medic wouldn't think he was by the time O'Doull got through with him.

Finding soldiers for a search party was the easiest thing in the world. He waved to the first squad he saw coming up the road and told them what he needed. The Army had made him a major so he could give enlisted men orders. "Right," said the corporal in charge of the squad. "So what do we do if we catch him laying this broad?"

"Throw cold water on him, pull him off, and haul his sorry ass back here," O'Doull replied angrily, which made the soldiers grin. They went off with a spring in their step and a gleam in their eye.

When they weren't back in half an hour or so—and when Donofrio, shamefaced or not, didn't show up on his own—O'Doull started to worry. He almost welcomed a man with a leg wound. Patching it up let him think about other things besides the medic and why he might be missing. Why the devil had he let Donofrio go? But he knew the answer to that: because Vince would have sulked and fumed for days if he hadn't, and life was too short. But if life turned out to be literally too short . . .

By the time another hour went by, O'Doull began to dread what would happen when the search party came back. Then they did. One look at the corporal's face told him he hadn't wasted his time worrying. "What happened?" he asked.

"Both dead," the noncom said grimly. "Beaten, stomped, kicked—you name it, they got it, the guy and the gal both. We found 'em in a field not far from the side of the road. The medic's holster was empty, so his pistol's gone. Some goddamn Confederate's got it now."

"Jesus!" O'Doull felt sick. He'd never been responsible for a man's death like this before. Plenty of wounded soldiers had died while he was working on them, but he was doing his goddamnedest to save them. Here, one word—*no*—would have saved Vince Donofrio. It would have, but he hadn't said it. He forced out the next question: "What now?"

"Sir, I've already talked to a line officer," the squad leader said. "We beat the bushes for the motherfuckers who did it. We take hostages. We put out the call for the guilty bastards to give themselves up. Then we blow the fuckin' hostages' heads off." He sounded as if he looked forward to serving in the firing squad.

"Jesus!" O'Doull said again. "How many people are going to die because Vince thought Billie Jean was cute?"

"She wasn't cute when we found her, sir," the corporal said. "They . . . Well, shit, you don't want to hear about that. But she wasn't. Neither was he."

O'Doull crossed himself. "I shouldn't have let him go. But he liked her looks, and I didn't think anything would happen this time, so—"

"You never think anything'll happen *this* time," the corporal said. "Only sometimes it does."

"Yeah. Sometimes it does." O'Doull covered his face with his hands. "Here's one I'll carry on my conscience the rest of my life." Yes, this was much worse than losing a patient on the table.

"We'll get 'em," the corporal said. "Or if we don't, we'll get enough of the bastards who might have done it to make the rest of the assholes around here think twice before they try anything like that again."

"Fat lot of good any of that will do Vince," O'Doull said.

"Sir, I'm sorry as hell about that. It's part of the war around these parts," the corporal said. "Sooner or later, I expect we'll put the fear of God into the Confederates."

That wouldn't do Vince Donofrio any good, either. O'Doull didn't say so—what was the use? The noncom saluted and led his squad away. Eddie came up to O'Doull. "Not your fault, Doc," he said. "You just did what anybody else would've done."

"I guess so," O'Doull said. "But if it went wrong when somebody else did it, it'd be his fault, right? So how come it's not mine?"

"You couldn't know he'd run into bushwhackers," the corpsman said.

"No, but I could know—hell, I did know—he might, and I let him go anyway. Shit." O'Doull wanted to get into the medicinal brandy, but he didn't think he deserved it. He wished a wounded man would come in so he'd be too busy to brood about what had happened—he could drown his sorrows in work as well as alcohol. But the poor slob who'd have to stop something so he could get busy didn't deserve that.

After a while, deserving or not, a soldier with a smashed shoulder came in. Acting as his own anesthetist again, O'Doull did what he could to clean out the wound and fix it up. Eddie assisted, long on willingness but not on skill. *Have to get a new senior medic*, O'Doull thought. He'd worked with Granny McDougald for a couple of years, with Vince Donofrio for only about three months. Now somebody else would have to figure out his quirks and foibles.

The local commandant wasted no time. Soldiers seized hostages that afternoon. They gave the men who'd ambushed Vince and Billie Jean forty-eight hours to surrender. If not . . . Well, if not it was a tough war all the way around.

"Has anybody ever given himself up?" O'Doull asked Major Himmelfarb, who'd sent out the ultimatum.

"It does happen once in a blue moon," the line officer answered. "Some of these bastards are proud of what they've done. They're willing—hell, they're eager—to die for their country." He shrugged. "We oblige 'em."

No one came forward to admit to killing Vince Donofrio and the girl whose finger he'd sewn up. Major Himmelfarb asked O'Doull if he wanted to watch the hostages die. He shuddered and shook his head. "No, thanks. I see enough bullet wounds every day. It won't bring Vince back, either."

"That's a fact." Major Himmelfarb looked as if he wanted to call O'Doull soft but didn't think he could. Instead, he went on, "Maybe it will keep some other dumb, horny U.S. soldier from getting his dick cut off. We can hope so, anyway."

"Right," O'Doull said tightly, wishing the other officer hadn't told him that. Sometimes you found out more than you wanted to know. He hoped the medic was dead by then.

U.S. custom was to assemble the people from the nearest town— here, it was Loganville, Georgia—to witness hostage executions and, with luck, to learn from them. Nobody in the CSA seemed to have learned much from them yet. O'Doull listened to one flat, sharp volley of rifle fire after another in the middle distance: twenty-five in all. Before they got to the last one, he did dip into the brandy. It didn't do a damn bit of good.

He kept wondering if Billie Jean's father or brothers or maybe even husband (had she worn a wedding ring?—he didn't remember, and Vince wouldn't have cared) would show up at the aid station. Then he wondered if those people were part of the crowd that had got the girl and the medic. Would they have lulled them into a false sense of security before springing the trap? He never found out.

Eddie stayed in the aid tent as his first assistant for three days. Then the replacement depot coughed up a new senior medic, a sergeant named, of all things, Goodson Lord. He was tall and blond and handsome—he really might have been God's gift to women, unlike poor Donofrio, who only thought he was.

O'Doull greeted him with a fishy stare. "How hard do you chase skirt?" he demanded.

"Not very much, sir," Lord answered. Something in his voice made O'Doull give him a different kind of fishy look: did he chase men instead? Well, if he did, he'd damn well know he had to be careful about that. Queers didn't have an easy time of it anywhere.

"Make sure you don't, not around here," was all O'Doull thought he could say. "The guy you're replacing did, and they murdered him for it." Sergeant Lord nodded without another word of his own.

When a U.S. soldier came in with a bullet in the hip, Lord proved plenty capable. He knew much more than Eddie, and probably more than poor Vince had. The aid station would run just fine. That was O'Doull's biggest concern. Everything else took second place, and a distant second to boot.

Armstrong Grimes and his platoon leader crouched—sprawled, really—in a shell hole northeast of Covington, Georgia. Armstrong was wet and cold. A hard, nasty rain had started in the middle of the night and showed no signs of letting up. The Confederates had a machine gun in a barn half a mile ahead. Every so often, it would fire a burst and make the U.S. soldiers keep their heads down.

"Wish we had a couple of barrels in the neighborhood," Armstrong said. "They'd quiet that fucker down in a hurry. Even a mortar team would do the trick."

"Well, it's not that you're wrong, Sergeant," Lieutenant Bassler replied. "But what we've got is—us. We're going to have to take that gun out, too. We leave it there, it stalls a battalion's worth of men."

"Yes, sir," Armstrong said resignedly. It wasn't that Bassler was wrong, either. But approaching a machine gun wasn't one of the more enjoyable jobs infantry got.

"For once, the rain helps," Bassler said. "Bastards in there won't be able to see us coming so well."

"Yes, sir," Armstrong said again. He knew what that meant. They'd be able to get closer to the gun before it knocked them down.

"You take your squad around toward the back of the barn," Bassler said. "I'll lead another group toward the front. We ought to be able to work our way in pretty close, and then we'll play it by ear."

"Yes, sir," Armstrong said one more time. He didn't have anything else to say, not here. Bassler wasn't just coming along. He'd given himself the more dangerous half of the mission. You *wanted* to follow an officer who did things like that.

"All right, then. I'll give you ten minutes to gather your men. We'll move out at"—Bassler checked his watch—"at 0850, and I'll see you by the barn."

"0850. Yes, sir. See you there." Armstrong scrambled out of the hole and wiggled off toward the men he led. The machine gun opened up on him, but halfheartedly, as if the crew wasn't sure it was really shooting at anything. He dove into another hole, then came out and kept going.

"Password!" That was a U.S. accent.

"Remembrance," Armstrong said, and then, "It's me, Squidface."

"Yeah, I guess it is, Sarge," the PFC answered. "Come on. What's up? We goin' after that fuckin' gun?"

"Is the Pope Catholic?" Armstrong said. "Our guys go to the right, the lieutenant goes to the left, and when we get close whoever sees the chance knocks it out. Will you take point?"

Squidface was little and skinny and nervous—he made a good point man, and a good point man made everybody else likely to live longer. But even the best point man was more likely to get shot than his buddies. He was there to sniff out trouble, sometimes by running into it.

"Yeah, I'll do it." Squidface didn't sound enthusiastic, but he didn't say no. "Who you gonna put in behind me?"

"I'll go myself," Armstrong said. "Zeb the Hat after me, then the rest of the guys. Or do you have some other setup you like better?"

"No, that oughta work," Squidface said. "If anything works, I mean. If the guys at the gun decide to go after us—"

"Yeah, we're screwed in that case," Armstrong agreed. "You got plenty of grenades? Need 'em for a job like this."

"I got 'em," Squidface said. "Don't worry about that."

"Good. We move at 0850."

Armstrong gathered up the rest of his squad. Nobody was thrilled about going after the machine gun, but nobody hung back, either. At 0850 on the dot, they trotted toward the barn. The rain had got heavier. Armstrong liked that. Not only would it veil them from the gunners, the drum and drip would mask the noise they made splashing through puddles.

Somewhere off to the left, Lieutenant Bassler's men were moving, too. *Maybe it'll be easy*, Armstrong thought hopefully. *Maybe the guys at the gun won't know we're around till we get right on top of them. Maybe—*

The gun started hammering. Despite the rain, Armstrong had no trouble seeing the muzzle flashes. They all seemed to be aimed right at him. He yipped and hit the dirt—hit the mud, rather.

Nobody behind him screamed, so he dared hope the burst missed the men he led, too. He peered ahead. He didn't see Squidface on his feet, but nobody with his head on straight would have stayed upright when the machine gun cut loose.

He hoped the platoon commander and his guys were taking advantage of all this. They could be getting close . . .

Then the hateful gun started up again. This time, it was aimed away from Armstrong and his squad. "Up!" he shouted. "Get cracking!" He splashed forward. And there was Squidface, up and running, too. Armstrong breathed a silent sigh of relief. He'd feared he would lope past the point man's corpse.

They'd got within a couple of hundred yards when the machine gun cut off once more. "Down!" Squidface yelled, and suited action to word.

Armstrong threw himself flat, too. Three seconds later, a bullet snarled through the place where he'd been standing. That made the hair on the back of his neck stand up. Somebody behind him yowled like a cat with its tail in a rocking chair—Whitey, he thought. His mouth shaped the word *Fuck*.

Three or four guys from Lieutenant Bassler's group opened up on the machine-gun crew—they could see the Confederates better than Armstrong and his squad could. Then another machine gun farther back opened up on them.

This time, Armstrong said, "Fuck," out loud. He might have known—and Bassler might have known, too—that the Confederates would have one gun covering another. Once the men in green-gray knocked out this one, they would have to stalk the next. And if they didn't take more casualties doing it, God would have doled out a miracle, and He was as niggardly with them as a quartermaster sergeant was with new boots.

As soon as the gun in the barn swung back to Lieutenant Bassler's men, Armstrong and his squad rushed it. They hadn't given themselves away by firing, so the gun farther back didn't know they were around—and the men they were attacking didn't realize how much trouble they were in till too late.

Squidface threw the first grenade. Armstrong's first flew at the same time as the PFC's second. The Confederate machine gunners howled. The gun got off a short burst. This time, two bullets came closer to Armstrong than they had any business doing. Another grenade knocked the machine gun sideways. The soldiers in butternut who could still fight grabbed for their personal weapons. None of them fired a shot. Armstrong's men made sure of that.

"Turn the gun around," Armstrong said. "We'll let the assholes at the next position farther back know their turn's coming up."

None of his men was a regular machine gunner. But if you could use a rifle, you could use a machine gun after a fashion. They'd all practiced with them in basic training. And the C.S. weapon was about as simple to use as a machine gun could be. Squidface aimed the gun while Zeb the Hat gathered fresh belts of ammunition.

"You know," Squidface said as he squeezed off a burst, "this goddamn thing has a bipod, too. We could take it off the tripod mount and bring it along with us."

"Are you volunteering?" Armstrong asked.

"Yeah, I'll do it," Squidface said. "Why the hell not? We sure get a lot of extra firepower, and we can probably liberate enough ammo to keep it fed."

"It's yours, then." Armstrong was all for extra firepower. If Squidface wanted to carry the machine gun instead of a lighter rifle, that was fine with him.

The Confederates back closer to Covington realized what machine-gun fire coming their way was bound to mean. They returned it. Armstrong flattened out like a nightcrawler under a barrel. The Confederates shot a little high, so nobody got hit.

"Way to go!" Lieutenant Bassler's voice came out of the rain. "Shall we stalk these next assholes, too?"

A gung-ho lieutenant was good. A lieutenant who got *too* gung-ho wasn't, because he'd get people killed. "Sir, I have one man wounded, maybe two," Armstrong answered. "Let's round up a mortar team and see if we can drop shit on the bastards instead."

When Bassler didn't say yes right away, Armstrong got a sinking feeling. The platoon commander was going to tell him no. That machine-gun crew up ahead would be waiting for the U.S. soldiers to come at them—not a chance in hell for surprise. Armstrong didn't want an oak-leaf cluster for his Purple Heart.

But before Lieutenant Bassler could issue what might literally have been a fatal order, a couple of Confederates fired short bursts from their automatic rifles in the direction of the gun Armstrong's squad had just captured. Nobody got hurt, but the U.S. soldiers hit the dirt again. Armstrong jammed an index finger up against the bottom of his nose to kill a sneeze. *Wouldn't get a Purple Heart for pneumonia*, he thought, *but I'd sure as hell end up in the hospital with it.*

The extra gunfire convinced Bassler he'd had a bad idea. "They've got a regular line up there," he said. "That gun's not just an outpost, the way this one was. No point slamming our faces into it—a mortar team's probably a better plan. Good thinking, Sergeant."

"Uh—thank you, sir," Armstrong answered. When was the last time an officer told him something like that? Had an officer *ever* told him anything like that? Damned if he could remember.

Squidface winked at him. "Teacher's pet."

"Yeah, well, up yours, Charlie," Armstrong replied. "You want to charge a machine-gun nest when Featherston's fuckers are waiting for you, go ahead. Don't let me stop you."

"No, thanks," Squidface said. "Already got my asshole puckered once today. That's plenty. Hell, that's once too many."

"Twice too many," Zeb the Hat said. "Why ain't we twenty miles back of the line, eatin' offa tablecloths an' screwin' nurses?"

" 'Cause we're lucky," Armstrong said, which drew a chorus of derisive howls. "And 'cause no nurse ever born'd be desperate enough to screw you, Zeb."

"Huh! Shows what you know, Sarge." Zeb the Hat launched into a story that was highly obscene and even more highly unlikely. It was entertaining, though, almost entertaining enough to make Armstrong forget he lay sprawled in cold mud with an enemy machine gun not nearly far enough away.

A few minutes later, mortar bombs started bursting somewhere near that C.S. gun. Through the driving rain, Armstrong couldn't tell how close they were coming. "Hey, you guys at the gun, fire off a burst," Lieutenant Bassler said. "Let's see if they answer."

"I'll do it if you want, sir," Squidface said, "but if I was a Confederate I'd sandbag and see if I could lure us in."

"Fuck me," Bassler said. "Yeah, you're right. Maybe we'd better sit tight for a while, wait till reinforcements come up."

Armstrong liked that order just fine. He drew back into the barn and lit a cigarette. It wasn't so bad in here. It was dry—though the roof dripped—and nobody was shooting at him right this minute. What more could you want? *A horny nurse*, he thought, and then, *Yeah, wish for the moon while you're at it.*

Jorge Rodriguez had a stripe on his sleeve. Making PFC meant he got another six dollars each and every month. It meant he got to tell buck privates what to do. And it meant the Confederate Army didn't care that he was a greaser from Sonora. He'd convinced the people above him that he made a pretty decent soldier.

Sergeant Blackledge treated him no different on account of his promotion. Blackledge treated everybody under him like dirt all the time. And not just people under him—the sergeant had threatened to shoot General Patton if he didn't quit slapping a soldier with combat fatigue. As far as Jorge was concerned, that took more guts than bravery against the damnyankees.

"Hey, Sarge!" Gabriel Medwick called as Jorge sewed on his stripe. "How come I don't get promoted, too?" He sounded more than half joking—he and Jorge were buddies. He was tall and blond and handsome: the Freedom Party ideal. Jorge was none of the above. They got on well anyhow.

"Next time we need a guy, I reckon you will," Blackledge answered. "In the meantime, don't get your balls in an uproar. You can't buy more'n a couple of extra fucks on a PFC's pay, so if you get too horny to stand it in the meantime, just pull it out of your pants and beat it."

That made Jorge snicker, but it shut Gabe up like a gag—and turned him sunset-red, too. He was as innocent as if he'd been born into the previous century; Jorge wondered if he'd heard about the facts of life before the Army grabbed him. Girls would have fallen all over him, too. Hardly any of the girls in Georgia wanted to look at Jorge, much less do anything else. He wasn't a nigger, but he wasn't exactly white, either.

Georgia girls might not think he was good enough to lay them, but they thought he was plenty good enough to keep the damnyankees away. He crouched in a muddy foxhole on Floyd Street, in front of what had been the Usher House. He gathered it had been a local landmark before the war came this way. But U.S. artillery and air strikes had accomplished its fall. Half a dozen columns had stretched across its front. Now they—and the house timbers—were knocked every which way, like God's game of pick-up-sticks.

Orders were to defend Covington to the last man. Sergeant Blackledge had some lewd remarks about orders like that. Jorge understood why, too. The veteran noncom had no problems about killing Yankees. He'd done a lot of it. He was much less happy about the prospect of getting killed himself. Who wasn't?

But Jorge could also see why the powers that be issued those orders. U.S. forces were curling down from the northeast. Every town they took cut off one more route into and out of Atlanta. Every advance they made brought more roads and railroad lines into artillery range. If they kept coming, Atlanta would fall—or else they would just strangle it and let it wither on the vine. The Confederacy had to stop them somewhere. Why not Covington?

Rising screams in the air made Jorge duck down low and fold himself up as small as he could. He didn't need the shouts of "Incoming!" to know artillery was on the way.

Most of it came down in back of the positions his squad was holding. In a way, that was a relief. It meant there was less risk of a round's butchering him right this minute. But it left him worried about what was coming next. Were the damnyankees trying to cut the town off from reinforcements? If they were, did that mean they'd try to smash through soon?

"Barrels!" somebody shouted. Jorge could have done without such a prompt answer to his question.

If the U.S. soldiers thought they could waltz into Covington, they had to change their minds in a hurry. A rocket took out the lead U.S. barrel, and an antibarrel cannon set two more on fire. Confederate artillery pounded the poor damned infantrymen loping along with the barrels. The rain kept Jorge from seeing them, but he knew they'd be there. U.S. attacks worked about the same as the ones his side used.

Enemy fire eased. "Taught 'em a lesson that time," Gabe Medwick said.

"*Sí.*" Jorge nodded. "Now what kind of lesson they gonna try and teach us?" He had a Sonoran accent, but his English was good.

"They've gotta know they can't drive us outa here as easy as they want to," his pal said.

"*Sí*," Jorge repeated, and he nodded again. "But they don't always gotta drive us out to make us move."

"Huh?" Medwick might be blond and brave and handsome, but there were good and cogent reasons why nobody had ever accused him of being bright. That was probably a big part of why Jorge had a stripe and he didn't.

Jorge didn't try to explain things to Gabe. Life was too short. If he was lucky, he was wrong, in which case the explanation would only be a waste of time anyhow. He just said, "Well, we find out," and let it go at that.

More U.S. artillery came down on Covington. A lot of it landed up toward the front line. Yes, the Yankees were annoyed that the defenders didn't lie down and quit. Before long, the shelling eased up again and a U.S. officer approached under a flag of truce. "What the hell you want?" Sergeant Blackledge yelled.

"You fought well," the lieutenant answered. "Your honor is satisfied. Throw down your weapons and surrender and you'll be treated well. If you keep fighting, though, you don't have a chance. We can't answer for what will happen to you then."

Blackledge had to wait for a Confederate officer to answer that; it wasn't his place. After a couple of minutes, somebody did: "We're ordered to hold this position. We don't reckon you can drive us out. If you want to try, come ahead."

The lieutenant in green-gray saluted. "You asked for it. Now you'll get it." He turned around and went back to his own lines.

"Hunker down, boys! Hunker down tight!" Sergeant Blackledge yelled. "We went and pissed the damnyankees off, an' they're gonna try and make us pay for it."

Jorge pulled his entrenching tool off his belt and went to work with it. What he could do to improve his foxhole wasn't much, though. What U.S. guns could do to wreck it was liable to be a lot more. And the enemy's cannon wasted little time before they started trying to knock Covington flat again. Jorge swore in English and Spanish when he heard gas shells gurgling in and people shouting out warnings. Gas wouldn't do as much in the rain as it would on a clear day, but he still had to put on his mask. Raindrops on the glass in front of his eyes made him seem to peer through streaked and splattered windows. Could he shoot straight? If he had to, he had to, that was all.

"Barrels!" That shout filled him with fear, because even with an automatic rifle he couldn't do anything about a barrel. He had to depend on others to take care of that part of the job—and if they didn't, he was dead even though he hadn't made any mistakes.

But they did. That antibarrel cannon knocked out two more U.S. machines in quick succession. The rest pulled back instead of charging into Covington.

"You can't answer," Sergeant Blackledge jeered. "You ain't got the balls to answer, you stinking Yankee cocksuckers." Talking through the mask, he sounded as if his voice came from the far side of the moon. That made him seem more scornful, not less.

No more barrels drew within range of the gun. U.S. infantry didn't swarm forward, either. Machine gunners and riflemen—and the artillery—made the Confederates keep their heads down. Some of the machine guns were captured C.S. weapons. Jorge knew the difference when they fired. His own side's guns spat far more rounds per minute than the ones the USA made.

Like Blackledge, he thought the U.S. lieutenant was trying to bluff the defenders of Covington out of a position from which they couldn't be forced. The truth turned out to be less simple. With all those shells landing close by, he didn't want to stick up his head and look around. But before long he had to—he could hear something going on to the south.

Because of what the rain was doing to the lenses on his gas mask, he couldn't see very far. But things weren't going well outside of town, though his ears told him more about that than his eyes could. Barrels were moving forward there—forward from the U.S. point of view, that is. They had plenty of artillery and small-arms support, too.

What kind of line did the CSA have south of Covington? Jorge didn't know. Up till now, he hadn't worried about it. He realized that maybe he should have. Heavy fire came from a little east of due south. After a while, it came from due south. After another little while, it came from west of due south.

You didn't have to be a professor with frizzy, uncombed hair and thick glasses to figure out what that meant. The damnyankees had tried to force a breakthrough there, and it looked as if they'd done it. The next interesting question was what they would do with it. They didn't keep anybody waiting long for an answer. Shells and machine-gun bullets came into Covington from the south as well as from the east and north. There was also firing from southwest of town, which wasn't good. If the defenders held their ground much longer, they'd be hanging on to a surrounded town. Those stories didn't have happy endings.

Other soldiers saw the same thing. They must have—otherwise, why would they start slipping out of Covington to the west? And why would Sergeant Blackledge watch them slip away without ordering them to stop or, just as likely, shooting them in the back?

"We gonna get orders to pull out, Sarge?" Gabriel Medwick asked.

"Beats the shit out of me," Blackledge answered. "If we don't, though, we'll spend the rest of the war in a POW camp . . . if the Yankees bother taking prisoners. If they don't, we'll be lucky if they waste the time to bury us."

Jorge didn't worry much about what happened to his body once he was done using it. But he wasn't—nowhere close. And dying to keep a third-rate town out of U.S. hands for a few extra minutes struck him as a waste of his precious and irreplaceable life. "When you gonna go, Sarge?" he called.

"Pretty damn quick," Blackledge said. "This place ain't worth throwin' myself down the crapper for. Unless somebody orders me to stay, I'm gone." And if somebody did order him, he might suddenly become hard of listening. It wouldn't surprise Jorge at all.

Before long, a worried-sounding lieutenant said, "We'd better pull back. If we don't, they're liable to cut us off."

"Would you believe it?" Sergeant Blackledge said. "Boy, if the officers can see it, you know it must be obvious."

Despite the noncom's sarcasm, Jorge felt better about pulling back with the lieutenant's permission. U.S. forces didn't make it easy. As soon as they realized the Confederates were withdrawing from Covington, men in green-gray pushed into the town from the northeast. Two mortar bombs burst closer to Jorge than he cared to think about. Fragments hissed and snarled past him. He felt a ghostly tug at his trouser leg, and looked down to discover a new tear. But he wasn't bleeding.

Things got more dangerous, not less, when he left Covington behind. The Yankees who'd broken through to the south lashed the fields
with gunfire. Jorge was glad to scramble into a truck and get out of
there much faster than he could have hoofed it.

Gabe Medwick sat across from him. "We got to hold 'em some-
wheres, or else we ain't gonna keep Atlanta," he said. He might not be
bright, but he had no trouble seeing that. Who would?

"How can we hold, they keep pounding on us like this?" Jorge
asked.

"Beats me." His buddy shrugged. "But if we don't, we won't just
lose Atlanta. We'll lose the damn war."

You also didn't need to be bright to see that. Neither Jorge nor any
of the other wet, weary soldiers in the truck tried to argue with him.
They'd got out of Covington alive. Right now, that seemed more than
enough.

First Sergeant Chester Martin looked at his company's new transport
with a raised eyebrow. Command cars, halftracks, guerrilla-style pickup
trucks with a machine gun mounted in the bed . . . anything that could
move pretty fast and shoot up whatever got in the way. They were going
to head east from Monroe, Georgia, till they ran into something tough
enough to stop them . . . if they did. The Great War hadn't been like this
at all. In those days, both sides measured advances in yards, not miles.

Lieutenant Boris Lavochkin, Martin's platoon commander, didn't
remember the Great War or give a damn about it. Chester was supposed to ride herd on him, as he had with other young lieutenants. It
wasn't easy with Lavochkin, who had a mind and a cold, hard will of
his own.

Chester suspected Lavochkin wouldn't stay a second lieutenant
long. He had higher rank written all over him—if he didn't stop a Confederate bullet. But one of the things that marked him for higher rank
was a propensity for going where enemy bullets were thickest. Chester
would have minded less had he not needed to go along.

"My platoon—listen up!" Lavochkin said. And it *was* his platoon,
which surprised Chester Martin more than a little. "We're going to go
out there, and we're going to smash up every goddamn thing we bump
into. We're going to show these sorry clowns that their government and
their troops aren't worth the paper they're printed on. And we're going

to show them what war is like. If they wanted one so bad, let's see how much they want it when it's in their own backyard."

A savage baying rose from the men. Lavochkin was an unusual leader. He didn't make his soldiers love him. He made them hate the other side instead. And he left them no doubt that he felt the same way—or that he'd make them sorry if they were soft or hung back.

"Nobody's going to mind if you bring back goodies, either," he finished. "Lavochkin's Looters, that's us! They'll be howling from New Orleans to Richmond by the time we get through with 'em!"

That got another fierce cheer from the men. They liked the idea of making the CSA pay for the war. They liked the idea of lining their own pockets while they did it, too. Chester caught Captain Rhodes' eye. They shared bemused grins. Captain Rhodes was a pretty damn good company CO, but he didn't know what to make of the tiger now under his command, either.

The soldiers piled into their motley assortment of transport. Martin would have liked to get into a command car with Lieutenant Lavochkin, but Lavochkin didn't want him that close at hand. He climbed into a halftrack instead. Yes, it was the lieutenant's show, all right.

Nobody seemed to expect a U.S. force to head east from Monroe. Morrell's troops had been using the town as a pivot point for the move to isolate Atlanta. They held off C.S. attacks from the north and, that done, wheeled around Atlanta instead of trying to break in. But with the main city in Georgia still in Confederate hands, no one in butternut was ready for raiders to strike in any other direction.

Every time the U.S. soldiers spotted an auto or truck on the road, they opened up with their machine guns. What .50-caliber slugs did to soft-skinned vehicles wasn't pretty. What they did to softer-skinned human beings was even uglier. The shock from one of those thumb-sized bullets could kill even if the wound wouldn't have otherwise.

And when Lavochkin's Looters and the rest of Captain Rhodes' company rolled into High Shoals, the first hamlet east of Monroe . . . It would have been funny if it weren't so grim. The locals greeted them with waves and smiles. It didn't occur to them that soldiers from the other side could appear in their midst without warning.

Lieutenant Lavochkin showed them what a mistake they'd made. He sprayed bullets around as if afraid he'd have to pay for any he brought back to Monroe. Women and children and old men ran screaming, those who didn't fall. Glass exploded from the front windows of the block-long business district. And Lavochkin howled like a coyote.

When he opened up, everybody else followed his lead. Grenades flew. A soldier with a flamethrower leaped out of a halftrack and shot a jet of blazing jellied gasoline at the closest frame house. It went up right away.

High Shoals had to be too small to have a militia of its own. There were probably as many U.S. soldiers as locals in the little town. In moments, though, two or three people found old Tredegars or squirrel guns and started shooting back. Chester spotted a muzzle flash. "There!" he yelled, and pointed toward the window from which it came. A machine gun and several rifles answered, and no more bullets came from that direction.

The raiders hardly even slowed down. Leaving ruin and death and fire behind them, they went on along the road toward Good Hope, a town that was about to see its name turn into a lie. Good Hope might have been a little larger than High Shoals, but the people there were no more ready for an irruption of damnyankees than their fellow Georgians farther west had been.

In Good Hope, all the U.S. machine guns opened fire at once. People fell, shrieking and writhing and kicking. They looked like civilians anywhere in the USA. One of the women who caught a bullet was a nice-looking blonde. *Waste of a natural resource*, Chester thought, and fired his rifle at a man with a big belly and a bald head with a white fringe of hair. Another round caught him at the same time as Chester's. He didn't seem to know which way to fall, but fall he did.

When the shooting started, some people came rushing out of houses and shops to see what was going on. People always reacted like that. It was the worst thing they could do, but a good many did. They paid the price for mistimed curiosity, too.

Lavochkin shot up the filling station. That got a good blaze going in nothing flat. He whooped as flames shot skyward from the pumps. "See how you like it, you bastards!" he yelled. "Hope your whole town burns in hell!"

As in High Shoals, a few determined people in Good Hope tried to fight back. Bullets came from upstairs windows and from behind fences. Overwhelming U.S. firepower soon silenced the locals' rifles and pistols. But one alert and determined man drove his auto sideways across the street to try to keep the green-gray vehicles from going any deeper into Georgia. He paid for his courage with his life. A fusillade of bullets not only killed him but flattened three of the tires on the motorcar.

And in the end he delayed the U.S. column only a few minutes. A halftrack rumbled forward and shoved the hulk out of the way. "Good thing we didn't set the son of a bitch on fire," Chester said. "Then we would've had to look for a way around."

"Screw it," said the soldier sitting next to him. "We would've found one. C'mon, Sarge. You think these sorry civilian assholes can stop us?"

"Doesn't look like it—that's for sure," Chester answered.

East of Good Hope, the column bumped into a platoon of short, swarthy soldiers in uniforms of a khaki yellower than the usual Confederate butternut. Mexicans, Chester realized, probably out chasing Negro guerrillas.

Like the locals, the Mexican troops took a few fatal seconds too long to realize the approaching soldiers weren't on their side. Some of Francisco José's men waved and took a few steps toward the command cars and halftracks.

"Let 'em have it, boys!" Captain Rhodes sang out. Everybody who could get off a shot without endangering U.S. soldiers in front of him opened up. The Mexicans went down like wheat before the harvester. A few tried to run. A few tried to shoot back. They got off only a handful of rounds before they were mowed down, too. A U.S. corporal yowled and swore and clutched his shoulder. Chester thought he was the first U.S. casualty of the day.

Southeast of Good Hope lay Apalachee. Rhodes ordered the U.S. vehicles to stop about a mile outside of town. Lieutenant Lavochkin's broad features clouded over. "You're not going to let this place off easy, are you, sir?" he demanded. "That's not what we're here for."

"I know what we're here for, Lieutenant. Keep your shirt on." The company commander seemed to enjoy putting Lavochkin in his place. Chester Martin would have, too, but it wasn't always easy for a noncom. Rhodes went on, "Mortar crews—out! Let's give them a few rounds from nowhere before we pay our respects. That should make them good and glad to see us when we roll into town."

As the men with the light mortars set up and started lobbing bombs towards Apalachee, Lieutenant Lavochkin smiled a smile Chester wouldn't have wanted to see aimed at him. Lavochkin pointed it toward the enemy, where it belonged. He gave Rhodes the most respectful salute Martin had ever seen from him.

Apalachee might have been an ants' nest that somebody had kicked when Captain Rhodes' company came in. People were running every which way. Wounded men and women screamed. A few buildings had chunks bitten out of them.

A middle-aged man in a business suit ran toward the lead command car. The left arm of his jacket was pinned up: he had no arm to fill it. "Thank God you're here!" he yelled. "We got a call from Good Hope that there were Yankees loose, and then they went and mortared us."

"How about that?" Boris Lavochkin took aim with the command car's machine gun.

"Uh-oh," the Georgian said: the last phrase that ever passed his lips. He started to turn away, which did no good at all. Lavochkin's burst almost cut him in half.

People shrieked and fled. Bullets and grenades made sure they didn't get far. Wails filled the streets. Chester shot a man who was reaching into the waistband of his trousers. Did he have a pistol stashed there? Nobody except him would ever know now. The bullet from the Springfield blew off the top of his head.

"This hardly seems fair," said the private next to Chester. "Not like we're fighting soldiers or anything."

"They're all the enemy," Chester answered, working the bolt and chambering a new round. "If they can't find enough soldiers to keep us from getting at civilians, what does that say?"

"I bet it says we're winning." The private grinned. He had a captured C.S. automatic rifle, and lots of magazines for it. Unlike Chester, he hardly bothered aiming. He just sprayed bullets around. Some of them were bound to hit something.

"I bet you're right." Chester Martin shot a man who drove his auto into range at exactly the wrong time. The fellow might not even have known U.S. soldiers were loose in Apalachee. He didn't get much of a chance to find out, either.

Lieutenant Lavochkin shot up another gas station—he seemed to enjoy that. This one rewarded him with a spectacular fireball. Had he been closer when he opened up, the flames might have swallowed his command car.

"Whoa!" shouted the kid next to Chester. "Hot stuff!"

"Yeah," Chester said. "We're hot stuff, and the Confederates can't do much about it, doesn't look like. If we had enough gas, I bet we could make it damn near to the ocean."

"That'd be something," the private said.

But things stopped being so much fun not long after they got out of Apalachee. An enemy barrel blew a command car into twisted, burning sheet metal. U.S. soldiers leaped out of the vehicles that carried them and stalked the metal monster. It wasn't a new model, but it was plenty tough enough. It wrecked another couple of vehicles and shot several soldiers before somebody clambered up on top of it and threw grenades into the turret. That settled that: the barrel brewed up.

"Fools," Boris Lavochkin said scornfully. "They didn't have infantry along to protect it."

"They probably didn't have any to spare," Chester said. Lavochkin thought that over. Then he smiled again. Any soldier in butternut who saw that smile would have wanted to surrender on the spot.

Flora Blackford found a place to sit on the Socialists' side of the aisle. Congressional Hall was always crowded during a joint session. President La Follette hadn't called many. He seemed to think actions spoke louder than words. Oddly, that made his words resonate more when he did choose to use them.

The Speaker of the House introduced him: "Ladies and gentlemen, I have the distinct honor and high privilege of presenting to you the President of the United States!"

Charlie La Follette took his place behind the lectern. The lights gleamed off his silver hair. Along with everybody else in the hall, Flora applauded till her hands were sore. La Follette was an accidental President, but he was turning out to be a pretty good one.

"Thank you, ladies and gentlemen. Thank you," he said. "I come before you today—I come before the people of the United States today—to help right a wrong that has continued in our country for too long.

"We do not have a large number of Negro citizens in the United States. Most Negroes in North America have always lived in the Confederacy. This is partly our own fault, as we have been slow to accept refugees from the oppression that has long existed there.

"Not caring for a man because of the color of his skin is one thing.

Leaving him to die in a country that hates him is something else again. It is a mistake, a reprehensible mistake, and not one we will continue to make. Any human being, regardless of color, is entitled to live free. I will ask that legislation be introduced in Congress to make sure this comes true.

"And, I fear, we have committed another injustice. For too long, we have believed that Negro men lack the courage to fight for their country. We have never conscripted them into the Army or even let them volunteer. In the Navy, we let them cook food and tend engines, but no more. This is not right, not if they are men like any others, citizens like any others.

"As if further proof were needed, colored guerrilla fighters in the Confederate States have shown beyond the shadow of a doubt that courage is not a question of black and white. Without their brave efforts, our war against Jake Featherston's vicious tyranny would be even harder and more perilous than it is.

"No law prevents the enlistment and conscription of Negroes into the armed forces of the United States. We have relied on long-standing custom instead. I say to you that this custom will stand no longer. By its dreadful example, the Confederacy shows us how evil prejudice of any sort is. This being so, I have today issued an executive order forbidding discrimination on the basis of race in the recruitment, training, and promotion of all U.S. military forces."

He paused there, perhaps wondering what kind of applause he would get. Flora clapped hard. So did almost all the Socialists and Republicans listening to President La Follette. And so did most of the Democrats in Congressional Hall. Flora was sure Robert Taft would have if a people bomb hadn't killed him; he was a conservative, yes, but one with a strong sense of justice. Only a few reactionaries, men who harked back to the days when their party dominated the states that became the CSA and the attitudes that went with those days, sat on their hands.

President La Follette beamed out at Congress. He must have got a better hand than he expected. Sounding relieved, he continued, "Under the terms of the executive order, Negro men from the ages of eighteen to forty-eight will have sixty days to register for conscription at the center nearest their homes. Once registered, they will be selected at random on the same basis as whites—and, for that matter, on the same basis as Orientals and Indians. Failure to register within sixty days will lead to the same penalties for them as for anyone else who tries to evade conscription."

Flora wouldn't have talked about penalties right after lifting the bar of discrimination. She didn't think Al Smith would have. Charlie La Follette didn't have such sure political instincts. If he did, he might have got elected on his own hook instead of being chosen to balance the Socialist ticket. Instincts or not, though, he was getting the job done.

If a bomb blew Jake Featherston to hell, how would the Confederate States fare under Don Partridge? As far as Flora could see, the Vice President of the CSA was a handsome, smiling, brainless twit. She suspected Featherston chose him as a running mate because he was a nobody: not a rival, not a threat. The previous Confederate Vice President had tried to murder his boss, and by all accounts damn near succeeded. Nonentities near the center of things were safer. As long as Jake Featherston survived, it didn't matter. His ferocious energy drove the CSA. But if he died . . .

Wishing he would made Flora miss a few words of President La Follette's speech. When she started paying attention again, he was saying, ". . . and 1944 is only two weeks away. It will be the fourth year of the war. But I pledge to you, people of the United States, it will also be the last! This is our year of victory!"

A great roar went up from the assembled Senators and Representatives. They sprang to their feet, clapping and cheering. No one hung back, not the most ardently revolutionary Socialists and not the most hidebound Democrats. The only alternative to beating Jake Featherston was losing to him, and he seemed to have gone out of his way to show the United States how horrid that would be.

"The birthday of the Prince of Peace is almost here," La Follette said after the Congressmen and -women reluctantly took their seats again, "and we shall have peace. That is my pledge to you. We shall have peace—and on our terms."

He got another stormy round of applause. If the United States won the war by this coming November, he would get more than that: he likely *would* get elected President on his own hook. And he would have earned it, too.

Flora wondered whether he would threaten to rain a new destruction on the Confederate States if they didn't give up, the way the Kaiser had warned Britain and France. But he kept silent there. Thinking about it, Flora decided it made sense. Jake Featherston knew what the United States was working on. He was working on the same thing himself. If he got it first, he might win yet. Every U.S. bombing raid on the C.S. uranium project made that less likely, but you never could tell. The Confederacy's rockets warned that its scientists and engineers were not to be despised, even if its leaders were.

"North America must have peace," was the way Charlie La Follette chose to finish. "Four times now, during one long lifetime, war has ravaged our continent. It must never come again—never, I say! Before the War of Secession, the United States stood off England in the fight that gave us our national anthem and defeated Mexico to plant our flag on the Pacific coast. We dominated the continent, being the sole power at its heart. And, when this cruel war ends at last, we shall do the same again!"

There! He'd said it! That was probably more important than obliquely warning the Confederates about uranium bombs. Charlie La Follette had declared there would be no more Confederates, no more CSA, when the war was over. If he could go down in history as the Great Reuniter, wouldn't he make people forget about Abraham Lincoln and the way the United States fell to pieces during his luckless term in office?

Senators and Representatives contemplating the end of the Confederate States cheered even louder than they had before. It wasn't given to many men to be in at the birth of something wonderful. If you couldn't do that, being in at the death of something foul was almost as good.

Congressmen and -women crowded up to congratulate the President as he stepped down from the rostrum. Flora started to, but then changed her mind. Charlie La Follette would know how she felt. And she wanted to find out what Jake Featherston had to say about his opposite number's speech. She didn't think she would need to wait very long.

But when she got to her office, Bertha waved a message form at her. "Mr. Roosevelt would like to see you as soon as you can see him, Congresswoman," she said.

"Is he coming here, or does he want me to go to the War Department?" Flora asked.

"He called right when the President finished. When I told him I expected you back soon, he said he was on his way," her secretary answered.

Roosevelt got there about fifteen minutes later. He wheeled himself into Flora's inner office and closed the door behind him. "What's going on, Franklin?" she asked.

"Well, I'm afraid I have bad news, and I wanted you to hear it straight from me," the Assistant Secretary of War said. "The Confederates landed raiders in Washington State—we think by submersible—and they fired a good many mortar rounds at the uranium project."

"*Gevalt!*" she exclaimed. "How bad is it?"

"They did some damage, damn them. We're still trying to figure out just how much," Roosevelt replied. "Two or three mortar bombs hit one of the dormitories, too. We lost some talented people, and they won't be easy shoes to fill."

"How close are we? Can we go on without them?"

Franklin Roosevelt shrugged broad shoulders. "We have to. And we're getting very close. I don't know how much this will delay us. I'm not sure it'll delay us at all. But I'm not sure it won't, either." He spread his hands. "We just have to see."

"What about the Confederate project? Are we delaying it?"

"If we're not, it isn't from lack of effort. That town will never be the same, and neither will that university. But they're burrowing like moles, putting as much as they can underground. That's delaying them all by itself. They haven't quit, though. I don't think that bastard Featherston knows what the word means."

"They won't get another chance to do this to us. They've already had too many," Flora said.

"Charlie made a good speech there," Roosevelt agreed. "I bet Jake Featherston's mad enough to spit rivets."

"Shall we see?" Flora reached for the knob on her wireless set. Even after it warmed up, static stuttered and farted as she turned the tuner to a frequency Featherston often used. The USA and CSA kept jamming each other's stations as hard as they could. Richmond's main transmitter, though, punched through the jamming more often than not.

Sure enough, the Confederate President came on the air right away. "I don't need to tell you the truth, on account of Charlie La Follette just did it for me," Featherston snarled. "The truth is, he aims to wipe the Confederate States clean off the map. Charlie La Follette thinks he's Abe Lincoln. Turned out Lincoln couldn't wipe us out. Old Charlie'll find out the hard way he can't, either. I know the Confederate people won't let the country down. They never have. They never will. And

Charlie La Follette will hear from us real soon now. You bet he will. So long."

He wasn't kidding. At least a dozen long-range rockets slammed into Philadelphia in the next few minutes. One of them missed Congressional Hall by alarmingly little. Flora felt the jolt in the soles of her feet. The rockets didn't announce themselves. They flew faster than sound, so the *boom!* when they went off was the first and only sign they were on the way.

After the salvo ended, Roosevelt said, "He can annoy us doing that, but he can't beat us. And we can beat him on the ground. And we are. And we will."

"But how much will be left of us by the time we do?" Flora asked.

The Assistant Secretary of War stuck out his chin. "As long as we have one man standing after he goes down, nothing else matters."

As long as the one man we have standing is my son, nothing else matters, Flora thought. But Franklin Roosevelt had a son in the Navy. Maybe he was thinking the same thing.

IV

Major Toricelli stuck his head into Abner Dowling's office. "Sir, you've got a call from Philadelphia."

"Do I?" Dowling viewed the prospect without delight. "What do they think I've gone and done now?" Calls from the War Department, in his copious experience, seldom brought good news.

But his adjutant said, "I don't *think* it's that kind of call, sir. It's General Abell. Shall I transfer it in here?"

"You'd throw a fit if I said no. So would he," Dowling said. A moment later, the telephone on his desk rang. He picked it up. "Abner Dowling here."

"John Abell, sir," said the voice on the other end of the line, and Dowling recognized the brainy General Staff officer's cool, cerebral tones. "I hope you're well?"

"Tolerable, General, tolerable," Dowling replied. "Yourself?"

"I'll last out the war," Abell said, which might have meant anything or nothing. "I have a question for you: how would you like to come back to the East and command an army in what we hope will be one of the decisive attacks of the war?"

How would you like to go to bed with a beautiful blonde who's passionately in love with you? Yes, there were dumber questions, but not many. "What's not to like?" Dowling asked.

And John Abell told him what there was not to like: "Your army-group commander would be General MacArthur."

"Oh," Dowling said. MacArthur had commanded a division in

George Custer's army in the Great War while Dowling was Custer's adjutant general. When MacArthur led an army in northern Virginia this time around, Dowling had commanded a corps under him for a while. The two men didn't get along well—which was, if anything, an understatement.

"We could use you back in Virginia, sir," Abell said. "You have experience with aggressive offensive action, and you have experience fighting Freedom Party Guards. You'd do the country a service if you came back."

"And what would I do to myself?" Dowling asked. Brigadier General Abell didn't answer; he had to figure that out on his own. "Who would take over for me here if I left?" he inquired. "Still lots of work that needs doing."

"We were looking at giving Colonel DeFrancis a star and putting him in charge of Eleventh Army," Abell said. "He should handle it, and his coming from the air-operations side of things would be an advantage on such a broad front. Or do you think I'm wrong?" *Is there anything about Terry DeFrancis we don't know?* he meant.

"No, I'm sure he'll do a bang-up job." Dowling had to answer that quickly and firmly, so Abell would have no doubts. "He's a fine officer, and he knows the situation here, so he won't have to waste any time figuring out what's going on. He's young to make general, but wars do that."

"So they do," said Abell, who, like Dowling, had waited a long time for stars. "I'll see you here in Philadelphia, then, as fast as you can come. Orders will be cut by the time you get to the airstrip outside of Snyder. Take care." He hung up without waiting for Dowling's good-bye.

"Pack a duffel, Angelo," Dowling called to his adjutant. "We're on our way to Philly, and then to Virginia."

"Who takes over here?" Toricelli asked.

"Terry DeFrancis," Dowling replied. "My guess is, his telephone's ringing right about now."

Sure enough, DeFrancis' auto pulled up in front of Eleventh Army headquarters just as Dowling and Toricelli were ready to leave for the airstrip. "Congratulations on getting back to the real war, sir!" DeFrancis called as he jumped out.

"Congratulations to you, General," Dowling said. They shook hands.

"I've got a hot transport waiting for you at the field," DeFrancis said. "It'll take you up to Wichita. I don't know what they've got laid on for you after that, but General Abell sure sounded like he wants you in Philadelphia fast as you can get there."

Dowling and Toricelli threw duffel bags with enough personal belongings to keep them going for a little while into a command car. After one more handshake with DeFrancis, Dowling told the driver, "Step on it!"

"Yes, sir!" The corporal needed no further encouragement. He drove like a bat out of hell—perhaps like a bat a little too eager to go back there.

The two-engined transport took off with an escort of four fighters. Terry DeFrancis hadn't mentioned that. Dowling was grateful all the same. U.S. air power dominated the skies in west Texas, but the Confederates still got fighters up in the air every now and then. Even a hot transport was no match for a Hound Dog.

Neither the Texas Panhandle nor western Sequoyah had suffered too badly in the war. The fighting in Sequoyah was mostly farther east, where the oil wells were. Where the oil wells had been, rather. The oil fields had changed hands several times during the war. Whenever they did, the side pulling out blew them up to deny them to the enemy. The conquerors would start making repairs and then have to retreat themselves—and carry out their own demolitions. By now, Sequoyah's oil wells were some of the most thoroughly liberated real estate on the face of the globe.

In the last war, Sequoyah had started out as Confederate territory. C.S. cavalry raids terrorized Kansas till the USA slowly and painfully overran that state's southern neighbor. These days, though, Wichita was a backwater. The arrival of a major general, even if he was only passing through on his way somewhere else, made airport personnel flabble.

"Your airplane is ready and waiting, sir!" said the major in command of the field.

"Thanks," Dowling said. "Where do I go from here?"

"Uh, St. Louis, sir," the major said. "Didn't they tell you?"

"If they had, would I be asking?" Dowling asked reasonably.

He got into St. Louis just as the sun was setting. That was a relief: he wasn't sure they would have turned on landing lights for his airplane. Confederate bombers from Arkansas came up often enough to leave blackout regulations tightly in place.

At the airport there, they offered him the choice of a Pullman berth on a fast train east or a layover and the first flight out in the morning. He chose the layover. A bed that didn't bounce and shake had its attractions.

He spent less time in it than he would have liked. The Confederates came over at eleven and then again at two. Instead of a bed that didn't bounce, Dowling got two doses of a chilly trench. Bombs whistled down and burst too close for comfort. He wondered if he would be able to fly out the next morning.

He did. The raid left the airport with a working runway, and didn't hit the airplane waiting to take him east. On the way, he got a bird's-eye view of what the war had done to the United States.

Only occasional craters showed on the ground till he flew over what had to be eastern Indiana. From there on, it was one disaster after another: deserted, unplowed farmland, with towns and cities smashed into ruins. How long would repairing the devastation take? How much would it cost? What could the country have done if it didn't have to try to put itself together again? He couldn't begin to guess. That was a question for politicians, not soldiers. But a soldier had no trouble seeing the USA—and the CSA, too—would have been better off without a war.

Though Dowling didn't see what had happened to the Confederate States, he knew that had to be worse than what he was looking at. "If they were smart, they would have left us alone," he said to Major Toricelli.

"If they were smart, they never would have elected that Featherston bastard," his adjutant replied. Dowling nodded—there was another obvious truth.

His airplane landed outside of Pittsburgh to refuel. As it spiraled down toward the runway, he got a good look at what the battle had cost the city. His first thought was, *Everything*. But that wasn't an obvious truth. Smoke rose from tall stacks—and from some truncated ones—from steel mills that were either back in business or had never gone out of business. Nobody had bothered repairing shell-pocked walls or, sometimes, roofs. Those could wait. The steel? That was a different story. Trucks on the roads, trains in the railroad yards, and barges on the rivers took it where it needed to go.

When he got out of the airplane to stretch his legs and spend a penny, his nose wrinkled. He'd expected the air to be full of harsh industrial stinks, and it was. He hadn't expected the stench of death to linger so long after the fighting ended.

"Not as bad as the graves outside of Camp Determination," Toricelli said.

"Well, no. I don't think anything in the whole world is that bad," Dowling replied. "But this is what the Great War battlefields were like. Most of the ones this time around aren't so foul. They move faster and cover more ground, so there aren't so many bodies all in the same place."

"Except here there are," his adjutant said.

Dowling nodded. "Yeah. Except here there are."

Philadelphia was another bomb-pocked nightmare of a city, another place where factories sent up defiant plumes despite the destruction. A green-gray motorcar met Dowling at the airport. "I'll take you to the War Department, sir," said the bright young captain who accompanied the enlisted driver.

"How bad are these long-range rockets we hear about?" Dowling asked as the auto picked its way through streets often cratered and rubble-strewn.

"They sure aren't good, sir," the captain answered. "First thing you know is, they go boom—and if you're there when they do, then you aren't any more."

That was convoluted, but Dowling got the message. Damage grew worse as the auto got closer to the center of town. A lot of the rockets seemed to have fallen there. Dowling saw the finned stern of one sticking up, and curved sheet metal from a couple of more.

The War Department had taken lots of near misses but no direct hits Dowling saw. He had to show his ID before they let him in. Even after he did, they patted him down. No one apologized—it was part of routine. The captain took him down to John Abell's office. "Good to see you, sir," Abell said, his usual bloodless tones sucking the warmth from the words.

"And you," Dowling replied, which wasn't entirely true but came close enough. He pointed to a map of Virginia on Abell's wall. "What are we going to do to them?"

Abell got up and pointed. "This is what we've got in mind."

Dowling whistled. "Well, whoever came up with it sure didn't think small."

"Thank you," Abell said. That made Dowling blink; the General Staff officer was more likely to see what could go wrong than what could go right. This scheme, though, definitely counted on things going right.

"You really think they're on their last legs, don't you?" Dowling said.

"Last leg," John Abell replied. "They're standing on it in Georgia. If we hit them here, too, the bet is that they fall over."

"It could be." Dowling hesitated, then said the other thing he thought needed saying: "Is General MacArthur really the right man to knock them over?"

"If you want command of the army group, sir, you won't get it." Now Abell's voice was as icy as Dowling had ever heard it, which said a good deal.

"No, no, no. I wasn't asking for myself. After a question like that, I wouldn't take it if you gave it to me on a silver platter," Dowling said. "But if we've got somebody better than that scrawny bastard handy, we ought to use him."

The General Staff officer relaxed fractionally. "Since you put it that way . . . Well, General Morrell is busy in Georgia, which is also of vital importance. And General MacArthur is the man on the spot, and familiar with conditions."

"All right," Dowling said. It wasn't, not really, but he'd made the effort. "When we're ready down there, I'll do everything I can."

Clarence Potter was so glad to get away from Georgia and George Patton that he almost didn't mind shuttling back and forth between Richmond and Lexington every few days. President Featherston couldn't seem to make up his mind whether he wanted Potter to pick up his work in Intelligence again or act as liaison with the uranium-bomb project.

Either way, Potter figured he was better suited to the work than he was to commanding a division under Patton. As far as he could see, the only things that suited a man to command a division under Patton were a rhino's hide and an uncanny ability to turn off one's brain. That probably wasn't fair—Patton had grievances with him, too. Potter didn't much care. *Not* dealing with Patton was such a pleasure.

Of course, not dealing with the general meant dealing with the President of the CSA—and, incidentally, with Professor FitzBelmont. But

Potter had been dealing with Jake Featherston since the Great War, and he scared the living bejesus out of the professor. He could handle both of those jobs without wanting to retread his stomach lining twice a day.

FitzBelmont was a man facing a problem all too common in the CSA these days: he was trying to do a key job without quite enough men or resources, and with the damnyankees pounding the crap out of him from the air. Back before the United States found out what was going on there, Washington University had been a lovely, leafy, grassy campus. Potter remembered what a joy coming to Lexington had been after the devastation visited on Richmond.

Lexington was making up for lost time these days. Everything except the uranium-bomb project had abandoned the university campus, which looked like a real-estate poster for a subdivision in one of the ritzier neighborhoods of hell. The slagged and cratered earth might have caught smallpox. Ruins of what had been elegant, graceful buildings, many dating back before the War of Secession, offered a sorry reminder of better times. Only the square, brutal simplicity of reinforced concrete, ton upon ton of it, had any hope of surviving the Yankees' nightly visits.

Down below that concrete, the pile was turning uranium into jovium, which was what FitzBelmont had christened element 94. Enough jovium would go boom, just like U-235. Making it go boom, though, wasn't so simple.

"With U-235, we could shoot a plug into a hole in a bigger chunk, and then everything would go up," FitzBelmont said.

"Why can't you do that with the jovium, too?" Potter asked.

"Our calculations show it would start going off too soon and get too deformed for a full blast," the physicist answered.

"Well, you seem to think you *can* make it go off," Potter said, and Henderson FitzBelmont nodded. Potter asked what looked like the next reasonable question: "How?"

"We have to slam a lot of pieces down into a sphere—that's what the math says," FitzBelmont replied. "It's harder than making a U-235 bomb would be, because it's so much more precise. But getting the jovium is easier, because we can chemically separate it from the uranium in the pile."

"My chemistry prof at Yale told me transmutation was nothing but a pipe dream," Potter said.

"Mine told me the same thing." FitzBelmont shrugged. "Sometimes the rules change. They did here. Transmutation isn't chemistry—it's physics."

"It could be black magic, and I wouldn't care," Potter said. "As long as we say, 'Abracadabra!' before the damnyankees do, nothing else counts."

"They're doing their best to make sure we don't. Are we doing the same to them?" the professor asked.

"What we can. Getting to Washington State isn't easy for us, and it got tougher after they went and grabbed Baja California from Mexico," Potter said. Henderson FitzBelmont looked blank. He was no military man. Patiently, Potter explained: "It makes it much harder for us to get ships and subs out of Guaymas. But we did it not so long ago, and we attacked their facility."

"And?" FitzBelmont asked eagerly.

"And past that I don't know," Potter admitted. "The attack went in—that's all I can tell you for sure. The United States keep real quiet about their project, same as we keep quiet about ours. We haven't picked up any leaks to let us know what we did—none I've heard, anyhow."

"We can't hit them the way they hit us," FitzBelmont said mournfully. "And it looks like they started work on this before we did."

Potter had been worrying about those very things for quite a while now. Except for getting the latest strike at the Yankee project started, he couldn't do much but worry. "That means we have to be smarter," he told the physicist. "We're up to that, aren't we? If we make fewer mistakes and don't get stuck in blind alleys, we can still win. You're as good as anybody they've got, right?" *You'd better be, or we're history.*

"Yes, I think so," FitzBelmont replied. "They may well have more highly competent people than we do, though. And I worry about Germany a good deal. The Kaiser's physicists, and the ones he can draw from Austria-Hungary, are the best in the world. Has the President been able to get any technical help from *our* allies?"

"If he has, he hasn't told me," Potter said. "I'll ask him next time I'm in Richmond."

That was only a couple of days later. Traveling inside Richmond was safer by day. U.S. airplanes mostly came at night. Confederate defenses and fighters still made daytime raids too costly to be common. The bombers had taken a terrible toll all the same. Intact buildings stood out because they were so rare. The streets were full of holes of all sizes. The smell of death floated through the air.

The grounds to the Gray House might have been hit harder than anything else in Richmond. The United States wanted Jake Featherston dead. They wanted to avenge Al Smith, and they thought the Confederacy would grind to a halt without its leader. Potter feared they were right, too, which made him leery of plots against Featherston.

After going underground, after a couple of unpleasantly thorough searches, he was escorted to the waiting room outside the President's office, and then into Featherston's presence. The President's secretary sniffed as she closed the door behind him.

"Lulu doesn't much fancy you." Jake Featherston sounded amused, which was a relief. "She doesn't reckon you think I'm wonderful enough."

How right she is. But saying that was impolitic. "The country needs you. I know it." Potter could tell the truth without giving away his own feelings.

"What's the latest from Lexington?" Featherston asked, letting Lulu go.

"They're doing everything they know how to do, and the United States are trying to make sure they can't," Potter answered. "Do you know what we did in Washington State?"

"Something," the President answered. "They've had repair crews in there—I know that for a fact. Don't know much more, though."

How did he know even that much? A spy on the spot? Reconnaissance aircraft? Intercepted signals? Whatever the answer was, the word hadn't come through Potter. "How are things in Georgia?" he asked. The wireless didn't say much, which was never a good sign.

"We're going to lose Atlanta," Featherston said bluntly. "They didn't want to come in, so they're sweeping around. They want to trap our army in there and grind it to pieces."

"For God's sake don't let them!" Potter exclaimed. The President had thrown away one army in Pittsburgh. Didn't he see he couldn't afford to do that again?

He must have, for he nodded. "We're pulling out. We're wrecking the place, too. They won't get any use from it when they get in." He paused. "When Patton challenged you to a duel, did you really choose flamethrowers?"

"Yes, sir," Potter answered. "For a little while, I thought he'd take me up on it, too."

"That wouldn't've been pretty, would it?" the President said. Potter shook his head; it would have been anything but. Featherston went on, "He was spitting rivets at you, though. Let me tell you, he was."

"Let him spit rivets at the damnyankees," Clarence Potter said. "It would hurt 'em a lot more than some of the other things he's tried."

"Yeah, I know." Featherston scowled. "But who have I got who'd do better?"

Potter grunted. That, unfortunately, was much too good a question. He found a question of his own: "If we can't lick the USA no matter who we've got in the field, why are we still fighting?"

"Well, for one thing, they want unconditional surrender, and I'll see 'em in hell first," Jake Featherston answered. "And, for another, the longer we hold on, the better the chance FitzBelmont and the other slide-rule boys have of blowing 'em a new asshole."

Reluctantly, Potter nodded. The Confederate States had shown they were too dangerous for the United States to give them another chance to rebuild and try again. It was a compliment of sorts, but one the Confederacy could have done without now. As for the other . . . "What if they get a uranium bomb first?"

"Then we're fucked." Featherston's response had, at least, the virtue of clarity. "Then we don't deserve to win. But that won't happen, so help me God it won't. We are going to lick those bastards right out of their boots. You wait and see."

When he said it, Potter just about believed it—a telling measure of how persuasive Featherston could be. But afterwards, coming up aboveground once more, seeing the devastation that had been a great city, Potter shivered. How often lately had Jake Featherston taken a good long look at what had become of his capital and his country?

That afternoon, Potter and Nathan Bedford Forrest III walked through the disaster that was Capitol Square. Washington's statue still survived; not even a mountain of sandbags had saved Albert Sidney Johnston's. "What the hell are we going to do?" the chief of the General Staff said—quietly, so no passerby could hear.

"What the hell can we do?" Potter answered. "We're stuck between the Yankees and Jake Featherston. If we dump Featherston—if we kill him, I mean, because he won't be dumped—the United States land on us with both feet. And if we keep fighting—"

"The United States land on us with both feet anyhow," Forrest finished bitterly.

"They won't let us quit," Potter said. "They aim to wipe us off the map, same as they did in the War of Secession."

"Featherston never should have started this damn war," Nathan Bedford Forrest III said.

"Oh, cut the crap . . . sir," Potter said. His superior gaped. Not caring, he went on, "You aren't mad at him for starting the war. You were all for it. So was I. So was everybody. You're just mad because we aren't winning."

"Aren't you?"

"Sure, but at least I know why. I—" Clarence Potter broke off.

"What?" Forrest said, but then he heard it, too: the distant rumble of artillery suddenly picking up. He frowned. His eyes, which were more like his famous great-grandfather's than any other feature, narrowed. "Damnyankees haven't done that much firing for quite a while."

"They sure haven't," Potter agreed. "I wonder if they think they can catch us with our pants down here because we've moved so much stuff to Georgia." *I wonder if they're right.* He didn't say that out loud. Nathan Bedford Forrest III had enough to worry about, and the same thought was bound to be going through his mind.

The chief of the General Staff stood there listening, his head cocked to one side. After a minute or so, he shook himself; he might almost have come out of a trance. "I'd better get back to the War Department, find out what the hell they're up to," he said.

"I'll come with you," Potter said. Forrest didn't tell him no, even though he didn't have a formal place there any more. The gunfire went on and on. Halfway back to the War Department building, both men broke into a trot.

Cassius and Gracchus strode through the streets of Madison, Georgia. They both wore U.S. Army boots on their feet and green-gray U.S. military-issue trousers. Only their collarless chambray work shirts said they weren't regular U.S. soldiers—those and their black skins, of course. Even the shirts had Stars-and-Stripes armbands on the left sleeve. The Negroes were at least semiofficial.

Gracchus carried a captured C.S. submachine gun; Cassius still had his bolt-action Tredegar. Both of them were alert for anything that looked like trouble. Madison had only recently fallen to the United

States. The whites here didn't like seeing their own soldiers driven away. They were even less happy about Negroes patrolling their streets.

A couple of days earlier, somebody'd fired at one of Gracchus' men. The guerrilla got his left hand torn up. Madison got a lesson, a painful one. The U.S. commandant, a cold-eyed captain named Lester Wallace, grabbed the first ten white men he could catch, lined them up against a brick wall, and had them shot without even blindfolding them first.

"Nobody fucks with anybody under U.S. authority in this town," he told the horrified locals in a voice like iron, while the bodies still lay there bleeding. "Nobody, you hear?"

"Jesus God, it was only a nigger!" a woman shrilled.

"Anybody who comes out with that kind of shit from now on, I figure you just volunteered for hostage duty," Wallace said. "Far as I can see, the black folks around here are worth at least ten of you assholes apiece—I mean at *least*. They didn't start murdering people for the fun of it. You 'Freedom!'-yelling cocksuckers did."

"We didn't know what happened to the colored folks who got shipped out," an old man quavered.

"Yeah—now tell me another one. You give me horseshit like that, you're a volunteer hostage, too," Captain Wallace said. "You didn't know! Where'd you *think* they were going, you goddamn lying bucket of puke? To a fucking football game?"

Cassius didn't know what he'd thought Yankees would be like. This chilly ferocity wasn't it, though—he was sure of that. A lot of U.S. soldiers hated the enemy with a clear and simple passion that shoved everything else to one side.

"You know, I never had much use for smokes," a skinny corporal who needed a shave told Cassius out of the blue one day. "But shit, man, if Featherston's fuckers have it in for you, you gotta have somethin' going for you."

Was that logical? Cassius wondered what his father would have thought of it. But there was a brutal logic that beat down the more formal sort. *The enemy of my enemy is my friend.* That was working here.

It had a flip side. *The friend of my enemy is my enemy.* As Cassius and Gracchus patrolled Madison, Cassius said, "Ain't never gonna be safe for niggers around here without Yankees close by from now on."

"Reckon not," Gracchus said, "but how safe was it for us 'fore the damnyankees done got here?"

That question answered itself. His family hauled out of church and taken off to a camp. His own life on the run ever since. The precarious life black guerrillas led, knowing there would be no mercy if they got caught.

"Well, you got me," Cassius said.

They tramped into the town square. A bronze plaque was affixed to a small stone pillar there. Somehow, the little monument had come through the fighting that leveled half the town without even a nick. Gracchus pointed to the plaque. "What's it say?" he asked. Cassius had taught him his letters, but he still didn't read well.

"Says it's the Braswell Monument," Cassius said. "Says in 1817 Benjamin Braswell done sold thirteen slaves after he was dead so they could use the money to educate white chillun. Says they raised almos' thirty-six hundred dollars. Ain't that grand?"

"Sold niggers to help ofays. That's how it goes, sure as hell." Gracchus strode up to the Braswell Monument, unbuttoned his fly, and took a long leak. "Show what I thinks o' you, Mr. Benjamin fuckin' Asswell."

A couple of white women with wheeled wire shopping carts were hurrying across the square. They took one look Gracchus' way and walked even faster. "They don't like your dark meat," Cassius said.

"My meat don't like them, neither," Gracchus replied. "I start fuckin' white women, I ain't gonna start fuckin' no ugly white women, an' they was dogs."

They hadn't been beautiful. Some Negroes in U.S. service didn't care. They took their revenge on Confederate women for everything Confederate men had done to them. A few U.S. officers reacted as badly to that as Confederate men might have. Not everyone in the USA loved Negroes, not by a long shot. But most men who wore green-gray uniforms hated the enemy worse than the blacks he'd oppressed.

"Know what I feel like?" Gracchus said as he and Cassius resumed their patrol. "I feel like a dog that jus' pissed somewhere to say, 'This here place mine.'"

"Dunno if it's yours or not," Cassius said. "Sure as shit don't belong to the Confederate ofays no mo'."

As if to emphasize that, the U.S. troops had run up a barbed-wire stockade just outside of Madison to hold C.S. prisoners of war. Cassius wasn't the only Negro drawn to that stockade as if by a magnet. Seeing soldiers in butternut—and, better still, seeing Freedom Party Guards in brown-splotched camouflage—on the wrong side of the wire, stuck inside a camp, disarmed and glum while he carried a weapon, was irresistibly sweet.

"They gonna reduce your population!" a Negro from a different band jeered at the POWs. "They gonna put you on a train, an' you ain't never gettin' off!"

Some of the captured Confederates looked scared—who could know for sure what the soldiers on the other side would do? Some swore at the black guerrilla. One stubborn sergeant said, "Fuck you in the heart, Sambo. They already put your nappy-headed whore of a mama on the train, and she deserved it, too."

A few seconds later, he lay dead, a bullet through his chest. A U.S. corporal, hearing the shot, came running. "Jesus!" he said when he saw the corpse. "What the hell'd you go and do that for?"

The Confederates in the stockade were screaming and pointing at the Negro who'd fired. The guerrilla was unrepentant. "He dogged my mother," he said simply. "Ain't nobody gonna dog my mother, 'specially not some goddamn ofay fuckhead."

"Christ, I'm gonna have to fill out papers on this shit," the noncom groaned. "Tell me what the fuck happened."

Several POWs tried to. They did their best to outshout the guerrilla who'd killed the sergeant. Cassius weighed in to balance them if he could.

"He said *that* to this guy?" the corporal said when he finished.

"He sure did," Cassius answered.

"Shit on toast," the noncom said. "He told me that, I bet I woulda blown his fuckin' head off." The POWs screamed at him, too. He flipped them off. "Listen up, assholes—something you better figure out. You lost. These guys"—he pointed at Cassius and the other Negro—"they won. Better get used to it, or a hell of a lot of you are gonna end up dead. And you know what else? Nobody's gonna miss you, either."

"We won't ever put up with bein' under niggers!" a captive shouted.

"That's right!" Two or three more echoed him.

"Then I figure you'll be underground." The corporal pointed to the corpse. "Take your carrion over to the gate. We'll put him where he belongs."

He got more curses and jeers, and ignored all of them. After he went away, the other Negro stuck out his hand to Cassius. "Thanks for backin' me. I'm Sertorius."

"My name's Cassius." Cassius took the proffered hand. As he had with Gracchus, he asked, "Reckon we ever be able to do anything down here without the Yankees backin' our play?"

"No," Sertorius said calmly. "But so what? Yankees don't come down here, fuckin' Confederate ofays kill us anyways. They really did take my mama, God damn them to hell an' gone."

"Mine, too, an' my pa, an' my sister," Cassius answered.

"How come they miss you?"

"On account of I didn't go to church. That's where they got everybody else."

"I heard stories like that before," Sertorius said. "If there's a God, He got Hisself a nasty sense o' humor."

"Reckon so." Cassius had wondered about God even before the ofays got his family. He'd always kept quiet, because he knew his mother didn't want him saying—or thinking—things like that. He had the feeling his father was sitting on the same kind of doubts. The older man never talked about them, either. One of these days, the two of them might have had some interesting things to say to each other. They never would now.

The black guerrillas had a camp alongside that of the U.S. soldiers who guarded the POWs and made sure the lid stayed on in Madison. They slept in U.S. Army tents, and used U.S. Army sleeping bags. Those gave them better, softer nights than they'd had most of the time on their own.

They got U.S. Army mess kits, too, and ate U.S. Army chow with the men from north of the Mason-Dixon line. They didn't have to wait till the soldiers in green-gray were served before they got fed. They just took their places in line, and the cooks slapped down whatever they happened to have. Sometimes it was good, sometimes not. But there was always plenty. For Cassius, whose ribs had been a ladder, that was plenty to keep him from complaining.

When he went into Madison, kids would ask, "Got any rations? Got any candy?"

No. Starve, you little ofay bastards. That was always the first thought that went through his head. But hating children didn't come easy. They hadn't done anything to him. And some of them looked hungry. He knew what being hungry was all about.

Then one of them called, "Hey, nigger! Got any candy?"

He didn't shoot the boy, who must have been about eight. That would have got him talked about. He did say, "You call me a nigger, brat, you can damn well starve for all I care."

The kid looked at him as if he were crazy. "Well, what are you if you ain't a nigger?"

"A colored fellow, or a Negro, or even a black man," Cassius answered. "Call somebody a nigger, it's an insult, like."

"You're a nigger, all right, an' you suck the damnyankees' cocks," the brat squeaked. He didn't get a handout from Cassius, or a lesson. He also still didn't get shot, but he came much closer to that than to either of the other two.

He'd likely feel the way he did till the day he died. So would countless others just like him. In the face of hate like that, what *were* the surviving Negroes in the CSA supposed to do? After the war ended, how could they settle down and make a living? If U.S. soldiers didn't back them, how long would they last? Not long—that seemed only too obvious.

And if U.S. soldiers did back them, the white majority—much larger now than before the murders started—would hate Negroes more than ever . . . assuming such a thing was possible.

"We is fucked," Cassius said sorrowfully. "We is *so* fucked."

"What? On account o' that ofay kid?" Gracchus said. "Little shithead run his mouth like that, he get hisself killed goddamn quick, an' nobody be sorry, neither."

"No, not on account o' him," Cassius said, which wasn't exactly true. "On account of everything." He started to explain, then gave up. What was the use? Once upon a time, he would have found a place in Augusta—not the place he would have had if he were white, but a place. He would have fit in. Now?

Now he carried a Tredegar, and he was ready to kill any white who got in his way. That too was a place . . . of sorts.

Chester Martin smoked a cigarette outside of Monroe, Georgia, and waited for the next raiding party to head east. The company-strength expedition had proved what the brass thought before—the Confederates hadn't had anything worth mentioning to oppose a U.S. thrust. Why not try it again, in greater strength?

To Chester, the answer seemed obvious enough. If you hit them there once, wouldn't they get ready to make sure you couldn't do it again?

Lieutenant Boris Lavochkin looked at him—looked through him—with those cold, pale Slavic eyes. "You're welcome to stay behind when we go, Sergeant," he said.

"You know I don't want to do that, sir," Chester said. "But I don't want to get my tit in a wringer, either, not when I don't have to."

"No guarantees in this business," Lavochkin said.

He wouldn't listen. Everything had come his way for a long time now. He thought it would keep right on happening. And he wasn't the only one. The brass never would have signed off on a raid if they didn't think it would fly. Maybe they were right. Chester could hope so, anyhow.

He did talk to Captain Rhodes, who, he was sure, knew his ass from his end zone. "If they're laying for us, sir, we'll be all dressed up with no place to go," he said.

"What do you think the odds are?" the company commander asked.

"Well, sir, we sure as hell won't take 'em by surprise twice," Martin answered.

"No, but how much can they do about it?" Rhodes said.

"Don't know, sir," Chester said. "I bet we find out, though. If I wanted to be a goddamn guinea pig, I would've bought myself a cage."

That made Captain Rhodes grin, but he didn't change his mind. "We've got our orders," he said. "We're going to go through with them. If we run into trouble, I expect we'll have backup. But I think we have a decent chance to bang on through, same as we did the last time around."

"Hope you're right, sir." Chester didn't believe it. Nobody above him cared what he believed. To the men in his platoon, he was God the Father to Lavochkin's Son and Rhodes' Holy Ghost. To the officers above him, he was just a retread with a big mouth. And the fellows with shoulder straps were the ones whose opinions mattered.

Two mornings later, the long, muscular armored column rolled down the road from Monroe to Good Hope, the same road the smaller raiding band had traveled not long before. Chester thought that might surprise whoever was in charge of the Confederate defenders. They wouldn't believe anybody could be dumb enough to hit them the same way twice running. Chester had trouble believing it himself.

They didn't run into any traffic on the way to Good Hope. They also didn't run into any ambushes, for which Chester was duly grateful. Maybe the C.S. brass really couldn't believe their foes would try the same ploy twice.

Good Hope looked like holy hell. Only a couple of people were on the street when the U.S. command cars and armored vehicles rolled in. The Confederate civilians didn't think the green-gray machines were on their side this time. They took one horrified look, screamed, and ran for their lives.

Maybe that did them some good; maybe it didn't. Machine guns and cannon cut loose as soon as the U.S. column came into the little town, and didn't let up till it rolled through. Martin looked back over his shoulder after he was outside of Good Hope. Clouds of smoke announced that raiders were on the loose. If the enemy had telephone and telegraph lines back up from the last assault, people were already letting C.S. military authorities know about the new one.

If there were any C.S. military authorities in this part of Georgia . . . Perhaps there weren't. Perhaps the Confederate States really were falling into ruin. Chester could hope so, anyhow.

Trouble came between Good Hope and Apalachee. The road went through some pine woods. The column stopped because a barricade of logs and rocks and overturned wrecked vehicles blocked it. Getting barrels up to knock the obstruction aside wasn't quick or easy, not with trees of formidable size alongside the narrow, badly paved road.

And as soon as the column bogged down, C.S. troops in the woods opened up with automatic weapons, mortars, and stovepipe rockets. Chester didn't think there were a whole lot of them, which didn't mean they didn't do damage. Several soft-skinned vehicles and a halftrack caught fire. Wounded men howled.

U.S. soldiers hit back with all the firepower they'd brought along: heavy machine guns and cannon on their vehicles, along with the rifles and automatic rifles and submachine guns the men carried. Nobody could come close to the column and live, which didn't help all that much when it wasn't going anywhere.

After half an hour or so, U.S. barrels did shoulder the roadblock out of the way. The column went on, minus the vehicles put out of action. When the soldiers got to Apalachee, they tore into it even more savagely than they had at Good Hope. Not much was left of the hamlet when they came out the other side.

Chester hoped they wouldn't duplicate the whole route from the last raid. That would give the Confederates more chances to bushwhack them, and would also mean they were tearing up more stuff they'd already wrecked once. He nodded in approval when they left the road and started cross-country, heading as close to due east as made no difference.

Whenever they came to a farmhouse, they shot it up. If the people who lived there made it very plain they were giving up—if they came out with hands high—the soldiers let them flee with the clothes on their backs. If they showed fight or even if they just stayed inside, they got no second chances.

A startling number of rural Georgians seemed to think a few rounds from a squirrel rifle or a shotgun would set the U.S. Army running. They paid for their education. None of them would ever make that mistake, or any mistake, again. Often, their families died with them.

"That's kind of a shame, sir," Chester said as a woman trapped in a burning farmhouse and likely wounded shrieked her life away.

"Think of it as survival of the fittest," Captain Rhodes replied. "If they're dumb enough to fire on us, they're too dumb to deserve to live."

"She probably didn't have a gun," Martin said.

The company commander shrugged. "She was dumb enough to marry somebody who did. We aren't here to talk to these people, Sergeant. We're here to teach 'em that fucking with the United States is as dumb as it gets."

Inside the farmhouse, cartridges started cooking off. The woman's shrieks mercifully faded. "I'd say she's got the point, sir," Chester said. "Fat lot of good it'll do her from here on out."

Before Rhodes could answer, Chester and he both heard airplane motors overhead. They expected U.S. fighter-bombers to pound whatever lay ahead of them. Then a fearsome scream rose with the rumble. Chester had heard that noise too many times, though not so often lately.

"Asskickers!" he yelled, and threw himself flat.

Anybody who could get to an automatic weapon opened up on the vulture-winged C.S. dive bombers. The Mules ignored the ground fire and planted their bombs in the middle of the thickest concentrations of vehicles they could find. One landed right on a halftrack. The fireball caught a couple of nearby soldiers and turned them into torches. The

Asskickers came back again to strafe the U.S. soldiers. Machine-gun bullets stitched the ground much too close to Chester. He scraped away with his entrenching tool, not that it would do a hell of a lot of good.

And then the dive bombers were gone. Captain Rhodes looked around at the damage they'd done. "Fuck," he said softly. "You all right, Chester?"

"Yeah." Martin scrabbled in his pockets for a cigarette. "Boy, I forgot how much fun that was."

"Me, too," Rhodes said. "We've got used to dishing it out. That's a lot more fun than taking it."

"Bet your ass—uh, sir." Chester needed three tries before he could strike a match; his hands were shaking. Then he held out the pack to Rhodes. The company commander didn't waste time trying to light one on his own. He just leaned close to Chester and started his the easy way.

Lieutenant Lavochkin came up. "We ought to push on, sir," he said. "We can do a lot more damage before nightfall."

He didn't care about the air attack. All he wanted to do was keep hitting the Confederates. That was either admirable or slightly insane, depending. Captain Rhodes sighed and blew out a ragged plume of smoke. "We'll see to the dead and wounded, and then we'll go on," he said.

Some of the dead didn't leave enough remains to bury. Maybe the Confederates would tear up the graves the men in green-gray quickly dug, but Chester could hope they wouldn't. Plenty of C.S. soldiers lay in U.S. soil, for the most part quietly.

When the war was over, they would probably sort all of that out. They'd done the same thing after the Great War. By all the signs, this war was bigger and nastier than the one that had lasted from 1914 to 1917. What would they call it when it was done? The Greater War? The Worse War? Right now, it was just the War, commonly with an obscene adjective stuck on in front.

They did roll on after an hour or so, and took a would-be Confederate ambush from behind. The enemy soldiers seemed highly offended at that—those who lived through the encounter, anyhow. U.S. soldiers took prisoners, as much to keep their intelligence officers happy as because they really wanted to. One of the men in butternut complained, "Y'all weren't suppose to come where you did."

"That's what she said," Chester answered, which left his buddies laughing and the POW shaking his head.

Home guards and Mexicans tried to make a fight in Stephens and Hutchings, two little towns in front of Lexington. They got blasted out of the way in short order in both places. They were brave, but bravery and small arms and a few mines didn't go very far against halftracks and barrels. The two villages went up in flames.

Lexington was a tougher nut to crack. The defenders had a couple of quick-firing three-inch guns, leftovers from a generation earlier. For all Chester knew, they'd been sitting on the courthouse lawn ever since. If they had, somebody'd kept them well greased. And some old-timer— *probably a guy a lot like me*, Chester thought—knew what to do with them. Shells rained down on the advancing U.S. soldiers.

But the Confederates didn't seem to have any armor-piercing ammunition. Those three-inchers weren't made for barrel busting, anyway. They did hurt some men on foot and in soft-skinned vehicles, but that was enough to make the soldiers in green-gray angry without being enough to stop them. As the December sun went down, Lexington got the same treatment as the two smaller towns in front of it.

The U.S. soldiers camped in the ruins. "See?" Lieutenant Lavochkin said. "Piece of cake."

"Expensive piece of cake . . . sir," Chester said woodenly.

Lavochkin shrugged. "They paid more than we did. And we can afford it better than they can."

Both those things were probably true. In the cold calculus of war, they were also probably the only things that mattered. A guy who'd just stopped shrapnel with his belly cared about none of that. Chester lit a Raleigh and thanked God he hadn't.

One of the first things Dr. Leonard O'Doull found out about Sergeant Goodson Lord was that he hated his name. "My mother's maiden name, and I've got it for my first one," the new medic said. "If I had a dime for every time I got called Good Lord, I'd be a goddamn millionaire."

"I believe it," O'Doull said. "Didn't your folks realize what they were doing?"

"I doubt it," Lord replied. "Neither one of 'em's got much of a sense of humor, I'm afraid."

"How about you?" O'Doull asked.

"Me, sir?" Sergeant Lord gave him a wry grin. "I earned mine the hard way. It was either laugh or murder some yokking asshole before I was twelve years old."

"Well, I spent a couple of years working with a guy who answered to Granny," O'Doull said. "If I say Good Lord every once in a while, I may not be talking to you."

"Can't ask for more," Lord said.

"And I'll tell you one more time—careful about the women around here."

"Hey, I like screwing—who doesn't?" the noncom said. "I hope I'm not too dumb about going after it."

He didn't seem to swish now, even if O'Doull had wondered before. He was on the young side of thirty. Most guys his age would have said the same thing—unless they came out and admitted that they thought with their dick. "*Try* not to get murdered," O'Doull said earnestly. "I hate breaking in a new guy every couple of months, you know what I mean?"

"Sir, I will do my best," Sergeant Lord said.

He did his best with the wounded, too. He was at least as good as Vince Donofrio had been, and he was plainly a better anesthetist. O'Doull still missed Granville McDougald, but Lord would definitely do.

And the wounded kept coming in as U.S. forces cut off one road into and out of Atlanta after another. O'Doull worked like a maniac to keep the hurt men from dying or getting worse right away, then sent them off to field hospitals farther back of the line.

He spent quite a bit of time patching up a sergeant's left hand, which had taken a bullet through the palm. "I *think* he'll have pretty good function there," he said when the surgery was done. "Hope so, anyway."

"I bet he will, Doc," Goodson Lord said. "You really do pay attention to the little stuff, and it matters. I've seen some guys just stitch up a wound like that and let it go. They figure the doctor in the rear'll take care of it, and sometimes they're right and sometimes they're wrong. Myself, I always thought it was a lazy, shitty thing to do."

"I'm with you. The more you do right the first time, as soon as you can, the less you have to be sorry for later," O'Doull said.

Sometimes you couldn't do much. The corpsmen brought in a soldier in the mottled camouflage uniform of a Freedom Party Guard; he'd been shot through the head. "Why did you bother?" Lord said after one look at the wound.

"Well, you never can tell," Eddie answered.

That was true. Every once in a while, O'Doull got a surprise. But he didn't think he would this time. The wounded man was barely breathing. His pupils were of different sizes and unresponsive to light, his pulse reedy and fading. Brains and blood and bits of bone dribbled out of a hole the size of O'Doull's fist.

"I can clean things up a little, but that's it," O'Doull said. "He's in God's hands, not mine." He didn't think God would hang on tight, either.

The Confederate died halfway through the cleanup. He gave a couple of hitching last breaths and then just—stopped. "That's a mercy," Sergeant Lord said. "Other mercy is, he never knew what hit him. How many bad burns have you seen, Doc?"

"One is a million too many," O'Doull answered, and the senior medic nodded. When O'Doull thought of those, he didn't think of seeing them, though. The smell, like pork left too long in the oven, rose up in his mind as vividly as if a burned barrelman lay on the table in front of him.

And they got themselves a different kind of casualty, one brought in not by the medics but by an irate platoon commander. "Sir, this sorry son of a bitch has the clap," the lieutenant said in a voice that seemed barely done changing. "Isn't that right, Donnelly?"

" 'Fraid so," Donnelly said. "Hurts like hell when I piss."

"Well, we can do something about that," O'Doull said; guys with VD were just as much out of the fight as if Jake Featherston's men had plugged them. "Drop your pants, Donnelly, and turn the other cheek."

"You gonna give me a shot?" the soldier asked apprehensively.

"Yup." O'Doull readied the needle—a big one.

"I thought you got pills for the clap." Donnelly might well be fearless in the field, but he sure wasn't here.

"You used to. This penicillin clears it up faster and better, though," O'Doull said. "Now bend over."

"You fuck around, Donnelly, I'll have you bend over and I'll kick your sorry ass—I won't stick it," the kid lieutenant said.

By the expression on Donnelly's face, he would rather have got a kicking than a shot. But he saw he had no choice. He yelped when the needle went home. O'Doull pushed in the plunger with a certain malicious glee. "For Chrissake, wear a rubber next time," he said.

"It's like screwing in socks," Donnelly whined.

"Well, your sweetheart sure gave you something to remember her by," O'Doull said. "What did you give her?"

"Four cans of deviled ham. She was skinny as all get-out. How was I supposed to know she'd give me a drippy faucet?"

"You're supposed to think about shit like that," his platoon commander snapped before O'Doull could say anything. "How many times did you hear about it in basic?"

"Yes, sir," Donnelly said. O'Doull had a good notion of what he *wasn't* saying: that the only thing he'd cared about was getting his jollies.

That was natural enough. Of course, so was running away if somebody started shooting at you. Soldiers could learn not to. They could also learn not to screw without being careful. They could, but this one hadn't.

"Clap isn't the only thing to worry about down here," O'Doull said. "Medic who worked with me got murdered for laying a Confederate woman."

"I wasn't worried about that, sir. I wasn't worried about anything," Donnelly said.

He wouldn't listen. O'Doull could see that. "Well, pull your pants up and get the hell out of here," he said. "If you come down with another dose, so help me God I'll find a bigger needle." The threat might work if anything did.

It made Donnelly look worried as he covered himself again, anyhow. The lieutenant kept barking at him as he led him away from the aid station. "How often does that happen?" Lord asked.

"Every now and again," O'Doull answered. "At least this guy didn't have a chancre."

"Penicillin'll do for syphilis, too," Sergeant Lord said.

"Sure a lot better than the chemicals full of arsenic we used before," O'Doull agreed. "And before that it was mercury and all kinds of other poison."

The senior medic made a face. "I think I'd rather have the pox. A lot of the time, something else would kill you before it got bad."

"Maybe," O'Doull said. "But maybe not, too. A lot of the time, you'd get sick over and over, one thing after another. They'd all be different. They'd all *look* different, anyhow. But they'd all have syphilis at the bottom. Damn thing's the great pretender."

"You know more about it than I do, sir," Sergeant Lord said. "I played the trombone before I got conscripted. I knew some guys who had it, and it didn't seem to bother them all that much."

"Seem to is right," O'Doull said, and then, "The trombone, eh? Have one with you?"

"Afraid not, sir. It's not like a flute or even the trumpet—not so easy to carry around."

"Too bad. Well, maybe you can liberate one."

"Maybe." Goodson Lord looked dubious. "I've seen fiddles and pianos and guitars in these pissant Confederate towns, but that's about it."

"Well, let the corpsmen know. Let the guys in front of us know," O'Doull said. "You'd be amazed at what they can come up with—besides the clap, I mean."

"If I want that, I'll get it myself," Lord said. O'Doull snorted.

Since the medic didn't seem to want to spread the word, O'Doull did it for him. Inside of three days, Eddie produced a horn. "Here you go," he said. "Merry Christmas."

"I'll be a son of a bitch," Goodson Lord said. He took the trombone and started to play. Notes smooth and mellow as butter filled the tent. They made the Army bugles O'Doull was used to seem like screeching blue jays by comparison.

"Wow!" Eddie said. "You really *can* play that so-and-so."

"You think I was lying?" Lord asked, lowering the trombone.

"No, not like that," Eddie answered. "But there's playing, and then there's *playing*, you know? You're really good!"

"Oh. Thanks." The corpsman's enthusiasm made the sergeant blink. He started to play some more.

He got about thirty seconds into a number from *Oh, Sequoyah!* before a corpsman brought in a man with a piece of shrapnel in his thigh. "You can blow that thing, man," the soldier said. "Can you keep playing while the doc works on me?"

"Sorry," Lord said after a quick look at the wound. "I think we're gonna have to knock you out."

"Aw, hell," the wounded man said. As far as Leonard O'Doull could remember, that was the first time he'd ever heard a man ask *not* to be anesthetized.

Sergeant Lord got the patient etherized on the table. O'Doull cut away the man's trouser leg and started cleaning out the wound and tying off bleeders. He could see the femoral artery pulsing in there, but it wasn't cut. If it had been, the man likely would have bled out before he got back to the aid station.

O'Doull sewed him up and injected him with penicillin and tetanus antitoxin. "These aren't so bad," he said. "He should heal up fine."

"You do like to work on 'em when they turn out that way," Lord agreed. "How many amputations have you done?"

"I couldn't even begin to count 'em. They're like burns: more than I ever wanted to, that's for damn sure," O'Doull said.

"Yeah, same here," Lord said. "They're easy to perform, they're fast, and the patient usually comes through 'em pretty well. But you know he'll never be the same afterwards, the poor bastard."

"Ain't it the truth?" O'Doull said sadly. "Most of the time when I do an amputation, I feel more like a butcher than a surgeon."

"That's about the size of it," Lord said.

O'Doull wished they hadn't been talking about it, because the very next man the corpsman carried in had a foot and lower leg smashed beyond the hope of saving. The doctor pulled out the bone saw and did what he had to do. As Sergeant Lord had said, the soldier would probably pull through. Whether he would be happy about it was a different question. O'Doull wasn't likely ever to learn his answer to it.

Fayetteville lay south and even a little west of Atlanta. A rail line ran through it. Once the U.S. Army got astride that line, it would pinch off one more Confederate artery into the beleaguered capital of Georgia. Lieutenant Michael Pound didn't think the enemy would be able to hold Atlanta much longer after that happened.

Being a platoon commander, Pound wore earphones more often than he wanted to. Instead of doing as he pleased, he had to keep track of what the other units in the regiment and the other barrels in his platoon were up to. He thought it cramped his style.

"Marquard's platoon has lost three barrels at square G-5," a voice from somewhere in back of the line intoned. "Need armor there to cover the infantry advance."

Pound checked the map. If his platoon was where he thought, they were right on the edge of G-5 themselves. "Pound here," he answered on the same frequency. "We can cover. Do you know why they lost them? Over."

He waited. He didn't have to wait long. "Roger your covering," the voice said. "Report is that the losses are due to enemy barrels. Over."

"What the hell's wrong with Marquard?" Pound asked, but not with the TRANSMIT key pressed. He happened to know that the other lieutenant had new-model machines. To his way of thinking, you had to be worse than careless to lose three in a hurry to C.S. barrels. You damn near had to be criminally negligent.

He wirelessed the news to the other four barrels in his platoon. By what their commanders said, they felt the same way. "We'll take care of it," one of the sergeants promised. "Those butternut bastards can kiss their butts good-bye."

"Damn straight!" Pound said. He led a bunch of hard-charging pirates, men who thought the same way he did. "Let's go get 'em. Follow me."

He led the platoon west and a little south, to come in where the luckless Marquard had got in trouble. He hadn't got far before realizing the trouble might not be what he thought. There sat a dead U.S. barrel in a field—not just dead but decapitated, for the turret lay upside down, about ten feet from the chassis.

"Fuck," Sergeant Scullard said. "Where'd they get a gun that could do that?"

"Good question," Pound said, which didn't answer the gunner. He got on the platoon circuit again: "Be careful, guys. Use all the cover you can. I think Featherston's fuckers just came up with something new."

For most of a year, the latest U.S. barrels had dominated the battlefield. If they couldn't do that any more . . . then everything got harder. Michael Pound approved of easy, not that the enemy cared.

He flipped up the lid to the cupola and stood up in the turret. He needed to be able to *see*; the periscopes built into the cupola just didn't do the job. There wasn't a lot of small-arms fire. If the C.S. gunners who nailed that U.S. barrel opened up on him with an automatic rifle or a machine gun . . . that was better than having them shoot at his barrel with whatever monster gun they had.

One of the other barrels in his platoon was about a hundred yards to his left. He saw a blast of flame burst from a thick stand of bushes, heard a thunderous roar, and a moment later watched the other U.S. barrel brew up. The men inside couldn't have had a chance—and that gun, whatever it was, would be aiming at him next.

"Front!" he bawled as he tumbled back into the turret.

"Identified," Scullard answered. "I'm going to give it AP. I think a hull's hiding in there."

"I don't know. I didn't see one." But Pound added, "If you got a better look, go with what you think."

Mouradian had already slammed the round into the breech. The gunner fired the piece. The cannon's bellow was slightly muffled inside the turret. Smoke and fire spurted from the heart of the bushes. Michael Pound whooped and thumped Sergeant Scullard on the back. "Gimme another round!" Scullard told the loader. He fired again. More flames burst from the bushes. *Shame Moses isn't here*, Pound thought.

"Sir, I think that son of a bitch is history," Scullard said.

"I think you're right," Pound said. "And if you weren't so quick—and if you weren't so sure about what was hiding there—we would be instead." He spoke into the intercom: "Move forward—carefully. I want to see what the hell we killed."

"Yes, sir," the driver answered.

By the time Pound's barrel drew near, the bushes were burning briskly. Through them, he got a pretty good look at a low hull, a turret as smoothly curved as a turtle's carapace, and a gun that looked as if it came off a destroyer.

"Fuck," Scullard said again. "Gonna be a ton of work killing these babies."

"We can do it. You did it," Pound said.

"I know," the gunner said. "But they can kill us, too, easy as you please. I hope the Confederates don't have a lot of 'em."

"Me, too," Pound admitted. "We can't go marching around like no gun can touch us any more—that's for sure." Sometimes U.S. new-model barrels, confident in their armor, would almost dare C.S. machines to shoot at them. If you did that against one of these barrels, they'd bury your ashes in a tobacco pouch.

He got on the wireless to pass what he'd found to division HQ. "Roger that," came the reply. "We've had a couple of other reports about them."

The soldier on the other end of the connection sounded calm and relaxed. Why not? He was well behind the line. "Why the devil didn't you pass the word along?" Pound yelled. "You damn near got me killed!"

"We said the losses were due to enemy barrels," the wireless man answered, as if that were enough. He probably thought it was.

Pound took off the earphones. "We can beat the enemy," he said to nobody in particular, "but God help us against our own side."

"Headquarters being stupid again?" Scullard asked sympathetically.

"They'd have to wise up to get to stupid." Warming to his theme, Pound added, "They've got their headquarters in their hindquarters."

"And we're the ones who'll end up paying for it," the gunner predicted.

"Guy in one of our uniforms coming up," Mouradian said.

That sent Pound out of the cupola again, a captured Confederate submachine gun at the ready. Just because somebody wore a U.S. uniform, he wasn't necessarily a U.S. soldier. But he stopped by himself before Pound could tell him not to come any closer. "You nailed that fucker," he said. His harsh accent claimed he was from Kansas or Nebraska, but that didn't prove anything, either.

"Yeah," Pound answered. "And so?"

"More of 'em around—bound to be," said the U.S. soldier—Pound supposed he was a U.S. soldier, anyhow. "Can you clear 'em out?"

"Who knows?" Pound didn't just look at the monstrous machine his barrel had just wrecked. He looked back at the U.S. barrel the Confederates had killed. Those were five men of his, five friends of his, gone in the wink of an eye. He hadn't had even a moment to grieve. He still didn't, not really.

"Those other guys, they walked into a buzz saw," the infantryman in green-gray said. "Bam! Bam! Bam! They went out one after another. I don't think they ever knew what got 'em."

Pound hoped the men in the barrel from his platoon didn't know what got 'em. Was that a 4½-inch gun on the C.S. machine? A five-incher? Whatever it was, it was devastating.

A Confederate machine gun started snarling. The foot soldier threw himself flat. Pound ducked down into the turret. He got on the platoon circuit with the survivors: "We're moving up. For God's sake, watch it. We aren't the biggest cats in the jungle any more."

How many of those big barrels did Featherston's men have? How fast were they? How maneuverable? How well did they do on bad ground? A barrel's engine could be as important a weapon as its gun. But the gun in that bastard . . .

"Kinda revs up the pucker factor, doesn't it, sir?" Scullard said, which came unpleasantly close to echoing Pound's thoughts.

"Maybe a little," he answered, his voice as dry as he could make it.

He didn't want to admit he was scared, but he couldn't very well deny it, either. He got on the wireless: "Any chance of sending up some more armor to G-5? We don't know what's ahead of us, and it feels pretty naked around here."

"Well, we'll see what we can do," said the wireless operator on the other end of the line. He was sitting in a chair under canvas somewhere. For all Michael Pound knew, he was eating bonbons and patting a cute nurse on the ass to hear her giggle. He wasn't up here at the sharp end of the wedge, wondering if he'd cook like a pot roast in the next few seconds.

Two rounds of HE silenced that chattering machine gun. The country was pine woods and little clearings. Pound stayed away from the clearings when he could and dashed across when he couldn't. Somewhere ahead lay the Georgia Southern line, somewhere ahead and to the right the unreduced town of Fayetteville. If everything worked, the enemy would have to abandon it along with Atlanta. Pound had been confident. He wished he still were.

He also wished the enemy were still counterattacking. That would have made things easier. Then those big honking barrels would have had to show themselves. As things were, they lurked in ambush. The only way to find one was . . . the hard way.

Having foot soldiers along came in handy. Pound waited in the woods while the men in green-gray trotted across a field. A big round of HE slammed into the poor bloody infantry. Some U.S. soldiers went flying, while others flattened out and dug in.

"See where that came from, sir?" Scullard asked.

"Bearing was almost straight ahead of us—behind that twisted tree with the chunk of bark missing," Pound answered, peering through the periscopes. "If he's smart, he'll back away—he ought to figure our guys have armor with 'em."

"Maybe he'll get greedy instead," the gunner said.

Pound wouldn't have, but the enemy crew did. They fired twice more at the infantrymen in the field. They had good targets in front of them, and they were going to take advantage of it. To give them their due, they didn't have any room to retreat, not if the CSA wanted to hang on to the railroad line.

"Identify 'em now, Mel?" Pound asked.

"Oh, hell, yes," Scullard said, and then, to the loader, "AP!" He added, "Be ready for another round as fast as you can. If the first one doesn't do the trick, we've got to try again."

"Right," Mouradian said.

If the second one doesn't do the trick, we've got to get away—if we can, Pound thought. The C.S. barrel would know where the shots were coming from, and would answer. Pound didn't want to be on the receiving end of that reply.

The gun spoke twice in quick succession. Scullard didn't wait to see if the first round hit before sending the second on its way. As soon as he'd fired both of them, Pound shouted, "Reverse!" The barrel jerked backward.

No enemy antibarrel rounds came after it. Pound popped out of the turret to see what they'd done to the C.S. barrel. Smoke rose from behind the tree, an ever-growing cloud. He spotted motion back there—somebody'd got out and was running away. That impressed him in spite of himself. His own barrel wouldn't have let anybody inside survive, not after it got hit twice. The Confederates had themselves some deadly dangerous new toys here. He hoped like anything they didn't have too many of them.

V

Irving Morrell posed for U.S. photographers in front of the Atlanta city hall. New Year's Day for 1944 was chilly and overcast, with the wet-dust smell of rain in the air. Morrell didn't care. He would have posed for these pictures in the middle of a deluge.

"A year ago, we were still mopping up in Pittsburgh," he said. "Now we're here. We've done pretty damn well for ourselves, by God."

"Did you expect the Confederates to evacuate the city?" a reporter asked.

"They were going to lose it either way," Morrell answered. "The question was, would they lose Atlanta, or would they lose Atlanta and the army that was holding it? They saved a good part of the army by pulling out."

They'd saved more than he wished they would have. They'd started the evacuation at night, and bad weather had kept U.S. fighter-bombers on the ground, so their columns hadn't got the pounding they should have. Patton's army was still a going concern, somewhere over near the Alabama border. Morrell didn't know what his C.S. opposite number would do with the men he had left, but he figured Patton would think of something.

A rifle banged, not too far away. Holdouts and snipers still prowled Atlanta. The Confederates had planted lots of mines. They'd attached booby traps to everything from fountain pens to toilet seats. The Stars and Stripes might fly here, but the town wasn't safe, and wouldn't be for quite a while.

"How much does this victory mean?" another reporter called.

"Well, the enemy will have a lot tougher time fighting the war without Atlanta than he would have with it," Morrell said. "It was a factory town and a transport hub, and now he'll have to do without all that."

The reporter waved at the wreckage. "Doesn't look like he could have done too much with it even when he had it."

"You'd be amazed," Morrell said. "We've seen how places that look beaten to death can go right on producing till they finally change hands."

A plaque on the bullet-pocked terra-cotta wall behind him said ATLANTA RESURGENS, 1847–1927. The city hall had gone up in the brief spell of prosperity that followed the CSA's devastating postwar inflation. Then the worldwide economic collapse sucked down the Confederacy along with almost everybody else, and paved the way for the rise of Jake Featherston.

"What do you aim to do now, General?" another reporter inquired.

By his earnest voice and expectant look, he really expected Morrell to answer in detail. Some reporters never did figure out that their right to a good story stopped where it began to endanger U.S. soldiers. As gently as he could, Morrell said, "Well, I don't want General Patton to read about it in tomorrow's paper, you know."

"Will you drive west into Alabama or east toward the Atlantic?" This fellow was stubborn or stupid or both.

"Yes," Morrell answered. The reporter blinked. Some of his colleagues, quicker on the uptake, grinned. Morrell said, "That's about all, boys. Happy New Year."

A few more flashbulbs popped. He didn't mind that—the Confederates already knew he was in Atlanta. Bodyguards closed up around him as the press conference ended. He didn't care for the guards, but he didn't care to get killed, either. Enemy snipers would have loved to get him in their sights.

The State Capitol wasn't far away. A lot of people on his staff had wanted him to make his headquarters there. He said no, and kept saying no till they believed him. Demolition men were still going through the building, which looked like a scaled-down version of the Confederate Capitol in Richmond—at the moment, including bomb damage. They'd already found a couple of dozen booby traps there . . . and how many had they missed?

A small, none too fancy house a couple of blocks away seemed a better, safer bet. The demolition experts had swept it, too, and found it clear. The Confederates didn't have enough ordnance or time to booby-trap *everything*, which came as a relief.

Morrell had other things to worry about, plenty of them. Sitting on his desk when he got back were photos of wrecked new-model C.S. barrels. By all reports, they were half a step ahead of the U.S. machines that had dominated the battlefield for most of 1943. How far could that race go? Would there be land dreadnoughts one day, with twelve-inch guns and armor thick enough to stop twelve-inch shells? You could build one now. What you couldn't build was an engine that would make it go faster than a slow walk—if it moved at all.

He was glad the reporters hadn't asked him anything about the new enemy machines. He wouldn't have had much of an answer for them, except to note that the Confederates didn't seem to have very many. How long would that last? *Hit Birmingham harder by air*, he wrote. Notes helped him remember the million things he had to do. They were already dropping everything but the kitchen sink on the town. Have to throw that in, too.

A large explosion stunned the air and his ears. He ducked, not that that would have done him any good had the blast been closer. He hauled out his notebook again. *Hit Huntsville, too*, he scribbled. Intelligence said the Confederates made their rockets there. Not many of them had crashed down on Atlanta yet, but how long would that last? Not long enough—he was dismally sure of it.

He was also sure he couldn't do a damn thing about the rockets except smash the factories that made them and the launchers that sent them on their way. Once they got airborne, there was no defense.

If Featherston had had them from the beginning . . . That would have been very bad. He was content to leave the thought there. Neither side had all of what it needed when the war began. Part of what the war was about was finding out what you needed. He'd heard rumors that higher-ups in Philadelphia were all excited about some fancy new explosive. Maybe that would end up meaning something, and maybe it wouldn't. They'd throw money and talent at it and see what happened next. What else could they do?

Another big boom rattled his nerves. He didn't know if the enemy was working on super-duper explosives. The ordinary sort people had been using since the end of the last century seemed plenty good enough.

Now he had to figure out what to do himself. The reporter had given him his two basic choices: he could keep his original plan of driving to the sea, or swing west against Birmingham and Huntsville. If the War Department ordered him to go west, he would, he decided. Otherwise, he wanted to cut the Confederacy in half. If the offensive in Virginia came to something, where would Jake Featherston run then? And could the Confederate West stand on its own for long without orders from Richmond—and without Featherston's ferocious energy available to stiffen spines? Finding out would be interesting.

An aide stuck his head into the bedroom Morrell was using for an office. "Sir, the mayor of Atlanta would like to speak to you."

"He would, would he?" Morrell said. "So he didn't run away with the Confederate army?"

"I guess not, sir."

"Well, send him in, then. Let's see what he's got to say for himself."

The mayor had gray hair and was skinny as a rail. He introduced himself as Andrew Crowley. When Morrell asked him why he hadn't fled, he answered, "I wanted to protect my people, so I chose to remain." He threw back his head, a gesture straight out of a corny movie.

"That's nice," Morrell said. "How many Negroes are you protecting?"

"I was speaking of Confederate citizens, sir," the mayor answered, "not of Confederate residents." One word made all the difference in the world.

"They all look like people to me," Morrell said.

"You don't understand the way we do things in this country," Crowley told him.

"Maybe I don't," Morrell allowed. "Of course, if you hadn't invaded mine I wouldn't be down here now. Since I am, I have to tell you that murder looks a lot like murder, no matter who you do it to. I haven't got a whole hell of a lot of sympathy for you, Mr. Mayor."

"We did what the government in Richmond told us to do," Crowley insisted. "Don't see how you can go and flabble about that."

"Yeah, sure. Now tell me you never once yelled, 'Freedom!' in all your born days."

Andrew Crowley's hollow cheeks turned red. "I—" He stopped. Maybe he'd been about to deny it. But how many people could give him the lie—to say nothing of the horse laugh—if he tried?

"Here's what's going on," Morrell told him. "We'll try to keep your people from starving. We'll try to keep them from coming down sick. If they stay quiet, we'll leave 'em alone. If they don't, we'll make 'em sorry. Shoot at a U.S. soldier, and we'll take twenty hostages and shoot 'em. Kill any U.S. soldier, and we'll take fifty hostages and shoot 'em. Kill a Negro, and it's the same price. Got that? Is it plain enough for you?"

"You're as cruel and hard as the government warned us you would be," Crowley whined.

"Tough beans, Mr. Mayor." Was Morrell enjoying himself playing the tyrant? As a matter of fact, he was. "Your soldiers were every bit as sweet in Ohio and Pennsylvania. Only difference now is, the shoe's on the other foot. Hope you like the way it feels."

"You've got to be kidding," the mayor said. "Fifty people for a worthless nigger? If that's not a joke, it ought to be."

"Chances are you don't need to worry about it much," Morrell said. "I bet you've taken most of yours off to be killed by now. Isn't that right?"

"Even if it is, the idea's ridic—" Crowley broke off several words too late. He went red again, this time at what he'd admitted by letting his mouth run free.

"Get out of my sight," Morrell said. "I don't think we've got much to say to each other. You wouldn't like it if I told you what I thought. Just get out before I chuck you in the calaboose."

Crowley got. This probably wasn't the interview he'd wanted to have. Morrell didn't intend to lose any sleep about that. He went into the bathroom and washed his hands. He wasn't Pilate, turning his back on the truth. He knew it when he ran into it, and its touch disgusted him.

He was glad he was only a soldier. He didn't have to try to figure out how to administer captured C.S. territory on any long-term basis. All he had to worry about was making sure the locals didn't give his men too much trouble. The War Department didn't care if he got rough doing it. That suited him fine, because the little he'd seen south of the Ohio inclined him to be gentle.

A long lifetime earlier, this had been part of the country he'd grown up in, the country he served. It wasn't any more. Nothing could be plainer than that. Attitudes toward the USA, attitudes toward Negroes . . .

Jake Featherston hadn't been in the saddle here for even ten years. But the hatreds he'd exploited and built on had been here long before he used them to such deadly effect. You couldn't create those out of nothing. Without them, the black rebellions during the Great War wouldn't have had such lasting and terrible aftereffects. Did whites here have guilty consciences? They had plenty to feel guilty about, that was for sure. If they didn't, the CSA's Negroes never would have launched uprisings almost surely doomed to fail.

Will the Confederates go on fighting for the next eighty years even if we wipe their country off the map? That was Morrell's greatest dread, and the greatest dread of everyone in the USA who thought about such things at all. The Mormons were bad. Canada gave every sign of being worse. But the Confederate States? If these people stayed determined, they could be an oozing sore for a long, long time.

If the United States *didn't* wipe their country off the map, wouldn't they start another big war in a generation? And wouldn't that be even worse?

George Enos, Jr., was a shellback. You couldn't get to the Sandwich Islands from Boston by sea without becoming a shellback. That gave him the privilege of harrying the poor, hapless polliwogs aboard the *Josephus Daniels*. The sailors who hadn't crossed the Equator before paid for the honor of swearing allegiance to King Neptune.

The poor polliwogs got sprayed with saltwater from the hoses. Some of them were painted here and there with iodine. The cook who doubled as a barber cut their hair in strange and appalling ways. One rating who was inordinately proud of his handlebar mustache got half of it hacked off. Anyone who squawked got thumped, too.

Sid Becker, a chief petty officer who might have been the hairiest man George had ever seen, played King Neptune. His mermaids had mop tops for wigs, inflated condoms for breasts, and some kind of padding to give them hips. They also had hellacious five o'clock shadows, no doubt to emulate their sovereign.

Polliwogs had to kiss each stubbly mermaid and then kiss King Neptune's right big toe, which was as hairy as the rest of him. George and the other shellbacks whooped as they gave out what they'd taken when they were initiated into the fraternity of the sea.

Sweetest of all, as far as George was concerned, was that Myron

Zwilling was a polliwog. King Neptune didn't respect rank or anything else; that was a big part of what made the ceremony what it was. The exec did have the sense to know he couldn't complain about anything that happened to him.

He didn't have the sense to know he ought to look as if he were enjoying it. He went through it with the air of a man who had no choice. George wondered if he was noting who did what to him for payback later. He wouldn't have been surprised—that seemed like Zwilling's style.

After crossing the Equator, the ship got back to work: keeping Argentine beef and grain from getting across the Atlantic, and keeping the Royal Navy from interfering. She could do the first on her own. For the second, she had help from a pair of escort carriers: the *Irish Sea* and the *Oahu*. The limeys had carriers in these waters, too. If one side's airplanes found the other . . . there would be a big brawl.

George was glad Captain Carsten gave the crews so much gunnery practice. The more time he put in as a loader, the faster he got. The more shells the twin 40mm mount threw, the better the chance it had of knocking down an enemy Swordfish or Spitfire before the airplane could perpetrate whatever atrocity its crew had in mind. Maybe even more than the other sailors in the gun crew, George liked that idea. They hadn't been attacked from the air when they couldn't shoot back. He had.

Having their own airplanes along enormously extended how far they could see. A wireless call sent the flotilla steaming south after a convoy more than a hundred miles away. The enemy freighters and their escorts would have got away if the baby flattops hadn't joined the destroyers and cruisers in the South Atlantic.

"Keep an eye peeled for subs," Swede Jorgenson warned as the *Josephus Daniels* picked up speed. The new gun chief added, "Be just like the limeys to have a couple traveling with the convoy just to fuck us over."

Even though the destroyer escort had its fancy new hydrophone, that struck George as good advice. He scanned the blue water for a telltale periscope. Maybe it wouldn't help, but it sure couldn't hurt. He didn't want to die the way his father had. He didn't want to die at all, but especially not that way.

Fighters and dive bombers streaked off the escort carriers. These new carriers didn't seem to have torpedo airplanes aboard. Scuttlebutt said the brass had decided they were sitting ducks, and dive bombers could do the job better.

Reaching the enemy convoy took a while. The *Oahu* and the *Irish Sea* slowed down the rest of the U.S. ships. The baby flattops were no faster than any of their predecessors. "Snails with flight decks," Jorgenson said scornfully.

"Yeah, but they're *our* snails with flight decks," George answered, and the crew chief grinned at him.

"Now hear this! Now hear this!" Lieutenant Zwilling said over the PA system. "Our aircraft report one enemy destroyer sinking and one on fire. The convoy is breaking up in flight. That is all." That was plenty to set sailors slapping one another on the back.

They steamed on. Then the *Josephus Daniels* and another destroyer escort pulled away from the ships that still stayed with the airplane carriers. "Something's going on," Jorgenson said.

"Do you think so, Sherlock?" Marco Angelucci said. The new shell-jerker laughed to take any sting from the words.

"Wish the exec or the skipper would tell us what," George said.

He'd hardly spoken before Zwilling came on the PA again. "We are in pursuit of a pair of enemy freighters that broke north from the pack of ships in the convoy. Our purpose is the capture or incapacitation of these vessels."

"Boy, the skipper wouldn't talk like that," Jorgenson said.

"No kidding," George said. "He'd say something like, 'We're after two of the bastards who're trying to get away. We'll take 'em or sink 'em.' "

The gun chief nodded. "Wonder how come the exec doesn't talk like that."

" 'Cause he talks through his ass instead of his mouth?" Angelucci suggested.

When the ship swung farther east, George wondered why. Was a U.S. airplane shadowing the freighters and wirelessing their moves back to the *Josephus Daniels*? That was the only thing that made sense to him.

Then he let out a catamount whoop. His finger stabbed toward the horizon. "Smoke!" he yelled.

Before long, the freighter making the smoke spotted the exhaust spewing from the *Josephus Daniels*' funnels. The other ship sheered away, trying to run. The destroyer escort was slow for a warship, but had no trouble overhauling her. The four-incher in the forward turret boomed, sending a shot across her bow. A moment later, the Argentine flag came down from the staff at the stern. Sailors along the rail waved whatever white rags and scraps of cloth they could get their hands on.

"We've got her!" Sam Carsten's voice boomed from the PA. "We're going to put a prize crew aboard her and take her back up to the USA. Whatever she's carrying, better we have it than the damn limeys."

"A prize crew?" Jorgenson laughed out loud. "That's something right out of pirate-ship days. I wonder if the guys still get a share of what she's worth."

"Is that what they used to do?" George asked. "How do you know about that old-time stuff?"

"There's this limey writer, or I guess maybe he's an Irishman. Anyway, his name's C. S. O'Brian. He writes about fighting Napoleon like you're there. You think swabbies got it bad now, you oughta read what it was like way back when."

"Loan me one," George said, and Jorgenson nodded.

Lieutenant Zwilling came down from the bridge to choose the prize crew. A chief came with him, to serve out submachine guns to the men he picked. If the sailors on the freighter—her name was the *Sol del Sud*—tried getting cute, they'd be sorry.

"All old shellbacks," George remarked as the sailors crossed to the *Sol del Sud*.

"You noticed that, too, eh?" Jorgenson said. Now George nodded. On one level, it made sense; men who'd crossed the Equator before likely had more experience than men who'd been polliwogs only a few days earlier. But wasn't the exec taking off men who'd given him a hard time when he was getting initiated? It sure looked that way to George.

As soon as the boats came back from the captured freighter, the *Josephus Daniels* hurried off after the other ship she'd been assigned. "Damn lumbering scow couldn't've got far," George said.

She hadn't. Before long, smoke came over the southeastern horizon. Again, the destroyer escort had no trouble running her down. Again, a shot crashed across her bow. She was the *Tierra del Fuego*, by looks a near twin to the *Sol del Sud*, but her captain seemed more stubborn. Another shot from the four-incher thundered past her, this one just in front of her bridge. "Next one we'll hit you with!" Carsten thundered over the PA. The *Tierra del Fuego* struck her colors.

Lieutenant Zwilling pointed at George. "Enos, go aboard her," he snapped. The CPO handed George a tommy gun and several drums of ammo.

George said the only thing he could: "Aye aye, sir." Maybe they'd take her back to Boston. He could hope so, anyhow. But yeah, the exec was clearing the destroyer escort of the people who'd had too good a time when he suffered with the other polliwogs.

One of the rubber-breasted mermaids and King Neptune himself were also in the prize crew: the CPO held command. When George told Becker what was going on, he shrugged and said, "I bet you're right, but I don't care. Zwilling ain't as smart as he thinks he is. I bring this baby in all right, maybe I go up through the hawse hole like the skipper. Only chance I got—I sure as hell can't pass the goddamn exam. Lord knows I've tried."

When George got up on the *Tierra del Fuego*'s deck, he eyed the sailors standing there. Would they give trouble, or were they just glad his ship hadn't sunk them? "Any of you guys speak English?" he asked.

Two men raised their hands—the skipper and a fellow with a lightning-bolt patch on his sleeve. *The wireless man*, George thought. "I do," the fellow said.

"Good. Tell your pals nobody's gonna hurt 'em as long as they do what we say," George said. "They'll be POWs in the USA, and they'll go home after the war." The wireless man rattled off some Spanish. A moment later, one of the sailors from the *Josephus Daniels* knocked him down and yelled at him, also in Spanish.

"Any of these assholes says anything with *puto* or *chinga* or *maricón* in it, beat the shit out of him, 'cause he's cussin' you," the sailor said. "They ain't gonna dick around with us." He spoke in Spanish to the would-be interpreter, then came back to English: "I told him to try it again, only not to get cute this time."

A couple of men from the destroyer escort's black gang went below to look at the engines. One of them came back up shaking his head. "They're oil-burners—she'd make even more smoke if they weren't," he reported. "But they're about as old as they can be and still burn oil. Ain't no surprise she couldn't outrun us."

Chief Becker took charge of the pistol and the couple of shotguns in the *Tierra del Fuego*'s arms locker. "Don't look like she ever had anything more," he said. "Enough to try and put down a mutiny, and that's about it."

At his orders, the freighter's sailors pointed her bow north and got her up to about eight knots. She lumbered along. George would rather have gone north aboard a fishing boat. It would have bounced worse, but it would have gone over the waves instead of trying to slice through them. He didn't look forward to riding out a gale in this wallowing tub.

Before long, they recrossed the Equator. Nobody asked whether any of the Argentine sailors were polliwogs. George didn't know whether the greasers talked about King Neptune. All he knew was that he had to keep an eye on them.

Day followed day. The chow on the *Tierra del Fuego* was different from what he would have eaten on the *Josephus Daniels*—not really better or worse, but different. He tried *yerba maté* tea. The stuff wasn't bad: better than he expected. It had more kick than regular tea, not so much as coffee.

If a British or Confederate seaplane spotted them flying the Stars and Stripes, they were history. George tried not to think about that. He blessed the fogs and mists that shrouded the *Tierra del Fuego* as she got farther north. They made navigation harder, but she was going by the seat of her pants anyway. When she came closer to the U.S. coast, no doubt she'd get an escort for the last leg of her journey. She'd need one, too.

In the meantime . . . In the meantime, it was just the ship and the sea. For George, that wasn't so bad.

Richmond. The front was Richmond. In the bunker under the ruins of the Gray House, Jake Featherston shook his fist toward the north and cursed a God Who seemed to be cursing him and the CSA.

Ever since the war started, people were saying that whoever could do two big things at once would win. The Confederacy had never managed it. Neither had the damnyankees . . . till now. They were still going great guns down in Georgia. And they were pushing out of the Wilderness and heading straight for the Confederate capital.

U.S. artillery hadn't fallen on Richmond yet. The ground between the Rapidan and the capital was likely the most heavily fortified stretch on the face of the earth. If the Yankees came, they had to come that way. Both sides knew it. Whatever artifice could do to stop them, artifice had done.

But along with artifice, the Confederate States needed men—men they didn't have. Too many soldiers had died in the Great War. Too many had died or gone off into captivity in Ohio and especially Pennsylvania this time around. And too many were doing everything they could to fight the USA farther south. That left a lot of the bunkers and gun emplacements between the Rapidan and Richmond nothing more than . . . what did the Bible call them? Whited sepulchers, that was it.

Featherston jumped when the telephone rang. He picked it up. "Yeah?" he said harshly.

"Lord Halifax on the line, sir," Lulu said.

"Put him through," Jake said at once. Was a rat deserting the sinking ship?

"Mr. President?" That plummy British accent.

"What's up?" Jake asked the ambassador. If Halifax *was* bailing out, he'd put a flea in the bastard's ear, all right.

"I have some papers you may perhaps be interested in seeing," the British ambassador said.

"Well, bring 'em on over, then," Jake told him. He was so relieved that Halifax was staying put, he couldn't refuse him anything.

When Halifax got there, it gave Jake an excuse to throw out Nathan Bedford Forrest III. He didn't want to listen to the chief of the General Staff anyhow; Forrest was too gloomy to be worth listening to. By the noises he made, he feared Richmond would fall. Even if that was true, Jake didn't want to hear it. So he bundled Forrest out and brought in the ambassador instead. "What's up?" he asked again.

Lord Halifax opened his fancy attaché case: buttery leather polished till it gleamed, with clasps that looked like real gold. He pulled out a document held together with a fat paper clip. "Here you are, Mr. President. I honestly didn't believe they would turn these loose, but they did. You must have made an even more favorable impression on the Prime Minister than I thought. He does admire a . . . purposeful man, no doubt of that."

Jake Featherston hardly heard him. He was flipping through the papers. He didn't understand more than one word in ten, and he didn't understand any of the math. But he knew the word uranium when he saw it. And he knew about element 94, even if the limeys were calling it churchillium and not jovium.

"Did your scientists name it after Winston because it's supposed to make a big boom when it goes off?" he asked with a sly grin.

"Officially, it's a compliment to his office. We call 93 mosleyium after the Minister of War," Halifax replied. "Unofficially . . . well, I shouldn't wonder if you're right."

"I'll get this to our people who can use it just as quick as I can," Jake said. "And I want you to thank Winston for me from the bottom of my heart. What he did here, it means a lot to the country and it means a lot to me personally."

"He found your point about the need to continue the struggle against the United States by any means necessary alarmingly persuasive," Lord Halifax said. "If you fail, Britain is most dismally surrounded by the Yankees and the Huns."

"How close are you to getting one of these bombs?" Jake asked.

The British ambassador shrugged narrow shoulders. "Haven't the foggiest, I'm afraid. Were I not ambassador to a country also taking part in this research, I doubt I should know there is any such thing as uranium."

"Mm—makes sense," Featherston allowed. That was the only reason the Confederate envoys in London and Paris knew about uranium and what you might be able to do with it. But they hadn't been able to pry anything out of England or France. He damn well had.

"Will you be able to hold Richmond, sir?" Halifax asked.

"Hope so," Jake said. "But even if we don't, we'll keep fighting. As long as we've got a puncher's chance, we'll hang on. And with this"— he tapped the document with a nicotine-stained forefinger—"we do."

"Very good," the British ambassador said. But he meant it the way limeys did, so it might have been *all right*. He didn't mean it *was* very good, just that he'd heard. "I shall convey your determination to London. Bombing is picking up there, I'm afraid, though it's not so bad as here."

"Damn squareheads have airfields closer to you now," Jake said. Lord Halifax looked like a man who'd just sat on a tack but was too polite to mention it. Featherston knew why. He hadn't been . . . diplomatic. *Well, too bad*, he thought. He'd told the truth, hadn't he? He'd told the truth all the time while he rose—it looked that way to him, anyhow. He didn't see any point to stopping now.

And he was telling the truth again. The Kaiser's forces had bundled the British out of northwestern Germany, out of Holland, and back into Belgium. They were threatening Ypres—universally pronounced *Wipers* by English-speakers—again, as they had in the Great War.

When it fell then, it was a sign that the Entente couldn't hold on against the Central Powers. If it fell this time around, it would be another verse of the same song.

"We are doing everything in our power to deny them the use of those air bases," Halifax said.

"Sure, sure." Jake nodded and smiled. He probably should have kept his mouth shut even if he did tell the truth. Didn't he owe Halifax that much? The ambassador—and his government, of course—had come through for the Confederacy in a big way. "Between us, your Lordship, sir, we'll lick the bad guys yet."

"Between us, yes. And the French and the Russians will have something to say about it as well." Lord Halifax grimaced again. "I worry about the Russians. Failure the last time around cost them the Ukraine and Finland and Poland and the Baltic states and a Red insurrection at least as unpleasant as yours." *He* was being diplomatic; the Tsar's fight against the Reds had been bigger and bloodier than anything the CSA went through. After a pause to light a Habana, he continued, "They're wavering again, I fear. When they couldn't beat the Germans, or even the Austrians . . . If they go out, heaven only knows what sort of upheaval will follow."

"Hell with that," Featherston said. "If they go out now, you and France get the shaft. The Kaiser can pull everything away from the east and shoot it all at you."

"Quite." British reserve had its uses. Lord Halifax got as much mileage from one soft-spoken word as Jake would have from five minutes of cussing. He rose and held out an elegantly manicured hand. "Always a pleasure, Mr. President. I do hope the document proves valuable to you."

"I'm sure it will be." *I'll know just how valuable by this time tomorrow,* Jake thought as he shook it. Aloud, he went on, "England's always been the best friend the Confederacy has. We know that, and we never forget it."

One more time, the truth. English recognition in 1862, English forcing of the U.S. blockade, had ensured the Confederacy's independence. English help during the Second Mexican War made sure the CSA got to keep Chihuahua and Sonora, even if an invasion of the USA from Canada came to grief in Montana.

Well, the Confederate States of America paid their debts to the UK in 1914. This time, no debt was involved: both countries wanted revenge against the enemies who'd beaten them. And remembering alliances past didn't mean you *had* to do anything but remember. Jake understood that perfectly well. Did Lord Halifax? No doubt; he was twisty as a snake.

As soon as the British ambassador bowed his way out, Featherston summoned a courier. The bright young lieutenant saluted. "Freedom!"

"Freedom!" Jake echoed. He handed the man the British document. "Get these pages photographed. As soon as you've done that, haul ass to Washington University in Lexington and deliver them to Professor FitzBelmont."

"Yes, sir." The courier hesitated. "If it's such a tearing hurry, sir, why wait for the photography?"

"Because this *has* to get through," Jake answered. "Even if something happens to you"—*even if the damnyankees roast you like a barbecued porker*—"FitzBelmont *has* to get it. So we make a copy before we send you off."

"All right, sir. I understand."

"Good. Tell the fellow in the photo lab to call me as soon as he does what he needs to do." With this document, Jake intended to take no chances whatever.

"Yes, sir," the lieutenant said again. He saluted and hurried away. He didn't even need to leave the armored underground compartment to find a photographic technician. Anything that had to do with running a country, you could do here.

Now he would have some idea of what was going on in Lexington. So would the man who photographed the pages. That worried Jake less than it would have a few months before. If one of them reported to the damnyankees . . . well, so what? The United States already knew the Confederate States were working on a uranium bomb. The United States knew where, too. Otherwise, they wouldn't have started pounding the crap out of Lexington. If they knew the limeys were helping out, how did that change things? Didn't it just give them a brand-new worry? It looked that way to Jake Featherston.

The courier hadn't been gone more than a couple of minutes before the telephone on his desk jangled again. He eyed it the way a man in the woods might eye a rattler with a buzzing tail. Unlike a man in the woods, he couldn't walk away from it no matter how much he wished he could.

He picked it up. "Featherston here . . . What the hell do you mean, they're over the North Anna?" He'd expected bad news—that was the kind that got to the President in a hurry. He hadn't expected news this bad, though. "How the devil did they do that? Which dumb-shit general had his thumb up his ass to let 'em? . . . Jesus Christ, they can't have *that* much armor—can they?" He sounded worried even to himself. That was no good. You needed to sound calm, even—no, especially— when you weren't.

He gave orders to try to stem the green-gray tide. The damn-yankees couldn't shell Richmond yet, no, but it wouldn't be long if they kept going like this.

"Over the North Anna. *Son* of a bitch," Jake muttered after he hung up. He started looking at the maps on his office walls in a new way. Richmond really might fall. And if it did, he needed somewhere else to go, a place from which he could keep fighting till FitzBelmont and the rest of the high foreheads came through.

He'd never thought it would come to this. He'd figured the United States would roll over and show their yellow belly when he cut them in half. When that didn't happen, he'd been sure losing Pittsburgh would make them quit. When they didn't lose Pittsburgh . . . About then, he realized he had a tiger by the tail.

Can't let go, he thought. And the Yankees had a tiger by the tail, too. If they didn't know that yet, they would. He nodded to himself. They sure as hell would. No matter where he had to do it from, he'd make them pay for every single thing they'd done to his country. He'd make them pay plenty.

Armstrong Grimes was happy as a clam in a country where they'd never heard of chowder. Along with the rest of his platoon, he tramped east toward the Savannah River and the sea. They'd told Lieutenant Bassler the Confederates didn't have a whole hell of a lot in front of them. So far, they looked to be right.

"Keep your eyes peeled, though," he warned the men in his squad. "Don't want to get your nuts shot off doing something dumb."

"Shit, Sarge, I don't want to get my nuts shot off doing something smart," Squidface said.

"You've got a point," Armstrong said. "Now put a hat on it."

The PFC flipped him off. He gave back the bird. When he took over the squad, the men had been wary about him. They'd come through a lot together, and they weren't about to trust somebody from the repple-depple till they saw he deserved it. By now, Armstrong had paid his dues and then some. He was part of the life of the platoon, somebody to razz and somebody to put them through their paces. They followed his orders not just because he had three stripes but because they'd seen he had a halfway decent notion of what he was doing.

Up ahead, a Confederate machine gun chattered. That tearing-sailcloth noise sobered people in a hurry. Men kind of hunched down to make themselves into smaller targets. They moved away from one another to make a burst less likely to take out several of them at once. Armstrong did all that himself, too, before he even thought about it. He knew his trade, the same as the other guys did.

Most of them did, anyhow. A couple were new men fresh out of the replacement depot. A tall, gangly kid called Herk had taken Whitey's place. He stared around in mild surprise when the soldiers around him spread out. Then a bullet cracked past his head. He knew what that meant, all right, and awkwardly dropped to the ground.

"You gotta move faster'n that, man," Armstrong told him. "Otherwise, you'll damn well stop one, and I ain't got time to nursemaid you."

"I'll try, Sarge." Herk was willing. He was just unskilled.

"Sure." Armstrong swallowed a sigh. He'd hit it, all right—he couldn't nursemaid the replacements. In a perfect world, they would have joined the unit when it got taken out of the line so the veterans got to know them a little bit. Here, it was baptism by total immersion. Experienced soldiers shied away from the new guys. Raw men didn't just get themselves maimed and killed; they also brought trouble down on their comrades, because the Confederates who aimed at them also hit guys near them.

If they made it through a couple of weeks of action, they learned the ropes and turned into decent soldiers. A lot of them didn't, though. Not too many Confederates stood in front of Armstrong's platoon right now. The ones who did knew their business. The only new Confederate soldiers were the ones who'd been too young for conscription when the war started.

From the ground, Herk asked, "We gonna go after that machine gun, Sarge?"

"Not if we can find a barrel or a mortar team to do it for us," Armstrong answered. "We want to lick these fuckers, yeah, but we don't want to pay too much while we're doing it."

"Now you hope the lieutenant feels the same way," Squidface said, his grin half sly, half resigned.

"Bet your ass I do." Armstrong could hope, anyhow. Lieutenant Bassler had pretty good sense . . . as far as lieutenants went. He didn't think he had an infinite supply of soldiers to do whatever he thought needed doing, and he didn't send his men anywhere he wouldn't go himself. Things could have been worse.

And they rapidly got that way. That rising howl in the air wasn't artillery. It was even worse. "Screaming meemies!" Squidface yelled while Armstrong was still sucking in wind to shout the same thing. Everybody who wasn't already on the ground threw himself flat. Armstrong got out his entrenching tool and started digging like a madman.

The salvo of rockets shrieked home before he'd thrown up more than a shovelful of red dirt. A couple of dozen of them slammed down within a few seconds. Armstrong got picked up and thrown around while chunks of jagged iron whined through the air. Whether he lived or died wasn't up to him; it was just luck one way or the other. He hated that more than anything else about combat. Sometimes whether you were a good soldier didn't matter worth a dime.

When he came down and stopped rolling, he looked around. There was Herk, blood running from his nose but otherwise seeming all right. There was Squidface, who hadn't even lost his cigarette. And . . . there was Zeb the Hat's head, attached to one shoulder and not much else. The rest of what was probably his body lay thirty yards away.

Herk got a good look at that and lost his breakfast. Armstrong had already seen a lot of bad things, but his stomach wanted to empty out, too. Squidface's lips silently shaped the word *Fuck*. Or maybe he said it out loud; Armstrong slowly realized he wasn't hearing very much.

Squidface said something else. Armstrong shrugged and pointed to his ears. The PFC nodded. He came over and bellowed, "He was a hell of a good guy."

"Yeah," Armstrong shouted back. "He was."

That was about as much of a memorial as Zeb the Hat got. Armstrong dragged his two pieces together so Graves Registration would know they went with each other. The surviving soldiers helped themselves to Zeb's ammunition and ration cans—he didn't need them any more. Armstrong took out his wallet and found his real name was Zebulon Fischer, and that he was from Beloit, Wisconsin. The billfold held only a couple of bucks. Had he had a real roll, Armstrong would have sent that to his next of kin.

More shrieks in the air announced another salvo of rockets. Armstrong went flat again. These screaming meemies came down off to the left, not all around him. He had more of a chance to dig in, and used it. The Confederates in this part of Georgia didn't seem inclined to let U.S. soldiers come any farther.

After the rockets slammed down, Armstrong breathed a sigh of relief: nothing bad had happened to him or his men. Then shouts came from the left. He needed a little while to make out what people were saying. The first salvo really had pounded the crap out of his hearing. After a while, though, he got the message: Lieutenant Bassler was wounded.

He swore. God only knew what kind of half-assed new man the repple-depple would cough up. Then somebody said, "Looks like you're in charge of the platoon, Sergeant."

"What the hell?" Armstrong said. Two of the other three sergeants were senior to him.

"Yeah, you are," the soldier insisted. "Same goddamn rocket got Borkowski and Wise. One of 'em's dead—looks like the other one'll lose a foot."

"Shit." Armstrong had got a platoon before, and the same way—everybody above him got wounded or killed. That was the only way a three-striper could command a platoon . . . or, if enough things went wrong, a company. He didn't really want the honor. As usual, nobody cared what he wanted.

"What are we gonna do?" the news bringer asked, something not far from panic in his voice. "We stay here, Featherston's fuckers'll just keep pounding the shit out of us."

"Tell me about it," Armstrong said unhappily. The Confederates would be loading up more screaming meemies right this minute. If he ordered a retreat, his own superiors would tear the stripes off his sleeve. They'd call him a coward, and he wouldn't be able to prove them wrong. Which left . . . "We gotta move up."

They would have to take out that machine gun now, like it or not. He didn't, but he was stuck. Squidface came to the same unwelcome conclusion: "That goddamn gun's gonna have to go."

"Uh-huh." Armstrong nodded. "You've got the squad for now."

"Fuck of a way to get it," Squidface said, but then he nodded, too. "You don't want the platoon, either, do you?"

"Not like this," Armstrong answered. "Keep the guys spread out. And watch that Herk, for Chrissake. He'll get his ass shot off before he knows what's what."

"I ain't his goddamn babysitter, for cryin' out loud." After a moment, Squidface nodded again. "Well, I'll try."

Armstrong hadn't gone very far before he realized the machine-gun emplacement could murder the whole platoon. It had an unobstructed field of fire to the west. No way in hell would they be able to sneak up on it. He yelled for the wireless man and got on the horn to regimental HQ: "This is Grimes, in charge of Gold Platoon, Charlie Company. We need a couple of barrels to knock out a nest at square, uh, B-9."

Some uniformed clerk well back of the line asked, "What happened to what's-his-name? Uh, Bassler?"

"He's down. I've got it," Armstrong growled. "You gonna get me what I need, or do I have to come back there and tear you a new asshole?"

"Keep your hair on, buddy," replied the fellow back at headquarters. "We'll see what we can do."

That wasn't enough to keep Armstrong happy—not even close. Yet another barrage of screaming meemies roared in. They were mostly long, but not *very* long. Armstrong damn near pissed himself. He knew plenty of guys who had. You didn't rag on them much, not if you had any sense. It could happen to you.

Half an hour later, after still more rockets—again, mostly long— the barrels showed up. Without getting out of the foxhole he'd dug, Armstrong pointed them toward the machine-gun nest. They clattered forward. The machine gun opened up on them, which did exactly no good. There was no place for advancing U.S. soldiers to hide. That also meant there was no place for C.S. soldiers with stovepipe antibarrel rockets to hide. The barrels shelled the machine-gun nest into silence.

"Let's go." Armstrong hustled to catch up with the barrels. So did his men. Anyone who'd been in action for even a little while knew armor made a hell of a life-insurance policy for infantrymen. It could take care of things that stymied foot soldiers—and it drew fire that would otherwise come down on their heads.

And the ground pounders were good for barrel crews' life expectancy, too. They kept bad guys with stovepipes and Featherston Fizzes from sneaking close enough to be dangerous. Barrels that got too far out in front of the infantry often had bad things happen to them before anybody could do anything about it.

"Come on, Herk!" Armstrong yelled, looking back over his shoulder and seeing that the new guy wasn't moving fast enough. "Shake a leg, goddammit!"

"I'm coming, Sarge." Yeah, Herk was willing. But he didn't understand why Armstrong wanted him to hurry up. He wasn't urgent and he wasn't alert. With the best will in the world, he was asking for trouble. Armstrong figured he'd buy a piece of a plot—or maybe a whole one—before he figured out what was what. Too damn bad, really, but what could you do?

Meanwhile, the Confederates with the screaming meemies were still lobbing them where the U.S. soldiers had been, not where they were now. Before long, the rocketeers would find out they'd goofed— with luck, when the barrels put shells or machine-gun bullets through them.

Armstrong trotted on. He heard a few bursts from up ahead, but nothing really bad. The bastards in butternut all carried automatic weapons. Nothing you could do about that. But if there weren't enough of them, what they carried didn't matter. And, right here, there weren't.

When Sam Carsten thought of prize crews, he thought about pigtailed sailors with cutlasses boarding sailing ships: wooden ships and iron men. But the *Josephus Daniels* was shorthanded because a couple of freighters that would have gone to England or France were bound for the USA instead.

Sam gave Lieutenant Zwilling the conn so he could straighten out some of the complications detaching men had caused. He was talking with a damage-control party—damage control being something about which he knew more than he'd ever wanted to learn—when Wally Eastlake, a CPO who'd played one of King Neptune's mermaids when the destroyer escort crossed the Equator, sidled up to him and said, "Talk to you for a second, Skipper?"

When a chief wanted to talk, listening was a good idea. "Sure," Sam said. "What's on your mind?"

Instead of answering right away, Eastlake drew himself out of earshot of the damage-control party. A couple of snoopy sailors started to follow, but the chief's basilisk stare made them keep their distance. In a low voice, Eastlake said, "Notice anything funny about the prize crews the exec took for those Argentine pigs?"

"Not a whole lot," Sam answered. "Mostly guys who've been in for a while, but that's more good than bad, you ask me. You need men with some experience when they go off on their own."

"If that was all, sure," Eastlake said. "But the guys who're gone, they're the ones who busted a gut laughing when he stopped being a polliwog. I'd be gone myself, I bet, except I was holding it in and busting up where it didn't show. Swelp me, Skipper, it's the God's truth." He drew a cross on his chest.

"Oh, yeah?" Sam said.

"Swelp me," the chief said again.

Carsten thought about it. He hadn't had much to do with the festivities. They were designed to let ratings get their own back. Even if the captain just watched, it dampened the fun. But he also had a pretty good notion of who'd enjoyed themselves most at Myron Zwilling's expense—and who'd had reasons for enjoying themselves. Eastlake was right—an awful lot of those people weren't on the ship any more. "Son of a bitch," Sam said softly.

"Yeah," Eastlake said. "I didn't think you noticed—you got bigger shit to worry about. But I figured you oughta know."

"Thanks—I guess." Now Sam had to decide what to do about it, or whether to do anything at all. Zwilling could deny everything and say he hadn't done it consciously. How would you prove he was lying? For that matter, maybe he wasn't. Or he could say he damn well had done it, and so what?

"You think I shoulda kept my big trap shut?" Eastlake asked.

"No. I'd rather know what's going on," Sam answered. "I'll take care of it." The CPO nodded. He didn't ask Sam *how* he'd take care of it, which was a good thing, because Sam still didn't know.

When he got back to the bridge, the exec was keeping station with the other warships in the flotilla. Zwilling was competent, precise, painstaking. The tip of his tongue stuck out of the corner of his mouth, as if he were a grade-schooler working on a big paper. He'd never be the shiphandler Pat Cooley was. He was plenty good enough to get the job done, though. Chances were he was better than Sam, who'd come to the wheel late. Whether he'd be better in an emergency, when instinct and balls could count for more than carefully acquired skill, was a different question.

"Anything interesting going on?" Sam asked.

"No, sir. All routine," Zwilling answered.

"All right. In that case, why don't you let Thad have it for a bit?" Sam nodded toward the Y-ranging officer. "He can use the practice. You never know what could happen if a British fighter or bomber chews up the bridge."

"Aye aye, sir." Zwilling stepped away from the wheel. Lieutenant Walters took it, a wide grin making him look even younger than he did most of the time.

Carsten gestured to the exec. "Come to my cabin, why don't you?" Yes, he was going to take the bull by the horns. He didn't know what else to do.

"Of course, sir." Zwilling's eyes narrowed. He knew something was up, but he couldn't very well say no.

The cabin, small for one man, was crowded with two. But, with the door closed, it was about the only place on the destroyer escort that offered reasonable privacy. Sam sat down on the bed and waved the exec to the metal chair, saying, "I've got a question for you."

"Sir?" Zwilling didn't show much. Well, with a superior getting ready to grill him, Sam would have shown as little as he could, too.

"When you picked prize crews for those freighters we nabbed, how did you go about it?"

Zwilling still didn't show much. He would have made a pretty fair poker player, and probably did. "I mostly chose men with above-average experience, sir. They'll be on their own going north. They'll need to be extra alert for enemy action, and for trouble from the sailors. New fish are less likely to do well in a situation like that."

"I see." Sam would have said the same thing. It was even likely to be true. But it wasn't likely to be the whole truth. With a sigh, Sam went on, "Did you also choose men who gave you a hard time when we crossed the Equator?"

Now the exec knew which way the wind was blowing. His mouth tightened. He hunched in on himself, just a little. But his answer was forthright: "Yes, sir. We're better off without some of those trouble-makers on board. That was a criterion of mine, too."

Thinking about the men who were gone, Sam shook his head. "They mostly aren't troublemakers, Mr. Zwilling. They have good records. They may not love you, but that's not the same thing."

By Zwilling's scowl, it was to him. "They're bad for discipline, sir. I'm not sorry to be rid of them."

"I'm sorry you used personal dislikes to influence what you did,"

Carsten said. "If I were you, I wouldn't do that again. I'm disappointed you did it once."

"If you're unhappy with me, sir, may I request a transfer off this ship?" Zwilling asked. "You need to have confidence in your executive officer."

He didn't say anything about his needing to have confidence in Sam. That would have been insubordinate, and he was a stickler for the proprieties. But it hovered in his tone and in the way he eyed Carsten.

With another sigh, Sam nodded. "Yes, I think that'll be best for everyone. This won't go in your papers. You didn't do anything against regulations. But you did something I don't fancy, and I won't try to tell you any different."

"Is that all, sir?" The exec's voice might have come from a machine.

"Yes, that's all. Go take the conn back." As far as the ship was concerned, Zwilling was fine. With the sailors, on the other hand . . . *And with me, too*, Sam thought sadly. There were skippers for whom Myron Zwilling would have been the perfect exec. Men who did things strictly by the book themselves would have been wild for him. But Sam flew by the seat of his pants. That drove Zwilling nuts, and the exec's insistence on routine grated on the mustang just as much.

Sam followed Zwilling back to the bridge. When the exec said, "I have the conn, Mr. Walters," the Y-ranging officer almost jumped out of his skin. Sam didn't blame him. Zwilling didn't sound like a machine any more. He sounded like a voice from beyond the grave.

Christ! Sam thought, now alarmed. *I hope he doesn't go hang himself from the first pipe fitting he finds.* He didn't want the exec dead, only off his ship and onto one where he fit better.

Thad Walters retreated in a hurry. His eyes asked Sam what had happened in the cabin. Sam couldn't tell him, even in private; that would have been monstrously unfair to Zwilling.

Then Sam shook his head. It wouldn't be so simple after all. Even now, people would be buzzing that Chief Eastlake had talked with him. And they would know all too soon that he and the exec had talked in his cabin. They would add two and two, sure as hell. And when Zwilling left the ship, Eastlake would be a power to reckon with indeed.

That wasn't good. You didn't want the crew thinking a CPO could hang an officer out to dry. Even more to the point, you didn't want a CPO thinking he could hang an officer out to dry. In this particular

case, it happened to be true, which only made things worse. Sam shook
his head again. Eastlake would have to go, too. That wasn't fair, but he
didn't see that he had any other choice.

He wished for word of an enemy convoy. He almost wished for
word of enemy aircraft on the way in. Anything that took his mind off
the ship's internal politics would have been nice. But no enemy
freighters came into sight. The sky remained clear of everything but the
sun. The only thing he had to worry about was Myron Zwilling steer-
ing the *Josephus Daniels* with a face that looked as if he were watching
his family tortured and killed.

Was I too hard on him? Sam wondered. He played back the conversation in his cabin inside his head. He really didn't think so. The
only other thing he could have done was pretend he didn't know anything about what Zwilling had pulled. And that wouldn't fly, because
Chief Eastlake *would* let the crew know he'd told Sam what was going
on. Their respect would get flushed right down the head.

And so would Sam's self-respect. He'd never been any damn good
at pretending. Oh, sometimes you had to. If you were dealing with a
superior you couldn't stand, a little constructive hypocrisy didn't hurt.
But that was about as far as he could make himself go. Ignoring this
would have felt like ignoring a bank robbery right under his nose.

Lieutenant Walters took a long look at his Y-ranging gear. The
screens must have been blank, for he stepped away from them and
over to Sam. In a low, almost inaudible voice, he asked, "Sir, what's
going on?"

Sam glanced at Lieutenant Zwilling. The exec didn't turn around.
Did his back stiffen, though? Was he listening? It didn't matter any
which way. Sam said what he would have said if Zwilling were down
in the engine room: "Nothing that's got anything to do with you."

"Yes, sir." The Y-ranging officer nodded, but he didn't go back to
his post. Instead, he asked, "Is it anything that will hurt the ship?"

Zwilling's ravaged voice and face made that query much too reasonable. But Sam didn't think he was lying when he shook his head.
"No, we'll be all right," he said. "It's . . ." He stopped. Even saying
something like *It's a personnel matter* went too far. Were he in the
exec's place, he wouldn't want anybody running his mouth about him.
"Just let it go, Thad. It'll sort itself out."

"I hope so, sir." Walters returned to his post. He'd needed nerve to
make even that much protest.

Muttering to himself, Sam turned away. He didn't like the idea of blighting Zwilling's career. He hadn't liked it back in New York City, and he liked it even less here. But try as he would, he didn't see what else he could do. Zwilling had made his bed; now he had to lie in it.

And what will the fancy-pants officers back in the USA think about me when they get wind of this? Sam wondered. Now that he'd been a lieutenant for a while, he wanted to make lieutenant commander. That would be pretty damn good for somebody who started out an ordinary seaman. Would the men who judged such things decide he could have handled this better?

After worrying at it and worrying about it for a couple of minutes, he shrugged. The ship had to come first. If the brass hats didn't care for what he'd done, he'd retire a lieutenant, and the world wouldn't end. When he first signed up, even CPO had seemed a mountain taller than the Rockies, but he'd climbed a lot higher than that.

So he'd go on doing things the way he thought he needed to. And if anybody away from the *Josephus Daniels* didn't like it, too damn bad.

The telephone on Jefferson Pinkard's desk jangled. He picked it up. "This is Pinkard."

"Hello, Pinkard," said the voice on the other end of the line. "This is Ferd Koenig, in Richmond."

"What can I do for you, sir?" Jeff asked the Attorney General, adding, "Glad to hear you still *are* in Richmond." From some of the things the papers were saying, the capital was in trouble. Since the papers always told less than what was really going on, he'd worried.

"We're still here. We aren't going anywhere, either," Koenig said. As if to contradict him, something in the background blew up with a roar loud enough to be easily audible even over the telephone. He went on, "We'll lick the damnyankees yet. You see if we don't."

"Yes, sir," Jeff said, though he'd already seen all the war he wanted and more besides in Snyder. Coming east to Humble was a wonderful escape. U.S. warplanes hardly ever appeared over the city of Houston (far, far away from the damnyankee abortion of a state that carried the same name) and had never been seen over this peaceful town twenty miles north of it.

"Wait till we get all our secret weapons into the fight," Koenig said. "We're already throwing those rockets at the USA, and we've finally got new barrels that'll make their best ones say uncle. Bigger and better things in the works, too."

"Sure hope so." From everything Pinkard could see, the Confederate States needed bigger and better things if they stood a chance of winning.

"Believe it. The President's promised we'll have 'em, and he keeps his word." Ferdinand Koenig sounded absolutely convinced, despite yet another big boom in the distance. He went on, "But there's something I need from you."

Of course there is. You wouldn't have called me if there wasn't, Jeff thought. Aloud, all he said was, "Tell me what."

"I want you to go through your guards. Anybody who's fit enough to fight, put him on a train for Little Rock. We'll take it from there," the Attorney General said.

"*Everybody* who's fit enough to fight?" Pinkard asked in dismay.

"That's what I said."

"Sir, you know a lot of my guys are from the Confederate Veterans' Brigades," Jeff said. Those were men the C.S. Army had already judged not fit to fight, mostly because of wounds from the Great War.

"Yes, I understand that. Sort through them, too. Some of 'em'll probably do—we aren't as fussy as we used to be," Koenig said. "But you've got plenty of Congressmen's nephews and Party officials' brothers-in-law. Come on, Pinkard—we both know how that shit works. But we can't afford it any more."

"Shall I get on the train myself, then?" Jeff asked. "Reckon I still know which end of a rifle's which."

"Don't be dumb," Koenig told him. "We've got to keep the camp running. That's damn important, too. Way things are, though, we need every warm body we can get our hands on at the front."

"Well, I'll do what I can, sir," Jeff said.

"I reckoned you would," the Attorney General replied. "Freedom!" The line went dead.

"Freedom," Jeff echoed as he hung up, too. Once the handpiece was back in the cradle, he added one more word: "Shit."

He wondered how few guards he could get away with sending. The men on the women's side, sure. They wouldn't be a problem. He could always replace them with dykes. Plenty of tough broads ready to send Negro women to the bathhouses. Plenty of tough broads *eager* to do it. And if some of them ate pussy in the meantime . . . well, hell, as long as the colored gals got what was coming to them sooner or later, Jeff supposed he could look the other way in the meantime. Yeah, lezzies were disgusting, but there was a war on, and you had to take the bad with the good.

Losing guards from the men's side would hurt more. He couldn't bring female guards over here. Some of them, the butch ones, would have liked it. But it would stir up trouble among the coons if he tried it, and it would stir up more trouble among his men. So he'd have to do some pruning, and then live with personnel being gone.

Congressmen's nephews. Party bigwigs' brothers-in-law. Sure, he had some guys like that. He didn't want to get rid of all of them. They were the young, the healthy, the quick here. You couldn't run a camp with a bunch of old farts who couldn't get out of their own way . . . could you? He hoped he wouldn't have to find out, and feared he would.

He got on the intercom, and then on the PA system, to summon Vern Green to his office. The guard chief got there about fifteen minutes later. "What's up, sir?" Pinkard told him what was up. He looked disgusted when he heard. "Well, for God's sake! They reckon our boys gonna win the damn war all by their lonesome?"

"Beats me," Jeff answered. "But when the Attorney General tells you you got to do this and that, you can't very well say no."

Green looked more disgusted yet, but he nodded. "I'll ask around," he said. "Maybe we can fix it." He had his own back channels to Richmond. Someone in the capital would be keeping an eye on Jeff for the government or the Party or both. Usually, that made the guard chief the camp commandant's rival. They both wanted to pull in the same direction today, though.

"Yeah, you do that," Jeff said. "But don't hold your breath. War news is bad enough, they'll be grabbing anybody they can get their hands on."

"Uh-huh," Green said. They both had to be careful when they talked about how things were going. Either could report the other for defeatism. But they couldn't afford to pretend they were blind, either. If the news were better, Richmond wouldn't be prying men loose wherever it could. The guard chief went on, "You got a roster handy?"

"Sure do." Jeff spread papers out on his desk. "I've made some marks already."

Green looked at them. He nodded. "What you've got makes sense. We can always come up with guards in skirts for the women's side."

"Just what I was thinkin'," Pinkard agreed. "The ones over here, though . . . That's gonna be a bastard. Bastard and a half, even."

"Yeah." The guard chief nodded again. "Some of these guys'll bawl like castrated colts when you tell 'em they got to go and fight the damnyankees. Some of their fathers'll bawl even louder."

"Tell me about it," Jeff said with a wry grin. "But I know what to do about that, damned if I don't. I'll just say, 'You want to squawk, don't you come squawkin' to me. Go squawk to Ferd Koenig, on account of he gave the orders. Me, I'm only doin' like he said.' "

Vern Green smiled a slow, conspiratorial smile. "Ain't gonna be a whole lot o' folks with the brass to try that."

"Hell, I wouldn't," Jeff said. "I know when I'm fightin' out of my weight. Anybody who wants to take a swing at it, well, good luck." He peered through his reading glasses at the roster. "Let's see how we can finish this off and still have enough left to do our jobs here."

Neither of them ended up happy about what they came up with. But they both agreed Camp Humble could go on reducing population without the guards they'd ship to Little Rock. Then they wrangled about who would announce the transfers. Jeff wanted the guard chief to do it. Green insisted the words had to come out of the commandant's mouth. In they end, they split the difference. Pinkard would announce the Attorney General's order, while Green read the names of the men who would go to Little Rock.

Even assembling the guards was tricky. Like any soldiers or bureaucrats, the men knew a break in routine was suspicious. To them, change was anything but good. And they started yelling their heads off when Jeff announced that Ferd Koenig required some of them to go to the front.

"Shut up!" Pinkard yelled, and his bellow was enough to rock them back on their heels and make sure they damn well *did* shut up, at least for a little while. Into that sudden, startled silence, he went on, "Y'all reckon I want to do this? You're out of your goddamn minds if you do. You reckon I've got any choice? You're just as crazy if you think so, and a lot stupider'n I figured you were."

"We won't go!" somebody yelled, and other guards took up the cry.

"Oh, yes, you will," Jeff said grimly. "I don't believe you catch on. You ain't just fuckin' with me, people. Y'all are fuckin' with Ferd Koenig and Jake Featherston and the Freedom Party and the Confederate government. You'll end up in the stockade, and then they'll ship your sorry asses to the front any which way. And if you don't end up in a penal battalion for raising a ruckus, then I don't know shit about how things work. And I damn well do."

A shudder ran through the guards. They didn't want to go to the front as soldiers. That was nasty and dangerous. But if you went to the front in a penal battalion, you were nothing but dead meat that hadn't got cooked yet. And they threw you straight into the fire.

"You still talkin' about not goin'?" Jeff asked. Nobody said anything this time. He nodded in something approaching satisfaction. "That's more like it. Maybe y'all ain't as dumb as you look after all. Hell, you go and mutiny, maybe they don't send you to the front at all. Maybe they just line you up and shoot you." He waited for another shudder, and got it. Then he went on, "Vern here'll read out the names of the men who're going to Little Rock. You hear your name, be ready to ship out tomorrow at 0600. You ain't ready, you got more trouble'n you know what to do with, I promise. Vern?"

One by one, the guard commander read the list of names. Some men who got called jerked as if shot. For a few, or more than a few, that was bound to be anticipation. Others cursed Green or the Freedom Party. And still others reacted with complete disbelief. "You can't do this to me!" one of them cried. "Do you know whose cousin I am?"

"You ain't Ferd Koenig's cousin, and you ain't Jake Featherston's cousin, either," Jefferson Pinkard said in a voice like iron. "And as long as you ain't, it don't matter for shit whose cousin you are. You got it?"

"You can't talk to me that way!" exclaimed the guard with the prominent—but not prominent enough—cousin.

"No? Seems like I just did," Jeff answered. "You can get on the train tomorrow morning, or you can go to the stockade now and get on another train after that. You just bet your ass you won't be happy if you do, though."

The cousin said not another word. Green went back to reading names. He got more howls of protest. Some guards did some virtuoso cussing. But nobody else said he wouldn't go. Nobody else said he had a relative important enough to keep him from going, either. As far as Jeff was concerned, that was progress.

He waited with the shivering guards the next morning. All but two of them were there. Those two had skipped camp. They'd be the military police's worry from now on. He figured the MPs would track them down and make them sorry. The train pulled in right on time, snorting up in the beginnings of morning twilight—sunup was still a ways away.

Doors opened. Glumly, the guards climbed up and into the passenger cars. When they'd all boarded, the train chugged off. Its light was dim. Even here, lights could draw U.S. airplanes. You didn't want to take chances you didn't have to.

After the train pulled away, Jeff went to the kitchen for fried eggs, biscuits and gravy, and coffee. He'd done his duty. He wasn't happy about it, but he'd done it. Pretty soon, Camp Humble would start doing its duty again, too. Even with a reduced guard contingent, the camp would keep on working toward making the Confederate States Negro-free.

That was damned important work. Jeff was proud to have a part in it. He just wished the damnyankees and the war wouldn't keep interfering.

VI

Lieutenant-Colonel Jerry Dover didn't have Atlanta to kick around any more. The senior supply officers there couldn't make his life miserable any more. They'd either fled or died or were languishing in U.S. POW camps. The Stars and Stripes flew over the capital of Georgia. And so . . .

And so . . . Alabama. Dover had never figured he would have to try to fight the damnyankees from Alabama. Now he could scream at Huntsville for not getting him what he needed.

It was less fun than screaming at Atlanta had been. The chief quartermaster officer in Huntsville was a brigadier general named Cicero Sawyer. He sent Dover anything he had. When he didn't send it, he didn't have it. Dover could complain about that, but Sawyer complained about it, too.

"Anything that comes from Virginia and the Carolinas, forget it," he told Dover on a crackling telephone line. "They can't get it here."

"Why not?" Dover demanded. "We've still got Augusta. We've still got Savannah. We've still got shipping. Damnyankees can't sink every freighter in the goddamn country."

"Reckon the big reason is all the shit that's going on up in Virginia right now," Sawyer said. "They want to hang on to every damn thing they can so they can go and shoot it at the Yankees there."

"Yeah, well, if they forget this is part of the country, too, pretty soon it won't be any more," Dover said. "Let's see how they like that."

"I know," Sawyer said wearily. "I've got two worries myself. I got to keep the soldiers supplied—that means you. And I've got to keep the rocket works going. We're hurting the USA with those things, damned if we're not."

"That's nice," Dover said. "In the meantime, I need boots and I need raincoats and I need ammo for automatic rifles and submachine guns. When the hell you gonna get that stuff for me?"

"Well, I can send you the ammunition," Brigadier General Sawyer answered. "That comes out of Birmingham, so it's no problem. The other stuff . . . Mm, maybe I can get some of it from New Orleans. Maybe."

"If you don't, I'm gonna have men coming down with pneumonia," Dover said. "Boots wear out, dammit, and they start to rot when it's wet like it is now. The guys who have shelter halves are wearing them for rain hoods, but they aren't as good as the real thing."

Sawyer sighed. "I'll try, Dover. That's all I can tell you. You aren't the only dumpmaster yelling his head off at me, remember."

"Why am I not surprised?" Dover hung up with the last word.

Dumpmaster was a word that fit him much too well right now. His supply depot was small and shabby. The nearest town, Edwardsville, was even smaller and shabbier. Close to a hundred years earlier, Edwardsville had been a boom town, for there was gold nearby. Then the mother lode in California shot the little Alabama gold rush right behind the ear. Some of the fancy houses built in Edwardsville's first—and last—flush of prosperity still stood, closed and gray and grim.

"Well?" Pete asked when Dover hung up.

"He promised us the ammo," Dover told the veteran quartermaster sergeant. "As far as the rest of it goes, we're screwed."

"Not us. We got the shit for ourselves," Pete said. Supply officers and noncoms lived well. That was a perquisite of the job. Pete went on, "It's the poor bastards a few miles east of here who get the wrong end of the stick."

Jerry Dover nodded unhappily. In the last war, the average Confederate soldier had been about as well supplied as his Yankee counterpart. Through the first couple of years of this fight, the same held true. But the Confederate States were starting to come apart at the seams, and the men were paying for it.

"Ammo's great," Pete went on. "What if everybody's too damn hungry and sick to use it, though?"

"I already told you," Dover answered. "In that case, we're screwed." He looked around to make sure nobody but Pete could hear before adding, "And we're liable to be."

Off to the northwest lay Huntsville, where the rockets came from. Off to the west lay Birmingham, where anything made of iron or steel came from. Off to the east lay damnyankees who knew that much too well. When they got ready to push west, could they go right on through the Confederates standing in their way?

Although Dover hoped not, he wouldn't have bet against it.

"How many niggers in these parts?" Pete asked, not quite out of a clear blue sky.

"Well, I don't exactly know," Dover answered. "I don't think I've seen any, but there could be some skulking around, like."

"Could be, yeah. I bet there are," Pete said. "I bet they get one look at what all we got here, then they light out to tell the Yankees."

"I bet you're right. We saw it often enough farther east," Dover said. "Maybe we ought to do some hunting in the woods around here." He remembered too well the black raiders who'd plundered his dump in Georgia.

"Maybe we should." Pete grinned. "I ain't been coon hunting since I was a kid."

"Heh." Dover made himself grin back. He'd heard jokes like that too many times to think they were very funny, but he didn't want to hurt Pete's feelings.

The hunt was no joke. Jerry Dover feared it was also no success. He couldn't get any front-line troops to join in, which meant he had to do it with his own men, men from the Quartermaster Corps. They could fight if they had to; they were soldiers. They'd had to a couple of times, when U.S. forces broke the lines in front of them. They hadn't disgraced themselves.

But there was a big difference between a stand-up fight and hunting down Negroes who didn't want to get caught or even get seen. Regular troops probably would have had a hard time doing that. It was more than the men from the supply dump could manage. They might have made the blacks shift around. They caught no one and killed no one. The day's only casualty was a corporal who sprained his ankle.

That evening, Birmingham caught hell. The bombers came right over the supply dump, flying from east to west. When the alarms went off, Dover scrambled into a slit trench and waited for hellfire and damnation to land on his head. As the Hebrews in Egypt must have done, he breathed a silent sigh of relief when the multi-engined Angels of Death passed over him, bound for other targets.

He felt guilty about that, and angry at himself, but he couldn't help it. Yes, the Confederacy was still going to get hurt. Yes, other men— and women, and children—were still going to get blown to bits. But his own personal, precious, irreplaceable ass was safe, at least till the sun came up.

He grimaced when he realized just how many U.S. airplanes were heading west. The damnyankees had loaded up their fist with a rock this time. Alabama boasted only two targets worth that much concentrated hate. The bombers' course told him they weren't bound for Huntsville. "Sorry, Birmingham," he muttered.

Birmingham, without a doubt, would be, and shortly was, even sorrier. He cowered in a trench more than seventy miles east of the city. Even from there, he could hear the bombs going off: a low, deep roar, absorbed almost as much through the palms of the hands and the soles of the feet as through the ears.

"Where the hell's our fighters?" Pete howled, as if Dover had a couple of dozen stashed away in the depot.

"We don't have enough," Dover answered. That had been true ever since the front lay up in Tennessee. It was more obviously, more painfully, true now. U.S. factories were outproducing their C.S. counterparts. Dover supposed U.S. pilot-training programs were outpacing their Confederate counterparts, too.

"How're we supposed to lick 'em if we can't go up there and shoot 'em down?" Pete wailed.

Jerry Dover didn't answer. The only thing he could have said was, *We can't.* While that was liable to be so, it didn't do anybody any good. If the writing was on the wall, Pete would be able to see it as well as anybody else.

The bombers didn't come back by the same route they'd taken going in. When Dover realized they weren't going to, he nodded in grudging respect. The Yankees weren't so dumb, dammit. C.S. antiaircraft guns would be waiting here for the returning airplanes. So would whatever night fighters the local Confederates could scrape up. Maybe Y-ranging gear could send the fighters after the U.S. bombers anyway. Dover hoped so. He was far from sure of it, though.

He wasn't sorry to climb out of the muddy trench. If chiggers didn't start gnawing on him, it would be nothing but dumb luck. Pete came out of his hole at about the same time. "Ain't this a fun war?" the sergeant said.

"Well, I could think of a lot of words for it, but I'd probably have to think a long time before I came up with that one," Dover answered.

"They knocked the shit out of Birmingham," Pete said.

"Can't argue with you."

Pete looked west, as if he could see the damage from where he stood. "You reckon the place can keep going after they hit it like that?"

"Probably," Dover replied. His eyes were well enough adapted to the dark to let him see Pete start. He went on, "Why not? We bombed plenty of Yankee towns harder than that, and they kept going. The USA hit Atlanta day after day, week after week, and it kept making things and shipping them out till just a little while before we finally lost it. Hard to bomb places back to the Stone Age, no matter how much you wish you could."

"Well, I sure as hell hope you're right." Pete pulled a pack of cigarettes from a breast pocket. He stuck one in his mouth and bent his head to light it. The brief flare of the match showed his hollow, unshaven cheeks. Remembering his manners, he held out the pack. "Want a butt, sir?"

"Don't mind if I do. Thanks." Dover flicked a lighter to get the proffered cigarette going. After a couple of drags, he said, "If they flatten Birmingham and Huntsville and maybe Selma, not many factory towns left between here and New Orleans."

"Yeah." Pete grunted. "Whole state of Mississippi's nothin' but farms, near enough. Farms and rednecks, I mean. Used to be farms and rednecks and niggers, but I reckon we took care o' most of the coons there. That's one good thing, anyways."

"Let me guess—you're not from Mississippi." Dover's voice was dry.

"Hope to shit I'm not, sir," Pete said fervently. "I came off a farm about twenty miles outside of Montgomery, right near the edge of the Black Belt. Well, it was the Black Belt then. Likely ain't no more."

"No, I wouldn't think so." Jerry Dover left it there. He thought the Confederacy had more urgent things to do than hunt down its Negroes. Jake Featherston thought otherwise, and his opinion carried a lot more weight than a jumped-up restaurant manager's. But if he'd put those coons into factories instead of getting rid of them, how many more white men could he have put into uniform? Enough to make a difference?

We'll never know now, Dover thought.

"You know how many Mississippians it takes to screw in a light bulb?" Pete asked out of the blue.

"Tell me," Dover urged.

"Twenty-seven—one to hold the bulb, and twenty-six to turn the house round and round."

Dover laughed his ass off—that one did take him by surprise. Here he was, his country crashing down around his ears, and he laughed like a loon at a stupid joke. If that wasn't crazy, he didn't know what would be. He didn't stop laughing, either.

When Jonathan Moss heard barrels clanking toward him, he feared it was all over. If the Confederates wanted to put that kind of effort into hunting down Spartacus' guerrilla band, they could do it. Moss knew that all too well. So did all the survivors in the band.

"Got us some Featherston Fizzes?" Spartacus called.

"We'd do better trying to hide," Nick Cantarella said.

"Ain't gonna hide from that many machines," the chieftain said, and Moss feared he was right. He went on, "We headin' fo' heaven, might as well send some o' them motherfuckers down to hell."

Moss wasn't so sure of his own destination, but he'd been living on borrowed time long enough that he didn't worry too much about paying it back. An old bolt-action Tredegar wasn't much use against a barrel, but he hoped a driver or a commander would be rash enough to stick his head out for a look around. If one of them did, Moss hoped to make it the last rash thing he ever tried.

There came one of the big, snorting monsters. Moss swore under his breath. The barrel was buttoned up tight. Just his luck to spot a crew who knew what they were doing. He also saw that barrel design had come a long way while he was on the shelf here in Georgia. This green-gray machine was different from any he'd seen before.

Green-gray . . . His eyes saw it, but his brain needed several seconds to process it, to realize what it meant.

His jaw had just dropped open when Nick Cantarella, a little quicker on the uptake, let out a joyously obscene and blasphemous whoop: "Jesus fuckin' Christ, they're ours!"

"Them's Yankee barrels?" Spartacus sounded as if he hardly dared believe it. Jonathan Moss knew how the guerrilla leader felt—he hardly dared believe it himself.

"Sure as shit aren't Confederate," Cantarella answered as two more machines rumbled down the road. The ground-pounder took a long look at them. "Wow," he breathed. "They've really pumped up the design, haven't they?"

"I was thinking the same thing. These look like they're twenty years ahead of the ones we were used to," Moss said. War gave engineering a boot in the butt. Moss thought of the airplanes he'd flown in 1914, and of the ones he'd piloted three years later. No comparison between them—and no comparison between these barrels and their predecessors, either.

If he walked out in front of them with a rifle in his hands, he'd get killed. The Negroes in Spartacus' band didn't have that worry. U.S. barrelmen, seeing black faces, would know they were among friends.

Again, the guerrillas figured that out at least as fast as he did. Several of them broke cover, smiling and waving at the oncoming barrels. The lead machine stopped. The cupola lid on top of the smooth rounded turret flipped up. "Boy, are we glad to see youse guys!" the barrel commander said in purest Brooklynese, his accent even stronger than Cantarella's.

"We's mighty glad to see you Yankees, too," Spartacus answered. "We gots a couple o' friends o' yours here." He waved for Moss and Cantarella to show themselves.

Cautiously, Jonathan Moss came out from behind the bush that had hidden him. The barrel's bow machine gun swung toward his belly button. A burst would cut him in half. He set down the Tredegar and half raised his hands.

"Who the hell are you?" the barrel commander asked. "Who the hell're both of youse?"

"I'm Jonathan Moss, major, U.S. Army—I'm a pilot," Moss answered. In scruffy denim, he looked more like a farmer—or a bum.

"Nick Cantarella, captain, U.S. Army—infantry," Cantarella added. "We got out of Andersonville, and we've been with the guerrillas ever since."

"Well, fuck me," the barrel commander said. "We heard there might be guys like you around, but I never figured I'd run into any. How about that? Just goes to show you. How long you been stuck here?"

"Since 1942." By the way Moss said it, it might as well have been forever. That was how he felt, too.

"Fuck me," the kid in the barrel said again. He looked around. "Gonna be some foot soldiers along any minute. We'll give you to them guys, and they'll do . . . whatever the hell they do with you. Clean youse up, anyway." That confirmed Moss' impression of himself. Cantarella looked even more sinister, because he had a thicker growth of stubble.

Sure enough, infantrymen trotted up a couple of minutes later. At least half of them carried captured Confederate automatic rifles and submachine guns. The lieutenant in charge probably wasn't old enough to vote. "Where are the closest Confederates?" he demanded, sticking to business.

"Down in Oglethorpe, other side o' the river," Spartacus answered. "They got some sojers there, anyways."

"You lead us to 'em?" the young officer asked.

Spartacus nodded. "It'd be my pleasure."

"All right. We'll clean 'em out—or if we can't, we'll call for the guys who damn well can." The lieutenant took a couple of steps towards Oglethorpe before he remembered he hadn't dealt with Moss and Cantarella. He pointed to one of his men. "Hanratty!"

"Yes, sir?" Hanratty said.

"Take these Robinson Crusoes back to Division HQ. Let the clerks deal with 'em." The lieutenant raised his voice: "The rest of you lazy lugs, c'mon! We still got a war to fight."

"Robinson Crusoes?" Moss said plaintively. The infantrymen tramped south, boots squelching through the mud. The barrels rumbled along with them. The Confederates in Oglethorpe were in for a hard time. Nobody paid any attention to the newly liberated POWs, not even the blacks with whom they'd marched and fought with for so long.

Well, there was Hanratty. "You guys were officers?" he said. Jonathan Moss managed a nod. So did Cantarella, who looked as stricken as Moss felt. Hanratty just shrugged. "Well, come on, sirs."

Still dazed, Moss and Cantarella followed. Moss had known the ropes with the guerrillas, and before that in Andersonville, and before that as a flier. Before long, he'd probably be in a situation where he knew them again. For now, he was in limbo.

Division HQ was a forest of tents a couple of miles to the north.

Hanratty turned his charges over to the sentries there, saying, "My outfit scraped up these two Crusoes running with the niggers. One's a major, the other one's a captain. They're all yours. I gotta get back to it—can't let my guys down." With a nod, he headed south again.

"Crusoes?" Moss said once more. Not even *Robinson Crusoe*s this time.

"That's what we call escaped POWs who've been on their own for a while, sir," the sentry said. Maybe he was trying to be kind, but he sounded patronizing, at least to Moss' ears. He went on, "You guys come with me, uh, please. I'll take you to the doc first, get you checked and cleaned up, and then they'll start figuring out what to do with you next."

"Oh, boy," Cantarella said in a hollow voice. Moss couldn't have put it better himself.

The doctor wore a major's gold oak leaves, but he didn't look much older than that kid lieutenant. He poked and prodded and peered. "Fleas, lice, chiggers, ticks," he said cheerfully. "You're scrawny as all get-out, too, both of you. Do a lot of walking barefoot?"

"Some, after our boots wore out and before we could, uh, liberate some more," Moss admitted.

"Hookworm, too, chances are. And some other worms, I bet." Yes, the doctor sounded like somebody in hog heaven. "We'll spray you and give you some medicine you won't like—nobody in his right mind does, anyway—and in a few days you'll be a lot better than you are now, anyhow. And we'll feed you as much as you can hold, too. How does that sound?"

"Better than the worm medicine, anyway," Moss said. "You make me feel like a sick puppy."

"You *are* a sick puppy," the doctor assured him. "But we'll make you better. We've learned a few things the last couple of years."

"When do we get back to the war?" Nick Cantarella asked. "If the United States are down here, Featherston's fuckers have to be on their last legs. I want to be in at the death, goddammit."

"Me, too," Moss said.

"When you're well enough—and when we make sure you are who you say you are." The doctor produced two cards and what looked like an ordinary stamp pad. "Let me have your right index fingers, gentlemen. We'll make sure you're really you, all right. And if you're not, you'll see a blindfold and a cigarette, and that's about it."

"If you think the Confederates would let somebody get as raggedy-assed as we are just to infiltrate, you're crazy as a bedbug, Doc," Cantarella said.

"Well, you aren't the first man to wonder," the doctor said easily.

For the next few days, Moss felt as if he'd gone back to Andersonville. He and Cantarella were under guard all the time. The food came from ration cans. The worm medicine flushed it out almost as fast as it went in. That was no fun. Neither was the idea that his own country mistrusted him.

At last, though, a bespectacled captain said, "All right, gentlemen—your IDs check out. Welcome back to the U.S. Army."

"Gee, thanks." Moss had trouble sounding anywhere close to enthusiastic.

The captain took his sarcasm in stride. "I also have the pleasure of letting you know that you're now a lieutenant colonel, sir—and you, Mr. Cantarella, are a major. You would have reached those ranks had you not been captured, and so they're yours. They have been for some time, which is reflected in the pay accruing to your accounts."

"That's nice." Moss remained hard to please. Nobody got rich on an officer's pay, and the difference between what a major and a light colonel collected every month wasn't enough to get excited about.

"When can we start fighting again?" Cantarella demanded, as he had before.

"You'll both need some refresher training to get you back up to speed," said the captain with the glasses. "Things have changed over the past couple of years, as I'm sure you'll understand."

"How much hotter are the new fighters?" Moss asked.

"Considerably," the captain said. "That's why you'll need the refresher work."

"Will I get back into action before the Confederates throw in the sponge?"

"Part of that will be up to you," the captain answered. "Part of it will be up to the Army as a whole, and part of it will be up to Jake Featherston. My own opinion is that you shouldn't waste any time, but that's only an opinion."

"We *are* going to lick those bastards?" Nick Cantarella said.

"Yes, sir. We are." The captain with the specs sounded very sure.

"What'll happen to Spartacus and his gang?" Moss asked, adding,

"They're damn good fighters. They wouldn't have stayed alive as long as they did if they weren't."

"We've started accepting colored U.S. citizens into the Army," the captain said, which made Moss and Cantarella both exclaim in surprise. The captain continued, "Since your companions are Confederates, though, they'll probably stay auxiliaries. They'll work with us, but they won't be part of us."

"And if they get out of line, you won't have to take the blame for anything they do." As a lawyer, Moss saw all the cynical possibilities in the captain's words.

The other officer didn't even blink. "That's right. But, considering everything the enemy has done to them, not much blame sticks to Negroes acting as auxiliaries in the Confederate States."

"Is it really as bad as that?" Having been away from even Confederate newspapers and wireless broadcasts since his escape, Moss had trouble believing it.

"No, sir," the captain said. "It's worse."

Somewhere ahead lay the Atlantic. Cincinnatus Driver had never seen the ocean. He looked forward to it for all kinds of reasons. He wanted to be able to say he had—a man shouldn't live out his whole life without seeing something like that. More important, though, was what seeing the ocean would mean: that the United States had cut the Confederate States in half.

He hadn't been sure it would happen. This thrust east across Georgia had started out in a tentative way. The United States was trying to find out how strong the Confederates in front of them were. When they discovered the enemy wasn't very strong, the push took on a life of its own.

And anywhere soldiers went, supplies had to go with them. They needed ammo. They needed rations. They needed gasoline and motor oil. Cincinnatus didn't like carrying fuel. If an antibarrel rocket—or even a bullet—touched it off . . .

"Hell, it's no worse than carrying artillery rounds," Hal Williamson said when he groused about it. "That shit goes up, you go with it."

He had a point. Even so, Cincinnatus said, "Artillery rounds blow, they take you out fast. You get caught in a gasoline fire, maybe you got time to know how bad things is."

"Well, maybe," the white driver said. "They give you a truckload, though, I figure it'll go off like a bomb if it goes."

"Mmm . . . maybe." Cincinnatus paused to light a cigarette. "Got us plenty o' cheerful stuff to talk about, don't we?"

"You wanted cheerful, you shoulda stayed home," Williamson said.

Cincinnatus grunted. That held more truth than he wished it did. But he said, "I tell you one cheerful thing—we're beatin' the livin' shit outa Featherston's fuckers. That'll do for me. Only thing that'd do better'd be beatin' the shit outa Featherston."

"Could happen," the other driver said. "You believe even half of what *Stars and Stripes* says, he won't be able to stay in Richmond much longer. Where's he gonna run to then?"

With another grunt, Cincinnatus replied, "You believe half o' what *Stars and Stripes* says, we won the goddamn war last year."

Hal Williamson laughed. "Yeah, well, there is that. Those guys lie like they're selling old jalopies."

"They got a tougher sell than that," Cincinnatus said. "They got to sell the war."

"Soon as the Confederates jumped into Ohio, I was sold," Williamson said. "Bastards tried to knock us flat and steal the war before we could get back on our feet again. Damn near did it, too—*damn* near."

He was right about that. "Same here," Cincinnatus said. " 'Course, they ain't as likely to shoot our asses off as they are with the kids in the front line."

"Still happens, though. You know that as well as I do. We've lost more drivers than I like to think about," Williamson said.

"Oh, yeah. I won't try to tell you anything different. All I said was, it ain't *as* likely, and it ain't," Cincinnatus said. He waited to see if the other driver would keep arguing. When Williamson didn't, Cincinnatus decided he'd made his point.

The next morning, he picked up a load of canned rations and headed for the front. He liked carrying those just fine. The soldiers needed them, and they wouldn't blow up no matter what happened. He couldn't think of a better combination.

About every third Georgia town had Negro guerrillas patrolling the streets along with U.S. soldiers. Whenever Cincinnatus saw some of them, he would tap his horn and wave. The blacks commonly grinned and waved back. "You a Yankee nigger?" was a question he heard again and again.

"I'm from Kentucky," he would answer as he rolled past. Let them figure that out. Yes, he'd grown up in the CSA, but he'd spent most of the second half of his life under the Stars and Stripes. His children were Yankees—no doubt about it. They even sounded as if they came from the Midwest . . . except when they got upset or angry. Then an accent more like his own would come out. But he was more betwixt and between than any one thing. He probably would be for the rest of his life.

U.S. authorities here took no chances. Bodies hung in almost every town square. That was supposed to make the living think twice about giving the USA any trouble. Seeing how much trouble the living gave the USA, Cincinnatus had his doubts about how much good it did. But those dead men wouldn't bother the United States again. He had no doubts about that at all.

Would the United States need to kill every white male in the Confederate States above the age of twelve? If they did need to, would they have the will to do it? Cincinnatus wasn't so sure about that, either. And even if the United States did set out to slaughter white male Confederates, wouldn't it be the same kind of massacre the Confederate whites had inflicted on their Negroes?

"Damn ofays have it coming, though," Cincinnatus muttered, there in the cab of his deuce-and-a-half.

Reluctantly, he shook his head. You couldn't play God like that, no matter how much you wanted to. Jake Featherston and the Freedom Party really and truly believed blacks had it coming, too. Nothing Cincinnatus had seen while stuck in Covington or while driving a truck through the wreckage of the CSA gave him any reason to think otherwise. Sincerity wasn't enough. What was? What could be?

"We got to stop killing each other. We *got* to," Cincinnatus said. Then he started to laugh. That would have been a fine thought . . . if he'd had it somewhere else, when he wasn't hauling food to soldiers dedicated to putting the Confederate States of America out of business for good.

The roads here didn't seem to be mined, the way so many had been in Tennessee. Up there, the enemy had known which way U.S. truck convoys were going. Here, they didn't. Cincinnatus wasn't sure U.S.

commanders knew where their forces were going from one day to the next. And if they didn't, how could the Confederates?

Every so often, snipers would take pot shots at the trucks from the woods. When they did, U.S. armored cars and halftracks lashed the pines with bullets. That took care of that . . . till the halftracks and armored cars drove on. Then, more often than not, the unharmed bushwhackers would climb out of their holes and start banging away at U.S. trucks again.

Cincinnatus watched the woods as closely as he watched the road, then. He kept a submachine gun on the seat beside him, where he could grab it in a hurry if he needed to. He didn't want to get shot, but he *really* didn't want to get captured. One of the bullets in the captured Confederate weapon might be for him if he had to use it that way.

He wondered how many movies he'd seen where the bad guy snarled, *You'll never take me alive, flatfoot!* He didn't think he was the bad guy in this particular melodrama, but the Confederate skulkers wouldn't feel the same way about him.

Everything went fine till the convoy got to Swainsboro, Georgia, not far from where the trucks would unload. The woods around Swainsboro were particularly thick. The town itself had a turpentine plant, a couple of planing mills, and a furniture factory to deal with the timber. In the cleared areas, farmers raised chickens and turkeys, hogs and goats. All in all, it was a typical enough backwoods Georgia town—or so Cincinnatus thought till a *big* bomb went off under a deuce-and-a-half a quarter of a mile in front of him. He was still in town; the other truck had just cleared Swainsboro.

The poor driver never knew what hit him. His truck went up in a fireball that would have been even bigger had he carried anything inflammable. Chunks of metal and asphalt rained down around Cincinnatus as he slammed on the brakes. Something clanged off a fender. Whatever it was, it sounded big enough to leave a dent. He was amazed his windshield didn't blow in and slash his face to ribbons.

No sooner had he stopped—just past the last buildings on the outskirts of town—than he grabbed for the submachine gun. He'd been through bombings before. Usually, the bomb was intended to stall the convoy so bushwhackers could hit it from the sides. His head swiveled. He didn't hear any gunfire, and wondered why not.

As the trucks ahead of him moved forward, he put his back in gear. An armored car went off the road to one side, a halftrack to the other.

The light cannon and machine guns the armored vehicles carried were potent arguments against getting gay with the convoy. Cincinnatus hoped they were, anyhow.

He ground his teeth when he had to leave the paving and go off into the mud to the side. The truck's all-wheel drive kept him from bogging down, but getting stuck was the least of his worries. If those bastards had planted more explosives next to the road . . . He'd seen that before, too.

He'd just got back up onto the road—and breathed a sigh of relief because he'd made it—when an antibarrel rocket trailing fire streaked out of the woods and slammed into the armored car's side. Those rockets were made to pierce much thicker armor than that. The armored car burst into flames.

Cincinnatus fired into the trees again and again. *Short bursts*, he reminded himself. The muzzle wouldn't pull up and to the right if he didn't try to squeeze off too many rounds at a time. That fire trail pointed right back to where the man with the launcher had to be. If Cincinnatus could nail him . . .

He growled out a triumphant, "Yeah!" when he did. A man in bloodied Confederate butternut staggered out from behind a loblolly pine and fell to his knees. Cincinnatus squeezed off another burst. The Confederate grabbed at his chest as he toppled. He lay there kicking. How many bullets did he have in him? Men often proved harder to kill than anyone who wasn't trying to do it would imagine.

This bastard, though, had surely killed everybody in the armored car. No hatches opened; no men got out. And the driver hadn't got out of the blasted truck, either. No way in hell he could have. So the Confederate had extracted a high price for his miserable, worthless life. If all his countrymen did the same . . .

But they couldn't. Cincinnatus had already seen as much. The enemy soldiers had the advantage of playing defense, of making U.S. forces come to them. But the United States also had an advantage. They could pick when and where to strike. And they could concentrate men and barrels where they thought concentrating them would do the most good. Breakthroughs were easier to come by in this war than they had been the last time around.

How many more would the USA need? Cincinnatus thought about that with half his mind while the rest got the truck rolling down the road again, and scanned the woods to either side. He'd spot the Confederates no doubt lurking in there only if they made a mistake—he knew that. Those bastards were human beings just like anybody else, though. They could screw up the same way U.S. soldiers could.

A good thing, too. Cincinnatus' shiver had nothing to do with the nasty weather. If the Confederates hadn't screwed up a couple-three times, they'd be ruling the roost now. A few Negroes still survived in the CSA. Had Jake Featherston won everything his heart desired, everything south of the border would be lily-white.

So . . . One more push into Savannah, and how long would the butternut bastards go on screaming, "Freedom!" with their goddamn country split in two? The United States could turn north and smash one half, then swing south and smash the other. Or maybe the body would die once the USA killed the head. Cincinnatus patted the submachine gun. He sure hoped so.

Jorge Rodriguez and Gabriel Medwick both sewed second stripes onto their sleeves. Jorge was lousy with a needle and thread; back in Sonora, sewing was work for women and tailors. He was surprised to find his friend neat and quick and precise. "How come you can do that so good?" he asked, ready to rag on Gabe.

"My ma learned me," Medwick answered matter-of-factly. "She reckoned I ought to be able to shift for myself, and knowing how to sew was part of it."

That left Jorge with nothing to say. Ragging on his buddy was one thing. Ragging on Gabe's mother was something else, something that went over the line. Instead of talking, Jorge sewed faster—not better, but faster. He wanted to get the shirt back on. Even sitting in front of a campfire, it was chilly out.

Artillery opened up behind him, from the direction of Statesboro. Covington was a long way northwest now, and long gone. Statesboro guarded the approaches to Savannah. The town wasn't that well fortified, not by what Jorge had heard. Why would it be? Back before the war, who would have imagined eastern Georgia would be crawling with damnyankees? Nobody in his right mind, that was for sure.

Imagine or not, though, U.S. soldiers swarmed through this part of the state. Everybody figured they were heading for Savannah. They'd been pushing the Confederates back toward the southeast for weeks. Where else would they be going?

Sergeant Hugo Blackledge appeared in the firelight. He had a gift for not being there one second and showing up out of nowhere the next: a jack-in-the-box with a nasty temper. He commanded the company these days. All the officers above him were dead and wounded, and replacements hadn't shown up. Jorge's promotion to corporal was older than Gabe's, even if their sets of stripes had both arrived at the same time. That meant Jorge had a platoon, while his friend only led a section.

"How's it feel, making like lieutenants?" Blackledge asked with a certain sardonic relish.

"Don't want to be no lieutenant," Gabriel Medwick said. "I got enough shit to worry about already."

"You said it," Jorge agreed.

As if to underline their worries, U.S. artillery came to life. Jorge listened anxiously, then relaxed as the shells roared over his head. That was counterbattery fire aimed at the C.S. guns. As long as the big guns shot at each other, as long as they left the front-line infantry alone, Jorge didn't mind them . . . much.

Sure enough, the U.S. shells came down well to the rear. Jorge finished sewing on his new stripes and put his shirt back on. Gabe, fussily precise, lagged behind.

"What are we gonna do?" Jorge said.

His buddy looked up from his sewing. "Fight the damnyankees. Keep fighting 'em till we chase 'em back where they came from."

"*¿Como?*" Jorge asked, startled into Spanish. The question sounded every bit as bleak in English: "How?"

"President'll figure out some kinda way." Medwick sounded a hundred percent confident in Jake Featherston.

Sergeant Blackledge lit a cigarette. "Don't get your ass in an uproar about that kind of shit, Rodriguez," he advised. "You can't do nothin' about it any which way. All we got to worry about is the damnyankees in front of us."

"That's bad enough!" Jorge exclaimed, because Blackledge made it sound as if the U.S. soldiers were nothing to worry about. Rodriguez wished they weren't but knew they were.

"Yeah, well, so what? You're still here. I'm still here. Hell, even pretty boy's still here." Blackledge blew smoke in Gabriel Medwick's direction.

"Up yours, too, Sarge," Medwick said without rancor. When he first got to know Blackledge, he wouldn't have dared mouth off like that. Neither would Jorge. And the formidable noncom would have squashed them like lice if they had dared. Now they'd earned the right, not least simply by surviving.

"All we can do is all we can do," Hugo Blackledge said. "We've put up a hell of a fight, seeing as they outweigh us about two to one."

"We'll lick 'em yet," Gabe said as he finally put his shirt back on.

"Uh-huh." Sergeant Blackledge nodded. Jorge had seen nods like that, from doctors in sickrooms where the patient wasn't going to get better but didn't know it yet. You kept his hope up as long as you could. Maybe it didn't do any good, but it didn't hurt, either. And he felt better, for a little while, anyway.

Jorge's dark eyes met the sergeant's ice-gray ones in a moment of complete mutual understanding. Gabe didn't get it, and probably wouldn't till Savannah fell, if then—and if he lived that long. The patient in the sickroom was the Confederacy. And chances were it wouldn't get better.

"Got another one of those Dukes?" Jorge asked Blackledge.

"Sure do. Here you go." The older man held out the pack.

Jorge got to his feet and walked over to take one. As he leaned forward so Blackledge could give him a light, he whispered, "We're fucked, *sí*?"

"Bet your sorry butt we are," Blackledge answered.

"Thanks." Jorge sucked in smoke. But he was more grateful for the candor than for the cigarette.

When morning came, he looked up the road along which he'd been retreating. A couple of dead Confederates lay there, about three hundred yards in front of the line. Nobody'd tried to retrieve their bodies. For one thing, it was too likely that U.S. snipers would shoot anyone who did. For another, C.S. engineers had booby-trapped the corpses. Any damnyankee who flipped them over looking for souvenirs would regret it.

Nobody'd set up a kitchen anywhere close by. Jorge made do with a ration can. It was U.S.-issue deviled ham, the favorite canned meal on both sides of the front. Jorge hadn't swapped cigarettes to get his hands on this one. He'd taken three or four cans off a dead Yankee. Looking at those bodies out there made him shake his head as he ate. Maybe he'd been lucky not to get blown to kingdom come.

It wasn't as if the damnyankees wouldn't have other chances.

Sooner or later—probably sooner—they would start pushing hard toward Savannah again. The only question was whether they'd do it right here or somewhere a little farther west. If they did it right here, Jorge knew he'd have to retreat or die. If they did it farther west, his choices would lie between retreating and getting cut off and trapped.

He didn't think the C.S. line could hold. As for counterattacks . . . Well, no. When a sergeant commanded a company, when a new corporal was leading a platoon, this army would have a devil of a time holding its ground. Pushing the enemy back seemed far beyond its power.

Too many damnyankee soldiers. Too many damnyankee barrels. Too many airplanes with the eagle and crossed swords. With Atlanta gone, with Richmond in trouble, with Birmingham getting pounded, how could the Confederacy reply?

No U.S. troops came close enough to try to plunder the booby-trapped corpses. That left Jorge more relieved than anything else. Advancing U.S. soldiers would have meant more hard fighting. He'd seen enough—more than enough, in fact—to last him a lifetime. He knew he hadn't seen the end of things here. Either he'd have to do more fighting or he'd have to fall back. Chances were, he'd have to do both. If he didn't have to do either one today, or maybe even tomorrow, so much the better.

Quiet lasted through the afternoon and into the evening. He smoked and ate and dozed and listened to the problems of a soldier in his platoon who had woman trouble back in North Carolina. Somebody'd sent Ray a letter that said his wife (or maybe fiancée; Jorge wasn't quite sure) was fooling around on him with a mechanic who was back there because he'd already lost an arm in the fighting.

"Shoulda blown off his shortarm instead," Ray said savagely. "What I want to do is, I want to go on home and take care o' that my own self."

"Well, you can't," Jorge said. "They catch you deserting, they shoot you. Then they hang up your body to give other people the message."

"It'd be worth it. Then Thelma Lou'd know how much I love her," Ray said.

Jorge wondered why he'd got stuck listening to this crap. He himself hadn't had a fiancée, let alone a wife, back in Baroyeca. The few times he'd lain down with a woman, he'd had to put money on the dresser first. But he was the platoon leader. That must have made him seem to Ray like someone who knew what he was doing. He wished he seemed that way in his own eyes.

He knew enough to be sure Ray was talking like a fool. Anybody who wasn't in love with Thelma Lou would have known that. "She just laugh when you get in trouble," Jorge said. "Then she go on fooling around with this asshole."

"Not if I kill him, she don't." Ray was as stubborn as he was stupid, which took some doing.

"Then she fool around with somebody else," Jorge said. "A gal who cheats on you once, she cheats on you lots of times. You don't get her back like she never screwed around at all." Ray's jaw dropped. Plainly, that had never crossed his mind. *Dumb as rocks*, Jorge thought sadly. He went on, "Or maybe this letter you got, maybe it's bullshit. Whoever sent it to you, there ain't no return address, right?"

"I dunno," Ray said, which covered more ground than he realized. "You might could be right, but I dunno. Kinda sounds like somethin' Thelma Lou'd go and do."

So why do you give a damn about her? Jorge didn't scream it, however much he wanted to. He could tell it would do no good. "You can't go nowhere," he said. "You don't want to let your buddies down, right?" Ray shook his head. He wasn't a bad soldier. Jorge pressed on: "You can't get leave, and there's lots of military police and Freedom Party men between here and your home town. So stay. All this stuff, if it really is anything, it'll sort itself out when the war's done. Why worry till then?"

"I guess." Ray didn't sound convinced, but he didn't sound like someone on the ragged edge of deserting, either.

Sergeant Blackledge swore when Jorge warned him of the trouble. "This ain't the first time he's had trouble with that cunt," he said. "But you were dead right—if he does try and run off, he ain't gonna get far, and he'll land in more shit than Congress puts out."

Half an hour after that, a captain and a second lieutenant and six or eight enlisted men showed up: a new company CO, a platoon commander, and some real live (for the moment, anyhow) reinforcements. Would wonders never cease? The captain, whose name was Richmond Sellars, walked with a limp and wore a Purple Heart ribbon with two tiny oak-leaf clusters pinned to it.

"I told 'em I was ready to get back to duty," he said, "so they sent my ass here." He pointed to the lieutenant, who had to be at least forty and looked to have come up through the ranks. "This is Grover Burch. Who's in charge now?"

"I am, sir. Sergeant Hugo Blackledge." Blackledge likely wasn't happy to see company command go glimmering. Jorge wasn't thrilled about losing his platoon. The good news was that he wouldn't have to listen to complaints like Ray's so much. They'd be Burch's worry, and Sergeant Blackledge's, too.

"Well, Blackledge, why don't you fill me in?" Sellars said. He'd seen enough to know he'd be smart to walk soft for a while.

The sergeant did, quickly and competently. He said a couple of nice things about Jorge, which surprised and pleased the new corporal. Then Blackledge pointed northwest. "Not really up to us what happens next, sir," he said. "The damnyankees'll do whatever the hell they do, and we've got to try and stop 'em. I just hope to God we can."

Forward to Richmond! That had been the U.S. battle cry in the War of Secession. It would have been the battle cry during the Great War, except the Confederates struck north before the USA could even try to push south. And in this fight . . .

In this fight, the CSA had held the USA in northern Virginia. The Confederate States had held, yes, but they weren't holding any more. Abner Dowling noted each new U.S. advance with growing amazement and growing delight. After U.S. soldiers broke out of the nasty second-growth country called the Wilderness, the enemy just didn't have the men and machines to stop them. The Confederates could slow them down, but the U.S. troops pushed forward day after day.

A command car took Dowling and his adjutant past burnt-out C.S. barrels. Even in this chilly winter weather, the stink of death filled the air. "I didn't believe I'd ever say it," Dowling remarked, "but I think we've got 'em on the run here."

"Yes, sir. Same here." Major Angelo Toricelli nodded. "They just can't hold us any more. They'll have a devil of a time keeping us out of Richmond."

"I hope we don't just barge into the place," Dowling said.

He glanced over at the driver. He didn't want to say much more than that, not with a man he didn't know well listening. His lack of faith in Daniel MacArthur was almost limitless. He'd served with MacArthur since the Great War, and admired his courage without admiring his common sense or strategic sense. He doubted whether MacArthur *had* any strategic sense, as a matter of fact.

"I've heard we're trying to work out how to get over the James," Major Toricelli said.

"I've heard the same thing," Dowling replied. "Hearing is only hearing, though. Seeing is believing."

A rifle shot rang out, not nearly far enough away. The driver sped up. Toricelli swung the command car's heavy machine gun toward the sound of the gunshot. He didn't know what was going on. He couldn't know who'd fired, either. The shot sounded to Dowling as if it had come from a C.S. automatic rifle, but about every fourth soldier in green-gray carried one of those nowadays—and the other three wanted one.

Toricelli relaxed—a little—as no target presented itself. "Back in the War of Secession, they would have had a devil of a time taking the straight route we're using," he remarked. "The lay of the land doesn't make it easy."

"Around here, the lay of the land's got the clap," Dowling said. His adjutant snorted. So did the driver. An adjutant was almost obligated to find a general's jokes funny. A lowly driver wasn't, so Dowling felt doubly pleased with himself.

He'd been exaggerating, but only a little. The rivers in central Virginia all seemed to run from northwest to southeast. Major Toricelli was right. Those rivers and their bottomlands would have forced men marching on foot to veer toward the southeast, too: toward the southeast and away from the Confederate capital.

But barrels and halftracks could go where marching men couldn't. And U.S. forces were pushing straight toward Richmond whether Jake Featherston's men liked it or not.

So Dowling thought, at any rate, till C.S. fighter-bombers appeared. The driver jammed on the brakes. Everybody bailed out of the command car. The roadside ditch Dowling dove into was muddy, but what could you do? Bullets spanged off asphalt and thudded into dirt. Dowling didn't hear any of the wet slaps that meant bullets striking flesh, for which he was duly grateful.

A moment later, he did hear several metallic *clang!*s and then a soft *whump!* That was the command car catching fire. He swore under his breath. He wouldn't be going forward to Richmond as fast as he wanted to.

He stuck his head up out of the ditch, then ducked again as machine-gun ammo in the command car started cooking off. Embarrassing as hell to get killed by your own ordnance. Embarrassing as hell to get killed by anybody's ordnance, when you came right down to it.

After the .50-caliber rounds stopped going off, Dowling cautiously got to his feet. So did the driver. Dowling looked across the road. Major Toricelli emerged from a ditch there. He wasn't just muddy—he was dripping. His grin looked distinctly forced. "Some fun, huh, sir?"

"Now that you mention it," Dowling said, "no."

"We'd better flag down another auto, or a truck, or whatever we can find," Toricelli said. "We need to be in place."

He was young and serious, even earnest. Dowling had been through much more. With a crooked grin, he replied, "You're right, of course. The whole war will grind to a halt if I'm not there to give orders at just the right instant."

Who was the Russian novelist who'd tried to show that generals and what they said and did was utterly irrelevant to the way battles turned out? Dowling couldn't remember his name; he cared for Russian novels no more than he cared for Brussels sprouts. With the bias that sprang from his professional rank, he thought the Russian's conclusions absurd. He remembered the claim, though, and enjoyed hauling it out to bedevil his adjutant.

"They do need you, sir," Major Toricelli said. "If they didn't, they would have left you in Texas."

"And if that's not a fate worse, or at least more boring, than death, I don't know what would be," Dowling said.

While he and Toricelli sparred, the driver, a practical man, looked down the road in the direction from which they'd come. "Here's a truck," he said, and waved for it to stop.

Maybe he was persuasive. Maybe the burning command car was. Either way, the deuce-and-a-half shuddered to a halt, brakes squealing. Over the rumble of the engine, the driver said, "You guys look like you could use a lift."

"You mean you're not selling sandwiches?" Dowling said. "Damn!"

The driver eyed his rotund form. "You look like you've had plenty already . . ." As his eyes found the stars on Dowling's shoulder straps, his voice trailed off. Too late, of course, and the glum look on his face

said he knew it. "Uh, sir," he added with the air of a man certain it
wouldn't help.

"Just get me to Army HQ in a hurry, and I won't ask who the hell
you are," Dowling said.

"Pile in. You got yourself a deal." Now the driver sounded like
somebody'd who'd just won a reprieve from the governor.

Before long, Dowling repented of the bargain. The trucker drove as
if he smelled victory at the Omaha 400. He took corners on two wheels
and speedshifted so that Dowling marveled when his transmission
didn't start spitting teeth from the gears. Other traffic on the road
seemed nothing but obstructions to be dodged.

"What are you carrying?" the general shouted. The engine wasn't
rumbling any more—it was roaring.

"Shells—105s, mostly," the driver yelled back, leaning into another maniacal turn. "How come?"

Major Toricelli crossed himself. Dowling wondered who was more
dangerous, the Confederate fighter-bomber pilot or this nut. Well, if the
shells went off, it would all be over in a hurry. Then, brakes screeching
now, the driver almost put him through the windshield.

"We're here," the man announced.

"Oh, joy," Dowling said, and got out of the truck as fast as he
could. Toricelli and the soldier who'd driven the command car also escaped with alacrity. The truck drove off at a reasonably sedate clip. The
madman behind the wheel probably felt he'd done his duty.

A sentry with a captured C.S. submachine gun came up. "I know
you, sir," he said to Dowling. "Do you vouch for these two?" The muzzle swung toward Toricelli and the driver.

Never saw 'em before. The words passed through Dowling's mind,
but didn't pass his lips. The sentry was too grim, too serious, to let him
get away with them, and too likely to open fire before asking questions.
"Yes," was all Dowling said.

"All right. Come ahead, then." The sentry gestured with his
weapon, a little more invitingly than he had before.

Familiar chaos enveloped Dowling as he stepped into the big tent.
The air was gray with tobacco smoke and blue with curses. People in
uniform shouted into telephone handsets and wireless sets' mikes. But
they just sounded annoyed or angry, the way they were supposed to
sound when things were going well.

He remembered headquarters in Columbus, back in the first summer of the war. He remembered the panic in officers' voices then, no matter how they tried to hold it at bay. They couldn't believe what the Confederates were doing to them. They couldn't believe anyone could slice through an army like a housewife slicing cheddar. They didn't know how to do it themselves, and so they'd figured nobody else knew, either.

They almost lost the war before they realized how wrong they were.

Now they knew what was what. Now they had the barrels and the bombs and the artillery and the men to turn knowledge into action. Better still, they had the doctrine to turn knowledge into *effective* action. Yes, they'd learned plenty of lessons from the enemy, but so what? Where you learned your lessons didn't matter. That you learned them did.

One of the men at a field telephone lifted his head and looked around. When he spotted Dowling, he called, "Message for you from General MacArthur, sir."

"Yes?" Dowling tried not to show how his stomach tightened at that handful of words. Daniel MacArthur often seemed incapable of learning anything, and the lessons he drew from what happened to him verged on the bizarre. His scheme to land men at the mouth of the James and march northwest up the river to Richmond . . .

I managed to scotch that one, anyhow, Dowling thought. *I earned my pay the day I did it, too.*

"Well done for your progress, and keep it up," the man reported. "And the general says he's over the Rapidan River east of Fredericksburg and rapidly pushing south. 'Rapidly' is his word, sir."

"Is it?" Dowling said. "Good for him!" The Confederates had given MacArthur a bloody nose at Fredericksburg in 1942. There wasn't much room to slide troops east of the town. Abner Dowling wouldn't have cared to try it himself. But if MacArthur had got away with it, and if he was driving rapidly from the Rapidan and punning as he went . . . "Sounds like Featherston's boys really are starting to go to pieces."

"Here's hoping!" three men in Army HQ said in one chorus, while another two or three added, "It's about time!" in another.

Dowling liked prizefights. People said of some boxers that they had a puncher's chance in the ring. If they hit somebody squarely, he'd fall over, no matter how big and tough he was. That was the kind of chance the CSA had against the USA. But when the United States didn't—

quite—fall over, the Confederate States had to fight a more ordinary war, and they weren't so well equipped for that.

Did Featherston have one more punch left? Dowling didn't see how he could, but Dowling hadn't seen all kinds of things before June 22, 1941. He shrugged. If the United States seized Richmond and cut the Confederacy in half farther south, what could Featherston punch with?

"Tell General MacArthur I thank him very much, and I look forward to meeting him in front of the Gray House," Dowling said. Forward to Richmond! Things really were going that way.

As far as Dr. Leonard O'Doull was concerned, eastern Alabama seemed about the same as western Georgia. The hilly terrain hadn't changed when he crossed the state line. Neither had the accents the local civilians used. Shamefaced U.S. soldiers caught social diseases from some of the local women, too.

This penicillin stuff knocked those down in nothing flat, though. It was better than sulfa for the clap, and ever so much better than the poisons that had been medicine's only weapons against syphilis.

"Move up, Doc!" a noncom shouted at O'Doull one morning. "Front's going forward, and you gotta keep up with it."

"Send me a truck, and I'll do it," the doctor answered. Sergeant Goodson Lord played a racetrack fanfare on his liberated trombone. The soldier who brought the news thumbed his nose at the medic. Grinning, Lord paused and returned the compliment, if that was what it was.

By now, O'Doull had moving down to a science. Packing, knocking down the tent, loading stuff, actually traveling, and setting up again went as smoothly as if he'd been doing them for years—which he had. He was proud of how fast he got the aid station running once the deuce-and-a-half stopped. And every forward move meant another bite taken out of the Confederate States.

He hadn't been set up again for very long before he got a hard look at what those bites meant. "Doc! Hey, Doc!" Eddie the corpsman yelled as he helped carry a litter back to the aid station. "Got a bad one here, Doc!"

O'Doull had already figured that out for himself. Whoever was on the litter was screaming: a high, shrill sound of despair. "Christ!" Sergeant Lord said. "They go and find a wounded woman?"

"Wouldn't be surprised, not by the noise," O'Doull answered. "It's happened before." He remembered an emergency hysterectomy after a luckless woman stopped a shell fragment with her belly. What had happened to her afterwards? He hadn't the faintest idea.

When he first saw the wounded person, he thought it was a woman. The skin was fine and pale and beardless, the cries more contralto than tenor. Then Eddie said, "Look what they're throwing at us these days. Poor kid can't be a day over fourteen."

This time, O'Doull was the one who blurted, "Christ!" That *was* a boy. He wore dungarees and a plaid shirt. An armband said, NATIONAL ASSAULT FORCE.

"You damnyankees here're gonna shoot me now, ain't you?" the kid asked.

"Nooo," O'Doull said slowly. He'd seen National Assault Force troops before, but they were old geezers, guys with too many miles on them to go into the regular Army. Orders were to treat them as POWs, not *francs-tireurs*. Now the Confederates were throwing their seed corn into the NAF, too.

"They said you'd kill everybody you got your hands on," the wounded boy said, and then he started shrieking again.

"Well, they're full of shit," O'Doull said roughly. He nodded to the stretcher-bearers. "Get him up on the table. Goodson, put him out."

"Yes, sir," Lord said. When the mask went over the kid's face, the ether made him think he was choking. He tried to yank off the mask. O'Doull had seen that before, plenty of times. Eddie and Goodson Lord grabbed the boy soldier's hands till he went under.

He'd taken a bullet in the belly—no wonder he was howling. O'Doull cut away the bloody shirt and got to work. It could have been worse. It hadn't pierced his liver or spleen or gall bladder. He'd lose his left kidney, but you could get along on one. His guts weren't *too* torn up. With the new fancy medicines to fight peritonitis, he wasn't doomed the way he would have been a few years earlier.

"I think he may make it." O'Doull sounded surprised, even to himself.

"I bet you're right, sir," Goodson Lord said. "I wouldn't have given a dime for his chances when you got to work on him—I'll tell you that."

"Neither would I," O'Doull admitted as he started closing up. His hands sutured with automatic skill and precision. "If he doesn't come down with a wound infection, though, what's to keep him from getting better?"

"*Then* we can kill him," Lord said. O'Doull could see only the medic's eyes over his surgical mask, but they looked amused. The kid had been so sure falling into U.S. hands was as bad as letting the demons of hell get hold of him.

"Yeah, well, if we don't kill him now, will we have to do it in twenty years?" O'Doull asked.

"He'll be about old enough to fight then," Sergeant Lord said.

That was one of too many truths spoken in jest. But what would stop another war between the USA and the CSA a generation down the road? After the United States walloped the snot out of the Confederates this time around, would the USA stay determined long enough to make sure the Confederacy didn't rise again? If the country did, wouldn't it be a miracle? And wouldn't the Confederates try to hit back as soon as the USA offered them even the smallest chance?

"Once you get on a treadmill, how do you get off?" O'Doull said.

"What do you mean, sir?" Lord asked.

"How do we keep from fighting a war with these sons of bitches every twenty years?"

"Beats me," the medic said. "If you know, run for President. I guaran-damn-tee you it'd put you one up on all the chuckleheads in politics now. Most of 'em can't count to twenty-one without undoing their fly."

O'Doull snorted. Then, wistfully, he said, "Only trouble is, I don't have any answers. I just have questions. Questions are easy. Answers?" He shook his head. "One reason old Socrates looks so smart is that he tried to get answers from other people. He didn't give many of his own."

"If you say so. He's Greek to me," Goodson Lord replied.

They sent the wounded Confederate kid off to a hospital farther back of the line—all the way back into Georgia, in fact. O'Doull, who had a proper professional pride in his own work, hoped the little bastard would live even if that meant he might pick up a rifle and start shooting at U.S. soldiers again twenty years from now . . . or, for that matter, twenty minutes after he got out of a POW camp.

The front ground forward. Before long, Birmingham would start catching it from artillery as well as from the bombers that visited it almost every night. O'Doull wondered how much good that would do.

The Confederates might be running short of men, but they still had plenty of guns and ammunition. The bombing that was supposed to knock out their factories didn't live up to the fancy promises airmen made for it.

Featherston's followers still had plenty of rockets, too. Stovepipe rockets blew up U.S. barrels. O'Doull hated treating burns; it gave him the shivers. He did it anyway, because he had to. Screaming meemies could turn an acre of ground into a slaughterhouse. And the big long-range rockets threw destruction a couple of hundred miles.

"Hell with Birmingham," Sergeant Lord said, picking screaming-meemie fragments out of the thigh and buttocks of an anesthetized corporal. "We've got to take Huntsville away from those fuckers. That's where this shit is coming from."

"No arguments from me." O'Doull held out a metal basin to the senior medic. Lord dropped another small chunk of twisted, bloody steel or aluminum into it. *Clink!* The sound of metal striking metal seemed absurdly cheerful.

"Well, if you can see it and I can see it, how come the brass can't?" Lord demanded. He peered at the wounded man's backside, then dug in with the forceps again. Sure as hell, he found another fragment.

"Maybe they will," O'Doull said. "They swung a lot of force south of Atlanta to make the Confederates clear out. Now we're better positioned to go after Birmingham than we are for Huntsville, that's all."

"Maybe." Lord sounded anything but convinced. "Me, I think the brass are a bunch of jerks—that's what the trouble is."

Of course you do—you're a noncom, O'Doull thought. He too was given to heretical thoughts about the competence, if any, of the high command. Yes, he was an officer, but as a doctor he wasn't in the chain of command. He didn't want to be, either. There often seemed to be missing links at the top of the chain.

Missing links . . . His memory went back to biology classes in college, in the dead, distant days before the Great War. He remembered pictures of low-browed, chinless, hairy brutes: Neanderthal Man and Java Man and a couple of others thought to lie halfway between apes and *Homo* laughably called *sapiens*. He imagined ape-men in green-gray uniforms with stars on their shoulder straps and black-and-gold General Staff arm-of-service colors.

The picture formed with frightening ease. "Ook!" he muttered. Sergeant Lord sent him a curious look. O'Doull's cheeks heated.

He also imagined hulking subhumans in butternut, with wreathed stars on their collars. Confederate Neanderthals also proved easy to conjure up. *A good thing, too,* O'Doull thought. *We'd lose if they weren't as dumb as we are.*

And wasn't Jake Featherston the top *Pithecanthropus* of them all? "Ook," Leonard O'Doull said again, louder this time. Then he shook his head, angry at himself for swallowing his own side's propaganda. Sure, Featherston had made his share of mistakes, but who in this war hadn't? The President of the CSA had come much too close to leading his side to victory over a much bigger, much richer foe. If that didn't argue for a certain basic competence, what would?

"You all right, sir?" Goodson Lord asked, real concern in his voice.

"As well as I can be, anyhow," O'Doull answered. What worried him was that Jake Featherston could still win. The Confederates had come up with more new and nasty weapons this time around than his own side had. The fragments Lord was cleaning up—another one clanked into the bowl—showed that. If the enemy pulled something else out of his hat, something big . . .

"Hey, Doc!" That insistent shout from outside drove such thoughts from his mind. No matter what the Confederates who weren't Neanderthals came up with, all he could do was try to patch up the men they hurt.

"You all right by yourself?" he asked Lord.

"I'll cope," the senior medic said, which was the right answer.

The new wounded man had had a shell fragment slice the right side of his chest open. The corpsmen who brought him in were irate. "It was a short round, Doc," Eddie said. O'Doull could all but see the steam coming out of his ears. "One of ours. It killed another guy— they'll have to scrape him up before they can bury him."

"That kind of shit happens all the time," another stretcher-bearer said.

"Happens too goddamn often." Yeah, Eddie was hot, all right.

"I think so, too." O'Doull had also seen too many wounds on U.S. soldiers inflicted by other U.S. soldiers. He hated them at least as much as Eddie did. All the same . . . "Let's get to work on him. The less time we waste, the better."

Collapsed lung, lots of bleeders to tie off, broken ribs. O'Doull knew what to expect, and he got it. The wound was serious, but straightforward and clean. O'Doull knew he had a good chance of saving the soldier. By the time he finished, he was pretty sure he had. If the war lasted long enough, the man might return to duty.

"Won't he be proud of his Purple Heart?" Eddie was a little rabbity guy. Somehow, that only made his sarcasm more devastating.

"He's here to get one, anyway," O'Doull said. "You told me he had a buddy who bought the whole plot, right?"

"Yeah." Eddie nodded.

"Well, this is better. This guy'll probably end up all right," O'Doull said. Eddie didn't answer, which might have been the most devastating comeback of all.

VII

When Cassius walked down the street, white people scurried out of his way. That still thrilled him. It had never happened before he started this occupation duty. His whole life long, he'd been taught to move aside for whites. Dreadful things happened to colored people who didn't.

Now he had a Tredegar in his hands and the U.S. Army at his back. Anybody who didn't like that—and there were bound to be people who didn't—and was rash enough to let him know it could end up suddenly dead, and no one would say a word. Other members of Gracchus' band had shot whites in Madison for any reason or none, and then gone about their business. Oh, the ofays in town flabbled, but who paid attention to them? Not a soul.

White women were particularly quick not just to get out of the way but to get out of sight. Cassius had seen that ever since he got here. Shooting wasn't the only revenge Negroes could take on their former social superiors. Oh, no—not at all.

Cassius scowled when he saw blue X's painted on walls. Those would come down or get painted over in a hurry—they were shorthand for C.S. battle flags. If a property owner didn't cover them up, U.S. soldiers would assume he was a Confederate sympathizer. They'd probably be right, too. Right or wrong, they'd make him sorry.

More than a few whites had already disappeared from Madison. The U.S. Army said they'd gone into prisons farther from the front. Negroes loudly insisted the U.S. soldiers had shipped them to camps.

Cassius had done it himself. He *wanted* the ofays quivering in their boots. They'd made him quiver too damn long.

They'd made him fight back, too. Tales of horror like that were liable to make the local whites fight back. Cassius didn't care. If the ofays wanted to try, they could. He figured the U.S. Army *would* start massacring them then.

And he would get to help.

He came to a street corner at the same time as another Negro marching from a different direction. "Mornin', Sertorius," he said. "How you doin'?"

"I's tolerable," his fellow guerrilla replied. "How 'bout yourself?"

"Could be worse," Cassius admitted. "We got us plenty o' grub, we got warm places to sleep, an' we got all the Yankees on our side. Yeah, sure enough could be worse."

"Amen," Sertorius said, as if Cassius were a preacher. "Couple months ago, things *was* worse." He wore a U.S. helmet, and made as if to tip it. Cassius returned the gesture with the cap he had on. "See you," Sertorius added, and went on marching his assigned route.

"See you." Cassius also walked on. Odds were they would see each other at the end of the day. They weren't living in fear, the way they had when they skulked and hid in the countryside. The ofays feared them now. Cassius liked that better. Who wouldn't?

And sometimes the ofays were starting to treat them with respect. A kid maybe eight or nine years old came up to Cassius. "Got any rations you can spare?" he asked, his voice most polite.

Cassius would have told a grown man to go to hell. A skinny kid, though, was a skinny kid. Cassius started to reach for one of the ration cans in his belt pouch. Then he took another look at the boy. His hand stopped. "You called me a goddamn nigger before," he said. "You said I sucked the damnyankees' dicks. Far as I'm concerned, you kin starve."

The white boy looked almost comically astonished. "I didn't mean it," he said, and smiled a winning smile.

How dumb was he? How dumb did he think Cassius was? That was the real question, and Cassius knew the answer—dumb as a nigger, that was what he thought. "Now tell me one I'll believe," Cassius said scornfully.

If looks could have killed, he would have fallen over dead on the spot. The white kid started to say something—probably something as sweet and charming as the insults he'd dealt out the last time he ran into Cassius. Then he glanced at the Tredegar and went away instead. That was the smartest thing he could have done. Cassius likely would have shot him if he'd run his mouth twice.

An old man came up behind him. "You won't even feed a little boy?" the geezer asked. "What's the world coming to?"

"I ain't gonna feed that little bastard no matter what the world's comin' to," Cassius answered. "Some other kid, maybe, but not him."

"Why not?"

"On account of he done called me a nigger and a cocksucker."

Well, you are a nigger. Cassius could see it in the old white man's shrewd gray eyes. The fellow had sense enough not to say it, though. And cocksucker was an insult to anybody. "Oh," was all that came out of the ofay's mouth. He walked on past Cassius, careful not to come close enough to seem threatening.

At noon, another black man took over Cassius' beat. Cassius went back to the tents outside of town to see if the U.S. Army cooks had any hot food. Sure enough, big kettles of chicken stew simmered over crackling fires. Cassius dug out his mess kit and got in line.

"How'd it go?" asked the white soldier in front of him. "Any trouble with the local yokels?"

"Nah." Cassius shook his head. But then he corrected himself: "Well, a little. This kid who don't like niggers—an' I *know* he don't like niggers—tried to bum food offa me."

"Hope you told him to fuck himself," the soldier said. "Little asshole can starve for all I care. Just save somebody on our side the trouble of shooting him once he grows up."

"You reckon another war's comin'?" Cassius asked as the line snaked forward.

"Shit, don't you?" the white man replied. "Sooner or later, we'll let these Confederate bastards back on their feet. A half hour after we do, they'll clean the grease off the guns they got stashed away and start greasin' us."

Was that savage cynicism or sage common sense? When it came to gauging the chances of peace and war, how much difference was there? Cassius didn't know. He did know Confederate whites despised both blacks and U.S. whites. He'd always known C.S. Negroes didn't love whites—and how little reason they had to love them. Now he'd

discovered that white soldiers from the USA couldn't stand Confederate whites, either. That was reassuring.

Plainly, quite a few soldiers in green-gray didn't like Negroes, either. But they hated Confederate whites more—at least while they were
down here. Confederate whites wanted them dead, and were willing—
no, eager—to pick up weapons and make sure they died. Negroes in
the CSA, by contrast, made natural allies. The enemy of my enemy . . .
is at least worth dishing out rations to, Cassius thought.

The cook loaded his mess kit with as much chicken stew as anybody else got. "Here y'are, buddy," he said, his lips barely moving because of the cigarette that dangled from the corner of his mouth.

"Thanks." Cassius moved on.

When he got a cup of coffee to go with the stew, he found it heavily laced with chicory. But it came from the same big pot—almost a
vat—that served the U.S. soldiers. No one was giving him particularly
lousy coffee. The good stuff was hard to come by—that was all. As
long as he got his fair share of what there was, he had no kick coming.

He made sure he washed his mess kit after he finished eating. The
U.S. Army came down hard on you if you didn't. One dose of a jowly
sergeant screaming in his face about food poisoning and the galloping
shits was enough to last him a lifetime. He did notice that the sergeants screamed just as loud at white men they caught screwing up.
Again, as long as they tore into everybody equally, Cassius could deal
with it.

Once he'd policed up—a term that had sounded funny when he
first heard it, but one he was used to now—he went over to the POW
camp outside of Madison. Watching Confederate soldiers behind
barbed wire was even more fun than looking at animals in cages had
been when his father took him to the zoo.

The Confederates were like lions—they'd bite if they got half a
chance. But he had claws of his own. The Tredegar's weight, which often annoyed him, seemed more like a safety net close to the prisoners.
"I had a gun myself, I'd shoot you for totin' that thing," a POW said,
shaking his fist.

"You could try," Cassius answered. "Some other ofays done tried
before, but I'm still here."

"You know what happens to uppity niggers?" the POW said.

"Sure do. They git shot." Cassius started to unsling the rifle. "Same thing happens to uppity prisoners." The Confederate shut up. Cassius let his hand drop.

Some of the other POWs weren't uppity. They were just hungry. They begged from U.S. soldiers, and they begged from Negroes, too. "Got any rations you don't need?" one of them asked, stretching out his hands imploringly to Cassius.

"You feed me if I was in there?" Cassius asked.

"Well, I hope so," the man answered after a perceptible pause for thought. "I'm a Christian, or I try to be."

"Reckon Jake Featherston's a Christian, too?"

"Sure he is," the POW said, this time without hesitation. "He loves Jesus, same as you'n me. Jesus loves him, too."

"Fuck you, you ofay asshole." Cassius turned away. "You can starve."

"You ain't no Christian," the Confederate called after him.

"If Jake Featherston is, I don't want to be." Cassius walked off. He wondered if the POW would cuss him out as he went. But the man kept quiet. A few untimely demises had convinced the C.S. prisoners that they needed to watch their mouths around the surviving Negroes.

Cassius' mother would have landed on him like a thousand-pound bomb if she heard him say he didn't want to be a Christian. She prayed even when things looked worst—no, especially when they did. And she got caught in church, and went straight from church to one of Jake Featherston's murder factories. What did that say about how much being a Christian was worth? Not much, not so far as Cassius could see.

Maybe she was in heaven, the way she always thought she would be. Cassius hoped so. He had trouble believing it, though. He had trouble believing anything these days.

He found Gracchus that evening. Gracchus thought about things, too. "You reckon we'll ever fit in again?" Cassius asked.

The former guerrilla leader didn't even pretend not to understand what he was talking about. "In Georgia? Naw." Gracchus shook his head.

"Don't just mean Georgia," Cassius said. "I mean anywhere. The Confederate ofays all hate us." He didn't love whites in the CSA, either, but he left that out of the mix, continuing, "Ofays from the USA don't all hate us, I reckon, but they's so different, ain't no way we belong in Yankeeland, neither. So what does that leave?"

"Nothin'." Gracchus managed a crooked grin. "When you ever know a nigger who had more'n dat?"

"You got somethin' there," Cassius admitted. His father had had more: a kingdom of the mind, a kingdom whose size and scope Cassius was only beginning to realize he'd never fully grasped. But what did all of Xerxes' quiet wisdom win him in the end? Only another place on the train bound for hell on earth. Cassius said, "I could kill ofays for the rest o' my life an' not even start payin' them fuckers back."

"It's a bastard, ain't it?" Gracchus said. "Maybe Jake Featherston wins, an' maybe he loses. But we-uns, we-uns already done lost." Cassius started to answer, but what could he say that Gracchus hadn't?

Yes, the front was Richmond. There had always been a danger in putting the Confederate capital so close to the U.S. border. Richmond made a magnet for U.S. ambitions. McClellan had threatened it in the War of Secession; a better general likely would have taken it then. Even in the Second Mexican War, the USA dreamt of marching in. During the Great War, the flood tide of green-gray had reached Fredericksburg on its way south before the Confederate government decided it had had enough.

And now . . . Now Jake Featherston was red-hot, almost white-hot, with fury, but not even his unending, unyielding rage could stiffen the Confederate armies north of the capital. "God damn it to hell!" he screamed at Nathan Bedford Forrest III. "We need to bring more men into the line up there!"

"Sir, we haven't got any more men to move," Forrest replied.

"Get 'em from somewhere!" Jake said.

"Where do you recommend, sir?" the chief of the General Staff asked. "Shall we pull them out of Georgia? Or maybe out of Alabama?"

"No! Jesus Christ, no!" Featherston exclaimed. "The fucking country'll fall apart if we do." The country was falling apart anyway, but he knew it would fall apart faster if he pulled soldiers away from the sectors where they were fighting hardest. "What have we got left in the Carolinas?"

"What was there is either up here or down in Georgia," Forrest replied. "It has been for weeks." He paused, then licked his lips and asked, "Are you sure you aren't overworked, Mr. President?"

"I'm tired of nobody doin' what needs doin'—I sure am tired o' that," Jake growled.

"That's . . . not quite what I meant, sir." Nathan Bedford Forrest III licked his lips again. "Don't you think the strain of command has been a little too much for you? Shouldn't you take a rest, sir, and come back to duty when you're refreshed and ready to face it again?"

"Well, I don't rightly know," Featherston said slowly. "Do you really reckon I'm off?"

"The war hasn't gone the way we wish it would have, and that's a fact." Forrest sounded relieved—and surprised—that Jake wasn't hitting the armored ceiling in fourteen different places. "Maybe somebody with a fresh slant on things can stop the damnyankees, or at least get a peace we can live with out of them."

"I suppose it's possible, but I wouldn't bet on it." Under the desk, out of the general's sight, Jake's left hand hesitated between two buttons. The first one, the closer one, would send the nearest guards rushing into the office. But the chief of the General Staff plainly had a coup in mind. If he hadn't suborned those guards, he wasn't worth the paper he was printed on. "Who do you have in mind to take over afterwards? You?" Keep the son of a bitch talking. Jake's finger came down on the other button.

"I'll take military command," Nathan Bedford Forrest III replied. "But I think Vice President Partridge is the better man to talk peace with the United States. Everything stays nice and constitutional that way." He was keeping Jake talking, too, waiting till his men got here to back his play.

You stupid piece of shit. Only way to get me out of this chair is to murder me. Featherston let a little anger show, but only a little—the sort he might show if he *was* thinking of stepping down. "Do you reckon even the Yankees are dumb enough to take Don Partridge seriously?" he demanded. "I sure as hell don't."

"If he's speaking in the name of the President, or as the President, they'll have to listen to him." Nathan Bedford Forrest's eyes kept slipping toward the door and then jerking back to Jake. The President of the CSA wanted to look that way, too, but he didn't. He had more discipline in his pinkie than Forrest did in his whole worthless carcass.

"So who all figures the country'd be better off without me?" Jake asked. "Don must be in on this, too, right? How about Clarence Potter?

He's a fellow with pretty fair judgment—always has been." He was also a fellow Featherston had suspected for years.

To his surprise, Forrest shook his head. "As a matter of fact, no. He thinks you're the best war leader we've got. I used to think so, too, but—"

He broke off. There was a commotion outside, shouts and screams and then a couple of gunshots and more screams and shouts. One of the bullets punched through what was supposed to be bulletproof glass in the door. Almost spent, it ricocheted off the wall above Jake's head and fell harmlessly to the floor.

An instant later, the door flew open with a crash. Four soldiers in camouflage uniforms burst into the President's office. Jake and Nathan Bedford Forrest III pointed at each other. "Arrest that man!" they both yelled.

Four automatic-rifle muzzles bore on the chief of the General Staff. So did the .45 Jake Featherston plucked from a desk drawer. "Hold it right there, traitor!" one of the soldiers roared.

"Freedom!" the other three shouted. They were Party Guards, not Army men. Nathan Bedford Forrest III seemed to notice that for the first time. His face turned gray as tobacco smoke. Jake Featherston watched with almost clinical interest. He'd never seen a man go that color before—not a live man, anyhow.

"How—?" Forrest gasped. That used up all the breath he had in him. He might have been a hooked crappie, drowning in air he couldn't breathe.

"What? You reckon I've only got one set of guards round this place?" Jake said. "You might be dumb enough to do something like that, but I sure ain't." He turned to the men who'd rescued him. "Make sure everything's secure down here. You find anybody you don't figure you can rely on, grab the son of a bitch. We'll sort out who's what later on. In the meantime, we squeeze answers out of this asshole. He'll sing. He'll sing like a fucking canary."

"You bet, boss." One of the Freedom Party Guards—a troop leader—grinned a sharp-toothed grin. "Once we get going, we can make a rock sing." The three-striper laughed.

So did Featherston. "He won't be a rock," he predicted. Part of him wanted to laugh at what an amateurish excuse for a coup Nathan Bedford Forrest III tried to bring off. Talking him into stepping down of his own accord! If that wasn't the dumbest thing in the world, Jake didn't know what would be. "Your granddad'd be ashamed of you," he told Forrest.

"Great-grandfather. And no, he wouldn't—he didn't like tyrants any better than I do," the suddenly former chief of the General Staff replied. He could talk a good game, but some games weren't about talk, and he'd never figured that out.

"Take him away," Jake said. He didn't want to argue with Forrest, and he didn't have to, either. But the other man hadn't the least idea what he meant. If the original Nathan Bedford Forrest planned a coup, he would have done it right. This smudgy carbon copy—hardly a Forrest at all in looks, except for the eyes—didn't know the first thing about how to manage one.

Away he went, perhaps too numb to realize yet what kind of hell he was heading for. Well, he'd find out pretty damn quick. The only thing that excused a plot was winning. Failure brought its own punishment.

Jake went out into the antechamber. Lulu sat at her desk as calmly as if two Army men didn't lie dead not ten feet away. "I knew you'd take care of that foolishness, Mr. President," she said. "Shall we call somebody to get rid of this carrion?"

"Mm—not quite yet," Featherston answered. "Let me bring in some more men I'm sure I can count on." The worst thing about having somebody mount a coup was being unable to trust the people around you afterwards.

But if he couldn't count on the Freedom Party Guards, he couldn't count on anybody—and if he couldn't count on anybody, Nathan Bedford Forrest III's strike would have worked like a charm. Jake went back to the telephone on his desk. Had Forrest had the brains to suborn the operator and keep the President from getting hold of loyal troops? That might make things dicey, even now.

But no. Within a minute, Featherston was talking with a regimental commander named Wilcy Hoyt, who promised to secure the Gray House grounds with his troops. "Freedom!" Hoyt said fervently as he rang off.

Would the men who backed Forrest fight? Would they try to take Jake out, reckoning it was their best chance? In their shoes, Featherston would have done that. He still had his .45. But the pistol was there to protect him against a visitor who turned out to be an assassin.

It wouldn't help much against a squad of soldiers determined to do him in.

As soon as he got off the telephone with Hoyt, he went out and grabbed an automatic rifle from one of the dead guards. Even that wouldn't do him as much good as he wished, but it was better than the pistol. If he had to go down, he aimed to go down fighting.

"Will there be more shooting, Mr. President?" Lulu asked.

"Well, I don't know for sure, but there may be," Jake answered.

"Hand me that other rifle, then," his secretary said.

Featherston stared at her as if she'd suddenly started speaking Swahili. "You know how to use it?"

"Would I ask if I didn't?" she said.

He gave her the Tredegar. She could handle it, all right. And two rifles blasting anybody who tried to break in were bound to be better than one. "Where the devil did you learn something like this?" Jake inquired.

"A women's self-defense course," Lulu answered primly. "I thought I'd be shooting at Yankees, though, not traitors."

"Rifle works the same either way," Jake said, and she nodded. He supposed she'd feared assaults on her virtue. His own view was that any damnyankee who tried to take it would have to be desperately horny and plenty nearsighted, too. He would never have said anything like that, though. He liked Lulu, and wouldn't hurt her for the world—which he wouldn't have said about most people he knew.

But the people who showed themselves at the doorway to the outer office were Freedom Party Guards: Featherston loyalists. Jake had the first few come in without their weapons and with their hands up. They obeyed. The obvious joy they showed at seeing him alive and in charge of things left him with no doubt that they were on his side.

When they'd set up a perimeter outside the office, he began to feel more nearly certain things were going his way. "Get me another outside line," he told Lulu. She nodded. Jake snorted in soft contempt. No, Nathan Bedford Forrest hadn't known thing one about running a coup. Well, too goddamn bad for him. Jake got down to business: "Put me through to Saul Goldman."

"Yes, Mr. President," Lulu said, and she did. That the Confederate Director of Communications remained free made Jake snort again. Didn't Forrest know you couldn't run a country without propaganda? Evidently he didn't. He'd left the best liar and rumormonger in the business alone. Had Saul said no, how would Forrest have publicized his strike even if he pulled it off?

No need to flabble about that now. "Saul? This here's Jake," Featherston rasped. "Can you record me over the telephone and get me on the air? We've had us a little commotion here, but we got it licked now."

"Hold on for about a minute and a half, sir," the imperturbable Jew replied. "I need to set up the apparatus, and then you can say whatever you need to." He took a bit longer than he'd promised, but not much. "Go ahead, Mr. President."

"Thank you kindly." Jake paused to gather his thoughts. He didn't need long, either. "I'm Jake Featherston, and I'm here to tell you the truth. Truth is that a few damn fools reckoned they could do a better job of running our precious country than me. Other truth is that the traitors were wrong, and they'll pay. Oh, boy, will they ever . . ."

Another new exec. Sam Carsten wondered what he'd get this time. He'd had one pearl of great price and one burr under the saddle. The powers that be might have told him to make do without. He could have done it, but it wouldn't have been any fun. He would have had to be his own ogre instead of playing the kindly, benevolent Old Man most of the time.

But a new officer had been chosen and brought down to the destroyer escort on a flying boat. And now Lieutenant Lon Menefee bobbed in the light swells of the South Atlantic as a real boat carried him from the seaplane to the *Josephus Daniels*.

"Permission to come aboard, sir?" he called when the boat drew up alongside the warship. By the matter-of-fact way he said it, the *Josephus Daniels* might have been moored in the Boston Navy Yard, not out on her own God only knew how many hundred miles from the nearest land.

"Permission granted," Sam said, just as formally. A rope ladder tied to the port rail invited Lieutenant Menefee upward. He stood up in the boat, grabbed the ladder, and climbed steadily if not with any enormous agility.

A couple of sailors stood by to grab him as he came over the rail. He turned out not to need them, which made Sam think better of him. "Reporting as ordered, sir," he said with a crisp salute.

"Good to have you aboard." Returning the salute gave Carsten the chance to look him over. He liked what he saw. Menefee was in his late twenties, with a round face, a solid build, and dark whiskers that said he might have to shave twice a day. His eyes were also dark, and showed a wry amusement that would serve him well . . . if Sam wasn't just imagining it, of course. Among the fruit salad on his chest was the ribbon for the Purple Heart. Pointing to it, Sam asked, "How'd you pick that up?"

"A Japanese dive bomber hit my destroyer somewhere north of Kauai," Menefee replied with a shrug. "I got a fragment in the leg. The petty officer next to me got his head blown off, so I was lucky, if you can call getting wounded lucky."

"All depends on how you look at things," Sam said. "Next to not getting hurt, getting wounded sucks. But it beats the hell out of getting killed, like you said."

"Yes, sir." Lieutenant Menefee cocked his head to one side. "I don't mean this any way bad at all, sir, but you aren't what I expected."

Carsten laughed. "If I had a nickel for every officer who served under me and said the same thing, I'd have . . . a hell of a lot of nickels, anyway. Who expects to run into a two-striper old enough to be his father?"

"That's not what I had in mind. Besides, I already knew you were a mustang," Menefee said. "But you're not . . ." He paused, visibly weighing his options. Then he plunged, like a man throwing a double-sawbuck raise into a poker game. "You're not a hardass, the way I figured you might be."

He had nerve. He had smarts, too. If that had rubbed Sam the wrong way, it could have blighted things between skipper and exec from then on out. But Menefee had it right—Sam *wasn't* a hardass, except every once in a while when he needed to be. "I hope not—life's mostly too short," he said now. "How come you had me gauged that way?"

"Well, I knew the executive officer you had before didn't last very long," Lon Menefee said. "If you're in my shoes, that makes you wonder."

"Mm, I can see that it would," Sam allowed. "Why don't you come to my cabin? Then we can talk about things without every sailor on the ship swinging his big, flapping hydrophones towards us."

"Hydrophones, huh?" Menefee's eyes crinkled at the corners. His mouth didn't move much, but Sam liked the smile anyway. "Lead on, sir. You know where we're going."

"I'll give you the grand tour in a bit," Sam said. "Come on."

After he closed the door to the captain's little cabin, he pulled a bottle of brandy and a couple of glasses from the steel desk by his bed. "Medicinal, of course," Lieutenant Menefee observed.

"Well, sure," Sam said, pouring. "Good for what ails you, whatever the devil it is." He handed the new exec one of the glasses. "Mud in your eye." They both drank. The brandy wasn't the best Sam had ever had—nowhere close. But it was strong, which mattered more. "So you want to hear about the old exec, do you?"

"If I'm going to sail these waters, sir, shouldn't I know where the mines are?"

"That seems fair enough," Sam said, and told him the story of Myron Zwilling. He finished, "This is just my side of it, you understand. If you listen to him, I'm sure you'd hear something different." One corner of his mouth quirked upward. "Yeah, just a little."

"I'll bet you one thing, sir," Menefee said: "*He* wouldn't figure the story had two sides. He'd tell me his was the only one, and he'd get mad if I tried to tell him anything different."

"I wouldn't be surprised," Sam said. Zwilling hadn't had any doubts. Sure as hell, that was part of his problem. "Do *you* see things in black and white, or are there shades of gray for you?"

"I hope there's gray," Menefee said. "Black and white make things easier, but only if you don't want to think."

That sounded like the right answer. But did he mean it, or was he saying what he thought his new skipper wanted to hear? *I'll find out*, Sam thought. Aloud, he said, "Things aboard ship are pretty much cut-and-dried right now. They'll stay that way, too, I hope, unless we need to pick another prize crew."

"I'll be all right with that," Menefee said. "I just got here, so I don't know who doesn't like me and who really can't stand me. Those are about the only choices an exec has, aren't they?"

"Pretty much," Sam said. "Is this your first time in the duty?"

"Yes, sir," the younger man replied. By the way he said it, a second term as executive officer wouldn't be far removed from a second conviction for theft. Maybe he wasn't so wrong, either. Didn't a second term as exec say you didn't deserve a command of your own?

"Just play it straight, and I expect you'll do fine," Carsten said, hoping he was right. "Pretty soon you'll have a ship of your own, and then somebody else will do your dirty work for you."

Menefee grinned. "I've heard ideas I like less—I'll tell you that. But I don't know. The war's liable to be over before they get around to giving me my own command, and after that the Navy'll shrink like nobody's business. Or do you think I'm wrong, sir?"

"It worked that way the last time around—I remember," Sam said. "This time? Well, who knows? After we get done beating the Confederates on land, we'll still need ships to teach Argentina a lesson, and England, and Japan. One of these days, the Japs'll have to learn they can't screw around with the Sandwich Islands."

"Can we go on with the little fights once the big one's over? Will anybody care, or will people be so hot for peace that they don't give a damn about anything else?"

"We'll find out, that's all," Sam said. The questions impressed him. Plainly, Lon Menefee had an eye for what was important. That was a good asset for an executive officer—or anybody else. "All we can do is what they tell us to do," Sam went on, and reached for the brandy bottle. "Want another knock?"

"No, thanks," Menefee said. "One's plenty for me. But don't let me stop you."

"I'm not gonna do it by myself." Sam put the bottle back into the desk drawer. He eyed Menefee, and wasn't astonished to find the new officer eyeing him, too. They'd both passed a test of sorts. The exec would have a friendly drink, but didn't care to take it much further than that. And Menefee had seen that, while Sam didn't live by the Navy's officially dry rules, he wasn't a closet lush, either. And neither of them had said a word about it, and neither would.

As the desk drawer closed, Menefee said, "Will you give me the tour, then, and let me meet some of the sailors who won't be able to stand me?" He spoke without rancor, and in the tones of a man who knew how things worked—and that they would work that way no matter what he thought about it. The slightly crooked grin that accompanied the words said the same thing. Sam approved, having a similar view of the world himself.

He took Menefee to the bridge first. Thad Walters had the conn, which meant a petty officer was minding the Y-ranging screens. The *Josephus Daniels* just didn't carry a large complement of officers. When Sam told the new exec that the chief hydrophone operator was a

CPO, Menefee raised one eyebrow but then nodded, taking the news in stride.

"Lots of antiaircraft guns. I saw that when I came aboard," Menefee remarked when they went out on deck.

"That's right, and I wish we carried even more," Sam said. "The only ship-to-ship action we've fought was with a freighter that carried a light cruiser's guns. We whipped the bastard, too." Sam remembered the pride—and the terror—of that North Atlantic fight. "Most of the time, though, airplanes are our number-one worry. Way things are nowadays, warships can't get close enough to shoot at other warships. So, yeah—twin 40mm mounts all over the damn place, and the four-inchers are dual purpose, too."

"Sure. They've got more reach than the smaller guns." Lieutenant Menefee nodded. "Things look about the same to me. If we don't find some kind of way to keep bombers off our backs, the whole surface Navy's liable to be in trouble."

"During the Great War, everybody flabbled about submersibles. This time around, it's airplanes. But as long as we bring our own air-planes with us, we can fight anywhere. And the carriers need ships to help keep the bad guys' airplanes away from them, so I figure we can keep working awhile longer, anyhow."

"Sounds good to me, sir." Menefee gave him another of those wry grins.

When they got to the engine room, the new exec started gabbing with the black gang in a way that showed he knew exactly what he was talking about. "So you come from engineering?" Sam said.

"Shows a little, does it?" Menefee said. "Yes, that's what I know. How about you, sir?"

"Gunnery and damage control," Sam answered. "We've got the ship covered between us—except for all the fancy new electronics, I mean."

"Most of the guys who understand that stuff don't understand any-thing else—looks that way to me, anyhow," Menefee said.

"Me, too," Carsten agreed. "If you can figure out all the fancy cir-cuits, doesn't seem likely you'll know how people work. I wouldn't want one of those slide-rule pushers in charge of a ship." But then he stopped himself, holding up his right hand. "Thad's an exception, I think. He can make the Y-ranging gear sit up and roll over and beg, but he's a damn good officer, too. You'll see."

"He's mighty young. He's had the chance to get used to it right from the start," Menefee said. Sam nodded, carefully holding in his smile. To his eyes, Lon Menefee was mighty damn young, too. But the new exec was right—there were degrees to everything. Young, younger, youngest. Sam couldn't hide the smile any more. Where the hell did *old fart* fit into that scheme?

Not Richmond, not any more. Richmond was a battleground. Basically, everything north of the James was a battleground—except for what had already fallen. And the damnyankees had a couple of bridgeheads over the river, too. They hadn't tried to break out of them, not yet, but the Confederates couldn't smash them, either. And so, when Clarence Potter left Lexington to report to Jake Featherston on what the physicists at Washington University were up to, he headed for Petersburg instead of the doomed capital of the CSA.

Getting to Petersburg was an adventure. Getting anywhere in the Confederacy was an adventure these days. But the Confederate States had hung on to equality in the air in northern Virginia, Maryland, and southern Pennsylvania longer than they had anywhere else. They'd hung on, and hung on, and hung on . . . till they couldn't hang on any more. That was how things stood now.

Antiaircraft guns still blazed away at strafing U.S. fighters and fighter-bombers. But antiaircraft guns were just annoyances. What really held enemy aircraft at bay were your own airplanes. And the Confederates didn't have enough to do the job any more.

His motorcar went off the road several times. It raced for a bridge once, and hid under the concrete shelter with bullets chewing up the ground to either side till the aerial wolves decided they couldn't get him and went off after other, easier game. Then, cautiously, the driver put the butternut Birmingham in gear.

"Some fun, huh?" Potter said.

The look the PFC at the wheel gave him told him how flat the joke fell. "Hope to Jesus whatever the hell you're doin' on the road is win-the-war important," the kid said. "If it ain't, we got no business travelin', on account of the damnyankees're too fuckin' likely to shoot our dicks off. Sir."

Potter wanted to clutch himself like a maiden surprised. The mere thought was appalling. Reality was worse. He'd seen it. He wanted no closer acquaintance with it than that. But he said, "It just may be, soldier. If anything can nowadays, it's got a pretty fair chance."

"Hope so," the driver said. This time, his suspicious stare was all too familiar. "How come you talk like a Yankee yourself?"

" 'Cause I went to college up there a million years ago, and I wanted to fit in," Potter replied. "And if I had a dime for every time I've answered that question, I'd be too rich to worry about an Army post."

"Reckon we'll go through security before we get real far into Petersburg." The driver sounded as if he was looking forward to it, which meant he didn't completely believe Potter. *And if I had a dime for that, too . . .* the Intelligence officer thought.

He figured Petersburg would be something out of Dante, and he was right. Soldiers and bureaucrats and civilian refugees thrombosed the streets. People moved forward by shouting and waving fists and sometimes by shooting guns in the air. Potter saw bodies hanging from lampposts. Some said DESERTER. Others said SPY. He felt the driver's eye on him, but pretended he didn't.

Sure as hell, there were security checkpoints almost every block. "Papers!" the soldiers or Freedom Party Guards—more and more Guards as Potter neared the center of town—would shout. The wreathed stars on his collar meant nothing to them. Considering that Nathan Bedford Forrest III and other high-ranking officers had risen against Jake Featherston, that made more sense than Potter wished it did.

Then a Freedom Party Guard checked off his name on a clipboard. "You're on our list," said the man in a camouflage smock. "You come with me right now." By the way he jerked the muzzle of his automatic rifle, Potter would be sorry if he didn't—although perhaps not for long.

"Where are you taking me?" Potter asked.

"Never mind that. Get out of your auto and come along," the Party Guard said.

Not seeing any other choice but starting a firefight he couldn't hope to win, Potter got out of the Birmingham. "Good luck, sir," the driver said.

"Thanks." Potter hoped he wouldn't need it, but it never hurt.

None of his escort—captors?—demanded the pistol on his belt. He wondered whether that was a good omen or simply an oversight. One way or the other, he figured he'd find out before long. "Now that we've got him, what the hell do we do with him?" another Party Guard asked.

The one who'd decided Potter was a wanted man checked the clip-board again. "We take him to the Lawn, that's what," he answered.

It meant something to the other Freedom Party Guard, if not to Clarence Potter. The security troops hustled him along. Nobody laid a finger on him, but nobody let him slow down, either: not quite a frog-march, but definitely something close.

The Lawn, on Sycamore near the corner of Liberty, turned out to be a tall red-brick house much overgrown by ivy. The grass in front of it had gone yellow-brown from winter cold. More Freedom Party Guards manned a barbed-wire perimeter outside the house. They re-lieved Potter of the .45 before letting him go forward. Before he could go inside, a stonefaced Army captain gave him the most thorough—and most intimate—patting down he'd ever had the displeasure to get.

"Do you want me to turn my head and cough?" he asked as the captain's probing fingers found another sensitive spot.

"That won't be necessary." The young officer didn't change ex-pression at all.

"Necessary . . . *sir*?" Potter suggested. He didn't usually stand on military ceremony, but he was sick and tired of being treated like a dangerous piece of meat.

He watched the captain think it over. The process took much longer than he thought it should have. At last, grudgingly, the man nodded. "You *are* on the list, and it looks like you're clean. So . . . it won't be necessary, sir. Are you happy . . . sir?"

"Dancing in the goddamn daisies," Potter replied.

That got the ghost of a grin from the young captain. "Go on in, then, sir." No audible pause this time. "The boss will take care of you."

"Who—?" Clarence Potter began, but the captain had already for-gotten about him. Somebody else was coming up to the Lawn, and needed frisking. Those educated hands had more work to do. Mutter-ing, Potter went on in. When he saw Lulu typing on a card table set up in the foyer, he figured out what was going on.

She paused when she recognized him. He almost laughed at the sniff she let out. She never had liked him—she never thought he was loyal enough to the President. But it wasn't funny any more. The way things were these days, suspicion of disloyalty was liable to be a capi-tal offense.

"General Potter," the President's secretary said.

"Hello, Lulu," Potter answered gravely. "Is he all right?"

"He's just fine." She got to her feet. "You stay right there"—as if he were likely to go anywhere. "I'll tell him you're here." The Confederate States of America might be going down the drain, but you couldn't tell from the way Lulu acted. She came back a moment later. "He wants to see you. This way, please."

This way took him through the living room, down a hall, past four more guards—any one of whom looked able to tear him in half without breaking a sweat—and into a bedroom. Jake Featherston was shouting into a telephone: "Don't just sit there with your thumb up your ass, goddammit! Hurry!" He slammed the handset down.

Lulu's cough said she disapproved of the bad language even more than of the man she escorted. "General Potter is here to see you, sir," she said. She still didn't care for Potter, though, not even a little bit.

"Thank you, darling," Jake said. Watching him sweet-talk his secretary never failed to bemuse Potter. He wouldn't have bet Featherston could do it if he hadn't seen it with his own eyes again and again. "Come in, Potter. Sit down." He pointed to a chair. "Lulu, hon, please close the door on your way out." *Please!* Who would have thought it was in the President's vocabulary?

Lulu gave Potter a fishy stare, but she did as Jake Featherston asked. "Reporting as ordered, Mr. President," Potter said, sinking into the overstuffed chair. It was all red velvet and brass nails, and looked like something from a Victorian brothel.

"How close are they to a uranium bomb?" Featherston didn't waste time or politeness on Potter. The President looked like hell: pale and haggard and skinny, with big dark circles under his eyes. How much did he sleep? Did he sleep at all? Potter wouldn't have bet on it.

"They're getting closer, sir," he answered. "They're talking about months now, not years—if the damnyankees' bombs don't set them back again."

"Months! Jesus Christ! We can't wait months!" Jake howled. "Haven't they noticed? This goddamn country's falling apart around their ears! Atlanta! Richmond! Savannah's going, and God only knows how long Birmingham will last. We need that fucker, and we need it yesterday. Not tomorrow, not today—yesterday! Months!" He rolled his eyes up to the heavens.

"Sir, I'm just telling you what Professor FitzBelmont told me," Potter said. "He also said that if you think you can find someone who'll do it better and faster, you should put him in charge."

Featherston swore. "There isn't anybody like that, is there?"

"If there is, Mr. President, I sure don't know about him," Potter answered. "Shall we try disrupting the U.S. program again?"

"What the fuck difference does it make?" Featherston said bitterly. That alarmed Potter, who'd never before heard him back away from anything. Even more bitterly, the President went on, "Shit, they're licking us without uranium bombs. I never would've reckoned they could, but they damn well are. Makes you wonder if we *deserve* to live, doesn't it?"

"No, sir. I have to believe that," Potter said. "This is my country. I'll do everything I can for it."

Featherston cocked his head to one side. "Ask you something?"

"You're the President, sir. How can I say no?"

"You sure never had any trouble before. But how come you didn't throw in with Bedford Forrest III and the rest of those bastards?"

"Sir, we're in a war. We need you. We need you bad. Whoever they brought in instead would have been worse. Chances are the Yankees wouldn't have made peace with him, either, not this side of—what do they call it?—unconditional surrender. That kills us. Way it looks to me is, we've got to keep fighting, because all our other choices are worse. Maybe the slide-rule brigade can save us. It's the best hope we've got, anyhow."

He realized he'd just admitted he knew about Forrest's plot, even if he hadn't gone along with it. If Jake wanted his head, he could have it. But that had always been true, ever since the Richmond Olympics. "Well, I get straight answers from you, anyway," the Confederate President said. "Listen, you go back and tell FitzBelmont I don't care what he does or who he kills—we've got to have that bomb, and faster than months. Get his head out of the clouds. Make sure he understands. It's his country, too, what's left of it."

"I'll do my best, sir. I don't know how much I can hurry the physicists, though," Potter said.

"You'd better, that's all I've got to tell you," Featherston said. Clarence Potter nodded. He'd seen the President of the CSA angry before—Jake Featherston ran on anger the way trucks ran on gasoline. He'd seen him gleeful. He'd seen him stubborn and defiant. But never—never till now, anyway—had he seen him desperate.

*   *   *

Next stop, Birmingham!" Michael Pound said exultantly. It wasn't spring yet, not even here in Alabama, where spring came early. It wasn't spring, no, but something even sweeter than birdsong and flowers filled the air. When Pound sniffed, he didn't just smell exhaust fumes and cordite and unbathed soldiers. He smelled victory.

The Confederates hadn't quit. He didn't think they knew the meaning of the word. Some of their terrifying new barrels came into the front line without so much as a coat of paint—straight from the factories U.S. bombers and now artillery were still trying to knock out. The crews who fought those shiny metal monsters were brave, no doubt about it. But all the courage in the world couldn't make up for missing skill.

And, while the Confederate machines trickled from their battered factories in dribs and drabs, U.S. production went up and up. Maybe a new C.S. barrel was worth two of the best U.S. model. If the USA had four or five times as many barrels where it mattered, how much did that individual superiority matter?

Not enough.

Pound guided his barrel past the guttering corpse of a machine that had tried conclusions with several U.S. barrels at once. That might have been a brave mistake, but a mistake it undoubtedly was. The Confederates had made so many big mistakes, they couldn't afford even small ones any more.

Somebody not far away fired an automatic rifle. Maybe that was a U.S. soldier with a captured weapon. On the other hand, maybe it was a Freedom Party Guard aiming at a barrel commander riding along with head and shoulders out of the cupola. Regretfully, Michael Pound decided not to take the chance. He ducked down into the machine.

"Where the hell are we, sir?" Sergeant Scullard asked. The gunner didn't get nearly so many chances to look around as the barrel commander did.

Despite having those chances, Pound needed to check a map before he answered, "Far as I can tell, we're just outside of Columbiana."

"And where the fuck's Columbiana?"

Unless you were born and raised in central Alabama, that was another reasonable question. "Twenty, maybe thirty miles from Birmingham, south and a little bit east," Pound said. "Town's got a munitions plant in it, run by the C. B. Churchill Company—that's what the map notes say, anyhow."

"Fuck," the gunner repeated, this time as a term of general disapproval. "That means those butternut assholes'll fight like mad bastards to keep us out."

"They've been fighting like mad bastards for almost three years," Pound said. "How much good has it done 'em? We're in the middle of Alabama. We've got 'em cut in half, or near enough so it makes no difference. If they had any brains, they'd quit now, because they can't win."

"Yeah, and then they'd spend the next hundred years bushwhacking us." Scullard was not in a cheerful mood.

Pound grunted. The gunner might have meant that for a sour joke. Even if he did, it made an unfortunate amount of sense. In a standup fight, the Confederacy was losing. But how much fun would it be to occupy a country where everybody hated your guts and wanted you dead? After the Great War, the United States hadn't enjoyed trying to hold on to Kentucky and Houston and Sequoyah. If the USA tried to hang on to the whole CSA . . .

"Well, nobody ever said the Army would go out of style any time soon," Pound said.

"A good thing, too," Scullard replied. "If we're in deep shit now, we'd be in a lot deeper without this baby." He rapped his knuckles on the breech of the barrel's main armament, adding, "I just wish we had more like it."

"They're coming," Pound said. "Maybe not as fast as if we'd started sooner, but they are. We can make more stuff than the Confederates can. Sooner or later, we'll knock 'em flat, and it's getting on toward sooner."

The words were hardly out of his mouth before a Confederate antibarrel rocket slammed into a U.S. machine a quarter of a mile away. The green-gray barrel brewed up, sending an enormous and monstrously perfect smoke ring up and out through the open cupola. Fire and greasy black smoke followed an instant later as the barrel slewed to a stop. Pound didn't think anybody got out.

He swore under his breath. The United States were making more stuff than the Confederate States could, yes. Sometimes, though—too damn often, in fact—the Confederates made better stuff. The automatic rifles their infantry carried, these antibarrel rockets, the screaming meemies that could flatten acres at a volley, the long-range jobs that reached into the USA . . . The enemy had talented engineers. Their cause stank like a dead fish, but they were good at what they did.

Scullard must have seen the U.S. barrel go up, too. "I hope we knock 'em flat sooner," he said. "That way, the mothers don't have the chance to come up with anything *really* nasty."

"Yeah," Michael Pound said. That marched with his own thoughts much too well.

Fields and forest surrounded Columbiana. Two routes led up to the town from the south: a county road whose thin blacktop coat the barrels' tracks quickly wrecked, and a railroad line maybe a hundred yards to the west. They were both nice and straight, and Pound couldn't have said which he distrusted more. They both let the Confederates see what was coming long before it got there.

And what they could see, they were too likely to be able to hit. That blazing barrel said as much. Of course, banging your way through the woods was asking to get nailed by some kid in butternut crouching behind a pine tree. You'd never spot him till he fired off his stovepipe, and that was too damn late.

Pound stood up in the cupola. He wanted to find out just how much U.S. armor was close enough to follow his platoon's lead. He hoped the other barrels would follow, anyway. If they didn't, he was liable to end up slightly dead.

Or more than slightly.

Sometimes, though, a barrel's engine was as important a weapon as its cannon. This felt like one of those times. Accidentally on purpose, he sent his orders over the all-company circuit instead of the one that linked him to his platoon alone: "Men, we are going to charge up this miserable little road as fast as we can go. We are going to blast anything that gets in our way, and we'll be inside Columbiana before Featherston's fuckers figure out what hit 'em." *I hope.* "Follow me. If this goes wrong, they'll get my barrel first." He switched to the intercom so he could talk to his driver: "You hear that, Beans?"

"Yes, sir." The driver's name was Neyer, but he rarely had to answer to it. His fondness for one particular ration can had given him a handle he'd keep till he took off his uniform . . . or till he got blown to smithereens, which might happen in the next couple of minutes.

Don't think about it, Pound told himself. *If you think about it, you'll get cold feet.* "Then gun it," he said. He was sure his own platoon would come with him. The rest . . . *Don't think about that, either.*

The engine roared. The barrel zipped forward. Flat out, it could do better than thirty. On rough ground, going like that would have torn out the kidneys of the men inside. On the road, it was tolerable . . . barely.

"Shoot first if you see anything," Pound advised, shouting over the noise.

"Going this fast, the stabilizer ain't worth shit," the gunner answered.

"Shoot first anyway. Even if you miss, you make the other guy duck. Then you can make your second shot count."

Scullard grunted. Pound knew damn well he was right, but he could see that it wasn't the sort of thing where you'd want to bet your life if you didn't have to.

As they neared Columbiana, they found there were Confederate soldiers on the road. The men in butternut hadn't figured the Yankees would be dumb enough or crazy enough to thunder down on them like that. The bow machine gun and the coaxial machine gun in the turret both started jackhammering. The C.S. troops scattered.

"Give 'em a couple of rounds of HE, too," Pound said. "Something to remember us by, you know?"

"Yes, sir!" Scullard said enthusiastically, and then, to the loader, "HE!"

The main armament thundered twice. A 3½-inch shell carried enough cordite to make a pretty good boom when it burst. One round went off in the middle of a knot of fleeing Confederates. Men and pieces of men described arcs through the air.

"Nice shot!" Pound yelled. Only later did he remember he was cheering death and mayhem. They were what he did for a living, his stock in trade. Most of the time, he took them for granted. He wondered why he couldn't quite do it now.

Then he did, because the barrel roared into Columbiana. He had no time to think about killing—he was too busy doing it. The barrel crew might have been an extension of his arm, an extension of his will.

"Where the hell is Lester Street?" he muttered. That was where the C. B. Churchill Company was, and had been since 1862. A glance through the periscopes built into the cupola told him what he needed to know. The biggest building in town, the one with the Stars and Bars flying over it, had to be the munitions factory. "Send a couple of HE rounds in there, too," he told the gunner. "Let 'em know they've just gone out of business."

"Right." But before Scullard could fire, machine-gun bullets rattled off the barrel's sides and turret, clattering but doing no harm. The bow gunner sent a long burst into a general store with a big DRINK DR. HOPPER! sign out front. Pound had tried the fizzy water, and thought it tasted like horse piss and sugar. The enemy machine gun abruptly cut off.

Boom! Boom! Pound watched holes appear in the munitions plant's southern wall. He giggled like a kid. Sometimes destruction for its own sake was more fun than anything else an alleged adult could do. He wondered whether Jake Featherston had an advanced case of the same disease.

And then he got more in the way of destruction than even he wanted. Maybe one of those HE rounds blew up something inside the factory. Maybe somebody in there decided he'd be damned if he let the plant fall into U.S. hands. Any which way, it went sky high.

Pound and his barrel were more than half a mile away. Even through inches of steel armor, the roar was overwhelming. The barrel weighed upwards of forty tons. All the same, the front end came off the ground. The machine might have been a rearing horse, except Pound was afraid it would flip right over onto its turret. Scullard's startled "Fuck!" said he wasn't the only one, either.

But the barrel thudded back down onto its tracks. Pound peered out through the periscopes again. One of the forward ones was cracked, which said just how big a blast that was. It must have knocked half of Columbiana flat.

"Well," he said, "we liberated the living shit out of this place."

Flora Blackford was listening to debate on a national parks appropriation bill—not everything Congress did touched on the war, though it often seemed that way—when a House page hurried up to her. His fresh features and beardless cheeks said he was about fifteen: too young to conscript, though the Confederates were giving guns to kids that age, using up their next generation.

"For you, Congresswoman," the page whispered. He handed her an envelope and took off before she could even thank him.

She opened the envelope and unfolded the note inside. *Come see me the second you get this—Franklin,* it said. She recognized the Assistant Secretary of War's bold handwriting.

Any excuse to get away from this dreary debate was a good one. She hurried out of Congressional Hall—leaving was much easier than getting in—and flagged a cab. The War Department was within walking distance, but a taxi was faster. When Franklin Roosevelt wrote, *Come see me the second you get this*, she assumed he meant it.

"Heck of a thing about this Russian town, isn't it?" the driver said.

"I'm sorry. I haven't heard any news since early this morning," Flora said.

"Bet you will." The cabby pulled up in front of the massive—and badly damaged—War Department building. "Thirty-five cents, ma'am."

"Here." Flora gave him half a dollar and didn't wait for change. A newsboy waved papers and shouted about Petrograd, so something *had* happened in Russia. Maybe the Tsar was dead. That might help the USA's German allies.

She hurried up the scarred steps. At the top, her Congressional ID convinced the guards that she was who she said she was. One of them telephoned Roosevelt's office, deep in the bowels of the building. When he'd satisfied himself that she was expected, he said, "Jonesy here'll take you where you need to go, ma'am. Somebody will check you out as soon as you get inside."

Check you out was a euphemism for *pat you down*. The tight-faced woman who did it took no obvious pleasure from it, which was something, anyhow. After she finished and nodded, Jonesy—who looked even younger than Flora's own Joshua—said, "Come along with me, ma'am."

Down they went, stairway after stairway. Her calves didn't look forward to climbing those stairs on the way up. Franklin Roosevelt had a special elevator because of his wheelchair, but no mere Congresswoman—not even a former First Lady—got to ride it.

"Here we go." Jonesy stopped in front of Roosevelt's office. "I'll take you up when you're done." *Don't go wandering around on your own.* Nobody ever came out and said that, but it always hung in the air.

The captain in the Assistant Secretary of War's outer office nodded to Flora. "Hello, Congresswoman. You made good time. Go right in— Mr. Roosevelt is expecting you."

"Thanks," Flora said. "Can you tell me what this is about?"

"I think he'd better do that, ma'am."

Shrugging, Flora walked into Franklin Roosevelt's private office.

"Hello, Flora. Close the door behind you, would you, please? Thanks." As always, Roosevelt sounded strong and jovial. But he looked like death warmed over.

He waved her to a chair. As she sat, she asked, "Now will you tell me what's going on? It must be something big."

"Petrograd's gone," Roosevelt said bluntly.

"A newsboy outside was saying something about that," Flora said. "Why does it matter so much to us? To the Kaiser, sure, but to us? And what do you mean, gone?"

"When I say gone, I usually mean *gone*," Franklin Roosevelt answered. "One bomb. Off the map. G-O-N-E. Gone. No more Petrograd. Gone."

"But that's imposs—" Flora broke off. She was as far from Catholic as she could be, but she felt the impulse to cross herself even so. She was glad she was sitting down. "Oh, my God," she whispered, and wanted to start the mourner's Kaddish right after that. "The Germans . . . Uranium . . ." She stopped. She wasn't making any sense, even to herself.

But she made enough sense for Roosevelt. He nodded, his face thoroughly grim. "That's right. They got there first. They tried it—and it works. God help us all."

"Do they have more of them?" Questions started to boil in Flora's head. "What are they saying? And what about the Russians? Have England and France said anything yet?"

"We got a ciphered message yesterday that made me think they were going to try it," the Assistant Secretary of War said. "They were cagey. I would be, too. Wouldn't be good to say too much if the other side is reading your mail, so to speak. And the Kaiser just talked on Wireless Berlin." He looked down at a piece of paper on his desk. " 'We have harnessed a fundamental force of nature,' he said. 'The power that sets the stars alight now also shines on earth. A last warning to our foes—give up this war or face destruction you cannot hope to escape.' "

"My God," Flora said, and then again, "My God!" Once you'd said that, what was left? Nothing she could see—not for a moment, anyhow. Then she did find something: "How close are we?"

"We're getting there," Roosevelt said, which might mean anything or nothing. The exasperated noise Flora made said it wasn't good enough, whatever it meant. Roosevelt spread his hands, as if to placate her. "The people out in Washington say we're getting close," he went on. "I don't know if that means days, weeks, or months. They swear on a stack of Bibles that it doesn't mean years."

"It had better not, not after all the time they've already used and all the money we've given them," Flora said. If not for the money, she never would have known anything about the U.S. project. And she found another question, one she wished she didn't need to ask: "How close is Jake Featherston?" Even with the Stars and Stripes flying in Richmond for the first time since 1861, she thought of the Confederacy boiled down to the terrifying personality of its leader.

So did Franklin Roosevelt, as his answer showed: "We still think he's behind us. We're plastering his uranium works every chance we get, and we get more chances all the time, because we're finally beating down the air defenses over Lexington. His people have put a lot of stuff underground, but doing that must have cost them time. If we're not ahead, he's got miracle workers, and I don't think he does."

"*Alevai*," Flora said, and then, "Do they have any idea how many dead there are in Petrograd?" Part of her wished she hadn't thought of that. Most of the dead wouldn't be soldiers or sailors. Some would be factory workers, and she supposed you could argue that the people who made the guns mattered as much in modern war as the people who fired them. All the generals did argue exactly that, in fact. But so many would be street sweepers and dentists and waitresses and schoolchildren . . . Thousands? Tens of thousands? Hundreds of thousands? From one bomb? "My God!" she exclaimed again.

Franklin Roosevelt shrugged the broad shoulders that went so strangely with his withered, useless legs. "Flora, I just don't know. I don't think anyone knows yet—not the Germans, not the Russians, nobody. Right now . . . Right now, the whole world just took a left to the chops. It's standing there stunned, trying not to fall over."

That wasn't the comparison Flora would have used, but it was vivid enough to make her nod. Before she could say anything—if she could find anything *to* say beyond one more "My God!"—the captain from the outer office came in and nodded to Roosevelt. "Sir, the Tsar just issued a statement."

"What did he say?" Roosevelt and Flora asked at the same time.

The captain glanced down at a piece of paper in his left hand. "He calls this a vicious, unholy, murderous weapon, and he condemns the massacre of innocents it caused." That went well with Flora's thoughts.

"Did he say anything about surrender?" Franklin Roosevelt asked.

"No, sir." The young officer shook his head. "But he did say God would punish the Kaiser and 'the accursed scientists and people of Germany'—his words—even if the Russian Army couldn't do the job."

"How can he keep fighting if Germany can drop bombs like that and he can't?" Flora asked, not really aiming the question at either Roosevelt or the captain. Was God listening? If He was, would He have let that bomb go off? "Moscow, Minsk, Tsaritsyn . . ." She ran out of Russian cities. She did, yes, but she was sure the Germans wouldn't.

"Russia always takes more losses than her enemies," the Assistant Secretary of War said. "That's the only way she stays in wars. But losses on that kind of scale? I don't think so, not for long."

"If the Tsar tries to go on fighting and the Germans drop one of those on Moscow, say, don't you think all the Reds who've gone underground will rise up again?" the captain asked. "Wouldn't you?"

"How many Reds *are* left?" Flora asked. "Didn't the Tsar's secret police kill off as many as they could after the last civil war?"

"They sure did," Franklin Roosevelt said, and the captain nodded. Roosevelt went on, "We know the secret police didn't get everybody, though. And the Reds are masters at going underground and staying there."

"They have to be, if they want to keep breathing," the captain added.

"So the short answer is, nobody—nobody on this side of the Atlantic, that's for sure—knows how many Reds there are," Roosevelt said. "Something like a uranium bomb will bring them out, though, if anything will."

"And if *it* doesn't kill them," the captain said. "Chances are, there are a lot of them close to Petrograd and Moscow."

Flora nodded. Those were the two most important Russian cities, and the Reds were like anybody else—they'd want to stay as close to the center of things as they could. Her thoughts went west. "England and France have to be shaking in their boots right now," she said. "Unless they've got bombs of their own, I mean."

"If they had them, they would use them," Roosevelt said. "The war in the west has turned against them—not as much as the war here has turned against the CSA, but enough. If the Kaiser's barrels really get rolling across Holland and Belgium and northern France, it won't be easy to stop them this side of Paris."

"Paris," Flora echoed. The Germans hadn't got there in 1917; the

French asked for an armistice before they could. Kaiser Wilhelm granted it, too. Looking back, that was probably a mistake. Like the Confederates, the French weren't really convinced they'd been beaten. "This time, the Germans ought to parade through the streets, the way they did in 1871."

"Sounds good to me," Roosevelt said. "Keep it under your hat, but I've heard Charlie La Follette's going to go to Richmond."

"Is it safe?" Flora asked.

"Not even a little bit, but he's going to do it anyhow," Roosevelt answered. "Abe Lincoln couldn't, God knows James G. Blaine couldn't, even my Democratic cousin Theodore couldn't, but La Follette can. And there's an election this November."

"Good point," Flora agreed. How many votes would each photo of President La Follette in the ravaged and captured capital of the Confederacy be worth? Maybe as many as the uranium bomb had killed, and that was bound to be a lot.

VIII

In! In! In!" Sergeant Hugo Blackledge bellowed. "Move your sorry asses before you get 'em shot off!"

Corporal Jorge Rodriguez hurried aboard the little coastal freighter. Fires in Savannah lit up the docks almost bright as day. Every so often, a flash and a boom would mark another ammo dump or cache of shells going up in smoke. The port was falling. Anybody who stayed to try to hold up the damnyankees would end up dead or a POW. Orders were to get out as many soldiers as could escape.

Nervously, Rodriguez looked up into the sky. If any fighters came over right now, they could chew his company to pieces. But they mostly stayed on the runways after dark. With a little luck, this ship—the *Dixie Princess*, her name was—would be far away from Savannah by the time the sun came up.

"Ever been on a boat before?" Gabe Medwick asked.

"No," Jorge admitted. "You?"

"A little rowboat, fishin' for bluegill an' catfish," his friend said. "This ain't the same thing, is it? Not hardly." He answered his own question.

Soldiers from eight or ten regiments—not all of them even from the same division—jammed the *Dixie Princess*. They eyed one another like dogs uncertain whether to fight. Sailors in gray dungarees elbowed their way through the butternut crush. They knew where they were going and what they were doing, which gave them a big edge on the troops they were carrying.

The rumble of the engines got deeper. Rodriguez felt the deck vibrate under his boots. The freighter pulled away from the pier and down the Savannah River toward the sea.

Only gradually did Jorge realize there were antiaircraft guns on deck. More sailors manned them. Some wore helmets painted gray. Others stayed bareheaded, as if to say a helmet wouldn't make any difference in what they did. A soldier near Jorge lit a cigarette.

"Kill that, you dumb dipshit!" Sergeant Blackledge yelled. "Kill it, you hear me? You want some damnyankee to spot your match or your coal? Jesus God, how fuckin' stupid are you, anyways?"

"All right, all right," the offender muttered. Down to the deck went the smoke. A boot mournfully crushed it out.

"Now, when it gets light y'all got to keep your eyes peeled for damnyankee submarines," Blackledge went on. "One of them fuckers puts a torpedo in our guts, it's a hell of a long swim to land, you know what I mean?"

"Boy," Gabriel Medwick muttered, "he sure knows how to make a guy feel safe."

Jorge laughed. That was so far wrong, it was funny. It would have been funny, anyway, if he weren't aboard this floating coffin. How many men were with him? He wasn't sure, but it had to be a couple of thousand. A damnyankee submersible skipper who sank the *Dixie Princess* would probably get the biggest, fanciest medal the USA could give out.

"You reckon it's true, what happened to that town in Russia?" somebody not far away from him asked.

"It's bullshit, you ask me," another soldier answered. "Damn Kaiser's just runnin' his mouth. Stands to reason—a city's too fuckin' big for one bomb to take out."

"You hear about that?" Medwick asked Jorge.

He nodded. "I hear, *sí*, but I don't know what to believe. What do *you* think?"

"I hope like anything it's bullshit," his buddy said. "If it ain't . . . If it ain't, we all got more trouble than we know what to do with. If the Germans have a bomb like that, if it's really real, how long before the Yankees do, too?"

"*¡Madre de Dios!*" Jorge crossed himself. "One bomb, one city? You couldn't fight back against something like that, not unless . . . Maybe we get those bombs, too."

"Maybe." Gabe seemed doubtful. "If we get 'em, we better get 'em pretty damn quick, that's all I got to say. Otherwise, it's gonna be too late."

He wasn't wrong, however much Jorge wished he were. The fall of Savannah meant the Confederate States were cut in half. People were saying that Richmond had fallen, too, and that Jake Featherston had got out one jump ahead of the U.S. soldiers coming in. Some people said he *hadn't* got out, but that didn't seem to be true, because he was still on the wireless.

What can I do about any of that? Jorge wondered. The only answer that occurred to him was, *Not much*. He yawned; it had to be somewhere not long after midnight. He couldn't even lie down and go to sleep: no room to lie down. He dozed a little standing up, the way only a tired veteran could.

Dawn was just painting the eastern horizon—all ocean, flat out to the edge of the world—with pink when he saw another ship ahead. No, it was a boat, much smaller than the *Dixie Princess*. It had a blinker that flashed Morse at the freighter. Up on the bridge, where no soldiers were allowed, a sailor—maybe an officer—answered back.

"What's going on?" Gabe Medwick asked around a yawn.

"Beats me," Jorge answered. "We just gotta wait and find out." If that didn't sum up a lot of soldiering, what did?

The *Dixie Princess* changed course and followed the smaller craft toward the low-lying coast ahead. Her guide zigged and zagged in a way that made no sense to Jorge. And whatever the guide did, the *Dixie Princess* did, too.

Then somebody said, "We better not hit one of them damn mines, that's all I got to say. That'd be worse'n getting torpedoed."

A light went on in Jorge's head. They had to be heading towards a port, one warded by mines to keep out U.S. warships. And the small boat knew the way through the floating death traps. Jorge hoped like hell it did, anyhow.

WELCOME TO BEAUFORT, a sign said. Jorge would have guessed the name was pronounced *Bofort*. What his guess was worth, he found out when a man with bushy white side whiskers called, "Welcome to Bewfort, y'all! Where d'you go from here?"

Jorge hadn't the faintest idea. Somebody—probably an officer—called, "Where's your train station?"

"Mile outside o' town," the old-timer said, pointing west. "We like our peace and quiet, we do. Ain't but one train a day anyways."

"Jesus H. Christ!" the officer exploded. "This is as bad as it would've been before the War of Secession!"

"No, sir." The white-whiskered man shook his head. "We had the hurricane back in '40, and the really bad one back in '93, an' we came through both o' them. And besides, we was full o' niggers in the old days. Ain't hardly got no more coons around now, though. Don't hardly miss 'em, neither. More room for the rest of us, by God."

Odds were the Negroes had done most of the hard work. Sailors had to jump down from the *Dixie Princess* and grab the mooring lines that bound her to the pier. Gangplanks thudded onto the rickety planking.

"Disembark! Form up in column of fours!" an officer shouted. "We will proceed to the railroad station and board transportation for Virginia!"

"Well, now we know what we're doing, anyway," Gabe Medwick said.

"*Sí*." Jorge nodded. "But one train a day? How big a train is it gonna be? How long we gonna have to wait?" He looked up at the sky, which was sunny and blue. "We ain't that far from Savannah, even now. What if a damnyankee airplane sees us? They come and drop bombs on our heads, that's what."

"Better not happen, that's all I've got to say." Medwick shivered at the idea, though the day felt more like spring than winter.

Down the gangplanks went the soldiers. As corporals, Jorge and Gabe tried to gather their squads together, but they didn't have much luck. The soldiers had got too mixed up in the desperate boarding in Savannah. "Hell with it," Sergeant Blackledge said—he was trying to gather a whole section, and having no more success than the squad leaders. "We'll sort things out when we get wherever the hell we're going."

They marched through Beaufort. Though it wasn't at all far from Savannah, the war might have forgotten all about it. Only some small, shabby houses with broken windows and with doors standing open spoke of the blacks who'd lived here till not long before.

Old men and those too badly maimed to fight—and a few women, too—crewed fishing and oystering boats. Truck gardens grew all around the town. Women and kids and the old and injured tended them, too.

At the station, the railroad agent stared at the long butternut column in unabashed horror. "What in God's name am I supposed to do with y'all?" he said.

"Get on the telegraph. Get trains down here, dammit," an officer answered. "We got out of Savannah. They want us up in Virginia. Fuck me if we're gonna walk."

"Well, I'll try," the agent said doubtfully.

"You better." The officer—he was, Jorge saw, a colonel, with three stars on each side of his collar—didn't even bother disguising the threat.

The agent clicked away on the telegraph. A few minutes later, an answer came back. "They'll be here in two-three hours," he reported.

Jorge would have bet that the time promised would stretch, and it did. The trains didn't get there till midafternoon. He had enough food in his pockets and pouches to keep from getting hungry before then, but he wondered if anybody would feed the soldiers on the way north. He wondered how bad the fighting would be, too. He'd served in Virginia before coming down to Tennessee. *Wherever things get tough, that's where they send me.* He was surprised at how little he resented that. It wasn't as if he were the only one in the same boat.

On the train, his two stripes won him a seat, even if it was hard and cramped. What with all the men standing in the aisles, he counted himself lucky. No matter how uncomfortable he was, he didn't stay awake long.

His eyes opened again when the train rolled through the town of St. Matthews. Except for a good many women wearing widow's weeds, the place seemed as untouched by the war as Beaufort. Jorge wasn't used to landscapes that hadn't been torn to bits. A town with all its buildings intact, without barricades and foxholes and trenches, seemed unnatural.

"It does, doesn't it?" Gabe Medwick said when he remarked on that. "It's like the place isn't important enough to blow up, almost."

Jorge hadn't looked at it quite like that, which didn't make Gabe wrong. He turned to ask one of the soldiers in the aisle what he thought, only to discover that the man was sound asleep standing up, much deeper under than Jorge had been on the *Dixie Princess*. How exhausted did you have to be to lose yourself so completely while you were upright?

After that, the train passed into North Carolina. There was a sign by the tracks that said so. The license plates on the autos went from white with blue letters and numbers to orange with black. Other than that, he couldn't see any difference. If the Confederate States had a safe haven, he was rolling through it.

Somebody at the front of the car dished out ration tins from a crate. They weren't good, but they were better than nothing. Drinks were bottles of Dr. Hopper, warm and fizzy. Jorge belched enormously.

Virginia was another sign at the border, and motorcar license plates with yellow characters on a dark green background. It was also, before long, the cratered, shattered, bombed-out landscape Jorge had grown used to. He nodded to himself. He knew what he'd be doing here.

R and R. Armstrong Grimes had gone out of the line in hostile country before. Did the people in Utah hate U.S. soldiers even more than the people here in Georgia did? He wouldn't have been surprised. But the locals here had nastier weapons with which to make their lack of affection known.

That meant Camp Freedom—the name had to be chosen with malice aforethought—had maybe the most extensive perimeter Armstrong had ever seen. Foxholes and barbed-wire emplacements and machine-gun nests and entrenchments gobbled up the fields for a couple of miles around the camp on all sides.

"Shit on toast," Squidface said as Armstrong's weary platoon made its way through the maze of outworks. "What all's inside here, the fucking United States mint?"

"They don't have soldiers, the bad guys go and take the mint away," Armstrong said.

"Well, yeah, Sarge, sure." Squidface spoke in calm, reasonable tones. "But they care about money, and they mostly don't care about us."

Armstrong grunted. It wasn't as if the PFC were wrong. Soldiers got the shitty end of the stick every day of the week, and twice on Sundays. If the other side didn't screw you, the assholes in green-gray who stayed safe behind the line would. The only people he trusted these days were smelly, dirty men in ragged uniforms that said they actually did some fighting. They knew what was what, unlike the jerks who campaigned with typewriters and telephones.

He didn't love MPs, either, not even a little bit. One of the snowdrops—he wore a white helmet and faggy white gloves—pointed and said, "Delousing station and showers are over that way. Where's your officer, anyway?"

"In the hospital." Armstrong jabbed a thumb at his own chest. "This is my outfit now."

The MP sniffed. A platoon with a sergeant in command couldn't be anything much, his attitude said. Somebody from the back of the platoon said, "Boy, Featherston's fuckers'd send him to Graves Registration in nothing flat."

"Who said that, goddammit?" the MP shouted. "I'll kick the crap out of you, whoever you are."

"Don't worry, Sergeant. I'll deal with him," Armstrong promised. All right, so the snowdrop wasn't yellow. But he didn't realize combat troops wouldn't fight fair. They'd ruin him or kill him, and then laugh about it. Getting away in a hurry was the best plan.

Back in the Great War, Armstrong's father said, delousing meant baking your clothes and bathing in scalding water full of nasty chemicals, none of which kept the lice down for long. The spray that a bored-looking corporal turned on the men now was nothing like that. But it had one advantage over the old procedure: it really worked.

There was nothing wrong with showering under scalding water. "Wish I had a steel brush, to get all the dirt off," Squidface said, snorting like a whale.

"Yeah, well, if you didn't have a goddamn pelt there, you could get clean easier," Armstrong said. Squidface was one of the hairiest guys he'd ever seen—he had more hair on his back than a lot of guys did on their chest. "If the Confederates ever kill you, they'll tan your hide for a rug."

"Ahh, your mother," Squidface said. Only somebody who'd saved Armstrong's bacon plenty of times could have got away with that. Squidface qualified. So did several other guys from the platoon.

After the shower, food. Along with canned rations, Armstrong had eaten a lot of fried and roasted chicken in the field—plenty of henhouses around, and you didn't need much more than a skillet or, in a pinch, a sharp stick to do the cooking. But this was fried chicken done right, not half raw and half burnt. The hash browns were crisp and just greasy enough, too. He couldn't remember the last time he'd seen a regular potato that didn't come out of a can. Yams and sweet potatoes were all right for baking, but they just didn't cut it when you sliced them up and put them in hot lard.

And apple pie! And vanilla ice cream on top! "Goddamn!" Squidface said reverently. "I think I just came in my pants."

"I know what you mean." The size of the bite Armstrong took would have made a boa constrictor jealous.

"I want a slice of cheese to put on my pie, not ice cream," Herk said. The replacement was a veteran now, entitled to a veteran's gripes—and entitled to get razzed like a veteran, too.

"Herk wants to cut the cheese." Squidface held his nose.

"You were the one who came in your pants," Herk retorted. "Me, I want a broad."

Up and down the long table, soldiers nodded solemnly, Armstrong among them. This camp had everything for giving soldiers a good time except a whorehouse. Bluenoses made sure the U.S. Army didn't officially sponsor any such thing. If you wanted a woman, you had to find your own—which could get you killed if you picked the wrong one, and could easily leave you with a disease that would land you in big trouble when the Army found out you'd caught it.

Squidface had several suggestions on how Herk could satisfy himself, each more alarming than the one before. "Shut up already," Armstrong said after a while. "You're making me lose my appetite."

"You better show up for sick call in the mornin', Sarge," Squidface said. "Something's sure as shit wrong with you."

The line for the nightly movie was almost as long as the one for a brothel would have been. Armstrong got a seat just before they showed the newsreel. "Here is the first film from ruined Petrograd!" the announcer said importantly.

Armstrong had seen plenty of ruined cities. He'd seen Provo and Salt Lake City, and you couldn't ruin a place any worse than they got ruined. Or he thought you couldn't, till the camera panned across what was left of Petrograd. The Russian town was *leveled*, all the way out to the horizon. When the camera got to something that stuck up from the devastation, it moved in for a closer look.

It was an enormous bronze statue of a man on horseback—or it had been. Now it looked melted, melted from the top down. Armstrong tried to imagine what kind of heat could have done such a thing.

"This was the statue of Peter the Great, who founded Petrograd," the announcer said. "Now he demonstrates the power of our allies' scientific accomplishments."

"Fuck our allies," Squidface said. "We don't get one of those ourselves pretty damn quick, the goddamn Kaiser'll drop one on Philly next."

That struck Armstrong as a pretty good guess. He made a guess of his own: "What do you want to bet Featherston's got guys in white lab coats working on one, too? With his fucking rockets, he could throw one anywhere in the USA."

"Shit." Squidface looked around, as if expecting one of those rockets to crash down any second now. "You're right."

As a matter of fact, Armstrong was wrong. The most powerful Confederate rockets reached only a couple of hundred miles. That meant they couldn't touch most of the USA, especially since the areas C.S. soldiers actually controlled shrank by the day. But, with a bomb like that, worry outran reality with ease.

"On our side of the Atlantic . . ." the newsreel announcer said. The screen showed the charred wreckage of gracious homes that had to date back to long before the War of Secession. It showed sunken ships in a bombed-out harbor district. It showed dirty, unshaven Confederate soldiers shambling off into captivity.

"We was there. We seen that," Squidface said.

"Better believe it," Armstrong agreed.

"On our side of the Atlantic, the capture of Savannah cuts the Confederate States in half," the announcer said proudly. "This on the heels of the loss of Richmond . . ."

The Stars and Stripes flew over the wreckage of the Confederate Capitol. U.S. soldiers prowled the cratered grounds of the Gray House, walking past twisted and overturned antiaircraft guns. Scrawny civilians got meals at a U.S. field kitchen.

"How long can the enemy hope to keep up his useless resistance in the face of overwhelming U.S. might?" the announcer asked, as if the soldiers watching the newsreel would be able to tell him.

The answer they were supposed to give him was, *Not very long.* Armstrong had seen enough propaganda to understand that. But this time the newsreel had outsmarted itself. The fearsome bomb that leveled Petrograd made you think twice. It made Armstrong think twice, anyhow. If the Confederates came up with one of those, or more than one, before the United States could, they were liable to win the war in spite of losing their capital and getting their country cut in half. Drop something like that on Philadelphia and New York and Boston, and the United States would really have something to worry about.

Drop one on Birmingham, Armstrong thought savagely. *Drop one on New Orleans. Drop one on fucking Charleston.* Like most people from the USA, he particularly despised the city where the War of Secession broke out.

After the newsreel came a short feature, with the Engels Brothers involved with an actor plainly meant to be Jake Featherston. "I'll reduce your population!" he yelled, which made the Brothers get into a ridiculous brawl to see which of them would be eliminated. That was all propaganda, too, but it was funny. Armstrong and Squidface grinned at each other in the darkness.

And the main feature was a thriller, with the Confederates after the secret of a new bombsight and the heroine thwarting them at every turn. She was pretty and she had legs up to there, which might have made Armstrong root for her even if she saluted the Stars and Bars.

After the feature, he got to lie down on a real bed. He hadn't done much of that lately—oh, a few times, when he flopped in a house some Georgians had vacated, but not very often. With snoring soldiers all around him, he could relax and sleep deep. Out in the field, he might as well have been a wild beast. The least little noise would leave him not just awake but with his heart pounding and with a rifle or a knife in his hand.

Bacon and eggs and more hash browns and halfway decent coffee the next morning were wonderful, too. So was eating them without peering this way and that, afraid of holdouts and snipers and his own shadow if it caught him by surprise.

"You know, this is pretty damn good. I could really get used to this." He was surprised at how surprised he sounded.

"It is, isn't it?" Squidface sounded surprised, too. Had he been in the war from the start? Armstrong didn't know. But he'd sure been in it long enough to turn into a vet.

"I think this is called peace. We used to have it all the time." Armstrong didn't think about those days very often. He'd gone from high school almost straight into the Army. He'd been a boy then. If he wasn't a man now, he didn't suppose he ever would be.

"Not quite peace," Squidface said. "No pussy around. We went through that when we got here."

"Well, yeah, we did," Armstrong admitted. "All right, it isn't quite peace. But it beats the shit outa where we were at before." Squidface solemnly nodded and stuffed another slice of bacon into his mouth.

They gave George Enos shore leave after he helped bring the *Tierra del Fuego* back to New York City. They gave it to him, and then they forgot about him. He grabbed a train up to Boston, had a joyous reunion with Connie and the boys, and set out to enjoy himself till the Navy decided what the hell to do with him next.

The Navy took so long, George wondered whether he ought to look for a slot on a fishing boat going out of T Wharf. He could have had one in a minute; the Navy had sucked in a lot of first-class fishermen. But he had plenty of money as things were, with so much back pay and combat pay in his pocket. And if he was out a few hundred miles from shore when he got called back to active duty, there would be hard feelings all around. His wouldn't matter. The Navy's, unfortunately, would.

He was back from church one Sunday morning when the telephone in his apartment rang. He'd found he liked Catholic services. He'd converted for Connie's sake, and never expected to take the rigmarole seriously. But the fancy costumes and the Latin and the incense grew on him. If you were going to have a religion, shouldn't you have one with tradition behind it?

"I bet that's my ma," Connie said as she went to answer the call. "She was saying she wants us over for dinner. . . . Hello?" The pause that followed stretched too long. As soon as she spoke again, her tone told George it wasn't her mother on the other end of the line: "Yes, he's here. Hold on. . . . George! It's for you."

"I'm coming," George said. Connie's stricken face told him who the caller was likely to be. He answered formally, something he rarely did: "This is George Enos."

"Hello, Enos. This is Chief Thorvaldson, at the Navy Yard. The *Oregon*'s going to put to sea day after tomorrow, and she's got a slot for a 40mm loader. You fit that slot, and you've had a long leave. Report aboard her by 0800 tomorrow."

"The *Oregon*. 0800. Right, Chief." George said what he had to say. Standing there beside him, Connie started to cry. He put his arm around her, which only made things worse.

"A battleship, Enos. You're coming up in the world," the CPO said. "You could hide your old destroyer escort in her magazines."

"Sure," George said, and hung up. He didn't much want to sail on a battleship. Like a carrier, it would draw enemy aircraft the way a dog drew fleas. But he couldn't do anything about that, either. With a sigh, he tried to smile at his wife. "We knew it was coming, babe. War's getting close to over, so I probably won't be gone real long now."

"I don't want you gone at all!" She clung to him fiercely. "And things can still go wrong at the end of a war. Look at your father."

He wished he'd never told her that story. Then he shrugged. He would have thought of it himself, too. He jumped when the telephone rang again. Connie picked it up. "Hello? . . . Oh, hi, Ma. God, I wish you'd been on the line a few minutes ago . . . Yes, we can come, but we can't stay late. George just got a call from the Navy . . . The *Oregon*. Tomorrow morning . . . 'Bye." She hung up. "Pa's got lobsters, so it'll be a good supper, anyway."

"Won't see them in the Navy," George agreed.

Lobsters, drawn butter, corn on the cob . . . It wasn't quite a traditional New England boiled dinner, which didn't mean it wasn't damn good. "Enjoy it, George," Connie's father said, sliding a Narragansett ale down the table to him. "Navy chow ain't even like what the Cookie makes on a fishing boat. I know that."

"It's the truth, Mr. McGillicuddy," George said sadly. He took a pull at the cold bottle of ale. It wasn't *bad*, but he'd had better. He didn't say anything about that. Narragansett went back further than he did. "How long have they been brewing this stuff, anyway?"

"It's been around about as long as I have, and I was born in 1887," McGillicuddy answered. "Can't tell you exactly, 'cause I wasn't paying much attention to beer back then, but that's about it, anyhow."

"Sounds right," George said. He was born in 1910, and Narragansett had been a Boston fixture his whole life long. He took another swig from the bottle.

What with all the food and the 'Gansett, he wanted to roll over and go to sleep when he and Connie and the boys got back to their apartment. But he wanted to do something else, too, and he did. Connie would have thought something was wrong with him if he hadn't. And

God only knew when he'd get another chance. "Gotta make it last," he said, lighting a cigarette to try to stretch the afterglow.

"I should hope so." Connie poked him in the ribs. "Don't want you chasing after chippies when your ship gets into some port that isn't Boston."

"Not me." George lied without hesitation. *Not very often, anyway*, he amended silently.

"Better not." His wife poked him again. "Give me one of those." He could reach the nightstand more easily than she could. He handed her the pack. They were Niagaras, a U.S. brand—they tasted of straw and, he swore, horse manure. But they were better than nothing. Connie leaned close to him for a light. He stroked her cheek. "Thanks," she said, whether for the smoke or the caress he didn't know.

He managed an early-morning quickie, too. Connie wouldn't have put up with that except on a day when he was shipping out. He kissed the boys good-bye—they bravely fought against the sniffles—and, duffel on his shoulder, headed across the Charles for the Boston Navy Yard.

Before he got in, Marine guards patted him down and searched the denim sack. Finding nothing more lethal than a safety razor and a clasp knife, they let him through. "Can't be too careful," one of the leathernecks said.

"Last week down in Providence, this shithead showed up in a lieutenant commander's uniform—he'd rolled the officer in an alley behind a bar. He blew up two guards—poor bastards—but he didn't get to the ships, and that's what counts."

"Story didn't make the news," George said.

"No—I guess they sat on it," the guard replied. "But one of the guys who bought a plot was my brother-in-law's best friend since they were kids. I knew Apple a little bit myself. He was a good guy."

"Apple?" George had heard a lot of nicknames, but that was a new one on him.

"Like a baby's arm holding one," the Marine explained. "Be some sad broads around, I'll tell you. Now pass on through."

Finding the *Oregon* was easy enough. George looked for the biggest damn ship tied up at any of the piers, and there she was: a mountain of steel bristling with guns of all sizes, up to the dozen fourteen-inchers of her main armament. She could smash anything that came within twenty miles of her—but, in these days of airplane carriers, how many enemy ships were likely to?

George shrugged; that wasn't his worry. He went up the gangplank and paused at the end. Catching the officer of the deck's eye, he said, "Permission to come aboard, sir?"

The OOD was a lieutenant. George had had a two-striper for a skipper before. "Granted," the name said. He poised pen and clipboard. "And you are . . . ?"

"George Enos, sir."

The officer checked him off the list. "You're new, then," he said, and George nodded. The OOD went on, "What was your previous duty? And your battle station?"

"I was on a destroyer escort, sir—the *Josephus Daniels*. My battle station was loader on a 40mm mount. When they ordered me to duty here, they said that was where you'd put me." He knew the powers that be would do whatever they damn well pleased, but he'd got his druthers in. "I can do just about anything if I have to. I was a fisherman before the war, and I came back to the USA in the prize crew of a freighter we took in the South Atlantic."

"Uh-*huh*. You realize we can check all this?"

"Yes, sir. It's all in my jacket, anyway." George wasn't talking about clothes, but about the paperwork any sailor carried with him.

"Uh-*huh*," the OOD said again. Then he turned and called, "Caswell!"

"Yes, sir?" A petty officer materialized behind him.

"Here's Enos. Put him on the number-three 40mm mount—he's a loader. Show him where he's supposed to go for general quarters and where he can sling his hammock."

"Aye aye, sir. Come on, Enos." Caswell had a thin, clever face and cold gray eyes. George didn't think getting him mad was a good idea. You'd pay for it, and you'd keep on paying, maybe for years.

He didn't want to get the senior rating mad at him any which way. "Show me where to go and what to do, and I'll go there and do it," he said. He'd hoped for a bunk, given the size of the battlewagon, but he could live with a hammock. It wasn't as if he hadn't had one before . . . and the *Oregon* would carry a much bigger crew than the *Josephus Daniels* did, too.

Caswell took him to his battle station first. That he still had his duffel slung over his shoulder seemed to mean nothing to the petty officer. Caswell wasn't carrying anything himself, after all. George could see right away that the 40mm mounts on the *Oregon*'s deck were added long after the ship was built. That was no surprise; every warship these days piled on as much AA as she could without capsizing. The number-three mount was on the port side, well forward.

George eyed the awesome bulk of the two triple fourteen-inch turrets not far away. "What's it like when they go off?" he asked.

"Loud," Caswell said, and said no more. *No shit*, George thought. That boom would probably blow the fillings out of your teeth, and maybe the hair off your head. He didn't want to think about the big guns going off when he had a hangover. If that didn't kill you, you'd wish it would.

He looked up and down the deck. Yeah, there was a lot of antiaircraft: 40mms, and .50-caliber and .30-caliber machine guns as well. And the five-inch guns of the secondary armament could fire AA rounds, too. "Anybody bores in on us, we can make him mighty unhappy," he remarked.

"We better," the petty officer replied. "We fuck up once, we're toast." That was nothing but the truth. A well-placed bomb could sink even this floating, fighting fortress. Caswell lit a cigarette. He didn't offer George one, but he did say, "Come on. I'll take you below."

There were bunks on the *Oregon*. But there were also lots of hammocks. Since George was a new fish here, his getting one was no man-bites-dog story. The sailors on either side of him seemed good enough guys—a hell of a lot friendlier than Caswell, that was for sure.

"Give me the straight skinny," George said to one of them, a broad-shouldered man who went by Country. "Is she a madhouse or is she a home?"

"She's a home . . . mostly." Country's harsh Midwestern accent said he hadn't grown up near the sea.

"Mostly? When do things go wrong?"

The other sailor tipped him a wink. "You'll find out," he said, and that was all George could get out of him.

Lieutenant-Colonel Jerry Dover looked around at the latest place his supply dump had come to rest. He looked at Pete, who'd done a hell of a lot of retreating with him. "From Edwardsville to Albertville," Dover said. "Reckon that'd make a good title for my memoirs when I write 'em up?"

"For your what?" The quartermaster sergeant gave him a blank look. "This Albertville place don't look like it's good for squat."

"It's bigger than Edwardsville," Dover said. Pete couldn't very well argue. Edwardsville had had only a couple of hundred people in it. Albertville, northwest of the other town—on the road to Huntsville, in other words—had three, maybe even four, thousand. It boasted a cotton gin and a cotton mill and a cottonseed-oil plant and a cornmeal mill. The local high school bragged about how it trained future farmers.

While Pete didn't argue, he didn't seem much impressed, either. "Horseshit's bigger'n dogshit, too, but shit's still shit, you ask me." He pulled out a pack of Raleighs. With Kentucky and Tennessee lost, with North Carolina cut off from Alabama, even good tobacco was getting scarce. Seeing Dover's longing expression, he gave his superior a smoke and a light. After his drag, he added, "And the Confederate States are in deep shit right now, and that's the God's truth."

"You think I'm gonna pat you on the ass and go, 'No, no, everything's fine,' you're out of your tree," Dover answered. "They're already knocking Birmingham flat. If we lose Huntsville, too . . ."

"We're fucked," Pete finished for him. "Without the rockets, we can't do *anything* against the damnyankees."

"Yeah." Jerry Dover smoked in quick, worried puffs. "If Birmingham and Huntsville go, what's left? New Orleans and Little Rock and Texas. God Himself couldn't lick the USA with New Orleans and Little Rock and Texas, and I bet He wouldn't be fool enough to try. Which is more than I can say for Jake Featherston."

Pete looked around nervously. "Jeez, sir, careful how you talk. You seen how many soldiers they've hanged from trees with DEFEATIST around their necks?"

"They won't hang me—or you, either," Dover said. "We're still doing our jobs—and we're doing 'em pretty goddamn well, too. That's a hell of a lot more than most people can say—including the President. Wasn't either one of us who lost Richmond."

"He says we'll get it back," Pete said.

"Freedom!" Dover replied—without a doubt, the most sardonic Party salutation in the history of the CSA. In one politically safe word, he called everybody who'd ever believed anything Jake Featherston said an idiot. He'd believed some of those things himself—not all of them, but some—so he knew he was an idiot, too.

Pete cocked his head to one side, like a bird dog taking a scent. "Firing's picking up at the front."

Jerry Dover listened, too. "Shit. You're right. Yankees are laying down more artillery than they've used for a while. If that doesn't mean another push is on its way . . ."

"Can't afford many more," Pete said.

"*Any* more," Dover corrected. "If they start shelling Huntsville *and* bombing it, how's it going to keep doing what it's got to do?"

Before Pete could answer, Dover's field telephone jangled. The noncom sketched a salute and ducked out of Dover's tent. "Albertville supply depot here," Dover said as he picked up the telephone. He listened, then answered, "I'm light on 105 shells, but I'll send you what I've got." He yelled for Pete to come back. Would Cicero Sawyer be able to get him more artillery rounds after he sent off what he had here? He had to hope so.

"I'll get 'em moving," Pete promised when Dover told him what he needed. "We don't have as many as I wish we did, though."

"Yeah, I know. I said the same thing," Dover answered. "Anything is better than nothing, though."

Was anything *enough* better than nothing? Dover didn't know. Once more, he had to hope. The telephone rang again, and then again. The soldiers farther forward sounded more and more desperate. "Things are falling apart up here!" one of them yelled.

"We can't hold!" another cried.

"I'll send what I can," Dover said, and rang up Huntsville. "Whatever you've got," he told Sawyer. "They're taking it on the chin here."

"I'll do what I can," Cicero Sawyer answered, sounding much like Dover himself. "We aren't getting stuff as fast as I wish we would, either."

"Great." Dover meant anything but what he said. "How are we supposed to fight a war if we don't have anything to fight with?"

"Good question," Sawyer said. "If you don't have any other good questions, class is dismissed." He hung up.

Swearing, so did Jerry Dover. After he finished cussing, he checked to see how many clips he had for his automatic rifle. He had the bad feeling he might need it before long.

The next time he saw Pete, he noticed the noncom was carrying a submachine gun. Pete's eyes went to his weapon, too. Neither of them said anything. If you didn't talk about what worried you, maybe it would go away and leave you alone.

Or maybe it wouldn't.

As he'd learned to do in the last war, Dover tracked the battle with his ears. He didn't like what he was hearing. The Yankees seemed to be pushing forward, straight toward his dump. And they seemed to be outflanking it on both sides.

A corporal came up to him. "Sir, shouldn't we be getting ready to pull out of here?"

"Yeah, I guess maybe we should." He'd had to move or abandon a lot of dumps in the Confederacy's grinding retreat. He wondered why he was dicking around with this one.

A staff car—a butternut Birmingham packed to the gills with officers and men—rattled up to the supply dump. "Get the hell out while you still can!" somebody yelled from inside. "The damnyankees're right on our ass!" The auto jounced away. The load it carried was too much for its springs.

Maybe the load Dover carried was too much for his. But he started shouting the orders he'd used so often before: "Set the time charges in the ammo! Start blowing up the supplies! Come on, dammit! We've got to get out of here, see where else we can make a stand."

Shells started landing close by. Then machine-gun bullets snapped and whined past his head—not aimed fire, not yet, but they meant U.S. soldiers sure as hell were too damn close. Before long, the Yankees *would* see what they were aiming at, and that wouldn't be good. And the rounds were coming in from three sides, not just from the front.

"Fuck," Dover muttered. He really had waited too long this time. He raised his voice to a shout: "Get out, men! Save yourselves!"

He'd just gotten in a truckload of new-model field telephones, lighter and better all around than the ones that had soldiered through the war. They still sat in their crates; he hadn't had a chance to send any of them forward yet. He shot them up, one short burst at a time. If his own side couldn't use them, he was damned if he'd let the bastards in green-gray get them.

"Come on, sir! Let's get out of here!" Pete sat behind the wheel of another military Birmingham. The irony of the auto's name struck home for the first time, here much too close to the city where it was made. Dover hopped in. Pete headed northwest, toward Huntsville.

They got maybe a quarter of a mile up one of the most godawful roads Dover's kidneys had ever met when a burst of machine-gun fire off to one side made the quartermaster sergeant grunt. Pete slumped over, half his head blown off. The Birmingham started limping as if it had a flat—later, Dover found out it had two. With no one controlling it, it slewed off the bumpy asphalt and hit a pine tree. Luckily, it wasn't going very fast. Dover was bruised and shaken, but not hurt. He bailed out.

"Hold it right there, motherfucker!" somebody with a U.S. accent yelled. "Drop that piece, or you're dead meat!"

Dover froze. He looked around wildly for somewhere to run, somewhere to hide. If he moved, the hidden Yankee could plug him before he took more than a couple of steps. Slowly and carefully, he set the automatic Tredegar on the ground. "I've got a pistol on my belt," he called. "I'm going to take it out and put it with the rifle."

"Don't get cute with it, asshole." That was another U.S. soldier, one with a deep bass rasp. Jerry Dover couldn't see him. "We got enough firepower to saw you in half like a fuckin' board."

"The last person who thought I was cute was my mother," Dover said, which won him raucous laughter from the unseen enemy troopers. Holding his .45 between thumb and forefinger, he laid it down next to the rifle. Then, without being asked, he raised his hands above his head. "You got me."

Not two but four U.S. soldiers cautiously came out of the bushes. Two of them had leaves and branches on their helmets, held in place with strips of inner tube. Two carried ordinary Springfields; one a heavy, clunky U.S. submachine gun; and one a captured C.S. automatic rifle. They all needed shaves. They smelled of old sweat and leather and tobacco and mud: like soldiers, in other words.

"Son of a bitch," one of them said as they drew near. "We got us a light colonel." The two stars on either side of Dover's collar weren't made to be visible from very far off. Why let snipers pick out officers the easy way?

"Cough up your ammo," said the guy with the Confederate weapon. Without a word, Dover gave him the clips he had left after shooting up the field telephones. His captors also relieved him of watch and wallet and cigarettes. He went right on keeping quiet. They weren't supposed to do that, but it happened all the time. And they didn't have to take him prisoner. He could end up dead if any one of them decided to pull the trigger.

"I guess we oughta send him back," said the one with the deep voice. He was a corporal, and one of the pair with leaves nodding above his head. "Officer like that, the guys in Intelligence can squeeze some good shit out of him."

"Maybe." The Yankee with the submachine gun aimed it at Dover's face. "Who are you, buddy? What do you do? C'mon. Sing."

"My name is Jerry Dover. I'm a lieutenant colonel." Dover rattled off his pay number. "I ran the supply dump back there by Albertville." According to the Geneva Convention, he didn't have to say that. Self-preservation argued it would be a good idea.

"Quartermaster, huh? No wonder you got good smokes," the one with the deep voice said. He turned to the guy with the automatic rifle. "Take him back to battalion HQ, Rudy. Don't plug him unless he tries to bug out."

"Gotcha," Rudy said. He gestured with the captured weapon. "Get movin', Pops. You run, it's the last dumbass stunt you pull."

"I'm not going anywhere, except wherever you take me," Dover said. He was so relieved not to get shot out of hand, he didn't even resent the *Pops*. He *was* old enough to be the damnyankee's father. "Will you please bury my sergeant there?" he asked his captors, pointing to the Birmingham. "He was a good man."

"We round up some more of you butternut bastards, they can take care of it," the corporal said. The Yankees weren't going to dig for an enemy themselves.

"Move it," Rudy said. Hands still high, Jerry Dover trudged off into captivity.

During the last war, Chester Martin remembered, the Confederates had seen the writing on the wall in northern Virginia. As the summer of 1917 went on, the spirit gradually leaked out of the men in butternut. They wouldn't stand and fight till they couldn't fight any more, the way they had earlier. They would throw away their rifles and put up their hands and hope their U.S. opposite numbers didn't murder them.

The same thing was happening in Georgia now. Even some of the

Freedom Party Guards had the message: the Confederate States weren't going to win this time around, either. Some of the men in brown-splotched camouflage smocks had a hard time surrendering. But then, anybody who tried to surrender to Lieutenant Lavochkin had a hard time.

Chester admired the platoon leader's courage. Past that . . . If everybody on the U.S. side were like Boris Lavochkin, the war probably wouldn't have been anywhere near so tough. But Chester didn't think he wanted to live in a country that produced a lot of men like that. Living with one of them was tough enough.

Getting to Savannah seemed to have amounted to the be-all and end-all of General Morrell's strategy. Once the port fell, once the sickle slice cut the Confederacy in half, things were confused for a while. The powers that be needed some time to figure out what to do next. After you went to bed with the girl of your dreams, what did you say when you woke up beside her in the morning?

Martin's platoon, along with the rest of the regiment and a couple of more besides, crossed the Savannah River and went up into South Carolina. The swamps on that side of the river seemed no different from the ones in Georgia. The people over there spoke with the same mushy drawl. They hated damnyankees just as much as the Georgians did, even if they hadn't been able to muster more than a few soldiers to try to keep the invaders in green-gray out of their state.

"South Carolina seceded first, boys," Captain Rhodes told the company. "This goddamn state got the CSA rolling. Been a hell of a long time since then, but we finally get to pay the bastards back."

As far as Martin was concerned, too much water had gone under the bridge to care about which drop went first. What difference did it make now? He despised all the Confederate states equally. Why not? Men from each and every one of them were equally eager to do him in.

What did give him chills were the empty villages through which his outfit passed. He'd seen the like in Georgia. Once upon a time—say, up until a couple of years earlier—Negro sharecroppers had lived in them. Those people were almost all gone. He would have bet dollars to doughnuts they were almost all dead. Before long, their flimsy shacks would crumble and fall down, and then who would remember that they'd ever lived here?

Local whites didn't want to. Lieutenant Lavochkin brought the mayor of a little town called Hardeeville to a nameless village a couple of miles away. The mayor didn't want to come; a rifle to the back of his head proved amazingly persuasive.

"What happened to these people?" Lavochkin demanded.

"Well, I don't rightly know." The mayor was a white-mustached fellow named Darius Douglas. He walked with a limp that probably meant he had a Purple Heart stashed in a drawer somewhere.

"What do you mean, you don't know?" Lavochkin rapped out. "You suppose they all decided to go on vacation at the same time?"

Douglas had fine, fair skin. When he turned red, the flush was easy to see. "Well, I reckon not," he admitted. "But a lot of 'em was gone a while back, off to towns and such. The fancier the farm machinery got, the fewer the niggers we needed."

"How come we didn't see 'em in Savannah, then?" The lieutenant's voice was silky with danger. "How come we don't see 'em anywhere? How many niggers you got in Hardeeville, damn you?"

"Don't have any, I don't reckon, but we never did," Darius Douglas answered. "Hardeeville, it's a white folks' town. Niggers came in to work, but they didn't live there. They lived in places like this here."

"Do you know what you are? You're a lying sack of shit, that's what," Lieutenant Lavochkin snarled. "If you came out and said, 'Yeah, we killed 'em, and I don't miss 'em a fucking bit,' at least you'd be honest. This way . . . Christ, you know what you assholes did, but it makes you jumpy enough so you don't want to own up to it, not when you're talking to people like me."

"I always knew damnyankees was nigger-lovers," the mayor of Hardeeville said. "Nobody else'd make such a fuss over a bunch o' damn coons."

"Yeah? So who's gonna make a fuss over you?" Lavochkin asked. Before Mayor Douglas could answer, the U.S. officer shot him in the face. Douglas dropped like a sack of beans in the middle of a muddy, overgrown street.

"Jesus!" Chester Martin exclaimed. "What the hell'd you go and do that for . . . sir?"

The platoon commander looked at him—looked through him, really. "You going to tell me he didn't have it coming?"

"Jesus," Martin said again. "I dunno. He didn't kill any of those coons himself, I don't think." The late Mr. Douglas was still twitching a little, and still bleeding, too. The iron stink of blood mingled with the foulness of bowels that had just let go.

"No, he didn't kill 'em. He just waved bye-bye when they went off to the camps," Lavochkin said. "All these Confederate cocksuckers did the same goddamn thing. Far as I'm concerned, they all deserve a bullet in the head."

As far as Martin was concerned, that had nothing to do with anything. "We deal with that after the war's over, sir. You start shooting civilians for the hell of it, we're going to have reprisals come down on our heads, and we need that kind of crap like we need a root canal."

Lavochkin grunted. "I'm not afraid of these assholes. They're whipped."

"How many replacements do we need right now?" Chester asked. The lieutenant grunted again. "They haven't all quit yet, so let's not fire 'em up. What do you say to that?"

He could tell what Lieutenant Lavochkin wanted to say. Lavochkin wanted to call him yellow, but damn well couldn't. Scowling, the lieutenant did say, "If I'm not a good boy, I don't get promoted, right? You think I give a flying fuck about that?"

Chester shrugged. He hoped Lavochkin did. It was the only hold he had on the cold-blooded young officer. Lieutenant Lavochkin liked killing too much, and Chester didn't know what he could do about it. Yeah, you killed in a war—that was what it was all about. But the guys who enjoyed it caused more trouble than they solved. Martin wondered whether the platoon commander needed to have an unfortunate accident.

He didn't let that show on his face. If he had, he was sure Lieutenant Lavochkin would have plugged him with as little remorse as he'd shot Darius Douglas. *If I have to take him out, I can't fuck up, 'cause I'll only get one chance*, Martin thought unhappily.

"Let's go back to Hardeeville," Lavochkin said, which was anything but a retreat.

"What will you say when the people ask what happened to the mayor?" Chester wondered.

"Shot resisting U.S. authority." The lieutenant's voice remained hard and firm. He didn't sound the least bit guilty. Chester wondered whether he knew how to feel guilty. The first sergeant wouldn't have bet on it. As far as Lavochkin was concerned, anything he did was right because he did it. How did that make him any different from Jake Featherston, except that Featherston had more scope for running wild than an infantry lieutenant did?

"Come on, you guys," Chester called to the men in the platoon. "You heard the lieutenant—we're heading back to Hardeeville. Keep your eyes open when we get there, in case of trouble." *In case the locals go nuts because we scragged the mayor.* He didn't say that, but he hoped the men could work it out for themselves.

Most of them seemed able to. They tramped back toward the little town as if advancing into battle. They moved in small groups, warily, keeping an eye out ahead and to all sides.

Hardeeville was a block of shops, a filling station, a saloon, and a few houses. Before the war, it might have held two or three hundred people. With the men anywhere close to military age gone, it was smaller than that now. When the mayor's wife saw the U.S. soldiers coming back without him, she screeched, "Where's Darius?"

"Dead," Lavochkin said flatly. "He resisted our authority, and—" Whatever he said after that, Mrs. Douglas' shriek smothered it. *She* made a fuss over the late mayor.

A shot rang out from one of the houses. A U.S. soldier went down, grabbing his leg. "Shit!" he yelled. Chester didn't think the cartridge was anything more than a .22, but that didn't mean it felt like a kiss.

Three soldiers with automatic rifles emptied their magazines into the front of the house. Glass and chunks of wood flew. A woman and a twelve-year-old boy staggered out. Both of them were bleeding. The boy still clutched the .22. He tried to raise it and shoot at the U.S. soldiers again, but he fell over instead, blood puddling under him.

"Fuck," said one of the men in green-gray. He was no happier about shooting a kid than anyone else would have been. Yeah, the kid had fired first. Yeah, he was an enemy. That didn't make it much better.

Had things ended there, they would have been bad. But they didn't. They got worse. Somebody fired from another house. A Featherston Fizz came flying out of nowhere and burst at the feet of a U.S. soldier. He screamed like a damned soul as flames engulfed him. And one of the old men in Hardeeville laughed.

"Take 'em out!" Lieutenant Lavochkin yelled. "Take 'em all out!"

Chester's first shot knocked over the old man who thought watching a Yankee burn was funny. His second shot hit the old woman next to the old man right in the middle of the chest. She crumpled before she had a chance to screech. Of course, Chester's wasn't the only bullet that hit her—not even close. All the soldiers in the platoon were letting go with everything they had.

They started throwing grenades into the houses closest to them. A couple of men had grenade launchers on their rifles. They lobbed grenades all over Hardeeville, almost at random. "It'll come down on somebody's head!" one of them whooped as he pulled the trigger and sent one off . . . somewhere.

The men and women and kids on the street went down as if scythed. Their dying cries—and the gunfire, and the grenades bursting randomly all over the little town—brought more people out to see what was going on. The U.S. soldiers shot them down, too.

It was madness, red-hot madness. Chester Martin felt it as he fired and reloaded, fired and reloaded, and slapped in clip after clip. He didn't know how many Confederates he killed. He didn't much care, either. Along with his buddies, he went through the town. By the time they got done, there wasn't much town left—it burned behind them. And just about everybody who'd lived in Hardeeville was dead.

Chester stood there shaking his head, like a man whose fever had suddenly broken. "Wow," he said, looking back on the devastation. "What did we just do?"

"Settled their hash," Lieutenant Lavochkin answered. "I don't think too much of this needs to go into the after-action report, do you?"

"Christ, no!" Chester thought about some of the things he'd just done. He wished he hadn't. He wished he hadn't done them, too. So, no doubt, did Hardeeville. Well, it was too late for him, and much too late for the little town. He had the rest of his life to try to forget. Hardeeville . . . didn't, not any more.

Confederate Connie was on the air again. To most people in the USA, the music the propaganda broadcaster played was hot stuff, at or past the cutting edge. Lieutenant Colonel Jonathan Moss—he was still getting used to the silver oak leaves on his shoulder straps—had heard stranger, wilder rhythms when Spartacus' guerrillas got their hands on a guitar and a fiddle.

Here he was, at a big air base just outside of Dayton, Ohio, not far from where the Confederates swarmed over the border not quite three years before. The base didn't exist then. Now, unless the Kaiser's airmen had something fancier, it was the biggest training center in the world.

The song ended. Like most of the other guys at the base, Moss thought listening to Confederate Connie was more fun anyway. She had a contralto like a wet dream.

"Well, you Yankee boys, aren't you proud of yourselves?" she said, as if she were waiting for you to get back into bed with her and didn't want to wait very long. She was probably fifty-five and frumpy, but she sure didn't sound that way. "Your *brave* soldiers went and wiped Hardeeville right off the map."

"Where the hell's Hardeeville?" somebody asked.

"Shut up," said Moss and two other men. Listening to Confederate Connie didn't just remind you why you fought. It reminded you why you were alive.

"That's right," she went on. "They marched into a defenseless town and they murdered everybody in it—men, women, children, everybody. Then they burned it down on top of the bodies. No more Hardeeville, South Carolina. Gone. Right off the map. Some fun, hey? Aren't you proud to live in a country that does stuff like that?"

Nobody could keep the men around the wireless set quiet after that. "Oh, yeah, like the CSA never murdered anybody!" a pilot said.

"Where's your coons, you lying cunt?" somebody else added.

"If they killed everybody, how come you know it happened?" demanded yet another flier.

Confederate Connie actually answered the last question, saying, "The Yankees missed a couple of women, though. They played dead in the blood and then got away. And now, to make you feel good about what your boys in green-gray managed to do, here's a tune by Smooth Steve and the Oiler Orchestra, 'How about That?' "

Music blared from the wireless, more of the syncopated noise the Confederates liked better than most people in the USA did. Jonathan Moss listened with at most half an ear. He wasn't the only one; plenty of people were still telling Confederate Connie what a liar she was.

Moss wasn't so sure. He'd heard enough war stories to believe a unit could go hog wild and massacre anybody who got in its way. He didn't believe troops would do anything like that just for the fun of it. If somebody in Hardeeville had fired at them, though . . . In that case, the town was what soldiers called shit out of luck. Probably all the men who'd torn up the place wished they hadn't done it—now. That was liable to be a little late for Hardeeville's innocent—and not so innocent—civilians.

A fellow with a bombardier's badge above the right pocket of his tunic said, "What's she getting her tit in a wringer for, anyway? I bet I blow up more people three times a week than those ground-pounders did. But I do it from twenty thousand feet, so I'm a fuckin' hero. It's a rough old war."

Along with the bombardier's badge, he wore the ribbons for a Purple Heart and a Bronze Star with an oak-leaf cluster. If he wasn't a hero, he would do till the genuine article came along. He also had a view of the war cynical enough to give even Moss pause.

The next morning, Moss got summoned to the commandant's office. He wondered how he'd managed to draw that worthy's notice, and what kind of trouble he was in. Major General Barton K. Yount was a sixtyish fellow who might have looked like a kindly grandfather if he weren't in uniform. "Have a seat, Moss," he said. His accent suggested he'd been born somewhere not far from here.

"Thank you, sir," Moss said cautiously, and sat with just as much care. *The condemned man got a hearty meal* went through his mind.

General Yount must have realized what he was thinking. "I didn't call you in here to ream you out, Colonel," he said. "I want to ask you a question."

"Sir?" The less Moss said, the less he might have to regret later on.

But Yount came straight to the point: "You've flown a lot of different airplanes, haven't you?"

"Well, yes, sir. I started with a pusher job in 1914, and I'm still doing it, so I must have, eh?"

"That's right." Yount smiled and nodded. "How would you like to add a turbo job to the list?"

A crazy grin spread across Moss' face. "Sir, I'd kill for a chance like that. Only reason I haven't is, I didn't know who needed bumping off."

Turbos were going to turn propeller-driven airplanes obsolete as soon as the boys with the slide rules and the thick glasses worked the gremlins out of them. They were already sixty or eighty miles an hour faster than the hottest prop-driven fighters. The drawbacks were unreliable engines and landing gear, among other things. Turbos were widowmakers on a scale that hadn't been seen since the early days of the Great War. Moss was one of thousands of pilots who didn't give a damn. He wanted that chance so bad he could taste it.

Major General Yount's smile got wider. He knew Moss was

kidding . . . up to a point. "You've got it, Colonel. You can call it a reward for a hard time, if you like. There's one thing I do have to warn you about, though."

"What? That it's dangerous? I already know, sir. I'm ready to take the chance."

"No, no." The training commandant shook his head. "I assumed you knew that. But you also have to know that for the time being we aren't using turbo fighters anywhere except above U.S.-occupied territory. If you get shot down or forced to crash-land because of engine trouble, we don't want this machinery falling into enemy hands. You must agree to that before you begin flight training here."

"Oh." Moss didn't try to hide his disappointment. "I wanted to go hunting."

"I understand that. You wouldn't be a good fighter pilot if you didn't. But I hope you follow the reasoning behind the order."

"Yes, sir," Moss said reluctantly. Even more reluctantly, he added, "All right, sir. I agree to the condition."

"Good. In that case, report to Building Twelve at 0730 tomorrow morning. You'll learn about the care and feeding of your new beast."

Several turbo fighters sat on the runway outside of Building Twelve. Moss got there early so he could walk around them before he went in. They looked weird as hell. The fuselage was almost shark-shaped. The wings swept back from root to tip. He'd never seen or imagined anything like that before. The turbos had no tailwheel. They sat on a nosewheel instead, so the fuselage rested parallel to the ground instead of sloping down from nose to tail. The engines sat in metal pods under the wings. Yeah, the new fighter was one peculiar bird. But the longer Moss stared, the more he nodded to himself. It might look different, but it also looked deadly.

He wasn't the only pilot giving the new airplanes a once-over. "Fly one yet?" he asked a much-decorated major.

"Yeah," the younger man answered.

"What's it like?"

"Like your first girl after you've been jacking off too goddamn long."

Moss laughed. That wasn't what he'd expected, but he liked the way it sounded. He went into the building to hear about the care and feeding of the Boeing-71, as the new turbo was officially known. The major doing the lecturing had some fresh and nasty burn scars on his left arm, and walked with a limp. Moss wondered if he'd got hurt in a turbo, but didn't ask. He didn't really want to know. Nobody else seemed curious, either.

He learned about the instruments, about the guns (four 30mm cannon in the nose—one hell of a punch), about the strange and temperamental landing gear, about what to do if an engine quit or caught fire, about what to do if both engines went out (not the most encouraging bit of instruction he'd ever had), about tactics against the Confederates' hottest prop-driven Hound Dogs, about everything he needed to know before he plopped his butt down in the cramped-looking cockpit.

He had to make himself listen. He knew he was hearing all kinds of stuff that would help keep him alive. He was a pro; he understood that. Even so, all he wanted to do was get in there and find out what the bird could do.

After what seemed forever and was only a week, he got his chance in a two-seat trainer. U.S. armies had driven the Confederates out of Petersburg. Birmingham and Huntsville were under artillery assault. Moss wondered if there'd be any enemy airplanes left for him to face when he finally went on duty in the new turbo—people were calling them Screaming Eagles, and the brass didn't seem to mind too much.

The noise inside the cockpit was different. He felt it all through his body instead of just hearing it. He gave the turbo some throttle. It raced down the runway—it needed half again as much tarmac as a prop job. As he came up to takeoff speed, the instructor said, "Ease the stick back. Not too much, now. You do everything by little bits with this baby."

"Right," Moss said, and then he was airborne. He gunned the turbo a little. When he felt what happened, he whispered, "Ohh." Sure as hell, the murmur wasn't much different from the one he'd made as he first slid into Beth Sullivan when he was seventeen. He'd forgotten you could mix so much delight and awe and astonishment.

The instructor chuckled. How many other pilots had made that same sound in his earphones? "It's something, isn't it?" he said.

"Wow," Moss answered, which wasn't a hell of a lot more articulate. After a moment, he tried again: "It's like angels are pushing."

"It is, isn't it?" Now the instructor sounded thoughtful; he hadn't heard that before, anyway. He paused for a moment, then said, "Remember, they can turn into devils in nothing flat if you screw up—or even if you don't. Sometimes only God knows why the engines flame out or throw a rotor or just up and quit. And if you don't want to be asking Him face-to-face, you've got to get out of the bird in a hurry."

"I understand," Moss said. The single-seat Screaming Eagle had one of the nicest cockpit canopies he'd ever seen, a sleekly streamlined armor-glass bubble. The trainer's canopy was longer and more bulbous, to accommodate the longer cockpit with two men. Could you yank it back quick enough to bail out? He hoped so.

At the instructor's command, he swung the turbo into a turn. You couldn't come close to turning as tight as you could in a prop job. But you wouldn't want to dogfight in a Screaming Eagle anyway, not when you could outdive, outclimb, and just plain outrun anything else in the air.

Landing with a nosewheel as the first flight ended felt strange, but he did it. He couldn't stop smiling when he got out of the fighter. If this wasn't love, what was it?

Georgia. Now Alabama. Cincinnatus Driver didn't care where they sent him. That he could drive through states which didn't come close to bordering the USA shouted louder than any words that the Confederacy was cracking up.

Enemy wireless programs still denied the obvious. They promised vengeance on the United States and swore C.S. victory lay right around the corner. "Those bastards are so full of bullshit, no fuckin' wonder their eyes are brown," Hal Williamson said. He paused to drag on a cigarette. The smoke, like the battery-powered wireless set, was loot from a captured Confederate supply dump. The enemy had destroyed what he could, but he'd had to retreat too fast to get rid of everything.

"We will take our revenge on the damnyankees!" the announcer brayed. "Our rockets will drop from the skies and punish them as they only dream of punishing us! We will wipe their corrupt and filthy cities off the map one after another!"

Cincinnatus lit up a Raleigh of his own. "Turn him off," he said. "Screechin' like that'll ruin my digestion."

"I hear you," Williamson said, and turned the power knob till it clicked. The ranting Confederate broadcaster—he must have studied at the Jake Featherston school of drama—fell silent. Williamson made as if to throw a rock at the set. "Goddamn lying cocksucker."

"Yeah," Cincinnatus said, and hoped he was right. U.S. newscasters went on and on about the German bomb that leveled Petrograd. If the Germans could do something like that, could the Confederates match them? You didn't want to think so, but was it impossible?

Hal's thoughts ran along a different train track: "Besides, where'll the dickheads get their rockets once we're done with Huntsville?"

"Yeah!" This time, Cincinnatus sounded much happier. Everybody knew the enemy rockets came from there. If the Confederates couldn't throw their superbomb at the USA, what good would it do them?

And, even before Huntsville got overrun, it was catching holy hell. Battery upon battery of 105s pounded away at the town. Their muzzle flashes brightened the horizon from the north all the way around to the southeast. The deeper *crump!* of bursting bombs said U.S. airplanes came over Huntsville, too. How anybody could go on working while high explosives were knocking his city flat was beyond Cincinnatus. The Confederates seemed intent on trying, though.

Before the drivers settled down for the night, they cut cards to see who would stand sentry when. Cincinnatus got a three-hour shift right at the start. That was good news and bad mixed together. He would have to stay awake longer when he was hungrier for sleep than for a good steak. But when he did climb into the cabin of his truck and roll up in blankets, he wouldn't have his sleep interrupted . . . unless Confederate raiders hit.

And they might. He knew that too well, which was why he carried his submachine gun with the safety off. C.S. regulars were thin on the ground. Raiders, damn them, popped out of nowhere. Some were bypassed soldiers, others civilians with a chip on their shoulder. If they could throw a few grenades or stitch a burst of automatic-weapons fire through a truck park, the damage they did more than paid for itself even if they got scragged.

A lot of the time, they didn't. They disappeared into the darkness and were never seen again. "Bastards," Cincinnatus muttered. His leg hurt. So did his shoulder. They did a lot of the time, even though he took enough aspirins to give himself a perpetual sour stomach. Run out in front of a motorcar and you weren't the same again afterwards.

He prowled around the parked trucks, doing his best to move quietly. Not far away, he heard a sound like crazy screeching. He froze for a second before realizing it was a raccoon. Those unearthly noises could get you going.

His wristwatch had numbers and hands that glowed in the dark.

When his stretch on patrol ended, he shook his replacement awake and curled up on the seat of his truck. Whatever happened from then till sunup happened without him.

Somebody had liberated a ham. Toasted over a fire, a thick slab of it was delicious, and beat the hell out of the canned scrambled eggs Cincinnatus also ate. The coffee tasted as if it was at least half chicory. He'd had blends like that when he lived in Covington. He was used to it; he even kind of liked it. Some of the white drivers grumbled.

Hal Williamson put things in perspective: "Shit, guys, it's better than no coffee at all." Nobody found any easy way to argue with that.

The drivers headed for the closest dump to load up with whatever the troops might need today (or whatever the quartermaster had, which wasn't always the same thing). Before they got there, a bird colonel in a command car waved them down. "You men have empty trucks, right?"

"Yeah? So?" the lead driver asked. Being technically a civilian, he could get away with things that would have put a soldier in the stockade. Cincinnatus was only two trucks behind, and could hear everything that went on between the driver and the officer.

That worthy didn't even blink at the near-insubordination. "So you're going to come with me instead of going wherever the hell you were going."

"We can't do that!" the lead driver exclaimed. "They'll have our heads."

"No, they won't," the colonel said. "Whatever you were doing, what I've got for you is more important. Unless you're on your way to pick up a bunch of those kraut superbombs, this trumps everything. And I will have your guts for garters if you fuck with me, buddy—I promise you that."

The lead driver considered, but not for long. "Colonel, you talked me into it," he said. Cincinnatus would have said the same thing; he didn't think the colonel was bluffing.

All the man said after that was, "Follow me." He got into the command car, nudged the driver, and took off. The truck convoy rumbled after him.

They headed straight for Huntsville—straight for the front, in other words. Cincinnatus began to wonder if the colonel wasn't one of those Confederate impostors who showed up every now and then. Even more than raiders, they caused trouble all out of proportion to their numbers. If this son of a bitch was leading a whole column of trucks into an ambush . . .

Cincinnatus glanced over to the submachine gun beside him. He had as many bullets as he could for the Confederates, and one more for himself afterwards. They wouldn't take him alive no matter what.

The command car pulled up in front of a nondescript factory building—or it would have been, except for the barbed-wire perimeter surrounding it. Soldiers stood at the doorway, soldiers in green-gray uniforms. Cincinnatus breathed a sigh of relief.

"Let them come out!" the colonel shouted. The soldiers waved and nodded. They threw the doors wide.

"Do Jesus!" Cincinnatus gasped. His next thought after an ambush had been that the USA might have overrun another camp where the Confederates got rid of their Negroes. He turned out to be wrong, but what he saw was just about as bad. He hadn't imagined anything could be.

The men who came shambling out were white. They wore striped uniforms, the way convicts had back when Cincinnatus was a kid. The trousers and shirts looked as if they were made for some much larger species. And so they had been—Cincinnatus didn't think any of these skeletons on legs weighed more than 120 pounds. Most of them weren't anywhere close to that. A powerful animal stench came from them.

"Do Jesus!" Cincinnatus said again. He was out of the truck and limping toward them before he thought about what he was doing. He had several ration cans in pouches on his belt. "Here!" he called, and tossed them to the closest captives.

He wasn't the only driver doing the same thing. Anyone who had enough himself—even someone who was only hungry—would have wanted to feed these bright-eyed walking skeletons.

But the food almost touched off a riot. The drivers didn't have enough with them to give everybody some. The starving men who didn't get any tried to steal from the ones who did. Finally, the U.S. guards had to break things up with rifle butts. "Hate to do it," one of them said. "It's like hitting your puppy 'cause he wants a bone. These guys can't help it—they're that hungry. But what can you do? Otherwise, we'll have an even bigger goddamn mess on our hands."

"You'll all get some soon!" the colonel shouted. "Honest to God, you will! That's what the trucks are here for—to take you to where there's food."

That turned the trick. The boneracks in stripes swarmed onto the trucks, which could hold many more of them than of human beings of ordinary dimensions. "Who are you poor bastards?" Cincinnatus asked.

"We're politicals," a scrawny man said, not without pride. "I'm a Whig. I was mayor of Fayetteville, Arkansas." He looked more like a disaster than a one-time public official. A weak breeze—never mind a strong one—would have knocked him over in a heap. "I didn't like the Freedom Party. Still don't, by God. And this is what it bought me."

"What were you doin' in there?" Cincinnatus asked. But the mayor of Fayetteville didn't hang around to chat. That might have cost him a place in a truck, and he wasn't about to take a chance.

One of the guards answered for him: "They were putting rockets together, that's what—the big mothers that go miles and miles. Featherston's fuckers figured they might as well work 'em to death as just shoot 'em."

"Oh," Cincinnatus said in a hollow voice. When the guard said *work 'em to death*, he wasn't kidding. Some of the men still coming out of the factory would plainly die before they got fed. The dreadful odor that accompanied them from the building said more than a few men were already dead in there.

And yet . . . What happened to these political prisoners was horrible, no doubt about it. But they still got to try to stay alive. Some of them might have staved off death since before the war began.

The Confederacy's Negroes never got even that much of a chance. They went into camps—and they didn't come out. The politicals who hated the Freedom Party still labored for the Confederate States. Negroes would have done the same . . . had anyone asked them to.

Nobody seemed to have. The Freedom Party and a lot of white Confederates wanted their Negroes dead—and they got what they wanted. As horrible as this was, it could have been worse. That was, perhaps, the scariest thought of all.

As Cincinnatus got back into the cab of his deuce-and-a-half, he also wondered whether that bird colonel would have made such a fuss if the rocket factory were full of Negro laborers. He shrugged; he couldn't be sure one way or the other. But if he had his doubts—well, who could blame him, considering all the things he'd seen, all the things he'd escaped?

None of which made the plight of the starving, stinking politicals who jammed the back of the truck anything less than dreadful. Yes, if they were black they would have been dead already. But they couldn't last long as things were. Cincinnatus put the truck in gear and drove them off toward whatever help the U.S. Army could give.

Even with no more than a scratch force of guards, Camp Humble went right on doing what it was designed to do: reducing population. Jefferson Pinkard was proud of that. He was proud of the men he had left, and he was proud of the way he'd designed the camp. It was so smooth, it almost ran itself. You just didn't need a whole lot of guards to herd Negroes from the trains to the trucks and bathhouses, and then to chuck bodies into the crematoria. Everything went as smoothly as it did in any other well-run factory.

Every few weeks, the latest batch of Negro trusties who thought they'd dodged death by playing along discovered they'd made their last mistake. The only thing Jeff kept on being unhappy about was the ovens. The company that made them had come out a couple of times to try to get them to perform better, but without much luck. Pinkard's conclusion was that the contractor had sold him a bill of goods from the start. The greasy black smoke that belched from the stacks and the burnt-meat stench that went with it were part of the operation, and he couldn't do a thing about it.

Trains still brought Negroes to the camp, trains from Alabama and Mississippi and Louisiana and Arkansas and Texas. He'd also had loads of blacks from Florida and Cuba arrive. The local authorities rounded up their Negroes and sent them to Houston or Galveston by ship. He'd heard reports that subs operating in the Gulf of Mexico had sunk some of those ships. That was funny, in a grim way: the damnyankees were doing some of the Confederacy's work for it.

The telephone on his desk rang. He scowled. Why couldn't people just leave him alone and let him take care of his job? It rang again. Scowling still, he picked it up. "Pinkard here," he rasped.

"This here's Lou Doggett, General," the mayor of Humble said. Pinkard wasn't a general; he had a Party rank instead. But he didn't argue. He'd been a PFC the last time around. If somebody wanted to call him *General*, he didn't mind a bit.

"What's up?" he asked now.

"Well, I'll tell you, General—the wind's blowing this way from your camp, and it's pretty bad," Doggett answered. "This ain't how you told me it was gonna be when you put that camp in."

"It ain't the way I thought it was gonna be, neither," Jeff answered. "But it's the way it is. I don't know what else I can tell you."

"If it don't get better pretty damn quick, I'm gonna talk to the Governor," the mayor warned.

Jeff Pinkard laughed. "Go right ahead. You do that. Be my guest. You reckon the Governor amounts to anything when you set him next to Ferd Koenig and Jake Featherston?"

To his surprise, the mayor of Humble answered, "Matter of fact, General, I sure do. Richmond's gone. Even if it wasn't, there's damnyankees in between here and there. What the hell can Koenig and Featherston do way out here?"

He might be right. A nasty chill of fear ran through Pinkard when he realized as much. Like any government, the Confederacy ran because people agreed it ought to. What happened if they stopped agreeing? What happened if Texas Rangers came out here with guns? How could you know ahead of time?

"Let me ask you a question, your Honor," Pinkard said heavily. "Who went down on his knees beggin' for me to put this here camp where it's at? Who damn near jizzed in his dungarees when I said I would? Was that anybody who looks like you?"

"That was then," Doggett returned. "You didn't tell me it was gonna stink the way it does and belch out black smoke you can see for miles."

"I didn't know, goddammit. Those bastards who put in the ovens and the stacks went and rooked me," Jeff said. "But even if it does stink, it's doing something the country needs. You gonna try and tell me I'm wrong?"

"Well, no. I got no more use for coons'n any other decent, God-fearing white man does," the mayor said. "But godalmightydamn, General, it sure *does* stink. Makes the whole town smell like a barbecue pit some stupid fool went and forgot about. You're in a fancy uniform, so you get to give orders. Me, I got voted in, and I got a hell of a lot of people here in Humble who sure ain't gonna vote for me again 'cause of that smell. I mean, gettin' rid o' niggers is one thing. Doin' it so you can smell 'em roast—that's a whole different story."

"You want to eat roast beef, but you don't want to butcher your cow," Jeff said. "Camp's gotta be somewhere. I liked it where it was at before, too, but the damnyankees went and ran us out of there. That ain't my fault."

"I didn't say it was, but it's another problem. Suppose we go and lose the war."

"That's defeatism," Jeff said automatically.

The mayor of Humble astonished him by replying, "Oh, cut the crap, General. We're fucked, and you know it as well as I do. Like I said, Richmond's gone. They chopped us in half in Georgia. The President's on the run. How are we gonna win? I wish we could, but I ain't a blind man. And suppose we lose, like I said. What if the damnyankee soldiers march in here and ask, 'What the devil were you doin' with a murder camp there on your doorstep, Mr. Mayor?' What do I tell 'em then, hey?"

"Fuck," Pinkard muttered under his breath. That was insubordination so bad, it was damn near treason. Or it would have been, if it weren't such a good question.

Suppose we do go and surrender. Suppose the Yankees do come marching in. What do I tell them? The only answer that came to mind was, *I was just doing what the bigwigs in Richmond told me to do.* Would they buy that? What would they do to him if they didn't?

"General? Hey, General! You there?" How long had Doggett been yelling in his ear? A little while, evidently. He'd had other things to worry about.

"Yeah? What is it?" he managed, dragging himself back to the business at hand.

"You don't get that camp cleaned up in jig time, I *will* talk to Governor Patman. You see if I don't."

"You'll be sorry if you do." Jeff thought he meant that, anyway. He knew damn well he had more firepower than the Texas Rangers could bring to bear against him. But whether his guards had the will to fight other Confederate white men . . . He wasn't so sure about that. He hoped like anything he wouldn't have to find out.

"If you're smart, General, you'll take off your uniform, put your wife an' young 'uns in a civilian motorcar, and head for some town where nobody knows your face. You think the damnyankees'll have questions to ask *me*? What'll they say to *you*?"

Pinkard hung up. He did it by sheer reflex. The mayor's thoughts didn't just run parallel to his. They'd got ahead of them on the same road. If U.S. soldiers came here, they *would* have things to say to him.

Unpleasant things.

"But I can't leave," he said aloud. No matter what the Yankees had to say to him, he was proud of everything he'd done here, and over in Snyder, and outside of Alexandria, too. He'd had an important job to do, and he'd done it well. If not for him, the whole population-reduction program would have been a hell of a lot less efficient. Didn't that count for anything?

The Attorney General thought so. Hell, the President of the Confederate States of America thought so. What else mattered?

Nothing else mattered—as long as his side was calling the shots. Never mind Texas Rangers. U.S. soldiers wouldn't like what he'd done. And the main reason they wouldn't like it—or so things seemed to him—was that his own side did.

"Fuck 'em," Jeff muttered. "Fuck 'em all."

He wondered whether Mayor Doggett would send cops around to give Edith and the boys a hard time. He didn't intend to put up with anything like that. Maybe his guards would have trouble against the Rangers. Against this little town's one-lung police force, though, they could start a reign of terror.

No sooner had that crossed his mind than the telephone rang again. He said some things that should have melted the glass out of the windows in his office. What did Doggett want now? "Pinkard here," he snarled.

"Jeff, it's me." That wasn't the mayor—it was Edith. "My pains have started. We're going to have us a baby."

"Oh, good God!" Jeff said, mentally apologizing to the Lord whose name he'd done worse than take in vain a moment before. "You ready to go down to Houston?"

"I sure am!" his wife answered. "Miss Todd next door, she'll take care of Willie and Frank till you can get home."

"I'll send a guard with an auto for you right away," Jeff said. He couldn't leave the camp himself right now, especially not after the brawl with the mayor. Humble wasn't big enough to boast a hospital of its own. But it was only twenty miles from Houston, so that shouldn't matter.

He summoned a reliable troop leader to drive one of the Birming-hams attached to Camp Humble. As he gave the three-striper his orders, he thought, *Damn, I wish Hip Rodriguez was still around to do this for me.* His old Army buddy would have done it right, one hundred percent guaranteed. Oh, Porter was more than reliable enough, but still. . . . As always, Pinkard knew a moment of pained incomprehension when he thought about Hipolito Rodriguez. What the devil made Hip eat his submachine gun? He was doing a good job, and doing a job that needed doing.

That was something to brood on as he poured himself a big snort from the highly unofficial bottle in a desk drawer. He couldn't have taken the whiskey along if he had torn himself away from this and gone to the hospital. What could he do in the waiting room, anyway? Worry. He could do that here, too. He could, and he did.

Dammit, what possessed Hip to do that? He didn't see any damnyankee writing on the wall; things were going well enough when he shot himself. Why, then? It was as if he'd suddenly decided he'd made some vast mistake, and blowing off the top of his head was the only way he could fix it.

"But that's crazy," Jeff said, taking a slug from the drink. "Just plain old crazy." It wasn't as if Hip didn't believe in getting rid of Negroes. He couldn't have had woman troubles, either. Jeff knew Hip got laid every once in a while on the women's side. Not many male guards didn't. (For that matter, the same was true of female guards.) He felt guilty about fooling around on his wife—Jeff remembered as much from the Great War. But he didn't feel all *that* guilty, which Jeff also knew.

So what went wrong, then? The obvious answer—that Hip couldn't stand killing people any more even if they were black—stared Pinkard in the face. It had ever since Rodriguez shot himself. And ever since then, Jeff had stubbornly refused to look at it.

He didn't change now. He'd come too far down this road to change . . . unless he put the barrel of a gun in his own mouth and pulled the trigger. He refused to look at doing that, either. Instead, he finished the drink and poured another one.

He kept on drinking for the next seven hours. The camp didn't fall to pieces in that time, which was just as well, because he wouldn't have cared if it had. He spilled whiskey when the telephone rang. "Pinkard here," he slurred.

"Congratulations, sir! Your wife is fine, and you've got a boy!" Troop Leader Porter said. "What'll you name him?"

"Raymond," Jeff answered at once—drunk or sober, he knew. "Raymond Longstreet Pinkard." He knew where he stood, too, even now.

* * *

Every time Irving Morrell came into Philadelphia, the city looked worse. The Confederates kept finding new ways to hit the de facto capital of the USA. U.S. forces had driven the Confederates from their own capital and held bridgeheads across the James. The rocket factories in Huntsville were history. But Jake Featherston's forces kept launching their damn birds. Not all of them had been driven out of range of Philly, not yet. Their bombers still managed to sneak up here by night, too. Fresh craters and wrecked buildings loudly insisted the war wasn't over yet.

But the people in Philadelphia had a jaunty spring in their step that wasn't there the last time Morrell came into town. Maybe it was all the general's imagination, but he didn't think so. Folks figured things were on the downhill slope. And, by God, they had plenty of good reasons to think so.

Not without pride, Morrell knew he'd given them more than a few of those good reasons himself.

His driver, a sergeant with a Purple Heart and three oak-leaf clusters—not the kind of decoration anybody in his right mind would want to win—said, "We've got those cocksuckers whipped, don't we, sir?"

"Well, we'd have to screw up pretty good to blow things now," Morrell allowed. "Are you on permanent light duty, Sergeant, or will you go back to the front? You're two wounds ahead of me, and I wouldn't wish that on anyone."

"I'll be at it again in a couple of weeks, sir," the noncom answered. "None of 'em's been real bad. I limp a little from the latest one, and I've lost a finger, but the other two . . . hell, I don't even notice 'em if I don't see the scars. For a guy who's not real lucky, I'm pretty lucky, you know?"

"Yeah," Morrell said, and he did. The way the sergeant put it was kind of loopy, but it made sense anyway. The Ford rolled past a wall with a few bomb scars and a big splash of dried blood. Morrell was afraid he knew what that meant: "People bomb?"

"Afraid so, sir. They think this one was a diehard Mormon. He took out four or five soldiers when he went."

"Damn," Morrell said. How long would the USA—and other countries all over the world—have to worry about people willing, even eager, to die for their cause? Get some dynamite, some nails or scrap metal, and there you were: your own artillery shell. And you could aim yourself better than the best gunner in the world. The assumption in war had always been that the other guy didn't want to die. How were you supposed to protect yourself against somebody who did?

"Mormons. Canucks. Confederates," the sergeant said mournfully. "Even what they call peace won't be the same."

"I was just thinking the same thing," Morrell said. "I don't know what to do about it. If you get any brainstorms, for Christ's sake tell the War Department. You'll be a captain faster than you can blink."

"No offense, sir, but I don't know if I want to be an officer." With some relief, the noncom hit the brakes in front of the War Department. "Here you go. You don't even have to tip me."

"Heh," Morrell said. He stepped between concrete barriers that kept autos from getting too close: they could carry a lot more explosives than mere people could. The War Department building had a big chunk bitten out of a corner. Those C.S. rockets weren't supposed to be real accurate, but one seemed to have landed right on the money.

Not even stars on his shoulder straps kept him from having to show his ID, or from getting patted down after he did. He submitted without a murmur; times were still dangerous. Once he'd placated the entrance dragons, an escort took him down to General Staff headquarters.

It hadn't been buried so deep the last time he came to the War Department. Of course, if it weren't now, it might have gone sky high when that rocket came down. "Here's General Abell's office, sir," the escort said. "Telephone when you need to come up again, and somebody will take you."

"Thanks," Morrell said. The kid gave him a crisp salute and hurried down the corridor. Morrell was much less eager to enter John Abell's sanctum, but he did.

"Welcome," the General Staff officer said with what passed for warmth from him. Brigadier General Abell sometimes reminded Morrell of a ghost mostly congealed into the real world. He was tall and thin and pale, and so cool of manner that he sometimes hardly seemed there at all. The General Staff suited him perfectly; he was a dab hand at moving divisions around, but would have been hopeless with dirty, smelly, wisecracking, foul-mouthed soldiers.

"Thanks," Morrell answered, and couldn't help adding, "See? It wasn't a two-year campaign after all."

"So it wasn't. Congratulations." Yes, Abell was in a gracious mood. "We managed to attrit the enemy so he couldn't resist with as much persistence as I thought he might utilize when we first broached the issue early last year."

Morrell distrusted officers who said *utilize* when they meant *use*. As for *attrit* . . . Well, obviously it came from *attrition*, but that didn't mean he ever wanted to hear it again. He managed a nod.

That seemed to satisfy John Abell. "The question now, of course, is, *Where do we go from here?*"

He could speak clear English when he wanted to. Why didn't he want to more often? "On the western flank, Birmingham and Huntsville are pretty much in the bag," Morrell said. "We're hitting Selma and Mobile hard from the air. We'll get to 'em before too long. New Orleans . . . Well, we can bomb it. If we smash the levees, we can flood a lot of it. But we won't get soldiers there any time soon."

"A reasonable estimate," Abell agreed. "And in the east?"

"I'm shifting most of the effort there up into South Carolina," Morrell replied. "Charleston, Columbia . . . If the General Staff has a different idea, I expect you'll let me know." He wondered if that was part of the reason he'd been summoned to Philadelphia. What did they think he would do if he stayed down in the Confederacy and got orders he didn't like? Set up on his own? He admired Napoleon as a soldier, but not as a politician.

"At present, no. That seems adequate, or more than adequate," John Abell said. He acted nervous, though.

For a moment, that made no sense at all to Morrell. The United States was manifestly winning the war. They'd cut the CSA in half. The campaign in Virginia was going well at last. Even the minor struggles in Arkansas and Sequoyah and west Texas all inclined toward the USA. So why wasn't Abell even happier?

Morrell didn't expect hosannas and backflips from the General Staff officer. He'd known Abell too long and too well for that. But still . . . Then a light went on, a light as bright and terrible as the sun. "That goddamn superbomb!" Morrell exclaimed. "How close is Featherston?" He didn't ask how close his own country was. That, he assumed, would be a secret more tightly held than the other.

"Ah. Good. You do understand the basic difficulty under which we labor," Abell said. "The answer is, we just don't know—and that is our principal area of concern at this point in time."

"I can see how it might be," Morrell said dryly. If the Confederates could blow a city off the map with one bomb, they hadn't lost yet, not by a long chalk. "We are trying to do something about this?"

"As a matter of fact, yes," John Abell said. "Before too much longer, the question may be moot, but at the moment it remains relevant."

And what was *that* supposed to mean? Were the United States about to capture the CSA's superbomb works? Or was his country close to getting a superduperbomb of its own? "Anything you can tell me without bringing the wrath of the great god Security down on your head?" Morrell inquired.

"Our own research along those lines is making good progress," Abell said, and not another word.

Even that much was more than Morrell expected. "Well, all right," he said, and took out two packs of Dukes. He pulled a cigarette from one and stuck it in his mouth; the other he tossed on Abell's desk. "Here you go. Spoils of war."

"Thanks." Abell opened the pack and held out a cigarette. Morrell gave him a light. The General Staff officer never went near the front. He probably got sick of the nasty U.S. tobacco—unless other officers who wanted to stay on his good side kept him in smokes. Maybe his desk was full of them. You never could tell.

"Those bombs are going to change the way we fight. They'll change the way everybody fights," Morrell said.

"We are commencing studies on that topic," Abell said.

"How? We don't know enough yet," Morrell said. "And that reminds me—how come the Kaiser hasn't flattened London or Paris? Did he only have the one bomb? How long till he gets another one?"

"I don't know the answer to *that*," Abell replied, "but I do have an idea why Petrograd went up in smoke and the Western capitals haven't."

"I'm all ears," Morrell said.

"Prevailing winds," Abell told him. "These bombs spew poison into the air, and the wind can carry it a long way. From Petrograd, the stuff goes deeper into Russia. From London or Paris, the Germans could give themselves a present."

"A present they want like a hole in the head," Morrell said. John Abell nodded. Morrell stubbed out his cigarette and shuddered. "That makes these damn things even worse than I thought."

"The only thing worse than using them on somebody is somebody else using them on you," Abell said.

"Have we stopped the Confederates from using one on us?"

"We hope so."

"What's that supposed to mean?" Morrell asked.

"They're working on this thing in a Virginia mountain town. We have bombed it so heavily, next to nothing is left aboveground," the General Staff officer replied.

Morrell had listened to a lot of presentations. He could hear what wasn't said as well as what was. "What are they doing underground?"

"Well, we don't precisely know." Abell sounded as uncomfortable as he ever did. "They've burrowed like moles since the bombing started. That's why I hope we've kept their program from producing a uranium bomb, but I can't be sure we have."

"Terrific," Morrell said. "How do we find out for sure?"

"If they use one on us, we failed," Abell said. "It's as simple as that, I'm afraid."

"Oh, boy," Morrell said in distinctly hollow tones. "That's encouraging." He looked up at God only knew how many feet of steel and concrete over his head. "If they drop one on Philadelphia, will it get us all the way down here?"

"I don't think they can do that, anyhow," Abell replied. "I'm told a uranium bomb is too heavy for any airplane they have. We're having to modify our bombers to carry the load."

"Mm. Well, I guess that's good news. So they've got to wait till their rockets get out of short pants, then? Or do they have an extra-special rocket ready to go?"

"We don't believe so," John Abell said. "But then, we didn't know about the ones they do have till they started firing them at us."

"Tell you one thing," Morrell said as he lit another cigarette. Abell made a questioning noise. Morrell explained: "You sure know how to cheer a guy up."

Yankee bombers still didn't come over Lexington, Virginia, very often in the daytime. C.S. fighters and heavy flak made that an expensive proposition. Clarence Potter thanked God for small favors. He would have thanked God more for big ones, but the Deity didn't seem inclined to give the Confederate States any of those nowadays.

A crane swayed a crate into the cargo bed of a truck that looked ordinary but wasn't. This machine had a very special suspension. Even so, the springs groaned as the crate came down.

Potter watched the loading process with Professor Henderson Fitz-Belmont. "You're sure this damn thing will work?" Potter said.

FitzBelmont looked at him. "No."

"Thanks a lot, Professor," Potter said. "You sure know how to cheer a guy up."

"Would you rather have me lie to you?" FitzBelmont asked.

"Right now, I really think I would," Clarence Potter told him. "I hate to try this if there's an even-money chance we'll get nothing but a squib."

FitzBelmont shrugged. "It's untested. Ideally, we would have more time and more weapons. Things being as they are . . ."

"Well, yes. There is that," Potter said. Just getting back to Lexington from Petersburg had been nightmare enough. "All right. We'll try it, and we'll see what happens, that's all. Wish us luck."

"I do," Professor FitzBelmont said. "In my own way, I'm a patriot, too." His way wasn't so different from Potter's. Neither man went around shouting, *Freedom!* They both loved the Confederate States all the same.

Potter climbed into the cab of the truck next to the driver, a sergeant. "We ready, sir?" the noncom asked in accents not much different from Potter's own.

"If we're not, we never will be—which is, of course, always a possibility," the Intelligence officer said. The sergeant looked confused. "We're ready, Wilton," Potter assured him. "Now we see what happens."

Several command cars and armored cars rolled north and slightly east with the special truck. Everybody in them spoke the same kind of English as Clarence Potter: all the men could pass for Yankees, in other words. Both sides had used that trick during the war whenever they thought they could get away with it. *One more time*, Potter thought. *It's coming down toward the end, but we're going to try it one more time.*

In the War of Secession, Stonewall Jackson had played the Shenandoah Valley like a master violinist. In his hands, it turned into a dagger, an invasion route aimed straight at the USA's heart. The same thing happened again during the Great War, with the Confederate charge that almost got to Philadelphia. After 1917, the United States occupied the northern end of the Valley and fortified it so the Confederate States couldn't try that again. And Jake Featherston didn't; he drove up through Ohio instead.

The Shenandoah Valley was also the CSA's granary. The United States, busy elsewhere and fighting for survival, hadn't tried to take the Valley away from the Confederacy. They had dropped a hell of a lot of incendiaries on it. One U.S. wag was supposed to have said that a crow flying up the Shenandoah Valley would have to carry its own provisions.

Things weren't quite so bad as that—but they sure weren't good. Potter drove past too many fields whose main crops were ash and charcoal, past too many barns and farmhouses that were nothing but burntout skeletons of their old selves. Even after a wet winter, the air smelled smoky.

He had bigger worries than the way the air smelled. The first time they came to a bridge, he said, "This is what they call a moment of truth."

"Sir?" Sergeant Wilton said. "They're supposed to have strengthened it."

"I know." Potter left it right there. The Confederate States were in their death agony. He knew it, even if Wilton didn't. Things that were supposed to get done might . . . or they might not. You never could tell. And if they didn't . . . *I'm screwed*, Potter thought. Only one way to find out. "Take it across," he said.

"Yes, sir." The driver did. The bridge held. Potter breathed a sigh of relief. Now—how many more bridges across the winding Shenandoah before they got to the head of the Valley? How many bridges beyond that? Again, only one way to find out.

They made it over, again and again. The truck's transmission and engine weren't happy; they'd been beefed up, too, but they were even more overstrained than the suspension. If the damn thing crapped out . . . well, they had some spare parts, but it wouldn't be good news.

Potter tensed again—for the millionth time—when they came into Luray, the northernmost town in the Valley the CSA held, just as the sun was setting. If things there weren't ready, they were screwed again. But the stuff they needed was waiting for them. Potter let out one more sigh of relief.

But for the caves outside of town and a nitrates plant that had drawn its share of U.S. bombs, Luray's chief claim to fame was a two-and-a-half-story brick courthouse near the center of town. Potter's convoy stopped there. A work crew dashed out and spread canvas over the truck and the vehicles accompanying it. Then, under that cover, they got to work, slapping green-gray paint over the butternut that had identified them. As soon as the paint was even close to dry, they put U.S. markings all over the machines. Those couldn't hide their Confederate lines, of course, but after almost three years of war both sides were using lots of captured equipment.

And the disguise didn't end with the truck and the armored cars and command cars. Potter and his comrades put on U.S. uniforms. He became a major, which suited him well enough. If the damnyankees captured him in their togs, they'd shoot him. He shrugged. At the moment, that was the least of his worries.

"You have the passwords and countersigns?" he asked the veteran first sergeant in charge of the unit there.

"Yes, sir, sure do. We went out and took a couple of prisoners less than an hour ago," the noncom answered. He was of about Potter's vintage, a man who'd been through the Great War and didn't flabble about anything. He gave Potter what he needed.

Potter wrote it down to be sure. "Thanks," he said. The retread sergeant nodded. The patch over his left eye and the hook sticking out of his left tunic cuff told why he was in a backwater like this. Despite them, he was a better man than most at the front.

The chameleon convoy rolled out of Luray before sunup. Potter wanted to get into U.S.-held territory while it was still dark. That would help keep his vehicles from giving themselves away right where people were most likely to get antsy about them.

Yankee country started just a couple of miles north of Luray. If somebody'd spilled the beans—not impossible with the CSA visibly coming to pieces—a couple of companies of real U.S. soldiers could have swooped down and ended a lovely scheme before it really got rolling.

But no. The sergeant's raid for prisoners hadn't even made the U.S. forces jumpy. Potter and his merry band got several miles into Yankee-land before they came to a checkpoint. The passwords he'd picked up in Luray worked fine. A kid second lieutenant asked, "What is all this crap, uh, sir?"

"Matériel captured from Featherston's fuckers," Potter answered crisply—he knew what the enemy called his side. "We're taking it north for evaluation."

"Nobody told me," the shavetail complained.

"It's a war," Potter said with more patience than he felt. "They wouldn't tell you your name if you hadn't had it issued ahead of time."

"No shit!" the lieutenant said, laughing. "All right, sir—pass on."

On they passed. The sun came up. They crossed over the Shenandoah again at Front Royal. Nobody on their side had specially reinforced that bridge. "Think it'll take the strain, sir?" Wilton asked.

"If they ever sent a barrel over it, it will," Potter said. "Barrels are a hell of a lot heavier than this baby."

They made it. They stopped at a fuel dump and gassed up, then went on. The farther they got from the front line, the less attention U.S. soldiers paid them. They just seemed to be men doing a job. One nine-year-old kid by the side of the road gaped, though. He knew they were driving C.S. vehicles—Potter could tell. He probably knew every machine and weapon on both sides better than the guys who used them did. Plenty of kids like that down in the CSA, too. It was a game to them. It wasn't a game to Clarence Potter.

Harpers Ferry. John Brown had come here, trying to start a slave uprising. Robert E. Lee led the men who captured him. And, three years later, Lee came through again on the campaign that won the Confederate States their independence. Maybe this trip north would help them keep it.

Over the Potomac. Into Maryland. Into the USA proper. Potter had come this way almost exactly thirty years earlier, with the Army of Northern Virginia's thrust toward Philadelphia. They'd fallen short then. Had they taken the de facto capital, they might have had a triumphant six weeks' war. Jake Featherston had hoped for the same thing this time around. What you hoped for and what you got weren't always the same, dammit.

Maryland looked prosperous; Pennsylvania, when they got there, even more so. Oh, Potter spied bomb damage here and there, but only here and there. This land hadn't been *fought over* the way so much of the CSA had. It had got nibbled, but not chewed up. The United States was too big a place for bombing alone to chew them up. Pittsburgh, now, Pittsburgh probably looked as if it had had a proper war, but Potter and his band of cutthroats headed east, not west.

Drivers in military vehicles coming the other way waved to him and honked their horns as they passed. He always waved back. They figured he was returning from the front with something important. Nobody bothered checking his papers or asking him where he was going or why. The United States *were* a big place. Once beyond the usual military zone, security for people who looked and sounded like U.S. soldiers eased off. He'd counted on that when he put this scheme together.

Jake Featherston wanted him to go all the way into downtown Philadelphia. He didn't intend to. There of all places, security would tighten up again. He couldn't afford to have anybody ask questions too soon. Some overeager goon with a Tommy gun or a captured automatic Tredegar could mess everything up if he got suspicious at just the wrong time.

No, not downtown. Potter stopped west of it, on the far side of the Schuylkill River. At his order, Wilton pulled into a parking lot. Potter ducked into the back of the truck and set two timers on the side of the crate—he wasn't going to take chances with only one. The driver, meanwhile, raised the hood.

"What's going on?" somebody called.

"Damn thing's broken down," Wilton answered. "We've got to round up a mechanic somewhere."

He and Potter jumped into one of the command cars. "Back the way we came," Potter said. "Fast as you can go." He eyed the man who'd questioned them. The fellow only shrugged and ambled into a shop. Maybe he'd seen breakdowns before.

"How long, sir?" asked the corporal behind the command car's wheel.

"Not long enough," Potter said. "Step on it."

Fifteen minutes later, the world blew up behind them.

Irving Morrell wasn't looking west when the bomb went off. He was standing at a counter, trying to decide between a chocolate bar and a roll of mints. All of a sudden, the light swelled insanely, printing his shadow on the wall in back of the sidewalk stand. The fat little old woman behind the counter screeched and covered her eyes with her hands.

"Good God!" Morrell said, even before the roar of the explosion reached him. His first thought was that an ammo dump somewhere had blown sky high. He didn't think of a bomb. The explosion seemed much too big for that.

He forgot about the candy and ran out into the street. Then he realized just how lucky he'd been, because a lot of windows had turned to knife-edged flying shards of glass. The magazine stand and snack counter where he'd been dithering didn't have a window of any sort, so he'd escaped that, anyhow.

He stopped and stared. He wasn't the only one. Everybody out there was looking west with the same expression of slack-jawed disbelief. No one had ever seen anything like that rising, boiling, roiling cloud before. How high did it climb? Three miles? Four? Five? He had no idea. The colors put him in mind of food—salmon, peach, apricot. The top of the cloud swelled out from the base, as if it were a toadstool the size of a god.

The roar came then, not just in his ears but all through his body. He staggered like a drunken man. But it wasn't his balance going; the ground shook under his feet. A blast of wind from nowhere staggered him. Also out of nowhere, rain started pelting down. The drops were enormous. They left black splashes when they hit the ground. When one hit his hand, he jerked in surprise—the rain was hot.

"Where's it at?" somebody asked.

"Across the river, looks like," a woman said.

It looked that way to Morrell, too. The rain shower didn't last more than a couple of minutes. It hadn't ended before he started trying to scrub the filthy drops from his skin. He remembered what John Abell had told him a few days before: uranium bombs put out poison. And what else could that horrible thing be? No ammunition dump in the world blew up like that.

How much poison was in the rain? How much was in that monstrous toadstool cloud? *Am I a dead man walking?* he wondered.

"We gotta go help," said the man who'd asked where the blast was. He hurried toward the Schuylkill River.

His courage and resolve shamed Morrell. Of course, the stranger—who was plump and fiftyish, with a gray mustache—didn't know what Morrell did. If ignorance was bliss . . .

After a moment's hesitation, Morrell followed. If he was already poisoned, then he was, that was all. Nothing he could do about it now. Overhead, that cloud grew taller and wider. Winds began to tear at it and tug it out of shape . . . and blow it toward downtown Philadelphia.

Crowds got worse the farther west Morrell went. Everybody was pointing and staring and gabbling. *You fools! Don't you realize you might all be dead?* No, Morrell didn't shout it out. But it filled his thoughts.

Damage got worse the farther west he went, too. All the windows that had survived years of Confederate air raids were blown out. Motorcars and trucks had windows shattered, too. Drivers, their faces masks of blood, staggered moaning through the streets. Many of them clutched at their eyes. Morrell knew what that was bound to mean: they had glass in them.

As he neared Philadelphia's second river, he saw buildings brutally pushed down and vehicles flipped onto their sides or upside down. Some men stopped to help the injured. Others pressed on.

And then Morrell got a chance to look across the Schuylkill. That part of the city was almost as heavily built up as downtown. Or rather, it had been. Next to Morrell, a skinny woman crossed herself. He felt like doing the same thing. Almost everything over there was knocked flat. A few buildings that must have been uncommonly strong still stood up from the rubble, but only a few.

A bridge across the Schuylkill survived, though it leaned drunkenly to one side. How long it would stay up, God only knew. People staggered across it from the west. Some had had the clothes burned off of them. Morrell saw several with one side of their face badly seared and the other fine: they must have stood in profile to the bomb when it went off.

"His shadow!" a dreadfully burned man babbled. "I saw his shadow on the sidewalk, all printed like, but not a thing left of George!" He slumped down and mercifully passed out. Morrell wondered whether he would ever wake. He might be luckier not to.

A loudspeaker started to blare: "All military personnel! Report at once to your duty stations! All military personnel! Report at once to—"

Morrell didn't exactly have a duty station. He headed back to the War Department. The catastrophe across the river was bigger than any one man. And he had a better chance of finding out what was going on at the military's nerve center.

So he thought, anyway. But one of the guards who patted him down asked, "What the hell happened, sir? Do you know?"

"Not exactly," Morrell answered. "I was hoping people here did."

Before a private took him down to John Abell's office, he paused in a men's room and washed off as much of the filthy rainwater as he could. "Why are you doing that, sir?" asked the kid, who went in with him.

"Just in case," Morrell answered. Getting rid of the horrible stuff wouldn't hurt. He was sure of that.

Abell always looked pale. He seemed damn near transparent now. He might have aged ten years in the few days since Morrell last saw him. "My God!" he said. "They beat us to the punch. I didn't think they could, but they did."

"Have you been up top?" Morrell asked. "Did you see it with your own eyes?"

"No." Abell had always wanted to deal with things from a distance. Was that a strength or a weakness? *Probably both at once*, Morrell thought. The General Staff officer went on, "How did they get it here? They couldn't have used an airplane—I swear to God they don't have a machine that can carry it. And our Y-ranging gear didn't spot a thing coming up from the south."

"They must have sneaked it in, God damn them," Morrell said. "Remember how they broke through in eastern Ohio? They had a whole battalion of guys in our uniforms, in our vehicles, who could talk like us. What do you want to bet they did the same damn thing again—and made it work?" He'd made it work himself, getting over the Tennessee River in front of Chattanooga.

Abell managed a shaky nod. Then he reached for a telephone. "With a little luck, they won't get away. We can shoot every last one of them if we catch them in our uniforms."

Morrell nodded. That was what the laws of war said. Whether the USA would want to shoot those Confederates if it caught them might be a different story. How much could they tell interrogators about their uranium-bomb project?

"We'd better catch them," Abell said as he slammed down the telephone after barking into it with unaccustomed heat. "They can't get away with that. How many thousands of people did they just murder?"

Would it have been better had the enemy dropped the bomb out of an airplane and then flown away? Would it have been better had he dropped ton after ton of ordinary bombs instead, or machine-gunned as many people as he'd killed in this one blast? Morrell found himself shaking his head. It wouldn't have been any better, but it would have been more familiar. That mattered, too. The uranium bomb was something brand new. Poison gas had carried some of that same whiff of horror during the last war. People took it for granted now.

Would they come to take uranium bombs for granted, too? How could they, when each one could devastate a city? And these were just the early ones. Would next year's model level a whole county, or maybe a state?

"My God," Abell said again. "Those stinking crackers . . . and they beat us. There won't be one stone left on top of another one by the time our bombers get through with Lexington—I'll tell you that."

The last time he and Morrell talked about uranium bombs, he'd waltzed around the name of the town where the CSA was working on them. This time, he'd slipped. He was human after all, and would probably have to do penance before the altar of Security the Almighty.

He realized as much a few seconds too late. "You didn't hear that from me," he said in some embarrassment.

"Hear what?" Morrell asked innocently.

"I wonder if we could drive down the Shenandoah Valley and take that place away from them," Abell said. Even though he was embarrassed, now that the cat was out of the bag he was letting it run around.

"Wouldn't take long to pull an assault force together." Morrell spoke with the assurance of a veteran field commander. "Don't know how hard the Confederates would fight back—hard as they can, I bet. Now that they've used one bomb, how long do they need to build another one?"

"That I can't tell you, because I don't know. I wouldn't tell you even if I did, but I don't," Abell said. "Days? Weeks? Months? Twenty minutes? I just have no idea."

"All right," Morrell said. The General Staff officer was liable to lie about something like that, but Morrell didn't think he was, not this time. He went on, "This would have been a lot worse if they'd brought it here by the government buildings instead of blowing it up across the river."

"I don't think they could have—it wouldn't have been easy, anyhow," Abell said. "We search autos and trucks before we let them in here. Auto bombs are bad enough, but put a couple of tons of high explosive in a truck . . ." He didn't finish, or need to. "One of those was plenty to make us clamp down."

"Good for you, then. You just saved the President and Congress and us. I mean, I hope you did." Morrell told him about the black rain. "Exactly how dangerous is that stuff, anyway?"

"We'll all find out. I don't know the details. I'm not sure anybody does." Abell looked down at his own soft, immaculately tended hands. "I do believe you were wise to wash off as much as you could. It's like X-rays: you want to keep the exposure to a minimum."

Morrell looked at his own hands and at his uniform, which still bore the marks of those unnatural drops. Were there little X-ray machines in them? Something like that, he supposed. Maybe there were more in the dust in the air. "We sure never learned any of this stuff at West Point," he said.

"Who knew back then?" John Abell said. "Nobody, that's who. Half of what we learned just went obsolete."

"More than half," Morrell said. "New rules from now on."

"If we live long enough," Abell said.

"Yeah. If." Morrell looked at his splotched uniform again. "I think the new Rule Number One is, *Don't get in a war with anybody who's got this damn bomb.*"

"A little too late for that now," the General Staff officer pointed out.

"Don't remind me," Morrell said.

I'm Jake Featherston, and I'm here to tell you the truth."

This wasn't the familiar studio in Richmond, from which Jake Featherston had bellowed defiance at the world since the days when he was a discredited rabble-rouser at the head of a withering Freedom Party. He had no idea whether that wireless studio still stood. He would have bet against it. Richmond had fallen, but the Confederates put up a hell of a fight before they finally pulled out.

Portsmouth, Virginia, then. It wasn't where Featherston wanted to be—he'd always wanted to broadcast in triumph from Washington, D.C., and Philadelphia. *And I will yet, goddammit*, he thought savagely. But Portsmouth would have to do for now. The station had a strong signal, and somehow or other Saul Goldman had patched together a web to send Jake's words all over the CSA—and up into Yankeeland, too. If Saul wasn't a wizard, he'd do till a real one showed up.

The speech. "Truth is, we just showed the damnyankees what we can do. Just like the Kaiser—one bomb, and *boom!* A city's gone. Philadelphia will never be the same." He didn't exactly say the uranium bomb (no, from the reports he got from FitzBelmont, it was really a jovium bomb, whatever the hell jovium was) had blown up all of Philly. If his Confederate listeners wanted to think he'd said that, though, he wouldn't shed a tear.

"Maybe St. Louis the next time. Maybe Indianapolis or Chicago. Maybe New York City or Boston. Maybe Denver or San Francisco. Who knows? But one bomb, and *boom!* No more city, whatever it is."

He didn't say when the next C.S. jovium bomb would go off. He had excellent reason for not saying anything about that: he had no idea. Henderson FitzBelmont didn't even want to guess. U.S. bombers were hitting Lexington harder than ever. Some of the bombs had armor-piercing noses, too, so they dug deep before going off. They were causing trouble.

But the CSA got in the first lick anyway!

"The damnyankees reckoned they had us down for the count," Jake gloated. "They forgot about how much we love . . . freedom! They'll never lick us, not while we can still load our guns and fire back. And we can."

As if on cue, cannon boomed in the distance. The studio insulation couldn't swallow all of that noise. Some were antiaircraft guns banging away at the U.S. bombers that constantly pounded the whole Hampton Roads area. And others were the big guns from the few surviving Confederate warships, now turned against land targets rather than enemy cruisers and destroyers. The damnyankees were pushing toward Portsmouth and Norfolk by land. Anything that could slow them down, the Confederates were using.

Since some of that artillery noise was going out over the air, Featherston decided to make the most of it. "You hear that, people?" he said. "That noise shows we *are* still in the fight, and we'll never quit. They say our country doesn't have a right to live. I say they don't have a right to kill it. They won't, either. If you don't believe me, ask what's left of Philadelphia."

He stepped away from the mike. Behind the glass wall that took up one side of the studio, the engineer gave him a thumbs-up. This wasn't the fellow he'd worked with for so long in Richmond, but some stranger. Still, Jake thought he'd given a good speech, too. Nice to find out other folks could tell.

"Well done, Mr. President," Saul Goldman said when Jake stepped out into the corridor. "What a speech can do, that one did."

"Yeah." Featherston wished the Director of Communications hadn't put it like that. What a speech could do . . . A speech might make soldiers fight a little longer. It might make factory hands work a little harder. All that would help . . . some.

No speech in the world, though, could take back Kentucky or Tennessee. No speech in the world could take back Atlanta or Savannah, or unsever the divided body of the Confederacy. No speech could take back the rocket works in Huntsville, and no speech could keep Birmingham from falling any day now.

No speech, not to put too fine a point on it, could keep the Confederate States of America from being really and truly screwed. "Dammit," Featherston said, "I didn't reckon things'd end up like this."

"Who would have, sir?" Goldman was loyal. Not only that, he didn't aspire to the top spot himself, maybe because he knew damn well no Confederate general or Party bigwig would take orders from a potbellied little Hebe. The combination—and his skill at what he did— made him invaluable.

They also meant Jake could talk more freely to him than to anyone else except perhaps Lulu. "No, this ain't how things were supposed to work," the President repeated. "Swear to God, Saul, if the Yankees lick us, it's on account of we don't *deserve* to win, you know what I mean?"

"What can we do? We *have* to win," Goldman said.

Featherston nodded. He had the same attitude himself. "We'll keep fighting till we can't fight any more, that's what. And we won't surrender, not ever," he said. "If we ever stop fighting, it'll only be on account of we got nobody left to fight with, by God."

The Director of Communications nodded. "You've always been very determined. I knew it right from the first time you started broadcasting on the wireless." He shook his head in wry wonder. "That's more than twenty years ago now."

"Sure as hell is," Jake said. You could see those years in Goldman's gray hair, in how little of it he had left, in his waistline and double chin. On the outside, time had dogged Featherston less harshly. He had lines on his face that hadn't been there then, and his hairline had retreated at the temples, too. But he remained whipcord lean; hate burned too hot in him to let him settle down and get fat. "And you know what?" he went on. "Even if the war turns out rotten, I've had a good life. I've done most of the things I always aimed to do. How many men can say that, when you get right down to it?"

"Not many," Goldman agreed.

"Damn right." Featherston paused to light a cigarette. He didn't like to smoke just before he went on the air; his voice was raspy enough anyway. "The folks who live down here after this war is over, whoever the hell they turn out to be, they won't have to worry about nigger trouble ever again, no matter what. And that's thanks to me, goddammit." He jabbed a thumb at his own chest.

"Yes, Mr. President."

But Goldman didn't sound happy. Jake had artilleryman's ear, and didn't hear so well as he had once upon a time. While he might miss words, though, he was still dead keen for tone. "What's eating you, Saul?" he asked.

"I guess it's the way you put it, sir," the Director of Communications said slowly. "I can see the Tsar talking about Jews like that, or the Ottoman Sultan talking about Armenians."

When nobody flabbled much about the way the Sultan got rid of his Armenians, that had encouraged Jake to plan the same for the blacks in the CSA. He'd said as much in *Over Open Sights*, too. Because he liked Goldman, he was willing to believe the other man had just forgotten. "The Tsar's a damn fool, even if he is on the same side as us," he said. "Jews are white men, dammit. And so are Armenians . . . I reckon. Can't talk about those folks the same way you do about niggers. Biggest mistake folks here ever made was shipping niggers over from Africa. Nobody ever tried to fix it . . . till me. And I damn well did."

Saul Goldman still didn't look convinced. Maybe his being Jewish was finally causing problems after all. His people had been persecuted unjustly. That might make it hard for him to see that Negroes really deserved what the Freedom Party was giving them. If he was getting pangs of conscience now, he'd sure taken his own sweet time doing it. Trains had been carrying blacks off to the camps since before the war started, and Saul's propaganda helped justify it to the Confederate people and to the world.

"C'mon outside," Jake told him. "Maybe you need some fresh air. It'll help clear your head."

"Maybe." Goldman didn't argue. Like anyone who bumped up against Jake Featherston, he'd soon come to realize arguing with him didn't do a damn bit of good.

It was a fine spring day. The savage heat and humidity that would close down soon hadn't yet descended on Portsmouth like a smothering blanket. A newly arrived hummingbird, ruby throat glittering, sucked nectar from a honeysuckle bush. The smell of growing things filled the air.

But so did nastier odors: the stench of death and the slightly less noxious stink of spilled fuel oil. Yankee bombers had been punishing Hampton Roads ever since the war began. They had reason to, damn them; this was the most important Confederate naval installation on the Atlantic coast.

As in Richmond, few buildings had survived undamaged. Not many warships were fit to put to sea from here, either. Salvage crews were clearing a sunken cruiser and destroyer from the channel. That steel would find another use . . . if the Confederacy lasted long enough.

It will, dammit, Featherston thought, angry at himself for doubting. The sun sparkled off the waves—and off the thin, iridescent layer of fuel oil floating atop them. A moored cruiser, laid up with engine trouble and bomb damage, let go with a salvo of eight-inch shells. They'd come down on the damnyankees' heads soon enough.

A few U.S. airplanes buzzed over Hampton Roads. Jake took that for granted nowadays. C.S. air power did what it could, but it couldn't do enough to hold the enemy at arm's length any more, not even above Virginia. By the sound of the engines, most of the engines were above Newport News, on the north side of the mouth of the James. Antiaircraft guns flung shells at them, but the bursts were too low to bring them down.

Jake pulled a notebook out of his breast pocket and wrote, *We need stronger AA*. The Confederate States needed lots of things right now. He had no idea when engineers could get around to designing a larger-caliber antiaircraft gun, let alone manufacture one, but it was on the list.

He looked down to put the notebook back in his pocket. That spared his eyes when a new sun sprang into being above Newport News, six or eight miles away from where he was standing. He suddenly had two shadows, the new one far blacker than the old. Slowly, the new shadow started to fade.

Saul Goldman had his hands clapped over his face—maybe he'd been looking the wrong way. Jake stared north in open-mouthed awe, even when a quick, fierce, hot blast of wind almost knocked him ass over teakettle. That toadstool cloud rising high into the sky was the most terrifying thing he'd ever seen, but it had a strange and dreadful beauty of its own.

Goldman took his hands away. He blinked. Tears ran down his face. "I can see you—sort of," he said. "Is . . . this what we did to Philadelphia?"

"Yeah." Jake's voice was soft and dreamy, almost as if he'd just had a woman. He might not have been able to stop the damnyankees from making their bomb, but in spite of everything he'd finished ahead of them. Both sides had staggered over the finish line. Still, the CSA won first prize.

"*Yisgadal v'yiskadash sh'may rabo . . .*" Saul went on in a language Jake didn't know.

The President of the CSA hardly noticed. He'd struck first, and he'd struck at the enemy capital. Newport News? He snapped his fingers. Who cared?

I'm Jake Featherston, and I'm here to tell you the truth." The voice coming out of the wireless set and the boundless arrogance it carried were absolutely unmistakable. The President of the CSA went on, "If the Yankees reckoned they'd blow me up when they dropped their fancy bomb, they reckoned wrong, and they went and killed a big old pile of innocent women and babies, the way the murderers always do."

"Damn!" Flora Blackford turned off the wireless in disgust. Blasting Jake Featherston off the face of the earth was the only way she saw to end this war in a hurry. Blasting Newport News off the face of the earth had its points, but it was only one town among many.

The lies Featherston could tell! To listen to him, the U.S. uranium bomb was designed solely to slaughter civilians. What about the one his men had touched off right across the Schuylkill from downtown Philadelphia? Well, that one was an attack against the U.S. government and military. It was if you believed Featherston, anyhow. Of course, if you believed Featherston there you also likely believed him when he said ridding his country of Negroes was a good idea, when he said the USA had forced him into war, and when he said any number of other inflammatory and improbable things.

If Jake Featherston said he believed in God, it would be the best argument Flora could think of for either atheism or worshipping Satan, depending. She nodded to herself and wrote that down on a notepad. It would make a good line in a speech.

One thing Featherston had said even before the U.S. uranium bomb went off did seem to be true, worse luck: the United States hadn't caught the Confederate raiders who'd brought the bomb north. Flora supposed those raiders wore U.S. uniforms and could sound as if they came from the USA. All the same, the Joint Committee on the Conduct of the War would have to look into the Army's failure to hunt them down.

But the Joint Committee had something else on the agenda this morning. They were going across the Schuylkill for a firsthand look at what the explosion of a uranium bomb was really like.

As she took a cab to Congressional Hall to meet with her colleagues, she couldn't help noticing that a lot of west-facing buildings had their paint scorched or seared off. On some, the paint had come through intact only in patterns: taller structures closer to the blast had shielded part of the paint but not all.

"They say we blew that Featherston item right off the map," the driver remarked. He seemed healthy enough, but he was at least ten years older than Flora, which put him in his mid-sixties at the youngest.

"It isn't true," she answered. "I just heard him on the wireless."

"Oh," the cabby said. "Well, that's a . . . darn shame. Don't hardly see how we'll get anywhere till we smoke his bacon."

"Neither do I," Flora said sadly. "I wish I did."

When the cab pulled up in front of Congressional Hall, she gave him a quarter tip, which pleased him almost as much as seeing Jake Featherston stuffed and mounted would have. "Much obliged, ma'am," he said, touching a forefinger to the patent-leather brim of his cap. He was grinning as he zoomed away.

Flora wasn't surprised to find Franklin Roosevelt there with the members of the Joint Committee. "First we'll see what one of these damn things can do," he said. "Then you'll rake me over the coals for not getting ours first and for not keeping the Confederates from finishing theirs."

"Did you think they could beat us to it?" she asked.

He shook his big head. "No. I didn't think they had a prayer, to tell you the truth. They're formidable people. All the more reason for squashing them flat and making sure they never get up again."

"Sounds good to me," Flora said.

They went to the Schuylkill in a bus. Two Army officers helped Roosevelt out of his wheelchair and into a seat, then manhandled the chair aboard. "Considering some of the terrain we'll be crossing, maybe I should have brought a tracked model," he said, sounding a lot more cheerful than Flora could have under the same circumstances.

The bus didn't cross at the closest bridge. Some of the steel supporting towers on that one had sagged a bit, and Army engineers were still trying to figure out whether it would stay up. The Joint Committee on the Conduct of the War had to chug north to find one that was sound. Then the bus went back south and west till wrecked buildings and rubble in the road made the driver stop.

"We're not quite a mile from the center of the blast," one of the officers said. "It gets worse from here."

He wasn't wrong. It got worse, and worse, and worse again. Before long, only what had been the stoutest, sturdiest buildings had any walls standing at all. Even they weren't just scorched but half melted in a way Flora had never imagined, much less seen.

One of the Army officers pushed Franklin Roosevelt forward. When the rubble got too thick to let the man advance with the Assistant Secretary of War, his colleague would bend and grab the front of the wheelchair. Together, the two would get Roosevelt over the latest obstacle and push him on toward the next.

Steel and even granite lampposts sagged like candles in the hot sun. How hot had it been when the bomb went off? Flora had no idea— some physicists might know. Hot enough, plainly. Hot enough and then some.

Somewhere between half a mile and a quarter of a mile from what the officers were calling ground zero, there was no sidewalk or even rubble underfoot. Everything had been fused to what looked like rough, crude glass. It felt like hard, unyielding glass under Flora's feet, too.

"My God," she said over and over. She wasn't the only one, either. She watched a Catholic Congressman cross himself, and another take out a rosary and move his lips in prayer. When you saw something like this, what could you do but pray? But wasn't a God Who allowed such things deaf to mere blandishments?

"Can the Confederates do this to us again?" someone asked Roosevelt.

"Dear Lord, I hope not!" he exclaimed, which struck Flora as an honest, unguarded response. He went on, "To tell you the truth, I didn't think they could do it once. But they've got an infiltrator—his name's Potter—who's so good, he's scary. We think he led their team. And so . . . they surprised us, damn them."

"Again," Flora said.

Roosevelt nodded. "That's right. They surprised us again. They almost ruined us when they went up into Ohio, and then they did . . . this. But do you know what? They're going to lose the war anyway, even if we didn't fry Jake Featherston like an egg the way he deserves."

"Why didn't we?" a Senator asked.

"Well, we had intelligence he was in the Hampton Roads area, and I still believe he was," Roosevelt replied. "But he wasn't right where we thought he was, which is a shame."

"Why didn't we catch the people who did this?" Flora said. "The ones who brought the bomb up here, I mean. The wireless has been saying we haven't, and I want to know why not. They can't play chameleon that well . . . can they?"

"It seems they can," Roosevelt said morosely. "Just before I joined you at Congressional Hall, I had a report that Confederate wireless is claiming the bombers got out of the United States. I can't confirm that, and I don't know that I'll ever be able to, but I do know we don't have them."

"Yes, I've heard the Confederates making the same claim." Flora kicked at the sintered stuff under her feet. "We don't have any witnesses, do we?"

"None who've come forward," Franklin Roosevelt said. "I'm sure there were some, but when a bomb like this goes off . . ." He didn't finish. Flora nodded anyhow. When a bomb like this went off, it took a whole neighborhood with it. Anyone who saw the truck—she supposed it was a truck—the bomb arrived in and wondered about it died in the blast.

"From now on, they'll be calling the police and the bomb squad any time anything bigger than a bicycle breaks down," a Congressman said.

"That's already happened," Roosevelt said. "It's got cops all over the country jumping like fleas on a hot griddle, but I don't know what we can do about it. People are nervous. And I'm afraid they've got a right to be."

"Anyone need to see anything else?" the Army officer behind him asked. When nobody said yes, the man started pushing Roosevelt back toward the bus.

The members of the Joint Committee on the Conduct of the War went back, too. The bus took them east over the Schuylkill to Philadelphia General Hospital, the closest one to survive the blast. The Pennsylvania Hospital for Mental and Nervous Diseases, only a couple of blocks from ground zero, was now as one with Nineveh and Tyre: a tallish lump in the melted glass, no more.

"I think you people are a bunch of ghouls to rubberneck here," a harried doctor said. "And I think you were crazy or stupid or both at once to rubberneck over there. Don't you know that goddamn bomb left some kind of poison behind? We've had plenty of people who weren't too bad, and then their hair falls out and they start bleeding internally—and out their noses and eyeballs and fingernails and, uh, rectums, too—and they just up and die. You want that?"

"Nobody told us," a Senator said faintly.

"*Nu?* Now I'm telling you," the doctor said. "And now I've got to do some work."

Hearing that was plenty for Flora, but some of her colleagues wanted to see what the doctor was talking about. She went with them, and ended up wishing she hadn't. People with ordinary injuries were heartbreaking enough, and the bomb caused plenty of those. If a window shotgunned you with knifelike shards of glass, or if your house fell down on you and you had to lie in and under the ruins till somebody pulled you out, you weren't going to be in great shape.

But there were others, worse ones, who made her have a hard time sleeping that night, and for several nights afterwards. The people with what the nurses called uranium sickness, which had to be what the doctor described. And the burns . . . There were so many burns, and such horrible ones. How many hands with fingers fused together did she see, how many faces with melted noses, how many moaning sufferers with eyes boiled out of their heads?

She was glad to escape. She didn't have the stomach for such things. One of her colleagues said, "Well, at least we've paid the Confederates back for this."

By then, the members of the Joint Committee on the Conduct of the War were climbing into their bus. Flora pointed back to the hospital. "I'm sure that makes the people in there very happy," she said.

The Congressman gave her an odd look. "I don't believe your

heart's in this any more," he said. "You've been a rock since the start. Why not now?"

"Because now I've seen the difference between enough and too much," Flora answered. "And what these bombs do is too much." She looked a challenge at him. "Go ahead—tell me I'm wrong." He didn't. He couldn't. She hadn't thought he would.

Abner Dowling had dreamt of seeing Richmond in his professional capacity ever since his West Point days. Those were long behind him now, but here he was, striding through the streets of the captured Confederate capital with not a care in the world . . . except for breaking his neck in the rubble, stepping on a mine, setting off a booby trap, or getting shot by one of the snipers who still haunted the ruins.

He turned to his adjutant. "You know, it's a funny thing," he said.

"What's that, sir?" Angelo Toricelli was sporting silver oak leaves instead of gold on his shoulders—the spoils of victory.

"We mashed this damn place flat, but next to what happened to Philadelphia and Newport News it's nothing but small change."

"Oh." The younger officer nodded. "Well, we had to do it the hard way, not all at once. If they'd held out a little longer, though . . ."

"Wouldn't have broken my heart," Dowling said. "I know that sounds cold, but it's the Lord's truth. A superbomb's about the only thing that would have got these people's attention."

As if to underscore the point, somebody with an automatic weapon opened up in the distance. Dowling started to dive for cover, then checked himself: none of the bullets came anywhere near. A shattered storefront nearby had FREEDOM! painted on it. That graffito and CSA were everywhere in Richmond. The locals didn't like the idea of living under the Stars and Stripes for the first time since 1861.

Something moved back behind the storefront. Dowling's hand dropped to the .45 on his belt. It wasn't much of a weapon against an automatic Tredegar, but it was what he had. Lieutenant Colonel Toricelli's pistol leaped from its holster. "Come out of there!" he barked.

The kid who did couldn't have been much above seven years old. He looked at the green-gray uniforms, then asked, "You a couple of nigger-lovin' damnyankees?" Before Dowling or Toricelli could answer, the kid went on, "Got any rations? I'm mighty hungry."

"Why should we feed you if you call us names?" Dowling asked.

"What names?" The little boy didn't get it. He'd probably never heard U.S. soldiers called anything else. He rubbed his belly. "Gimme some rations. Y'all got any deviled ham?"

"Here, kid." Toricelli took a can out of a pouch on his belt and tossed it to the boy. "Now you got some. Scoot." The boy disappeared with his prize. Looking faintly embarrassed at himself, Toricelli turned to Dowling. "Maybe he'll grow up civilized."

"Yeah, maybe," Dowling said, "but don't hold your breath."

High overhead, a swarm of bombers flew south like wintering birds. Below the James, the Confederates still fought as stubbornly as they could. If they wouldn't give up, what was there to do but keep pounding them till they didn't have any choice? Dowling wished he could see something, but he couldn't.

"Once we win, do we really want to try to run this place?" he asked, speaking more to God than to his adjutant.

But his adjutant was the one who answered: "What choice have we got, sir?"

Dowling wished he knew what to say to that. If the USA beat the CSA, what happened next? As far as Dowling could see, the USA had two choices. The United States could leave an independent Confederacy, or they could reunite North America under the Stars and Stripes. An independent Confederacy was dangerous. What had just happened to Philadelphia told how dangerous it was.

But if Virginia returned to the USA . . . well, what then? If all these states that had been their own nation for eighty-odd years returned to the one from which they'd seceded, wouldn't they spend years trying to break away again? Wouldn't there be guerrillas in the mountains and the woods? Wouldn't there be people bombs in the cities? Wouldn't the locals send Freedom Party bastards to Congress, the way Kentucky and Houston had between the wars?

"Winning this goddamn war will be almost as bad as losing it would have been," Dowling said in a voice not far from despair.

"That crossed my mind, too, sir," his adjutant said. "How many of these sons of bitches will we have to kill?"

"As many as it takes," Dowling answered. "If we don't kill any more than that just for the fun of it, our hands are . . . pretty clean, anyway."

He had to look around to orient himself. The United States had knocked most of Richmond flat, while the Confederate defenders had flattened much of the rest. They'd fought hard. They never seemed to fight any other way. But there hadn't been enough of them to keep U.S. soldiers from breaking in.

Jefferson Davis. Robert E. Lee. Stonewall Jackson. Old Pete Longstreet. Woodrow Wilson. The famous Confederates of ages past had to be spinning in their graves—unless U.S. bombs had already evicted them. A pity Jake Featherston wasn't spinning in his. Well, the time for that was coming.

"You know, sir, in a way they're lucky here," Lieutenant Colonel Toricelli said.

"Oh, yeah? How's that?" Dowling asked.

"It's like I said before—if they'd kept fighting a little longer, they *would* have had a uranium bomb come down on their heads. Then they'd think what's left here was paradise by comparison."

"Well, you're bound to be right about that," Dowling said. "Except most of them wouldn't be doing any thinking—"

"Like they do anyway," his adjutant put in.

That stopped him, but only for a second. "Because they'd be dead," he finished. A lot of them already were. The stench in the air left no doubt of that.

Stench or no stench, though, he'd done something a lot of the most important people in U.S. history never managed. He'd remembered long-gone Confederate dignitaries before. Now Lincoln and McClellan, James G. Blaine and John Pope, and Teddy Roosevelt and George Custer sprang to mind. Not a one of them had ever set foot in Richmond. *But here I am, by God!* Dowling thought proudly.

"General! Hey, General Dowling, sir!" somebody behind him yelled. "Guess what, sir!"

"That doesn't sound so good," Angelo Toricelli said.

"No, it doesn't." Slowly, ponderously, Dowling turned. "I'm here. What is it?"

"Guess what?" the soldier said again, but then he told what: "We just found a whole family of nig—uh, Negroes, all safe and sound."

"Well, I'll be damned," Dowling said. A few blacks had come out of hiding when U.S. soldiers entered Richmond, but not many. After the uprising here, Jake Featherston's goons had been uncommonly thorough. Every surviving Negro seemed a separate surprise. "Who are they? How did they make it?"

"They were servants to some rich guy before the war," the soldier answered. "Carter, I think his name was, from the Tarkas estate. Or maybe I've got it backwards—dunno for sure, sir. But anyway, he and his people have been hiding them ever since colored folks started having trouble here."

"How about that?" Lieutenant Colonel Toricelli said. "Just when you think they're all assholes, somebody goes and does something decent and fools you."

"They're human beings," Dowling said. "They aren't always the human beings we wish they were, but they're human beings." He raised his voice to call to the soldier: "Send this Carter fellow to my headquarters. I'd like to talk to him."

"Will do, sir," the man replied.

Dowling's headquarters were in a tent in Capitol Square, not far from the remains of the statue of Albert Sidney Johnston. George Washington's statue, smothered in sandbags, still stood nearby. He got back there just before Jack Carter arrived. The Virginian was tall and trim and handsome, with gray eyes, black hair, and weathered features; he looked to be some age between thirty-five and sixty. "Welcome," Dowling told him. "I'd like to shake your hand."

Carter looked at him—looked through him, really. "I'm sorry, General, but I don't care to shake yours."

This wasn't going to go the way Abner Dowling had thought it would. Whatever Carter was, he wasn't the U.S. liberal somehow fallen into the CSA Dowling had thought him to be. "Maybe you'll explain why," the U.S. soldier said.

"Of course, sir. I'd be glad to," Jack Carter replied. "My chiefest reason is that I am a Confederate patriot. I wish you were hundreds of miles from here, suing for peace from victorious Confederate armies."

"That's nice," Dowling said. "Jake Featherston wishes the same thing. He won't get his wish, and you won't get yours. Santa Claus doesn't have those in his sack."

"Jake Featherston. Do me the courtesy, if you please, of not mentioning that name in my presence again." Carter's loathing might have been the most genteel Dowling had ever met, which made it no less real.

"Sorry about that. He's still President of the Confederate States."

"He's an upstart, a backwoods bumpkin. His father was an overseer." Jack Carter's lip curled. That was one of those things people talked about but hardly ever saw. Dowling saw it now. Carter went on, "My family has mattered in this state since before the Revolution."

A light went on in Dowling's head. "*That's* why you saved your Negroes!"

"Yes, of course. They've served us for as long as we've served Virginia. To lose them to the vulgar excesses of that demagogue and his faction . . ." Carter shook his head. "No."

"*Noblesse oblige*," Dowling murmured.

"Mock me if you care to. We did what we thought right for them."

Dowling wasn't sure whether he was mocking or not. Without a doubt, Carter had risked his own life and his family's to protect those of his servants. That almost required admiration. And yet . . . "Did you do anything for other colored people, Mr. Carter?"

"That was not my place," Carter said simply. "But you'll find I was not the only one to take the measures I thought necessary."

He was bound to be right. Some other whites had hidden Negroes and helped them escape the Freedom Party's population reductions. Some had, yes, but not very many. "Maybe you'd better go," Dowling said.

Jack Carter took a step back. "You thought we might be friends because of what I did. I assure you, sir, I am more sincerely your enemy than Jake Featherston ever dreamt of being. Good day." He bowed, then stalked out.

He might be a more sincere enemy, but Jake Featherston made a more dangerous one. Carter was content to abhor from a distance. Featherston wasn't. He wanted to kill what he didn't like, and he was much too good at it.

A sergeant with the wireless patch on his left sleeve burst into the tent. "Paris, sir!" he exclaimed.

"Paris?" Dowling's first thought, absurdly, was of Helen of Troy.

The sergeant set him straight: "Yes, sir! Paris! The Kaiser just blew it to hell and gone. Eiffel Tower's nothing but a stump, the report says!"

"Jesus Christ!" Dowling said, and then, "Will anything still be standing by the time this damn war gets done?"

Nobody messed with Lavochkin's Looters as they fought their way up the South Carolina coast toward Charleston. Nobody shot at them from ambush. Nobody gave them any guff when they went through a town. Confederate soldiers who surrendered to them seemed pathetically grateful to have the chance.

"You see?" Lieutenant Boris Lavochkin said. "You *can* put the fear of God in these assholes. You can, and we did."

Chester Martin didn't answer that. He pretended he didn't hear it. He wished he could pretend he'd had nothing to do with the massacre in Hardeeville. But he had. He was no damn good at lying to himself. Even if he were, the nightmares that tore apart even his exhausted sleep would have made him stop trying.

He wasn't the only one who had them. Several guys in Lavochkin's platoon were jumpier than a cat at a Great Dane convention. Some replacements knew what was going on as soon as they came in. "Aren't you the guys who—?" they would say, and stop right there.

Others, more naïve or less plugged in, tried to figure out what was going on. They usually said something on the order of, "How come you guys are so weird?"

If anything bothered Lieutenant Lavochkin, he didn't show it. If anything, he was proud of what had happened in Hardeeville. "Nobody fucks with my outfit," he would tell anyone who wanted to listen. "I mean nobody. You fuck with us, tell the carver what you want on your goddamn headstone, 'cause you are all over with."

Captain Rhodes kept shaking his head. "I never expected anything like this to happen to me," he said one evening. He and Chester had got outside of some pretty good cherry brandy a Confederate had left behind. Booze blunted nightmares.

"War's a filthy business," Chester said. "God knows I saw that the last time around. I think the trenches were even worse than what we're doing now. For fighting in, I mean."

"Yeah, for fighting in," the company CO agreed. Or rather, half agreed, for he went on, "But what happened in Hardeeville, that wasn't fighting. That was just . . . murder for the fun of it. And what the Confederates are doing in those goddamn camps, that isn't fighting, either. That's murder for the fun of it, too, 'cause the smokes can't fight back. This war's filthier than the last one was. The horrible stuff then just kinda happened, 'cause they couldn't help it. This time, they're making it horrible on purpose."

He knew about the last war from what he'd read and what people told him. He wasn't anywhere near old enough to have fought in it. "You have a point, sir," Chester said. "Some of a point, anyway." Disagreeing too openly with a superior didn't do. But he damn well *had* been through the Great War. "What about the guys who started using gas? You think they weren't being horrible on purpose?"

"Well, you got me there," Rhodes admitted. Chester liked shooting the bull with him not least because he would admit somebody else had a point. He didn't have anything close to Boris Lavochkin's messianic confidence in his own rightness . . . and righteousness. What was Lieutenant Lavochkin but a scale model of Jake Featherston?

Featherston had flushed a whole country down the toilet. Lavochkin had only a platoon to play with—so far. But Chester was part of the platoon. If the lieutenant threw it away, the first sergeant went with it.

He didn't want to think about that, so he took another swig. Yeah, cherry brandy made a good thought preventer. The bottle was damn near empty. He passed it to Captain Rhodes, who put the kibosh on *damn near*.

"Charleston up ahead," Chester said. "Won't be long now."

"One more city," Rhodes said.

"Oh, it's more than that." Chester knew he sounded shocked. But Rhodes would have gone to school in the lull of the 1920s. Back then, nobody thought you needed to remind anybody of just how and why the USA and CSA got to be mortal foes. They would stay peaceful and live happily ever after. And if pigs had wings . . .

Chester remembered his own school days, before the Great War. They pounded you over the head with the War of Secession then. They kept saying that one day the USA would pay the CSA back. And the United States did. And then the Confederate States had some backpaying to do. *And that's how come I'm sitting on my ass somewhere south of Charleston*, Chester thought.

"I wouldn't mind marching through there," he said. "Give them one in the eye for Fort Sumter, you know?"

"Well, yeah," Rhodes said. But it didn't mean so much to him. Martin could tell. He didn't have that *This is where it all began, and we'll damn well end it here, too* kind of feeling. Maybe Lieutenant Lavochkin would. Or maybe he hated the whole Confederacy equally. All things considered, Chester didn't want to ask him.

He woke with a headache the next morning. Strong coffee and a couple of aspirins helped. Incoming artillery, on the other hand . . . Even now, the Confederates counterattacked whenever they thought they could drive their foes back a couple of miles. A U.S. machine gun opened up no more than twenty yards from Chester. His head didn't explode, which only proved he was tougher than he thought.

Then he had to do some shooting of his own, and that was even worse. A lot of the Confederates didn't hit the dirt as fast as they should have. *New men*, Chester thought with an abstract sympathy that didn't keep him from killing them as fast as he could. They would have done the same to him if they could. But they'd got thrown into the fight too soon to know what they were doing, and a lot of them would never have the chance to learn now.

U.S. armor rattled up to put the final quietus on the Confederate attack. A couple of barrels had Negroes riding on them. The blacks had probably shown the barrel crews shortcuts through the coastal swamps. One of them gleefully blazed away at the men in butternut with a submachine gun. The cannons' bellow made Chester dry-swallow three more aspirins.

The barrels pushed past the U.S. foot soldiers and went after the Confederates. "Come on!" Lieutenant Lavochkin yelled. "Follow me! We don't leave them to do the work by themselves." He jumped out of his hole and loped along with the green-gray machines.

No matter what Chester thought about him, he was dead right there. Armor and infantry worked better as a team than either one did by itself. "Come on, guys!" Chester scrambled from his foxhole—he wasn't limber enough to leap the way the lieutenant did. "Let's go get those bastards!"

Some Confederates stayed stubborn to the end, took a few Yankees with them, and died. Some gave up as soon as they could. Most of those lived; killing in cold blood a poor, scared kid who only wanted to quit didn't come easy. The ones who hesitated were lost.

A youngster with a face full of zits and enormous gray eyes full of terror threw down his submachine gun and raised his hands high over his head. "Don't shoot me, Mr. Damnyankee!" he blubbered to Chester. He couldn't have been more than sixteen. "I give up!"

Chester gestured with the muzzle of his rifle. As it pointed to the young soldier's midsection, a dark stain spread across his crotch.

"Oh, Jesus!" he wailed. "I went and pissed myself!"

"It happens," Chester said. He'd done it himself in two wars now, but he wasn't going to tell that to a kid he was capturing. He gestured with the rifle again. "Go on back there, and they'll take care of you one way or another."

"Thank you! Thank you! God bless you!" Hands still high, the boy trudged off toward the rear.

And, one way or another, they would take care of him. Maybe they'd take him all the way back to a POW camp. Or maybe they'd just shoot him. Whatever they did, it wasn't Chester's worry any more.

The damned Confederates kept fighting as hard as they could. Chester captured another guy who had to be older than he was. The National Assault Force soldier had lost his upper plate, and talked as if he had a mouthful of mush. "Maybe we fought each other the lasht time around," he said.

"Could be," Chester allowed. "I was on the Roanoke front, and then in northern Virginia. How about you?"

"Nope. I wash in Tenneshshee," the Confederate retread said. "Never reckon you bashtards'd get into Shouf Carolina."

"You fuck with us, Pops, and that's what happens," Chester told him. "Go on back to the rear. They'll deal with you."

"Uh-huh," the old-timer said bleakly. Unlike the kid, he knew what could happen to him. But he went. He'd passed the first key test: he hadn't got killed out of hand. All the others would be easier. Of course, you only had to fail one and that was all she wrote.

"Come on!" Lieutenant Lavochkin shouted. "We push hard, we'll be in Charleston tomorrow! Maybe even by sundown!" Chester thought he was right, too. Try as they would, the Confederates didn't have enough to stop the men in green-gray.

All of which turned out to have nothing to do with anything. The wireless man shouted for Captain Rhodes: "Sir, we've got a stop order! Nobody's supposed to advance past map square Gold-5."

"Oh, yeah?" the company CO said. "Let me talk to Division." He talked. He listened. He talked some more. Then he did some shouting of his own: "All troops halt! I say again, all troops halt! We have to stop right here."

"No!" Lieutenant Lavochkin said. "We've got 'em licked! The brass can't screw us out of this."

"Lieutenant, the halt order comes straight from the War Department," Captain Rhodes said. "You can write 'em a nasty letter when this is all over, but for now we are damn well going to halt."

"No!" Lavochkin repeated.

"That is an order, Lieutenant." Rhodes' voice turned icy. "From the War Department and from me. Is that plain enough? Next stop, the stockade."

"They can't keep us out of Charleston!" Lavochkin raged. "The enemy hasn't got a chance! The dumbshit brass hats in Philly don't know diddly-squat. I'm going forward anyway, and taking my men with me. We'll see you in Charleston, too."

"No, sir," Chester Martin said. Lavochkin stared at him, caught between fury and astonishment. But a first sergeant was there to keep a lieutenant in line. Chester went on, "I think we better follow the order."

"You'll pay for this, Sergeant," Lavochkin said.

Chester shrugged. Slowly and deliberately, he sat down on the muddy ground and lit a cigarette. "I'll take my chances . . . sir." He wondered whether Lavochkin would go on by himself. The rest of the platoon was stopping. The lieutenant's face had murder all over it, but he stopped, too.

He fumed and swore for the next three hours. "God damn it to hell, I could have been in Charleston by now. We all could," he said. Chester didn't think so, but the lieutenant wasn't so far wrong. Why *had* the brass called a halt with the city so close?

When the fireball rose over Charleston, when the toadstool cloud—weirdly beautiful and weirdly terrifying—rose high above the town where the War of Secession started, he understood. So did Captain Rhodes. "Lieutenant, do you really want to get any closer to that place?" Rhodes asked.

"Uh, no, sir," Boris Lavochkin answered in an unwontedly small voice.

"Do you think following orders might be a good idea every once in a while, even if you don't happen to like them personally?" Captain Rhodes persisted.

"Uh, yes, sir."

"Congratulations. That *is* the right answer, Lieutenant. Do you realize you and whoever you dragged with you would have ended up dead if you did manage to break into Charleston?"

"Uh, yes, sir," Lavochkin said again, still more softly than usual.

"Then remember that, goddammit," Rhodes barked.

"Yes, sir," the young lieutenant said one more time. And no doubt he would . . . for a while. How long? *Not long enough, I bet*, Chester Martin thought.

Portable wireless sets would have been a lot better if they lived up to their name. Luggable was more like it, as far as Leonard O'Doull was concerned. The damn things were too damn big and too damn heavy, and so were the batteries that powered them. Those batteries didn't last long enough, either.

Still, having a wireless set was better than not having one, especially since U.S. Wireless Atlanta went on the air. USWA had the power to punch through all the jamming the Confederates put out, and it brought the word—or the U.S. version of the word—into the heartland of the CSA: over near Birmingham, for instance.

It also gave U.S. personnel something to listen to besides Confederate Connie. Her sultry voice kept reminding O'Doull he'd been away from home too damn long. He knew she told lies every time she opened her mouth. Like hundreds of thousands of other guys, he kept listening to her anyway. She sounded like bottled sex.

When he said something like that one evening, Eddie nodded. Then the corpsman said, "She's probably sixty and fat and ugly."

"Yeah, she probably is—life works that way too goddamn often," O'Doull agreed. "But she sure *sounds* hot."

"She doesn't do that much for me," Sergeant Goodson Lord said.

O'Doull reached for his wrist. "Do you have a pulse, man?" Sergeant Lord jerked his arm away. Not for the first time, O'Doull wondered whether the senior medic was a fairy. How could you like women and not like Confederate Connie?

Eddie looked at his wristwatch. "Seven o'clock," he said. "Time for the news." He switched the wireless from Confederate Connie's music to USWA.

He couldn't have timed it better if he tried for a week. "Hello," said a deep voice with a distinctive U.S. accent. "I'm Eric Sevareid, and I'm here to tell you the *real* truth." All the men in the aid station grinned. How many times over how many years had they heard Jake Featherston open up a can of worms with that bullshit?

"Hope the Confederates listen up," Goodson Lord said. "They'd better." He might be a queer, but if he was, he was a patriotic queer. *Long as he doesn't grab* my *ass, I can live with that*, O'Doull thought, and felt proud of his own tolerance.

"Today, President La Follette again called for the surrender of the Confederate States," Sevareid said on the wireless. "In his words, 'Only by quitting the war now can the CSA hope to escape destruction of a sort the world has never seen before. Newport News and Charleston are just the beginning. We *will* put an end to this evil regime one way or another. Which way that will be is the only thing left for existing Confederate officials to decide.'"

"That's telling 'em!" Eddie said. He was as mild and inoffensive a little guy as ever came down the pike, but he hated the CSA. He wouldn't have had to see so much misery if not for Jake Featherston.

"Featherston's reply was, 'We aren't going to lay down for the United States, and they can't make us do it,'" Sevareid continued. "He is believed to have broadcast that reply from somewhere in North Carolina. Richmond, of course, is in U.S. hands. Featherston narrowly escaped the Newport News bomb, and U.S. forces are now pushing toward Hampton Roads. Before long, he will be a president without a country." The broadcaster's voice showed unmistakable satisfaction.

"In the European half of the war, German drives against Russia continue," Sevareid said. "The Tsar's army shows signs of disintegration, but Petrograd Wireless—now broadcasting from Moscow after the destruction of Petrograd—denies reports that the Tsar is seeking an armistice from Germany."

"If Russia bails out, England and France are done," Lord opined.

"France is about done anyway," Eddie said. "Bye-bye, gay Paree." He waved.

Half a lifetime spent in the Republic of Quebec speaking French almost all the time made O'Doull look at France differently from most Americans. It was the sun around which Quebec revolved whether they were on the same side or not. And when the heart of the sun was torn out . . .

"Despite the loss of Paris, France also denies any plan to leave the conflict," Eric Sevareid said. "The new King of France, Louis XIX, vows revenge against Germany. And Winston Churchill was quoted by the BBC as saying, 'We can match the Hun bomb for bomb. Let him do his worst, and we shall do our best. With God's help, it will be good enough.'"

"With him and Featherston, the bad guys have all the good talkers," Sergeant Lord said. "Doesn't seem fair."

"Churchill's a better speaker than Featherston any day," O'Doull said. "He's not such a bastard, either."

"That's what you say, Doc," Eddie put in. "Ask the Kaiser, and I bet he'd tell you different."

Since he was bound to be right—what did the Kaiser care about the CSA?—O'Doull didn't argue with him. He gave his attention to the wireless: "Japan has sent Russia an ultimatum over several Siberian provinces. If the Tsar's forces do not evacuate them, the Japanese threaten to take them by force."

"Wait a minute!" Lord said. "The Japs and the Russians are on the same side."

"They're on the same side against us," Leonard O'Doull said. "Otherwise? Forget it. The Japs already screwed England in Malaya. They've got Australia sweating bullets. They're the ones who've done the best for themselves in this war. If they'd driven us out of the Sandwich Islands, nobody could ever touch 'em."

"Won't be easy, even the way things are," Eddie said.

"They haven't used any of these new superbombs yet," O'Doull said. "I wonder how close they are to building one."

"Well, if they weren't working on 'em before, they sure as hell are now," Goodson Lord said. That was another obvious truth.

Back before the Pacific War, people in the USA would have wondered whether the Japanese were smart enough to do something like that. Not any more. The Pacific War was a push, or as close as made no difference, but Japan bombed Los Angeles while the United States never laid a glove on the home islands. This time around, the United States hadn't tried breaking through the Japs' island barricade, either. All the fighting had been on U.S. soil and in U.S. waters. The United States was too busy fighting for their life against the Confederacy to give Japan more than a fraction of their attention.

It had been quiet up at the front. Suddenly, it wasn't any more. Machine guns and automatic weapons started banging away. "It's getting dark outside!" Lord exclaimed. "What the hell do they think they're shooting at?"

"They don't care," O'Doull answered. "Somebody imagined he saw something, and as soon as one guy starts shooting they all open up."

"We better get up there," Eddie told his fellow corpsmen. They scurried out of the aid station. Before long, they'd likely be back with wounded men.

Eric Sevareid went on talking about the world and the USA. He had a good wireless voice, a voice that made you think he was your friend even though you'd never met him and never would. You wanted to believe what he said. You wanted to believe what Jake Featherston said, too, even after you knew what a liar he was. If he didn't believe it himself, he put on one hell of an act.

"Will the corpsmen be able to find us in the dark?" Goodson Lord asked.

"Don't know," O'Doull answered. "But I'll tell you something— I'm not gonna put on a light. If our own side doesn't shoot us because of it, the enemy would."

Not even fifteen minutes later, he heard the too-familiar shout of "Doc! Hey, Doc!" from somewhere off to the left.

"Hey, Eddie!" he yelled back. A battery of 105s was thundering behind the U.S. lines. Pretty soon, C.S. artillery would open up, too, or they'd start shooting off screaming meemies, and then hell really would be out to lunch.

In the meantime . . . "We got a sucking chest, Doc!" Eddie said.

O'Doull swore. That was a bad wound, one that would kill the soldier who had it unless everything went right—and might kill him anyway. "How are we fixed for plasma?" he asked Sergeant Lord.

"We've got enough," Lord answered.

"Good," O'Doull said. "Grab a big needle—chances are we'll want to pour it in as fast as we can."

Sweat made the corpsmen's faces shine when they brought in the wounded soldier. Heat and humidity were starting to build toward summer. O'Doull noticed only out of the corner of his eye; most of his attention focused on the corporal on the stretcher. The man had bloody foam on his lips and nostrils. Sure as hell, he'd taken one through the lung.

"Get him up on the table," O'Doull told the corpsmen. To Goodson Lord, he said, "Get him under."

"Right," Lord said. He jammed the ether cone down on the noncom's face as soon as the corpsmen put him in position. The plasma line went in next. The corporal already seemed unconscious, so O'Doull started cutting even before the anesthetic would have fully taken hold. Seconds counted here.

When he opened the guy up, he found the chest cavity full of blood. He hadn't expected anything different. He had a fat rubber tube ready to go to siphon it out of there. How bad was the wound? Did he have time to tie off the major bleeders in the lung, or would he have to do something more drastic?

He needed only a moment to decide he couldn't do anything that took a long time. His vorpal scalpel went snicker-snack and took out the bottom two lobes of the right lung. That left him with just a few vessels to tie off, and he knew where they were—he didn't have to go looking for them. You could live with a lung and a third. You could live with one lung if you had to, though you wouldn't have an easy time if you did anything strenuous for a living.

With the worst of it done, he repaired the wound in the corporal's back. "What's his BP?" he asked as he worked.

"It's 95 over 68," Goodson Lord answered, checking the cuff. "Not real great, but it's pretty steady, anyway."

"All right." O'Doull dusted the inside of the chest cavity with sulfa powder, then started closing up. He'd read in a journal that the powder probably helped less than people said it did. He used it anyhow. Why not? It wouldn't hurt.

"What do you think?" Sergeant Lord asked while he finished. He left a honking big drain in the incision. That could come out later.

"If shock doesn't get him, if he doesn't hemorrhage . . ." O'Doull shrugged, wishing for a cigarette. "I've done what I can. Maybe he'll make it. I can hope so, anyway." The corporal would be dead for sure if he hadn't got here. If he lived—*If he lives, score one for me*, O'Doull thought. That wasn't a bad feeling to have, not even a little bit.

LIEUTENANT Michael Pound had fought through the Battle of Pittsburgh. He'd seen what a city looked like after two armies jumped on it with both feet. Now, on the outskirts of Birmingham, Alabama, he was seeing it again.

Confederate General Patton was holed up inside Birmingham, and he wasn't coming out. The USA had forced him out of Atlanta, but he refused to pull what was left of his army out of the Alabama factory town. He refused to surrender, too. "If you want me, come and take me," he told the U.S. officers who went in to parley with him.

"I don't want to dig the son of a bitch out a block at a time," Sergeant Mel Scullard grumbled. "Expensive goddamn real estate, y'know?"

"Yeah." Pound nodded. "Maybe we won't have to."

"How come, sir?" the gunner asked. "Can't just leave him there."

"No, but if we gave one to Newport News and we gave one to Charleston, how long will it be before we give one to Birmingham, too?" Pound said.

Scullard laughed a particularly nasty laugh. " 'Bye, George!" he said, waving. "See you in hell, like you deserve!"

"That'd be pretty good, all right," Joe Mouradian agreed. "But what if they blow us up, too? We ain't that far outside of town ourselves."

"Urk." Pound hadn't thought of that. The more he did, the more it worried him. The brass would be eager to get rid of Patton. After Jake Featherston and maybe Ferdinand Koenig, he was the most dangerous character the Confederacy had. If one of those superbombs took him out but hurt or maybe killed some of their own guys, how much would the fellows back in Philadelphia care? Not a whole hell of a lot, not unless a dedicated cynic like Michael Pound missed his guess.

He stuck his head out of the cupola for a quick looksee. He wasn't sure what a superbomb could do to Birmingham that lots and lots of ordinary bombs and artillery shells hadn't already done. The place had been torn up and burned more times than anybody could count. Everything that wasn't green was gray or black, and just about all the walls he could see either listed or had chunks bitten out of them or both.

But the remnants of Patton's Army of Kentucky still lurked in the ruins. They were stubborn men with automatic weapons and stovepipe rockets. They wouldn't be winkled out easily or cheaply. Maybe a superbomb could get rid of them the way DDT got lice out of clothes.

As if to prove the Confederate States were still in business, somebody squeezed off a burst from one of their carnivorous machine guns. Pound ducked down into the barrel. He didn't want to win a Purple Heart, not this late in the game. He didn't want to buy a plot, either.

"Anything worth going after, sir?" Scullard asked.

"Not . . . right this minute," Pound answered. He prided himself on being an aggressive soldier. And he was still ready to go forward whenever anybody told him to. Without anything obviously urgent ahead, though, he was just as well pleased to sit tight.

This must be what the end of the war feels like, he thought. Yeah, you were still willing. But how eager were you when pushing too hard might get you killed just when things wound down?

Sitting tight didn't mean sticking his head in the sand like an ostrich. Standing up in the open cupola wasn't smart right now. All right—next best thing, then. That was looking out through the periscopes built into the cupola. He couldn't see as much with them as he could head and shoulders above there, but . . .

"Powaski!" he shouted to the bow gunner and wireless man. "Ten o'clock! Somebody sneaking up on us, maybe 150 yards!"

"I'm on it," Powaski answered over the intercom. The bow gun wasn't useful very often. Pound had heard talk that the next generation of barrels would dispense with it and go with a four-man crew instead of five. This once, though, it was liable to be a lifesaver.

It started to chatter now. Pound watched tracers spang off brickwork and fly every which way. The turret hummed as Scullard traversed it so he could bring the coaxial machine gun—and maybe the cannon, too—to bear.

Like any well-trained gunner, Powaski squeezed off short bursts. You didn't want to burn out your machine-gun barrel and have to change the son of a bitch. But the butternut bastard behind the bricks got the bow gunner's rhythm quicker than he had any business doing. As soon as Powaski eased off the trigger after a burst, he popped up and let fly with a stovepipe rocket.

"Aw, shit!" Pound said. It was a long shot for one of those babies. Maybe this one would fall short or fly wide left or right like a bad field goal . . .

Maybe it would, but it didn't. It caught the barrel right in the glacis plate. The thick armor there nearly kept the hollow-charge warhead from penetrating. *Nearly* mattered with everything but horseshoes and hand grenades—and, it turned out, hollow-charge warheads, too.

Powaski and Neyer both screamed. Pound didn't think either of them had a prayer of getting out. And inside a barrel, nine million different things could catch fire, especially when a white-hot gout of flame played across them.

Pound screamed himself: "Out!" Some of the things that could catch fire were his boots and his coveralls. They could, and they did. He screamed again, without words this time. Then he shot out through the cupola. He never remembered opening it, but he must have.

Next thing he knew, he was on the ground beside the burning barrel, on the ground and rolling away. Mel Scullard had got out, too. More of his clothes than of Pound's were burning.

Drop and roll and beat out the fire. That was what they taught you. Doing it while you were actually burning . . . Well, if you could do that, you were disciplined indeed. Michael Pound surprised himself— he was. He got some more burns on his hands putting out his boots and the legs to his coveralls, but he did it.

Easy, when it's either that or make an ash of yourself, he thought, and started to laugh. Then he realized it wasn't just his clothes—he'd been on fire, too. He howled like a wolf instead.

A foot soldier in green-gray ran up to Mel Scullard with a bucket of water and put him out. Scullard was already shrieking—yes, he'd got it worse than Pound. "Corpsman!" the soldier yelled, and then, "Hold on for a second, buddy, and I'll give you a shot."

What about me? Pound wondered. He fumbled for the wound kit on his belt. That was a brand new hell—an inferno, in fact—because his hands *were* burned. He managed to get out the syringe and stick himself. He wanted instant relief. Hell, he wanted a whole new carcass. Every second he had to wait seemed an eternity. *Maybe this is what Einstein means about relativity.*

Inside the burning barrel, ammunition started cooking off. He hoped it wouldn't keep medics back. The first team that got there carried Sergeant Scullard away. "We'll be right back for you, pal," a little bespectacled guy called to Pound. He didn't wait for an answer.

Right back turned out to be something more like fifteen minutes. By then, the morphine syrette had kicked in. It didn't make the pain disappear, but did shove it into a dark closet so Pound didn't have to give all of his attention to it. Anything was better than nothing.

Here came that same stretcher team. "Ease onto the litter, there," the little guy said—he seemed to be in charge. He looked at Pound's legs with experienced eyes. "Not *too* bad."

"It's never too bad when it happens to somebody else," Pound snarled, in no mood for sympathy.

The little guy blinked, then nodded. "Well, I'm not gonna tell you you're wrong." He turned to the other bearers. "On three . . . One . . . Two . . . Three!" Up went the stretcher.

"How come we get the heavy guy *after* the light one, Eddie?" a bearer grumbled.

" 'Cause we're lucky, that's why," said the guy with the glasses. "Come on. Let's move."

They took Pound back to an aid station a few hundred yards behind the line. Morphine or no morphine, he yelled and swore whenever a stretcher-bearer missed a step. He felt ashamed at being such a slave to pain, which didn't mean he could do anything about it.

Red crosses flew everywhere on and around the aid-station tent, which didn't keep bullet holes from pockmarking the canvas. "Doc's still busy with your buddy," Eddie said. "Want another shot?"

"Yes, please!" Pound said, in lieu of grabbing him by the shirtfront and making him use the syrette. He hardly noticed the bite of the needle. The second shot really did send the pain off into some distant province.

He thought so, anyway, till they picked him up again and lugged him inside. That hurt in spite of all the morphine. "How's Mel?" he asked the doctor, who was scrubbing his hands in an enameled metal basin.

"He's the other burned man?" The doctor had a funny accent, half New England, half almost French-sounding. He waited for Pound to nod, then said, "I think he'll make it. He won't be happy for a while, though." He turned to Eddie. "Get this one up on the table, and we'll see how happy he'll be."

"Right, Doc," Eddie said.

Somebody—a medic, Pound supposed—stuck an ether cone over his face. The gas didn't just smell bad; it smelled poisonous. Even as consciousness faded, he tried to tear off the cone. They wouldn't let him.

When he woke up, his legs hurt so bad, he wasn't sure he'd really been anesthetized. But he lay in a bed somewhere that wasn't the aid station. His groan brought a real, live female nurse. She wasn't beautiful or anything, but she was the first woman from the USA Pound had seen in a devil of a long time. "In pain?" she asked briskly.

"Yes," he said, thinking, *What the hell do you expect?*

Even though she'd asked a dumb question, she had the right answer: "I'll give you a shot." As she injected him, she went on, "The tannic-acid dressings do hurt, I know, but you'll heal much better because of them. Your burns won't weep so much, and you're less likely to get infected."

"Oh, boy," Pound said. Everything else seemed secondary to the way he felt. He tried to look around, but his eyes weren't tracking real well yet. "Is Mel Scullard here?" he asked, adding, "He's my gunner."

"Yes, he's three beds down," the nurse said. "He hasn't regained consciousness yet."

Poor Mel. He did *get it worse than I did,* Pound thought. Then the morphine started to kick in. It struck faster now than it had right after he got burned. Maybe that meant he wasn't fighting so much pain. He could hope so, anyhow. "Ahh," he said.

"We have to be careful with this stuff," the nurse told him. "We don't want you getting hooked."

Right then, Pound couldn't have cared less if he had to stick a needle in his arm every hour on the hour for the rest of his life. If it made him stop hurting, that struck him as a good deal. Down underneath, there wasn't much difference between people and animals. War brought that out all kinds of ways. Pound wished like anything he hadn't found out about this one at firsthand.

The officers' POW camp to which the Yankees took Jerry Dover was somewhere not far from Indianapolis. The train trip that brought him there wasn't much fun, but it was instructive just the same. Confederate wireless went on and on about all the sabotage that raiders behind U.S. lines were still perpetrating in Georgia and Tennessee and Kentucky.

Well, maybe they were. Even so, the train didn't have to stop once. It didn't even have to slow down. As far as Dover could tell, it didn't make any detours. Yes, bridges and overpasses were guarded. Yes, concrete blockhouses with machine guns sticking out of them protected some stretches of track. But trains seemed to get wherever they needed to go, and to get there on time.

Jerry Dover's train also had no trouble crossing the Ohio. All the bridges across what had been the C.S.–U.S. border should have been prime targets. They probably were. If this one, near Evansville, had ever been hit, it had also been efficiently repaired.

Evansville itself had been bombed. But it hadn't been flattened, the way so many Confederate cities were. It lay in the western part of Indiana, well away from the early thrust north that almost won the war for the CSA.

"They should have done a better job here," complained the artillery captain sitting next to Dover.

"It's a big country," Dover said. "They couldn't get all of it."

"Well, they should have," the younger man repeated glumly.

He wasn't wrong. But if the United States turned out to be too big to let the Confederacy smash them all up, didn't that go a long way toward explaining why the war was going as it was? It sure looked that way to Dover.

Actually reaching the camp also told Dover his country was fighting out of its weight. He knew how the CSA housed prisoners of war. The Confederacy's camps were no sturdier than they had to be, because his country had nothing to spare. They probably didn't break Geneva Convention rules—you didn't want to give the enemy an excuse to take it out on POWs from your side—but he would have been amazed if they didn't bend them.

Camp Liberty! (with the exclamation point—a sardonic name if ever there was one) wasn't like that. Dover wouldn't have wanted to assault it with anything less than an armored brigade. It didn't just have a barbed-wire perimeter: it had a wall and a moat, with barbed wire on top of the wall and outside the machine-gun towers beyond the water. You got in there, you weren't going anywhere.

Inside, the buildings were as solid as if they were meant to last a hundred years. Yes, Indiana had harder winters than Georgia, but even so. . . . The lumber and the brickwork and the labor the United States could afford to lavish on a place like this were daunting.

If the military clerk who signed him in were twenty-two years old and fit, Jerry Dover really would have been alarmed. But the man had to be at least sixty-five, with a white Kaiser Bill mustache the likes of which Dover hadn't seen since he quit fighting the damnyankees in 1917. Didn't this guy know they were as out of fashion as bustles? Evidently not; he seemed proud of his.

"You're in Barracks Twelve, and you'll sleep on cot seventeen," the clerk declared in harsh Midwestern tones. "Numbers are large. I don't think you can miss 'em."

After that, Dover felt he ought to get lost on general principles. He couldn't, though, because the Yankee was right. Directional signs told you just where everything was. Barracks 12 was a brick building with a poured-concrete floor. Starting a tunnel and keeping it hidden would be a bitch, or more likely impossible.

Two stout coal-burning stoves sat there to heat the hall in winter. A wireless set was playing an insipid Yankee tune when Dover walked in. The Confederates punished POWs for clandestine wirelesses. U.S. authorities equipped the halls with them. That was daunting, too.

A colonel in his late thirties ambled up to Dover. "Howdy. I'm Kirby Smith Telford," he said, Texas in his voice and in his name. "I'm the senior officer hereabouts. They caught me outside of Chattanooga late in '43."

Jerry Dover introduced himself. "They shot up my command car and got me in front of Huntsville," he said. "I was up near Chattanooga, too. Had to clear out my supply dump quick as I could when the damnyankees' paratroops came down."

"Yeah, that screwed everything up, all right." Telford watched him with a blue-eyed directness that looked friendly but, Dover realized, wasn't. "You sound like you've been around. I reckon somebody in here'll be able to vouch for you."

"Vouch for me?" Dover echoed. "I'm a POW, for crying out loud. What the hell else am I gonna be?"

He didn't think the colonel would have an answer for him, but Kirby Smith Telford did: "Maybe a Yankee plant. They try it every now and then, see what they can find out about us. Pretty soon you'll find out who you can talk in front of and who you've got to watch yourself with. I don't mean any offense, Colonel—don't get me wrong—but right now I don't know you from Adam, so I'll be careful what I say around you."

"However you please. I don't mean any offense, either, but right now I don't know how much difference it's gonna make," Dover said.

Telford's face clouded. "That's defeatist talk," he said stiffly.

"I've got news for you, Colonel. The damnyankees didn't capture me outside of Huntsville because we're winning."

The senior officer turned away from him without another word. Dover contemplated winning friends. He'd just lost one. Even if somebody did vouch for him now, Telford wouldn't want much to do with him. *Well, too goddamn bad*, Dover thought. *If he doesn't like the truth, he can read a novel.*

He found cot 17. It was a better bed than the one he'd had in his own tent. It had a footlocker underneath. Dover didn't have much to stick in there, not after the soldiers who caught him relieved him of his chattels personal. They hadn't shot him, and they could have. Next to that, robbery was a detail.

He stretched out on the cot. He'd been sitting up ever since he got on the train somewhere near the Alabama–Georgia border. Two minutes later, he was snoring.

What might have been the voice of God—if God talked like a Yankee—blasted him awake: "Supper call! Supper call!" The camp had a PA system! He was sure the Confederates had never thought of that.

Supper wasn't fancy, but it wasn't bad: fried chicken, green beans (overcooked, of course—the ex-restaurateur did notice that), and French fries. You could take seconds. The apple pie for dessert was actually pretty good. Dover turned to the captain sitting next to him and said, "Hell of a note when the enemy feeds us better than our own side did."

"Yeah." The younger officer—except for some other obvious retreads, all the men in here were younger than Dover—looked surprised. "Hadn't thought about it like that, but you're right."

If I am, what does it mean? Dover didn't like any of the answers that occurred to him. The most obvious one was the one that was probably true. The United States were enough richer than the Confederacy that they didn't have to worry about pennies and dimes. They could afford to do little things like build sturdy POW camps and give enemy soldiers decent rations. The CSA couldn't. The Confederates had enough trouble taking care of their own men.

Nothing to do after supper but troop back to the barracks hall. A couple of card games got started. Two officers bent over a chess set. By the way they shot pieces back and forth as the game opened, they'd already played each other a great many times.

Dover played a fair game of checkers, but chess had never interested him. He figured he'd play poker or bridge one of these days, but he didn't feel like it now. He went up to Kirby Smith Telford, who was reading a news magazine and shaking his head every now and then. "Can I get some paper and a pencil?" Dover asked. "I'd like to let my family know I'm in one piece."

"They'll have a Red Cross wire by now," Telford said, which was likely true, but he handed Dover a sheet of cheap stationery imprinted CAMP LIBERTY!, an envelope, and a pencil. "Don't seal it when you're done," he warned. "Censors look over everything you write."

"I reckoned they would," Dover said. After more than ten years of Freedom Party rule in the CSA, he took censorship for granted. No reason the damnyankees wouldn't have it, too. "Thanks," he added, and went back to his own cot.

As he went, he felt Colonel Telford's eyes boring into his back. Did the other officer think he hadn't been respectful enough? Did they worry about that crap here? If they did, why, for God's sake? What difference did it make now? As for Dover, he'd cussed out generals. He was damned if he'd get all hot and bothered about somebody whose three stars didn't even have a wreath around them.

He wished he could have grabbed some table space. Writing at the cot was awkward, but he managed. *Dear Sally*, he wrote, *I bet you will have heard by now that I'm a POW. I'm up here in the USA, in Indiana. I'm not hurt. They're treating me all right. I love you and the kids. I'll see you when the war is over, I guess. XOXOXOX—Jerry.*

He looked at the letter. After a shrug, he nodded. It said everything he needed to say. He couldn't see anything the censor would flabble about. He folded the paper, put it in the envelope, and wrote his home address on the outside. No matter what Telford had said, he started to lick the glue on the flap, but caught himself in time. *I'm a creature of habit, all right*, he thought.

Somebody turned on the wireless. Women sang about war bonds in yapping Yankee accents. They wouldn't have made Dover want to buy. When the advertisement ended, an announcer said, "And now the news."

None of the news was good, not if you were a Confederate POW. Dover assumed U.S. broadcasts bent things the same way his side did. But you could bend them only so far before you started looking ridiculous. When the newsman said Birmingham was surrounded, it probably was. When he said U.S. soldiers had freed more starving political prisoners from rocket factories on the outskirts of Huntsville, they probably had. Using politicals for work like that sounded like something the Freedom Party would do. So did starving them.

And when the fellow said the Tsar was asking the Kaiser for an armistice, how could you doubt him? After Petrograd went up in smoke, Russia had hung on longer than Jerry Dover thought it could. But all good things came to an end. England and France would be in even more trouble now that Germany didn't have to fight on two fronts.

Two Confederate cities had already gone up in smoke. So had a big part of Philadelphia. The war on this side of the Atlantic sounded like a game of last man standing. Who could make superbombs faster? Who could get them where they needed to go? How long could the poor bastards on the other side stand getting pulverized?

Odds were the United States could make bombs faster. They made everything else faster. Odds were the USA could deliver the goods, too. How long could even Jake Featherston stay stubborn when death rained down on his country from the skies?

Camp Liberty! Dover winced. Odds were he'd get his liberty back when his country finished losing the war.

XI

Jonathan Moss savored the feeling of being at a forward air base again. He was a little southwest of Atlanta—not too far from where he'd pounded the ground with Gracchus' guerrillas. Comparing what he could do now with what he'd done then was funny, in a macabre way. The new turbo fighter could take him as far in an hour as he could march in a month.

Every time he flew off towards Alabama, he hoped to pay the Confederates back for all the time away from his specialty they'd cost him. The pilot who'd shot him down might have killed him instead. So might the soldiers who'd taken him prisoner. He didn't dwell on that. Resenting them for turning him into a guerrilla helped keep and hone his fighting edge.

His biggest trouble these days was finding someone to fight. The Confederates didn't—couldn't—put up many fighters any more. He had a pretty good notion of what his Screaming Eagle could do, but he wanted to put it through its paces against the best opposition the enemy could throw at it.

If the turbo wasn't going after the latest souped-up Hound Dogs or Razorbacks or Mules, it didn't have much point. It carried enough firepower to make a fair ground-attack aircraft, but only a fair one: it went so fast and covered so much ground, it couldn't linger and really work over a target. It had bomb racks, but using it as a fighter-bomber struck Moss as the equivalent of using a thoroughbred to pull a brewery wagon. Sure, you could do it, but other critters were better suited to the job.

And so he wished the United States had come up with it a year and a half earlier. It would have swept Confederate aircraft from the skies. As things worked out, enemy airplanes were few and far between anyhow, but getting them that way had taken a lot longer and cost a lot more.

His pulse quickened when he spotted a pair of Hound Dogs well below him. The newest Confederate aircraft got a performance boost by squirting wood alcohol into the fuel mix. They were a match for any U.S. piston-engined fighter. They weren't a match for a turbo—not even close.

He gave the fighter more throttle and pushed the stick forward. As he dove, he wondered what kind of pilots sat in those cockpits. These days, the Confederates had two types left: kids just out of flight school who might be good once they got some experience but didn't have it yet, and veterans who'd lived through everything the USA could throw at them and who'd be dangerous flying a two-decker left over from the last war.

The way these guys stuck together, leader and wingman, told him right away that they'd been through the mill. So did the speed with which they spotted him. And so did the tight turns into which they threw their aircraft. The one thing a turbo couldn't do was dogfight a Hound Dog. You'd get in trouble if you tried. They'd turn inside you and get on your tail in nothing flat.

Even if they did, they wouldn't stay there long. In a turbo, you could run away from anything in the world except another turbo.

Moss climbed again for a new pass. The Hound Dogs dove for the deck. He followed them down, smiling when his airspeed indicator climbed over 500. No piston job could touch that, not even diving for all it was worth.

They knew he was after them, all right. They stuck together all the same. Yes, they'd been flying together awhile, or more than awhile. He had to guess which way they'd break when he got close. He chose right, and that was right. They started to turn so they could shoot back at him, but his thumb had already come down on the firing button atop the stick.

When the cannon boomed, pieces flew from the C.S. wingman's Hound Dog. The pilot struggled for control and lost. The fighter spun toward the ground. The pilot wouldn't have an easy time bailing out.

Meanwhile, though, the leader was shooting at Moss. Well, he was trying to: your sights wouldn't let you lead a turbo airplane. It just flew too fast. The leader's tracers went behind the turbo as it zipped past him.

Swinging through as tight a turn as he could make, Moss came back at the C.S. fighter. The Hound Dog didn't want any more of him. Its pilot wanted nothing more than to escape. And he did, too, getting down to treetop height and dodging and jinking in a way Moss couldn't hope to match.

"All right, buddy—I'll see you some other time." Inside his cockpit, Moss sketched a salute. That was a good flyer over there on the other side. Yeah, he was a Confederate son of a bitch, but he made one hell of a pilot.

Time to break off, then. When Moss pulled back on the stick, the turbo seemed to climb hand over hand. No prop job could come close to matching that performance. You had to trade speed for height, but the turbo had so much speed that it sacrificed much less than a Hound Dog or similar U.S. fighter. If Moss could have seen this in 1914 . . .

He'd flown a two-decker pusher when the Great War broke out. That was the only way anyone had figured out to get a machine gun firing straight ahead. No interrupter gear to fire through the spinning prop, not yet. Moss laughed. That technology was turning obsolete right before his eyes.

He hadn't had a wireless in his pusher, either. He hadn't had an enclosed cockpit, let alone oxygen. He hadn't worn a parachute. If he went down, he was a dead duck. And, with an airplane made of wood and canvas and glue and wire, with an engine almost aggressively unreliable, plenty of those early airplanes did go down, even with no enemies within miles.

He laughed once more. Now he sat behind sheet metal and bulletproof glass in an armored seat. He could fly more than twice as high as that pusher could have gone. But he still flew, or flew again, with aggressively unreliable engines. Maybe he could bail out now if they went south on him. On the other hand, maybe he couldn't.

Finding the airstrip from which he'd taken off was another adventure. Just any old field wouldn't do. The turbo had a high takeoff and landing speed. It needed a lot of runway. One that was fine for prop jobs likely wouldn't let him land.

Instead of the base, he spotted another airplane: a Confederate

Grasshopper buzzing along over U.S. territory to see what it could see. Grasshoppers were marvelous little machines. They could hover in a strong headwind and land or take off in next to nothing. For artillery spotting or taking out casualties or sneaking in spies or saboteurs, they couldn't be beat. Moss knew that several captured specimens were wearing the U.S. eagle over crossed swords instead of the Confederate battle flag.

The guy in this one saw him coming before he got close enough to fire. It scooted out of the way with a turn no honest fighter could match. Try to shoot down a Grasshopper whose pilot knew you were there and you'd end up talking to yourself. It was like trying to kill a butterfly with an axe.

More for the hell of it than any other reason, Moss made another pass. With effortless ease, the Grasshopper evaded him again. He didn't even bother opening fire. And the observer in the back of the light airplane's cockpit squeezed off a burst at him with his pintle-mounted machine gun. None of the tracers came close, but the defiant nose-thumbing—it couldn't be anything else—tickled Moss' funny bone. He would have had a better chance against the Grasshopper in his 1914 Curtiss pusher than he did in a Screaming Eagle.

He made it back to the airfield and eased the turbo down to the ground. You had to land gently. The nosewheel was less sturdy than it should have been; sometimes it would break off if you came down on it too hard. The first couple of pilots who'd discovered that would never learn anything else now.

"How'd it go?" a groundcrew man asked as Moss climbed down from the cockpit.

"Nailed a Hound Dog," he answered. The groundcrew techs cheered. Somebody pounded him on the back. He went on, "His buddy dove for the deck and got away—bastard was good. And I made a couple of runs at a Grasshopper, but *ffft!*" He squeezed his thumb and forefinger together, miming a watermelon seed squirting out between them.

"Take an even strain, Colonel," a groundcrew man said. "Those suckers'll drive you bugshit." The others also made sympathetic noises.

"How'd she perform?" another tech asked.

"Everything went fine this time around." Moss banged a fist off the side of his head in lieu of knocking wood. "Engines sounded good, gauges looked good all the way through, guns behaved themselves, nosewheel wasn't naughty." He turned to eye it. There it was, all right, looking as innocent as if its kind never, ever misbehaved. No matter how innocent it looked, he knew better.

Leaving the Screaming Eagle to the men who fed and watered it, he walked over to the headquarters tent to report more formally. His flight suit kept him warm up over thirty thousand feet. Here in the muggy warmth of Georgia spring, he felt as if it were steaming him.

Colonel Roy Wyden ran the turbo squadron. He was a boy wonder, just past thirty, with the ribbons for a Distinguished Service Cross and a Bronze Star among the fruit salad on his chest. When Moss told him he'd knocked down a C.S. fighter, Wyden reached into his desk drawer and pulled out a bottle and two glasses. He poured a couple of knocks of good Tennessee sipping whiskey—spoil of war—and said, "Way to go."

"Thank you, sir." Moss tasted the drink and added, "*Thank* you, sir." Wyden grinned at him—and seemed even younger. Moss went on, "I went after a Grasshopper, too, but he got away a lot easier than the Hound Dog's buddy."

"Those goddamn things. There ought to be a bounty on 'em," Wyden said. "A Screaming Eagle isn't exactly the weapon of choice against them, either."

"Tell me about it!" Moss exclaimed. "He fired at me. I never laid a glove on him. He's back there somewhere laughing his ass off."

"They'll drive you to drink, all right." As if to prove it, Wyden sipped from his own whiskey. He glanced over to Moss. "Does that Hound Dog make you an ace in both wars?"

"No, sir. I made it the first time, but I've only got three this round," Moss said. "I spent too damn long on the shelf in Andersonville and then running around with the black guerrillas."

"You ought to get some credit for that. It's not like you didn't hurt the Confederates while you were doing it."

"The war on the ground's an ugly business." Some of the memories that surfaced in Moss' mind made him finish his drink in a hurry. "*Our* war with the CSA is ugly. The one the Negroes are fighting . . . No quarter on either side there. And what Featherston's fuckers would have done to me for fighting on the Negroes' side—"

"Better not to think about that," Wyden broke in.

"Yeah. I know. Just staying alive took luck. If the Confederates hadn't had all of their regulars fighting the USA, they would've hunted us down pretty damn quick. Jake should've started in on his blacks sooner, or else left them alone till after the war. Trying to get rid of them at the same time as he was fighting us only screwed him up."

"He figured he'd whip us quick and then take care of the smokes." Wyden got outside the last of his drink. "Tough shit, Eliot."

For some reason, Moss thought that was the funniest thing he'd ever heard. He started giggling. Nobody in the guerrilla band, not even Nick Cantarella, would have made that kind of joke. Moss hadn't known how much he missed it till he heard it again.

When George Enos saw land off the *Oregon*'s port bow, he realized how much the war had changed. That was the coast of North Carolina out there. Even six months earlier, coming so close would have been asking to get blown to pieces. Now some of the big wheels back in Philadelphia thought the Navy could get away with it.

George hoped like hell they were right.

Two battleships, two heavy cruisers, two escort carriers to give them air cover, the usual destroyers and supply ships that accompanied a flotilla: now they were paying a call on the Confederate States. The gamble was that the Confederates couldn't pay a return call on them.

"Listen up, guys," said Wally Fodor, the chief in charge of George's antiaircraft guns. "We can put a hell of a lot of shells in the air. No goddamn Asskicker's gonna make a monkey out of us, right?"

"Right!" the gun crew shouted. George didn't know about the other guys, but he was as pumped up as he would have been if he were playing in a big football game. That was for glory and for cash, though. He was playing for his neck here.

Dive bombers roared off the baby flattops' decks. They would send a message to a state that had mostly been shielded from the war ever since it started. U.S. fighters circled overhead. Any Confederate airplanes that tried to visit the flotilla would get a warm reception.

Smoothly, almost silently, the *Oregon*'s forward pair of triple turrets swung so the big guns bore to port. The barrels elevated a few degrees. "Brace yourselves!" Fodor yelled. He covered his ears with his hands and opened his mouth wide to help equalize the pressure inside his head.

In the nick of time, George did the same. The guns thundered, right over his head. He staggered—he couldn't help it. He felt as if somebody'd dropped a boulder on his noggin. In spite of his precautions, his ears wanted to move to a far country where things like this didn't happen. "Wow!" he said.

Shore had to be twenty miles away, maybe more. Some little while went by before the distant roar of bursting fourteen-inch shells came back to George's abused ears. He was amazed he heard them—or anything else.

"Good morning, Morehead City!" Wally Fodor whooped.

George imagined people going about their business, probably not even suspecting anything was wrong, when all of a sudden—*wham!* Fourteen hundred pounds of steel and high explosive coming down on your head could ruin your whole day.

The guns bellowed again. When George reached for his ears this time, it was to see if they were bleeding. They didn't seem to be. He couldn't imagine why not. The other battleship—she was the *Maine*—was firing, too. Those detonations were just loud. Or maybe his ears were so stunned that nothing this side of cataclysmic really registered.

"Well, if they didn't know we were in the neighborhood before, they damn well do now," Tom Thomas said. People mostly called the shell-jerker Ditto; George wondered what the devil his parents were thinking of.

More booms said the latest shells were striking home—or maybe those were bombs from the carriers' airplanes. Smoke began to rise from the shore. The cruisers from the flotilla had to get closer to land than the battlewagons before opening up. Their eight-inch main armament didn't have the range of the bigger ships' heavier guns. Before long, they started firing, too.

"This is so neat!" Ditto said. "Ever think we could get away with shore bombardment?"

"We ain't got away with it yet," Fodor answered. George Enos was thinking the same thing. But he was the new kid on the block, so he kept his mouth shut. The gun chief went on, "When we steam out of aircraft range, then I'll be happy. And even after that there's fuckin' subs."

The main armament fired again. *Fired* was the word, too. The gouts of flame that shot from the muzzles were almost as long as the gun barrels. If God needed to light a cigar, this was where He'd do it.

Up above the bridge, the Y-ranging antenna spun round and round, round and round. It would spot enemy airplanes on the way in, anyway.

How much good that would do . . . Well, knowing the bastards were coming was better than not knowing they were.

Inshore from the *Oregon*, not far from the cruisers, a tall column of water suddenly sprang into being. A moment later, another one appeared, even closer to the U.S. warships.

"What the hell?" somebody said. "Those aren't bombs—we woulda got the word the bombers were loose."

"They must have shore guns," Wally Fodor said. "Soon as we spot the flashes, they're history. And they'll have a bitch of a time hitting us. We can move, but they're stuck where they're at."

A few more rounds fell near the cruisers. Then, as abruptly as they'd begun, they stopped. Either the Confederates had given up or U.S. gunfire put their cannon out of action. George neither knew nor cared what the right answer was. As long as those guns kept quiet, that suited him fine.

Then the PA system came to life with a crackle of static: "Now hear this! Now hear this! Enemy aircraft approaching from the north! Expect company in five or ten minutes!"

George's stomach knotted. *Here we go again*, he thought. He'd had a ship sunk under him; he knew disasters could happen. He didn't want to remember that, but he didn't see how he could help it, either.

"Just like a drill," Chief Fodor said. "They haven't got us yet, and we aren't about to let 'em start. Right?"

"Right!" the gun crew shouted again. George was as loud as anybody. How loud he yelled made no difference in the bigger scheme of things, but it wasn't bad if it helped him feel a little better.

Some of the fighters that had been circling over the ships zipped away to see if they could meet up with the intruders before the C.S. airplanes got the chance to intrude. Others held their stations. If the enemy bombers got past the first wave of fighters, they still wouldn't have a free run at the flotilla.

"You've been through this before, right?" Fodor asked George. "I mean for real, not just for practice."

"Sure, Chief," George answered. "I've got it from the Japs and Featherston's fuckers and the limeys. I don't like it, but I can do it."

"That's all you need," the gun chief said. "I thought I remembered you lost your cherry, but I wanted to make sure."

Airplane engines scribed contrails across the sky. *Their wakes*, George thought. But the comparison with ships misled. It wasn't just that airplanes were so much faster. They also moved in three dimensions, not just two like surface ships.

A destroyer's antiaircraft guns started going off. So did the heavy cruisers'. Then George saw a couple of gull-winged ships that looked only too horribly familiar. "Asskickers!" he yelled, and his wasn't the only cry that rose.

One of the slow, ungainly Confederate dive bombers went down trailing smoke a moment after he shouted. It splashed into the Atlantic a mile or so from the *Oregon*, and kicked up more water than the shells the coastal guns had fired.

The other C.S. Mule bored in on the battleship. The *Oregon* heeled in as tight a turn as she could make, but she was large and cumbersome and much less nimble than, say, the *Josephus Daniels* would have been. That made her action less evasive than George wished it were.

He didn't have much time to worry about it. "Commence firing!" Wally Fodor shouted. The shell-jerkers started passing George ammo. He fed the twin 40mms' breeches like a man possessed. Casings leaped from the guns and clattered on the deck. Bursts—puffs of black smoke—appeared all around the attacking airplane.

But it kept coming. The bomb under its belly dropped. The Asskicker zoomed past, hardly higher than the tops of the battleship's masts. The bomb burst on the ocean, less than fifty yards from the *Oregon*.

Water hit George like a fist in the face. Next thing he knew, he was flat on his back, partly on the deck, partly on Ditto Thomas, who'd stood right behind him. "Get—*glub!*—offa me, goddammit!" Thomas spluttered, spitting out what looked like about half of the ocean.

"Yeah." George scrambled to his feet and gave Ditto a hand to haul him up, too. Ditto rubbed at his eyes. George's also stung from seawater. The other men from the gun crew were picking themselves up. Wally Fodor had a cut on his ear that bloodied the shoulder of his tunic. Could you get a Purple Heart for something like that? George wouldn't lose any sleep over it, and he didn't think Wally would, either.

At that, the number three mount got off lucky. Guys were down at the next 40mm mount, too, only they weren't getting up again. A fragment of bomb casing had taken off one sailor's head like a guillotine blade. Another man was gutted as neatly as a fat cod on a fishing trawler. But cod didn't scream and try to put themselves back together.

And you couldn't gaff a sailor and put him on ice in the hold, though it might have been a mercy.

Stretcher-bearers carried him below. The *Oregon* boasted not one but two real doctors, not just a pharmacist's mate like the *Josephus Daniels*. Could they do anything for a guy with his insides torn out? Doctors were getting smarter all the time, and the fancy new drugs meant fever didn't always kill you. Even so . . .

George didn't get the chance to brood about it. "Come on!" Fodor yelled. Did the CPO even know he was wounded? "Back to the gun! We may get another shot at the sonsabitches!"

Suddenly, though, the sky seemed bare of Confederate aircraft. One limped off toward the north, toward land, trailing smoke as it went. The rest—weren't there any more. A rubber raft bobbed on the surface of the Atlantic: somebody'd got out of one of them, anyhow.

The *Oregon*'s main armament boomed out another thunderous broadside. Half a minute later, the *Maine* also sent a dozen enormous shells landward. The air attack had made them miss a beat, but no more.

"Jesus!" George said, his ears ringing. "Is that the best those sorry suckers can do?"

"Sure looks like it." Chief Fodor sounded surprised, too. He noticed the blood on his shoulder, and did a professional-quality double take. "What the fuck happened here?"

"Maybe a splinter nicked you, or maybe you got hurt when the water knocked you down," George answered.

"I be damned," Fodor said. "I always heard about guys getting hurt without even knowing it, but I figured it was bullshit. Then it goes and happens to me. I be damned."

A U.S. destroyer steamed toward the downed Confederate flier. Somebody on the destroyer's deck threw the man a line. He didn't climb it. After a minute or so, a sailor went down into the raft with him and rigged a sling. The men on deck hauled the Confederate up—he must have been wounded. He was probably lucky not to be strawberry jam. Then they lowered the line to their buddy. Up he swarmed, agile as a monkey.

The big guns on both battlewagons bellowed again. If that was all the Confederates could do to stop them . . . If that was all, the Confederacy really was coming apart at the seams.

* * *

Paperwork. Jefferson Pinkard hated paperwork. He'd never got used to it. He didn't like being a paper-shuffler and a pen-pusher. He could manage it, but he didn't like it. Working in a steel mill for all those years left him with the driving urge to go out there and *do* things, dammit.

To soothe himself, he kept the wireless going. If he listened with half an ear to one of the Houston stations playing music, he didn't have to pay so much attention to all the nitpicking detail Richmond wanted from him. Muttering, he shook his head. No, not Richmond. Richmond was gone, lost, captured. Jake Featherston and what was left of the Confederate government were somewhere down in North Carolina now, still screaming defiance at the damnyankees and at the world.

Camp Humble went right on reducing population. Trains still rolled in from Louisiana and Mississippi and Arkansas and east Texas. Ships brought Negroes from Cuba to the Texas ports. He aimed to go right on doing his job till somebody set over him told him to stop.

Without warning, the song he was listening to broke off. An announcer came on the air: "We interrupt this program for a special proclamation from the Governor of the great state of Texas, the Honorable Wright Patman. Governor Patman!"

"What the—?" Jeff said. Something had hit the fan, that was for damn sure.

"Citizens of Texas!" Governor Patman said. "A hundred years ago, this state was an independent republic, owing allegiance to no nation but itself. We joined first the USA and then the CSA, but we have never forgotten our own proud tradition of . . . freedom." That was the Party slogan, yeah, but he didn't use it the way a good Party man would.

Jeff muttered, "Uh-oh." No, he didn't like the way Patman used it at all.

Sure as the devil, the Governor of Texas went on, "The Confederate government has brought us nothing but ruin and a losing war. The United States have already stolen part of our territory and revived the so-called state of Houston that blighted the map after the last war. They have killed our soldiers, bombed our cities, and ruined our trade. The Confederate government is powerless to stop them or even slow them down."

"Uh-oh," Pinkard said, and then, for good measure, "Aw, shit."

"Since the Confederate government cannot protect us, it is no

longer a fit government for the great people of Texas," Governor Patman said. "Accordingly, by my order, the state of Texas is from this day
forward no longer part of the so-called Confederate States of America.
I hereby restore the Republic of Texas as a free and independent nation,
on an equal footing with the Confederate States, the United States, the
Empire of Mexico, and all the other free and independent nations of
the world.

"As my first act as provisional President of the Republic of Texas,
I have asked the government of the United States for an armistice. They
have recognized my administration—"

"Jesus! I fuckin' bet they have!" Jeff exclaimed. What a mess! And
he was, literally, in the middle of it.

"—and agreed to a cease-fire. All Texas soldiers are ordered to no
longer obey the so-called Confederate authorities. All other Confederate troops within the borders of the Republic of Texas may hold in
place and be disarmed by Texas authorities, or may withdraw to territory still under the rule of the so-called Confederate States. The United
States have agreed that the forces of the Republic of Texas are not
obliged to hinder this retreat, nor will we—so long as it remains peaceful and orderly. U.S. forces reserve the right to attack retreating C.S.
forces, however, and neither will we interfere with them on the ground,
in the air, or at sea.

"At this point in time, that is all. As peace returns at last after the
madness of the Featherston administration, I call on God Almighty to
bless the great Lone Star Republic of Texas. Thank you, and good afternoon."

"That was Governor—uh, excuse me, President—Wright Patman
of the, uh, Republic of Texas." The wireless announcer sounded as
flummoxed as everybody else had to be. He went on, "President Patman has brought peace to Texas, and what could be a more precious
gift?"

"He's bugged out on the war, that's what he's done, the goddamn
traitor son of a bitch!" Jeff Pinkard shouted, as if Patman and the announcer were there to hear him.

He remembered what Mayor Doggett had told him to do if the
damnyankees got close: take his family and get the hell out in a civilian
auto and civilian clothes. The advice looked a lot better now than it had
then. But Raymond was tiny, and Edith still wasn't over birthing him,
and . . .

The telephone rang. If that was Edith, and she'd listened to the wireless . . . "Pinkard here."

It wasn't Edith. It was Vern Green, and *he'd* listened to the wireless. "Fuck a duck!" the guard chief cried. "What the hell are we gonna do, sir? Can we get outa here? The damnyankees'll crucify us if they catch us."

"They're still way the hell over on the other side of the state," Jeff said uneasily.

"All the better reason to get out now, while we still can," Green said. "That asshole Patman, he's surrendering to them, near as makes no difference. There'll be U.S. soldiers all over Texas fast as they can move."

Part of Jeff said Vern Green was flabbling over nothing. There wouldn't be U.S. soldiers *all over* Texas no matter what—the state was too damn big for that. But there might be U.S. soldiers here at Camp Humble in the next day or two. The Yankees wanted this place closed down, and they wanted that bad.

He'd never dreamt he would have to worry about something like this. "Anybody who wants to disappear, I won't say boo," he said slowly. "Do what you think you gotta, that's all. Hell, you may be right."

"Much obliged, sir," Green said, and hung up. Jeff knew what that meant: he planned on bailing out.

How much did what he planned matter? A guard knocked on Jeff's door. When the camp commandant let him in, the man said, "Sir, there's a Texas Ranger captain named Hezekiah Carroll out there, and he wants to see you."

Pinkard didn't want to see the biblically named Texas Ranger. What choice did he have, though? "All right," he growled. "Bring him on in."

Carroll was tall and weathered and tough-looking. But if he was as tough as he looked, why wasn't he in the Army? Before Jeff could ask him, he said, "You will have heard of the reestablishment of the Republic of Texas?"

"Yeah, I've heard of it. Getting out while the getting's good, are you?" Jeff said.

"Yes," Carroll answered baldly. "You will also have heard that Confederate troops may evacuate?"

"I heard that, too, all right," Jeff allowed. "What about it?"

"It doesn't mean you. That's part of the deal Governor—uh, President—Patman cut with the Yankees," Carroll said. "They say Confederate combat soldiers are welcome to leave. But you people—they want y'all. Crimes against humanity, they call it."

"Oh, my ass!" Pinkard exploded. "You gonna tell me you're sorry we're taking care of our nigger troubles? Yeah, sure—go ahead. Make me believe it."

Captain Carroll turned red. All the same, he said, "What I think hasn't got diddly-squat to do with it. I know damn well this is the best deal Texas can get. If you and your people try to evacuate this camp, we will stop you, and that's the God's truth."

"Christ! I never thought my own side would fuck me!" Jeff tried to figure out what to do. With all the machine guns in the guard towers, he could hold off the Rangers, or anybody else who didn't have artillery, for a long time. But what good did that do him when he needed to get the hell out of here?

None. Zero. Zip.

Maybe he could mount machine guns in some of the camp trucks and shoot his way past the Rangers. Yeah, it might work once, but it was more than a hundred miles from Humble to the Louisiana border. Could he win a running fight? Not a chance in church, and he knew it.

"I am a citizen of the Republic of Texas, and my country has an armistice with the USA," Carroll said. "I have to abide by the terms of the armistice, and I will. I'm only following orders, same as you were doing here. But the country that gave you orders is going down the crapper, and mine's just getting started."

Only following orders. That was the main defense Pinkard had if he ever did get in trouble for what the camps did. It sounded pretty goddamn hollow when somebody else threw it in his face.

"Listen—let's do it like this." He wasn't used to pleading; he hadn't had to do it for a lot of years. He gave it his best shot, though: "We can keep it unofficial. Let us slide on out of here a few at a time—how's that? Then nobody'll be any wiser when we're gone, nobody'll get in any trouble, and we can get back to doing what needs doing once we're somewhere that's still fighting." He didn't even cuss out Wright Patman, no matter how much he wanted to.

But Hezekiah Carroll shook his head. "Sorry about that—I *am* sorry about that. I would if I could, but I can't, so I won't. I don't reckon you understand how bad the damnyankees want you. They told the—the President they would bomb the living shit out of Austin if you got away."

"They're a bunch of nigger-lovers, that's why! And you're throwing in with 'em!" Jeff couldn't keep his temper down forever.

"What we are is out of the war. You think we want the damnyankees dropping one of those superbombs on Dallas? You think we want 'em to drop one on Houston or Austin or San Antone? You better think again, buddy."

"But— But— Christ on His cross, you're cutting the CSA off from Sonora and Chihuahua. You can't do that!"

"No, huh? Just watch us," Captain Carroll said. "White folks don't need all those greasers around anyway. If Francisco José wants 'em back, he's welcome to 'em, far as I'm concerned."

Realization smote Pinkard. "If we were smokin' *their* sorry asses, I bet you'd let us go!" he said.

Carroll neither affirmed nor denied. He just said, "Things are the way they are. And so you know, the Yankees are flying in a team to take charge of this place. They ought to be landing in Houston pretty soon. Won't be more than a couple of hours before they're here. Whatever you've got to say from now on, you can say to them." He left the office without a salute, without a nod, without a backwards glance.

Vern Green burst in a moment later. "What are we gonna do?" he cried.

Jeff told him what the Texas Ranger had said. "If you and the guards still want to try and skip, I still won't say boo," he finished. "Maybe you'll get away, maybe you'll get your ass shot off. I don't know one way or the other. With Edith and the kids here, I'm fuckin' stuck."

"Damnyankees'll hang you," Green warned.

"How can they? I was doing what Ferd Koenig told me to do," Jeff said. "Could I say, 'No, we got to treat the niggers better'? He'd shoot me if I did. 'Sides, the job needed doing. You know it as well as I do."

"Sure. But the Yankees won't." Green sketched a salute. "I am gonna try and get away. Wish me luck."

"Luck," Jeff said. Not much later, he heard spatters of gunfire in the near distance. He had a couple of drinks at his desk.

Two and a half hours after that, a man in a green-gray uniform with gold oak leaves on his shoulder straps walked in. "You're Brigade Leader Pinkard?" he asked in U.S. accents.

"That's right," Jeff said, a little surprised the Yankee officer got the Party title right.

"Major Don Little, U.S. Army," the other officer said, and then, "You're under arrest."

Artillery fire came down near Armstrong Grimes' platoon—not *real* close, but close enough to make them pucker some. Through the man-made thunder, Squidface said, "How come we ain't in Texas?"

"How come you ain't a beautiful woman?" Armstrong answered. "How come you ain't even an ugly woman, for cryin' out loud? If you didn't know how to handle a gun, you'd be fuckin' useless."

"Ah, you've been talkin' to my old man again," Squidface said in mock disgust.

He remained stubbornly male. And central Alabama, where the war was very much alive, remained nothing like the state—or even the Republic—of Texas, where it had died. Instead, soldiers on both sides were doing the dying here. The Confederates didn't have enough to keep the United States away from Selma and Montgomery, but they didn't seem to know it yet.

Armstrong didn't mind showing them. He did mind getting killed or maimed on a bright spring day when the air smelled green and the birds sang and the bastards in butternut couldn't possibly win even if they wiped out every U.S. soldier south of Birmingham. Why couldn't they see the shit had hit the fan and just give up? That would have suited him fine.

But the Confederates down here were a stubborn bunch. They didn't just fight back—they kept throwing in local counterattacks. A little farther east, one of those had driven U.S. forces back ten or fifteen miles before it finally ran out of steam. By now, the enemy had lost all that ground again, and more besides. He'd thrown away men and barrels he couldn't possibly hope to replace. What the hell was the point? Armstrong couldn't see it.

Some of the shells from his latest barrage sounded funny. So did the bursts they made when they hit the ground. "Oh, for Chrissake!" Armstrong said, almost as disgusted with the men he was facing as he had been when he fought the Mormons. He raised his voice: "Gas!" he yelled. "They're throwing gas at us!" Why were they bothering? What was it supposed to prove?

He put on his mask. It was annoying. It was inconvenient. If they wanted to attack here, they'd have to wear masks, too, and be annoyed and inconvenienced. And his own side's gunners would probably give them a big, lethal dose as soon as they found out this crap was going on. *Serve 'em right*, Armstrong thought, sucking in air that smelled like rubber instead of spring.

Off to the left, somebody—he thought it was Herk, but how could you be sure when a guy was talking through a mask?—shouted, "Here they come!"

Armstrong peered in that direction through porthole lenses that needed cleaning. Sure as hell, the Confederates *were* pushing forward, their foot soldiers backed up by a couple of assault guns and one of their fearsome new barrels. Somebody must have fed their CO raw meat.

A U.S. machine gun started chattering. The masked soldiers in butternut dove for cover. The barrel's massive turret swung toward the machine-gun nest. The main armament fired once. Sandbags and somebody's leg flew through the air. The machine gun fell silent.

That did the Confederates less good than it would have earlier in the war. Armstrong had a captured automatic rifle. Squidface had his own gun. Herk was banging away with a C.S. submachine gun. Plenty of other captured weapons and U.S.-issue Tommy guns gave the guys on Armstrong's side a lot more firepower than they would have had even a year earlier.

Mortar rounds started landing among the unhappy C.S. soldiers, too. Armstrong whooped. "See how you like it, you bastards!" he shouted. "It's better to give than to receive!" Then a U.S. barrel put an AP round through an assault gun's glacis plate. The assault gun slewed sideways, sending greasy black smoke high into the sky. He whooped again. That pillar of smoke marked four men's funeral pyres. They weren't his buddies, so he didn't care.

A moment later, the other assault gun hit a mine and stopped with a track blown off. That was the signal for every U.S. barrel in the neighborhood to open up on it. It didn't last long—what could have? Recognizing the minefield, the enemy barrel's crew also stopped. A couple of rounds hit it, but bounced off. Armstrong stopped whooping and swore. AP rounds *could* penetrate those monsters—he'd seen it happen. But it didn't happen all the time.

And the metal monster started picking off U.S. barrels, one after another. Its big gun could penetrate any U.S. machine's frontal armor with no trouble at all. Still swearing, Armstrong wished for a stovepipe rocket like the ones Jake Featherston's men carried. If any of those had been captured, they didn't seem to be in the neighborhood. Too bad.

How come the Confederates get all the good stuff first? he wondered. They did, damn them. They'd carried automatic weapons against Springfields. They had the screaming meemies and the stovepipe anti-barrel rockets and the long-range jobs. They even used the superbomb first.

And a whole fat lot of good it did them, because there weren't quite enough of them anyway, not if they wanted to conquer a country that could put three times as many soldiers in the field. He supposed Featherston's fuckers got the fancy weapons because they really needed them. The USA muddled along with ordinary stuff, and eventually got the job done.

The local Confederate attack bogged down when the big, nasty barrel stopped going forward. The C.S. infantry knew they couldn't push their foes out of the way without armor support. They went to ground and dug in. Artillery and mortar rounds rained down on them. Dig as they would, their holes weren't so good as the ones they would have had in prepared defensive positions.

Two fighter-bombers zoomed in and ripple-fired rockets from underwing racks. One of those, or maybe more than one, hit the C.S. barrel. The rocket got through the armor where the AP rounds hadn't. The barrel started to burn. Somebody bailed out of the turret. Every U.S. soldier around fired at the barrelman, but Armstrong thought he made it to cover. *Too bad*, he thought.

Whistles blew. Somebody who sounded like an officer yelled, "Let's push 'em back, boys! With their armor gone, they won't even slow us down." Then he said the magic words: "Follow me!"

If he was willing to put his ass on the line, he could get soldiers to go with him. "Come on!" Armstrong called, scrambling out of his own scrape in the ground. "Let's go get 'em! We can do it!"

And damned if they couldn't. Oh, some of the Confederates fought. There were always diehards who wouldn't quit till the last dog was hung. But there weren't very many, not this time around. Some of the men in butternut drew back toward their own start line. Others raised their hands as U.S. soldiers drew near.

"Don't shoot me! Sweet Jesus, buddy, I don't want to die!" an unshaven corporal called to Armstrong. Another Confederate soldier near him also held his hands high.

"Waddaya think?" Armstrong asked Squidface.

"We can take 'em down the road," Squidface answered.

"'Bout what I figured," Armstrong agreed. He raised his voice: "Herk! Take these guys down the road."

"You sure, Sarge?" Herk asked.

"Yeah—go on. Go deal with 'em," Armstrong said.

"Right." Herk gestured with his captured weapon. "Come on, you two." The Confederate soldiers eagerly went with him. After he led them around behind some trees, the submachine gun stuttered out two short bursts. He came back. "It's taken care of," he said.

"Attaboy. C'mon. Let's go," Armstrong told him. If you told one of your men to take somebody back, you really meant to make a prisoner of him. If you told your guy to take him down the road . . . Well, it was a hard old war. Sometimes you didn't have the manpower or the time to deal with POWs. And so—you didn't, that was all.

Somebody up in the middle of the fighting was on the horn to U.S. artillery. The USA didn't have screaming meemies, but battery after battery of 105s did a hell of a job. The barrage moved in front of the advancing soldiers, and fell with terrible power on the line from which the Confederates had jumped off. They couldn't hold that line, not with the men they had left after the counterattack failed. They would have done better not to try to hit back at the U.S. forces.

Sunset found Armstrong and his men several miles farther south than they had been at daybreak. He camped in an empty sharecropper village. He'd seen a lot of those here. This was supposed to be the Black Belt, the heart of Alabama Negro life. But the heart had been ripped out of the state.

Or so he thought, till a sentry said, "Sarge, we got niggers comin' in—maybe half a dozen."

"Fuck me," Armstrong said. That didn't happen every day. "Well, go on, Snake—bring 'em in. We can spare the rations for 'em."

"Right," Snake said—he had a rearing rattler tattooed on his left forearm. He came back a few minutes later with two skinny black men, an even skinnier woman, and three kids who were nothing but skin and bones . . . and, in the firelight, eyeballs and teeth.

The soldiers gave them food, which got their immediate undivided attention. After the Negroes had eaten enough to blunt the edge of their hunger, Armstrong asked, "How'd you people stay alive?"

"We hid. We stole," one of the men answered. His accent was so thick, Armstrong could hardly follow him.

"Now we is free again," the woman said. "Now we kin live again."

"Long as they's sojers here. Long as they's Yankees here," the second man said. "Reckon the white folks here'd get rid of us pretty damn quick if they seen a chance."

Armstrong reckoned the Negro was right. Not many white Confederates seemed unhappy about what had happened to the blacks who'd lived alongside them. The only thing the whites were unhappy about was losing the war.

"What is we gonna do?" the first man asked, as if a kid sergeant from Washington, D.C., had answers for him.

"Hang around with soldiers as much as you can. We won't screw you," Armstrong said, although he knew some of the guys in the platoon liked Negroes no better than most Confederates did. And some of the guys *would* want to screw the woman. Yeah, she was skinny as a strand of spaghetti. Yeah, she was homely. Yeah, she might have VD. If she stayed around very long, somebody would make a pass at her. And trouble would follow, sure as night followed day.

They can hang around with soldiers, Armstrong decided, *but they won't hang around with my platoon. I'll send 'em to the rear, let somebody else worry about 'em.* He nodded to himself. That definitely sounded like a plan.

And when he put it to the Negroes, they didn't squawk a bit. "Rear sounds mighty good," the first man said. "We done seen us enough fightin' to las' us fo' always." All the other blacks solemnly nodded.

Come to that, Armstrong had seen enough fighting to last him for always, too. *Maybe*, he thought hopefully, *I won't have to see much more.*

There was a poem about the way the world ended. Jorge Rodriguez hadn't had as much schooling as his folks wished he would have. When you grew up on a farm in Sonora, you didn't get a whole lot of school-ing. But he remembered that poem—something about not with a bang but a whimper.

He knew why it came to mind now, too. He was thinking that the fellow who'd written that poem didn't know what the hell he was talk-ing about.

Buckingham, Virginia, wasn't a whole lot more than a wide spot in the road. It didn't even have a gas station, though it did boast a couple of hotels that dated back to before the War of Secession. It lay west and a little south of Richmond, and Jorge's outfit had orders to hold it in spite of everything the damnyankees could do.

The indomitable Hugo Blackledge had charge of the company—all the new officers were either casualties or missing in action. Jorge led one platoon, Gabe Medwick another. Blackledge looked around at Buckingham. "We'll dig in," he said. "We'll fight as long as we can, and then we'll pull back and fight somewhere else. This chickenshit hole in the ground ain't worth dyin' for, and that's the God's truth."

"That's not what the high command told us." Medwick sounded worried.

"They ain't gonna kill us for moving back after we fight," Jorge as-sured him. "They're too fucked up for that. But I think the sergeant, he's right. We make a big stand here, the damnyankees blow us up for sure." His wave encompassed the country town. "And for what, *amigo*? For what?"

Gabe had no answer for that. Nobody who'd done any fighting would have. Buckingham would have fallen a while ago if the main Yankee thrust from Richmond hadn't gone southeast, through Peters-burg toward Hampton Roads. But the United States had enough men to push west, too . . . and the Confederacy, by all the signs, didn't have enough men to stop them.

Still, if you weren't going to surrender you had to try. Somebody's rear-guard action up ahead gave the company a couple of hours to en-trench and to eat whatever rations and foraged food they happened to have on them. A command car towing an antiaircraft gun came through town. Sergeant Blackledge flagged it down. "Got any armor-piercing rounds?" he asked.

"A few," one of the gunners answered.

"Good," Blackledge said. "Stay here. You'll have a better chance to use 'em than you would have wherever the hell you were going." He didn't quite aim his automatic rifle at the command car, but he looked ready to. Jorge was one of the men who stood ready to back his play.

The gunner didn't need long to figure out what was what. "You talked us into it," he said after a barely perceptible pause. "Show us where to set up."

He and his crew had just positioned the gun when U.S. 105s started landing on Buckingham. The first few fell short, but the rest came down right in the middle of town. Huddling in a foxhole, Jorge knew what that meant: the Yankees had a forward artillery observer hidden in the trees somewhere, and he was wirelessing the fall of the shot back to the batteries that were firing. Killing him would have been nice, but who could guess where he lurked?

Fighter-bombers worked Buckingham over next. They dropped bombs. They fired rockets. And they dropped fish-shaped pods of jellied gasoline, as if the town were under attack by flamethrowers from the sky. Some burned men screamed. Some, Jorge feared, never got the chance. One of the fine hotels from before the days of the War of Secession went up in flames. It had lasted for a century, but no longer.

After the damnyankees softened up the town, infantry and armor came forward. Why do things the hard way when you could take it easy? That was what the U.S. officer in charge must have thought, anyhow.

But nothing turned out to be easy for the men in green-gray. That antiaircraft gun knocked out two barrels in quick succession. The others pulled back in a hurry. Machine-gun and automatic-weapons fire sent U.S. foot soldiers diving for cover. The Confederates in Buckingham raised a defiant cheer.

If they'd had barrels of their own, if they'd had air support, if they'd had more ground-pounders, they could have driven the enemy back toward the James. If they'd had all those things here, they also would have had them lots of other places. The war would have looked very different.

Since they didn't have any reinforcements, they had to wait for the U.S. forces to regroup and take another crack at Buckingham. "Pull back into the woods south of town!" Sergeant Blackledge called. "We'll let them beat on the place while it's empty, then move back into our old holes and give 'em a surprise."

Smoke from the burning buildings in Buckingham helped screen the withdrawal from Yankee observers. And Blackledge knew just what was coming. More shells, more bombs, more rockets, and more napalm descended on Buckingham. Jorge crossed himself. He was glad to crouch half a mile away from all that destruction.

As soon as the last fighter-bombers roared off to the north, Sergeant Blackledge yelled, "C'mon! Hustle up! We gotta get back to our places before the enemy infantry starts moving up!"

Trotting forward, Jorge saw that the antiaircraft gun wouldn't stop any barrels this time around. It lay upside down, the tires on the gun carriage all burnt and melted and stinking. How many stovepipes did the company have? He swore under his breath. The cannon could kill from much farther away than one of those rockets.

At least no jellied gasoline smoldered in his foxhole. He slid down into it and waited for the push that was bound to come. He felt more resigned than afraid. He wondered why. Probably because he'd been in lots of other bad spots. What was one more? *My grave, it could be.*

Not far away, Gabe Medwick was praying. His version of the Lord's Prayer had words a little different from Jorge's. *Protestant*, the Sonoran thought condescendingly. But both versions meant the same thing, so how much did the words really matter?

"Hang in there, boys," Hugo Blackledge said. "We been screwin' so long with a limber dick, why the fuck *can't* we row the damn boat with a rope?" In spite of himself, Jorge laughed. Sometimes obscenity wasn't so far from prayer.

Here came the damnyankees again. They were more cautious this time—they didn't want another bloody nose. The Confederates in Buckingham held their fire till the enemy soldiers and fighting vehicles got very close. Then they all opened up at once. Howls of dismay from the U.S. soldiers said they'd hoped it would be easy this time. No matter what they hoped, it wasn't.

A lancehead riding a shaft of fire, a stovepipe rocket incinerated a green-gray barrel. But other U.S. machines sensibly stayed out of stovepipe range. They raked Buckingham with high-explosive rounds and machine-gun bullets. That let Yankee infantry grab a toehold on the north side of town—not enough Confederates could put their heads up to stop the enemy.

And the Yankees pushed forward to either side of Buckingham, too. There weren't enough men in butternut to hold them back. "Hey, Sarge!" Jorge called urgently. "We done what we could do here, *sí*?"

"Bet your ass." Blackledge raised his voice to a formidable roar:

"Back! Back, goddammit! We'll make another stand at the next town south, wherever the fuck it is!"

Disengaging under fire wasn't easy, either. A less experienced outfit might not have been able to bring it off so neatly. But Jorge had plenty of practice making a getaway from overwhelming U.S. strength. So did his buddies. They left the wounded behind for the Yankees to take care of. That gave the hurt soldiers a better chance than they would have had if they got dragged along. The men in green-gray mostly fought fair.

The ground rose south of Buckingham. No roads led south, only tracks and game trails. The soldiers trudged past a couple of farms carved out of the forest. A woman in homespun stared at them from a cornfield. Was that a pipe in her mouth? Damned if it wasn't. Jorge hoped the Yankees wouldn't shell her farm trying to kill the retreating C.S. soldiers.

On he went. Armor wouldn't have an easy time coming after him, anyhow. Artillery started probing for the Confederates. Suddenly, Jorge hated the trees. Air bursts were deadly, and the only thing you could do to protect yourself was dig in with a roof over your head. Any hanging branch might touch off a shell and rain fragments down on you.

A hundred yards away from him, Gabe Medwick fell with a wail, clutching his arm. "No!" Jorge yelled, and rushed over to his friend. When he got there, he saw Gabe had a leg wound, too. With the best will in the world, the kid from Alabama couldn't go on.

"Hurts," Gabe got out through clenched teeth.

"I bet it does." Jorge clumsily injected him with morphine, then bandaged the wounds. The leg wasn't too bad. The arm . . . Jorge hoped Gabe would keep it, but it looked pretty chewed up. "The Yankees, they take care of you," Jorge said, feeling helpless.

"Don't want nothin' to do with no damnyankees." Gabe sounded like a petulant child.

"Here." Jorge gave him his canteen and some rations. "You sit tight and yell for them when they get close. *Buena suerte, amigo.*" He hurried away, not knowing what else to say.

Before long, Jorge got to pick up a canteen from a man an air burst had shredded. There were worse things than getting wounded. The flies were just starting to gather on one of those things.

Jorge stumbled up to the top of the line of hills and then down the other side. The company, what was left of it, was hopelessly scattered.

Through a break in the trees, Jorge caught a glimpse of a town down below. "That place is where we're going!" Hugo Blackledge yelled. "We'll form up there and figure out what the hell to do next."

What *could* they do? Jorge had no idea. But he had a target now, somewhere to go. As he picked his way through thicker stands of timber, the town disappeared, but he could always find it again. It looked bigger than Buckingham, not that that was saying much.

When he drew closer, he got a glimpse of armor in the town. He'd wondered when he would see more of it. Hell, he'd wondered if the Confederates had any armor left in central Virginia. There were already soldiers in the streets, too. Maybe the CSA could throw one more rally together. Even after you thought your side had done everything it could, it kept surprising you.

The first few men from the company, Jorge among them, had come out onto open ground within a quarter of a mile of the town when Sergeant Blackledge let out a theatrical wail of despair: "They're Yankees!"

And they were. They even had some sort of portable PA system. "Surrender!" somebody blared. "Surrender or die! First, last, and only warning! There is no escape!"

There wasn't, either. The barrels and the automatic weapons ahead could tear the dismayed Confederates to pieces. They'd lost their last race with the enemy. Blackledge set down his automatic rifle and walked into captivity with his hands and his head high.

If he can do it, so can I, Jorge thought. He laid his weapon on the ground and walked toward the waiting U.S. soldiers. One of them pointed into the town. "Line up by the courthouse," he said, not unkindly. "Some trucks'll take you off to prison camp."

"All right." Jorge pointed back the way he'd come. "We left wounded in the woods. My buddy's there."

"We'll get 'em—don't flabble about it. You move along now."

Dully, Jorge obeyed. The men with whom he'd endured so much tramped through the late-afternoon stillness in the little town of Appomattox—a sign on the courthouse gave him the name of the place—toward the end of the war.

Things were quiet outside of Birmingham, and inside, too. Cincinnatus Driver approved of that. After all the shells that had flown back and forth, a truce was holding now. A U.S. officer had gone into Birmingham to confer with C.S. General Patton.

None of the drivers, of course, knew what the U.S. officer would tell the surrounded general. That didn't stop them from guessing. "If he don't quit, I bet we drop a superbomb on him," Cincinnatus said.

"Sounds good to me," Hal Williamson said. Several other men nodded. Williamson went on, "All the trouble Patton's caused, we ought to drop a bomb on the fucker anyway."

More nods, Cincinnatus' among them. "I wonder when he'll come out," the Negro said. The officer, a major, had gone in not far from their encampment. If he came out the same way, maybe he would tell them what was what. You could hope so, anyway.

"How long d'you think he'll give Patton?" somebody asked.

"I wouldn't give him long," Williamson said. "If it's surrender or get one of those bombs in the kisser, what does he need to figure out?"

Cincinnatus lit a cigarette. Not even tobacco smoke soothed him much. He wanted to know what was going on there inside the battered heart of the Confederate industrial town.

So did the other drivers. "That Patton's a stubborn bastard," one of them said. "What if he doesn't give in?"

"His funeral, in that case," Cincinnatus said, and then, "Couldn't happen to a nicer fella. . . . Well, it could happen to Jake Featherston, but I reckon that's comin', too."

Williamson pointed into the ruin that was Birmingham. "Here comes our guy," he said. "And look! He's got one of those butternut bastards with him."

Sure enough, two men came out of the city, each of them carrying a large flag of truce. The C.S. officer looked clean and neat despite the disaster that had befallen the place he was defending. He also looked as unhappy as if he were burying his only son. That told Cincinnatus most of what he needed to know.

"They givin' up, suh?" he called to the U.S. officer, the rising lilt in his voice saying he already had a good notion of the answer.

All the drivers burst into cheers when the major nodded. "They sure are," he answered, "or it looks that way, anyhow. We've still got a few little things to iron out—that's why Captain Monroe is with me."

The Confederate started to give the men standing near the big green-gray trucks a polite nod. Then he saw Cincinnatus among them. "You have those damned black terrorists here?" he demanded of the officer in green-gray.

"I ain't a guerrilla." Cincinnatus spoke for himself. "I don't blame those folks for risin' up—don't get me wrong—but I ain't one of them. I'm a citizen of the USA, and proud of it, too."

"That's telling him!" Hal Williamson said.

Captain Monroe looked even more mournful than he had before. The U.S. major, whose name Cincinnatus still didn't know, grinned from ear to ear. "You asked, Captain," he said. "Now you know."

"It's still wrong," Monroe said stubbornly. "Niggers got no business fighting."

"You call me nigger again, you ofay asshole, you ain't gonna last to dicker your goddamn surrender," Cincinnatus said. Captain Monroe's jaw dropped all the way to his chest. He couldn't have been more astonished if an Army mule had cussed him out.

"Somebody doesn't seem to agree with you," the U.S. major observed. "And since he's here, maybe he's got a point, you know?"

Monroe shook his head. Cincinnatus hadn't expected anything different. Speaking of Army mules . . . When it came to the Confederates' views of Negroes, they could have given the beasts mulishness lessons.

As the two officers went back to confer with U.S. higher-ups, Hal Williamson thumped Cincinnatus on the back. "That butternut bastard can't make nasty cracks about you!"

"He better not," Cincinnatus said. "The guys who can talk are the guys who end up winnin'. You lose, you got to listen to the fellas on the other side doin' the braggin'."

"That's us!" Two drivers said it at the same time. Cincinnatus nodded.

After that, with the ceasefire holding, the drivers had nothing to do but sit around and smoke and eat and play cards. Cincinnatus didn't mind, not even a little. Nothing could go wrong while he was in the middle of a big U.S. army. Nobody was likely to shoot at him from ambush. His truck wouldn't hit a mine and explode in flames. And they gave him the same combat bonus for this as they did for driving through bushwhacker country.

Three hours later, the U.S. major and C.S. Captain Monroe returned, both of them with their white flags. The officer in green-gray was all smiles, while Monroe, his shoulders slumped, his head bowed, showed nothing but gloom.

"It's all over," the U.S. major said. "They'll come out. One more nail in the coffin, and a big one, too."

"Did you have to say that?" Monroe barked.

"I'm sorry, Captain, but will you tell me it's not the truth?" the major asked. The Confederate officer didn't answer, which in itself told everything that needed telling. The major nodded to the group of truck drivers. "We gave them one thing: Patton gets to address his men after they lay down their arms."

"Why not?" Cincinnatus said. "Talk is cheap." His pals laughed. The U.S. major didn't, but mostly, Cincinnatus judged, to keep from offending his C.S. counterpart. As for Captain Monroe, his glare said Cincinnatus belonged in a camp even if he was a U.S. citizen. Cincinnatus scowled back, remembering how close he'd come to ending up in one. How many other Negroes from Covington's barbed-wire-enclosed colored district were still alive? Any? He just didn't know.

The two officers went back into Birmingham. Cincinnatus listened to shouts, some of them amplified, inside the city. *Spreading the word*, he judged. After another hour or so, Confederate soldiers started coming out. They weren't carrying weapons, and they held their hands above their heads. A few had bits of white rag tied to sticks. They were skinny, and their uniforms had seen a lot of wear, but, like Captain Monroe, they all looked surprisingly well bathed and well groomed. Patton was supposed to be a stickler for stuff like that.

They weren't shy about scrounging ration tins from anybody in green-gray they saw. "Thanks, pal," one of them said when Cincinnatus tossed him a can. Then the man did a double take at his dark skin. He looked at the can. "Yeah, thanks," he repeated, and went on.

"Wow," Hal Williamson said. "This place made half the shit they threw at us, seems like. And now it's out of business." He mimed swiping the back of his hand over his forehead in relief.

"So where do we drop the superbomb we were gonna put here?" another driver asked.

"New Orleans. Gotta be New Orleans." The answer came to Cincinnatus as soon as he heard the question. "Satchmo won't like it, but too bad for him."

"No offense, Cincinnatus, but I don't much care for the music he plays," Hal said.

Cincinnatus shrugged. "Well, I can see that, 'cause it ain't what you're used to. Me, I grew up in the CSA, so it sounds right to me. And he's damn good at what he does, whether you like it or not."

"So is Jake Featherston," Williamson said, which was true but not exactly a compliment. Cincinnatus thought about rising to it and arguing for real, but why? When a whole Confederate army was surrendering, what point to a dumb little quarrel?

More and more soldiers in butternut and Freedom Party Guards in camouflage uniforms trudged out of Birmingham. The Party guards looked even sorrier about giving up than the Army men did. Had they seen any chance to fight on, they would have grabbed it. But they didn't—even they knew the jig was up.

Hall nudged Cincinnatus. "Look! That's Patton! That has to be Patton."

"Sure does," Cincinnatus said. Nobody else would have worn a chromed helmet with wreathed stars picked out in gold. Nobody else would have worn not one but two fancy six-shooters, either. Patton's look of loathing made everything from the other soldiers and the Freedom Party Guards seem downright benign by comparison.

Patton already had U.S. soldiers walking along watching him as if he were a lion in a zoo—a dangerous beast that couldn't hurt anybody any more. Cincinnatus and the rest of the drivers fell in with them.

The Confederate soldiers—now the Confederate POWs—stood in rough ranks in a battered, cratered field. U.S. troops, many armed with captured automatic weapons, guarded them. More U.S. soldiers rubbernecked like Cincinnatus. Engineers had set up a microphone in front of the prisoners. The U.S. commander was a long-faced, bald brigadier general named Ironhewer; he waited by the mike for Patton's approach.

Patton saluted him with immense dignity. General Ironhewer returned the military courtesy. Patton took off his pistols and handed them, still holstered, to Ironhewer. This time, the U.S. general saluted him first. He gave the ceremonial weapons to an aide, then went up to the microphone.

"Men of the Army of Kentucky," he said in Midwestern accents, "General Patton has asked leave to speak to you one last time. As this battle ends, as peace between our two countries draws near, I did not see how I could refuse him this privilege." He nodded to the C.S. commander. "General Patton."

Ironhewer stepped away from the microphone and Patton took his place. "Thank you, General, for the courtesy you have shown me and the kindness you are showing my men," he said, his voice thick with unshed tears. He needed a moment to gather himself before continuing. "Soldiers, by an agreement between General Ironhewer and me, the troops of the Army of Kentucky have surrendered. That we are beaten is a self-evident fact, and we cannot hope to resist the bomb that hangs over our head like the sword of Damocles. Richmond is fallen. The cause for which you have so long and manfully struggled, and for which you have braved dangers and made so many sacrifices, is today hopeless.

"Reason dictates and humanity demands that no more blood be shed here. It is your sad duty, and mine, to lay down our arms and to aid in restoring peace. As your commander, I sincerely hope that every officer and soldier will carry out in good faith all the terms of the surrender.

"War such as you have passed through naturally engenders feelings of animosity, hatred, and revenge. But in captivity and when you return home a manly, straightforward course of conduct will secure the respect even of your enemies." Patton paused. He brushed a hand to his eyes, then went on. "In bidding you farewell, rest assured that you carry with you my best wishes for your future welfare and happiness. I have never sent you where I was unwilling to go myself, nor would I now advise you to a course I felt myself unwilling to pursue. You have been good soldiers. Preserve your honor, and the government to which you have surrendered can afford to be and, I hope, will be magnanimous."

Still very erect, he saluted his men. Some of them cried out his name. Others let loose with what they still called the Rebel yell. Tears now streaming down his face, Patton waited for the tumult to die down a little. Then he stepped into the ragged ranks of the rest of the POWs.

Defeated Confederate soldiers shook his hand and embraced him. Cincinnatus watched them with a little sympathy—but not much. "We done licked 'em here," he said to Hal Williamson. "Now we got to finish it everywhere else."

XII

Did taking your own airplanes with you mean a flotilla could operate close to enemy-held land? It hadn't at the start of the war, as Sam Carsten remembered too well. Land-based C.S. airplanes badly damaged the *Remembrance* when her bombers struck at Charleston.

Well, all kinds of things had changed since then. Charleston was no more—one bomb from a (land-based) airplane had seen to that. And the fleet approaching Haiti had not one airplane carrier but half a dozen. Only one of those was a fleet carrier, newer and faster and able to carry more airplanes than the *Remembrance* had. The others were smaller, and three of them slower. Still, together they carried close to three hundred airplanes. If that thought wasn't enough to give the Confederate defenders on the western part of the island of Hispaniola nightmares, Sam didn't know what would be.

He had a few nightmares of his own. The Confederates still had airplanes on Haiti, in the Bahamas, and in Cuba. They had submersibles and torpedo boats. They had a sizable garrison to hold Haiti down and to keep the USA from using the Negro nation as a base against them in the Caribbean. They had . . .

"Sir, they have troubles, lots of them," Lon Menefee said when Sam flabbled out loud. "All those colored folks on these islands hate Jake Featherston like rat poison. Why, Cuba—"

"I know about Cuba," Sam broke in. "The *Josephus Daniels* ran guns in there a couple of years ago, to give the rebels a hand."

"Well, there you go, then." The new exec damn near dripped confidence. "Besides, they may have airplanes, but have they got fuel? We've been pounding their dumps and hitting the shipping from the mainland. We can do this. I honest to God think we can, sir."

"Hey, here's hoping you're right," Carsten said. It wasn't just that Menefee was a kid, because he was plenty old enough to have served through the whole war. But he wasn't the Old Man. The *Josephus Daniels* was Sam's responsibility. If anything went wrong, the blame landed squarely on him. Command made you the loneliest, most worried man in the world—or at least on your ship. The poor son of a bitch in charge of the destroyer half a mile away knew what you were going through, though. So did the sub skipper who was trying to send you to the bottom.

Bombers and covering fighters roared off the carriers' flight decks. Squadron after squadron buzzed off toward the southwest, toward Cap-Haïtien and Port-au-Prince. More fighters flew combat air patrol above the fleet.

Battleships' guns roared. The battlewagons didn't rule the fleet the way they had when Sam enlisted back before the Great War started. But their big guns still reached far enough and packed enough punch to make them great for shore bombardment.

Sam's gaze went forward, to one of the *Josephus Daniels'* pair of four-inch guns. His smile was fond but wry. That gun could shoot at enemy aircraft from longer range than the twin 40mms that had sprouted like mushrooms everywhere there was free space on the deck. For shore bombardment . . . Well, you'd better be hitting some place where the bad guys couldn't hit back.

Slow, squat, ungainly landing craft surged forward. The troops on them were going to take Haiti away from the Confederate States. If everything went right they were, anyhow. If the operation went south, every skipper in the fleet and every brass hat up to and including the Secretary of the Navy would testify under oath before the Joint Committee on the Conduct of the War.

"Anything?" Sam asked Thad Walters.

The Y-ranging officer shook his head. "I've got our aircraft on the screen, sir, but I'm not picking up any bandits."

"I'll be damned." Sam glanced over to Lon Menefee. "Maybe you're right. Maybe the butternut bastards are further gone than I thought."

"Sure hope so," Menefee said. "Tell you one thing: when the Marines and the Army guys go ashore, their venereal rate's gonna climb like one of those fighters. Lots of infected people in Haiti, and the gals there'll be mighty glad to see 'em."

"Well, with the spiffy new pills and shots we've got, it's not as bad as it used to be. Still not good," Sam added hastily—you couldn't sound complacent about VD. The idea of lying down with a colored woman didn't drive him wild. But if you were a horny kid and there were no white gals for three islands around, you'd take whatever you could get. He remembered some of his own visits to brothels full of Chinese girls in Honolulu during the last war.

A yeoman came up onto the bridge. "Carriers report airplanes heading our way from Cuba, sir."

"Thanks, van Duyk," Sam said. Carriers had stronger Y-ranging sets than his ship did.

The men already stood at battle stations. Sam passed the word that the enemy was on the way. After he stepped back from the PA microphone, Lon Menefee said, "Well, we're not first on their list, anyhow."

He was bound to be right about that. The Confederates would want to hit airplane carriers and battlewagons and, he supposed, landing craft before they bothered with a lowly destroyer escort. All the same, Sam said, "If we end up on their plate, they won't send us back to the kitchen. And we don't want to get loose and sloppy, either."

"You've got that straight, sir," Menefee said at once.

"That's what she said," Sam answered, and the exec snorted. Overhead, some of the fighters from the CAP streaked off toward the west. Was that a good idea? If more enemy aircraft came at the fleet from another direction, from the Bahamas or from Haiti itself, they might catch the ships with their pants down.

These days, battles mostly happened out of sight of one side's fleet or the other's. This one might start out of sight of both. And that record would be hard to top, unless one of these days you got a fight something like the Battle of the Three Navies back in Great War days.

"I have bandits on the screen, sir," Lieutenant Walters reported. "Bearing 250, approaching . . . well, pretty fast. Looks like they're about ten minutes out. Our boys are on 'em."

"Thanks, Thad," Sam said, and passed the word to the crew. Then he asked, "Any sign of bandits from some different direction?"

Walters checked his screens before answering, "No, sir."

Sam grunted. That sounded more like what he'd hoped than what he'd expected. Echoing his thoughts, Lon Menefee said, "The Confederates really must be at the end of their tether."

"Well, maybe they are. Who woulda thunk it?" Sam called down a speaking tube to the hydrophone station in the bowels of the ship: "Hear anything, Bevacqua?"

"Not a thing, sir," the CPO replied. "Nothin' but our screw and the ones from the rest of the fleet. Jack diddly from the pings when I send 'em out."

"All right. Thanks. Sing out if you do, remember."

"Better believe it, sir," Bevacqua said. "It's my ass, too, you know."

Hearing that float out of the speaking tube, Menefee raised an eyebrow. It didn't faze Sam a bit. "Is he wrong?" he asked. The exec shook his head.

Another destroyer escort off to the west started firing. A moment later, so did the *Josephus Daniels*. "They're going after the carriers," Sam said, watching the Confederate airplanes.

"Wouldn't you?" Menefee asked.

"Maybe. But if I could tear up the landing craft, I might want to do that first. This is about Haiti, after all," Sam said. If it was about the island any more. For all he knew, it might have been about hurting the United States as much as the Confederacy could, and nothing more than that. On such a scale, carriers were likely to count more than landing boats.

But not many C.S. airplanes came overhead. Sam didn't know how many had set out from Cuba, but he would have bet a lot of them never made it this far. The CAP was doing its job.

The yeoman hurried back up to the bridge. "Our men are ashore, sir," he said. Sam sent the news out over the loudspeakers. The crew cheered and whooped. Van Duyk didn't go away. "There's more news, sir," he added in quieter tones.

"What's up?" Apprehension gusted along Sam's spine.

"Hamburg's gone, sir," van Duyk answered. "One of those bombs."

"Jesus!" Sam said. Churchill hadn't been kidding, then. England had caught up with the Germans, or at least come close enough to wreck a city. "What does the Kaiser say?"

"Nothing yet, sir," van Duyk said. "But I sure wouldn't want to be living in London right now."

"Me, neither," Sam agreed. "Or anywhere else a German bomber could get to." Or a British bomber . . . Did the limeys have aircraft that could lug what had to be a heavy bomb across the Atlantic to New York City? Did they have bombers that could fly across the Atlantic almost empty and pick up their superbombs in the CSA? That would be easier—if the Confederates had any new superbombs to pick up. All kinds of unpleasant possibilities . . .

And he couldn't do a goddamn thing about any of them. All he could do was clap his hands when the forward four-inch gun turned a C.S. bomber into a smear of smoke and flame in the sky.

Abruptly, it was over, at least around the *Josephus Daniels*. He couldn't spot any more Confederate airplanes above the ship. The gunners went on shooting awhile longer. They didn't believe in taking chances.

"Boy," Lon Menefee said. "I hope the guys going ashore have as easy a time as we did."

"Yeah, me, too," Sam said. "You would've thought the Confederates could throw more at us."

"A year ago, they could have," the exec said. "Two years ago, they were throwing the goddamn kitchen sink."

Carsten nodded. For the first year of the war, things had looked mighty black. Pittsburgh said the CSA wouldn't be able to conquer the USA. Till then, even that was up in the air. If the Confederates had taken it and gone on toward Philadelphia— But they hadn't. They couldn't. And afterwards it became clear they'd thrown too much into that attack, and didn't have enough left to defend with.

That was afterwards, though. At the time, no one had any idea whether they would fall short. What looked inevitable after the fact often seemed anything but while shells were flying and people were dying. By how much *did* the Confederates fall short in Pittsburgh? Sam didn't know, and he wasn't sure anyone else did. All the same, he would have bet the answer was on the order of *only a little bit*.

Lon Menefee's thoughts ran in a different direction: "Wonder how many smokes our guys'll find alive on Haiti."

"Hadn't worried about that." Sam bared his teeth in what was anything but a smile. "They would've had guns—they were a country before the butternut bastards jumped on 'em. I hope they gave Featherston's fuckers a good big dose of trouble." No, he didn't particularly love

Negroes, but he didn't want to see them dead, either—especially if they were making the Confederates sweat.

Cassius hadn't thought patrolling Madison, Georgia, and keeping white folks in line could get dull, but it did. Anything you did over and over got dull. Well, he didn't suppose screwing would, but he hadn't done enough of that to count as "over and over." A few hasty grapples with women who'd been part of Gracchus' band at one time or another were the sum of his experience.

He knew just enough to know he wanted to know more.

And he knew enough to be worried about whether he'd ever get the chance for it. One muggy evening at supper, he asked Gracchus, "Where we gonna find us some nice gals to marry?"

The guerrilla chief looked down at his mess kit, as if hoping one would turn up there. But he had the same roasted pork ribs and sweet potatoes and green beans as Cassius—only those, and nothing more. "Beats me. Beats the shit outa me," he said heavily. "Most of the niggers left alive down here is the ones in the bands. Ain't a hell of a lot of gals who wanted to pick up a Tredegar."

"Don't I know it! Sometimes I gets so horny, can't hardly stand it," Cassius said. "Plenty of white women left with no husbands on account of the war . . ."

"Good fuckin' luck! Good *fuckin'* luck!" Gracchus said. "Yeah, plenty o' white widows. An' you know what else? They's sorry their husbands is dead. An' they's even sorrier we *ain't.*"

Cassius wished he thought the older man were wrong. Unfortunately, he didn't. A shortage of black women and a shortage of white men should have had an obvious solution. Before the war, during the war, saying that where any white could hear him would have got him a one-way ticket to the graveyard. Would things be any different once the CSA finally threw in the sponge? *Fat chance*, he thought.

"Be a few gals don't care what color man they got, long as they got one," Gracchus predicted. "A few—the ones who git horny the same way a guy does. But even supposin' you find one, where you gonna set up housekeepin' wid her? Any place you try, how long 'fore the neighbors burn your house down, likely with the both of you in it?"

"The Yankees—" Cassius began.

Gracchus shook his head. "Yankees can't be everywhere. 'Sides, most of 'em don't want us messin' wid no white women, neither. They kin use us, yeah. But they ain't gonna stick their necks out fo' us when they don't got to, and you kin bet your ass on dat. Hell, you mess wid a white woman, you *is* bettin' your sorry ass on dat."

"Shit," Cassius said, again not because he thought Gracchus was wrong but because he didn't. "Maybe we go up to the USA, then. Got to be some colored gals there who'd give us the time o' day."

"Might not be too bad, if the Yankees let us," Gracchus allowed. "But we ain't U.S. citizens any more'n we's Confederate citizens. We don't belong nowhere. You don't believe me, go ask a white man."

Once more, he made more sense than Cassius wished he did. Every time you tried to get around what Jake Featherston and the Freedom Party had done to Negroes in the Confederate States, you banged your head into a stone wall instead.

The next morning, a couple of Confederate privates and a corporal came up to Cassius as he was on patrol. None of them was carrying a weapon. When they saw him, they all raised their hands and stood very still. "Don't shoot, pal," the corporal said. "We're just lookin' for somebody to surrender to, that's all. Reckon you're it."

Had they worn the camouflage of the Freedom Party Guards, Cassius would have been tempted to plug them no matter how they tried to sweet-talk him. Who could guess what guards were doing when they weren't fighting the Yankees? Cassius could, for one. Maybe they were closing Negroes up behind barbed wire. Or maybe they were shoving them into the hell-bound trains from which nobody came back. It wasn't by accident that Freedom Party Guards had a tough time giving themselves up to the U.S. Army's new black auxiliaries.

But these three were just in ordinary butternut. If they'd gone out of the way to give Negroes a hard time, it didn't show. And the noncom hadn't been dumb enough to call Cassius *boy*. He gestured with his rifle. "Y'all come with me. POW camp's right outside of town. You don't give nobody trouble, you'll be all right."

"Had enough trouble," the corporal said, and both privates nodded. The two-striper went on, "Me, I got a Purple Heart and two oak-leaf clusters. One more wound and I'm a goddamn colander. Enough is enough. Damnyankees wouldn't be here in the middle of Georgia if we weren't licked."

"Damn right." If the Yankees weren't here, Cassius probably

wouldn't have been, either. Sooner or later, the militias and the Mexicans would have squashed Gracchus' band. "Get movin'. Keep your
hands high, and don't git close enough to make me jumpy, or you be
mighty sorry."

"You got the piece," the corporal said. "You call the shots."

As they tramped through Madison, the other two soldiers opened
up a little. One was from Mississippi, the other from Arkansas. They'd
had enough of the war; they were heading home. Cassius thought they
were nuts to try to get through two states full of U.S. soldiers, but they
weren't the first men to tell him a story like that. As Confederate armies
came apart at the seams, as men thought of themselves ahead of their
country once more, the whole thrashing corpse of the CSA seemed full
of people in uniform on the move. Some were trying to get somewhere,
like these. Others were trying to get away either from Confederates
who didn't want them deserting or from U.S. soldiers who had reason
to want to catch them.

"Never reckoned we'd get whupped," the corporal said mournfully. "First time I got shot was in Ohio. Second time was in Pennsylvania. Third time was in Tennessee, just outside of Chattanooga. Things
weren't going so good by then."

"I suppose I can see how you'd say that," Cassius allowed. "But if
you was a colored fella here in Georgia, things never went good. Ain't
many of us left alive."

"We were up at the front, fighting the damnyankees. We didn't
know nothin' about none o' that," the private from Arkansas said
quickly. Too quickly? Cassius wasn't sure. He did know the U.S.
guards at the POW camp questioned new prisoners about what they'd
done before they got caught. Every so often, they arrested somebody
and took him away for more grilling.

"Nabbed yourself some more of these sorry sacks of shit, did
you?" a U.S. sergeant in Madison called to Cassius, and gave him a
thumbs-up. Cassius waved back.

"He's got no cause to call us that," the C.S. corporal said. "I
wouldn't call him that if I went and captured him—and I got me a few
damnyankees during the war."

The private from Mississippi nodded. "*You* didn't cuss us when
you caught us," he said to Cassius. "Your mama must've learned you
manners."

"She did." Cassius' eyes suddenly stung. "And then you goddamn ofays went an' shipped her to a camp, an' my pa, an' my sis, too, an' I reckon they's all dead now."

None of the Confederate soldiers said much after that, which was smart of them. And yet the Mississippian had a point of sorts. Cassius *hadn't* cursed the Confederates when they gave themselves up to them. Some of that was because swear words weren't enough to let him tell them what he thought of them. But some of it was because Confederate whites and Confederate blacks understood one another in ways U.S. whites never would. They might not like one another—hell, they might and often did hate one another. But they and their ancestors had mostly lived side by side for hundreds of years. Each knew how the other ticked.

"Score three for the good guys!" a guard outside the POW compound called as Cassius brought the captives up to the entrance.

"I leave these fellas with you?" Cassius asked.

"Yeah, I'll take care of 'em from here on out," the guard replied. He carried a submachine gun, a heavy U.S. Thompson. It would do the job if it had to. "C'mon, you lugs," he told the Confederates. "This is the end of the line for you."

"I don't mind," the corporal said. "Like I told this fella here"—he nodded toward Cassius—"I already been shot three different times. I'm still here. I'm still walkin'. One more, maybe my luck woulda run out."

"Damn war's over with," one of the privates added. "We lost. Ain't much point to fighting any more."

"You guys aren't so dumb," the U.S. soldier said. "Kick you in the teeth often enough and you get the idea." He led them off into captivity. They didn't seem the least bit sorry to go. They'd managed to give up without getting killed. And the chow inside the barbed wire was bound to be better than what they'd scrounged on their own. How much food the Yankees took for granted had already astonished Cassius. The men in butternut were scrawny enough to make him sure it would amaze them, too.

Cassius went back on patrol. Unlike the POWs, he had to earn his victuals. And damned if another pair of Confederate soldiers didn't come into Madison an hour and a half later. They'd also made sure they weren't carrying weapons before they showed themselves.

Seeing Cassius—and seeing his rifle—they wasted no time raising their hands. "We ain't people bombs or nothin', Rastus," one of them said. "Cross my heart we ain't." He lowered his right hand for a moment to make the gesture.

"My name ain't Rastus," Cassius retorted. But, again, as long as they didn't wear camouflage or call him *nigger* or *boy*, he was willing if not precisely eager to let them give up.

The same soldier in green-gray still stood at the entrance to the POW camp when Cassius brought in his next set of captives. "Son of a bitch!" the Yankee said. "You're turning into a one-man gang!"

"They know they's licked," Cassius said. "Don't bother 'em to give up now, like maybe it did befo'."

"That's about the size of it," one of the Confederates agreed. "What's the point to gettin' shot now? Sure ain't gonna change how things turn out."

"You got that right, anyway," the U.S. soldier said. "Well, come on. We'll get you your rooms at our hotel, all right. You can have the caviar or the pheasant under glass. The barmaid'll be along with the champagne in a few minutes, but it costs extra if you want her to blow you."

Both men in butternut stared. So did Cassius; the Yankee's deadpan delivery was mighty convincing. Then the Confederates started to laugh. One of them said, "Long as I don't get blown *up*, that's all I care about right now."

"Amen!" said the other new POW, as if responding to a preacher in church.

On that kind of simple level, Cassius had no trouble understanding and sympathizing with them. When he tried to fathom their cause, though . . . *If they had their way, I'd be dead, same as the rest of my family. How can they want that so bad? I never done nothin' to them.*

They didn't care. They feared Negroes might do something to them, and so they got in the first lick. That was Jake Featherston all the way—hit first, and hit hard. But he hadn't hit the United States quite hard enough. He got in the first lick, but they were getting the last one. *And I'm still here, too*, Cassius thought. *You may not like it, you ofay asshole, but I damn well am.*

Sitting in the Humble jail was a humbling experience for Jeff Pinkard. Even if the Republic of Texas had seceded from the Confederate States, the guards at the jail were all U.S. military policemen. They wore

green-gray uniforms, white gloves, and white helmets with MP on them
in big letters. They reminded him of a lot of the men who'd guarded
Camp Humble and the other camps he'd run: they were tough and
brave and not especially smart.

They wouldn't let his wife or stepsons in to see him. They wouldn't
let him see his new baby. All he had for company was Vern Green; the
guard chief moped in the cell across the hall.

Three hulking U.S. MPs came for Jeff early in the morning. They
all carried big, heavy U.S. submachine guns. "Come on, Pinkard," one
of them—a sergeant—said, his voice cold as Russian Alaska.

Jeff thought they were going to take him outside and shoot him.
Who was there to stop them? Not a soul. He fought to keep a wobble
out of his voice when he said, "I want to talk to a lawyer."

"Yeah? So did all the coons you smoked. Come on, asshole," the
MP said. One of his buddies unlocked the cell door. Jeff came. Fear
made his legs light. All he could do was try not to show it. If you were
going to die anyway, you wanted to die as well as you could.

He squinted against the sun when they led him out of the jail. He
hadn't seen so much sunshine since they locked him up. Looking back
at the jail building, he saw the U.S. and Texas flags flying side by side
above it. His mouth tightened. Both those flags reminded him of the
Stars and Bars; both, now, were arrayed against it.

Barbed wire and machine-gun nests and armored cars defended the
jail and the buildings close to it. Seeing Jeff glance at the new fortifica-
tions, the MP sergeant said, "Nobody's gonna spring you from this
place, so don't get your hopes up."

"Way you've got it set up, you must reckon an awful lot of folks
want to," Jeff replied. The noncom scowled at him but didn't answer.
Jeff smiled to himself—that shot must have got home.

What had been a bail bondsman's office down the street from the
jail now had U.S. soldiers standing guard in front of it. The Lone Star
flag might fly over the jail, but Pinkard didn't see any Texas Rangers.
The damnyankees were running this show. He didn't think that was
good news for him.

One of the guards opened the door. "Go on in," the MP sergeant
said.

"What happens when I do?" Jeff asked suspiciously.

"The bogeyman gets you," the MP snapped. When Jeff neither
panicked nor asked for any more explanation, the Yankee gestured

impatiently. "Just go on. You wanted a lawyer. They're gonna give you one. More than you deserve, if anybody wants to know what I think."

Pinkard didn't give a rat's ass for what the MP thought. A lawyer was more than he'd thought he would get from the U.S. authorities. Of course, having one and having one who'd do any good were two different critters. He was playing by Yankee rules now, and he knew damn well they'd be stacked against him.

In he went, before the snooty sergeant could tell him again. Sitting at what had been the bondsman's desk was a skinny fellow with curly red hair, a big nose, and a U.S. major's gold oak leaves. "You're Jefferson Pinkard?" the man asked.

"That's right." Jeff nodded. "Who're you?"

"My name is Isidore Goldstein," the major answered. *I figured he was a hebe*, Jeff thought. *Well, chances are he's smart, anyway.* Goldstein went on, "I'm part of the Judge-Advocate's staff. I'm an attorney specializing in military law. I will defend you to the best of my ability."

"And how good are you?" Pinkard asked.

"Damn good, matter of fact," Goldstein said. "Let's get something straight right now: I didn't want this job. They gave it to me. Well, that's how it goes sometimes. I don't like you. No—I despise you. If you've done one percent of what they say you've done, I'd stand in the firing squad and aim at your chest. And we both know you've done a hell of a lot more than that."

"If you're *my* lawyer, why do they need some other asshole to prosecute me?" Jeff said.

He surprised a laugh out of Goldstein. The Yankee lawyer—the Yankee Jew lawyer, almost a stock figure in Confederate movies about the depravities of life in the USA—said, "But you gotta understand something else, too. My job is defending people. Guilty people need lawyers. Guilty people *especially* need lawyers. Whatever they let me do, I'll do. If I can get you off the hook, I will. If I can keep 'em from killing you, I will. That's what I'm supposed to do, and I'll damn well do it. And like I say, I know what I'm doing, too."

Pinkard believed him, not least because Goldstein plainly didn't care whether he believed him or not. "So what are my chances, then?"

"Shitty," Goldstein answered matter-of-factly. "They've got the goods on you. They know what you did. They can prove it. You get rid of that many people, it's not like you can keep it a secret."

"Everything I was doing, I was doing 'cause I got orders from

Richmond to take care of it," Jeff said. "Far as the laws of my country went, it was all legal as could be. So what business of your country is it what I was doing inside of mine?"

"Well, that's one of the arguments I aim to use," Isidore Goldstein said. "You're not so dumb after all, are you?"

"Hope not," Jeff said. "How come you reckoned I was?"

"One way to do what you did is just do it and never think about it at all," the U.S. attorney said. "I figured you might be like that, where you'd go, 'Yeah, sure,' and take care of things, like. But you've got too many brains for that—I can tell. So why *did* you do it?"

" 'Cause the niggers were screwing my country. Honest to God, they were. First time I went to combat in 1916, it wasn't against you Yankees. Oh, hell, no. I was fightin' the damn coons in Georgia after they rose up and stabbed us in the back."

Goldstein pulled a notebook out of his left breast pocket and wrote something in it. "Maybe that will help some. I don't know, but maybe," he said. "The charge, though, is crimes against humanity, and that can mean whatever the people who make it want it to mean."

"Sounds chickenshit to me," Jeff said. "They gonna make believe the niggers weren't up in arms against our government long before we went to war with the USA? They can do that—I sure can't stop 'em—but they're a pack of goddamn liars if they do."

The military attorney did some more scrawling. "Maybe you want to forget the word *nigger*."

"How come?" Pinkard asked, genuinely confused.

"Because you hammer another nail into your coffin every time you say it," Goldstein answered. "In the United States, it's an insult, a fighting word." The idea that Negroes could fight whites without having the whole country land on them with both feet deeply offended Jeff. He was shrewd enough to see saying so wouldn't do him any good. He just nodded instead. So did Isidore Goldstein, who went on, "And they'll say things were so bad for the colored population in the Confederate States under Freedom Party rule that it had no choice but to rebel."

"Well, they can can say any damn thing they want," Jeff replied. "Saying something doesn't make it so, though."

" 'I'm Jake Featherston, and I'm here to tell you the truth,' " Goldstein quoted with savage relish. "Yes, we've noticed that."

"Oh, yeah. You damnyankees never once told a lie. And every one of you just loves coons, too. And I bet your shit don't stink, either."

"All of which would be good points except for two minor details." The lawyer ticked them off on his fingers: "First one is, the United States are going to win and the Confederate States are going to lose. Second one is, you really are responsible for upwards of a million deaths."

"So what?" Jeff said. That made even Goldstein blink. Angrily, Pinkard said it again: "So what, goddammit? Who gave the orders to drop those fucking superbombs on our cities? You think that asshole ain't a bigger criminal than me? You gonna hang him by the balls? Like hell you will! Chances are you'll pin a medal on the motherfucker instead."

"Again, two minor details," Goldstein said. "First, you used the superbomb before we did—"

"Yeah, and I wish we woulda started a year ago," Jeff broke in. "Then you'd be laughing out of the other side of your face."

Goldstein continued as if he hadn't spoken: "And, again, we're winning and you're not. You might do well to sound sorry for what you've done and to blame it on Featherston and on Ferdinand Koenig. I'm afraid I don't think it will do you much good, but it may do you some."

"You want me to turn traitor," Jeff said.

"I'm trying to tell you how you have some small chance of staying alive," Isidore Goldstein said. "If you don't care, I can't do much for you. I'm very much afraid I can't do much for you anyhow."

"I'll tell you what I'm sorry about. I'm sorry we lost," Pinkard said. "I'm sorry it comes down to me havin' to try and beg my life from a bunch of damnyankees. Seems like I got a choice between dyin' on my feet and maybe livin' on my knees. You had a choice like that, Mr. Smartass Lawyer, what would you do?"

"I don't know. How can any man know for sure before he has to find out the hard way?" Goldstein said. "But I'm still Jewish. That says I likely have some stubborn ancestors up in the branches of my family tree."

Jeff hadn't thought of it like that. He didn't exactly love Jews. But, like most Confederates, he aimed the greater portion of his scorn at Ne-groes and a big part of what was left at Mexicans. (He wondered what Hip Rodriguez would do in a mess like this. He didn't think Hip would crawl; greaser or not, Hip was a man. But why—*why*, dammit?—did he go and eat his gun?)

"There you are, then," Jeff said.

"Yeah, here I am. And here you are, and how the hell am I supposed to defend you?" Goldstein shook his head. "I'll give it my best shot. Better than you deserve, too. But then like I said, it's the guys who don't deserve a defense who deserve it most of all."

What was that supposed to mean? Jeff was still chewing on it when the U.S. MPs took him back to jail. He looked around as he walked, hoping for a glimpse of Edith. No luck. Wherever she was, she wasn't close by. He wondered whether he'd ever see her again. If the Yankees hanged him, would they be cruel enough to keep her away even then? He never wondered what the Negroes on their way to his bathhouses thought of him.

These days, the Joint Committee on the Conduct of the War had less to do. Congress had set it up to hold the Army's feet to the fire—and the Navy's, too. With the war almost won, the Senators and Representatives didn't have much to criticize. Flora Blackford wished the super-bomb had vaporized Jake Featherston—but so did the Army. Sooner or later, it would catch him. Either that, or he'd die fighting to escape capture. Flora didn't much care which, as long as the world was rid of him.

A Senator was grilling a Navy captain about why the United States was having so much trouble matching the new German submersible designs. Those promised a revolution in submarine warfare once the USA got them right. That hadn't happened yet.

"Isn't it a fact, Captain Rickover, that the German Navy has had these new models in service for almost a year?"

"Yes, but we only got the plans a few months ago," Rickover answered. *You tell him*, Flora thought: the captain was a Jew, one of the few to rise so high. He had no give in him, continuing, "We'll get the boats built faster than the *Kriegsmarine* did, but we can't do it yesterday. I'm sorry. I would if I could."

"I don't need you to be facetious, Captain."

"Well, I don't need you to play Monday-morning coach, Senator, but the rules are set up to let you do that if you want to."

"Mr. Chairman, this witness is being uncooperative," the Senator complained.

"I am not," Rickover said before the chairman could rule on the dispute. "The distinguished gentleman from Dakota—a state famous for its seafaring tradition—wants the Navy Department to accomplish the impossible. The merely improbable, which we've done time and again, no longer satisfies him."

The Senator from Dakota spluttered. The chairman plied his gavel with might and main. Before Flora found out how the exciting serial ended, a page hurried up to her and whispered, "Excuse me, Congress-woman, but you have a telegram."

"Thank you." Flora stood and slipped out. *Escaping this nonsense is a relief, nothing else but,* she thought.

Then she saw the kid in the Western Union uniform, darker and greener than the one soldiers wore. When a messenger boy waited for you, did you really want the wire he carried? Too often, it was like see-ing the Angel of Death in front of you. Her hand shook a little as she reached out for the flimsy yellow envelope.

"Much obliged, ma'am," he said when she gave him a quarter. He touched two fingers to the brim of his cap in a sort of salute, then hur-ried away.

She had to make herself open the envelope. The blood ran cold in her veins—it almost didn't want to run at all—when she saw the tele-gram was from the War Department. *The Secretary of War deeply re-grets to inform you . . .* Tears blurred the words; she had to blink several times before she could see to go on. *. . . that your son, Joshua Blackford, was wounded in action on the Arkansas front. The wound is not believed to be serious, and a full recovery is expected.* The printed signature of a lieutenant colonel—an assistant adjutant general—followed.

"How bad is it, ma'am?" the Congressional page asked.

"Wounded," Flora answered automatically. "The wire says they think he'll get better."

"I'm glad to hear it," the page said. If the war went on another year—which didn't seem likely—he might be in uniform himself. He probably had friends who already were. Did he have any who'd been unlucky? Flora didn't want to ask.

She hurried over to the bank of telephones down the hall from the committee meeting room. Instead of calling Lieutenant Colonel Pfeil, whose signature probably went out on dozens of wires a day, she rang up Franklin Roosevelt. In one way, a wounded private was no concern of his. But when the wounded private was the son of a Congresswoman who was also a former First Lady and who was friends with the Assistant

Secretary of War . . . Maybe Roosevelt would know more than he might if she were calling about Private Joe Doakes.

She got through in a hurry. "Hello, Flora." Roosevelt didn't sound as ebullient as usual, so he probably knew something. "Yes, I had heard. I'm sorry," he said when she asked.

"What happened?" she demanded.

"Well, this is all unofficial, because I'm not supposed to keep track of such things, but I understand he's lost the middle finger on his left hand," Roosevelt said. "Bullet or a shell fragment—I don't know which, and I'm not sure anyone else does, either. Not a crippling wound . . . Um, he isn't left-handed, is he?"

"No," Flora said. She didn't know whether to be relieved it wasn't worse or horrified that it had happened at all. She ended up being both at once, a stew that made her heart pound and her stomach churn.

"That's good. If he isn't, I'd say it's what the men call a hometowner."

"A hometowner." She'd heard the phrase, too. "*Alevai*," she said. "By the time he gets well, the war will be over, won't it?"

"We sure hope so," Roosevelt answered. "Nothing is ever as sure as we wish it would be, but we hope so."

"Do you know where he is? The wire didn't say."

"I don't know, but I'm sure I can find out for you. Are you in your office?"

"No, I'm at a telephone outside the committee meeting room. But I can get there in five minutes."

"All right. Let me see what I can find out, and I'll call you back." The Assistant Secretary of War hung up.

Flora ducked back into the meeting room to explain what had happened. The Senators and Representatives made sympathetic noises; a lot of them had fought in the last war, and several had sons at the front this time around. Captain Rickover gave her his best wishes from the witness stand.

The telephone was ringing when she hurried into her office. Bertha stared in surprise. "Hello, Congresswoman! How funny you should walk in. Mr. Roosevelt is on the line for you."

"I'll take it right here," Flora said, and grabbed the handset away from her secretary. "Hello, Franklin! Here I am."

"Hello, Flora. Joshua is in the military hospital in Thayer, Missouri, which is right on the border with Arkansas."

"Thayer, Missouri," Flora repeated. "Thank you." She hung up, then turned to Bertha. "Get me to Thayer, Missouri, as fast as humanly possible."

That turned out to be a flight to St. Louis and a railroad journey down from the big city. Bertha squawked till she found out why Flora needed to make the trip. Then she shut up and arranged the tickets with her usual competence.

Landing in St. Louis, Flora saw to her surprise that it had been hit almost as hard as Philadelphia. The war in the West never got the press things farther east did. But Confederate bombers still came up to strike St. Louis, and long-range C.S. rockets fired from Arkansas had hit the town hard.

The train ride southwest from St. Louis to Thayer was . . . a train ride. Every few miles, a machine-gun nest—sometimes sandbagged, more often a concrete blockhouse—guarded the track. Here west of the Mississippi, spaces were wide and soldiers thin on the ground. Confederate raiders slipped north every now and again. The Joint Committee on the Conduct of the War would have had something sharp to say about that . . . if it hadn't had so many other bigger things closer to home to worry about.

Thayer had gone up as a railroad town. It had flourished, in a modest way, as a cross-border trading center—and then suffered when the war strangled the trade that kept it going. The military hospital on the edge of town put a little life back into the economy—but at what a cost!

Joshua wasn't in his bed when Flora got there to see him. She feared something had gone wrong and he was back in the doctors' clutches, but the wounded man in the bed next to his said, "He's playing cards in the common room down at the end of the corridor, ma'am."

"Oh," Flora said. "Thank you."

When Flora walked in, Joshua held five cards in his right hand. Bandages swathed the left. He put down the cards to toss money into the pot. "See your five and raise you another five." Then he looked up from the poker game. "Oh, hi, Mom," he said, as if they were bumping into each other back home. "Be with you in a minute. I have to finish cleaning Spamhead's clock."

"In your dreams, kid. I'll raise you five more." Another greenback fluttered down in the center of the table. The sergeant called Spamhead did have a square, very pink face. He seemed to take the nickname for granted. Flora wouldn't have wanted to be called anything like that.

He won the pot, too—his straight beat Joshua's three tens. Joshua said, "Oh, darn!" All the other poker players laughed at him. What would he have said if his mother weren't there to hear it? Something spicier, no doubt. He stood up from the table and walked over to Flora. "I didn't think you'd get here so fast."

"How are you?" Flora asked.

Joshua raised his wounded hand. "It hurts," he said, as he might have said, *It's sunny outside*. "But not too bad. Plenty of guys here are worse off. Poor Spamhead lost a foot—he stepped on a mine. He's lucky it wasn't one of those bouncing ones—it would've blown his balls off. . . . Sorry."

"It's all right," Flora told him. "How else can you say that?" *Spamhead got mutilated, and Joshua think's he's lucky. I can see why, but* . . . "What does your doctor say?"

"That it was a clean wound. That it's nothing much to flabble about. That—"

"Easy for him to say," Flora broke in indignantly. "He didn't get hurt."

"Yeah, I know. I thought of that, too," Joshua said. "But he's seen plenty worse, so it's not like he's wrong, either. I'll heal from this, and I'll heal pretty fast. The only thing I won't be able to do that I could before is give somebody the finger with my left hand."

"Joshua!" Flora wasn't exactly shocked, but she was surprised.

Her son grinned sheepishly, but not sheepishly enough—he'd done that on purpose. "I didn't even think of it," he said. "The medic who took me back to the aid station was the one who said it first."

"Terrific. Now I know who to blame." Flora sounded as if she were about to haul that medic up before the Joint Committee on the Conduct of the War. She was tempted to do it, too. She recognized abuse of power when she saw it, which didn't mean it failed to tempt her.

Maybe Joshua saw the temptation gleaming in her eyes, for he said, "Somebody else would've come up with it if he hadn't. I would have myself, I bet—it's the way soldiers think."

"Terrific. I don't want you thinking like that," Flora said. Joshua didn't answer. He just looked at her—looked down at her, to remind her he was taller, to remind her he was grown if not grown up, to remind her that he didn't care how she wanted him to think. He would think the way he chose, not the way she did. She squeezed him, careful of the gauze-shrouded hand. "I'm glad you're going to be all right. I'm gladder than I know how to tell you."

"Sure, Mom." Joshua took it for granted. Flora didn't, couldn't, and knew she never would. She started to cry. "I'm fine, Mom," Joshua said, not understanding at all. He probably was. Flora knew too well that she wasn't.

Ever feel like a piece on a chessboard, sir?" Lon Menefee asked.

Sam Carsten nodded. "Now that you mention it, yes." The comparison wasn't one he would have made himself. Poker, pinochle, and checkers were more his speed. He knew how the different chessmen moved, but that was about it.

But the *Josephus Daniels* sure was making a long diagonal glide across the board of the Atlantic right now. Something big was in the wind. The Navy Department had found a more urgent assignment for her than protecting the carriers that protected the battlewagons that bombarded the coast of Haiti while Marines and soldiers went ashore.

"I'm sure not sorry to get out of range of land-based air," he said. "Even with our own flyboys overhead, I don't like that for hell."

"Worked out all right," Menefee said.

Sam had to nod. "Well, yeah. When the butternut bastards on the island saw they wouldn't be able to hold us, they couldn't give up fast enough."

The exec laughed. "D'you blame 'em?"

"Christ, no!" Sam said. "If they didn't surrender to us, the Haitians would've got 'em. They weren't up for that." Haiti had won its freedom from France in a bloody slave revolt that shocked the South a century and a half before. What the Negroes there now would have done to the Confederate soldiers they caught . . . Carsten's mouth tightened. "The blacks probably wouldn't have treated Featherston's fuckers any worse than they got treated themselves."

"Yes, sir," Menefee said, "but that covers one hell of a lot of ground."

"Mm." Sam let it go at that. Again, the exec wasn't wrong. The Confederates had set up one of their murder factories outside of Port-au-Prince. At first, they'd just killed Haitian soldiers and government officials. Then they'd started in on the educated people in the towns:

folks who might give them trouble one of these days. Before long, all you needed was a black skin—and how many Haitians didn't have one of those?

"They'll pay," Menefee predicted. "If we can arrest the guys who ran that camp in Texas, we can do the same with the sons of bitches in the Caribbean."

"I expect you're right," Sam said. A wave rolling down from the north slapped the *Josephus Daniels*' port side and made the destroyer escort roll a little. She was heading east across the ocean as fast as she could go, east and north. Musingly, Sam went on, "I wonder how long we'll stay out of range of land-based air."

"You think U.S. troops will land on Ireland the way we did on Haiti, sir?" Menefee asked. "That'd be a rougher job. Logistics are worse, and the limeys aren't knocked flat the way the Confederates were."

"It's one of the things I'm wondering about," Sam answered. "The other one is, what's the Kaiser going to do now? Yeah, England dropped a superbomb on Hamburg, but how many more does Churchill have? You don't want to piss the Germans off, because whatever you go and do to them, they'll do to you doubled and redoubled." He wasn't a great bridge player, either, but he could talk the lingo.

"Beats me," Menefee said. "I expect we'll find out before too long."

The *Josephus Daniels* remained part of the flotilla that had landed troops on Haiti. Sam felt a certain amount of satisfaction because the destroyer escort wasn't the slowest ship in it—the baby flattops were. He wouldn't have done without them for the world; if he really was sailing against the British Isles, he wanted all the air cover he could get. In fact, he wanted even more air cover than that.

Summer in the North Atlantic was much more pleasant than winter. Days were longer, seas were calmer, and the sun was brighter. Lon Menefee tanned. Sam reddened and burned and wore his hat whenever he went out on deck. He exchanged resigned looks with the handful of sailors who came close to being as fair as he was.

Nobody on the destroyer escort was eager to run into the Royal Navy. Britain's fleet didn't have the worldwide reach it had enjoyed before the Great War. Where it still went, though, it remained a highly capable outfit.

A destroyer off on the other side of the flotilla heard, or thought she heard, a submersible lurking in the sea. She prosecuted the sub with a shower of ashcans. There was no triumphant signal showing the enemy boat—if it was an enemy boat—had gone to the bottom. Sam didn't much care. As long as the sub couldn't launch torpedoes, he stayed happy.

He began haunting the wireless shack, as he'd done aboard several other ships, he'd served. He noticed he wasn't the only one; all the officers and chiefs seemed to be waiting for the other shoe to drop.

But he was asleep in his cabin when it did. The clatter of running feet on the steel of the corridor floor woke him a split second before someone pounded on the door. "It's open!" he called, turning on the lamp and sitting up in his narrow bed. He didn't have two more sailors right over his head, the way he did when he first put to sea.

Yeoman van Duyk burst into the cabin. "They've gone and done it, sir!" he said, his voice cracking with excitement.

"Who? The Germans?" Sam asked around a yawn. A hot flask full of coffee stood on the steel nightstand. He grabbed for it—he didn't think he'd need to worry about sleep any more tonight. "London?"

"Yes, sir." Van Duyk nodded. "And Brighton, and Norwich—all at the same time, or close enough."

"Sweet Jesus!" Sam exclaimed. As he poured from the hot flask, he found himself wanting to improve the coffee with a slug of medicinal brandy. He didn't, not with the rating standing there. "Did they get Churchill? Did they get the King?"

"I took this off the German wireless, sir, so they don't know," van Duyk answered. "No word from the BBC yet."

"All right. Thanks." Sam's guess was that the Prime Minister and King Edward and his family would have got out of London even before the RAF hit Hamburg. They had to know the Kaiser would land a superbomb there sooner or later. "What else did the Germans say?"

"That they had more where those three came from, and that they were ready to knock England for a loop if that was what it took to get the limeys out of the war."

"Jesus!" Sam said again. "How much of this poor, sorry world's gonna be left if we keep blowing chunks of it off the map?"

"Beats me, sir," van Duyk said. "I better get back to the shack." He sketched a salute and disappeared.

"And I better get my ass up to the bridge," Sam said, even though nobody was there to hear him. He put on his shoes and jacket; he'd slept in the rest of his clothes. He'd look a little rumpled, but the world wouldn't end.

The exec had the conn when Carsten came in. "You heard, sir?" Menefee asked.

"You bet I did," Sam answered. "Three at once? They must be turning those bastards out in carload lots."

"They're lucky they didn't get one of their bombers shot down."

"Damn right they are. I bet they snuck 'em in as part of a big raid. That way, the limeys couldn't know which machines to go after. Maybe they had fighters flying escort, too—with the Y-ranging sets they've got nowadays, you can see what you're going after even at night."

"Makes sense." The exec nodded. "You've been thinking about this."

Sam gave him a crooked grin. "Didn't know it wasn't in the rules. But you're right—I have. I figured the Kaiser had to hit back. If I was him, how would I go about it?"

"What will England do now?" Menefee wondered.

"Depends on how many bombs she's got, I suppose," Sam said. "If she has more, she'll use 'em. If she doesn't . . . How can she go on?"

"Beats me," Menefee said.

"Hell, if it wasn't for Churchill, I bet England would have quit already," Sam said. "Him and Featherston—the other side's got the stubborn so-and-sos."

"Now we hope he's dead," the exec said.

"Amen." Sam and Thad Walters spoke at the same time. They looked at each other and grinned.

But Churchill wasn't dead. He went on the BBC about half an hour later. Van Duyk called Sam down to the wireless shack. The British Prime Minister was speaking from "somewhere in the United Kingdom." He sounded furious, too. "If the Hun thinks we are beaten, let him think again," he thundered. "We shall avenge this monstrous crime. Even now, the Angel of Death unfolds his wings over a German city I do not choose to name. With weeping and repentance shall the Kaiser rue the day he chose to try conclusions with us."

"Wow!" Sam said. "Too bad he's not one of the good guys—he gives a hell of a speech."

"Yes, sir." Van Duyk turned the dial on the shortwave set. "Sounds like the Germans are going to get hit right about now. Let's see what they have to say."

He found the English-language German wireless. "There is a report of what may have been a superbomb explosion between Bruges and Ghent, in Belgium," the announcer said, only the slightest guttural accent betraying his homeland. "One of our turbo-engined night fighters brought down a British bomber in approximately the same location. If the Angel of Death sought to spread his wings over Germany tonight, he fell short by a good many kilometers."

Van Duyk whooped. "Up yours, Winston!" Sam said. He hurried up to the bridge to spread the news.

"Oh, my," Lon Menefee said. "Well, how many more cards do the limeys have?"

"We'll find out," Sam said. "Stay tuned for the next exciting episode of 'As the World Goes up in Smoke,' brought to you by the Jameson Casket and Mortuary Company. Our slogan is 'You're going to die sometime—why not now?'"

"Ouch!" Lieutenant Walters said.

"Lord, it's the way things look," Carsten said wearily. "This can't go on much longer—can it?" He sounded as if he was pleading—and he was.

"Ask Featherston. Ask Churchill," Lieutenant Menefee said. "They're the ones who have to quit."

"Can't happen soon enough," Sam said. "It's pretty much pointless now. We know who won. We know who lost. Only thing we don't know is how many dead there are." He paused. "Well, maybe Churchill has enough bombs left to force a draw. Doesn't look like Featherston does."

"I just don't want to see a bomber coming over *us* at thirty thousand feet, that's all," Walters said.

"Yipes!" Ice walked up Sam's spine. "I didn't even think of that." He made as if to look at the sky. No CAP at night. It wouldn't be flying anywhere near so high, anyway. Who'd ever imagined you might need to? But a superbomb didn't need to score a direct hit to ruin a warship. He wanted to turn around and run for home. But he couldn't, and the *Josephus Daniels* steamed on.

This is going to hurt a little."

Michael Pound had come to hate those words, because a little always turned into a lot. He'd never imagined changing dressings on his burned legs could hurt so much. And, at that, there were plenty of guys who had it worse than he did. Some of the badly burned men—pilots and other aircrew, most of them, and a few soldiers from barrels with them—needed morphine every time they got fresh bandages. He didn't, not any more.

He missed the stuff now that he wasn't getting it, but not enough to make him think he'd turned into a junkie. It did do more against pain than whatever else they had; codeine wasn't much stronger than aspirin by comparison. He could bear what he had to live with, though. When he heard other men howling, he understood the meaning of the phrase *it could be worse*.

The military hospital was somewhere near Chattanooga. Formidable defenses kept snipers and auto bombs at bay. From what everybody said, holding the CSA down was proving almost as expensive as conquering the damn place had been. That wasn't good, but Pound couldn't do anything about it.

He got his Purple Heart. He got a Bronze Star to go with his Silver Star. He didn't particularly think he deserved one, but nobody asked him. He got promoted to first lieutenant, which thrilled him less than the brass who gave him a silver bar on each shoulder strap probably thought it would. And he got a letter from General Morrell. Morrell wasn't just an old acquaintance—he was a friend, despite differences in rank. And he'd been wounded, too. A letter from him really did mean something.

"You should do very well, Lieutenant," a doctor told Pound one day. "A lot of third-degree burns are much deeper, and impair function even when they heal well. You'll have some nasty scars, but I don't think you'll even limp."

"Terrific," Pound said. "How would you like it if somebody said something like that about your legs? Especially when you were hurting like a son of a bitch while he did it?"

The doctor pulled up the left sleeve of his white coat. His arm had scars that made nasty look like an understatement. "I was in a motorcar crash ten years ago," he said. "I know what I'm talking about—and now we can do things for burns they didn't dream of back then."

"Can you use your hand?" Pound asked.

"Thumb and first two fingers," the doctor replied. "The tendons and nerves to the others are pretty much shot, but I've got the important ones, anyhow. You don't have that worry—I know your toes work."

"Uh-huh," Pound said unenthusiastically. He knew they worked, too; the therapists made him wiggle them. That made him forget about the rest of his pain—it felt as if a flamethrower were toasting them.

"Just hang on," the doctor said. "It's a bitch while it's going on, but it gets better. You have to give it time, that's all."

Pound couldn't even tell him to go to hell, because the other man had been through what he was in the middle of now and had come out the other side. "It *is* a bitch," was as much as he thought he could say.

"Oh, I know," the doctor answered quietly. "I still miss the needle sometimes, but I'll be damned if I go back to it . . . and you can take that any way you please." He nodded and walked on to the next patient.

He looked like such a mild little fellow, too: the kind who slid through life without anything much ever happening to him. Which only proved you never could tell. Michael Pound had seen that plenty of times with soldiers he got to know. He wondered why he was so surprised now.

He wished he could get up and do things, but he was stuck on his back—or sometimes, to stave off bedsores, on his stomach. The therapists said he could put weight on his feet in a couple of weeks. He looked forward to that, and then again he didn't. Till you'd been through a lot of pain, you didn't understand how much you wanted to stay away from more.

In the meantime, he had magazines and newspapers and the handful of books in the hospital library. He voraciously devoured them. He also had the wireless. He would have listened to news almost all the time. The other guys in the ward plumped for music and comedies and dramas. Pound endured their programs—he couldn't try throwing his weight around, not unless he wanted everybody else to hate him. But the news was all that really mattered to him.

Sometimes the other burned men gave in to him, too, especially in the middle of the night when they were all too likely to be awake and when the regular programs were even crappier than they were the rest of the time. And so he was listening to a news program when a flash came in.

"We interrupt this broadcast," said the man behind the mike. "This just in from the BBC—the Churchill government has fallen. Parliament voted no confidence in the Churchill-Mosley regime that has run the United Kingdom for more than ten years. Pending elections, a caretaker government under Sir Horace Wilson has been formed. Wilson has announced that his first action as Prime Minister will be to seek an armistice from the Kaiser."

The room erupted. A nurse rushed in to quiet the whoops and cheers. When she found out what had happened, she let out a whoop herself.

"They only had two!" Pound said.

"Two what?" the nurse asked.

"Two bombs," Pound and two other guys said at the same time. Pound went on, "They had two, and the second one didn't go off where they wanted it to, and that was it. Now the Germans can blow up their cities one at a time, and they can't hit back."

"Wow," the nurse said. "Are you a general? You talk like a general."

"I'm a lieutenant," he answered. "I've got gray hair 'cause I was a sergeant for years and years. They finally promoted me, and they've been regretting it ever since."

She laughed. "You're funny, too! I like that."

He wished he had a private room. Maybe something interesting would have happened. The ward didn't even boast curtains around the beds. Whatever they did to you, everybody else got to watch. After a while, you mostly didn't care. This once, Pound might have.

"Only Featherston left," said the man in the next bed.

"What do we do when we catch him?" somebody asked.

"String him up!" The answer came from Pound and several other wounded soldiers at the same time. It also came from the nurse. She suggested stringing the President of the CSA up by some highly sensitive parts of his anatomy. Coming from most women, that would have shocked Pound. He'd seen that nurses had mouths at least as raunchy as those of soldiers. It made sense: nurses saw plenty of horrors, too.

"My God," someone else said. "The war really is just about over."

Nobody made any snide comments about that. Maybe the other men in the ward had as much trouble taking it in as Michael Pound did. The war had consumed his whole being for the past three years—and before that, when he'd been down in Houston before it returned to the CSA, he might as well have been at war.

He wondered what he'd do when peace finally broke out. Would the Army want to keep a first lieutenant with gray hair? The service needed some grizzled noncoms; they tempered junior officers' puppyish enthusiasm. But he'd never be anything more than a junior officer himself, and he was much too goddamn old for the role.

If they turned him loose, if they patted him on the back and said, *Well done—now we'll go use up somebody else*, what the hell would he do then? He had no idea. The thought was frightening enough. The Army had been his life since he was eighteen years old.

They couldn't just throw him out . . . could they?

"Shit," another burned man said. "This fuckin' war's never gonna be over—excuse my French, miss."

"I've heard the words before," the nurse said dryly.

The soldiers laughed. The one who'd been talking went on, "It won't be. Honest to God, it won't. Maybe the Confederate government finally surrenders, yeah, but we'll stay on occupation duty down here forever. Lousy bushwhackers and diehards won't start singing 'The Star-Spangled Banner' tomorrow, and you can take that to the bank. We have grandchildren, *they'll* be down here shooting at waddayacallems—rebels."

Three or four guys groaned, probably because they thought the burned man was likely to be right. Michael Pound felt like cheering, for exactly the same reason. He didn't—everybody else would have thought he was nuts. But he felt like it. If the war, or something a lot like the war, went on and on, the Army wouldn't have any excuse to throw him out on his ear.

Well, it wouldn't have any excuse except maybe that he'd made himself too obnoxious for the brass to stand. Not without pride, he figured he was capable of that.

"Once we get done licking the Confederates, do we go after the Japs next?" asked the guy in the next bed.

If the General Staff of the burn ward of the military hospital outside Chattanooga had their way, the answer to that one was no. Pound wouldn't have minded seeing the Sandwich Islands, but not as a way station to a battle somewhere even farther off in the Pacific. The Japs had their sphere, and the United States had theirs, and as long as neither side poached on the other that was fine with him.

He did say, "I bet they're working overtime in Tokyo, trying to figure out how to build a superbomb."

"Wouldn't you be?" said the soldier next to him.

"You bet I would," Pound answered. "As long as we've got it and they don't, it's a club we can use to beat them over the head. I bet the Tsar's telling all his scientists they're heading for Siberia if they don't make one PDQ, too. If the Germans have one and the Russians don't, they're in big trouble."

He wondered whether Austria-Hungary would try to make one. Berlin was the senior partner there, and had been since the early days of the Great War. Germany had saved Austria-Hungary's bacon against the Russians then, and again this time around. But Vienna had some clever scientists, too. You never could tell, Pound decided with profound unoriginality.

"Before long, everybody and his mother-in-law's going to have those . . . miserable things." A soldier had mercy on the nurse's none-too-delicate ears. "How do we keep from blowing each other to king-dom come?"

That was a good question. It was probably *the* question on the minds of the striped-pants set these days. If the diplomats came up with a halfway decent answer, they would earn their salaries and then some.

Michael Pound thought about the CSA's rockets. If you could load superbombs onto bigger, better ones, you could blow up anybody you didn't like, even if he didn't live next door. Wouldn't that be fun?

Could you make a rocket shoot down another rocket? Airplanes shot down airplanes . . . some of the time, anyhow. Why shouldn't rockets shoot down rockets . . . some of the time, anyhow? Would that be enough? Pound had no idea, which left him in the same leaky boat as everybody else in the world.

XIII

Jake Featherston felt trapped. The skies over North Carolina had been lousy with damnyankee fighter-bombers coming down from the north. Now that he'd crossed into South Carolina, the skies were lousy with damnyankee fighter-bombers coming up from the south. He and the handful of loyalists who clung to him through thick and thin moved by night and lay up by day, like any hunted animals.

Only chunks of the Confederate States still answered to the Confederate government: pieces of Virginia, North Carolina, and South Carolina; the part of Cuba that wasn't in revolt; most of Florida; most of Sonora and Chihuahua (which, cut off by the goddamn treasonous Republic of Texas, might as well have been on the far side of the moon); and a core of Mississippi, Louisiana, and most of Arkansas. If the war would go on, if the war could go on, it would have to go on there.

One thing wrong: Jake hadn't the faintest idea how to reach his alleged redoubt. "What are we going to do?" he demanded of Clarence Potter. "Jesus H. Christ, what *can* we do? They're squeezing us tighter every day, the bastards."

"O God! I could be bounded in a nutshell and count myself a king of infinite space, were it not that I have bad dreams," Potter answered.

"What the hell is *that*?" Jake said.

"Shakespeare. *Hamlet.*"

"Hot damn! I don't need to go back to school now, thank you kindly." Featherston glared at the longtime foe who'd done him so much good. "What are you doing here, anyway? Why don't you give yourself up to the USA? You can tell 'em you've hated my guts since dirt."

"If things were different, I might," Potter said calmly. "But I'm the guy who blew up Philadelphia, remember. And I did it wearing a Yankee uniform, too."

"I'm not likely to forget." Jake's laugh was a hoarse, harsh bark. "You got out again, too, in spite of everything. I bet those sons of bitches are shitting rivets on account of it."

"Bad security," Potter said. "If we had another superbomb, we could get it up there."

That made Featherston cuss. They would have another bomb in a few months—if the United States didn't overrun Lexington first, which seemed unlikely. Henderson FitzBelmont had moved heaven and earth to make one superbomb. Now, when the CSA needed lots of them, he got constipated. You couldn't count on anybody—except yourself. Always yourself.

"But now the United States want to kill me worse than you ever did," Potter went on. "And they've got an excuse, because I wore their uniform. So in case they find out who I am, I expect I'm dead. Which means I'm all yours, Mr. President."

"All mine, huh? Then why the devil ain't you a redheaded gal with legs up to here?"

"You can't have everything, sir. You've still got Ferd Koenig along for the ride, and you've still got Lulu."

She sat in a different motorcar, parked under some trees not far away. Jake looked over in that direction to make sure she couldn't overhear before he said, "She's a wonderful woman in all kinds of ways, but not that one. I do believe I'd sooner hump me a sheep."

"Well, she doesn't do anything for me, either, but she worships the ground you walk on," Potter said. "God knows why."

"Fuck you, too," Featherston said without rancor. "She's a good gal. I don't want to make her unhappy or anything, so she better not hear that from you."

"She won't. I don't play those kinds of games," Potter said, and Jake decided to believe him. The Intelligence officer wasn't usually nasty in any petty way. After a moment, Potter went on, "You know, you're right—you *are* nice to Lulu. You go out of your way to be nice to Lulu. How come you don't do that with anybody else?"

There was a question Jake had never asked himself. Now he did, but he only shrugged. "Damned if I know, Potter. It's just how things worked out, that's all. I like Lulu. Rest of the world's full of assholes."

"I wish I could tell you you were wrong," Potter said. Airplanes droned by overhead—Yankee airplanes. They were going to hit something farther north. Columbia was already in U.S. hands, so they could drop their load on North Carolina and then land in Virginia. With a sigh, Potter asked, "How are we going to make it out West? Do you think we can get an Alligator to land anywhere near here? Do you think it could fly across Georgia and Alabama without getting shot down?"

"Wouldn't bet on it," Jake answered mournfully. "What I was thinking was, if we put on civvies and make like we're a bunch of guys who gave up, we can say we're going home and sneak across what the damnyankees are holding, and they won't be any wiser. How do you like it?"

Potter pursed his lips. "If we can't get an Alligator, maybe. If we can, I believe I'd sooner fly at night and take the chance of getting blown out of the sky."

Jake scowled at him. Potter looked back unperturbed, as if to say, *Well, you asked me.* He was one of the few men who never sugarcoated their opinions around the President of the CSA. Reluctantly, Featherston respected him for that. And he was too likely to be right, damn him. "I'll see what we can come up with," the President said.

When his shrunken entourage drove into Spartanburg, South Carolina, he found the colonel in charge of the town's defenses lost in gloom. "Damnyankees are on the way, and to hell with me if I know how to stop 'em," the officer said.

"Do your best," Jake answered. "Now let me get on the horn to Charlotte." That was the closest place where he thought he was likely to find a transport. And he did. And, after some choice bad language, he persuaded the authorities there to fly it down to Spartanburg.

"If it gets shot down—" some officious fool in Charlotte said.

"If it doesn't get here, *you'll* get shot down." Jake wasn't sure he could bring off the threat. But the jerk up in Charlotte couldn't be sure he couldn't.

The Alligator landed late in the afternoon. Ground crew personnel swarmed out with camouflage nets to make it as invisible as they could. "Do we really want to do this?" Ferd Koenig asked.

"If you don't, then stay here," Featherston answered. "Say hello to the U.S. soldiers when they catch you." The Attorney General bit his lip. He got on the airplane with everybody else.

"Don't know exactly how we'll land if we have to do it in the dark," the pilot said.

"You'll work something out," Jake told him.

"Well, I sure as hell hope so." But the pilot didn't sound too worried. "One thing—if I think this is crazy, chances are the damnyankees will, too. Maybe we'll surprise 'em so much, we'll get through 'em just like shit through a goose."

"Now you're talking. You take off in the wee small hours," Jake said. "Fly low—stay under the Y-ranging if you can. Goddammit, we aren't licked yet. If we can just make the enemy see that occupying our country is more expensive than it's worth, we'll get their soldiers out of here and we'll get a peace we can live with. May take a while, but we'll do it."

He believed every word of it. He'd been fighting his whole life. He didn't know anything else. If he had to lead guerrillas out of the hills for the next twenty years, he was ready to do it. After so many fights, what was one more? Nothing to faze him—that was for sure.

After they got airborne, the pilot asked, "Want me to put on my wing lights?"

"Yeah, do it," Jake answered. "If the Yankees see 'em, they'll reckon we're one of theirs. I hope like hell they will, anyway."

"Me, too," the pilot said with feeling, but he flicked the switch. The red and green lights went on.

The Alligator droned south and west—more nearly south than west at first, because neither the pilot nor Jake wanted to come too close to Atlanta. If U.S. forces would be especially alert anywhere, they both figured that was the place.

Looking out of one of the transport's small side windows, Jake had no trouble figuring out when they passed from C.S.- to U.S.-held territory. The blackout in the occupied lands was a lot less stringent. The Yankees didn't expect Confederate bombers overhead, damn them. And the worst part was, the Yankees had every right not to expect them. The Confederacy didn't have many bombers left, and mostly used the ones it did have in close support of its surviving armies.

Turbulence made the Alligator bounce. Somebody gulped, loudly. "Use the airsick bag!" three people shouted at the same time. The gulper did. It helped—some.

And then turbulence wasn't the only thing bouncing the Alligator. Shells started bursting all around the airplane. Suddenly, the road through the air might have been full of potholes—big, deep ones. A major general who wasn't wearing a seat belt went sprawling.

"Get us the fuck out of here!" Jake yelled. If Lulu sniffed or squawked, he didn't hear her.

Engines roaring, the transport dove for the deck. The antiaircraft guns pursued. Shrapnel clattered into the wings and tore through the fuselage. Somebody in there shrieked, which meant jagged metal tore through a person, too.

"We're losing fuel!" the pilot shouted. "Lots of it!"

"Can we go on?" Jake had to bellow at the top of his lungs to make himself heard.

"Not a chance in church," the pilot answered. "We'd never get there."

"Can you land the son of a bitch?"

"If I can't, we're all dead," the man answered. Jake remembered that he hadn't been thrilled about landing at night even in Confederate-held territory. How much less enthusiastic would he be about a nighttime emergency landing on enemy soil? *I told him to put on the wing lights*, Jake thought. *Did it matter? Too goddamn late to worry about it now.*

He hated having his fate in somebody else's hands. If he was going out, he saw himself trading bullets with the damnyankees and nailing plenty of them before they finally got him. This way . . . *Dammit, I'm a hero. The script isn't supposed to work like this.*

"Brace yourselves!" the pilot shouted. "Belts on, everybody! I'm putting it down. I think that's a field up ahead there—hope like hell it is, anyway. Anybody gets out, let Beckie know I love her."

One of the engines died just before the Alligator met the ground—that was one hell of a leak, all right. The transport was built to take it and built to land on rough airstrips—but coming down in a tobacco field with no landing lights was more than anybody could reasonably expect.

But it got down. It landed hard, hard enough to make Jake bite the devil out of his tongue. One tire blew. The Alligator slewed sideways. A wingtip dug into the ground. The transport tried to flip over. The wing broke off instead. The fire started then.

"Out!" the pilot screamed. "Out now!" The airplane hadn't

stopped moving, but nobody argued with him. Jake was the second man out the door. He had to jump down to the ground, and turned an ankle when he hit. Swearing savagely, he limped away.

"Fuck!" he said in amazement. "I'm alive!"

Clarence Potter wondered how many nasty ways he could almost die. This blaze was a lot smaller than the radioactive fire he'd touched off in Philadelphia, but it was plenty big enough to give a man an awful fore-taste of hell before it finally killed him. To the poor chump roasting, how could any fire be bigger than that?

He heard Jake Featherston's obscene astonishment from not far away. It summed up how he felt, too. He'd scrambled away from the burning Alligator right after the President of the CSA. Was everybody out? He looked at the pyre that had been a transport. Anybody who wasn't out now never would make it, that was for damn sure.

"Where the hell are we?" Ferdinand Koenig's deep voice came from over to the right.

"Somewhere in Georgia—I can't tell you anything else." That was the pilot. Nobody would have to deliver his message to Beckie . . . yet.

But they weren't free and clear, not by a long shot. "Let's get out of here," Potter said. "This field will be swarming with Yankees in noth-ing flat."

Some of the Confederate big shots weren't going anywhere. "I think my leg is busted," said the general who'd replaced Nathan Bed-ford Forrest III as chief of the General Staff. Potter couldn't remember his name; as far as Potter was concerned, the officer wasn't worth re-membering. "I'm not going anywhere quick."

"You can surrender, Willard. Don't reckon they're shooting soldiers—only politicians," Jake Featherston said. "Just don't tell 'em I'm around."

"I wouldn't do that, sir," Willard said. *First name or last?* Potter wondered. Hell, it didn't matter to anybody but Willard any more.

"General Potter is right," Saul Goldman said. Potter blinked. He hadn't even known the Director of Communications got on the Alliga-tor. Goldman was so quiet and self-effacing, he could disappear in plain sight.

Lulu was hurt, too, hurt badly. "I don't want the Yankees to get me, Mr. President," she told Jake. "Will you please shoot me and put me out of my misery?"

"I don't want to do that!" Featherston exclaimed.

"Please," Lulu said. "I can't go on. It's the last thing you can do for me, since . . . Oh, never mind. You didn't care about that, not with me."

She knew what she was talking about. Jake had put it more pungently the afternoon before, but it amounted to the same thing. The President of the CSA muttered to himself. He started to turn away, then turned back. Potter had rarely seen him indecisive—wrong often, sometimes disastrously so, but hardly ever at a loss. "Christ," he said under his breath.

"Hurry," Lulu said. "You can't stay here."

Potter hadn't imagined he would find Lulu agreeing with him, either. "Christ," Jake said again, a little louder this time. Then he yanked the .45 out of the holster he always wore. He fired, and whispered, "Sorry, Lulu," as he did. "Come on!" Now he almost shouted. "Let's get the fuck away from here."

They stumbled and limped through the field. The only light came from the burning Alligator, and they were trying to put it behind them as fast as they could. "That must have been hard, sir," Potter said after a while: cold comfort, he realized as soon as he spoke, if any at all.

"Feels like I just shot my own luck," Featherston answered, his voice rough with—tears? "That make any sense at all to you?"

"Sense? No," Potter answered. As the President glared at him, he added, "I understand what you mean, though. Let's hope you're wrong, that's all."

"Yeah. Let's." Jake's voice stayed harsh. "You know what? You're liable to be our ace in the hole. We do run into damnyankees, you can talk for us, make 'em think we're on their side."

"I hope I can, anyhow," Potter said. He'd done it up in the USA. If he couldn't do it again—they were up the well-known creek, that was all. "I hope I don't have to. I hope there aren't any Yankees within miles."

"That'd be nice." Featherston didn't sound as if he believed it was likely. Since Potter didn't, either, he would have let it rest there. But Featherston went on, "Best thing we can do is get into some town the Yankees didn't bother garrisoning. We borrow a couple of motorcars from loyal people, we can head west. . . . Wish to hell I knew just where we were at."

Potter did. They were in trouble, that was where. Jake Featherston yelled for the pilot and asked him. "Somewhere east of Atlanta—can't tell you closer," he replied. "I was going to fly south a little while longer, then swing west. That's about as good as I can do right now. Beg your pardon, sir, but I'm fuckin' surprised I'm in one piece."

"You did good, son," Jake said—he was never shy about patting small fry on the back. That was probably one of the things that had helped him rise and kept him on top. "Yeah, you did good. So where's a town?"

"Let's find a road," Potter said. "Sooner or later, a road's got to take us into a town." He didn't say what kind of town a road would take them into. They just had to trust to luck on that. No sooner had the thought crossed his mind than Featherston's mournful comment followed it.

He found the road by the simple expedient of stepping down into it. He came closer to hurting himself then, than he had in the Alligator's crash-landing. "Which way?" Ferdinand Koenig asked. *North or south, east or west?* was supposed to follow that question, but Potter had no idea which direction was which. Evidently, neither did anyone else.

But there was the moon, a thin waning crescent, so that had to be the east. Which meant the North Star should be about . . . there. And there it was, with the rest of the Little Dipper curling from it.

Jake Featherston worked it out at the same time as Potter did. "This way," he said, pointing. "We'll keep on heading south, see what the hell happens." He'd most likely spent more time in the field than anybody else here. He would be able to figure out which way was which as soon as he set his mind to it.

Down the road they went, a ragged squad, some hale enough, others limping. Most of them had pistols; one officer carried an automatic Tredegar. If Yankee soldiers came on them, they wouldn't last long. Potter understood that perfectly well. He wondered how many of the others did.

He also wondered how long they could keep going. Sooner or later, their minor injuries would catch up to them. And more than a few of them were, to put it politely, not men accustomed to taking much exercise. Ferd Koenig, in particular, resembled nothing so much as a suet pudding in a gray Freedom Party uniform.

Potter realized they should have changed into civilian clothes before they got on the Alligator. Too late to worry about that now. Too late to worry about lots of things now. *Would I be here if I'd managed to shoot Jake at the Olympics?* No, of course he wouldn't; the President's bodyguards would have gunned him down. But maybe the country wouldn't have been in the mess it was in.

Or maybe it would have—how could you tell? The Vice President in those days hadn't been an amiable nonentity like Don Partridge. Willy Knight of the Redemption League wanted to do a lot of the same things Jake Featherston did. The only reason he didn't get a chance was that the Freedom Party grew bigger faster. A couple of years later, he came close to assassinating Jake himself.

And close counted in . . . ? Horseshoes and hand grenades, was the soldiers' joke. Knight disappeared off the face of the earth after that. Potter supposed he'd died in one camp or another. Or maybe he just got summarily killed and dumped in the James. Any which way, he was gone.

"Can we get away?" somebody asked.

"Believe it," Jake Featherston said instantly. "If you believe it, you can do it. That's what life's all about. Believe it hard enough, work for it with everything you've got, and you'll get it. Look at me."

He was right—and he was wrong. He'd climbed from nowhere to the top of the heap in the CSA. He'd run the country for ten years. And now the Confederate States of America—*are getting it, all right*, Clarence Potter thought. *Nice to know I can still make stupid jokes at a time like this.*

Off in the distance, like the roar of faraway lions, he heard the rumble of truck motors. They neared far faster than lions would have, and they were likely to be far more dangerous. "Hit the dirt!" Potter sang out.

The Confederate dignitaries scrambled off to the side of the road and hid behind bushes and in ditches. It would have been funny if it weren't so grim. *This* was what the Confederate States of America had come down to: a dozen or so frightened men hiding so the damn-yankees wouldn't catch them.

One after another, the heavy trucks pounded past. Exhaust stank in Potter's nostrils. He got a glimpse of soldiers in green-gray in the rear compartments and heard a couple of windswept snatches of bad language in U.S. accents. Then, after a few seconds that were among the longest of his life, the last deuce-and-a-half was gone.

"God damn them, they'll find Willard, and that'll spill the shit in the soup," Jake Featherston said. Potter wouldn't have put it the same way, which didn't mean he disagreed with the President. Jake went on, "We *got* to make it to a town quick, grab us some autos, and get the fuck out of here." That also seemed like good advice.

"Let's get moving," the pilot said. He was younger than just about everybody else there—and also the man the Yankees were least likely to shoot out of hand if things went wrong.

Move they did. Fifteen minutes later, they all hid and flattened out as more trucks growled up the road. These machines had an ambulance with them, which likely meant the Yankees had indeed found the head of the C.S. General Staff. Would they rough Willard up? Would he keep quiet if they did? *Next episode of the serial*, Potter thought.

He began to pant. His feet started hurting—he was wearing dress shoes, not marching boots. The sky lightened in the east. "Where the hell's that town?" somebody said, voice numb with fatigue. "Feels like we've been going down this goddamn road forever."

"Couldn't have said it better myself," Potter said. He was definitely getting a blister on his left heel. If it worsened, he wouldn't be able to keep up. The damnyankees would catch him—and, he suspected, that would be that in short order.

Featherston pointed. "Sign up ahead." Half an hour earlier, they wouldn't have seen it till they were right on top of it.

Potter, with his weak eyes, would have been one of the last men to be able to read it. Somebody called out the name of the town on the sign and said it was a mile and a half off, so he didn't have to.

"Where the hell are we?" Ferd Koenig demanded—the name meant as little to him as it did to Potter.

"Smack in the middle of Georgia," Jake answered confidently. Did he carry a map of the CSA in his mind detailed enough to include a nowhere of a place like this one? Potter wouldn't have been surprised. Jake knew all kinds of strange things, and remembered almost everything he heard. That wasn't the problem. The problem was, he'd come up with too many wrong answers from what he knew—or maybe, if you went and aimed the CSA at the USA, there weren't any right ones.

Cassius yawned. He hadn't been on patrol all that long, but the anti-aircraft fire woke him up ahead of when he would have had to crawl out of the sack anyway. He wondered what the hell was going on. The Confederates hadn't sent any airplanes over Madison for quite a while.

He yawned again and shook his head. For all he knew, somebody'd got a wild hair up his ass and started shooting at a Yankee airplane, or maybe at something imaginary. You never could tell with something like that.

"Anything goin' on?" he asked Gracchus when he replaced the other Negro at the north end of town.

"More guns an' tracers an' shit than you can shake a stick at," the older man replied.

"I knew *that*," Cassius said. "Got me up early. See a real airplane, though?"

"Not me," Gracchus said. "*Somethin'* funny goin' on, though. They wouldn't've sent out so many sojers in trucks if there wasn't."

"Soldiers?" Cassius echoed. Gracchus nodded. "Huh," Cassius said. "Bet you're right, then. They got somethin', all right, or they think they do."

"I know what I's gonna get me." Gracchus yawned till his jaw seemed ready to fall off. "Gonna get me some shut-eye, is what. You kin march around the nex' few hours an' earn your vittles. I's gone." He patted Cassius on the back and headed off toward the Negro guerrillas'—the Negro auxiliaries', now—camp.

All mine, Cassius thought, and then, *Hot damn*. By now, the whites in Madison were pretty well cowed. They hadn't given any real trouble for several weeks.

That thought had hardly crossed his mind when he heard somebody's voice in the distance, floating through the clear, quiet early morning air. He started to bark out a challenge—it was still before the Yankees' curfew lifted. Then he looked north along the highway that led down from Athens. Damned if at least a dozen ofays weren't heading his way.

The rosy light of dawn showed them well enough. Cassius didn't think they could see him: he stood in the deep shadow of some roadside pines. He scurried behind one of them. Challenging that many men when he was by himself didn't seem like a good idea. Maybe they were Yankees, in which case a challenge would be pointless. If they weren't, they were trouble. That many Confederates wouldn't be running around together at daybreak unless they were trouble.

He waited and watched as they got closer. He almost relaxed—they were in uniform, and who but U.S. soldiers would be in uniform around here? But then he saw that the uniforms were gray and butternut, not green-gray. He wanted to scratch his head, but he stood very still instead. Whoever these people were, he didn't want them spotting him. One of them carried a better rifle than his, and almost all of them had holsters on their belts.

"Come on, goddammit," a rangy, middle-aged man up near the front of the pack said loudly. "We're almost there."

That voice . . . Cassius knew it instantly. Anyone in the CSA would have. Anyone black in the CSA would have reacted as he did. The Tredegar leaped to his shoulder. He could almost fire over open sights—the range couldn't have been more than a hundred yards. He'd never aimed so carefully in all his life. Take a breath. Let it out. Press the trigger—don't squeeze.

"Get us some motorcars, and—" the rangy man went on as the rifle roared and bucked against Cassius' shoulder. The bullet caught the fellow right in the middle of the chest. He got his left foot off the ground for one more step, but he never finished it. He crumpled and fell instead.

Cassius worked the bolt and fired again, as fast as he could. Jake Featherston jerked before his face hit the asphalt. While he was lying there, Cassius put another bullet into him. This one made red bits spurt from his head. Cassius chambered one more round. When you were shooting a snake, you didn't know for sure what it took to kill him.

One of the men in butternut knelt by the President of the CSA. The just-risen sun shone from his spectacles and their steel frames. He leaned toward Jake Featherston. Cassius could easily have shot him, too, but waited instead to see what happened next. The bespectacled man started to feel for Featherston's wrist, then shook his head, as if to say, *What's the use?* When he rose, he seemed suddenly old.

The rest of the Confederates might have turned to wax melting in the sun, too. When Cassius saw they slumped and sagged, he began to believe Jake Featherston was dead—began to believe he'd killed him. Were the tears in his eyes joy or sorrow or both at once? Afterwards, he never knew.

"Y'all surrender!" he shouted blurrily, and fired another shot over the Confederates' heads.

As if on cue, Gracchus ran up the road from Madison. Four or five white men in green-gray pounded after the Negro. One by one, the

Confederates standing in the roadway raised their hands above their heads. The officer with the automatic Tredegar carefully set it on the tarmac before he lifted his.

Only then did Cassius step out from behind the tree. Gracchus skidded to a stop beside him. "Who is them ofay shitheads?" the guerrilla chief panted.

"Dunno. Big-ass ol' Confederates, that's all I kin tell you," Cassius said. "But I just shot me Jake motherfucking Featherston. That's him on the ground there, an' he's dead as shoe leather."

"No," Gracchus whispered. The U.S. soldiers heard Cassius, too. They stared north toward the knot of Confederates and the corpse in the road. Then they stared at Cassius.

"Kid, I'd give my left nut to do what you just done," one of them said.

"My right nut," said another.

"Do you know how famous you just got?" a third one added.

"It doesn't matter," Cassius said. "He killed my whole family, the son of a bitch. Shooting's too good for him, but it's all I could do. I heard his voice, and I knew who it was, and then—*bang!*"

Gracchus set a hand on his shoulder. "You got that, anyways. Rest of us, we don't got nothin'. He done kilt all our famblies. But you kilt him? You really an' truly did?" His voice was soft with wonder.

"I sure did." Cassius sounded amazed, too, even to himself. "Now I want to see him dead."

He walked forward, his rifle still at the ready in case any of the men ahead tried something. He had only one round left in the clip, but he wasn't too worried about that, not with Gracchus and those U.S. soldiers to back him up.

Flies were already starting to buzz above the blood pooling around the corpse in the roadway. Cassius stirred the body with his foot. Jake Featherston's lean, hungry face stared sightlessly up to the sky. A fly landed on his cheek. It crawled over to the rill of blood that ran from the corner of his open mouth and began to feed.

"Well, you did it. You just sank the Confederate States of America." The officer with glasses talked like a Yankee. But he wore a C.S. uniform with, Cassius saw, a general's wreathed stars on his collar. He took off his spectacles and wiped his eyes with his tunic sleeve. "Jake Featherston was a son of a bitch, but he was a great son of a bitch— and you killed him."

He looked as if he wanted to say more. Telling off somebody with a Tredegar was never a good idea, though.

Another man, a heavy fellow in a gray Party uniform, figured that out, too. He said, "Who would've reckoned a . . . colored kid could do in the President?" The pause meant he'd almost said *nigger*, or more likely *goddamn nigger*, but he swallowed anything like that before it got out.

"Who the hell are you people, anyway?" one of the U.S. soldiers— a sergeant—demanded.

"Ferdinand Koenig, Attorney General, CSA," the heavy man answered. Cassius almost shot him, too. Koenig ran the camps. He was Jake Featherston's enforcer. But shooting anybody with his hands up wasn't so easy.

"Clarence Potter, brigadier general, CSA," said the man with glasses.

"Christ!" the sergeant in green-gray said. "You're on our list! You're the asshole who blew up Philly!"

"You know that?" Potter blinked, then actually bowed. "Always an honor to be recognized," he said. Cassius found himself surprised into admiration. Potter had style, in a cold-blooded way.

The other Confederates gave their names and ranks. The only one Cassius had heard of was Saul Goldman, whom he thought of as the Confederacy's chief liar. But the rest were all big shots, too, except for a young captain with a pilot's wings on the right breast pocket of his tunic.

"Do Jesus!" Gracchus said. "There here's 'bout what's left o' the Confederate gummint, ain't it?"

"Where's what's-his-name? The Vice President?" The U.S. sergeant snapped his fingers. "Partridge in a pear tree—him?"

Even with their cause in ruins and themselves in captivity, several of the Confederates smiled at that. A couple of them even laughed. "The Vice President isn't with us," General Potter said. "If you look under a flat rock, you'll find a lizard or a salamander or something. It's bound to be just as smart as Don."

"Jesus, Potter, show a little respect," Ferd Koenig said. "He's President now, wherever he is."

"Only proves we're screwed, if you ask me," Potter said calmly.

Three command cars rumbled up from Madison: probably called

by wireless. Their machine guns added to the U.S. firepower. A photographer jumped out of one of them. "Godalmightydamn," he said, aiming his camera at the corpse in the road. "That really is the motherfucker, ain't it?" He took several pictures, then looked up. "Who punched his ticket for him?"

Gracchus gave Cassius a little shove. "This fella right here."

A flashbulb went off in Cassius' face. He saw green and purple spots. "Way to go, sonny. You just turned famous, know that? What's your name, anyway?"

"Cassius," he answered. Now two people, both white, had thrown fame in his face. "I'm Cassius. I don't care nothin' about famous. Only thing I care about is, that bastard's dead an' gone."

"You may not care about famous, buddy, but famous is gonna care about you," the photographer predicted. "Bet your ass it will. You're gonna be the most famous smoke in the whole goddamn US of A."

Smoke wasn't exactly an endearment, but Cassius was too dazed to get very upset about it. More command cars and a halftrack came up the road. Some of the people who got out were soldiers. Others were reporters. When they found out Cassius had shot Jake Featherston, they all tried to interview him at once. They shouted so many questions, he couldn't make sense of any of them.

Some of the reporters started grilling the captured Confederates, too. The prisoners didn't want to talk, which seemed to upset the gentlemen of the press.

Cassius kept looking at the body every so often. *I did that*, he told himself. *I really did.*

"Don't pay these mouthy fools no mind," Gracchus advised him. "You don't got to say nothin' to 'em if you don't care to. You *done* somethin' instead."

It wasn't enough. If Cassius could have killed Jake Featherston five million or six million or eight million times, it might have come close to being enough. But he'd done all he could do. He made himself nod. "Yeah," he said.

Not far outside of Pineville, North Carolina, Irving Morrell stood up in the cupola of his barrel for what he hoped was the last time in the war. Sweat ran down his face. He was glad to escape the iron oven in

which he'd ridden north. The cease-fire continued to hold. With a little luck, it would soon turn into something more like a real peace.

A monument of piled stone, two or three times as tall as a man,
marked the place where James Polk had been born. Since Polk was
President of the United States before they split into two countries, this
seemed a good place for the representatives of those two countries to
meet.

Close to the monument stood what could only have been a Negro
sharecropper's cabin. It was empty now, windows broken, door hanging half open. If meeting at Polk's birthplace symbolized something,
that deserted cabin meant something else altogether. Where were
the blacks who'd called it home? Anywhere on this earth? Morrell
doubted it.

The sergeant in charge of another U.S. barrel peered up the road
toward Charlotte with field glasses. He waved to Morrell. "Here they
come, sir!"

"Thanks," Morrell said.

A moment later, his own Mark One eyeball picked up the approaching autos. As they got closer, he saw that the Confederates were
scrupulously abiding by the terms of the cease-fire agreement. All three
motorcars were unarmed. The first flew a large white flag from its wireless aerial. So did the third. The middle auto had two aerials. One flew
the Stars and Bars, the other the flag of the President of the Confederate States.

Morrell's barrel was flying the Stars and Stripes from its antenna.
That guided the Confederates to the proper machine. He could have
blown them to hell and gone. Even now, when they were giving up, the
temptation was very real. Instead, he climbed down from the barrel as
the Confederate motorcars stopped under his guns.

A Confederate officer—a general, Morrell saw—got out of the lead
motorcar. He walked up to Morrell and saluted stiffly. "Good day,
sir," he said. "I recognize you from many photographs. My name is
Northcote, Cyril Northcote. After the, ah, recent unfortunate events, I
have the dubious privilege of being the senior General Staff officer not
in captivity."

Morrell returned the salute. "Pleased to meet you, General Northcote."

"Meaning no disrespect to you, sir, but I'm afraid I can't say the
same," Northcote answered bleakly.

"Well, General, under the circumstances, I don't see how I can take offense at that," Morrell said.

"Yes. Under the circumstances." Northcote spoke as if each word pained him. The door to the middle C.S. motorcar opened. A young-looking blond man in a sharp gray civilian suit came out. General Northcote waved to him and he came forward, his perfectly shined shoes flashing in the bright sun. Machinelike, Northcote said, "General Morrell, it is my duty to present to you the President of the CSA, Mr. Don Partridge. Mr. President, this is U.S. General Irving Morrell."

"Mr. President," Morrell said formally. He did not offer to shake President Partridge's hand—he was under orders from Philadelphia to do no such thing.

Partridge's hand did start to rise, but fell back like a dead thing when he realized no handshake would be forthcoming. Close up, his round face didn't just look young. It looked boyish, as if none of the past three years of struggle had registered with him or on him at all. How was that possible? Morrell didn't know, but it seemed to be.

"General," Partridge said, and managed a nod.

Morrell nodded back; he had no orders against that. "Mr. President, you have come here under the terms of the cease-fire now in place to agree to the unconditional surrender of all forces still under command of the Confederate States of America. Is that correct?" He sounded like a man speaking from a script, and he was.

President Partridge had to work to manage another nod. "Yes. That's right." He sounded surprised and hurt, as if wondering how fate—and Morrell—could do such a thing to him.

"All right, then. I have the terms of the surrender here." Morrell took two copies of the document from his left breast pocket and unfolded them. "I would like to go over them with you before you sign so no one can say afterwards that there was any misunderstanding. Is that agreeable to you, sir?"

"Have I got a choice?" Don Partridge sounded bleak, too.

"Only going on with the war," Morrell answered.

"Then I haven't got a choice." Partridge sighed. "Go ahead, General. We can't fight any more, or I wouldn't be here."

Morrell thought that had been true ever since Savannah fell, if not since Atlanta did. But Jake Featherston kept the Confederacy going months longer than anybody would have imagined, and what he did to

Philadelphia . . . *He may have killed me yet, even if it takes years.* Well, it was over now, thank God.

"All right. Here we go—Article One says you surrender unconditionally to the United States all forces on land, at sea, and in the air who are at this date under Confederate control," Morrell said.

Don Partridge nodded. "That's what I'm here for." Under his breath, he added what sounded like, "Goddammit." Morrell pretended not to notice.

"Article Two says your high command will immediately order all Confederate authorities and forces to cease operations on Thursday, July 14, 1944, at 1801 hours Eastern Summer Time: today at a minute past six," the U.S. general went on. "Your forces will hold in place. They will hand over weapons and equipment to U.S. local commanders. No ship or aircraft is to be scuttled or damaged. Machinery, armaments, and apparatus are to be turned over undamaged. This specifically includes your superbomb works in Lexington. Is that plain enough for you?"

"I understand you," Partridge said. "We won't do any damage to them. Your bombers have already done plenty, though."

"Make sure you don't use that as an excuse for any sabotage there," Morrell warned. "My government is very, very serious about that. If your people get cute, they'll be sorry."

"They're already sorry," the President of the CSA said. "We'll go along."

"You'd better. Now—Article Three. At that same time—6:01 today—all your camps killing Negroes are to cease operations," Morrell said. "Camp authorities are to make every effort to feed their inmates. U.S. supply convoys will reach them as soon as possible. Camp personnel will surrender to the first U.S. officers who arrive. Anyone who flees instead of surrendering will be liable to summary execution—we'll shoot the bastards on sight. Have you got *that*?"

"I've got it," Don Partridge answered. "Some of them will likely take their chances anyway."

He was bound to be right there. Even so, Morrell went on, "That brings us to Article Four. Your high command will at once issue orders to the appropriate commanders that they obey any commands issued by the U.S. War Department and carry them out without argument or comment. All communications will be in plain language—no codes."

"Agreed." By the way he spat it out, the word seemed to taste bad in Partridge's mouth.

"Good." Again, Morrell left the new and unhappy Confederate President what little pride he could. "Article Five says that a final political settlement may supersede this surrender."

That got him a glare. "When you decide how you want to carve us up, you'll go ahead and do it, you mean," Partridge said.

Yes, Morrell thought. Aloud, he said, "Sir, I'm only a soldier. I don't have anything to do with that." *Yeah, I'll pass the buck.* "Article Six now. If your high command or any forces under your control fail to act in accordance with this surrender, the War Department will take whatever punitive or other action it deems appropriate. If you disobey or fail to comply, we will deal with you in accordance with the laws and usages of war."

"You won. We lost. You'll do whatever you damn well please," Don Partridge said.

"That's about the size of it, sir," Morrell agreed. "And if there's any doubt or dispute about what these terms mean, the decision of the United States will be final." He handed Partridge both copies of the instrument of surrender. "Have you got a pen?"

"Yes." Partridge took one from an inside pocket. He read the terms to make sure they said what Morrell claimed they did. Maybe he wasn't so dumb as people in the USA thought. Maybe he'd been playing possum to make sure Jake Featherston didn't do unto him as he'd done unto Willy Knight. Chances were it wouldn't matter now one way or the other. Biting his lip, Partridge signed. He thrust one copy back at Morrell. "Here."

"Thank you." Morrell tried to stay what the diplomats called correct. *We hate each other, but we don't let it show.* "Do you have wireless equipment to let you relay the news of the surrender to your commanders so they can issue the appropriate orders? You are welcome to use U.S. equipment if you don't."

"I do, thank you very much," Partridge replied. *So there*, Morrell thought. The President of the CSA went back to his motorcar. Morrell watched him talk into a microphone in there.

Morrell made small talk with General Northcote till Partridge got out again. Then he asked, "All taken care of?"

Don Partridge nodded. "Yes. You will have full cooperation from all our officials. And now, if you will excuse me, I'd like to get back up to Charlotte and do what I can to keep things running."

"Um—I'm afraid not," Morrell said.

"Pardon me?" Partridge raised a pale eyebrow.

"I'm afraid not," Morrell repeated, more firmly this time. "You have surrendered—the Confederate States have surrendered—unconditionally. There is no Confederate government right now, sir. There isn't anything, not till the United States say there is."

"What does that make me, then?" President Partridge demanded.

"My prisoner, sir," Morrell answered.

He'd captured a swarm of prisoners in the course of two wars. He'd never had one cuss him out with the virtuoso splendor Don Partridge showed. Partridge must have listened to his boss a lot; by all accounts, Jake Featherston could swear like a muleskinner. Morrell let Partridge have his say. Why not? In the end, it made no difference. The USA had the firepower, and the CSA didn't.

"At a minute past six tonight, Mr. President, it's all over," Morrell said when Partridge finally ran down. "They'll remember you as the man who made peace."

"They'll remember me as the man who threw in the sponge," Partridge said. "Or else they won't remember me at all." Considering how little he'd done up till now, Morrell reflected, he might well be right.

The Confederates in front of Lavochkin's Looters weren't giving up without a fight. They kept firing even after word came that the Confederacy was giving up. Chester Martin stayed deep in his muddy foxhole. He was damned if he wanted to get hurt when it didn't mean a thing. He just looked at his watch every now and then and waited for 6:01 to roll around.

Lieutenant Boris Lavochkin still gave the impression of eating too much raw meat. "If those assholes fire even one shot—even one—after surrender time, we're going to roll on over them and clean them out!" he shouted.

We? You and your tapeworm? Martin wondered. Didn't the lieutenant know he was the only one who still felt like fighting? Maybe he didn't, because he went right on yelling. But if he wanted to charge the C.S. position at 6:02, he'd do it by himself. Martin would have bet everything he owned on that.

The second hand spun round and round. The minute and hour hands didn't seem to want to move, but they did. And when 6:01 came,

Chester Martin lit a Raleigh and blew out a grateful cloud of smoke. "Son of a bitch!" he said. "I made it."

He still didn't straighten up or show himself. For all he knew, his watch was a couple of minutes fast. Then he heard a picket call, "Goddamn—they're coming out!" The man sounded awed, not blasphemous.

Chester decided he could look out. Men in butternut were coming through the bushes, their hands high, their eyes either empty or else burning with hate. "Well, you've got us," one of them said, spitting a stream of tobacco juice off to the side. "And a hell of a git you've got."

He had a point. The Confederates were scrawny and filthy and ragged. Quite a few of them were walking wounded. They looked more like hoboes in uniform than soldiers. But they could fight. Through two wars, Chester had never found any reason to doubt that.

"Give 'em rations, boys," Captain Rhodes called. "It's all over now." Lieutenant Lavochkin, Chester was sure, would never have said any such thing.

Once you got up into your fifties, you didn't scramble out of a foxhole. You emerged with dignity. Coming into the open with the enemy in sight seemed dangerous, wrong, unnatural. Chester remembered that from 1917, too.

He caught the eye of the closest Confederate soldier—a kid who couldn't have been more than sixteen. "Want some chow?" he asked.

"Much obliged," the youngster answered. Martin tossed him a can. As he caught it, he said, "What'll y'all do with us now?"

"Beats me," Chester said. "Make sure we've got all your weapons, I bet—we have to take care of that. Then? Who knows? Somebody up top'll tell us, and we'll do it, whatever it turns out to be."

"You did this before, didn't you? You coulda fought against my pa, too," the young Confederate said as he used the key to get the lid off the can.

"Yeah, well, we had to lick you people twice." Chester wondered whether the kid even heard him. He was shoveling canned beef stew—which tasted like tire tread in mud gravy—into his mouth with his dirty fingers. It wasn't one of the better U.S. rations, but the new POW didn't care.

Not far away, Captain Rhodes was talking with a Confederate sergeant with a beer belly and gray stubble. The guy could have been a defeated butternut version of Martin himself—he was plainly a retread. "Take me to your demolitions people," Rhodes was saying. "We want to make sure we get your explosives under control."

"Well, I'll do it, but we don't have a hell of a lot of that stuff left," the veteran noncom said.

"Cut the shit, Charlie," Rhodes told him, which was almost exactly the thought going through Chester's mind. "You figure you're gonna squirrel that crap away for people bombs and auto bombs and toys like that? You better think twice, that's all I've got to say. We *will* take hostages—lots of 'em. We'll shoot 'em, too. If there's not a white man left alive from Richmond to Key West, nobody in the USA's gonna shed a tear. You can take that to the bank."

The sergeant glared at him with undisguised loathing. "I believe you. You damnyankees are all a bunch of nigger-lovers."

"I know one nigger I love right now—the kid who shot Jake Featherston," Captain Rhodes answered. "Get it straight, Sergeant. Your government's surrendered. If it hadn't, how long did you have to live? A couple of days, maybe—not much more. After that, we would've flattened you like a steamroller. If you fuck with us now, we will anyway. And you know what else? We'll enjoy doing it, too."

Chester stared. No, that wasn't Boris Lavochkin with an extra bar on each shoulder strap. Captain Rhodes was usually a pretty mild fellow. Usually, yeah, but not always. He meant every word of this.

And the C.S. sergeant knew it, too. "Well, come on, then," he said. "I'll take you to 'em. Just don't blame me if they ain't got everything you want."

"I'll blame somebody—that's for damn sure." Rhodes looked around. His eye lit on Chester. "Gather up a squad, Sergeant, and come along. We may need to do some persuading here."

"Sure will, sir." Martin rounded up a dozen men, just about all of them with automatic weapons instead of Springfields. They followed Captain Rhodes behind what had been the enemy line.

That was scary, especially with the sun sinking in the west. If somebody hadn't got the word or just didn't give a damn . . . Chester was sure there would be little spasms of fighting for days. He didn't want to get stuck in one, that was all. And he didn't want them to turn into a full-scale rebellion against the U.S. occupiers. If they did, the USA really might have to kill piles and piles of Confederate hostages. He didn't look forward to that. No matter what Captain Rhodes said, he didn't think it would be fun.

Not all the Confederate soldiers had put down their arms yet. The men in butternut scowled at the men in green-gray. Nobody did more than scowl, though. The enemy troops had to know about the surrender, even if they didn't like it.

"If we were as big as the United States, we would've whipped y'all," a corporal said.

"If pigs had wings, we'd all carry umbrellas," Chester answered. "You so-and-sos shot me twice. That's enough, goddammit. I don't want your kids trying to shoot my kid."

The U.S. soldiers walked past a battery of worn-looking 105s. Rhodes told off four or five men to take charge of the guns and their ammunition. "God only knows what a son of a bitch with an imagination can do with an artillery shell," he remarked. Chester could think of a few things, all of them unpleasant. He was sure real explosives people could come up with a lot more.

He chatted with the Confederate veteran, who turned out to have also fought on the Roanoke front in the Great War. "Yeah, that was pretty bad, all right," the other sergeant said. "I got hit twice—a bullet once, a shell fragment in the foot the other time."

"I got it once then and once this time around," Chester said. "Lucky, if you want to call it that. Shit, we both lived through two rounds, so we are lucky."

"Plenty who didn't—that's for damn sure." The Confederate pointed. "The people your captain's looking for are just ahead there."

As a matter of fact, they weren't—they'd bugged out. But they'd left their stock in trade behind in earthwork revetments roofed with planks and corrugated sheet iron. Captain Rhodes set a guard over the explosives and fuses and blasting caps. Shaking his head, he said, "How many setups like this are there all over the CSA? How many'll get emptied out before our guys show up? How much trouble is that gonna cost down the line?"

Lots. Quite a few. Quite a bit. Chester had no trouble finding answers for questions like that. He looked around. This wasn't good guerrilla country—too flat and too open. Other places, though . . .

Hearing them talking, an armed Confederate ambled up to see

what was going on. His eyes widened. "Jesus!" he yipped. "You're damnyankees!"

Chester grinned at him. "Nothing gets by you, does it?"

He stopped grinning a second later, because the Confederate soldier aimed a submachine gun at his midsection. "Hold it right there! Y'all are my prisoners."

"Oh, for Christ's sake!" Captain Rhodes said, though Chester noted that he kept his hands away from his .45. "Don't you know your side surrendered?"

"My ass!" the man in butternut said. "We'd never do anything like that."

"Go find some of your buddies," Chester said. "Talk to them. We aren't bullshitting you, man. How'd we get so far behind your line if we were just sneaking around?"

"Beats me." The enemy soldier gestured with the submachine gun. "You come with me. If you're lyin', you'll be sorry."

"However you want." Chester never argued with a man who could kill him. "Let's go. I won't even get mad after you find out what's what."

The other man turned out not even to know Jake Featherston was dead. He no more believed that than he believed his country had surrendered. And, no doubt to drive Chester crazy, they couldn't find anybody else in butternut. That veteran sergeant had disappeared—with luck to head for a POW camp, without it to go off and make trouble.

At last, just as the sun was setting, they found another Confederate soldier. To Chester's enormous relief, he had got the news. " 'Fraid the Yankee's tellin' you the truth," he said to his countryman. "It's all over. We're licked."

"Son of a bitch bastard!" Chester's erstwhile captor said. "If that ain't the biggest crock o' crap . . . We weren't even losing."

"Hello—this is South Carolina. What am I doing here if you guys are winning?" Martin asked. The Confederate gaped at him as if that had never once crossed his mind. Chester got the idea not a whole lot of things had crossed the other fellow's mind. "Why don't you hand me that piece so my guys don't shoot you for having it?"

Reluctantly, the soldier in butternut gave him the submachine gun. Even more reluctantly, he raised his hands. "My pappy's gonna whup me when he finds out I quit," he said glumly.

"Not your fault," Chester said. "The whole CSA gave up."

"Pappy won't care," the soldier predicted. "He'll whup me any old way."

"Did he fight in the last war?" Chester asked.

"I hope to shit he did!"

"Then he gave up once himself. Tell him so."

"Like he'll listen. You don't know Pappy."

As far as Chester was concerned, that was just as well. "Let's go back to the explosives shed," he said. "I want my captain to know you found out we weren't pulling your leg."

"Still can't hardly believe it. And the President bought a plot?" The Confederate shook his head. "Holy fuckin' shit!"

He could cuss as much as he pleased. Chester had his weapon. He remembered the Navy guys who'd got torpedoed after the cease-fire in the Great War. Thank God he hadn't gone that way himself!

George Enos, Jr., was thinking of his father as the *Oregon* steamed toward the surfaced Confederate submarine. That bastard of a sub skipper hadn't wanted to quit when the Great War ended, so he'd fired one last spread of torpedoes—and little George grew up without a man around.

This submersible was playing by the rules. It had surfaced and broadcast its position by wireless. Now it was flying a large blue flag in token of surrender. Men in dark gray uniforms stood on the conning tower and on the deck, though nobody went near the deck gun. Taking on a battlewagon with that little excuse for a weapon was closer to insane than anything else, but you never could tell.

A lieutenant with a bullhorn strode up to the *Oregon*'s bow. "Ahoy, the Confederate sub!" he bawled. "Do you hear me?"

On the sub, a fellow in a dirty white officer's cap raised a loudhailer to his own lips. "I hear you," he answered. "What are your instructions?"

"Have you jettisoned your ammunition?"

"Yes," the Confederate answered.

"Have you removed the breechblock from your gun?"

"Done that, too."

"Are the pistols out of your torpedoes? Are the torpedoes rendered safe?"

"Yes. We've followed all the surrender orders." The enemy officer didn't sound happy about it.

"Do you have any mines aboard?" asked the lieutenant on the *Oregon*.

"No—not a one."

"All right. We are going to send an officer and a CPO to inspect your boat before we give you your sailing instructions for Baltimore. Stand by to receive a boarding party."

"Very well," the Confederate skipper said. "But if the surrender order didn't tell us we had to do exactly what you tell us, I would have something different to say to you."

"You would be trying to sink us, and we would be dropping depth charges on your head," the U.S. lieutenant said. "Things are what they are, though, not what you wish they were."

"And ain't that the sad and sorry truth?" the sub skipper said. "We will receive your boarders—we won't repel them." That made George think of pigtailed sailors with bandannas and cutlasses, and of clouds of black-powder smoke. No more, no more.

The officer who crossed to the submersible was barely old enough to shave. The chief might have been his father, as far as years went. George knew what would happen. The ensign would write up the inspection report, and the chief would tell him what to say.

They came back after a couple of hours. The ensign was nodding and grinning, but George kept his eyes on the CPO. When he saw that the senior rating seemed satisfied, he relaxed. Nobody on that sub would give the U.S. Navy any more trouble.

After talking with the ensign (and also glancing at the chief), the lieutenant picked up his bullhorn again. "You are cleared to proceed to Baltimore. Keep flying your blue flag by day, and show your navigation lights at night."

"Understood," the C.S. skipper said.

As if he hadn't spoken, the lieutenant went on, "Remain fully surfaced at all times. Report your position, course, and speed every eight hours. All wireless transmissions must be in plain language. A pilot will take you through the minefields. Obey any instructions you may receive from U.S. authorities."

"We'll do it," the Confederate replied. "Is there anything else, Mommy, or can we go out and play now?"

Several U.S. sailors snickered, George among them. The lieutenant went brick red. "No further instructions at this time," he choked out.

The C.S. skipper doffed his cap in sardonic salute, then disappeared down the hatch into the submarine. It moved off to the northwest, in the direction of Chesapeake Bay.

The lieutenant was still steaming. "If I ever run into that son of a bitch on dry land, I'll punch him in the nose," he ground out.

"Take an even strain," said the chief, who'd gone aboard the Confederate submarine. "We won. They lost. Let him talk as big as he wants—it doesn't change what really matters."

"No, but it makes me look like a jerk. All I was doing was making sure he understood the surrender terms. We don't want the kind of trouble we had the last time around."

"I should say we don't." The CPO looked this way and that till he spotted George. "Here's Enos. He knows more about that kind of shit than you and me put together. His old man was on the *Ericsson*, and his ma's the gal who went down to the CSA and plugged the skunk who put her on the bottom."

"Really?" The lieutenant, unlike the chief, didn't know George by sight. At a quick gesture from the CPO, George took half a step away from the twin 40mm mount. The lieutenant said, "You're Sylvia Enos' son?"

"Yes, sir." George was always pleased when somebody remembered his mother's first name.

"I read her book," the officer said. "It was one of the things that made me decide to join the Navy. I thought I ought to help do things right, so people like her didn't have to pick up guns and take care of it themselves."

"Yes, sir," George repeated, less enthusiastically this time. Whenever he thought about *I Shot Roger Kimball*, he couldn't help also thinking about the hard-drinking hack who did the actual writing. His mother should have known better than to have anything to do with Ernie except for the book. She should have, but she hadn't, and so she was dead, and so was he. And if Ernie hadn't shot himself, George would gladly have killed him.

The lieutenant seemed to run out of things to say, which might have been a relief for him and George both. "Well, carry on, Enos," he said, which was strictly line-of-duty. He hurried back toward the *Oregon*'s towering bridge. George returned to the gun mount.

Some of the men on the gun crew already knew who he was and who his mother had been. Unlike the lieutenant, they also knew better than to make a fuss about it. "Officers," one of them said sympathetically.

"Yeah, well . . ." George spread his hands. "What can you do?"

"Jack diddly," the other sailor said. "Put up with 'em the best way you can. Try not to let 'em fuck you over too bad."

"They're like women," a shell-jerker said. "You can't live with 'em, and you can't live without 'em, neither."

"Nope." George shook his head. "If you could get pussy from officers, they'd be good for something. Way things are, too many of 'em are—"

"Good for nothing!" Three guys on the crew said the same thing at the same time. They grinned at one another, and at George. The banter about what officers would be like if they were equipped the way women were went on and on. It got louder and more hilarious and more obscene with each succeeding joke as each sailor tried to top the fellow who'd gone before him.

George's grin stretched wider and wider. It wasn't just that the guys were funny. Everybody was all loosey-goosey. Unless some Confederate diehard hadn't got the word, nobody would be shooting at the *Oregon* or bombing her or trying to torpedo her. They'd made it through the war.

"Now all we got to worry about is the crappy cooks in the galley," George said.

"See? They should be broads, too," one of the other guys put in. "Then they'd know what they were doin'."

"And if they did feed us somethin' shitty, they could really show us they was sorry," somebody else said. It went on from there.

They spotted another surfaced submarine later that day. This one flew the Union Jack, not a blue surrender flag like the Confederate boat. "I have no quarrel with you gentlemen," the captain called through a loudhailer, "but I will not go to one of your ports. I have received no such orders. We have an armistice with Germany and you, but we have not surrendered."

"We can blow you out of the water," warned the U.S. officer with whom he was parleying.

"No doubt," the British sub skipper replied politely. "But we have done nothing provocative, and have no intention of doing any such thing. Are you really so eager to put the war on the boil again?"

Muttering, the young U.S. officer got on the telephone to the bridge. He was muttering louder when he hung up. "You may proceed," he told the Royal Navy officer.

"Thanks ever so." The limey actually tipped his cap. "May we meet again—and not in our professional capacities."

"We ought to blow him up anyway," the U.S. officer growled—but not through the bullhorn.

Sailors in the British submarine were bound to be thinking the same thing about the *Oregon*. As long as the boat stayed surfaced and didn't aim either bow or stern at the battleship, George figured he wouldn't flabble. If the submarine dove . . .

It didn't, not till it was out of sight. George hoped the *Oregon*'s Y-ranging set watched it even farther than that. Since no Klaxons hooted, he supposed everything stayed hunky-dory. Thinking about women officers was a lot more fun than worrying about getting sunk.

"I bet the limeys never do surrender, not the way the Confederates did," Wally Fodor said. The gun chief went on, "I bet they just bail out of the fight on the best terms they can, same as they did in the last war. Long as they got their navy in one piece, they're still a going concern."

"Till somebody drops a superbomb on their fleet, anyway," George said.

"Yeah, but the Kaiser's got to be sweating about how big Japan's getting. Hell, so do we," Fodor persisted. "The Japs don't have the superbomb yet, so England's the only one who can give 'em a hard time— unless we want to go through the Pacific one goddamn island at a time."

Nobody at the twin 40mm mount wanted anything like that. George, who'd already had a long tour in the Sandwich Islands, *really* didn't want anything like that. He'd paid all the dues against Japan he felt like paying.

"Tell you one thing," he said. "All this bullshitting is a lot better than sweating out bombs and torpedoes for real."

"Amen!" That went up from several sailors at once.

"We licked Jake Featherston, and the limeys look like they've had enough, anyway," George went on. "Pretty soon, we'll be able to get our old lives back again." Did he look forward to going after cod from T Wharf? He wasn't so sure about that, but coming home to Connie more often sounded mighty good.

XIV

Dr. Leonard O'Doull donned a professional scowl and glared at the unhappy young PFC standing in front of him. "That's one of the most disgusting chancres I've ever seen," he growled. It was red and ugly, all right, but he'd run into plenty just like it. The kid didn't have to know that, though.

Quivering, the PFC said, "Sorry, sir." He looked as if he was about to cry.

"Were you sorry while you were getting it?" O'Doull asked.

"Uh, no, sir." The youngster in green-gray turned red.

"Why the hell didn't you wear a rubber?"

"On account of I didn't figure I needed to. She was a *nice* girl, dammit. Besides, it feels better when you're bareback."

It did. O'Doull couldn't quarrel about that. He could ask, "And how does it feel now?" The PFC hung his head. O'Doull went on, "Do you still think she was a nice girl?"

"No, sir," the kid said, and then, apprehensively, "What are you going to do to me, sir?"

"Me? I'm going to fix you up, that's what." O'Doull raised his voice: "Sergeant Lord! Let me have a VD hypo of penicillin."

"Coming up, Doc." Goodson Lord produced the requisite syringe.

The PFC stared at it with something not far from horror. "Jeez Louise! You could give an elephant a shot with that thing."

"Elephants don't get syphilis. Far as I know, they don't get the clap, either." O'Doull nodded to the kid, who wasn't far wrong there, either—it was a big needle. "Bend over."

Most unwillingly, the U.S. soldier obeyed. "Shit," he muttered. "I went through the last year and a half of the war. I got a Purple Heart. And I'm more scared of your damn shot than I was of the screaming meemies."

He wasn't the first man to say something like that. With bullets and shells and rockets, you could always think they'd miss. When somebody aimed a hypodermic at your bare ass, he'd damn well connect.

And O'Doull did. The PFC let out a yip as he pressed home the needle and pressed in the plunger. "You get one on the other side three days from now. If you don't show up, you're in a lot more trouble than you are for coming down venereal. You got that?"

"Yes, sir," the kid said miserably. "Can I go now, sir?"

He really did want to escape if he was that eager to return to the clutches of his regular superiors. O'Doull couldn't do anything but stick him, but they could—and would—give him hell. Still, he wasn't quite finished here. "Not yet, son. You need to tell me the name of the woman you got it from, where she lives, and the names of any others you've screwed since. We don't want 'em passing it along to any of your buddies, you know."

"Oh, hell—uh, sir. Do I gotta?"

"You sure do. VD puts a man out of action just as much as a bullet in the leg does. So . . . who was she? And were there any others?"

"Damn, damn, damn," the PFC said. "There's just the one, anyway. Her name is Betsy, and she lives a couple of miles from here, on a farm outside of Montevallo."

Montevallo was a pissant little town south of Birmingham. It boasted a small college for women; O'Doull had wondered whether the soldier got his disease from a student with liberal notions. Evidently not. Montevallo also boasted a large oak called the Hangman's Tree, which had come through the war undamaged. The doctor wondered whether the tree and the college were related. The PFC wouldn't know about that, though.

"You have a last name for Miss Betsy?" O'Doull asked. The soldier shook his head. O'Doull sighed. "One of the things you'll do between now and when I stick your ass again is take some men and get her and bring her back here so we can treat her, too. Got that?"

"Yes, sir." It was hardly more than a whisper.

"You'd better have it. And *now* you can go," O'Doull said. The PFC slunk away. O'Doull sighed. "Boy, I enjoyed that."

"I bet," Sergeant Lord said. "Still, it beats the crap out of trying to take out a guy's spleen, doesn't it?"

"Well, yeah," O'Doull admitted. "But damn, we've had a lot of venereals since the shooting stopped." He sighed one more time. "Don't know why I'm so surprised. The guys can really go looking for pussy now, and the Confederate women know they've lost, so they'd better be nice to our troops. But I keep thinking about Donofrio, the medic you replaced. VD isn't the only thing that can happen to you."

"You told me about that before," Lord said, so politely that O'Doull knew he'd told him at least once too often. The medic went on, "I'm not going to make a fuss about any silly bitch down here."

"Well, good," O'Doull said, and wondered if it was. Would Goodson Lord make a fuss about a silly boy instead? O'Doull hoped not. If the sergeant was queer, he seemed to be discreet about it. As long as he stayed that way, well, what the hell?

Betsy came in the next day, cussing out the soldiers who brought her in a command car. She was about eighteen, with a barmaid's prettiness that wouldn't last and a barmaid's ample flesh that would turn to lard before she hit thirty. "What do you mean, I got some kind of disease?" she shouted at O'Doull.

"Sorry, miss," he said. "Private, uh, Eubanks"—he had to remember the soldier's name—"says you left him a little present. We can cure you with a couple of shots."

"I bet he didn't catch it from me. I bet the dirty son of a bitch got it somewhere else and gave it to me!" she screeched.

From the freshness of the U.S. soldier's chancre, O'Doull doubted that. Out loud, he said, "Well, you may be right," which was one of the useful phrases that weren't liable to land you in much trouble. It didn't matter one way or the other, anyhow. "I'm going to need to examine you, maybe draw some blood for a test, and give you a shot, just in case."

"What do you mean, examine me? Examine me *there*?" Betsy shook her head, which made blond curls flip back and forth on either side of her face. She would have seemed more alluring—to O'Doull, anyway—if she'd bathed any time lately. "You ain't gonna look up my works, pal, and that's flat, not when I never set eyes on you till just now. What kind of girl d'you reckon I am?"

Had O'Doull told the truth there, he would have had to listen to more screeching. "This is a medical necessity," he said. "I'm a doctor. I'm also a married man, in case you're wondering."

Betsy tossed her head in splendid scorn. "Like that makes a difference! I know you're just a dumb damnyankee, but I didn't think even damnyankees were that dumb."

O'Doull sighed. It *didn't* make any difference; he'd seen as much plenty of times in Rivière-du-Loup. He wished he were back there now. Better—*much* better!—sweet Nicole than this blowsy, foul-mouthed gal. "Get up on the table, please," he said. "No stirrups, I'm afraid. It wasn't made with that in mind."

"Stirrups? What the hell are you talkin' about?" Betsy said. "And I done told you I don't want to get up there."

O'Doull's patience blew out. "Your other choice is the stockade," he snapped. "Quit fooling around and wasting my time."

"Oh, all right, goddammit, if I gotta." Betsy climbed onto the table and divested herself of her drawers. O'Doull put on rubber gloves. He felt as if he needed them more here than with most of the ordinary war wounds he'd treated. "Having fun?" she asked him as he got to work.

"In a word, no," he answered, so coldly that she not only shut up with a snap but gave him a fierce glare, which he ignored. He went on, "You've got it, all right. You ought to thank your boyfriend for getting you over here."

"Not likely!" she said, and added some verbal hot sauce to the comment.

"However you please," O'Doull told her. "Roll over onto your stomach so I can give you your first shot." Goodson Lord ceremoniously handed him a syringe.

"Will it hurt?" she asked.

"A little." O'Doull jabbed the needle home. She yipped. He didn't care. "You need to come back in three days for your second injection," he told her.

"What happens if I don't?" Betsy sure hadn't said no to PFC Eubanks—or, odds were, to a lot of guys before him—but she was co-operating with O'Doull as little as she could.

"Two things," O'Doull said. "We come and get you, and we tell your folks and everybody in Montevallo how come we came and got you."

"You wouldn't do that!"

"When it comes to getting rid of VD, we'll do whatever it takes. Dammit, this is for your own good."

"Then how come it hurts?" Betsy whined.

"If we didn't treat you, you'd hurt more down the line," O'Doull said. Actually, a lot of syphilis patients didn't have symptoms for years after the primary lesions went away. Some never did. But syphilis was also the great pretender; a lot of ills that seemed to be other things really went back to the spirochete that caused it. If you could get rid of the germ, you needed to.

"Might as well get used to it, Doc," Sergeant Lord advised. "This is what we'll see from here on out—guys with drippy faucets, guys in auto crashes, every once in a while a guy who steps on a mine or something."

"Could be worse," O'Doull said. "Long as we don't start having lots of guys who guerrillas shot, I won't kick."

"Amen to that," the medic said.

"Can I go now?" Betsy asked, much as her boyfriend in green-gray had.

"Yes, you can go," O'Doull answered. "If you don't come back for your next shot, remember, we'll make you sorry you didn't."

"I won't forget," she said sullenly. "My pa, he'll kill me if he finds out." By the way she scurried away from the aid tent, she meant that literally.

"Wonder how many round-heeled broads we'll give the needle to," Lord said.

"Quite a few, I bet," O'Doull said. "And if it's going to be that kind of practice, you can handle it as well as I can." He was thinking about home again. He wasn't a career soldier; he had a life away from the Army. He had it, and he wanted to go back to it.

Goodson Lord gave him a shrewd look. "Won't be too long before they start figuring out how to turn people loose, I bet. You paid your dues and then some."

"Yeah." O'Doull nodded. *And once I get back into the Republic of Quebec, they'll never pry me out again.* There had been times when his practice in Rivière-du-Loup bored him. He hadn't been bored the past three years. Scared out of his mind? Astonished? Appalled? All of those, and often, but never bored. He was amazed at how wonderful ennui seemed.

* * *

Abner Dowling stared at Lexington, Virginia, with nothing less than amazement. He turned to his adjutant and said, "Damned if it doesn't look like they used a superbomb on this place."

Lieutenant Colonel Toricelli nodded. "Yes, sir. The fun we had getting here should have given us a hint, I suppose."

"Fun? Heh. That's one word for it, I guess," Dowling said. As the crow flew, Lexington was only about 110 miles from Richmond. Dowling wished he'd flown from the capital—the former capital?—of the CSA. He'd gone by command car instead, and the roads were disastrously bad . . . which said nothing about the wrecked bridges and the places where mines were still being cleared. What might have been a two-and-a-half-hour drive ended up taking a day and a half.

Something moved in the rubble. At first he thought it was a stray dog. Then he realized what it really was: a possum. It looked like a cat-sized rat that had got its nose stuck in a pencil sharpener. The long, bare pinkish tail seemed vaguely obscene. Lieutenant Colonel Toricelli was looking in the same direction. "If that's not the ugliest thing God ever made, damned if I know what is," he said.

"Now that Jake Featherston's dead, I agree with you," Dowling said, which jerked a laugh from the younger man.

Washington University lay on the north side of town. U.S. soldiers who'd come down from the north right after the surrender were already thick on the ground there. The only way you could tell the university grounds from the rest of Lexington these days was that they'd taken an even heavier pounding from the skies.

It didn't do enough, dammit, Dowling thought. In spite of everything that came down on their heads, the Confederate physicists managed to put together a superbomb. Abstractly, Dowling admired the achievement. Staying abstract when they'd blown a big chunk of Philadelphia off the map wasn't so easy, though.

The surviving physicists were housed in tents surrounded by barbed wire and machine-gun nests. A U.S. colonel named Benjamin Frankheimer was in charge of them. Before he let Dowling in to talk with the prisoners, he checked with the War Department.

"Weren't you told to expect me?" Dowling asked.

"Yes, sir," Frankheimer replied. "But we haven't met, and I wanted to make sure they confirmed that a man of your description went with your name."

"You're . . . a careful man, Colonel."

"Taking care of people who know this kind of stuff, I need to be, sir." Frankheimer scratched his nose. It was much the most prominent feature on his face: he was little and skinny and looked very, very Jewish. Dowling guessed he'd got this job because he was a scientist himself . . . till he noticed the fruit salad on the colonel's chest. It showed he'd won a Distinguished Service Cross, a Silver Star with oak-leaf cluster, and a Purple Heart with oak-leaf cluster. Frankheimer had had himself a busy war.

"Well?" Dowling said. "Am I who I say I am?"

"Oh, yes, sir. No doubt about it," Frankheimer answered. "You're free to go in and do whatever you need to do—now."

"Thanks." Dowling sounded less sarcastic than he might have. The men inside this heavily guarded compound weren't just dynamite—they were a hell of a lot more explosive than that, and they'd proved it.

He wasn't astonished when he and Lieutenant Colonel Toricelli had to surrender their sidearms before going in, either. He didn't think of physicists as tough guys, but you never knew. If the fellows with the white lab coats and the slide rules didn't have the chance to grab any weapons, they wouldn't be tempted.

The first man he saw inside the compound sure didn't look like a tough guy. The fellow was about fifty, on the skinny side, and walked with a limp and a cane. "Can you tell me where Professor FitzBelmont is?" Dowling called to him.

"That tent there." The middle-aged man pointed.

"Thanks." Dowling ducked inside.

He recognized FitzBelmont right away; the photos he'd studied were good likenesses. Tall, tweedy, bespectacled: he *looked* like a physicist, all right. He gave Dowling a grudging nod. "Pleased to meet you," he said, and then, "I've already met a lot of U.S. officers"—so he probably wasn't *very* pleased.

"Come outside with me, Professor," Dowling said. "We've got some talking to do."

"If you like," FitzBelmont said. "But anything you say to me, my colleagues can also hear. What are you going to do with us, anyway?"

"Well, that's one of the things I'm here to talk about," Dowling answered. "More than a few people in Philadelphia who want to string you up by the thumbs, paint you with gasoline, and light a match. Then there are the ones who think that's too good for you."

Some of the scientists and technicians in there with FitzBelmont flinched. He didn't. "I don't understand why," he said. "We were serving our country in the same way that your scientists were serving the United States. If your service is permitted, even heroic, why shouldn't ours be, as well?"

He had a scientist's detachment—or maybe he was just a natural-born cold fish. "There is a difference, Professor," Dowling said.

"I fail to see it," Henderson FitzBelmont said.

"Why am I not surprised?" Lieutenant Colonel Toricelli murmured.

"Hush," Dowling said, and then, to FitzBelmont, "It's simple. I'll spell it out for you. We won. You lost. There. Is that plain enough?"

"To the victors go the spoils?" FitzBelmont said. "Is that what this war was about?"

"That's part of it. If you don't believe me, ask Jake Featherston," Dowling answered. FitzBelmont turned red, so maybe at one point or another he *had* asked the late, unlamented President of the CSA. Dowling continued, "The other part is, now you can't go on murdering your own smokes any more."

FitzBelmont got redder. "I didn't know anything about that."

"I ought to kick your scrawny ass for lying, you miserable son of a bitch," Dowling said with weary revulsion. "If I had a dime for every Confederate shithead who told me the same thing, I'd be too rich to wear this uniform—you'd best believe I would. Where the hell did you think all the coons in fucking Lexington disappeared to? You think somebody swept 'em under the goddamn rug?"

"I never even considered the issue," Professor FitzBelmont said.

Dowling almost did haul off and belt him. But the way FitzBelmont said it gave him pause. Unlike most of his countrymen, the physicist might have been telling the truth. From the reports the USA had on FitzBelmont, he had trouble noticing anything bigger than an atomic nucleus.

"How many millions did they do in, Angelo?" Dowling asked.

"Best guess right now is about eight million, sir," his adjutant replied. "But that could be off a million either way, easy."

"And you never considered the issue?" Dowling tried to wither Henderson FitzBelmont with his scorn.

"I'm afraid not," FitzBelmont said, unwithered. "We had no Negroes at all involved in the project. Even our cooks and janitors were whites or Mexicans. Negroes were deemed to be security risks, and so we did not see them. It's as simple as that, I'm afraid."

The Confederates had good reason to think Negroes might be security risks. Blacks had brought the USA lots of good intelligence data. Dowling didn't know how much in the way of physics a cook or janitor could understand. Understand it or not, anybody could steal papers, though. Which reminded him . . .

"Under the terms of the surrender, you're supposed to keep all your paperwork intact. You've done that?"

"What survives of it, yes, certainly."

"What's that mean?" Dowling demanded.

"You ought to know," Professor FitzBelmont said. "Your airplanes have been bombing Lexington for the past year. Do you think you didn't do any damage? You'd better think again."

"Huh," Dowling said. The Confederate physicist had a better excuse than *The dog ate my homework*. He and his pals could have destroyed anything, and then blamed it on U.S. bombers. Dowling didn't know what he could do about it, either.

"It is possible for you to expect too much of us, you know," FitzBelmont said.

"Maybe. I'm not the expert," Dowling agreed. "But you will be interrogated by people who are experts—I promise you that. Even if your paperwork is gone, they'll figure out what you were up to. And yes, you're obliged to cooperate with them."

"If we don't?" the physicist asked.

Dowling made hand-washing motions. "God help you, in that case. You can bet your bottom dollar nobody else will."

"You have an unpleasant way of making your point," Professor FitzBelmont said.

"Thank you," Dowling answered, which stopped FitzBelmont in his tracks.

After a moment, the physicist asked, "When will they let us go?"

"Beats me," Dowling answered cheerfully. "Suppose you'd won. When would you have let our superbomb people go? Ever?"

"I . . . don't know," the Confederate scientist said slowly. That, at least, struck Dowling as basically truthful. Henderson FitzBelmont went on, "Surely you understand that we can't be dangerous to the

United States without facilities like the ones we had here. You can't make a superbomb with a blackboard and chalk."

"I don't know anything about that. It's not my call to make, anyhow," Dowling said. "My job is to make sure you're here, to make sure you're well protected, and to put you at the disposal of our scientists when they get around to needing you. I'm taking care of that right now."

"How about making sure we're well treated?" FitzBelmont asked.

"Believe me, Professor, you are," Dowling said. "You have shelter. You have enough to eat. You have a doctor and a dentist when you need one. Compared to the average white man in the CSA these days, you're in hog heaven. Compared to the average Negro in the CSA . . . Hell, you're alive. That puts you ahead of the game right there."

Professor FitzBelmont looked severe. "If that's a joke, General, it's in poor taste."

"Who's joking?" Dowling said. "You're the one who didn't look at what was going on with your Negroes, you say? We're going to hang some of the bastards who did that to them. Crimes against humanity, we're calling it. Considering what happened in Philadelphia, you ought to thank your lucky stars we aren't charging you with the same thing . . . yet."

"How could you do that when your own scientists built the bombs that blew up Newport News and Charleston? Where is the justice there?"

Dowling shook his head. FitzBelmont really didn't get it. "How much justice would you have given our guys if you won? As much as you gave your own smokes? We don't need justice, Professor—I told you that once already. We may use it, but we don't need it. We damn well won."

Colonel Roy Wyden eyed Jonathan Moss with what looked like real sympathy. "What are we going to do with you?" Wyden asked.

"Beats me, sir," Moss answered. "Not much call for a fighter jockey any more, is there? Especially one who's my age, I mean."

"I'm sorry, but there isn't," Wyden said. "Your file shows you weren't in the military straight through. What did you do between the wars?"

"I'm a lawyer, sir."

Wyden brightened. "Well, hell, you'll make more money after you muster out than you're pulling down now."

Moss laughed harshly. "It ain't necessarily so. My specialty was occupation law. For one thing, the Canadian uprising's still going. For another, they'll change all the rules once they finally do knock it flat. And, for another, I don't want to go back to it anyway. A terrorist blew up my wife and my daughter. Maybe the bomb was meant for me—I don't know. But that's the big reason I rejoined. So I don't really have anywhere else to go."

"Jesus! I guess you don't. I'm sorry. I didn't know your story," Wyden said.

"Not like I'm the only one who's had the roof fall in on him," Moss said. "I'll land on my feet one way or another."

"If you think you will, chances are you're right," Wyden said. "Let me make a few telephone calls for you, see if I can line something up."

"What have you got in mind?" Moss asked.

"I don't want to tell you yet, in case it doesn't pan out," Wyden answered. "Are you willing to give me a couple of days to see if it will?"

"Sure. Why not?" Moss managed a wry grin. "It isn't like I've got a hell of a lot of other stuff going on." He left Colonel Wyden's tent more intrigued than he'd thought he would be.

Wyden didn't summon him back for three days. When he did, he came straight to the point: "How would you like to go to the Republic of Texas?"

"To do what?" Moss inquired.

"They're going to try the bastards who ran Camp Determination and then Camp Humble," Wyden answered. "They've got guys lined up from here out the door to prosecute them, but their number one defense lawyer, a guy named Izzy Goldstein, was in an auto wreck last week. He's in the hospital, pretty torn up—no way he'll be able to fill that slot now. So they're looking for a legal eagle. Are you game?"

Moss whistled softly. "I don't know. I mean, I think those guys are guilty as shit. Don't you?"

"Of course I do," Wyden answered. "You're the lawyer, though. Don't guilty people deserve to have somebody on their side, too?"

That was a commonplace argument in law school. Moss had always believed it there. He'd acted on it, too, when he was doing occupation law up in Canada. A lot of his clients there weren't guilty of anything worse than falling foul of U.S. occupation procedures. This . . . This was a different story. "Only thing worse would be defending Jake Featherston himself."

"Funny you should mention that," Wyden answered. "The people I talked to said they were gonna shoot him without trial if they caught him. That colored kid just took care of it for them, that's all. Look, you don't have to do this if you can't stomach it. I'm not giving you orders or anything—I wouldn't, not for this kind of thing. But you were at loose ends, and it's military justice, so you're qualified, you know what I mean? Your call. One of the guys there remembers you from Canada. He said you were a son of a bitch, but you were a smart son of a bitch."

"From a military prosecutor, that's a compliment . . . I guess," Moss said. Colonel Wyden grinned and waited. Moss lit a Raleigh to help himself think. "Damn," he muttered, sucking in smoke. He blew it out in what was at least half a sigh. "Tell you what. Why don't I go over there and talk to one of those assholes? If I decide to take it on, I will. If I don't . . . I won't, that's all." The Army couldn't put much pressure on him. If it did, he'd damn well resign his commission. Then he'd have to figure out what to do with the rest of his life as a civilian, that was all.

Roy Wyden nodded. "Sounds fair enough. If you do tackle it, you'll be doing them a favor, not the other way around. I'll cut you orders for transit to Houston—the city, not the state. That's gonna confuse the crap out of people for a while."

And so Jonathan Moss found himself riding a train across Alabama, Mississippi, and Louisiana. It was, perhaps, the most surreal journey of his life. He passed through the part of the Confederacy that the United States hadn't occupied during the war. Not many soldiers in green-gray had entered that part of the country yet. It felt very much like going into enemy territory.

The Confederate States still felt like a going concern there, too. The Stars and Bars flew from flagpoles. Soldiers in butternut still carried weapons. Nobody gave him any trouble, though, for which he was duly grateful.

His train had an hour's layover in Hattiesburg, Mississippi. He got out to stretch his legs and grab a sandwich and a Dr. Hopper—he'd spent enough time in the CSA to get used to the stuff. When he came back to the platform, he found three or four Confederate soldiers facing off with a squad of men in green-gray who'd just got off a truck. Plainly, the U.S. troops were there to let the town know things really had changed and the surrender was no joke.

Just as plainly, the C.S. soldiers didn't want to believe it. "Well, hell," one of them said, "y'all may have whupped those sorry bastards back East, but you never licked us." His pals nodded.

As if by magic, all the U.S. soldiers brought up their weapons at the same time. Their sergeant stepped forward and shoved the mouthy Confederate to the floor. He kicked him in the ribs—probably not hard enough to break any, but not with any token little thump, either. "How about now, fucker?" he asked. "Have we licked you yet, or do we have to blow your goddamn head off to get the message across? Talk fast, or you're dead meat."

"Reckon . . . maybe . . . I'm licked," the man in butternut wheezed.

"Bet your sweet ass you are." The sergeant kicked him again, then stepped back. "Get it straight—you fuck with us, we make you sorry you tried, on account of we'd sooner kill you than look at you."

As long as U.S. forces felt that way, Moss judged, they at least had a chance of staying ahead of any Confederate insurgency. The soldier in butternut struggled to his feet. His buddies helped him get away from the men in green-gray. All the new occupiers looked ready to spray bullets around the train station. They grinned at Moss. "We showed him!" one of them crowed.

"You bet," Moss replied, and their grins got wider. What would they say if they found out he was heading west to see if he wanted to defend the Confederate officers who ran a murder factory? Nothing he wanted to hear—he was sure of that. And so he didn't tell them.

When he passed from Louisiana to Texas, the Lone Star flag replaced the Stars and Bars. He wondered how long the United States would go on letting the Texans pretend they were independent. Recognizing their secession from the CSA had been a useful way to get them out of the war, but he didn't think it was likely to last.

A Texas Ranger stood on the platform holding a small cardboard sign with his name on it. When Moss admitted who he was, the Texan—who was short and wiry, going dead against the image the men of his state liked to put across—said, "I'm here to take you to the city jail, sir."

"Then let's go," Moss answered.

The Ranger didn't have much to say. Houston seemed almost intact. Not many Confederate cities were farther from U.S. bomber bases. People on the street wore old, shabby clothes, but they didn't look hungry.

"How do you feel about working with the United States?" Moss asked when the auto—a Confederate Birmingham—stopped in front of the red-brick fortress that housed prisoners.

"Sir, where we were at, it looked like the best thing to do." With that less than ringing endorsement, the Texas Ranger killed the engine. He hopped out and held the door open for Moss.

U.S. officers meticulously checked Moss' ID and then patted him down before admitting him to the building. He got checked and searched again when he went into the visitors' room. A tight steel mesh separated his side from that of the man he might be representing.

In came Jefferson Pinkard. The fellow who'd run Camp Determination and Camp Humble was about Moss' age. He had a big, burly frame: muscles with a lot of fat over them. He looked tough, but not vicious. Moss knew how little that proved, but found it interesting all the same.

Pinkard was giving him the once-over, too. "So the damnyankees found another bastard willing to speak up for me?" he asked in a Deep-South drawl.

"I don't know that I am yet," Moss answered. "Why did you want to kill off as many Negroes as you could?"

Had Pinkard denied it, Moss would have walked out. He didn't, though. He said, "Because they were enemies of my country. They were shooting at us before we started fighting you Yankee bastards."

"Men, women, and children?" Moss said.

"They're black, they don't like us," Pinkard said. " 'Sides, what business of yours is it, anyway? They were Confederate niggers. We can do what we damn well please in our own country. Far as I know, we didn't do anything to coons from the USA."

As far as Moss knew, that was true. He thought it was Pinkard's strongest argument. A country was sovereign inside its own borders, wasn't it? Nobody had gone after the Ottoman Sultan for what he did to the Armenians or the Tsar for pogroms against Jews . . . or the United States for what they did to their Indians. But . . . "Nobody ever made camps like yours."

"Nobody ever thought to." Jefferson Pinkard didn't sound repentant—he sounded proud. "Fuck, you assholes are gonna hang me. You won, and I can't do shit about it. But the only thing I was doing was, I was doing my job. I did it goddamn well, too."

"I read that the mayor of Snyder killed himself after he got a look at the mass graves your camp had there," Moss said.

"Some people are soft," Pinkard said scornfully. "Yeah, we lost the war. But we'll never have to worry about niggers down here, not the way we did before. Hell, you can even ask these chickenshit Texas traitors—they'll tell you I'm all right in their book. I helped clean out Texas along with the rest of the CSA. You can defend me or not, however you please. I know what I did, and I'm damned if I'm sorry."

You're damned, all right, Moss thought. Did guilty people really and truly need lawyers just like anybody else? Did he want to be one of them? There were all kinds of ways to go down in history. Was this the one he really had in mind?

If he didn't do it, who would? Whoever it was, would the fellow do as good a job as Moss would himself? He had to doubt it, especially with the Army's chief defense lawyer already down for the count. He didn't believe anybody could get Pinkard off, but he'd always enjoyed giving military prosecutors a run for their money.

In the end, that—and being at loose ends as a pilot with the war over—decided him. "Do you want me to defend you? I'll give it my best shot."

"D'you reckon you can get me loose?" Pinkard asked. "Or was I right the first time?"

"Long odds against you, mighty long. Anybody who tells you different is lying, too, just so you know."

The camp commandant grunted. "Fuck. It looked that way to me, too, and to that Goldstein guy, but I was hoping maybe you saw it different. But, shit, even if you don't, Colonel Moss, I'm mighty glad to have you. Do whatever the hell you can, and see if you can embarrass 'em before they put a noose around my neck."

He didn't have unreasonable expectations, anyhow, which was the start of being a good client. "I think we've got ourselves a deal," Jonathan Moss said. Because of the wire screen, they couldn't even shake on it.

*   *   *

A lot of the Confederate officers at Camp Liberty! sank into despair when they finally believed their country had surrendered. Most of the ones who took the surrender hardest had been in there longest. They hadn't seen the disasters of the past year and a half with their own eyes. Jerry Dover had. He knew damn well that the Confederate States were licked.

"Yeah, we lost," he'd say whenever somebody asked him about it—or sometimes even when nobody did.

"Why don't you soft-pedal the doom and gloom, Dover?" Colonel Kirby Smith Telford asked him. The senior C.S. officer was convinced Dover wasn't a Yankee plant, which didn't mean he was happy with him. "People already feel bad enough without you rubbing it in."

"Christ on a crutch, it's over. We're licked," Dover said. "How can it be doom and gloom after we're doomed?"

"Keeping our chins up means we can respect ourselves," Telford answered. "It makes U.S. forces respect us more, too."

That last might even have been true. It left Dover no happier. "What difference does it make?" he demanded. "We don't even have a country any more. The United States are occupying the whole CSA. Far as I can see, that turns us into damnyankees."

"My ass," Telford said. "I'll see them in hell before I bow down and worship the goddamn Stars and Stripes."

"Yes, sir. I feel the same way," Dover said. "Only problem is, as long as we feel that way, why should the Yankees let us out of this place?"

"Why? Because the war's over, dammit, that's why." But not even Kirby Smith Telford could make himself sound as if he thought that was reason enough.

The U.S. authorities showed no signs of letting their commissioned POWs go free. After a few days, Colonel Telford asked them why not. The answer he got left him scowling.

"They say they're investigating to see if they need to charge any of us with this 'crimes against humanity' crap," he reported.

Jerry Dover didn't like the sound of that. It struck him as being vague enough to let the United States do whatever they pleased. "What exactly do they mean by that?" he asked.

"Well, what they were mostly talking about with me was finding out whether we ever gave niggers up to the people who shipped 'em off to the camps," Telford answered.

"Oh." Dover relaxed. About the most hideous thing he'd done as a quartermaster officer was send gas shells up to the front. Since the damnyankees had used gas themselves, they couldn't very well get their bowels in an uproar about it . . . unless they felt like getting their bowels in an uproar. If they did, who was going to stop them?

Nobody this side of the Kaiser, that was who.

Someone said, "They can't treat us this way," so maybe he thought he *was* the Kaiser, or else somebody even more important.

Kirby Smith Telford looked bleak and sounded bleaker. "Not much we can do about it. Not anything we can do about it, far as I know. If they decide to line us up and shoot us, who's going to complain to them?"

"It ain't right," the other Confederate officer said. Telford only shrugged.

Who'd complained when the Confederacy got rid of its Negroes? Dover knew he hadn't. He also knew his fellow officers wouldn't appreciate his pointing that out. Sometimes the smartest thing you could do was just keep your big mouth shut. Dover, a man who liked to yell at people, had been a long time learning that. He had the lesson now, though.

One by one, the officers in his barracks hall got summoned to their interrogations. A few left Camp Liberty! not much later. The rest stayed where they were, fuming and cursing their damnyankee captors. Dover wondered how smart the victors were. If these POWs hadn't been embittered Yankee-haters who would do anything they could to hurt the USA once they finally got free, they were more likely to turn into men with views like that the longer they sat and stewed.

Of course, maybe the U.S. authorities didn't intend to let them go at all. Dover imagined stooped, white-haired POWs dying of old age as the twentieth century passed into the twenty-first. He shivered. Not even the Yankees could stay vengeful for upwards of half a century . . . could they?

They seemed to be questioning prisoners in roughly the order the Confederates had been captured. That meant Jerry Dover had quite a while to wait. He was perfectly willing to be patient.

Kirby Smith Telford came back from his grilling hot enough to cook over. "I'm a special case, the sons of bitches say," he rasped.

"How come?" Dover asked. "You were just a combat soldier, right? Why are they flabbling about you, then?"

"On account of I'm from Texas, that's why," Telford answered. "From the goddamn traitor Republic of Texas, now. If I'm gonna get outa here, I have to swear to be loyal to a country"—he made as if to spit at the very idea—"that betrayed the country I grew up in."

"You could just ask them to ship you back to some other part of the CSA," Dover said.

"I tried that. It only made things worse," Telford said bleakly. "They reckoned I said that because I wanted to raise trouble for them. I didn't mean it that way—not then I didn't. But Jesus God! If I get out of here now . . ." He didn't say what he would do then. What he didn't say, nobody could report to the authorities. Dover didn't have much trouble figuring it out, though.

"Probably should have done whatever they told you to do, and then gone on about your business afterwards," he said.

"Yeah. I figured that out, too, only not quick enough to do me any goddamn good." Kirby Smith Telford sounded almost as disgusted at himself as he did at his Yankee interrogators.

Dover's turn came about a week later, on a summer day as hot and sticky as any in Savannah. The officer who questioned him was a major about half his age, a fellow named Hendrickson. He had a manila folder with Dover's name on it. It was fat with papers. Dover wondered whether that was a good sign or a bad one.

"You were in the Quartermaster Corps," Major Hendrickson said. He had a prissy little hairline mustache that didn't go with the shape of his face.

"I sure was," Dover said.

"You were taken outside of Huntsville."

"That's right."

"You fought in the Great War, but you're not career military."

"Right again." This ground seemed safe enough.

Hendrickson lit a cigarette—a nasty U.S. brand. He didn't offer one to Dover. Instead, he went through some of the papers in the folder. "Tell me what you did between the wars."

"I managed a restaurant in Savannah, Georgia," Dover replied. Hendrickson asked him for the name of the place. "The Huntsman's Lodge," Dover said, wondering why that could possibly matter.

It seemed to; Major Hendrickson grunted and checked something off. Dover tried to see what it was, but he couldn't read upside down well enough to tell. The interrogator went on, "Did you employ Negroes in this restaurant?"

"Yeah," Dover said. "Cooks and waiters and cleanup crew. Couldn't hardly get along without 'em."

"We don't seem to have any trouble," Hendrickson said primly. Dover only shrugged; he didn't care how damnyankees ran their eateries. The interrogator riffled through his papers some more. "Was one of these Negroes a man named, uh, Xerxes?"

He botched the name, so Dover almost didn't recognize it. "Xerxes?" He said it the right way, as if the first X was a Z. "Yeah, he worked for me for years. Hell of a smart guy. Probably would've been a lawyer or a Congressman if he was white. But how the devil did you know that?"

Annoyingly, Hendrickson answered a question with another question: "Do you remember his son's name?"

"Have to think about that—I only met him a couple of times. He was . . . Cassius. How come?" Before the Yankee major answered, Dover's jaw dropped. "Sweet suffering Jesus! Not *that* Cassius?" The U.S. wireless wouldn't shut up about the Negro who'd shot Jake Featherston.

Major Hendrickson nodded. "The very same. And it just so happened your name came up a couple-three times when we questioned him."

"Oh, yeah?" Dover had never imagined his fate could rest on a black man's—hell, on a black kid's—word. "What'd he have to say?"

Before answering, Hendrickson shuffled papers, even though he had to know already. Dover wanted to clout him, but made himself sit tight. "He said you treated his old man pretty decent. Said you saved his whole family from a cleanout once. Is that a fact?"

"Yeah." Dover didn't want to make a big deal out of it now. He'd saved Scipio and his family—and several other colored workers and theirs—as much to keep the Huntsman's Lodge going as for any other reason. But this U.S. soldier didn't need to know that. "What about it?"

"Well, it means you aren't real likely to be a hardcore Freedom Party man," Hendrickson said. "Will you swear an oath to live peacefully in Georgia and not to cause trouble for the United States if we let you go?"

"Major, I have lived through two wars now. I have had enough trouble to last me the rest of my days," Dover said. "Read me out your oath. I will swear to it, and I will live up to it."

"Raise your right hand," Hendrickson said. Dover did. The oath was what the U.S. soldier said it was. Dover repeated it, swore to it, and then signed a printed copy in triplicate. "Show one copy to U.S. military authorities on request," Hendrickson told him. "We will give you the balance of your back pay and a train ticket to Augusta. You can wear your uniform, but take off your rank badges before you leave the camp. The C.S. Army is out of business."

Kirby Smith Telford scowled at Dover as he packed a meager duffel and took the stars off his collar. Other POWs eyed him with varying mixtures of envy and hatred. He didn't care. He was going home.

A young captain looked at Cincinnatus from across a no-doubt-liberated card table that did duty for a desk. "You are Cincinnatus Driver," he said.

"Yes, sir. I sure am," Cincinnatus agreed.

"You have been serving as a civilian truck driver attached to the U.S. Army since the end of 1942," the captain said.

"That's right, too. Did the same thing in the las' war," Cincinnatus said.

"Yes—so your records indicate. According to your superiors, you always performed your duties well, in spite of your physical limitations."

"Always done the best I could," Cincinnatus answered. "I had to stick around when it got tight—couldn't hardly run."

"You're probably eager to return to your family in, uh, Des Moines"—the captain had to check Cincinnatus' papers before naming his home town—"now that we have achieved victory."

Cincinnatus nodded. "Sure am. You know anybody who ain't?"

To his surprise, the officer took the question seriously. "There are always some who are more comfortable in the Army. They don't have to think for themselves here—they just have to do as they're told. And they never have any doubts about who's on their side and who isn't."

The young officer was probably right. No, he was bound to be right. "Hadn't thought of it that way, sir," Cincinnatus said. "But me, I'm a big boy. I can take care of myself, and I can make up my own mind. And if the government's ready to muster me out, I'm real ready to go home."

"That's what you're here to arrange," the captain said. "I have your final pay warrant here, and I have a train ticket to get you home."

"Ask you a favor, sir?"

"I don't know. What is it?"

"Can you arrange my train route to take me through Covington, Kentucky? I was born and raised there, and I want to see if any of my people in the colored quarter came through in one piece."

"It's irregular. It's an extra expense . . ." The officer in green-gray frowned, considering. "Let me talk to my superiors. You may have to stay in Alabama an extra day or two while we set things up—if they approve, that is."

"I don't mind," Cincinnatus said. "Not even a little bit."

He stayed an extra three days, in fact. The rest of the drivers in his unit headed for home long before he did. Hal Williamson shook his hand and said, "Good luck to you, buddy. Goddamn if I didn't learn something from you."

"What's that?" Cincinnatus asked.

"Colored guys—you're just like anybody else, only darker," Hal answered.

Cincinnatus laughed. "Shit, I'll take that. Good luck to you, too, man."

He got the travel orders he wanted. Back in Confederate days, he would have had to ride in a separate car. No more. Some white passengers looked unhappy at sharing a row with him, but nobody said anything. That suited him well enough. He didn't ask to be loved: only tolerated.

The Stars and Stripes flew over Covington. A blue X that stood for the C.S. battle flag showed up on walls all over town. So did the word FREEDOM! The CSA had lost the war, but not everybody had given up.

Buses were running. He took one east from the train station to the colored quarter by the Licking River, or what was left of it. He sat up near the front of the bus, the first time he'd been able to do that here regardless of whether Covington flew the Stars and Stripes or Stars and Bars.

Not all the fences and barbed wire that sealed off the colored quarter had come down yet. But ways through the stuff were open now. Cincinnatus got off the bus a couple of blocks from Lucullus Wood's barbecue place. If anyone had come through what the Confederates did to their Negroes, he would have bet on the Red barbecue cook.

Houses and shops stood empty. Windows had broken panes; doors sagged open. Leaves drifted on lawns. Ice shivered up Cincinnatus' spine. What was that fancy word people used when they talked about dinosaurs? This place was *extinct*.

A stray cat darted across the street and behind some untrimmed bushes. Cats could take care of themselves without people. Cincinnatus didn't hear any barking dogs. He should have, if the colored quarter had any life left to it.

When he saw somebody else on the street, he jumped in surprise and alarm. It was an old white man in a cool linen suit, his white hair shining under his Panama hat. The white man seemed as startled to spot a Negro as Cincinnatus was to see him. Then, all of a sudden, he wasn't. "I might have known it would be you," he said. "You're tougher to kill than a cockroach, aren't you?"

"Go to hell, Bliss," Cincinnatus said wearily. "Lucullus still alive?"

"His place looks as dead as the rest of this part of town," Luther Bliss answered. The longtime head of the Kentucky State Police sighed. "I tried to get him out once they closed off the colored quarter, but I couldn't do it. Don't know what happened to him, but I'm afraid it's nothing good. Damn shame."

"They go and kill everybody?" Cincinnatus asked. "They really go an' do that?"

"Just about," Bliss said. "And you were in bed with 'em for a while. Doesn't that make you proud?"

"Fuck off and die," Cincinnatus said coldly. "I was never in bed with the goddamn Freedom Party, and you know it."

Luther Bliss spat. "Maybe. I never knew anything about you for sure, though. That's how come I never trusted you."

Cincinnatus laughed in his face. "Don't give me that shit. You never trusted your own grandma."

"If you'd known the old bat, you wouldn't've trusted her, either. She was an evil woman." Nothing fazed Bliss. His mournful hound-dog eyes pierced Cincinnatus. "So you drove a truck, did you?"

"Keepin' tabs on me?"

"Damn straight I was," Bliss replied. "You deserve it. But things are all over now. The United States won, and if we kill enough Confederates to keep the rest quiet we'll do all right."

He waited. Cincinnatus laughed again. "What? You reckon I'm gonna argue with you? We better kill a lot of them bastards. Otherwise, they'll be killin' us too damn soon."

"Well, we agree about something, anyway," Luther Bliss said. "I hope to God I never see you again. You gave me too much to worry about—more than Lucullus, even. He was smarter than you, but I always knew where he stood. With you, I had to wonder."

"You son of a bitch," Cincinnatus said. "You kept me in jail for two years. Wasn't for that Darrow ofay, you never woulda let me out."

"I still say I was doing the USA a favor by keeping you in." Nothing would ever make Bliss back up or admit he might have been wrong, either.

The two men warily sidled past each other. Cincinnatus went on toward the barbecue shack. He didn't trust Bliss' word about anything—he had to see with his own eyes. But the secret policeman wasn't lying here. The place Lucullus had taken over from his father sat quiet and deserted. Oh, the building still stood, but piles of dead leaves and broken windows said no one had come here for a long time. Even the wonderful smell that had always wafted from the shack was gone. You could gain weight just from that smell. No more, dammit. Nothing in Covington would ever be the same.

Sighing, Cincinnatus walked on to the house his father and mother had shared till she passed away. He'd lived there himself, getting over his accident, helping to take care of her as she slid deeper into senility, and then simply trapped in Covington. The house was still standing, too. Cincinnatus supposed his father still owned it. Even with a shell hole in the front yard and a little shrapnel damage, it was bound to be worth something.

Who would want to buy a house in the colored district, though? How many Negroes would want to live here, even with Covington passed back to the USA? How many Negroes were left to live in Covington and all the other towns that had flown the Stars and Bars? Not enough. Nowhere close to enough. Would whites eventually settle in this part of town, too? Or would they tear everything down and try to pretend Negroes had never been a part of life south of the Mason-Dixon Line and the Ohio?

Cincinnatus couldn't know which, but he sure knew which way he'd bet.

Sore and sad, he walked on through the almost-deserted quarter instead of heading back to the bus stop and the train ride on to his family. His feet knew where he was going better than his head did. Before long, he found himself in front of the Brass Monkey. He'd drowned a lot of sorrows in that bar while he was stuck here.

He almost jumped out of his shoes when a voice floated out through the door: "C'mon in! We're open!"

"Do Jesus!" Cincinnatus walked inside. There was no electricity, so his eyes needed a little while to adjust to the dimness. A black man sat at the bar, nursing a whiskey. Another one stood behind it, fanning himself. It was the same bartender who'd been there before. "Didn't reckon I'd see you alive," Cincinnatus remarked.

"I could say the same thing about you," the man answered. "When the *po*lice done took you away, I reckoned you was dead meat."

"I was on a list," Cincinnatus said.

"Figured you was. That's why they took you away."

"No, a different kind o' list. They went an' exchanged me an' my pa fo' a couple of Confederates who got stuck up in the USA."

"Lucky," the bartender observed.

"Yeah, I reckon," Cincinnatus said. "How'd you get by?"

"Me? I was lucky a different kind o' way." The bartender fanned harder and didn't go on.

The black man at the bar said, "Cambyses, he done the butternut bastards enough favors, they didn't take him off to no camp."

"Shut your mouth!" the bartender squawked indignantly.

"Shit, don't make no difference now," the other man said. "Me, I done the same damn thing. I ain't what you call real proud o' myself, but I ain't dead, neither, an' a hell of a lot o' folks is."

Cincinnatus had been about to buy himself a drink—he could have used one. Instead, he turned around and walked out. Had those two Negroes survived by ratting on their fellows? He'd always wondered about Cambyses, and he seemed to have been right to wonder. Had they bought their lives at too high a price?

They wouldn't say so. As for Cincinnatus, he was mostly surprised the Confederates had let them live. Maybe the whites just hadn't had time to kill them before Covington fell. How many Negroes down here had made the same Devil's bargain to survive? He was heading back to Des Moines, back to the USA. He thanked God he wouldn't have to find out.

* * *

With a wheeze that said it might not get much farther, the train stopped at the little station in Baroyeca. Jorge Rodriguez wore his butternut uniform, shorn of his stripes and all Confederate insignia. It was all the clothing he had. He'd been living on the ration cans the Yankees gave him when they let him out of the POW camp. If he never ate anything that came from a tin can again, he wouldn't be sorry. He was even sick of the famous deviled ham. Enough was enough, and then some.

Jorge was the only one who got off at Baroyeca. There on the platform stood his mother, his brother Pedro, and his sister Susana and two of her little children. Jorge hugged everybody and kissed everybody and slapped Pedro on the back. His older brother had been a POW much longer than he had.

"Do you know when Miguel is getting home?" Jorge asked.

Their other brother had been captured, too, and wounded as well. Pedro shook his head. "I haven't heard anything. One of these days, that's all."

"Soon, God, please." Their mother crossed herself.

When Jorge saw the *alcalde*'s house, he saw the Stars and Stripes flying above it. "Even here!" he said in dismay.

"Even here," Pedro agreed. "We lost. You can get into big trouble if you show the Confederate flag. All we can do is what the Yankees tell us—for now."

He sounded as if he was ready to pick up the fight again if he ever saw the chance. Jorge wasn't so sure. He'd seen a lot more war than his brother had—enough to satisfy him for a long, long time, if not forever. As long as you could live your life, how much difference did it really make which flag flew over the *alcalde*'s house?

There was Freedom Party headquarters, where his father spent so much time. It stood empty, deserted. "What happened to *Señor* Quinn?" Jorge asked.

"He went off to war himself, when things got hard and they started calling in older men," his mother answered. "After that, nobody here knows. He hasn't come back—I know that."

"Maybe he will," Jorge said. Who could guess how long all the Confederate soldiers would need to come home, especially if they lived in out-of-the-way places like Baroyeca? Maybe Robert Quinn lay in a U.S. hospital. Maybe he was still in a camp. As the war ran down and surrender finally came, the Yankees took prisoners by the tens, maybe by the hundreds, of thousands.

"Let's go home," his mother said. Actually, what she said was *Vamos a casa*. She mixed English and Spanish indiscriminately. Most people her age did. Jorge and Pedro smiled at each other. They'd used more English even when they lived here. Since going into the Army, the only time Jorge had spoken any Spanish was when he ran into another soldier from Sonora or Chihuahua. Even then, he and the other man would mostly speak English so their buddies from the rest of the CSA wouldn't tab them for a couple of dumb greasers.

Home was a three-mile walk. Jorge carried his little nephew part of the way. After a sixty-pound pack and a rifle on his back, Juanito didn't seem to weigh much. It was hot, but Jorge was used to heat. The air was dry, anyhow; he wouldn't have to wring himself out when he got to the farmhouse.

"Better weather than farther east," he said, and Pedro nodded.

A black-headed magpie-jay sat on a power line and screeched at the people walking by below. Jays in the rest of the CSA were smaller, with shorter tails. They didn't sound the same—but they did sound like cousins.

When he got to the farmhouse, it seemed smaller than he remembered. It also seemed plainer and poorer. He hadn't thought anything of the way he lived before he went into the Army. People who lived around Baroyeca either scratched out a livelihood from farms like this one or went into the mines and grubbed lead and silver—never quite enough silver—out of the ground.

By local standards, his family was well off. They had running water and electricity, though they hadn't when Jorge was younger. They'd talked about getting a motorcar. Jorge had needed to go up into the rest of the CSA, the part where everyone spoke English all the time, to realize how much he'd grown up without. If nobody around you had it, though, you didn't miss it.

"Like old times, having two of my sons home and the third one on the way." His mother was invincibly optimistic. He thought so, anyhow, till her face clouded and she went on, "If only your father were here to see it."

"*Sí*," Jorge said. Nobody seemed to want to say any more than that. Hipolito Rodriguez's death, so far from all his family, would cast a shadow over them for the rest of their lives. *Why* had he shot himself? He'd been doing work he thought the country needed, and doing it for his Army buddy from the last war. What could have gone wrong?

It was almost as if he'd listened to Yankee propaganda about the camps, and that even before there was much Yankee propaganda. If *mallates* were people like anybody else, then putting them in those camps was wrong. If. No matter what the damnyankees said, Jorge had trouble believing it. Most Confederate citizens would. His father would have—he was sure of that.

Could something he saw, something that happened at the camp, have changed his mind? Jorge also had trouble believing that. And, with no way to look inside his father's mind and understand what he was thinking, it would stay a mystery forever.

His mother cooked tacos stuffed with shredded pork and spices fiery enough to make his nose run—he wasn't used to them any more. He ate and ate. Yes, this kind of food beat the devil out of canned deviled ham. And there were *chicharrones*—pieces of pigskin fried crisp and crunchy that gave your teeth a workout.

"This is wonderful," Jorge said. "I ate boring food so long, I forgot how good things could be."

His older brother laughed. "I said the very same thing when I got here—didn't I, *mamacita*?"

"Yes, exactly the same thing," Magdalena Rodriguez answered.

"Let's hope we can hear Miguel say it, too," Susana said.

"And soon, please, God," their mother said. Someone knocked on the door. "It's the postman." She got up to see what he had.

There were a couple of advertising circulars and a large envelope that looked official. And it was: it came from something called the U.S. occupying authority in the former state of Sonora. Magdalena Rodriguez fought through the pronunciation of that. When she opened the envelope and unfolded the piece of paper inside, she made a face.

"All in English," she said.

"Let me see." Jorge could read English well enough. And, in fact, the paper was aimed at Pedro and him. He frowned at the eagle in front of crossed swords on the letterhead; people using that emblem had done their level best to kill him. Now they were telling him what he had to do as a returned prisoner of war.

And they weren't kidding around, either. Returned POWs had to report to the *alcalde*'s office once a week. They had to renounce the Freedom Party. They had to report all meetings of more than five people they attended.

Pedro laughed when Jorge said that. "More than five people here now," he observed. "Do we report this?"

"I wouldn't be surprised," Jorge said. He kept reading. Returned POWs could not write or subscribe to forbidden literature. They couldn't keep weapons of caliber larger than .22—either pistols or longarms.

"I'm surprised they let you have any," his sister said when he read that.

"Somebody who was writing the rules had to know every farm down here has a varmint gun," Jorge said. His father had taught him to shoot, and to be careful with firearms, when he was a little boy. "If they said we couldn't keep guns at all, we wouldn't pay any attention to them. They think this keeps them out of trouble."

"You can kill somebody with a .22," Pedro said.

"Sure," Jorge agreed. "But you have to hit him just right."

"Are you sure they really let us out of the camps?" his brother asked.

He shrugged. "We're here. This isn't so good, but they'll get tired of it after a while. They have to. How many soldiers can they put in Baroyeca?"

"As many as they want," Pedro said.

But Jorge shook his head. "I don't believe it. They'd have to stick soldiers in every little town from Virginia to here. Even the Yankees don't have that many soldiers . . . I hope."

Pedro thought about it. "Mm, maybe you're right. The war is over. The Yankees will want to go home, too."

"Sure they will. Who wouldn't?" Jorge said. "Being a soldier is no fun. You march around, that's not so bad. But when you fight, most of the time you're bored and uncomfortable, and the rest you're scared to death."

"And you can get hurt, too," their mother said softly, and crossed herself again.

Jorge and Pedro had both been lucky, coming through the war with nothing worse than a few scratches. Their brother hadn't. The roll of the dice, the turn of the card . . . Some guys had a shell burst ten feet away from them and didn't get badly hurt. Some turned into hamburger. Who could say why? God, maybe. From everything Jorge had seen, He had a rugged sense of humor.

One of these days, he wanted to talk that over with Pedro—and with Miguel, too. Not here, though. Not now. Not with their mother listening. She believed, and she hadn't seen so many reasons not to believe.

Well, all that could wait. It would have to, in fact. "How is the farm?" he asked his mother. He would be here for a long time. This was what counted now.

"Not so bad," she answered, "but not so good, either. We all did everything we could. With so many men in the Army, though"—she spread her hands—"we couldn't do everything we wanted to. The livestock is all right. The crops . . . Well, we didn't go hungry, but we barely made enough to pay for the things we need and we can't get from the land."

"It's about what you'd expect," Pedro said. "If we work hard, we can bring it back to the way it was before the war—maybe better. If the Yankees let us, I mean."

"I think maybe they will. They don't care so much about us—we're too far away," Jorge said. "Virginia, Tennessee—they really hate the people there. And Georgia, too. I think they'll come down on them harder and leave us alone unless somebody here does something stupid like try to rise up."

Pedro didn't say anything. Jorge realized that wasn't necessarily good news. No, his brother hadn't seen so much fighting as he had. Maybe Pedro was still ready for more. Jorge knew damn well he wasn't. Bombers dropping loads on Baroyeca, without even any antiaircraft to shoot back? Believe it or not, the mere idea made him want to cross himself.

XV

People in the United States said Washington, D.C., had Confederate weather. Armstrong Grimes' father, who was from Ohio, said so all the goddamn time. Armstrong had always believed it. Why not? His old man wouldn't waste time and effort lying about anything so small.

But now Armstrong was stuck in southern Alabama in the middle of summer, and he was discovering that people in the USA didn't know what the hell they were talking about. He'd already found that out about his father—what guy growing up doesn't?—but discovering the same thing about the rest of the country came as a bit of a jolt.

Every day down here was like a bad day back home. It got hot. It got sticky. And it never let up. U.S. soldiers gulped salt tablets. When the sweaty patches under their arms dried out—which didn't happen very often—they left salt stains on their uniforms. He itched constantly. Prickly heat, athlete's foot, jock itch . . . You name it, Armstrong came down with it. He smeared all kinds of smelly goop on himself. Sometimes it helped. More often, it didn't.

And there were bugs. They had mosquitoes down here that could have doubled as fighter-bombers. They had several flavors of ferocious flies. They had vicious little biting things the locals called no-see-'ems. They had chiggers. They had ticks. They had something called chinch bugs. The Army sprayed DDT on everything and everybody. It helped . . . some. You would have had to spray every square inch of the state to put down all the nasty biting things.

Local whites hated the men in green-gray who'd whipped their armies and made them stop killing Negroes. Bushwhackers shot at U.S. soldiers. You looked sideways at every junked motorcar by the side of the road. It could go boom and take half a squad with it.

The U.S. Army didn't waste time fighting fair, not after the surrender. Every time a U.S. soldier got shot, ten—then twenty—Confederates faced the firing squad. The number for an auto bomb started at a hundred and also quickly doubled.

Armstrong hadn't been on any firing squads while the war was going on. Now, with three stripes on his sleeve, he frequently commanded one. The first couple of times he did it, it made his stomach turn over. After that, it turned into routine, and he got used to it.

So did the soldiers who did the shooting. They went about their business at the same time as they argued about whether it did any good. "Just makes these motherfuckers hate us worse," Squidface opined.

"They already hate us," Armstrong said. "I don't give a shit about that. I just don't want 'em shooting at us."

"If we don't get the assholes who're really doin' it, what do we accomplish?" Squidface asked. "Shootin' little old ladies gets old, you know?"

"We shoot enough little old ladies, the ones who're left alive'll make the trigger-happy guys knock it off," Armstrong said.

"Good fuckin' luck." Squidface was not a believer.

Armstrong trotted out what he thought was the clincher: " 'Sides, we kill all the whites down here, nobody'll be left to go bushwhacking, right?"

"Shit, now you're talkin' like a Confederate nigger," Squidface said. "We do that, won't be *anybody* left alive down here."

"Wouldn't break my heart." Armstrong wiped his face with his sleeve. The sleeve came away wet—big surprise. "Best thing they could do with this country is give it back to the possums and the gators."

Squidface laughed, but he wouldn't give up on the argument— what better way to kill time? He suggested a reason to leave some Confederates alive: "Nobody gets laid any more if we kill all the women. Some of the ones we grease are cute. That's a waste of good pussy."

"How come you haven't come down venereal yet?" Armstrong asked.

"Same reason you haven't, I bet," Squidface answered. "I'm lucky. And when I figure maybe I won't be lucky, I'm careful. The broads down here, they're nothin' but a bunch of whores."

"They lost," Armstrong said, which went a long way towards explaining things. He added, "A lot of 'em, their husbands or boyfriends aren't coming back, either."

He supposed he had been lucky. He'd got an education down here that was a hell of a lot more enjoyable than anything they'd tried to cram down his throat in high school. He hadn't cared about English lit or medieval history or practical math. This—this was stuff he wanted to learn.

The one thing he was glad about was that none of the women who'd enlightened him had come before his firing squad. That would have been worse than embarrassing, and it might have landed him in trouble. Orders against what the brass called fraternization had gone out. Getting anyone to listen to them was another story.

"Far as I'm concerned, it's the same now as it was when we were shooting at each other," he said. "I just want to serve out my hitch, take off the goddamn uniform, go back home, and figure out what the hell to do with the rest of my life."

"Want to hear somethin' funny?" Squidface said.

"I'm all ears," Armstrong answered.

"Me, I'm thinkin' about turning into a lifer."

"Jesus Christ! C'mon with me, buddy. I'm taking you to the aid station. You're down with something worse than the clap. You've got softening of the brain, damned if you don't."

"Nah. I been thinkin' about it," Squidface said. "Thinkin' hard, too. Say I go back to Civvy Street. What's the best thing that can happen to me?"

"You get out of the Army," Armstrong answered at once.

"Yeah, and then what? Best thing I can see is, I spend the next forty years working in a factory, I find some broad, we have some kids and get old and fat together. Big fucking deal, pardon my French."

That was, in broad outline, the future Armstrong saw for himself, too. It didn't seem so bad—but, when Squidface laid it out, it didn't seem so good, either. But when the other choice was staying in . . . "Would you rather get your balls shot off instead? I already got one Purple Heart. That's about five too many."

"It won't be as bad now as it was," Squidface said. "What I figure is, if I stay in, I can end up a top kick pretty goddamn fast. They're gonna lose all kinds of senior noncoms—some of those sorry assholes are Great War retreads, and they ain't gonna stick around. People'll call me First Sergeant Giacopelli, not Squidface. I'll get to tell lieutenants where to head in. Even captains won't look at me like I'm dogshit on the bottom of their shoe. I'll have more fruit salad on my chest than the mess hall has in cans."

"You're gonna do what you're gonna do," Armstrong said. "Don't figure I can talk you out of it. Hell, I wish you luck, if it's what you really want. But I'm not gonna go that route."

"You'll end up in an office somewhere, with a secretary to blow you if your wife won't. You're a smart guy," Squidface said. "I'm just a sap from the wrong side of the tracks. Army's the first place I ever got anything like a square deal."

"If I'm so smart, what am I doing here?" Armstrong asked. Squidface laughed. Armstrong wished he hadn't made the crack about secretaries. His own father had worked in a Washington office since time out of mind. Armstrong didn't have any reason to think his old man was unfaithful, but now he'd wonder. That wasn't so good.

Then somebody let out a yell, and Armstrong and Squidface both jumped up to see what was going on. The guy who yelled was a captain. Seeing Armstrong, he said, "Gather up your platoon, Grimes, and take 'em into Hugo. We've got trouble there."

"Yes, sir," Armstrong said, and then, "Can you tell me what kind of trouble, so they know what to look out for?"

"There's a gal says a nigger raped her. He says she gave it up, and she only started yelling when somebody saw him leaving her house. All the white folks in town want to hang him up by the nuts. Before we got down here, they'd hang a coon for whistling at a white woman, let alone fucking her."

"What are we supposed to do, exactly?" Armstrong asked.

"He's in the town jail. Don't let 'em haul him out and lynch him. We're still figuring out what really happened—trying to, anyway. So that's what's going on. Go deal with it. Do whatever you have to do to hold the jail. White folks here have to know we're the law in these parts nowadays. They aren't. Got it?"

"Yes, sir," Armstrong replied—the only possible answer. *Go deal with it*, he thought. *Right*. Turning to Squidface, he said, "Let's round 'em up."

"Sure, Sarge." Squidface said the only thing *he* could.

They tramped into Hugo in full combat gear, weapons loaded and ready. Finding the jail was the easiest thing in the world—it was the building with the mob in front of it. A squad of scared-looking U.S. soldiers in the jail looked as if they didn't think they could hold the mob out if it attacked. They might well have been right, too.

"Break it up there!" Armstrong yelled from behind the crowd of irate Alabamans. "Go home!"

They whirled, almost as one. For a second, he wondered if they would charge his men. The sight of so many more soldiers in green-gray—and so many automatic weapons—seemed to give the locals pause. "We want the nigger!" one of them yelled. Then they all took up the cry: *"We want the nigger!"*

"Well, you aren't gonna get him," Armstrong said. "He's ours to deal with, once we work out what really went on. You people go on home. First, last, and only warning: we start shooting, we don't quit."

"What he done to that white gal, just killin's too good for him!" shouted a man with a gray mustache stained by tobacco juice. "We're gonna—"

"You're gonna shut the fuck up and go home right now, or you're gonna end up dead," Armstrong broke in. "Those are the only choices you got. *We'll* deal with the colored guy, or maybe with the whore he was trickin' with." That caused fresh tumult. He silenced it by chambering a round. The harsh *snick!* cut through the crowd noise like a sharp knife through soft sausage. "Enough of this shit," Armstrong said. "Beat it!"

He wondered if they would rush him in spite of everything. He also wondered if he and his buddies could shoot enough of them to break the rush before they got mobbed. Then, sullenly, the crowd dispersed. They were willing to kill to defend Confederate womanhood, but less enthusiastic about dying for it.

"Whew!" Armstrong said.

"Yeah." Squidface nodded. "Ain't you glad the war's over?"

"Christ, we almost started it up again," Armstrong said. "And you want to keep on doing crap like this? You gotta be out of your tree."

"Hey, I won't be bored, anyway," Squidface made light of it, but he wasn't about to change his mind. "Got a butt on you?"

"Sure." Armstrong handed him a pack. "Wonder if that coon really did give her the old what-for?"

"Who cares?" Squidface paused to flick his Zippo, sucked in

smoke, and went on, "Way I look at it is, all the shit these white Freedom Party assholes gave the spades, who gives a shit if they get some of their own back eight inches at a time?"

"Mm, you've got something there." Armstrong lit a cigarette, too. "Besides, I bet she's ugly." He and Squidface both laughed. Their side had won. They could afford to.

Cassius had wondered about a lot of things in his life. Whether he would be famous never made the list. A Negro in the CSA had no chance at all of reaching that goal, so what point to wondering about it?

All he had to do, it turned out, was be a halfway decent shot. Knock one man over, and his own world turned upside down and inside out. No, he hadn't expected that. He hadn't even imagined it. None of which kept it from happening.

First, U.S. officers inside Madison grilled him. He told his story. There wasn't much of a story to tell: "Soon as I seen it was Jake Featherston, I shot the son of a bitch. Shot him some more once he was down so's he wouldn't get up no mo'."

"What'll we do with him?" one officer asked another over Cassius' head. They might as well have been talking about somebody in the next county.

"Hell, I don't know," the second Yankee answered. "If it was up to me, though, I'd put him up for a Congressional Medal of Honor."

"Can't," the first officer said.

"Why the hell not?"

"He isn't a U.S. citizen."

"Oh." The second officer laughed sheepishly. "Yeah. You're right. But he just did more for us than a fuck of a lot of guys who are."

One thing that happened because he'd shot Jake Featherston was that he didn't have to go out on patrol any more. He didn't have any more duties at all, in fact. He could eat as much as he wanted and sleep as late as he wanted. If they'd issued him a girl, he would have had the whole world by the short hairs. And if he'd asked, they probably would have. But he didn't think of it, and no one suggested it, so he did without.

A few days later, a newsreel crew filmed him. He told them the same story he'd given the Army officers. One of them asked, "Did you feel you were taking revenge for all the Negroes Jake Featherston hurt?"

"He didn't hurt 'em, suh—he done *killed* 'em," Cassius answered. "My ma an' my pa an' my sister an' Lord knows how many more. Can't hardly get even for all that jus' by killin' one man. He needed killin'—don't get me wrong. But it ain't enough—not even close."

"Why didn't you get taken with the rest of your family?" asked the white man from the USA.

"On account of I didn't go to church on Sunday. That's where they got grabbed."

"Do you think God was saving you for something else?"

"Beats me," Cassius answered. "Plenty of other times I could've got killed, too."

"What are you going to do now?"

Cassius spread his hands. "Suh, I got *no* idea."

Plenty of other people had ideas for him. Next thing he knew, he was on a train heading for the USA. He'd never ridden on the railroad before, and he would have gone hungry if one of the whites escorting him hadn't taken him to the dining car. The food was good—better than U.S. Army chow. It didn't measure up to what the Huntsman's Lodge or his mother had made, but he didn't figure anything ever would, not this side of heaven.

He took some satisfaction in seeing what the USA had done to the CSA—and the Carolinas had been a Confederate redoubt till late in the war. As he passed through Virginia, he saw what the United States had done where they weren't fooling around. He saw white people living in the midst of the rubble. They were filthy and grubby and scrawny. He'd gone through that himself. He might have been sorry for them . . . if he'd seen more than a tiny handful of blacks living alongside them. Since he didn't, he stifled whatever sympathy he would have felt.

Then he crossed into the USA. Another country! Not only that, a country where they just treated Negroes . . . not too well. His father had always been cynical about the United States. Compared to what Cassius had survived, though, being treated . . . not too well looked pretty goddamn good.

The United States didn't look so good. The part he saw, the stretch between the Maryland-Virginia border and Philadelphia, looked almost as bomb-pocked and trampled as the land farther south had. He wondered how any part of this poor battered continent would ever climb back to its feet again.

He saw the edges of what the superbomb had done to Philadelphia.

The edges were bad enough. What were things like at the center, where the bomb went off? Maybe not knowing was better.

They put him up in a hotel not far from Congressional Hall. "Anything you want—anything at all—you just telephone and ask for it," a bright young lieutenant said. "They'll bring it to you."

"Thank you kindly," Cassius said, and then, "Show me how to work the telephone, suh, please."

"You never used one before?" The officer, who couldn't have been more than a year or two older than Cassius, blinked.

"No, suh," Cassius answered. "Weren't more than a couple in the Terry—where I come from—even before things got bad. After that, we didn't have nothin'."

"All right." The white man—he was blond and blue-eyed and handsome; in the CSA, he might have become a Freedom Party Guard—showed him what to do. "You know about hot and cold water taps, right?"

"Well, we always had to heat our own, but I can cipher out what's hot and what's cold. An' we had the bathroom down the hall. Mighty nice, puttin' it right here."

"I bet. My folks grew up in a place like that. I'm lucky I didn't have to. They'll be delivering a dress uniform for you tonight, too. You go up to Congress tomorrow, so they can thank you for getting rid of Featherston."

"Oh, my," Cassius said.

He tried the telephone, and ordered a steak and fried potatoes. Fifteen minutes later, somebody knocked on the door. A white man in a fancy getup a lot like what Cassius' father had worn brought in a tray. "Here you are, sir," he said in a funny foreign accent. Cassius understood tips. They'd given him pocket money, so he handed the waiter fifty cents. With a nod and a smile, the man left. *I did that right*, Cassius thought.

Again, the food reminded him Army cooks didn't know everything there was to know. Was it as good as what the Huntsman's Lodge made? Pretty close, if it wasn't.

He'd just finished eating when the uniform arrived. It fit perfectly. How did they do that? Did they measure him while he wasn't looking? The fabric was buttery soft. The only differences from a real U.S. Army uniform were plain brass buttons and no U.S. on his collar. He had an auxiliary's armband instead. Well, he was one.

His visit to Congress passed in a blur. Dozens of people shook his hand. One of them, he realized just after it happened, was the President of the USA. Charlie La Follette didn't look nearly so fierce as Jake Featherston. But he'd won. *And I helped*, Cassius thought dizzily.

He got dizzier a moment later. Along with a resolution expressing the Thanks of Congress, they gave him a reward—$100,000, tax-free. The Congresswoman who made a speech about that was Flora somebody. Afterwards, she told him, "If you like, I'll find someone you can trust to help you look after the money. You don't want to waste it." Then she smiled. "Or maybe you do—I don't know. But it would be a shame."

"Thank you, ma'am. Reckon I take you up on that." Cassius had never imagined so much money. But he remembered how his folks always squeezed every penny to get by. He didn't think he wanted to waste this, not when it could set him up for life. *Maybe waste a little*, he thought.

He gave wireless interviews. He talked to Bill Shirer and Eric Sevareid and Walter Winchell. He could hardly understand Winchell's rapid-fire, slang-filled New York accent. If he hadn't heard a few soldiers talking that way, he probably wouldn't have been able to follow at all.

Each broadcaster asked the question a different way, but they all wanted to know the same thing: what did killing Jake Featherston feel like? The more he told the story, the further from the reality of it he felt.

A few days later, as if remembering it had overlooked something, Congress voted Cassius a fresh honor: it declared him a citizen of the United States. He felt more excited than someone from, say, the Empire of Mexico might have. Up till now, he'd never been a citizen of any country. Negroes in the CSA were residents, but they didn't have the rights citizens did.

The Congresswoman who'd offered to help him sent over an accountant: a thin, quiet man named Sheldon Klein. He always wore a glove on his left hand. Cassius watched it and saw only his index finger and thumb move, so he probably had some kind of war wound there.

"Yes, if we invest in bonds and some carefully chosen stocks, we can provide you with a very decent income without touching your principal at all," he said.

"My what?" Cassius asked.

"Your principal. That means the basic amount of money you have now. It will still be there, and you can live off what it earns," Klein answered. He didn't say, *You dumb nigger*. He didn't even act as if he thought it.

"Any chance I can make more money?" Cassius asked.

"I'm sure you will," the accountant said. "There will probably be a book about you, and a film as well. The fees from those you can either spend as they come in or add to the nest egg and make your investment income larger. And nothing stands in the way of your pursuing an education and having a career like anyone else."

Cassius hadn't even thought about that. "What about—?" He brushed a couple of fingers across the black skin on the back of his other hand.

"A difficulty. Not an impossible difficulty, not in this country," Sheldon Klein replied. "If you work hard, you can overcome it. And, if I may speak frankly, even people who dislike most Negroes will go out of their way for the man who rid the world of Jake Featherston."

That wasn't fair, which didn't mean he was wrong. "Don't like to take advantage," Cassius said slowly.

"If you can, if you aren't hurting anybody—why not?" Klein said. "You spent your whole life up till now disadvantaged, didn't you? You were a Negro in the Confederate States, so of course you did. Do you even read and write?"

"Yes, suh. My pa, he learned me. He knew . . . all kinds of things." Cassius realized he had no idea just how much his father knew. He'd never had the chance to find out. Even having his letters made him stand out in the Terry.

He also saw he'd surprised Klein. "All right. That will help you, then," the white man said. "The stronger your foundation, the bigger the house you can build on it."

"Reckon you're right." Something else occurred to Cassius. "What do you make out of this?"

"Off of you? Not a dime. Congresswoman Blackford would skin me if I charged you," Klein answered. "I may get some extra business when people find out I work for you, but that's a different story. Oh, and just so you know—it's easy for an accountant to steal from you. Every so often, you should pay somebody else to check up on what I do."

Cassius started to say he was sure he wouldn't need to. Then he saw Klein was telling him he shouldn't be sure of things like that. And the accountant wouldn't be the only one who could screw him if he wasn't careful. So he nodded back and said, "Thanks. Reckon I will." By the way Sheldon Klein nodded, he'd passed a small test—or maybe not such a small one.

Sam Carsten remembered coming home after the last war. He'd been a petty officer on the *Dakota* then, and eager to learn more about the strange and exciting new world of naval aviation. He'd been on the *Remembrance* when the new airplane carrier launched. After some detours, he'd been aboard her when she got sunk, too.

Coming home with the *Josephus Daniels* was different. She was *his*. He wondered what the Navy would do with her after the war. She'd done everything they asked of her while the country needed ships. When you got right down to it, though, she couldn't do any one thing very well.

And he wondered what the Navy would do with him after the war. A middle-aged lieutenant up through the hawse hole . . . He might have had a better chance of hanging on if he'd stayed a CPO. The Navy needed grizzled old chiefs. Grizzled old midgrade officers? That was a different story, too.

Since he couldn't do anything about it, he tried not to worry. He steered the destroyer escort to her berth in the Boston Navy Yard himself. By God, he could get the job done. As sailors on the pier caught lines and made her fast, he nodded to Lon Menefee and said, "Well, we made it."

"Yes, sir." The exec nodded. "In style, too."

"As much as the old beast has." Was Sam talking about the ship or himself? Even he wasn't sure.

Men who'd got leave happily hurried off the destroyer escort. A lot of them wouldn't stay in the Navy much longer. They would pick up the threads of the lives they'd led before they put on the uniform. Sam couldn't very well do that. He'd cut those threads thirty-five years before. But if they put him on the beach he'd have to find something else to do.

He wished he had any idea what.

"She's in your hands for a bit, Lon," he said. "I get to go talk to a board."

"All things considered, I think I'd rather have a tooth pulled," Menefee said judiciously. "Matter of fact, I'm sure of it."

"Ha! Your time will come, and soon, too." Sam wasn't kidding. The exec was still in his twenties. He had plenty of time to climb the links in the chain of command. Carsten wished he did himself.

That was one wish he wouldn't get. At least he had sense enough to know it. He set his cap at the proper angle, left the bridge, and then left the *Josephus Daniels*. A commander who couldn't be much older than Lon Menefee started to salute him, then jerked his arm down. Without smiling, Sam did salute the younger man. That kind of thing happened all the time when you had more wrinkles than stripes.

Two younger but senior officers did salute him before he got to the meeting room where he supposed he would hear his fate. As was his habit when they did that, he returned the salutes with an admiral's dignity. If one of his stripes were of thick gold . . . *If I had an admiral's pay!* he thought. You couldn't get rich in the service no matter what, not if you were honest, but if you won flag rank you did pretty well for yourself.

He laughed, which made a passing sailor give him a funny look. A lieutenant's pay was nothing to speak of, but he had a fair bit of money sitting in one account or another. When had he had time to spend any of it?

When he walked in to face the board, one of the men on it was a rear admiral and two were captains, all about his age. The last fellow was also a four-striper, but of much more recent vintage, his handsome face unlined, his brown hair unfrosted with gray. He grinned, jumped to his feet, and held out a hand. "Hello, Sam!" he said. "How are you?"

"Mr. Cressy!" Sam exclaimed. "Good to see you!" He shook hands with the former exec of the *Remembrance*. "You're going up as fast as I thought you would, sir. Is that the ribbon for a Navy Cross?"

Dan Cressy looked embarrassed. "I was lucky."

"You're lucky you're alive. That's one of the ways you get a Navy Cross," the rear admiral said. He turned back to Sam. "Take a seat, Lieutenant Commander Carsten."

"Lieut—" Sam blinked. "Thank you, sir!" Two and a half stripes! He'd made it at last! Wonder filled him as he sat down. He'd climbed about as high as a mustang could hope to get. But he couldn't relax even now. The Navy might be giving him a pat on the back at the same time as it was giving him a kick in the ass. A promotion on the way out the door was anything but unheard of.

"You had yourself a busy war," the rear admiral observed. "Captain Cressy's told us part of the story, and your record since you got a ship of your own speaks for itself."

"I took her where I got sent, sir," Carsten answered. "I did what my orders told me to do. I'm just glad we didn't get cut up too bad doing it."

"Your attitude does you credit," one of the senior captains said. "Captain Cressy predicted you would tell us something like that."

"He should talk. 'I was lucky'!" Sam glanced toward Cressy. "No offense, sir, but you sandbag like a son of a gun."

"I don't know what you're talking about," Cressy said, deadpan. Everybody laughed.

The rear admiral returned to business. "You had a little trouble with your previous exec, Carsten. How does Lieutenant Menefee suit you?"

"He's a fine officer, sir," Sam said quickly—he didn't want to screw Menefee. "I recommend him without reservation. That's the short answer. Details are in his fitness reports, but it all boils down to the same thing."

"Short answer will do for now." The rear admiral nodded to one of the captains, who wrote something down. The admiral's sea-gray eyes swung back to Sam. "Where do you see yourself going from here?"

"As long as it's in the Navy, sir, I'll take a shot at whatever you want to give me," Sam replied.

"We've heard that before," said the captain, who was taking notes.

"Haven't we just?" the rear admiral agreed. "I don't think the Navy's going to shrink the way it did after the last war. We've got the Japs to keep an eye on, God only knows how friendly Germany will stay, and we really are going to sit on the Confederates—and the damn Canucks—this time around. We won't leave you on the beach."

"That's mighty good to hear, sir," Sam said. "Will Congress give us the money we need to do all that good stuff?"

The rear admiral glanced over to Captain Cressy. "Well, you were right. He's plenty sharp."

"I said so, didn't I?" Cressy returned.

"You sure did." The flag officer gave his attention back to Sam. "They will for this year, anyhow, because we're still running on war appropriations. What happens after that . . . I've never believed in borrowing trouble. Have you?"

"Only when I worry about my ship," Sam answered.

All the senior officers sitting across from him nodded. "There is that. Yes, indeed. There is that. You understand what command's all about, all right. Suppose we give you a choice. You can keep the *Josephus Daniels* and go on occupation patrol in Confederate waters. Or, if you'd rather, you can have a real destroyer out in the Sandwich Islands. I don't know what kind of duty that would be. Technically, we're still at war with the Empire of Japan, but it looks like we'll let things peter out on the *status quo ante bellum*, same as we did the last time around. You may end up gathering moss out there. If you go down to the Confederacy—to the South, I suppose I ought to call it, since we're going to try to hold on to it . . ."

"If I go down there, it won't be dull, whatever else it is," Sam finished for him.

"Well, yes," the rear admiral said. "That's how it looks."

"I'll hang on to the DE, sir," Sam said. "If I were Captain Cressy's age, I'd take the bigger, newer ship. It'd look spiffier in my service jacket. But I figure I can do more good keeping the Confederates in line. The Pacific war . . ." He shook his head. "The supply lines are just too damn long to let either side fight a proper war out there."

"That's how it's been so far, anyhow," Captain Cressy said. "If we get airplanes that can carry a superbomb from Midway, say, to the Philippines—"

"Or if they get one that can carry a superbomb from Guam to Honolulu," the rear admiral broke in.

"Or if either side gets a bomber that can fly a superbomb off an airplane carrier," Sam said.

"*There's* a cheerful thought. With these new turbos, it'll probably happen in the next few years," the rear admiral said. "Or else the smart boys'll make the bombs smaller, so the prop jobs we've already got can carry them. Interesting times, interesting times." However interesting they might be, he didn't sound as if he looked forward to them.

Sam understood that, because he knew he didn't. "Sir, how the heck is the Navy going to fight a war when one airplane with one bomb can knock out a flotilla?"

"You want the straight dope?" the rear admiral asked.

"Yes, sir!" Sam said eagerly.

"All right. The straight dope is, right now nobody has the faintest idea in the whole wide world. If you've got any hot suggestions, put 'em down in writing and send 'em to the Navy Department. They'll go into the mix—you bet your sweet ass they will."

"The only idea I've got about a superbomb is, being under it when it goes off is a bad plan."

"You're even with everybody else, Sam," Captain Cressy said. "Hell, you're ahead of some people. There are officers and civilians in Philadelphia who think the Kaiser is our buddy and the Japs don't know how to build superbombs, so why worry?"

"I believe you. Even though it's Philadelphia, I believe you," Sam said. "Some people don't believe things are real till they happen to them. And if a superbomb happens to you, it's too late."

"Sometimes you can talk till you're blue in the face, and it doesn't do you one damn bit of good. Makes you wonder." The rear admiral shook his head. "All right. We'll cut orders for you, and we'll get your ship refitted. And congratulations again, Commander."

"Thank you, sir!" Sam got to his feet and saluted. Hearing it that way sounded even better. It was as if he'd got the whole third stripe, not just half of it. Most of the time, people didn't bother calling you *Lieutenant Commander*, any more than they bothered calling you *Lieutenant, Junior Grade*. Sam knew all about that. He'd been a j.g. for a long time.

Two and a half stripes! And they still had a slot for him! He really hadn't expected the one, and he'd flabbled about the other. Once he got back to his ship, he owed all the officers drinks. Well, he could take care of that. He could tie one on if he felt like it—he'd earned the right. *Maybe I will*, he thought. *When am I ever going to have another promotion party?* The answer to that was all too plain. Never.

Somebody said you could never go home again. Back in Augusta, Georgia, Jerry Dover would have said that whoever it was had a point. The city he came back to wasn't the one he'd left when he joined the Confederate Army.

When he left, the war hadn't touched Augusta. Negro rebels had set off auto bombs in town, but that was different. So was the isolation of the Terry from the white part of town. Whites and Negroes had always lived apart. Barbed wire between them didn't seem to matter so much—not if you were white, anyhow.

Everything had got shabby even before he joined up. Nobody put any effort into keeping things neat; that all went into doing whatever it took to beat the damnyankees. Well, the whole damn country did whatever it took to beat the damnyankees, and that turned out not to be enough.

And now the whole damn country was paying for it.

Augusta sure was. The Stars and Stripes flew over city hall for the first time in more than eighty years. The Yankees had captured the town more or less by sideswipe in their drive down the Savannah River to the port of the same name. They'd bombed it a few times, but the Confederates didn't make a stand here. Jerry Dover had seen what happened to places where one side or the other made a stand. He thanked heaven Augusta wasn't one of them.

Incidental damage was bad enough. Streets had craters in them. Walls had chunks bitten out of them. Most windows stared with blind eyes. The smell of death was old and faint, but it was there.

His family had survived. His house was—mostly—intact. He supposed he ought to thank heaven for all that, too. As a matter of fact, he did. But he would have liked things better if the town and the way of life he'd liked so well had come through the war in one piece.

They hadn't. It wasn't just that U.S. soldiers tramped through the streets of Augusta now. The life, the energy, were gone from the city. Like the rest of the CSA, it had done everything it knew how to do. It didn't know how to do anything any more.

So many men were missing. A lot were dead. A lot were maimed. Some remained in U.S. POW camps, though every day more came back on the train. But even the ones who were there seemed missing in action. After a losing war, how could you give a shit about putting things back together and making a living again?

Jerry Dover was one of the most hardheaded, practical men around. *He* had a hell of a time giving a rat's ass about what happened next. And if he did, what about his countrymen? He saw what about them. They came back, and they had no idea what the hell to do after that.

A lot of them drank. Good booze was in short supply, and hideously expensive when you could find it. There was plenty of rotgut and moonshine, though. The Yankees didn't mind if taverns opened up. Maybe they figured drunks would be too bleary to bother them. And maybe they were right.

Maybe they weren't, too. Some of the drunken ex-soldiers didn't care what happened to them any more. They would pick a fight for the sake of picking it. The Yankees, who weren't *ex*-soldiers, had a simple rule: shoot first. Augusta crackled with gunfire. The U.S. soldiers often didn't bother burying corpses. They left them on the sidewalk or in the gutter to warn other hotheads.

Because the United States played by the Geneva Convention rules and paid him at the same rate as one of their officers, Dover had money in his pocket when he got home. Green money—U.S. money—was in desperately short supply in the conquered Southern states. No one knew what brown money—Confederate cash—was worth any more, or whether it was worth anything. In the bad days after the Great War, one U.S. dollar could have bought billions, maybe trillions, of Confederate dollars. It wasn't that bad now, but it wasn't good. Not even the occupying authorities seemed sure what to do about the currency of a defunct country.

Putting all that together made leaving the house an adventure every time Jerry did it. He needed to look for work; his greenbacks wouldn't last forever, or even very long. But he was lucky if he could get more than a couple of blocks before jumpy kids in green-gray challenged him.

On a typical hot, muggy afternoon, a Yankee corporal barked, "Hey, you!"

"Yes?" Dover stopped in his tracks. He didn't want to give the soldiers any excuse to do something he'd regret later.

"You fight in the war?" the corporal snapped.

"Yes," Dover said.

The noncom held out his hand. "Let's see your release papers."

"I'm going to reach into my left trouser pocket to get them out," Dover said. He waited till the U.S. soldier nodded before moving. When he did, he moved slowly and carefully. He showed the Yankee he was holding only papers. "Here."

"Gimme." The corporal examined the papers and then sent Dover a fishy stare. "You were a light colonel, and they let you go anyway?"

"No, not me. I'm still back in Indianapolis," Dover answered.

"Funny guy. I'm laughing my ass off," the U.S. soldier said. Dover's big mouth had got him into trouble before. *When will I learn?* he wondered unhappily. The soldier in green-gray went on, "How come they turned you loose? And don't get cute with me, or you'll be sorry."

"I was only in the Quartermaster Corps. And I signed the papers that said I wouldn't give any more trouble. Hell, I know we lost. You guys wouldn't be here if we didn't," Dover said.

"Bet your balls, buddy." The corporal scratched his bristly chin. "Doesn't seem like enough, somehow. Not a lot of officers released yet."

"Well, there is one thing more," Dover admitted reluctantly.

"Yeah?"

"The guy who shot Jake Featherston, his father used to work in the restaurant I managed. Maybe he said I wasn't a total bastard."

"Maybe he was lying through his teeth. Or maybe you are." The corporal gestured with his tommy gun. "C'mon with me. We'll get this shit sorted out."

"Right," Dover said, resignation in his voice. If he said no, he'd get shot. So they went to the corporal's superiors. Dover told his story over again. A U.S. second lieutenant with more pimples than whiskers called somebody on a field telephone. The kid—he had to be younger than the corporal—talked, listened, and hung up.

"They'll get back to us," he said.

"What am I supposed to do in the meantime?" Dover asked.

"Wait right here," the baby-faced officer answered. Dover didn't say anything, but he couldn't have looked very happy. The lieutenant said, "What's the matter, Pops? You got a hot date stashed somewhere?"

"No," Jerry Dover said with a sigh. His last "hot date," down in Savannah, had blackmailed him and was probably some kind of Yankee spy. That didn't mean sitting around in a green-gray tent made his heart go pitter-pat with delight. Since his other choices seemed to be the stockade and the burial ground, he sat tight.

After a while, they gave him a couple of ration cans. He ate without another word. He'd had U.S. rations plenty of times during the war and in the POW camp. Eating them in his home town added insult to injury.

After two and a half hours, the field telephone rang. The lieutenant picked it up and listened. "Really?" he squeaked in surprise. "All right—I'll take care of it." He hung up and eyed Jerry. "Your story checks out."

"It should. It's true," Dover said.

"I know that—now. I wouldn't've believed it before." The junior officer scribbled something on Dover's papers. "There. I've written an endorsement that should keep them from hauling you in again."

"That'd be nice," Dover said, and then, belatedly, "Thanks." Maybe the endorsement would do some good, maybe it wouldn't. But at least the kid with the gold bars made the effort. Dover supposed a lot of Yankees would have laughed to see him get in trouble time after time. He put the papers back in his pocket.

"You're done here," the lieutenant said. "You can go."

"Thanks," Dover said again, and ambled off.

He got stopped one more time before he made it to the Huntsman's Lodge. This U.S. patrol didn't haul him in, so maybe the lieutenant's endorsement really did help. Stranger things must have happened, though Dover had a hard time thinking of one.

The Huntsman's Lodge was open for supper. That didn't surprise Jerry Dover; the fancy places always made it. Most of the customers were U.S. officers. Some of them were eating with pretty girls who definitely didn't come from the USA. That didn't surprise Jerry Dover, either. It was the way the world worked.

Most of the waiters and busboys were Mexicans. The ones who weren't were whites: a couple of sixteen-year-olds and a couple of old men. That was a revolution; in the prewar CSA, most whites would sooner have died than served anyone.

One of the Mexicans recognized Dover. The short, swarthy man came over and shook his hand. "Good to see you again, *Señor*," he said.

"Good to be seen, by God," Dover answered. "Willard Sloan still running things here?"

"*Sí*—uh, yes. I take you to him."

Dover grinned. "You reckon I don't know the way, Felipe?"

All the same, he let the waiter escort him to the tiny, cramped office where he'd put in so many years. Seeing Sloan behind *his* battered desk was a jolt. The current manager of the Huntsman's Lodge was in his late forties, with a lean face, a bitter expression, and hard blue eyes. When he sat behind the desk, you could hardly tell he used a wheelchair. His legs were useless; he'd got a bullet in the spine during the Great War.

He eyed Jerry Dover with all the warmth of a waiter eyeing a patron sliding out the door without paying his check. "Think you can take my job away from me, do you?" he said.

"That's not what I came here for," Dover answered, which was at least partly true. "Just . . . wanted to see how things were. I spent a lot of years here, you know."

"Yeah," Sloan said glumly. "Owners know you're back yet?"

"No," Dover said.

"Maybe I ought to plug you now, then." Sloan sounded serious. Did he keep a pistol in a desk drawer? The way things had gone in the CSA, maybe it wasn't such a bad idea. The cripple gave Dover another wintry stare. "Or maybe I just ought to shoot myself, save somebody else the trouble."

"Hey, I only want to get . . . started over." Dover didn't want to say *get back on my feet again*, not to a man who never would. "Doesn't have to be here."

"But this'd suit you best." Willard Sloan didn't make it a question.

"If you've done a halfway decent job since I left, the owners'll keep you on," Dover said. "I bet they're paying you less than they paid me." Would he work for less than he had before? Damn right he would. But he didn't tell Sloan that.

"Yeah, they jewed me down pretty good," the present manager agreed. "What can you do, though?"

"Not much," Dover said. What could *he* do? He could let the owners know he was around. He'd likely taken care of that just by showing up here. If they wanted him back, they'd get word to him—and too bad for Willard Sloan. If they didn't . . . he'd have to figure out something else, that was all.

Thick wire mesh in the Houston jail's visiting room separated Jefferson Pinkard from the new damnyankee officer the U.S. authorities had chosen to defend him. As he had with Isidore Goldstein, he growled, "Dammit, I didn't do anything in your country. I didn't do anything to anybody from your country. I didn't do anything the people in my country didn't want me to do, either."

The damnyankee—he was called Moss, and he was about as exciting as his name—shook his head. "None of that counts. They're charging you with crimes against humanity. That means you should have known better than to do that stuff even if they told you to."

"My ass," Jeff said angrily. "Goddamn coons always hated the Confederate States. They fucked us when they rose up in the last war.

Hell, first time I went into action, it wasn't against you Yankees. It was against Red niggers in Georgia. You reckon they wouldn't've done it again? Like hell they wouldn't. Only we didn't give 'em the chance this time around."

Moss shook his head again. "Women? Children? Men who never did anybody any harm? You won't get a court to buy it."

"Well, shit, tell me something I don't know," Pinkard said. "You assholes are gonna hang me. Anything I say is just a fuckin' joke, far as you're concerned. Why'd they even bother giving me a new lawyer when Goldstein got hurt? Just to make it look pretty, I bet."

"I wish I could tell you you're wrong," Moss replied, which took Jeff by surprise. "Chances are they *will* hang you. But I'll fight them as hard as I can. That's my job. That's what lawyers do. I'm pretty good at it, too."

Jeff eyed him through the grating. He still wasn't much to look at: a middle-aged man who'd been through the mill. He did sound like somebody who meant what he said, though. Jeff knew professional pride when he heard it. He thought Moss *would* do the best job he could. He also thought it wouldn't do him one goddamn bit of good.

"Can you give me anything to show there were Negroes you didn't kill when you could have?" Moss asked. "That kind of thing might help some."

"Nope." Pinkard shook his head. "I did what I was supposed to do, dammit. I didn't break any laws."

"How many Negroes went through your camps?" Lieutenant Colonel Moss asked. "How many came out alive? How many had trials?"

"Trials, nothing," Jeff said in disgust. "Trials are for citizens. Niggers aren't citizens of the CSA. Never have been. Never will be now, by God." He spoke with a certain doleful pride. He'd helped make sure of that.

"Even there, you're wrong," Moss said. "There were Negro citizens in the Confederate States—the men who fought for them in the Great War. They went into your camps just like the rest. U.S. authorities can prove that."

"Well, so what? They were dangerous," Jeff insisted. "You leave out the ones who learned how to fight, they're the bastards who'll give you grief down the line. When we take care of stuff, we do it up brown."

The Yankee sighed. "You aren't making it any easier for me—or for yourself."

"What the hell difference does it make?" Pinkard demanded. "You said it yourself—they're gonna hang me any which way. I'll be damned if I give 'em excuses. I did what I was supposed to do, that's all."

"Are you sorry you did it?" Moss said. "You might be able to persuade them to go a little easier on you if you make them believe you are."

"Easy enough to leave me alive?" Jeff asked.

"Well . . ." The military attorney hesitated. "You are the one who started using trucks to asphyxiate Negroes, right? And you are the one who started using cyanide in the phony bathhouses, too, aren't you?"

"How'd you know about the trucks?" Jeff asked.

"There's a Confederate official in Tennessee named . . ." The lawyer had to stop and check his notes. "Named Mercer Scott. He told us you were responsible for coming up with that. Is he lying? If he is, we have a better chance of keeping you breathing."

Jeff considered. So Mercer was singing, was he? Well, he was trying to save his neck, too. Chances were he wouldn't be able to do it, not when he ran Camp Dependable after Jeff moved on to Camp Determination. The trucks first showed up at Camp Dependable. They made life a lot easier for guards than taking Negroes out into the swamps and shooting them. Was the mechanic who'd made the first one still alive? Jeff didn't know. It probably didn't matter. Other guards back at the camp by Alexandria would be able to back Mercer up. As for the cyanide, he had plenty of correspondence with the pest-control company that made it. If he tried to deny things there, he was screwed, blued, and tattooed.

And so, with a heavy sigh, he shook his head. "No, I did that stuff, all right. I did it in the line of duty, and I don't need to be ashamed of it."

"You were trying to kill people as efficiently as you could," Moss said.

"I was trying to dispose of niggers as efficiently as I could, yeah," Pinkard said. "They were a danger to the Confederate States, so we had to get rid of 'em."

"Jake Featherston could have settled on redheads or Jews just as easily," the lawyer said.

"Nah." Jeff shook his head. "That's just stupid. Redheads never did anything to anybody. And Jews—hell, I don't have a lot of use for Jews, but they pulled for us, not against us. Look at Saul Goldman."

"He's under arrest, too," Moss said. "They'll hang him for all the lies he told and all the hatred he stirred up."

Jefferson Pinkard laughed. "You dumbass Yankees reckon we need to get talked to to hate niggers? We can take care of that on our own, thank you kindly. And so can you-all. Otherwise, you would've opened up the border and let 'em all in back before the war. Sure as hell didn't see that happening."

Moss wrote himself a note. "I'll bring it up at the trial. Some of the Negroes' blood is on our hands."

"Think it'll help?" Jeff asked.

"No," Moss said. "It'll just make the judges mad, because they'll aim to lay all the blame on you. But I'll get it on the record, anyhow."

"Hot shit," Jeff said.

The lawyer shrugged. "I can't promise to get you off the hook, not when I don't have a chance in church of delivering. They're going to do what they're going to do. I can slow them down a little and piss them off a little, and that's about it."

"It ain't fair," Jeff said. "You can't blame me for doing what my country wanted me to do. It's not like I broke any of my laws. You're changing the rules after the game is over."

"You're probably right, but so what?" Moss answered. "Millions of people are dead. Millions of people got killed for no better reason than that they were colored. The government of the USA has decided that that's a crime regardless of whether it broke Confederate law or not. I can't appeal against that decision—they won't let me. I have to play by the rules they give me now."

"Well, I had to play by the rules they gave me then. What's the goddamn difference?" Jeff said.

Moss reached into his briefcase and pulled out some photographs. He held them up so Pinkard could see them. They showed the crematorium at Camp Humble and some of the mass graves back at Camp Determination. "This is the difference," Moss said. "Doesn't it mean anything to you?"

"It means they're gonna fuck me," Jeff said. "That lousy crematorium never did work the way it was supposed to."

"I know. I've seen your letters to the company that built it," Moss said. "The people in charge of that company are also charged with crimes against humanity. The whole Confederacy went around the bend, didn't it?"

"Nope." If Jeff admitted that, he admitted he'd done something wrong. No matter what the damnyankees thought, he was damned if he believed it. "We were just taking care of what we had to do, that's all."

The U.S. officer sighed. "You don't give me much to work with, but I'll do what I can."

He sounded as if he meant it, anyhow. "Thanks," Jeff said grudgingly.

"Right." Moss put papers back into the briefcase, closed it, pushed back his chair, and got up. "We've done about as much as we can today, looks like."

He left. He *could* leave. Guards took Jeff back to his cell. He wasn't going anywhere, not until the damnyankees decided it was time to try him and hang him. The unfairness of it gnawed at him. When you won the war, you could do whatever you goddamn well pleased.

He imagined the Confederate States victorious. He imagined Jake Featherston setting up tribunals and hanging Yankees from Denver to Bangor for all the nasty things they'd done to the CSA after the Great War. There'd be Yankee bastards dangling from every lamppost in every town. Well, he could imagine whatever he pleased. Things had worked out the other way, and the sons of bitches from the USA were getting a brand new chance to work out on the Confederacy.

Where was the justice in that? Nowhere, not as far as he could see.

Of course, he couldn't see very far, not where he was. He could see lots and lots of iron bars, a forest of them. They weren't even damnyankee iron bars. They came to his eyes courtesy of the city of Houston. What mattered, though, was his own cell. It boasted a lumpy cot, a toilet without a seat (God only knew what kind of murderous weapon he could have come up with if they'd given him a toilet seat), and a cold-water sink. He knew why he didn't get hot water—that would have cost money, heaven forbid.

And he was an important prisoner, too. He had the cell to himself. Most cells held two men. He wouldn't have minded the company, but worrying about what he wanted wasn't high on anybody's list. Well, his own, but nobody gave a rat's ass about that any more. He'd been a big wheel for a long time. He'd got used to shoving Army officers around and arguing with the Attorney General. Now he might as well have been a coon himself, up on a drunk-and-disorderly rap.

Except they wouldn't hang a coon for that. They were going to hang him higher than Haman.

An attendant brought him a tray of food. He'd gone to jail in Birmingham a few times in his younger days. The chow then had been lousy. It still was.

"Sorry, buddy," the attendant said. "If it was up to me, I'd give you a fuckin' medal for what you did with the nigs."

"A medal doesn't do me a hell of a lot of good," Jeff said. "Can you get me out of here instead?"

The attendant shook his head. "Nope. No chance. Too many Yankees around. They'd hang me right alongside of you, and I got five kids."

Jeff could see the fear in his eyes. He would have said no if he were a fairy with no kids and no hope of any. The attendants were locals. Even though Texas was calling itself the Republic of Texas these days, they loved blacks no more than any other white Confederate did. But they loved their necks just fine. Nobody would help an important prisoner, nobody at all.

My name is Clarence Potter," Potter told the U.S. interrogator in Philadelphia. "My rank is brigadier general." He rattled off his pay number. "Under the Geneva Convention, that's all I've got to tell you."

"Screw the Geneva Convention," the interrogator answered. He was a major named Ezra Tyler, a real Yankee from New England. "And screw you, too. You blew up half of Philadelphia. And you did it wearing a U.S. uniform. You get caught after that, the Geneva Convention won't save your sorry ass."

"You won. You can do whatever you want—who's going to stop you?" Potter said. "But you know you used U.S. soldiers in C.S. uniforms in front of Chattanooga—other places, too. And you dropped two superbombs on my country, not just one. So who do you think you're trying to kid, anyway?"

Major Tyler turned red. "You're not cooperating."

"Damn straight I'm not," Potter agreed cheerfully. "I told you—I don't have to. Not legally, anyway."

"Do you want to live?"

"Sure. Who doesn't? Are you people going to let me? Doesn't seem likely, whether I cooperate or not."

"Professor FitzBelmont doesn't have that attitude."

"Professor FitzBelmont isn't a soldier. Professor FitzBelmont knows

things you can really use. And Professor FitzBelmont is kind of a twit."
Potter sighed. "None of which applies to me, I'm afraid."

"A twit?" One of Tyler's eyebrows rose. "Without him, you
wouldn't have had a superbomb."

"You're right—no doubt about it," Potter said. "Put a slide rule in
his hands and he's a world beater. But when he has to cope with the ordinary world and with ordinary people . . . he's kind of a twit. You
didn't have much trouble getting him to open up, did you?"

"That's none of your business," the interrogator said primly.

Henderson V. FitzBelmont, in his tweedy innocence, wouldn't have
known what Tyler meant, but Potter did. "Ha! Told you so."

"He . . . appreciates the delicacy of his position. You don't seem
to," Tyler said.

"My position isn't delicate. In international law, I'm fine. Whether
you care about international law may be a different story."

"We're treating you as a POW for the time being. You weren't *captured* in our uniform. You'll have a trial," Major Tyler said. "But if we
charge you with crimes against humanity—"

"Will you charge the Kaiser? What about Charlie La Follette? Like
I said, you used two superbombs on us. We only had one to use on
you."

"That's different."

"Sure it is. You won. I already told you that, too."

"Not what I meant, dammit." Tyler went red again. "We dropped
ours out of airplanes, the way you would with any other bomb. We
didn't sneak them over the border under false pretenses."

"Over, under, around, through—so what?" Potter said. "Shall I
apologize because we didn't have a bomber that would carry one of the
goddamn things? I'm sorry, Major—I'm sorry we didn't have more,
and I'm sorry we didn't have them sooner. If we did, I'd be interrogat-
ing you."

Ezra Tyler changed the subject, which was also the victor's privilege: "Speaking of crimes against humanity, General, what did you
know about your government's extermination policy against your Negroes, and when did you know it?"

Fear trickled through Potter. If the Yankees wanted C.S. officials
dead, they could always throw that one at them.

"All I knew was that I was involved in sniffing out the Negro uprising in 1915—which really did happen, Major, and which really did go a long way toward losing us that war. And I know there was a black guerrilla movement—again, a real one—before the start of this war. Those people were not our friends."

"Do you think your government's policy had anything to do with that?"

Of course I do. You'd have to be an idiot not to. I'm not that kind of idiot, anyway. Aloud, Potter said, "I'm a soldier. Soldiers don't make policy."

"Yes, you are a soldier. You returned to the C.S. Army after the 1936 Richmond Olympics, where you shot a Negro who was attempting to assassinate Jake Featherston."

"That's right."

"Before that time, you opposed Featherston politically."

"Yes, I was a Whig."

"You traveled to Richmond for the Games. You had a gun. You were close to a President you opposed. Did you go there intending to shoot him yourself?"

"It's not illegal to carry a gun in the CSA, any more than it is here. The language in our Constitution comes straight from yours." For the past eight years, Potter had been automatically saying no to that question whenever it came up. Saying yes would have got him killed—an inch at a time, no doubt. He needed a deliberate effort of will to tell the truth now: "Scratch that, Major. Yes, I went up there with that in mind. Maybe things would have gone better if I did it, or if I let the coon do it. They couldn't have gone much worse, could they? But it's a little late to worry about it now."

Major Tyler grunted. "Well, maybe. After all, of course you'd make that claim now. Amazing how many Confederates always hated Jake Featherston and everything he stood for—if you ask them, anyhow . . . What's so funny?"

Potter's laughter was bitter as wormwood. He'd lied convincingly enough to make a connoisseur of liars like Jake Featherston believe him. All the other Confederate big shots had, too. Now he was telling the truth—and this damnyankee wouldn't take him seriously. If he didn't laugh, he would cry.

"You can believe whatever you want—you will anyhow," he said. "I believe plenty of people who yelled, 'Freedom!' when that looked like the smart thing to do will tell you now that they never had anything to do with anything. They know who's on top and who's on the bottom. Life is like that."

The major wrote something in his notebook. "You're so cynical, you could go any way at all without even worrying about it. Down deep, you don't believe in anything, do you?"

"Fuck you, Tyler," Potter said. The Yankee blinked. Potter hadn't lost his temper before. "Fuck you in the heart," he repeated. "The one woman I ever really loved, I broke up with on account of she was for Featherston and I was against him."

"Will she testify to that?" the interrogator asked.

"No. She's dead," Potter answered. "She was in Charleston when your Navy bombers hit it back in the early days of the war." He barked two more harsh notes of laughter. "And if she were there at the end, she would have gone up in smoke with the rest of the city because of your superbomb."

Major Tyler gave him a dead-fish look. "You're in a poor position to complain about that, wouldn't you say?"

"Mm, you may be right," Potter admitted. That made the Yankee blink again; he didn't know Potter well enough to know his respect for the truth. *Who does know me that well nowadays?* Potter wondered. He couldn't think of a soul. That bespoke either a lifetime wasted or a lifetime in Intelligence, assuming the two weren't one and the same.

"If we were to release you, would you swear a loyalty oath to the United States?" the interrogator asked.

"No," Potter said at once. "You can conquer my country. Hell, you did conquer my country. But I don't feel like a good Socialist citizen of the USA. I'd say I was sorry I don't, only I'm not. Besides, why play games? You aren't going to turn me loose. You're just looking for the best excuse to hang me."

"We don't need excuses—you said so yourself, and you were right," Tyler replied. "Let me ask you a slightly different question: would you swear not to take up arms against the USA and not to aid any rebellion or uprising against this country? You don't have to like us for that one, only to respect our strength. And if you violate that oath, the penalty, just so you understand, would be a blindfold and a cigarette—a U.S. cigarette, I'm afraid."

"Talk about adding insult to injury," Potter said with a sour smile. "Yes, I might swear that oath. There's no denying we're knocked flat.

And there's also no denying that pretty soon I'll get too old to be dangerous to you with the worst will in the world. Things will go the way they go, and they can go that way without me."

"By your track record, General, you could be dangerous to us as long as you're breathing, and I think we'd be smart to make sure you don't sneak a telegraph clicker into your coffin," Ezra Tyler said.

"You flatter me," Potter told him.

"I doubt it," the U.S. officer replied. "If we were to release you, where would you go? What would you do?"

"Beats me. I spent a lot of years as a professional soldier. And when I wasn't, in between the wars, I lived in Charleston myself. Not much point going there, not unless I want to glow in the dark." Potter took off his glasses and polished them with a handkerchief. It bought him a moment to think. "Why are you going on and on about turning me loose, anyway? Are you trying to get my hopes up? I've been on the other end of these jobs, you know. You won't break me like that."

If they started getting rough . . . He had no movie-style illusions about his own toughness. If they started cutting things or burning things or breaking things or running a few volts—you didn't need many—through sensitive places, he would sing like a mockingbird to make them stop. Anybody would. The general rule was, the only people who thought they could resist torture were the ones who'd never seen it. Oh, there were occasional exceptions, but the accent was on *occasional*.

Major Tyler shrugged. "Our legal staff has some doubts about conviction, though we may go ahead anyway. If you were captured in our uniform . . . But you weren't."

"Don't sound so disappointed," Potter said.

"What did you think when that colored kid shot President Featherston?" the Yankee asked out of a blue sky.

"I didn't know who did it, not at first," Potter answered. "I saw him fall, and I . . . I knew the war was over. He kept it going, just by staying alive. If he'd made it to Louisiana, say, I don't think we could have beaten you, but we'd still be fighting. And I'd known him almost thirty years, since he was an artillery sergeant with a lousy temper. He made you pay attention to him—to who he was and to what he was. And when he got killed, it was like there was a hole in the world. We won't see anyone like him any time soon, and that's the Lord's truth."

"I say, thank the Lord it is," Tyler replied.

"He damn near beat you. All by himself, he damn near did."

"I know. We all know," Tyler said. "And everybody who followed him is worse off because he tried. He should have left us alone."

"He couldn't. He thought he owed you one," Potter said. "He was never somebody who could leave anybody alone. He aimed to pay back the Negroes for screwing him out of a promotion to second lieutenant—that's how he looked at it. He wanted to, and he did. And he wanted to pay back the USA, too, and you'll never forget him even if he couldn't quite do it. I hated the son of a bitch, and I still miss him now that he's gone." He shook his head. Major Tyler could make whatever he wanted out of that, but every word of it was true.

XVI

The doctor eyed Michael Pound with a curious lack of comprehension. "You can stay longer if you like, Lieutenant," he said. "You're not fully healed. You don't have to return to active duty."

"I understand that, sir," Pound answered. "I want to."

He and the doctor wore the same uniform, but they didn't speak the same language. "Why, for God's sake?" the medical man asked. "You've got it soft here. No snipers. No mines. No auto bombs or people bombs."

"Sir, no offense, but it's boring here," Pound said. "I want to go where things are happening. I want to make things happen myself. I needed to be here—I needed to get patched up. Now I can walk on my hind legs again. They can put me back in a barrel, and I'm ready to go. I want to see what the Confederate States look like now that they've surrendered."

"They look the way hell would if we'd bombed it back to the Stone Age," the doctor said. "And everybody who's left alive hates our guts."

"Good," Pound said. The doctor gaped. Pound condescended to explain: "In that case, it's mutual." He held out his hospital-discharge papers. "You sign three times, sir."

"I know the regulations." The medical man signed with a fancy fountain pen. "If you want a psychological discharge, I daresay you'd qualify for that, too."

"Sir, if I want a discharge, I'll find a floozy," Pound said. As the doctor snorted, Pound went on, "But you've even got things to really cure VD now, don't you?"

"As a matter of fact, we do. Curing stupidity is another story, worse luck." The doctor kept one copy for the file and handed back the rest. "Good luck to you."

"Thanks." Pound took the papers and limped across the street to the depot there for reassignment.

"Glutton for punishment, sir?" asked the top sergeant who ran the Chattanooga repple-depple. He was not far from Pound's age, and had an impressive spread of ribbons on his chest—including one for the Purple Heart with two tiny oak-leaf clusters on it.

"Look who's talking," Pound told him. The noncom chuckled and gave back a crooked grin. Pound asked, "What have you got for me?"

"Armor, eh?" the sergeant said, and gave Pound a measuring stare. "How long did you wear stripes on your sleeve instead of shoulder straps?"

"Oh, a little while. They finally promoted me when I wasn't looking," Pound said.

"Thought that was how things might work." The sergeant didn't have to be a genius to figure it out. A first lieutenant with graying, thinning hair and lines on his face hadn't come out of either West Point or the training programs that produced throngs of ninety-day wonders to lead platoons. Every so often, the school of hard knocks booted out an officer, too. The sergeant shuffled through papers. "What's the biggest outfit you were ever in charge of?"

"A platoon."

"Think you can swing a company?"

Pound always thought he could do anything. He was right more often than he was wrong, which didn't stop him from occasionally bumping up against a hard dose of reality. But, since he would never again be able to get back to the pure and simple pleasures of a gunner's job, he expected he could handle a larger command than any he'd had yet. "Sure. Where is it?"

"Down in Tallahassee, Florida," the personnel sergeant said. "Kinda tricky down there. They didn't see any U.S. soldiers during the war, so a lot of them don't feel like they really lost."

"No, huh?" Pound said. "Well, if they need lessons, I can give 'em some."

"There you go. Let me cut you some orders, then. I'll send a wire to the outfit down there, tell 'em they've got their man. And we'll give you a lift to the train station." The sergeant sketched a salute. "Pleasure doing business with you, sir."

"Back at you." Pound returned the military courtesy.

Seeing the train gave him pause. It said—screamed, really—that the fighting wasn't over yet. A freight car full of junk preceded the locomotive. If the track was mined, the car's weight would set off the charge and spare the engine. There was a machine gun on the roof of every fourth car, and several more gun barrels stuck out from the caboose. You didn't carry that kind of firepower unless you thought you'd need it.

He already knew what Georgia looked like. He'd helped create that devastation himself. He was moderately proud of it, or more than moderately. He changed trains in Atlanta. Walking through the station hurt, but he didn't let on. Released Confederate POWs in their shabby uniforms, now stripped of emblems, also made their way through the place. They were tight-lipped and somber. Maybe the people in Tallahassee didn't know the CSA had lost the war, but these guys did.

The new train also had a freight car in front and plenty of guns up top. Pound looked out on wrecked vehicles and burnt farmhouses and hasty graves—the detritus of war. He thought the devastation would have a sharp edge marking the U.S. stop line, but it didn't. Bombers had made sure of that. Towns had got leveled. Bridges were out. He sat there for several hours waiting for the last touches to be put on repairs to one.

"Why don't we go back or go around?" somebody in the car asked.

"Because that would make sense," Pound said, and no one seemed to want to argue with him.

He got into Tallahassee in the late afternoon, then, and not the morning as he'd been scheduled to do. It wasn't remotely his fault, but he didn't think it would endear him to his new CO, whoever that turned out to be.

A sergeant standing just inside the doorway held a sign that said LIEUTENANT POUND. "That's me," Pound said. "Sorry to keep you waiting."

"It's all right, sir. I know the railroads on the way down here are really screwed up," the noncom said. "I've got an auto waiting for you. Can I grab your duffel? Colonel Einsiedel said you were coming off a wound."

"Afraid I am." Pound took the green-gray canvas sack off his shoulder and gave it to the sergeant. "Sorry to put you to the trouble, but if you're kind enough to offer I'll take you up on it."

"Don't worry about it, sir. All part of the service." The sergeant was in his early twenties. He'd probably been a private when the war started, if he'd been in the Army at all. Michael Pound knew what his curious glance meant. *You're the oldest goddamn first looey I ever saw.* But the man didn't say anything except, "I've got it. Follow me."

The motorcar was a commandeered Birmingham. The sergeant drove him past the bomb-damaged State Capitol and then north and east up to Clark Park, where the armored regiment was bivouacked. It wasn't a long drive at all. "Tallahassee's the capital of Florida, isn't it?" Pound said. "I thought there'd be more of it."

"It's only about a good piss wide, sure as hell," the sergeant agreed. "Christ, the Legislature only meets for a coupla months in odd-numbered years. We had to call 'em back into session so we could tell 'em what to do."

"How did they like that?" Pound asked.

"Everybody hates us. We're Yankees," the sergeant said matter-of-factly. "But if anybody fucks with us, we grease him. It's about that simple. All of our barrels have a .50-caliber machine gun mounted in front of the commander's cupola, and we carry lots of canister, not so much HE and AP. We're here to smash up mobs, and we damn well do it."

"Sounds good to me." Pound had wished for a machine gun of his own plenty of times in the field. Now he'd have one—and a .50-caliber machine gun could chew up anything this side of a barrel. And if God wanted a shotgun, He'd pick up a barrel's cannon firing canister. Canister wouldn't just smash up a mob—it would exterminate one.

Barbed wire surrounded Clark Park. So did signs with skulls and crossbones on them and a blunt warning message: HEADS UP! MINES! U.S. guards carrying captured C.S. automatic rifles talked to the sergeant before swinging back a stout, wire-protected gate and letting the Birmingham through.

"Had trouble with auto bombs or people bombs?" Pound asked. "Do they shoot mortars at you in the middle of the night?"

"They tried that shit once or twice, sir," his driver answered. "When we take hostages now, we're up to killing a hundred for one.

They know we'd just as soon see 'em dead, so they don't mess with us like they did when we first got here. Now they've seen we really mean it."

"That sounds good to me, too." Pound was and always had been a firm believer in massive retaliation.

The sergeant drove him up to a tent flying a regimental flag—a pugnacious turtle on roller skates wearing a helmet and boxing gloves—that looked as if some Hollywood animation studio had designed it. Colonel Nick Einsiedel looked as if some Hollywood casting office had designed him. He was tall and blond and handsome, and he wore the ribbons for a Silver Star and a Purple Heart.

"Good to have you with us," he told Pound. "I did some asking around—you've got a hell of a record. Shame you didn't make officer's rank till the middle of the war."

"I liked being a sergeant, sir," Pound said. "But this isn't *so* bad." As Einsiedel laughed, he went on, "How can I be most useful here, sir?"

"That's the kind of question I like to hear," the regimental CO replied. "We're trying to be tough but fair—or fair but tough, if you'd sooner look at it that way."

"Sir, if I've got plenty of canister for the big gun and a .50 up on my turret along with the other machine guns, you can call it whatever you want," Pound said. "The people down here will damn well do what I tell 'em to, and that's what counts."

Colonel Einsiedel smiled. "You've got your head on straight, by God."

"I've been through the mill. Maybe it amounts to the same thing."

"Wouldn't be surprised," Einsiedel said. "One thing we don't do unless we can't help it, though—we don't send a barrel out by itself. Too many blind spots, too good a chance for somebody to throw a Featherston Fizz at you."

That didn't sound so good. "I thought the locals were supposed to be too scared of us to try any crap," Pound said.

"They are—supposed to be," the regimental CO answered. "But in case they aren't, we don't want to lead them into temptation, either. Does that suit you?"

"Oh, yes, sir. I want to know what I'm getting into, that's all," Pound said.

Einsiedel gave him a crooked grin. "Whatever you get into down here, make sure you go to a pro station afterwards, 'cause chances are you'll end up with a dose if you don't."

"Understand, sir," Pound said, thinking back to his joke with the doctor before he got released. "Uh—is there an officers' brothel in town?"

"Officially, no. Officially, all the brown-noses back up in the USA would pitch a fit if we did things like that. Unofficially, there are two. Maude's is around the corner from the Capitol. Miss Lucy's is a couple of blocks farther south. I like Maude's better, but you can try 'em both."

"I expect I will. All the comforts of home—or of a house, anyway," Pound said. Colonel Einsiedel winced. Pound figured he'd got off on the right foot.

Like most Congressional veterans, Flora Blackford spent most of her time in Philadelphia. As summer swung towards autumn every other year, though, she went back to the Lower East Side in New York City to campaign for reelection. And this was a Presidential election year, too.

She thought Charlie La Follette ought to win in a walk. But the Democrats had nominated a native New Yorker, a hotshot prosecutor named Dewey, to run against him. Dewey and his Vice Presidential candidate, a blunt-talking Senator from Missouri, were running an aggressive campaign, crisscrossing the country saying they could have handled the war better and would ride herd on the beaten Confederacy harder. President La Follette and his running mate, Jim Curley of Massachusetts, had to content themselves with saying that the Socialists damn well *had* won the war. Would that be enough? Unless people were uncommonly ungrateful, Flora thought it would.

Normally, she wouldn't have wanted to see Congressman Curley on the ticket. He came straight from the Boston machine, an unsavory if effective apparatus. But Dewey's would-be veep was a longtime Kansas City ward heeler, and the Kansas City machine was even more unsavory (and perhaps even more effective) than Boston's.

Visiting Socialist Party headquarters felt like coming home again. The only difference from when she worked there thirty years earlier was that the butcher's shop underneath the place was owned by the son of the man who'd run it then. Like his father, Sheldon

Fleischmann was a Democrat. And, like his father, he often sent cold cuts up anyhow.

The district had changed. Far fewer people here were fresh off the boat than had been true in 1914. Native-born Americans tended to be more conservative than their immigrant parents. All the same, Flora worried more about the national ticket than her own seat. The fellow the Democrats had nominated, a theatrical booking agent named Morris Kramer, had to spend most of his time explaining why he hadn't been in uniform during the war.

"He's got a hernia," Herman Bruck said. He'd been a Socialist activist as long as Flora had. "So all right—they didn't conscript him. But do you think anybody wants a Congressman who wears a truss?"

"If he didn't wear it, his brains would fall out," somebody else said. That got a laugh from everyone in the long, smoky room. Half the typewriters stopped clattering for a moment. The other half wouldn't have stopped for anything this side of the Messiah.

"I won't give him a hard time for not going into the service," Flora said. "The voters know the story." If they didn't know it, she *would* make damn sure they found out before Election Day. "I want to show them what having somebody who's been in Congress for a while means to them."

"Well, you've got a chance to do that," Bruck said.

"I know," Flora answered unhappily. During the Great War, C.S. bombers hardly ever got as far north as New York City. They did little damage on their handful of raids. It wasn't like that this time around, worse luck.

Most of the Confederates' bombs had fallen on the port—most, but far from all. Some rained down on the city at random. In a place so full of people, the bombardiers must have assumed they would do damage wherever their explosions came down—and who was to say they were wrong?

Flora's district had suffered along with the rest of New York. Bombs had blown up apartment buildings and clothing factories and block after block of shops. Incendiaries had charred holes in the fabric of the city. Rebuilding wouldn't be easy or quick or cheap.

One advantage incumbency gave Flora was her connections down in Philadelphia. If she asked for money to help put her district back together, she was more likely to get it than a Congressman new in his seat.

Her campaign posters got right down to business when they talked about that. DO YOU WANT A NEW KID ON YOUR BLOCK? they asked, and showed Morris Kramer in short pants pulling a wheeled wooden duck on a string. That wasn't even remotely fair, but politics wasn't about being fair. Politics was about getting your guy in and keeping the other side's guy out. Once you'd done that, you could do all the other neat stuff you had in mind. If you stood on the sidelines looking longingly toward the playing field, all the neat ideas in the world weren't worth a dime.

"We want to make this district a better place than it was before the war," Flora said to whoever would listen to her. "Not the same as it used to be, not just as good as it used to be. Better. If we can't do that, we might as well leave the ruins alone, to remind us we shouldn't be dumb enough to fight another war."

Herman Bruck brought a blond kid in a captain's uniform up to her one afternoon at the Socialist Party headquarters. "Flora, I'd like you to meet Alex Swartz," he said.

"Hello, Captain Swartz," Flora said. "What can I do for you?" She had no doubt that the earnest young officer with a roll of papers under one arm was on the up and up. Whether Herman Bruck had an ulterior motive in introducing him . . . Well, she'd find out about that.

"Very pleased to meet you, ma'am," Alex Swartz said. He had broad, Slavic cheekbones and a narrow chin, giving his face a foxy cast. "I graduated from Columbia with a degree in architecture two weeks before the war started. I'm on leave right now—in a week, I go back down to occupation duty in Mississippi. But I wanted to show you some of the sketches I've made for how things might look once we put them back together."

"I'd like to see," Flora said, not exaggerating too much. If the sketches turned out to be garbage, she could come out with polite nothings, let the captain down easy, and then get on with her reelection campaign and with taking care of the damage in the district.

But they weren't garbage. As he unrolled them one by one and talked about what he had in mind, she saw she wasn't the only one who'd been thinking along those lines. The sketches showed a more spacious, less jam-packed, less hurried place than the one her constituents lived in now.

"This is a lot like what I have in mind," she said. "I particularly like the way you use green space, and the way you don't forget about theaters and libraries. The next question is, how much does it all cost?" That was the one that separated amateurs from professionals. She wouldn't have been surprised if Alex Swartz hadn't worried about it at all.

He had, though. "Here—I've made some estimates," he said, and pulled a couple of folded sheets of paper from his left breast pocket. "Not cheap, but I hope not too outrageous."

"Let's have a look." Flora peered through the bottoms of her bifocals. She found herself nodding. Captain Swartz had it just about right—what he was proposing wasn't cheap, but it wasn't too expensive, either. If you wanted to do things right, you had to spend some money. "Not bad, Captain. Not bad at all."

"Do you think . . . there's any chance it will happen?" he asked.

"There's some chance that some of it will," she answered. "I can't say any more than that. Nothing the government touches ever ends up looking just the way you thought it would before you started—you need to understand that right from the beginning, or else you start going crazy."

Swartz nodded. "Got you."

"Are you sure? You'd better, or you'll end up very disappointed. Most things end up as compromises, as committee decisions that don't make too many people too unhappy. Some good stuff goes down the drain. So does some crap. Which is which . . . depends on who's talking a lot of the time."

"Getting some of this built is better than leaving it all as pretty pictures," Captain Swartz insisted. "Pretty pictures are too easy."

"That sounds like the right attitude," Flora said.

"One thing you find out pretty darn quick in the Army—you won't get everything you want," Swartz said.

"It's no different in politics," Flora said. "We don't always have to shoot at people to make that clear, though, which is all to the good."

Captain Swartz looked about sixteen when he grinned. "I bet." Then the grin slipped. "Didn't I hear your son got wounded? How's he doing?"

"He's getting better," Flora answered. "It was a hand wound—nothing life-threatening, thank God." And it kept him out of action while the war finally ran down. Maybe it kept him from stopping something worse. She could hope so, anyway. Hoping so made her feel not quite so bad when she thought about what *did* happen to Joshua.

"Glad to hear it," the architect said. "I admire you for not keeping him out of the Army or getting him a job counting paper clips in Nevada or something. You would've had the clout to do it—I know that."

"Captain, I'll tell you what isn't even close to a secret. I'm his mother, after all. If he'd let me do something like that, I would have done it in a heartbeat," Flora answered. "But he didn't, and so I didn't. If, God forbid, anything worse would have happened, I don't know how I would have looked at myself in a mirror afterwards."

"Well, I can see that," Alex Swartz said. "But I can see how he feels about it, too. You don't want to think your mother's apron strings kept you out of danger everybody else had to face."

"No, and you don't want to get killed, either." Flora sighed. "He came through it, and he didn't get hurt too bad. That means I don't hate myself . . . too much." She tapped an unrolled drawing with the nail of her right index finger. "I really think you're on to something here with these sketches. I hope we can make some of them more than sketches, if you know what I mean. The district will be better off if we can."

His eyes glowed. "Thank you!"

"You're welcome," she said. "Remember, I grew up here, in a cold-water flat. We're too crowded. I like the open space that's part of your plan. We need more of it here. We'd be better off if the whole district had more, not just the parts the Confederates bombed."

"Using war as an engine for urban improvement—" Captain Swartz began.

"Is wasteful," Flora finished for him. She didn't know if that was what he was going to say, but it was the truth. She went on, "But if it's the only engine we've got, *not* using it would be a crime. And the way things are on the Lower East Side, I'm afraid it is."

"If I got out of the Army before Election Day, I was going to vote for you anyway," he said. "Now I want to vote for you two or three times."

From behind Flora, Herman Bruck said, "That can probably be arranged."

"Hush, Herman," Flora said, though she knew he might not be kidding. She turned back to Captain Swartz. "Instead of doing that, take your plans to Morris Kramer. If he wins, he can do his best to push them through, too. And they're important. They ought to go forward regardless of politics." Did she really say that? Did she really mean it?

She nodded to herself. She did. When it came down to the district, you could . . . every once in a while.

From Virginia all the way down to Florida—except the area around Lexington, Virginia, which was the most special of special cases— Irving Morrell's word was law. *Military governor* was a bland title, but it was the one he had. In the Roman Empire, he would have been a pro- consul. That held more flavor, at least to him. A Roman, to whom Latin came naturally, might have disagreed.

Morrell had always had a bitch of a time with Latin. He set up shop in Atlanta. It was centrally located for his current command, and it also hadn't taken the pounding Richmond had. One of these days, the states under his jurisdiction might rejoin the USA. That was the long-term outlook in Philadelphia. Morrell would believe it when he saw it. Right now, his main job was making sure smoldering resent- ment didn't burst into flaming revolt.

Thick tangles of barbed wire strengthened by iron and concrete pillars made sure autos couldn't come within a couple of hundred yards of his headquarters. No auto bomb was going to take out the whole building. Everyone who approached on foot, male or female, was me- thodically searched.

Security was just as tight at other U.S. headquarters throughout the fallen Confederacy. Neither that nor brutal retaliation for attacks had kept a couple of colonels and a brigadier general from joining their an- cestors.

"And these people are supposed to become citizens?" Morrell said to his second-in-command. "How long do they expect us to wait?"

"The French and Germans don't love each other, either," Harlan Parsons replied.

"But they both know they're foreigners," Morrell said. "The Con- federates speak English. These states used to belong to the USA. And because of that, the bigwigs in Philadelphia think it can happen again, easy as pie. And I've got one thing to say to that: bullshit!"

"You get to try to make it work," Brigadier General Parsons said. "Aren't you lucky . . . sir?"

"Yeah. I'm lucky like snow is black," Morrell answered.

His number two sent him a quizzical look. "You're the first officer I ever heard who used that line and wasn't Jewish."

"I knew I stole it from somebody. I forgot who," Morrell said.

The telephone on his desk rang. Parsons picked it up. "General Morrell's office." Maybe he could protect his superior from the slings and arrows of outrageous—or outraged—idiots. Here, though, he listened for a little while and then said, "I'll pass you through. Hold on." Putting his hand over the mouthpiece, he told Morrell, "It's Colonel Einsiedel, down in Tallahassee."

"Thanks." Morrell took the telephone. "Hello, Colonel. What's gone wrong now?" He assumed something had. People didn't call him to talk about the weather.

Sure enough, the local commander said, "We're facing a boycott here. All the locals are pretending we don't exist. And they aren't going into any of the stores that sell to us. Some of the merchants are starting to feel the pinch."

"That's a new one," Morrell said. "Any violence?"

"Not aimed at us," Colonel Einsiedel answered. "They may have used some strong-arm tactics to get their own people to go along. What are we supposed to do about it?"

"Ignore them. Wait it out," Morrell said. "What else is there?"

"Some of the storekeepers don't want to sell to us any more," the colonel said. "They're trying to get out of the deals they made. It's hard to blame them. If they keep doing business with us, they starve."

"You can't let 'em get away with that. If you do, this time tomorrow there won't be a shop in the old Confederacy where we can buy anything. We aren't niggers, and our money's good."

"Yes, sir. We'll try," Einsiedel said. "One of my lieutenants said we ought to shoot any storekeeper who won't sell to us."

Morrell laughed. "Damned if that doesn't sound like Michael Pound."

"How the devil did you know, sir?" The colonel in Florida sounded flabbergasted.

"You mean it is?" Morrell laughed again. "Well, I can't say I'm surprised. I've known Pound for twenty-five years now. He has a straightforward bloodthirstiness that would scare the crap out of any General Staff officer ever born. He's not always right, but he's always sure of himself."

"Boy, you can say that again," Einsiedel said. "All right, sir. We'll see what we can do to nip this stuff in the bud."

"Don't be too gentle," Morrell said. "We won the war. If they think they're going to win the peace, they can damn well think again."

"I sure hope so," Colonel Einsiedel said, which wasn't exactly the encouraging note on which Morrell would have wanted the conversation to end. But the colonel hung up after that, so Morrell couldn't pump him any more without calling him back. Deciding that would make more trouble than it saved, Morrell put the handset back into its cradle instead.

"Boycott, huh?" Brigadier General Parsons said. "That's . . . different."

"Yeah. It lets them annoy us without giving us a good excuse to shoot them," Morrell said. "Some of them are still fighting the war, even if they don't carry guns any more. Every time they make us blink, they figure they've won a battle."

"So we don't blink, then," Parsons said.

"That's about the size of it." Morrell hoped he could get his own officers to go along. Not all of them would see that this was a problem.

Michael Pound did, by God! Morrell smiled and shook his head. Pound saw problems and solutions with an almost vicious clarity. As far as he was concerned, everything was simple. And damned if watching him in action didn't make you wonder whether he had it right and everybody else looked at the world through a kaleidoscope that made everything seem much more complicated than it should have.

The telephone rang again. "General Morrell's office," Harlan Parsons said. This time, he didn't hesitate in answering on his own hook: "That's right. As of the surrender, Negroes have the same rights on ex-Confederate territory as whites do. Anyone who tries to go against that goes up against the U.S. government. . . . Yes, that includes intermarriage, as long as the people involved want to go through with it."

After he hung up, Morrell asked, "Where?"

"Rocky Mount, North Carolina," his second-in-command answered. "Nice to know there are still some Negroes there."

"Still *some* Negroes all through the CSA," Morrell said. "Just not many." He'd heard so many stories of survival by luck and by stealth and by guerrilla war that they started to blur. He'd heard some of survival by the kindness of whites, but fewer than he wished he had.

"Featherston turned a whole country upside down and inside out," Parsons said. "It'll never be the same down here. Never. How many dead?"

"Six million? Seven? Ten?" Morrell shrugged helplessly. "I don't think anybody knows exactly. Maybe they can figure out how many Negroes the Confederates shipped to their camps. I bet it'd be easier to count how many are left now, though. Then subtract from how many there were before the Freedom Party started killing them, and the number you get is how many bought a plot."

"Those Freedom Party bastards had to be out of their skulls," Parsons said: far from the first time Morrell had heard that opinion. "Imagine all the effort they put into killing colored people. All the camps they had to build, all the trains they had to use . . . They would have done better if they aimed that shit at us."

"They would have done a hell of a lot better if they'd put their Negroes into factories to make stuff to throw at us, or if they put them in uniform and pointed them at us," Morrell said. "Or that's how it looks to me, anyhow. But they saw it different. Far as Featherston was concerned, getting rid of Negroes was every bit as important as whaling the snot out of us."

Parsons spiraled a forefinger by his right ear. "Out of his skull," he repeated.

"Yeah, I think so, too—most of the time. But for people who were crazy, they sure went at it like they knew what they were doing." Morrell shivered. "Those camps ran like barrel factories. Negroes went in, and corpses came out. If that was what they were aiming for, they couldn't have done a smoother job."

"I know. Those phony bathhouses, so the colored people wouldn't know they were gonna get it till too late . . ." Parsons shuddered, too. "But don't you have to be crazy to *want* to do something like that?"

"When the Ottomans started killing Armenians after the Great War, I sure thought so," Morrell answered. "Maniacs in fezzes . . . But shit, the Confederates aren't *that* different from us, or they weren't till they started yelling, 'Freedom!' all the damn time. Biggest difference is, they had lots of Negroes and we only had a few. So could *we* do something like that, too?"

Harlan Parsons looked horrified. "Christ, I hope not!"

"Yeah, well, so do I," Morrell said. "But what's that got to do with anything? If we decide we can't stand Negroes or Jews or Chinamen or whoever the hell, do we fish the designs for these asphyxiating trucks out of the file and start making our own?"

"I don't *think* so, sir," his second-in-command replied. "For one thing, the Confederates went and did that. Maybe we can learn our lesson from them."

"Here's hoping." Morrell nodded. "You might have something there. I sure hope you do. Who'd want to go down in history as the next Jake Featherston?" He answered his own question: "Nobody. I hope."

"Now if only the people down here could get it through their damn thick heads that what the Freedom Party did was wrong," Parsons said.

"If they would have thought it was wrong, it never would have happened in the first place," Morrell said. "If they hadn't voted Featherston in, or if they hadn't let him go after the colored people . . . They did, though. And you said it, General. This is a whole different landscape here now."

How *would* the area that had made up the CSA get along without Negroes to do the jobs whites didn't want or felt to be beneath their dignity? He'd already seen part of the answer. Lots of Mexicans had come north to work in the fields and to wait tables and cut hair and clean house. Unless the USA posted machine guns every few hundred yards along the Rio Grande, the Mexicans would keep on coming, too. They could do less and get more money for it here than they could in Francisco José's ramshackle empire. Without machine guns, how were you going to keep them away?

Well, that wasn't his worry. The Secretary of State and the Secretary of the Interior and the Secretary of War would figure out what to do about it, and then they'd tell him. And then he would have to do it— or try to, if it turned out to be one of the stupid orders that came out of Philadelphia every now and then.

Bang! When Morrell heard that noise, he ducked first and thought later. So did Harlan Parsons. Nothing else happened, though. Parsons straightened with a sheepish smile. "I *think* it was only a backfire."

"I think you're right," Morrell said. "That's a relief, isn't it? One of these days, we may even be able to hear that noise without flinching."

"One of these days—but not soon," Parsons said.

Morrell nodded. The war hadn't just changed the Confederate States. It had changed his own country. And it had changed *him*, and changed every soldier on both sides who came through alive. Starting at loud noises was the least of it. The last time around, one Confederate soldier came out changed enough to convulse his country a generation later. Who would change things this time around—and how?

*   *   *

Congratulations, Dr. O'Doull! Congratulations, Lieutenant Colonel O'Doull!" Colonel Tobin said. He was the U.S. officer in charge of this part of Alabama, and he was proud of it, God help him. He handed Leonard O'Doull the little velvet box containing a lieutenant colonel's silver oak leaves as if it were the Holy Grail.

"Thank you, sir." O'Doull was much less impressed. He also suspected Tobin had chosen to promote him to try to persuade him to stay in the Army. If so, the man was barking up the wrong tree. "Sir, I've been away from my family a long time now. With the war over and done, I'd like to arrange to return to civilian life."

"So would we all," Tobin said. "But you can't deny soldiers are still getting wounded, can you? And you can't deny they're coming down with, uh, unpleasant diseases, either." He didn't want to come right out and say VD.

"No, sir. I can't deny any of that. Still, it is peacetime—formally, anyhow. And with our new antibiotics, a medic can do just as much for syphilis and gonorrhea as I can."

Colonel Tobin winced when he heard the names. But he didn't retreat. "I'm very sorry, but the United States still need you. You did sign up to serve at the country's pleasure, you know."

That was a trump against most men in U.S. service. Against Leonard O'Doull? Not necessarily. "Sir, meaning no disrespect, but I'm going to have to get hold of my government and see what it thinks of your refusing to discharge me."

"*Your* government?" Tobin had bushy eyebrows, and got a good theatrical effect when he raised one. "You have a different one from everybody else's?"

"Yes, sir," O'Doull said, which made the colonel's eyebrow jump again—this time, O'Doull judged, involuntarily. He pulled a maroon passport out of his trouser pocket. "As you see, sir, I'm a citizen of the Republic of Quebec. Actually, I have dual citizenship, but I've lived in the Republic since the last war. I met a girl up there, and I stayed and started a practice in Rivière-du-Loup."

"Good God. Let me see that." Tobin took the Quebecois passport as if it were a poisonous snake. He found the page with O'Doull's picture and grunted in surprise, as if he truly hadn't expected to see it there. Shaking his head, he handed the passport back. "You'd better get hold of your officials. If they write me and say they want you to go on home, I have a reason to turn you loose. Till then, though, you're a U.S. military physician, and we do need your services."

Damn, O'Doull thought. He had no idea whether the authorities in the Republic would send that kind of letter. But he couldn't deny that Colonel Tobin was playing by the rules. "All right, sir. I'll do that, then." O'Doull put the passport back in his pocket. Colonel Tobin seemed glad to see him go.

"Well, Doc? Any luck?" Goodson Lord asked him when he got back to the aid station.

"Depends on what you mean." O'Doull displayed his new rank insignia. Sergeant Lord shook his hand. "As for getting out," O'Doull went on, "well, yes and no. If I can get a letter from my mommy—I mean, from my government—Tobin will have a real, live piece of paper to give him an excuse to turn me loose. Till then, I'm here."

"Hope like hell they give it to you," Lord said. "If I had an angle like that, you bet your sweet ass I'd use it. Playing a horn beats the crap out of this."

"You're a good medic," O'Doull said.

"Thanks. I try. Some guy comes in bleeding, you don't want to let him down, you know what I mean?" Lord said. "Even if I am halfway decent, though, it's not like I want to do it the rest of my life."

"That seems fair," O'Doull allowed.

He wondered how long the United States would be able to occupy the Confederate States. The government might want to do it, but the soldiers on the ground were a lot less enthusiastic. They chafed under the discipline they'd accepted without thinking when their country was in peril.

They drank whatever they could get their hands on. They got into brawls with the locals and with one another. Despite all the thunderous orders against fraternizing with Confederate women, they chased skirt as eagerly as they would have back home. And what they chased, they caught. They caught all kinds of things—the penicillin they got stuck with testified to that.

"I don't know what the hell her name was," said a private most unhappy about his privates—he had one of the drippiest faucets O'Doull had ever seen. "It was dark. She said, 'Five dollars,' so I gave it to her. Then she gave it to me."

"She sure did. Bend over. I'm going to give it to you, too," O'Doull said. The soldier whined when the shot went home. O'Doull persisted: "Where was this? At a brothel? We need to know about those."

"No . . ." The soldier sighed with relief as the needle came out. "I was going back to my tent after I stood sentry, you know? And she called, and I felt like it, so I paid her and I screwed her in the bushes. And the bitch gave me something to remember her by."

O'Doull sighed. "Oh, God, I am so tired of this."

"Yeah, well, let me tell you somethin', Doc—it's even less fun on this end of the needle." The soldier did up his pants. "Is that it? Am I done?"

"No. You have to come back in three days for another shot," O'Doull answered. The other man groaned. O'Doull felt like groaning himself. *This is why I need to get out of the Army*, he thought glumly. "And I have to see your dogtags. Your superiors in the line need to know you came down venereal."

The soldier with the clap *really* didn't like that. If Goodson Lord and Eddie hadn't opportunely appeared, he might have stormed out of the aid station and forgotten about the second half of his cure. Eddie held a wrench; Sergeant Lord had a tire iron. O'Doull got the information he needed.

As soon as he'd written that down, he started in on the letter to the powers that be in the Republic of Quebec. Finding an envelope for it was easy. Coming up with a postage stamp wasn't. Soldiers in Confederate territory who were writing to the USA got free franking. Writing to Quebec, O'Doull didn't, and he'd used his last stamp a few days before on a letter to Nicole. He thought about using Confederate stamps, but they'd been demonetized. Eventually, a mail clerk came up with the requisite postage, and the letter went on its way.

And then he forgot about it. He went back to being a busy Army doctor, because an auto bomb killed several U.S. soldiers and wounded two dozen more. He hated auto bombs. They were a coward's weapons. You could be—and, if you had any brains, you were—miles away when your little toy went off. And you could laugh at what it did to the people you didn't like.

Digging jagged chunks of metal out of one soldier after another, O'Doull wasn't laughing. He didn't think the locals would be laughing very long, either, even though they probably were right now. "How many hostages will the authorities take after something like this?" he asked.

"Beats me," Goodson Lord answered. "But they'll shoot every damn one of 'em. You can bet your last nickel on that."

"I know. And that will make some diehard mad enough to build another bomb, and then it just starts up again. Ain't we got fun?" O'Doull said.

"Fun. Yeah," Lord said. "How's this guy doing?"

"We would have lost him in the last war—this kind of belly wound, peritonitis and septicemia would have got him for sure. But with the antibiotics, I think he'll pull through. His colon's more like a semicolon now, but you can live with that."

"Ouch!" Lord said. The pun seemed to distress him more than the bloody work he was assisting with. He'd done the work lots of times. The pun was a fresh displeasure. O'Doull had pulled it on Granny McDougald before, but not on him. *I'm getting old*, he thought. *I'm using the same jokes over and over.*

After he'd repaired as best he could the wounded who were brought to him, he took a big slug of medicinal brandy, and poured another for Goodson Lord. He wouldn't have done that during the fighting. No telling then when more casualties were coming in, and he'd wanted to keep his judgment as sharp as he could. Now he could hope he wouldn't have anything more complicated than another dose of clap to worry about for a while.

He lit a cigarette. It was a Niagara, a U.S. brand, and tasted lousy. But the C.S. tobacco firms were out of business—for the moment, anyway. Bad smokes beat no smokes at all.

Puffing on a Niagara made him think of heading north again, out of the USA and back to the country he'd adopted. Living in the Republic of Quebec meant returning to a backwater. Things happened more slowly there. Movies got to Rivière-du-Loup months, sometimes years, after they were hits in the United States. Most of them were dubbed into French; a few had subtitles.

O'Doull's English would have got even rustier than it had if not for the need to read medical journals and try to keep up with the miracles happening in the USA—and the miracles the USA imported from Germany. Back before the United States fostered Quebecois independence, Canada tried ramming English down the locals' throats. Older people still remembered the language, but not fondly. Younger ones wanted nothing to do with it.

He could live with that if he had to. He had lived with it, for years.

You took the bad with the good wherever you went. By now, his college French had picked up enough of the local accent to let people who didn't know him think he was born in *La Belle Province* himself. Of course, not many people in Rivière-du-Loup didn't know him. As far as he was concerned, that was part of the good.

"Penny for 'em," Sergeant Lord said.

"Thinking about going home again," O'Doull answered.

"Figured you were," Lord said. "You're right here, but your eyes were a million miles away."

"Better than the thousand-yard stare the poor mudfoots get when they've been through the mill," O'Doull said. Lord nodded. They both knew that look too well.

O'Doull stubbed out the cigarette and lit another one. He'd done something useful today, anyhow. If Colonel Tobin had sent him home, it would have been up to Goodson Lord. The guy with the shrapnel might have died then. Granny McDougald could have pulled him through, but O'Doull didn't think Lord was up to it.

But if the Confederates kept a rebellion smoldering for years, was that reason enough for him to stay down here till it finally got stamped out, if it ever did? He shook his head. He'd paid all the dues he felt like paying—more than he'd had to pay. He wasn't so goddamn young any more. He'd had that thought not long before, too. He wanted the rest of his life for himself.

Whether the U.S. Army or the authorities in the Republic wanted him to have it might be a different question. Well, he'd done what he could along those lines. Off in the distance, a train whistle blew. He smiled. If all else failed, he could hop a freight. What did the the soldiers say when you came out with something stupid? *And then you wake up*—that was it.

Doctor Deserts! Heads for Home in Spite of Orders! He saw the headlines in his mind's eye. Yes, it would be a scandal. It would if they caught him, anyhow. If they didn't, he was home free. The Republic wouldn't extradite him—he was sure of that.

Stop it, he told himself. *You'll talk yourself into it, and then you'll really be up the creek.*

Seventeen days after he wrote his letter, one with a Quebecois stamp came back. He opened the envelope with a strange mix of apprehension and anticipation. If they said no . . . But if they said yes . . . !

And they did! In stilted English, a bureaucrat in Quebec City proclaimed that he was a valuable medical resource, and vitally needed to serve the populace of Rivière-du-Loup. He grinned from ear to ear. He'd been called a lot of things before, but never valuable, let alone a medical resource. He hurried off to show Colonel Tobin the letter.

Jonathan Moss didn't like Houston. It was even hotter and muggier than Georgia and Alabama, and that was saying something. New Orleans was supposed to be just as bad, or maybe worse, but you could have a good time in New Orleans. If you could have a good time in Houston, Moss hadn't found out how.

Defending a man he loathed sure didn't help. Defending a man who might be the biggest murderer in the history of the world made things worse. And defending a man who might be the biggest murderer in the history of the world and didn't seem the least bit sorry about it, who seemed proud of what he'd done, made things *much* worse.

Defending Canadians who'd fallen afoul of occupation authorities was worth doing. This, on the other hand . . . Moss wished Major Isidore Goldstein hadn't smashed his stupid motorcar and himself. Then *he* would be going through the torments of the damned right now. Moss would rather have been flying turbo fighters, even though there was no one to fly them against any more. Would he rather have been sitting on the shelf? Sometimes he thought yes, sometimes no.

Pinkard's trial, and that of guard chief Vern Green, and those of several other guards from Camp Humble and its predecessor farther west, went on in what had been the Confederate District Courthouse in Houston. The exterior was modeled after the Parthenon: all elegant columns. But it was built from cheap concrete, not marble, and it was starting to crumble in Houston's savage weather.

Filling in for Confederate judges were U.S. Army officers. They'd shot down Moss' arguments for getting Jefferson Pinkard off the hook one after another. No, he couldn't claim Pinkard was only acting on orders from Richmond.

"The charge is crimes against humanity," said the chief judge, a craggy brigadier general named Lloyd Meusel. "The defendant is assumed to have been aware that, regardless of orders, it is illegal and criminal to have murdered innocent people in literally carload lots by various ingenious methods and then either burying them in mass graves or burning them so that their passing became a stench in the nostrils of mankind forever."

"Dammit, they weren't all that innocent," Pinkard said—he wouldn't keep his mouth shut, which was something any defendant needed to know how to do. "Plenty of rebels—and they all hated the CSA."

And, of course, that gave the military prosecutor, a bright young major named Barry Goodman, the chance to pounce. He grabbed it. "May it please the court," he said, "how many of the Negroes who passed through these extermination camps were tried and convicted of any crime, even spitting on the sidewalk? Is it not a fact that the only thing they were guilty of was being colored, and that this became a capital crime in the Confederate States?"

General Meusel leaned over backwards to be fair. "Well, Major, we are here to determine whether that is a fact. We can't assume it ahead of time."

"Yes, sir," Goodman replied. "I will endeavor to demonstrate and document its truthfulness. I believe I can do that."

Jonathan Moss believed he could, too. Moss had seen the photographs taken outside of Snyder, and the documents captured from the meticulous files kept at Camp Humble. They offered overwhelming evidence of what the CSA had done. And Goodman put them into evidence, again and again.

He had letters where the gasketing of trucks was said to be tightened up "to improve their asphyxiating efficiency." Jefferson Pinkard's initials said he'd read and approved—and approved of—those letters. Goodman had other letters about the construction of the bathhouses at Camp Humble, and about the airtight doors that made sure Negroes didn't escape from the "termination chambers." He had letters to and from the people who provided the cyanide for the termination chambers. And he had a small mountain of letters complaining about the shoddy workmanship and design of the crematoria of Camp Humble.

Just listening to those letters being read into evidence pissed Pinkard off. Jonathan Moss could tell. And it wasn't because his client had written them. It was because Pinkard still wanted to slug the bastards who'd sold him a bill of goods about the body-burning ovens and their smokestacks.

After court adjourned that day, Moss badly needed a drink. Soldiers in U.S. uniform were not welcomed with open arms in most of

Houston's watering holes. Out of consideration for that fact, the Army had set up an officers' club and one for enlisted men in the courthouse basement. Moss hied himself thither for a snort.

Barry Goodman was already down there, working on a double whiskey over ice. That looked so good, Moss ordered the same thing. "Every day when General Meusel turns us loose, I feel like I ought to go back to the barracks and take a bath," he said.

"Tell me about it!" the prosecutor exclaimed. "You've got it worse than I do, Counselor, because at least I'm on the side of the angels this time, but I am so sick of wading through this shit . . ."

"You know what the worst part is?" Moss paused to drink so the whiskey would put a temporary shield between him and his current duty.

"I'm all ears," Goodman said.

"Talk about wading through shit? We've barely got our feet wet. We ought to hang the Cyclone people—they knew what the cyanide was going for. We ought to hang the people who fixed up the trucks, and the people who made the bathhouses, and the engineers who designed the airtight doors, and the ones who designed the heavy-duty crematoria, even if they didn't know what the hell they were doing—"

"Did you see your client, Colonel? He still hates those people for botching the job," Goodman broke in.

"I know, I know," Moss said wearily. "But you can't put *that* into evidence, thank God."

"Like I need to," Goodman said, which was nothing but the truth. He added, "Besides, d'you think the judges didn't notice?"

"They did." Moss knocked back the drink and signaled for another. As the uniformed bartender made it, he went on, "And we need to hang the guys who built the crematoria, and the guys who installed them, and . . . Where does it end, Major? Does anybody down here have clean hands?"

"Good question." The prosecutor finished his drink. He also waved for a refill. "We can't kill all of them, though. I don't think we can, anyway. If we do, how are we better than they are?"

"If we don't, plenty of guilty bastards walk," Moss said. "When I was in Alabama, occupation officials were already starting to slide around the ban on using Freedom Party personnel to run things. All the people with brains and energy were in the Party, they said. Those were the people who could get things done. So they used them, and they bragged about how things were coming back to life."

The bartender brought them their fresh drinks and took away the empty glasses. Goodman stared down into his whiskey as if hoping for answers there, not just surcease. He shook his head. "I don't know what you can do. A lot of them are going to get off, and they'll brag about what they did till they're old and gray."

"Except when Yankees are around," Moss said. "Then they'll swear up and down that they didn't know what was going on. Some prick will probably write a book that shows how they didn't really massacre their Negroes after all."

"Oh, yeah? Then where'd the smokes go?" Goodman asked. "I mean, they were there before the war, and then they weren't. So what happened?"

"Well, we killed a bunch of 'em when we bombed Confederate cities." Moss was a well-trained attorney; he could spin out an argument whether he believed in it or not. "Some died in the rebellion. Some went up to the USA. Some died of hunger and disease—there *was* a war on, you know. But a massacre? Nah. Never happened."

Barry Goodman's mouth twisted. "That's disgusting. That'd gag a maggot, damned if it wouldn't."

"Bet your ass," Moss said. "You think it won't happen, though? Give it twenty years—thirty at the outside."

"Disgusting," Goodman repeated. "Well, we're gonna hang some people, anyway. Better believe we are. Maybe not enough, but some. And Pinkard's one of 'em."

"I've got to do everything I can to stop you," Moss said. "And I will."

"Sure." Major Goodman didn't despise him for playing on the other side, the way several military prosecutors up in Canada had. That was something, anyhow. "You have a job to do, too. But they aren't just asking you to make bricks without straw. They're asking you to make bricks without mud, for cryin' out loud."

Since Moss knew exactly the same thing, he couldn't very well argue. He just sighed. "I'd feel better about defending him if he thought he was a murderer, you know? If he felt bad about it, if he felt guilty about it, he'd be somebody I could give a damn about. I'd *want* to get him off the hook. It wouldn't be just an assignment. But as far as he's concerned, everything he did was strictly line of duty, and every one of the Negroes he got rid of had it coming."

"I know. I've seen the documents, and I've seen him in court. What he was doing, it was a job for him. He turned out to be good at it, so they kept promoting him." Goodman shook his head. "And look where he ended up."

"Yeah. Look." Moss looked at his glass. It was empty again. How did that happen? Two quick doubles were making his head spin, so that was how it happened. If he got another one . . . If he got another one, he'd stagger back to BOQ, and he'd need aspirins and coffee in the morning. His client deserved better than that. On the other hand, his client also deserved worse than that. He glanced over to Goodman. "I'll have another one if you do." That would even things up—and salve his conscience.

The prosecutor laughed. "I was going to say the same thing to you. I need another one, by God." They both waved to the barkeep. Stolidly, the enlisted man built two more doubles.

Moss got about halfway down his before a really ugly thought surfaced. "What if *we* elected somebody because he wanted to get rid of all the people with green eyes in the country? Do you think he could find guys like Pinkard to do his dirty work for him?"

Barry Goodman frowned. "It'd be harder," he said slowly. "We haven't hated people with green eyes since dirt, the way whites hate blacks in the CSA."

"Yeah, that's true." Moss conceded the point. Why not? They weren't in court now. "All right—suppose we elected a guy who wanted to get rid of our Negroes, or our Jews. Could he get help?" Was Goodman Jewish? With a name like that, maybe yes, maybe no. His looks didn't say for sure, either.

Whatever he was, he answered, "I'd like to tell you no, but I bet he could. Too damn many people will do whatever the guy in charge tells 'em to. They figure he knows what he's doing, and they figure they'll get in trouble if they don't go along. So yeah, our Featherston could get his helpers. Or do you think I'm wrong?"

"Christ, I wish I did," Moss answered. "But the Turks did it to the Armenians way back when, and the Russians have been giving it to the Jews forever. So it's not just the Confederates going off the deep end. They were more efficient about it than anybody else has been, but we could do that, too."

"Now we've got this big, ugly, bad example staring us in the face,"

Goodman said. "Maybe it'll make everybody too ashamed to do anything like it again. I sure want to think so, anyhow. It'd give me hope for the goddamn human race."

"I'll drink to that. To the goddamn human race!" Moss raised his glass. Goodman clinked with him. They drank together.

U.S. authorities in Hugo, Alabama, took their own sweet time about trying the Negro accused of raping a white woman there. They wanted to let things calm down. Armstrong Grimes approved of that. He'd managed to stave off one riot in front of the jail. He knew he might not be so lucky the second time around.

He'd lost his enthusiasm for the uniform he wore. He'd gone through the whole war from start to finish. All right, fine. He'd seen the elephant. He'd got shot. He'd paid all the dues anybody needed to pay. As far as he was concerned, somebody else could come down and occupy the CSA.

The government cared for his opinion as much as it usually did. It already had him down at the ass end of Alabama, and it would keep him here as long as it wanted to. If he didn't like it, what could he do about it? Not much, not when his only friends for hundreds of miles were other U.S. soldiers in the same boat he was.

So all right. He was stuck here. But he was damned if he'd give the U.S. Army a dime's worth more than he had to. Sitting quiet and not stirring up the locals looked mighty good to him.

To his surprise, Squidface stayed all eager-beaver. "You outa your mind?" Armstrong asked the Italian kid. "The more you piss these people off, the more likely it is somebody'll shoot at you."

"Somebody's gonna shoot at us. You can bet your ass on that," Squidface answered. "But if we keep these shitheads off balance, like, it'll be penny-ante stuff. We let 'em start plotting, then half the fuckin' state rises up, and we have to level everything between here and the ocean to shut it down. You know what I'm sayin', man?"

Armstrong grunted. He knew, and didn't like knowing. He wanted to think like a short-timer, somebody who'd escape from the Army soon. To Squidface, who wanted to be a lifer, the problem looked different. Squidface wanted long-term answers, ones that would keep this part of Alabama not quiet but quieter for years to come. Armstrong didn't give a damn what happened in 1946 if he'd be out of here by 1945.

If. That was the question. The Army seemed anything but eager to turn soldiers loose. Despite taking hostages, despite shooting lots of them, it hadn't clamped down on the diehards in the CSA. No matter what the surrender orders said, everybody knew Confederate soldiers hadn't turned in all their weapons or all their explosives. And they were still using what they'd squirreled away.

"You think they can make us sick enough of occupying them, we give it up and go home?" he asked Squidface.

The PFC's mouth twisted. "Fuck, I hope not. We'll just have another war down the line if we do. And they gotta have more guys down here who know how to make superbombs. Genie's out of the bottle, like. So if it's another war, it's a bad one."

"Yeah." Armstrong agreed unenthusiastically, but he agreed. "But if they hate us forever and shoot at us from behind bushes forever, how are we better off? It's like a sore that won't scab up."

"Maybe if we kill enough of 'em, the rest'll figure keeping that shit up is more trouble than it's worth." Squidface had an odd kind of pragmatism, but Armstrong nodded—he thought the same way.

Two days later, a sniper killed a U.S. soldier. When that happened these days, people in Hugo tried to get out of town before anybody could grab them as hostages. The occupying authorities discouraged that by shooting at them when they saw them sneaking off.

Armstrong ended up leading a firing squad. The rifles issued to the men doing the shooting had one blank round per squad per victim. If you wanted to, you could think that maybe you hadn't really killed anybody. You could also think you could draw four to a king and end up with a royal flush. By the time you'd pulled the trigger twenty times, your odds of innocence were about that low.

After the shootings, a U.S. officer spoke to the people left in Hugo: "Get it through your heads—we *will* punish you. If you know beforehand that somebody's going to shoot at us, you'd better let us know. If you don't, we'll keep shooting people till we run out of people to shoot."

Armstrong got drunk that night. He wasn't the only one from the firing squad who did. He hated the duty. Shooting people who could shoot back was one thing. Shooting blindfolded people up against a wall? That was a different business, and a much nastier one.

"No wonder those Confederate assholes invented all those fancy ways to kill niggers," he said, very far in his cups. "You shoot people day after day, you gotta start going bugfuck, don't you?"

"Don't sweat it, Sarge," said Squidface, who'd also poured down a lot of bad whiskey. "You're already bugfuck."

"You say the sweetest things." Armstrong made kissing noises.

For some reason—no doubt because they were smashed—they both thought that was the funniest thing in the world. So did the other drinkers. Pretty soon everybody was pretending to kiss everybody else. Then somebody really did it, and got slapped. That was even funnier— if you were drunk enough.

Nothing seemed funny to Armstrong the next morning. Strong coffee and lots of aspirins soothed his aching head and gave him a sour stomach instead. He got a different kind of headache when he went into Hugo to buy a ham sandwich for lunch instead of enduring rations.

"I don't want your money," said the man who ran the local diner. "I don't want to serve you. I don't aim to serve any Yankee soldier from here on out, but especially not you."

"What did I do?" Armstrong was still hung over enough to be extra grouchy. *I don't need this shit*, he thought unhappily.

"You told those bastards to shoot my brother-in-law yesterday, that's what. Your damn captain made me watch you do it, too. I ought to feed you, by God, and put rat poison in your sandwich. I'd do it, too, if you bastards wouldn't murder more folks who never done you no harm."

"You're gonna get your ass in a sling," Armstrong warned. All he wanted was a sandwich, not an argument.

"I ain't hurting nobody," the local said. "I don't aim to hurt nobody, neither. But I don't want Yankee money any more. I don't reckon anybody in this here town wants Yankee money any more."

If he hadn't said that last, Armstrong might have walked out in disgust. As things were, he growled, "Conspiracy, huh? You *are* gonna get your ass in a sling." He didn't just walk out; he stomped out.

And he reported the conversation to the first officer he found. "A boycott, eh?" the captain said. "Well, we'll see about *that*, by God!"

They did, in short order. By the end of the week, nobody in Hugo would sell U.S. soldiers anything. On Friday, an edict came down from the military governor in Birmingham. It banned "failure to cooperate with U.S. authorities." If you tried going on with the boycott, you'd go to jail instead.

Naturally, the first question that went through Armstrong's mind was, "If a girl doesn't put out, can we arrest her for failure to cooperate?"

"Sure, Grimes," said the major who was getting the troops up to speed on the new policy. "Then you can arrest yourself for fraternizing."

"Ah, hell, sir," Armstrong said. "I knew there was a snatch—uh, a catch—to it."

"Thank you, Karl Engels," the major said dryly. "Can we go on?" Armstrong nodded, grinning. Karl was his favorite Engels Brother. He'd even talked about growing a long blue beard and joining the comedy troupe himself.

Maybe the people who joined the boycott figured they were safe because they weren't doing anything violent. The failure-to-cooperate order was announced over bullhorns and posted in notices nailed to every telegraph pole in the towns where boycotters were trying to show their displeasure.

As soon as somebody said he wouldn't sell a soldier something after that, the offender disappeared. "Where you taking old Ernie?" a local asked Armstrong when he was one of the men who arrested the man who ran the Hugo diner.

"To a camp," Armstrong answered.

"A camp? Jesus God!" The local went pale.

Armstrong laughed a nasty laugh. "What? You think we're gonna do to him like you did to your niggers? That'd be pretty goddamn funny, wouldn't it?"

"No," the local said faintly.

"Well, I don't think we'll waste his sorry ass—this time," Armstrong said. "But you bastards need to get something through your heads. You fuck with us, you lose. You hear me?" When the Alabaman didn't answer fast enough to suit him, he aimed his rifle at the man's face. *"You hear me?"*

"Oh, yeah." The local nodded. He was old and wrinkled himself, but he was game. "I hear you real good."

"You better, Charlie, 'cause I'm not bullshitting you." Armstrong lowered the weapon.

And the boycott collapsed even faster than it had grown. Some of the men and women who got arrested came back to Hugo. Others stayed disappeared. Armstrong didn't know what happened to them. His best guess was that they *were* in prison camps somewhere. But he couldn't prove that the United States weren't killing them the way the Confederate States had killed Negroes. Neither could the locals. It made them uncommonly thoughtful.

"See?" Squidface said. "This is how it's supposed to work. We keep these bastards on their toes, they can't do unto us."

"I guess," Armstrong said.

The next day, a land mine ten miles away blew a truck full of U.S. soldiers to kingdom come. U.S. authorities methodically took hostages, and shot them when the fellow who'd planted the mine didn't come forward. Rumor said that one of the soldiers who'd done firing-squad duty shot himself right afterwards.

"Some guys just can't stand the gaff," was Squidface's verdict.

"I guess," Armstrong said. "But I don't like firing-squad duty myself. I feel like a goose just walked over my grave."

That was the wrong thing to say around Squidface, who goosed him. The wrestling match they got into was more serious—more ferocious, anyhow—than most soldierly horseplay. Squidface eyed a shiner in a steel mirror. "You really do have this shit on your mind," he said.

Armstrong rubbed bruised ribs. "I fuckin' told you so. How come you don't listen when I tell you something?"

" 'Cause I'd have to waste too much time sifting through the horseshit," Squidface answered, which almost started another round.

But Armstrong decided his ribs were sore enough already. "They let soldiers vote, who'd you vote for?" he asked.

"Dewey," Squidface answered at once. "He's got a chickenshit mustache, but the Dems wouldn't've been asleep at the switch the way the Socialists were when Featherston jumped on our ass. How about you?"

"Yeah, I guess," Armstrong agreed. "I bet the Socialists'd pull us out of here faster, though."

"Just on account of you think like a short-timer doesn't make you one," Squidface said. Armstrong sighed and nodded. Wasn't *that* the truth?

XVII

Hey, Chester!" Captain Hubert Rhodes called. "C'mere a minute."

"What's up, sir?" Chester Martin asked.

"Got something from the War Department that might apply to you," the company commander answered. "You're over fifty, right?"

"Yes, sir," Martin answered. "And some of the shit I've been through, I feel like I'm over ninety."

"Well, I can understand that." Rhodes took a piece of paper out of his tunic pocket. He was in his early thirties, at the most—he didn't need to put on glasses before he read something. "Says here the Army is accepting discharge applications from noncoms over fifty who aren't career military. That's you, right?"

"Yes, sir," Chester said again. "Jesus! Have I got that straight? They'll turn me loose if I ask 'em to?"

"That's what it says. See for yourself." Rhodes held out the paper.

Chester's current reading specs had cost him half a buck at a local drugstore. He'd lost track of how many pairs of reading glasses he'd broken since reupping. These weren't great, but they were better than nothing. He read the order, wading through the Army bureaucratese. It said what Captain Rhodes said it said, all right. "Where do I get this Form 565 it talks about?" he asked. "Or is the catch that they haven't printed any copies of it, so I'm screwed regardless?"

Rhodes laughed, for all the world as if the Army would never pull a stunt like that. But then, like a magician with a top hat, he pulled out a rabbit—or rather, a Form 565. "Came with the bulletin. I wish I could talk you into sticking around, but I know I'd be wasting my breath."

" 'Fraid so, sir. I got shot once in each war. Nobody can say I didn't do my bit. I have a wife and a life back in L.A. I want to get back while I've still got some time left." Chester looked at the form. "I've got to get my immediate superior's signature, huh? Well, Lieutenant Lavochkin won't be sorry to see me go—I've cramped his style ever since he got here."

"Good thing somebody did, at least a bit," Rhodes said. Both men laughed, more than a little uneasily. Chester didn't want to think about the massacre he'd been part of. Officially, Rhodes didn't know about that. But what he knew officially and what he knew were different beasts. He went on, "If Boris gives you any trouble, send him to me. I'll take care of it."

"Thank you, sir. I appreciate it, believe me," Chester said. "I'm gonna hunt him up right now. Sooner I get everything squared away, happier I'll be."

"All right." Rhodes stuck out his hand. "It's been a pleasure serving with you, and that's the God's truth."

"Thanks," Chester repeated as they shook. "And back at you. The lieutenant . . ." He shrugged. No, he wouldn't be sorry to say good-bye to the lieutenant.

He found Boris Lavochkin right where he thought he would: on the battered main street of Cheraw, South Carolina. Lavochkin carried a captured automatic Tredegar and looked extremely ready to use it. By the way he eyed Chester as the veteran noncom approached, he might not have minded using it on him. Lavochkin didn't like getting his style cramped.

Chester pretended not to notice. "Talk to you a second, sir?"

"You're doing it," Lavochkin answered, and lit a cigarette. He didn't offer Chester one, and Chester wasn't sure he would have taken it if Lavochkin had.

"Right," Chester said tightly. He explained about the War Department ukase, and about Form 565. "So all I need is your signature, sir, and pretty soon I'll be out of your hair for good."

"You're bugging out?" Boris Lavochkin didn't bother hiding his scorn.

"Sir, I've put in more combat time than you have," Martin answered. "Like I told Captain Rhodes, I've got a life outside the Army, and I aim to live it. I've seen as much of this shit as I ever want to, by God."

"Suppose I don't sign your stupid form?"

"Well, sir, I've got three things to say about that. First one is, you better go talk to Captain Rhodes. Second one is, you damn well owe me one, on account of I kept you from killing all of us when we super-bombed Charleston. And the third one is, you can bend over and kiss my ass."

Lavochkin turned a dull red. Chester stood there waiting. He had a .45 on his belt; few U.S. soldiers ever went unarmed in the former CSA, peace or no peace. But the lieutenant could have shot him easily enough. Lavochkin didn't, even if the Tredegar's muzzle twitched. He was a bastard, but a calculating bastard. "Give me the damn thing. It'll be a pleasure to get rid of you," he snarled.

"Believe me, sir, it's mutual."

Leaning the automatic rifle against his leg, Lavochkin pulled a pen from his left breast pocket and scribbled something that might have been his name. He thrust Form 565 back at Chester. "There!"

"Thank you, sir." Chester's voice was sweet—saccharine-sweet. Boris Lavochkin gave him a dirty look as he took the signed Form 565 back to Captain Rhodes.

Rhodes signed, too, and without kicking up any fuss. "I'll send this back to regimental HQ, and they'll move it on to Division," he said. "And then, if all the stars align just right, they'll ship you home."

"Thanks a million, Captain." When Chester spoke to Hubert Rhodes, he sounded as if he meant it, and he did.

"You don't owe the country anything else, Chester," Rhodes said. "I'd like you to stick around, 'cause you're damn good at what you do, but I'm not gonna try and hold you where you don't want to be."

"That's white of you." Martin listened to what came out of his mouth without thought. He shook his head. "There's an expression we have to lose."

"Boy, you said it." Rhodes nodded. "Especially down here, where the whites aren't on our side and the Negroes are—what's left of 'em."

"Yeah," Chester said grimly. Some Negroes had come out of hiding now that U.S. troops were on the ground here. Some more, skinny as pipe cleaners, had come back from the camps in Texas and Louisiana and Mississippi. Back before the Freedom Party got its massacre going,

South Carolina had had more blacks than whites. It sure didn't any more—not even close.

The ones who had lived through everything wandered around like lost souls. Chester couldn't blame them. How could they rebuild their shattered lives in towns and countrysides where whites had shown they hated them? Chester wouldn't have wanted to try it himself, and he was a middle-aged man with a decent education and a considerable sense of his own worth. What chance did an illiterate sharecropper or his barefoot, maybe pregnant wife have?

While he was wondering about that, a white man in a snappy suit approached him and Hubert Rhodes and said, "Talk to you, Captain?"

"You're doing it," Rhodes said. "What's on your mind?"

"My name is Walker, Nigel R. Walker," the man said. "Up until the surrender, I was mayor of Cheraw. Now there's some foolish difficulty about letting me go back to my proper function in the community."

Rhodes looked at him—looked through him, really. "You were a Party member, weren't you, Mr. Nigel R. Walker?"

"Well, sure," Walker said. "Membership for officials was encouraged—strongly encouraged."

"Then you're out." Rhodes' voice was hard and flat. "No Freedom Party members are going to run things down here any more, and you can take that to the bank. Those are my orders, and I'm going to follow them."

"But you're being unreasonable," Walker protested. "I know of several towns in this state where men with much stronger Party ties than mine are very actively involved in affairs."

Chester knew of towns like that, too. Some occupying officials wanted to put things back together as fast as they could. They grabbed the people who were most likely to be able to do the job. If some of those people had screamed, "Freedom!" for a while, they didn't care. They thought of themselves as efficiency experts. What Chester thought of them wasn't fit to repeat in polite company.

"I know some U.S. officers are skirting those orders," said Captain Rhodes, who felt the same way he did. "And if they can do that with a clear conscience, then they can. I can't. I can't come close. As far as I'm concerned, you disqualified yourself when you joined that pack of murderous goons. Is that plain enough, Mr. Nigel R. Walker, sir, or shall I tell you what I really think of you?"

"I'm going to take my objections to your superiors, Captain." Walker strutted off, his stiff back radiating anger.

Rhodes sighed. "He should have asked Lavochkin—Boris would have plugged him. You see, Chester? He *is* good for something."

"Damned if you're not right," Martin said. "The nerve of this asshole, though!"

"He was a big fish in a little pond," Rhodes said, and Chester nodded—nothing except possibly the Apocalypse would ever make Cheraw a big pond. Rhodes went on, "He thinks he has the right to go on being a big fish."

"Ought to ship him to one of those camps. That'd teach him more about rights than he ever dreamt of, the fucker," Chester said savagely.

"Yeah." The company commander sighed again. "He may even be a decent guy. For all I know, he is. Plenty of people *did* join the Party because it was a meal ticket. I've never heard any Negroes claim he was especially bad. But I've never heard 'em say he was especially good, either. To me, that means he's tarred with the Party brush. He might not have done anything much, but he didn't try to stop anything, either. So screw him."

"No, thanks—too damn ugly," Chester said. Rhodes laughed. Chester started thinking of Rita. He'd been a good boy ever since he put the uniform back on, and he knew his right hand better than he'd ever wanted to.

One day followed another. The weather started turning cool and nasty. That was what Chester thought at first, anyhow. Then he realized that, compared to what he would have had to put up with in Toledo, it was pretty damn good. He'd lived in Los Angeles long enough to get spoiled.

He felt more alert now than he had since the very last days of the war. He didn't want to get hurt just when he was about to head home. Well, he didn't want to get hurt any old time, but he especially didn't want to get hurt now. And he knew too well that he could. Cheraw was no more reconciled to the Stars and Stripes than any other part of the dead but still writhing CSA. Locals probed every day to see how much they could get away with. U.S. authorities clamped down hard. That only gave the locals more reasons to hate damnyankees—as if they needed them.

At last, his discharge orders came. So did a travel voucher that would send him up to Philadelphia and then across the country through U.S. territory. He couldn't have been happier: the sooner he left the Confederacy forever, the happier he'd be.

He was painfully hung over when he boarded the northbound train—but not too hung over to notice the machine guns it carried. He hoped it wouldn't have to use them; they might make his head explode. Captain Rhodes and a bunch of guys from his platoon—a lot of them the worse for wear, too—saw him off. Lieutenant Lavochkin didn't. Chester didn't miss him.

Rhodes and the soldiers waved and shouted as the whistle screeched and the train pulled out of Cheraw. "Lucky stiff!" somebody called. *Yeah*, Chester thought, gulping three aspirins. He was going home.

Abner Dowling knew more about uranium than he'd ever imagined he would. Before the war, he wasn't sure he'd ever heard of the stuff. Oh, maybe in chemistry, back in the dark ages around the turn of the century. Yes, it was an element. So what? You didn't do experiments with it, the way you did with copper and sulfur and things like that.

And he knew about saturnium and jovium, which was what the Confederate physicists called elements 93 and 94. Just to confuse the issue, U.S. scientists had named the same elements neptunium and plutonium. He gathered they had different handles in every country that had found them. Back in the vanished days when he was at West Point, no one had dreamt they existed.

"Boy, I didn't know how obsolete I was till I got here," he complained to Angelo Toricelli. "Most of what I thought I knew turns out not to be so, and stuff I never imagined is what really counts. You can't win."

"Sir, if it makes you feel any better, I didn't learn this stuff in school, either," his adjutant answered.

That *did* make Dowling feel better. Misery, or at least confusion, loved company. "After they reassign us, you know, they'll have to put permanent bloodhounds on us, to make sure nobody knocks us over the head and hijacks us on account of what we know," he said.

"Maybe, but maybe not," Toricelli said. "I mean, you can bet your bottom dollar that everybody who wants a superbomb either has one by now or is already working on one as hard as he can. What do those people need with us?"

"Go ahead. Be that way!" Dowling said. "But if I catch you talking to a Jap in glasses or a beautiful Russian piano player, you'll be in more trouble than you can shake a stick at, and you'd better believe it."

"I'd like to talk to a beautiful Russian piano player," Toricelli said wistfully. "Hell, I'd like to talk to a beautiful piano player from Seattle."

If you were a career officer, you often didn't have time to find a wife. Dowling never had, and he was far from alone in the fraternity of war. George Custer had made it work—although Dowling often thought George was the steed Libbie rode to glory. Irving Morrell was married, too, and by all accounts happily. It could happen. Odds against it were longer than they were in a lot of trades, though.

"Just as long as you don't say too much to a beautiful piano player from Lexington," Abner Dowling warned.

"I wouldn't do that, sir." His adjutant sounded hurt. "Besides, I haven't seen a gal here I'd want to give the time of day to."

Dowling nodded. "I know what you mean." He didn't suppose Confederates were uglier or handsomer than U.S. citizens, taken all in all. But the war had hit hard here, especially in the last few months, when the USA tried to blast Lexington flat to keep the CSA from building a superbomb. It didn't work, but it did take its toll on the locals. People hereabouts still looked haggard and hungry. The Shenandoah Valley was some of the richest farmland in the world, but it got hit, too . . . and not so many folks were left to raise crops, either.

"And even if I did find a woman I liked here, well, I might want to lay her, but I don't think I'd ever marry a Confederate," Toricelli said. "I'd wonder why she wanted to marry me, and all my superiors would wonder whether I'd gone out of my mind."

He wasn't wrong. A marriage like that could blight his hopes for promotion. It could also blight his life if it didn't work, and it was much too likely not to. Even so . . . Dowling said, "You wouldn't be the first, you know. We've already had a couple of petitions from enlisted men to let them marry local girls."

"I'd better know, sir," his adjutant said. "That paperwork crosses my desk before it lands on yours."

"Yes, yes." Dowling didn't want the younger man to think he was forgetting things like that. As soon as they started believing you were past it, you were, whether you knew it or not. Hastily, Dowling went on, "I'm the one who has to decide, though. That's one more thing they didn't teach at West Point. Does this PFC really have good reason to marry a Virginia woman? Should I ship him back to the USA instead? Or should I just hose him down with cold water till he comes to his senses?"

"Cold water would put a lot of these proposals or propositions or whatever they are on ice," Lieutenant Colonel Toricelli said gravely.

Dowling sent him a severe look. Toricelli bore up under it like the soldier he was. Dowling said, "If I do let them get married and things go sour, they'll blame me. Plenty of perfectly normal marriages go bad, God knows. Usually it's nobody's fault but the bride and groom's. Figure anybody would remember that?"

"Fat chance," Toricelli said. "Sir."

"I know. But the one where the guy knocked the gal up . . . I am going to approve that one, hell with me if I'm not. If I say no, her father's liable to use a shotgun on our soldier, and then we'll have to take hostages, and it'll just be a goddamn mess. I'll pay for an unhappy marriage to stay away from firing squads."

"That makes sense, sir," Toricelli said. "Kind of a cold-blooded way to look at things, but it makes sense."

"You get as old as I am, if you're hot-blooded you're either dead or you're George Custer, one," Dowling said. "I know damn well I'm not Custer—thank God!—and I wasn't dead last time I looked. So . . . I try not to blow my cork unless my cork really needs blowing."

His adjutant returned a sly stare. "Like with General MacArthur, right?"

"I won't waste my time answering that, even if it is true." Dowling stood on his dignity, a shaky position for a man of his bulk.

Before his adjutant could call him on it, a noncom stuck his head into the office and said, "Sir, that professor guy wants to see you."

"FitzBelmont?" Dowling asked.

The sergeant nodded. "That's him."

Dowling didn't want to see the physicist. He said, "Send him in," anyway. Sometimes what you wanted was different from what you needed. If this wasn't one of those times, he could have the pleasure of throwing Henderson FitzBelmont out on his ear.

When FitzBelmont came in, he looked as angry and as determined as a professorial man could. "General, when am I going to get my life back?" he demanded. "It is now almost four months after the surrender, but your interrogators continue to hound me. To be frank, sir, I am tired of it."

"To be frank, sir, I don't give a flying fuck." Abner Dowling didn't blow his cork, but he didn't need to waste politeness on FitzBelmont, either. "When you went to work for Jake Featherston, you sold your soul to the Devil. Now you've got to buy it back, one nickel at a time. If the boys aren't finished with you, too bad. You have a train to catch, or what?"

"I would like to be a normal human being in a normal country, not a . . . a bug under a microscope." The professor didn't have the force of personality to hold anger together very long. His voice went high and shrill and petulant.

"Sorry, but that's what you are. Get used to it," Dowling said. "You're going to be under the microscope for the rest of your life. You're too dangerous for us not to keep tabs on you. If you don't believe me, ask what's left of Philadelphia."

"I can't do that again. You've made very sure I can't," FitzBelmont said. "And some of your interrogators are nothing but idiots. You know more about the physics of fission than they do."

"God help them if that's true." Dowling hadn't known anything about 235 and 238 and the other magic numbers till this assignment landed on him. He hoped he'd learned enough to be effective, but he wouldn't have sworn to it.

"Well, it is," Professor FitzBelmont said. "One imbecile asked me why we didn't use iron instead of uranium. It was easier to find and to make, he said, and much cheaper, too. The frightening thing is, he was serious."

"And the answer is . . . ?" Dowling asked.

"Very simple, General. I'm sure you can figure it out for yourself: you can do whatever you please to iron, but you'll never make a super-bomb out of it. The same goes for lead or gold or most other things you can think of."

"Not all of them?" Dowling said sharply.

Professor FitzBelmont hesitated. "If I didn't know for a fact that your physicists were already working on this, I wouldn't say a word. Not ever."

"Well, you already did. Now go on," Dowling told him.

"It's theoretically possible, using isotopes of hydrogen with a superbomb for a fuse, you might say, to make a bomb a thousand times as powerful as the ones we have now, a bomb that burns the way the sun burns—a sunbomb, you might say."

"A thousand times as strong as a superbomb?" Dowling's mind bounced off that like a rotary saw recoiling from a spike driven into a tree trunk. "Good God in the foothills! You could blow up a thousand Philadelphias or Petrograds?"

"You could blow up an area more than thirty times as wide as the area those bombs destroyed," FitzBelmont said. "Area varies as the square of the diameter, of course."

"Of course," Dowling agreed in a hollow voice. "So a . . . a sun-bomb could pretty much blow Rhode Island off the map?"

"How big is Rhode Island?" By the way FitzBelmont said it, he didn't waste time keeping track of U.S. geography.

"I don't know exactly," Dowling said. "A thousand square miles—maybe a little more."

Henderson FitzBelmont got a faraway look in his eyes. *Doing the math*, Dowling realized. FitzBelmont finally nodded. "Yes, that's about right. One of those bombs should destroy most of it. Why do you have such a small state?"

"Beats me." Dowling couldn't recall enough colonial history to come up with the reason. It didn't matter, anyhow. What did matter . . . "How long would it take to build one of these sunbomb things?"

"I don't know," FitzBelmont said. "I would be surprised if anyone had them in five years. I would be surprised if no one had them in twenty-five."

"Good God!" Dowling said again. If God wasn't in the foothills, He was probably running for them. The general tried to imagine a world where six or eight countries had sunbombs. "How would you fight a war if a bunch of your neighbors could blow you into next week if you got frisky?"

"General, I wouldn't," FitzBelmont said bleakly. "Whether that will stop the politicians . . ."

"Ha!" Dowling stabbed out a forefinger at him. "You've got your nerve saying something like that after you went and worked for Jake Featherston."

The professor turned red. "He led my country in time of war. What should I have done? *Not* helped him?"

That wasn't a question with a simple answer. Had the CSA won,

U.S. scientists would have asked Confederate interrogators the same thing, hoping to stay out of trouble. *Yeah, but we weren't gassing our own people by the millions,* Dowling thought. To which victorious Confederates would have replied, *So what?* And if all or even most physicists felt the way FitzBelmont did . . . The world was in big trouble, in that case.

When Jorge Rodriguez could, he walked into Baroyeca to meet the train. He couldn't always. Farm work had no peaks and valleys, the way soldiering did; you needed to keep at it every day. The damnyankees still hadn't let Miguel out of their POW camp. Jorge hoped he was all right. Maybe he'd been wounded, and word never got to Sonora. Maybe he was dead, and word never got here. He hadn't written since the end of the war, and things inside the CSA were falling apart by then.

But maybe he would get off the train one afternoon, good as new or somewhere close. The hope kept Jorge walking. He'd seen enough to know you never could tell. And if he stopped in at *La Culebra Verde* for a glass of beer before he came home, well, it was nothing his father hadn't done before him.

Every so often, nobody got out when the train stopped in Baroyeca. It wasn't a big city, and never would be. If not for the silver and lead mines in the hills back of town, it wouldn't have been a town at all. When the mines closed between the wars, the town almost died. Even the trains stopped coming for a while.

Jake Featherston had fixed that. He'd fixed lots of things. You couldn't say so, not unless you wanted to get in trouble with the Yankees. Jorge had enough sense to keep his *boca cerrada*. A couple of people who didn't . . . disappeared.

One afternoon, a tall, balding fellow whose remaining hair was yellow mixed with gray stepped down and looked around in wonder. Anybody with that coloring and those beaky features stood out in swarthy, *mestizo*-filled Baroyeca.

"*Señor* Quinn!" Jorge exclaimed—not his brother, but another familiar face he hadn't seen for a long time.

"*Hola*," Quinn said, and then went on in his deliberate, English-accented Spanish: "You're one of Hip Rodriguez's boys, but I'm damned if I know which one."

"I'm Jorge," Jorge answered in English. "Pedro's back, too. I was hoping Miguel would be on the train. That's why I came. But the damnyankees are still holding him. How are you, *Señor* Quinn?"

"Tired. Whipped," Quinn said. "Just like the rest of the country." The train pulled out of the station, heading south. Quinn and Jorge both coughed at the dust it kicked up.

Jorge looked around. Nobody was in earshot. In a low voice, he asked, "Are you going to start the Freedom Party up again, *Señor* Quinn?"

"Not officially, anyway. I'd put my neck in the noose if I did," Quinn answered. He'd lived in Baroyeca a long time, building the Party up from nothing and nowhere. Also quietly, he continued, "As far as *los Estados Unidos* know, I'm nothing but another POW. If they find out I was an organizer, God knows what they'll do to me."

"They won't hear from me," Jorge promised. "My father, he always thought you were a good man."

"Well, I always thought he was a good man, too," Robert Quinn said. "I was sad to hear he'd passed away, and even sadder to hear how. I've wondered about that a lot, and it doesn't make much sense to me."

"It doesn't make much sense to anybody." Jorge didn't mention Camp Determination. The way things were nowadays, you kept your mouth shut about what went on in places like that. What could his father, a good Party man, have seen or felt that made him decide those camps weren't doing the right thing? It had to be something on that order. Jorge was sure no personal problem would have made Hipolito Rodriguez eat his gun.

"Tell you what," Quinn said, still softly. "If nobody down here rats on me, well, we'll see what we can do if the damnyankees step on our toes too hard. We may not be able to hold meetings and stuff, but that doesn't mean the Freedom Party's dead. It's not dead unless we decide it's dead. How's that sound?"

"Good to me." Jorge didn't say *Freedom!* or ¡*Libertad!* or give the Party salute. You were asking for trouble if you did things like that. But he knew he wouldn't be the only one watching the United States to see what they did.

And he also knew the United States would be watching Baroyeca, as they would be watching all of the CSA, or as much of the country as they could. If they sensed trouble, they would land on it with both feet.

You played the most dangerous game in the world if you even thought about rising up against the damnyankees.

"Can I buy you a glass of beer, *Señor* Quinn?" Jorge asked.

"No, but you can let me buy you one, by God," the Party organizer answered. "I've got plenty of money, believe me. Some of the people who think they can play poker haven't got the sense God gave a duck."

Jorge smiled. "All right. Do you remember where *La Culebra Verde* is?"

"I'd damn well better," Quinn said. "*¡Vámonos, amigo!*"

It was dark and cool and quiet inside the cantina. A couple of men looked up from their drinks when Jorge and Robert Quinn walked in. It stayed quiet in there, but now the silence was one of suspense. Slowly and deliberately, the bartender ran a damp rag over the counter in front of them. "What can I get for you, *señores*?" he asked.

"*Dos cervezas, por favor.*" Quinn set a U.S. half-dollar on the bar. He sat down on a stool. Jorge perched next to him. The bartender made the silver coin disappear. He drew two beers and set them in front of the new customers.

"Thanks." Jorge put down another quarter. "One for you, too, or whatever you want."

"*Gracias.*" Bartenders didn't always want the drinks customers bought them. This time, though, the man in the boiled shirt did pour himself a beer.

"*¡Salud!*" Quinn raised his glass. He and Jorge and the bartender drank. "*Madre de Dios*, that's good!" Quinn said. Was he even a Catholic? Jorge didn't know. He'd never worried about it till now.

One of the men at a table in the back raised a finger to show he and his friends were ready for a refill. The bartender filled glasses and set them on a tray. A barmaid picked them up and carried them off, her hips swinging. Jorge followed her with his eyes. So did Robert Quinn. They grinned at each other. Once you got out of the Army, you remembered how nice it was that the world had pretty girls in it.

As the beers emptied, the bartender murmured, "Good to have you back, *Señor* Quinn. We didn't know if we would see you again."

"Good to be back," Quinn said. "There were some times when I wondered whether anybody would see me again, but war is like that."

"*Sí.*" Jorge remembered too many close calls of his own. The man behind the bar was about his father's age. Had he fought in the Great War? Jorge didn't know; again, he'd never wondered till now.

"What are we going to do here, Jorge?" Robert Quinn asked. "Are you ready to live quietly under the Stars and Stripes? Or do you remember what your country really is?" He hadn't been so bold in the train station. Could one beer have done it to him?

Jorge looked down at his glass. He looked around the cantina. His mind's eye took in the rest of Baroyeca and the family farm outside of town. All that made him feel *less* determined than he had over at the station. "*Señor* Quinn," he said sadly, "I have seen all the fighting I want to see for a long time. I am sorry, but if the damnyankees do not bother me, then I do not care to bother them, either. If they do bother me, the story will be different."

"Well, that's a fair answer," Quinn said after silence stretched for more than half a minute. "You've done your soldiering. If you don't want to do it again, who can blame you? I wish you felt different, but if you don't, you don't." He drained his glass and strode out of *La Culebra Verde*.

"Did you make him unhappy?" the bartender asked.

"I'm afraid I did. He doesn't want the war to be over, but I've had enough. I've had too much." He wondered how Gabe Medwick was getting along. He hoped the U.S. soldiers had picked up his wounded buddy back in the Virginia woods. Was Gabe back in Alabama by now, or did he still languish in a POW camp like Miguel?

And what about Sergeant Blackledge? Jorge would have bet anything that he was raising trouble for the Yankees wherever he was. That man was born to bedevil anybody he didn't like, and he didn't like many people.

The bartender drew another beer and set it in front of Jorge. "On the house," he said. "I don't want to go to the hills. I don't want the United States shooting hostages here. I don't want to be one of the hostages they shoot. *Por Dios*, Jorge, enough is enough."

"Some men will eat fire even if they have to start it themselves," Jorge said, looking at the door through which Robert Quinn had gone.

"He will find hotheads. People like that always do. Look at Jake Featherston." The bartender never would have said such a thing while the Freedom Party ruled Baroyeca. It would have been worth his life if he had. He went on, "I don't think anyone will speak to the *soldados* from *los Estados Unidos* if *Señor* Quinn stays here quietly. But if he goes looking for stalwarts . . . Then he's dangerous."

Was the bartender saying he would turn in Robert Quinn if Quinn tried to raise a rebellion? If he was, what was Jorge supposed to do about him? Kill him to keep him from blabbing? But that was raising a rebellion, too, and Jorge had just told Quinn he didn't want to do any such thing.

He also didn't want to sit by while something bad happened to his father's old friend. Sometimes nothing you did would help. He had the feeling that that was true for much of the CSA's last war against the USA.

He also had the feeling it would be true if Confederates tried to mix it up with the USA in the war's aftermath. Yes, they could cause trouble. Could they cause enough to make U.S. forces leave? He couldn't make himself believe it.

When he came back to the farm alone late that afternoon, his mother's face fell, the way it always did when he came back alone. "No Miguel?" she asked sadly.

"No Miguel. I'm sorry, *mamacita*." Then Jorge told of meeting Robert Quinn as the Freedom Party man got off the train.

His mother only sniffed. Next to her missing son, a man who wasn't from the family didn't cut much ice. The news excited Pedro, though. "Does he want to—?" He didn't go on.

"Yes, he does," Jorge answered. "I told him I didn't." He spoke elliptically, as Pedro had, to keep from making their mother flabble.

Pedro looked discontented. But Pedro hadn't done a whole lot of fighting. He'd spent most of the war behind barbed wire. He didn't have such a good idea of what the United States could do if they decided they wanted to. Jorge did. What he'd seen in Virginia as the war wound down would stay with him for the rest of his life. The overwhelming firepower and the will to use it scared him more than he was willing to admit, even to himself.

"What are we going to do? Sit here quiet for the rest of our lives?" Pedro asked.

"You can do what you want," Jorge answered. "Me, I'm going to stay on the farm and see how things go. We have a crop this year, and that's enough for now. If things change later, if the United States make life too hard to stand . . . Then I'll worry about it. Not until."

"What kind of patriot are you?" his brother asked.

"A live one," Jorge answered. "That's the kind I want to go on being, too. *Los Estados Confederados* are dead, Pedro. Dead. I don't think they'll come back to life no matter what we do."

"You think we're beaten."

"*Sí.* That's right. Don't you?"

Pedro didn't answer. He stormed out of the farmhouse instead. Jorge started to go after him, then checked himself. His brother could figure out what was going on without him. Jorge hoped he could, anyhow.

T he *Oregon* cruised off the Florida coast. The weather was fine. It felt more like August than October to George Enos. Back home in Boston, the leaves would be turning and it would be getting cold at night. Everything stayed green here. He didn't think autumn would ever come.

All the same, he didn't want to stay stuck on the battleship the rest of his life. He wanted to get home to Connie and the boys. Fighting in a war was one thing. Yeah, you needed to do that; he could see as much. Occupation duty? As far as he was concerned, they could conscript somebody else for it.

He griped. Most of the sailors on the *Oregon* who weren't career Navy guys were griping. Griping let off steam, and did no other good he could see. Nobody who mattered would pay attention. Nobody who mattered ever paid attention to ratings. That was how the Navy operated.

"Hey, you sorry bastards are stuck," Wally Fodor said. "We can't just pretend the fucking Confederates'll be good little boys and girls, the way we did the last time around. We know better now, right?"

"All I know is, this ain't what I signed up for," George answered. "I got a family. My kids hardly remember who I am."

"As soon as you swore the oath and they shipped your sorry rear end to Providence, they had you. They had you but good," the gun chief said. "You might as well lay back and enjoy it."

"I've been screwed long enough," George said. "Too damn long, to tell you the truth. I want to go home. I'm not the only one, either— not even close. Congress'll pay attention, whether the brass does or not."

"Don't hold your breath—that's all I've got to tell you." Fodor gave what was much too likely to be good advice.

In the meantime, there was Miami, right off the starboard bow. If anybody got out of line, the *Oregon*'s big guns could smash the city to bits. That was what battleships were good for nowadays: blasting the crap out of people who couldn't shoot back. In the Great War, they'd been queens of the sea. Now they were afterthoughts.

"Think we'll get liberty?" one of the shell-jerkers asked, a certain eagerness in his voice. Miami had a reputation almost like Habana's. Didn't hot weather produce hot women? That was how the stories went, anyhow.

George didn't know whether to believe the stories. He did know he'd been away from Connie long enough to hope to find out if they were true. He could hope it would be his last fling before he went back to his wife for good. That would help him feel not so bad about doing what he wanted to do anyway.

But Wally Fodor repeated, "Don't hold your breath. Besides, do you really want to get knocked over the head if you go ashore? They don't love us down here. Chances are they're never going to, either."

"Hey, I don't care about love," the shell-jerker said. "Long as I can get it in, that's good enough." Laughter said it was good enough for most of the gun crew.

They didn't get liberty. They did get fresh produce. Boats came alongside to sell the battleship fruit and meat and fish. Fresh orange juice and lemonade appeared in the galley. So did fresh peas and green beans, and salads with tender lettuce and buttery avocados and tomatoes and celery. The sailors ate fried shrimp and fried fish and spare ribs and fried chicken.

George had to let his belt out a notch. The chow beat the hell out of any Navy rations he'd had before. Bumboats brought out fresh water, too, enough so the crew didn't have to use seawater and saltwater soap when they showered. If that wasn't a luxury, he'd never known one. Peace had its advantages, all right.

He'd just stripped off his uniform to get clean when an enormous explosion knocked him ass over teakettle. "The fuck?" he said, which was one of the more coherent comments from the naked sailors.

Klaxons hooted. He ran for his battle station without thinking about his clothes. Bodies lay on the deck. He'd worry about them later. Right now, he had a job to do, and he could do it with pants or without. He wasn't the only naked man heading for duty—not even close.

Petty Officer Fodor had a cut on his face and another one on his arm. He didn't seem to notice either one. "They blew up a goddamn bumboat," he said. "Right alongside us, they blew up a goddamn bumboat."

"They're idiots if they did," George said. The *Oregon*, like any modern battleship, had sixteen-inch armor belts on either side to protect against gunfire and torpedoes. They weren't perfect, as the melancholy roll of torpedoed battlewagons attested. But they were a hell of a lot better than nothing. A blast that might have torn a destroyer in two dented the *Oregon* and killed and hurt people exposed to it without coming close to sinking her.

"This is the captain speaking!" the PA blared. "Odd-numbered gun stations, aid in casualty collection and damage assessment. Even numbers, hold your posts."

As the skipper repeated the order, George and the other men from his twin-40mm mount dashed off to do what they could for the sailors who hadn't been so lucky. There were a lot of them: anybody who'd been on deck when the bumboat exploded was down and moaning or down and thrashing or down and not moving at all, which was worst.

Some of the paint was burning. Men already had hoses playing on the fires. The stink made George's asshole pucker. When your ship got hit, that odor was one of the things you smelled. And he almost fell on his face skidding through a puddle of seawater from the firefighters.

He knelt by a burned man who was clutching his left shoulder. "C'mon, buddy—I'll give you a hand," he said.

"Thanks." The wounded sailor groped for him. "Sorry. I can't see a goddamn thing."

"Don't worry about it. The docs'll fix you up." George had no idea whether they could or not. The other man's face didn't look good, which was putting it mildly. "Your legs all right? I'm gonna get you on your feet if I can."

"Give it a try," the injured man said, which might have meant anything. He groaned and swayed when George hauled him upright, but he didn't keel over again. George got the fellow's good arm around his own shoulder. He also got blood on his own bare hide, but that was something to flabble about later.

Helping the other sailor down three flights of steep, narrow steel stairs when the poor guy couldn't see where to put his feet was an adventure all by itself. George managed. Other sailors and groups were carrying injured men and trying to get them down in stretchers without spilling them out.

In the sick bay and in the corridors outside it, the battleship's doctors and pharmacist's mates were working like foul-mouthed machines. One of the mates took a quick look at the sailor George had brought down. "Put him there with them," he said, pointing to a group of other men who were hurt but not in imminent danger of dying. "We'll get to him as soon as we have a chance to."

"Good luck, pal," George said as he eased the wounded sailor down. It was painfully inadequate, but it was all he could offer.

"Thanks. Go help somebody else," the other man said. Somebody— maybe a pharmacist's mate, maybe a rating one of the doctors had dragooned—stuck a needle into him. Morphine sure wouldn't hurt.

George was helping to get another injured man down to first aid when someone said, "I wonder what we'll do to Miami for this."

"Blow the fucking place off the fucking map," the wounded sailor said. That sounded good to George. He'd heard of people bombs and auto bombs, but a boat bomb? The son of a bitch who thought of that one had more imagination than he knew what to do with. George hoped he'd been on the boat and pressed the button that blew it up. If he had, maybe the scheme would die with him.

Or was that too much to hope for?

"Hell of a note if we've got to inspect every boat that brings us supplies," a CPO said. "Sure looks like we will, though."

When George got down to sick bay this time, he noticed a group of badly hurt men nobody was helping. They had to be the ones the doctors thought wouldn't get better no matter what. No time to waste effort on them, then. That was cruel logic, but it made sense.

The *Oregon*, he learned later, lost 31 dead and more than 150 wounded. In response, the U.S. Army seized 1,500 Miamians. Some of the attempted seizures turned into gun battles, too. The locals knew what the soldiers were coming for, and weren't inclined to give themselves up without a fight. Because of the casualties the Army took rounding up the hostages, it rounded up more hostages still.

Guns aimed toward the city, the *Oregon* sailed close inshore. The sharp, dry *crack!*s of rifle volleys came across the water, one after another after another. They got the message across: if you messed with the USA, you paid. And paid. And paid.

Some of the sailors weren't satisfied even so. "We ought to blast the shit out of that place," Wally Fodor said. "Those assholes fucked with us, not with the Army. We ought to give them a fourteen-inch lesson."

"Sure works for me," George said. All right, so battleships were shore-bombardment vessels these days. There was a shore that needed bombarding, and it was lying there naked and undefended in front of them.

But the order didn't come. The men pissed and moaned. That was all they could do. They couldn't open up on Miami without orders. Oh, maybe they could—the men on the smaller guns, anyhow—but they were looking at courts-martial and long terms if they did. Nobody had the gall to try it.

Discipline tightened up amazingly. They'd taken it easy after the Confederate surrender. They didn't any more. You never could tell what might happen now. George would have bet skippers and execs all around the fleet were preaching sermons about the battleship. That was just what he wanted, all right: to serve aboard the USS *Object Lesson.*

"Isn't it great?" he said to Fodor. "All those guys are going, 'See? You better not be a bunch of jerkoffs like the clowns on the *Oregon.* Otherwise, the Confederates'll blow your nuts off, too.'"

"Yeah, that's about the size of it, all right," the gun chief agreed. "They can fix up the scar on the side of the ship and slap fresh paint all over the place, but the scar on our reputation ain't gonna go away so fast. Goddamn Confederate cockknockers took care of that in spades."

"Fuck it," George said. "I just want to get back to Boston in one piece. Goddamn war was supposed to be over months ago."

"You think we were down here for no reason?" Fodor patted the gun mount. "I wish they would've lined up the hostages right there on the beach. Then we coulda opened up on 'em with the 40mms. Boy, we would've gone through 'em in a hurry."

"Yeah." George hadn't thought of the antiaircraft guns as weapons that could substitute for a firing squad. But Wally Fodor wasn't wrong. "You turn these babies on people, you know what you've got? You've got Grim Reapers, that's what."

"I like it," Fodor said, and damned if he didn't show up the next day with a can of white paint and some stencils. GRIM REAPER 1 went on the right-hand gun barrel, GRIM REAPER 2 on the gun on the left. "Way to go, Enos. Now they've got names."

"Oh, boy." George tried not to sound too gloomy. He was stuck on the *Oregon*, though, and he wished to God he weren't.

After so long in the war zone, Cincinnatus found Des Moines strange. Sleeping in his own bed, sleeping with his own wife—that was mighty good. Getting used to a peacetime world wasn't so easy.

He flinched whenever an auto backfired or a firecracker went off. He automatically looked for somewhere to hide. He noticed white men half his age doing the same thing. They noticed him, too. "You go through the mill, Pop?" one of them called when they both ducked walking down the street after something went boom.

"Drove a truck all the way through Kentucky and Tennessee and Georgia," Cincinnatus answered. "Wasn't right at the front, but I got bushwhacked a couple-three times."

"Oughta do it," the white man agreed. "I was in Virginia, and I got shot. Then they sent me to Alabama. I don't think I'll ever stop being jumpy."

"Man, I know what you mean," Cincinnatus said with feeling. They gave each other waves that weren't quite salutes as they passed.

Cincinnatus knew just where he was going: to the recruiting station where he'd signed up to drive a truck. It was right where it had been. UNCLE SAM STILL NEEDS YOU! said the sign out front. He went inside.

Damned if the same recruiting sergeant wasn't sitting in there, doing paperwork with a pen held in a hook. The man looked up when the door opened. "Well, well," he said, smiling. "I know you, and your name will come to me in a second if I let it. You're Mr.—Driver."

"That's right, Sergeant." Cincinnatus smiled, too. "I first came in here, I called you *suh*."

"You didn't know the ropes then. I see you do now," the noncom answered. "I'm glad you came through in one piece. I bet you cussed the day you stuck your nose in here plenty of times."

"Best believe I did," Cincinnatus said. "You mind if I sit down?"

"Not even a little bit. I remember you had a bad leg. And you can see I'm busy as hell right now, right?" The sergeant got to his feet. "Can I grab you a cup of coffee?"

"I'd thank you if you did," Cincinnatus replied. "Stuff's startin' to taste good again."

"We're getting real coffee beans for a change, not whatever kind of crap we were using instead," the recruiting sergeant said. "You take cream and sugar?"

"Both, please." Cincinnatus hesitated. "You know, I never learned your name the las' time I was here."

"I'm Dick Konstam—a damn Dutchman, but at your service. You've got a fancy handle. I remember that, but you'd better remind me what it is."

"Cincinnatus—that's me. . . . Thank you kindly." Cincinnatus sipped from the paper cup. The coffee was strong, but it hadn't been sitting on the hot plate long enough to get bitter yet. He took another sip. Then he asked the question he'd come here to ask: "Sergeant Konstam—uh, Dick—how the hell do I get myself to fit back into things? Wasn't near so hard the last time around."

Konstam paused to light a cigarette. It was a Niagara. He made a sour face. "Tobacco still sucks." He blew out smoke. "You sure you want to talk about that with me, Cincinnatus? What makes you think I've got any answers?"

"You done it yourself. And you've seen plenty of other fellows come and go through here," Cincinnatus said. "If you don't know, who's likely to?"

"Well, I hated everything and everybody when I caught this." Sergeant Konstam held up the hook. Cincinnatus nodded; he could see how that might be so. The white man took another drag—he handled a cigarette as deftly as a pen. After he exhaled a gray stream of smoke, he went on, "But life is too short, you know? Whatever you've got, you better make the most of it, you know?"

"Oh, yeah. I hear that real good," Cincinnatus said.

"Figured you did. You're a guy who busts his hump. You made something out of yourself, and that's pretty goddamn tough for somebody your color. Probably a lot easier to be a shiftless, no-account nigger the way most people expect."

"Know somethin'?" Cincinnatus said. The sergeant raised a questioning eyebrow. Cincinnatus explained: "Think maybe this is the first time I ever heard a white man say *nigger* an' I didn't want to punch him in the nose."

"Yeah, well, some colored guys *are* niggers. It's a shame, but it's true. And some Jews *are* kikes, and some Dutchmen *are* goddamn fuckin' squareheads—not me, of course." Konstam flashed a wry grin. "We got rid of all those assholes, we'd be better off. Good fuckin' luck, that's all I got to tell you. We're stuck with 'em, and we just have to deal with 'em the best way we know how."

"Like them Freedom Party goons," Cincinnatus said.

Sergeant Konstam nodded. "They fill the bill, all right. Only good thing about them is, we *can* shoot the fuckers if they step out of line. Nobody's gonna miss 'em when we do, either."

"Amen," Cincinnatus said. "If I was whole myself . . ." He didn't want to go on and on about his physical shortcomings, not when he was talking to a mutilated man. "My work was messed up after I got back from Covington. Ain't gonna get no better now."

"Remind me what line you were in."

"Had me a hauling business. Had it, yeah, till before the war. Damned if I know how to put it back on its feet now. Ain't got the money to buy me a new truck. Even if I did, I need somebody to give me a hand with loadin' an' unloadin' now."

"Got a son?" Konstam asked.

"Sure do," Cincinnatus said, not without pride. "Achilles, he graduated high school, an' he's clerking for an insurance company. He don't want to get all sore and sweaty and dirty like his old man. And you know what else? I'm damn glad he don't."

"Fair enough. Good for him, and good for you, too. Insurance company, huh? He must take after his old man, then—wants to make things better for himself any way he can. Maybe his kids'll run a company like that instead of working for it."

"That'd be somethin'. Don't reckon it'd be against the law up here, the way it would in the CSA. Don't reckon it'd be easy, neither. Achilles' babies, they're half Chinese."

Konstam laughed out loud. "Ain't that a kick in the head! Who flabbled more when they got hitched, you and your wife or your son's new in-laws?"

"Nobody was what you'd call happy about it," Cincinnatus said. "But Achilles and Grace, they get on good, and it ain't easy stayin' mad at people when there's grandbabies. Things are easier than they were a while ago, I got to say that."

"Glad to hear it." Dick Konstam whistled through his teeth. "I wasn't exactly thrilled when one of my girls married a Jewish guy. Ben hasn't turned out too bad, though. And you're sure as hell right about grandchildren." His face softened. "Want to see photos?"

"If I can show you mine."

They pulled out their wallets and went through a ritual as old as snapshots. If people had carried around little paintings before cameras got cheap and easy, they would have shown those off, too. Cincinnatus and the sergeant praised the obvious beauty and brilliance of each other's descendants. Cincinnatus didn't think he was lying too hard. He hoped Dick Konstam wasn't, either.

The sergeant stuck his billfold back in his hip pocket. "Any other problems I can solve for you today, Mr. Driver?"

He hadn't solved Cincinnatus' problem. He had to know it, too. But he had helped—and he sounded like a man who wanted to get back to work. "One more thing," Cincinnatus said. "Then I get out of your hair. How can I keep from wantin' to hide behind somethin' every god-damn time I hear a loud noise?"

"Boy, you ask the tough ones, don't you?" Konstam said. "All I can tell you is, don't hold your breath. That took me years to get over. Some guys never do. Poor bastards stay nervous as cats the rest of their days."

"Don't want to do that." But it might have more to do with luck than with what he wanted. Slowly and painfully, he got to his feet. "I thank you for your time, Sergeant, an' for lettin' me bend your ear."

"Your tax dollars in action," Konstam replied. "Take care of your-self, buddy. I wish you luck. You haven't been back all that long, re-member. Give yourself a chance to get used to things again."

"I reckon that's good advice," Cincinnatus said. "Thank you one more time."

"My pleasure," the sergeant said. "Take care, now."

"Yeah." Cincinnatus headed for home. A work gang with paste pots were putting up red, white, and blue posters of Tom Dewey on anything that didn't move. HE'LL TELL YOU WHAT'S WHAT, they said.

They were covering up as many of Charlie La Follette's Socialist red posters as they could. Those shouted a one-word message: VIC-TORY!

Cincinnatus still hadn't decided which way he'd vote. Yes, the So-cialists were in the saddle when the USA won the war. But they also helped spark it when they gave Kentucky and the state of Houston back to the CSA after their dumb plebiscite. The promise of that vote helped get Al Smith reelected in 1940.

The colored quarter in Covington was empty because of the plebiscite. If Cincinnatus wanted to, he could blame the auto that hit him on the plebiscite. Oh, he might have had an accident like that here in Des Moines chasing after his senile mother. He might have, yeah. But he *did* have it down in Covington.

How much did that count? He laughed at himself. It counted as much as he wanted it to, no more and no less. Nobody could make him vote for the Socialists if it mattered a lot in his own mind. Nobody could make him vote for the Democrats if it didn't. "Freedom," he murmured—in the real sense of the word, not the way Jake Featherston used it. Cincinnatus grinned and nodded to himself. "I'm here to tell you the truth." The truth was, he was free.

When he got back to the apartment, he found his wife about ready to jump out of her skin with excitement. Half a dozen words explained why: "Amanda's fella done popped the question!"

"Do Jesus!" Cincinnatus sank into a chair. When he left Des Moines not quite two years earlier, his daughter hadn't had a boyfriend. She did now. Calvin Washington was a junior butcher, a young man serious to the point of solemnity. He didn't have much flash—hell, he didn't have any flash—but Cincinnatus thought he was solid all the way through. "She said yes?"

Elizabeth nodded. "She sure did, fast as she could. She thinks she done invented Calvin, you know what I mean?"

"Expect I do." Thoughtfully, Cincinnatus added, "He's about the same color she is."

"Uh-huh." His wife nodded again. "It don't matter as much here as it did down in Kentucky, but it matters."

"It does," Cincinnatus agreed. That an American Negro's color did matter was one more measure of growing up in a white-dominated world, which made it no less real. Had Calvin been inky black, Cincinnatus would have felt his daughter was marrying beneath herself. He didn't know whether Amanda, a modern girl, would have felt that way, but he would have. Were Calvin high yellow, on the other hand, he might have felt he was marrying beneath himself. Since they were both about the same shade of brown, the question didn't arise. "When do they want to get hitched?" Cincinnatus asked.

"Pretty soon." Elizabeth's eyes sparkled. "They're young folks, sweetheart. They can't hardly wait."

"Huh," Cincinnatus said. It wasn't as if his wife were wrong. Whether he was ready or not, the world kept right on going all around him.

*   *   *

The first thing Irving Morrell said when he got into Philadelphia was, "This is a damned nuisance."

John Abell met him at the Broad Street station, as he had so many times before. "If you want to get it quashed, sir, I'm sure we can arrange that."

"No, no." Regretfully, Morrell shook his head. "The man's a cold-blooded son of a bitch, but even a cold-blooded son of a bitch is enti-tled to the truth."

"Indeed," the General Staff officer murmured. Abell was a cold-blooded son of a bitch, too, but one of a rather different flavor. He had two virtues, as far as Morrell could see: they were on the same side, and Abell didn't go around telling the world how goddamn right he was all the time. Right now, he asked, "Shall I take you over to BOQ and let you freshen up before you go on?"

Morrell looked down at himself. He was rumpled, but only a little. He ran a hand over his chin. Not perfectly smooth, but he didn't think he looked like a Skid Row bum, either. He shook his head. "No, let's get it over with. The sooner it's done, the sooner I can head west and see my wife and daughter."

"However you please," Abell said, which meant he would have showered and shaved and changed his uniform first. But he left the ed-itorializing right there. "My driver is at your disposal."

"Thanks." Morrell followed him off the platform.

They didn't have far to go. Morrell didn't have to look at the slagged wreckage on the other side of the Schuylkill, which didn't mean he didn't know it was there. Its being there, in fact, was a big part of why he was here.

There was no fresh damage in Philadelphia now that the war was over. Some of the wrecked buildings had been bulldozed, and the rub-ble hauled away. Repairmen swarmed everywhere. Glass was beginning to reappear in windows. "Looks . . . neater than it did before," Morrell remarked. "We're starting to come back."

"Some," Abell said. "It won't be the way it was for a long time. As a matter of fact, it will never be the way it was."

"Well, no. You can't step into the same river twice." Some Greek had said that a couple of thousand years before Morrell. He didn't re-member who; John Abell probably did. Morrell, no great lover of cities, didn't much care how Philadelphia rose again. As long as it had peace in which to rise, that suited him.

The War Department had set up a Tribunal for Accused Confederate War Criminals in a rented office building not far from the government buildings that dominated the center of town. Despite the stars on Morrell's shoulder straps and those on John Abell's, getting in wasn't easy. Security was tight, and no doubt needed to be.

A neatly lettered sign outside a meeting room turned courtroom said UNITED STATES OF AMERICA VS. CLARENCE POTTER, BRIGADIER GENERAL, CSA. "I would never tell you to perjure yourself," Abell said as they paused outside the door, "but I wouldn't hate you if you did, either."

"I'm Irving Morrell, and I'm here to tell you the truth," Morrell said. Abell winced. Morrell went on in.

Inside the makeshift courtroom, everyone except a few reporters and the defendant wore green-gray. The reporters were in civvies; Clarence Potter had on a butternut uniform that, even without insignia, singled him out at a glance. Morrell knew of him, but had never seen him before. He was a little older and more studious-looking than the U.S. officer expected, which didn't mean he wasn't dangerous. He'd already proved he was.

His defense attorney, a U.S. major, got to his feet. "Since General Morrell has chosen not to contest our subpoena, I request permission to get his remarks on the record while he is here."

He faced a panel of five judges—a brigadier general sitting in the center, three bird colonels, and a lieutenant colonel. The general looked over to the light colonel who seemed to be the prosecutor. "Any objections?"

"No, sir," that officer replied. *I'm stuck with it*, his expression said.

"Very well," the chief judge said. "Come forward and be sworn, General Morrell, and then take your seat."

When Morrell had taken the oath and sat down, Potter's defense counsel said, "You are aware that General Potter is on trial for conveying the Confederate superbomb to Philadelphia while wearing the U.S. uniform for purposes of disguise?"

"Yes, I know that," Morrell said.

"This is considered contrary to the laws of war as set down in the 1907 Hague Convention?"

"That's right."

"Had the Confederates ever used soldiers in U.S. uniform before?"

"Yes, they had. Their men in our uniforms helped get a breakthrough in eastern Ohio in 1942. They even picked men who had U.S. accents. It hurt us."

"I see." The defense attorney looked at some papers. "Were the Confederates alone in using this tactic?"

"No," Morrell said.

"Tell the court about some instances when U.S. soldiers under your command used it."

"Well, the most important was probably the 133rd Special Reconnaissance Company," Morrell replied. "We took a page from the CSA's book. We recruited men who could sound like Confederates. We armed them with Confederate weapons, and put them into Confederate uniform."

"Where did you get the uniforms?" asked the major defending Potter.

"Some from prisoners, others off casualties," Morrell said.

"I see. And the 133rd Special Reconnaissance Company was effective?"

"Yes. It spearheaded our crossing of the Tennessee in front of Chattanooga."

"Surprise and deception made it more effective than it would have been otherwise?"

"I would certainly think so."

"Thank you, General. No further questions."

The chief judge nodded to the prosecutor. "Your witness, Colonel Altrock."

"Thank you, sir." Altrock got to his feet. "You say you were imitating Confederate examples when you dressed our men in enemy uniform, General?"

"I believe that's true, yes," Morrell said.

"Would you have done it if the enemy hadn't?" Altrock asked.

"Objection—that's a hypothetical," the defense attorney said.

After the judges put their heads together, their chief said, "Overruled. The witness may answer the question."

"Would I? Would we?" Morrell pursed his lips. "Probably. It's too good a move—and too obvious—to ignore."

"No further questions," Altrock said. One had done him enough damage.

"Anything on redirect?" the chief judge asked Potter's lawyer, who shook his head. The judge nodded to Morrell. "You are dismissed, General. We appreciate your testimony."

Clarence Potter spoke for the first time: "If I may say so, I appreciate it very much." His own accent might have inspired him to dress up Yankee-sounding Confederates in U.S. uniforms.

"I don't love you, General, but if they hang you it should be for something you did and we didn't." Morrell got to his feet. He nodded to the judges and left the courtroom.

John Abell wasn't waiting there any more. Morrell hadn't expected him to hang around. The driver was. "Where to, sir?" he said. "Wherever you need to go, I'll take you there."

"Back to the train station, quick, before somebody else here decides he needs me," Morrell answered. "By God, I *am* going to see my wife and daughter."

The driver grinned. "I know how you feel, sir. Let's go."

Two and a half hours later, Morrell was on a train bound for Kansas City. He traveled through the stretches of western Pennsylvania, Ohio, and eastern Indiana that had seen the hardest fighting inside the USA. Looking out the window at the devastation was like falling back in time. Down in the occupied Confederacy, hardly anyone looked out of train windows. What people saw there was too likely to hurt. The United States was luckier, but this one stretch of terrain had suffered as much as any farther south.

Morrell breathed easier when he neared Indianapolis. C.S. bombers had hit the city, but nowhere near as hard as they'd pummeled Washington and Baltimore and Philadelphia. And the only soldiers in butternut who'd made it to Indianapolis went into the POW camps outside of town. Some of them still languished there. Most had gone home by now. Some of the ones who had would make U.S. authorities sorry they'd ever turned them loose. Morrell was as sure of that as he was of the scars on his thigh and shoulder, but what the hell could you do?

St. Louis had taken a beating, and Missouri went up in flames whenever war broke out. Even three generations after the War of Secession, it had some stubborn Confederate sympathizers. Lines were fluid in the West, too; C.S. raiders had little trouble sneaking up from Arkansas and raising hell.

Kansas City and Leavenworth, as well as the fort nearby, had also suffered. But, as the war went on, the Confederates found troubles of their own closer to home. Morrell knew Agnes and Mildred had come through without a scratch. To him, selfishly, that was all that mattered.

They were waiting for him when he got off the train. Agnes was about his age, but her black hair showed not a streak of gray. Maybe that was a miracle; more likely it was dye. Morrell didn't care either way. His wife looked damn good to him, and she had ever since they met at a dance right here in town.

He was amazed at how shapely Mildred had got. She was nineteen now, but the years had gone by in a blur for him. He eyed Agnes in mock severity. "You've been feeding her again," he said sternly. "Didn't I warn you about that? See what happens?"

"I'm sorry, Irv." Agnes sounded as contrite as he was angry—which is to say, not very.

"Daddy!" Mildred was just plain indignant.

He gave her a kiss. "It's good to see you, sweetheart. You've grown up as pretty as your mother." That he meant. Mildred was certainly better off with Agnes' looks than with his own long-faced, long-jawed countenance. He wasn't an ugly man, but a woman with features as harsh as his wouldn't have been lucky.

"How long can you stay?" Agnes asked.

"They promised me a couple of weeks, but you know what Army promises are worth," Morrell answered. The rueful twist to his wife's mouth said she knew much too well. He went on, "We'll just have to make the most of the time, however long it turns out to be."

"Of course we will." Agnes looked at Mildred. "That's good advice any old time." She had her own bitter experience; she'd lost her first husband in the early days of the Great War.

Mildred wasn't impressed. With a toss of the head, she said, "I thought I graduated from high school."

Morrell started to give her a swat on the behind for sass, but checked himself. She was too big these days for a man to spank. He contented himself with asking, "Have you been giving your mother lip all the time I've been gone?"

"Every single minute," Mildred answered proudly. That took the wind out of his sails.

"Let's go home," Agnes said. "We have a lot of catching up to do." She winked at Morrell. He grinned. He looked forward to trying to catch up, anyhow.

All over the country—and all over the wreck of the CSA, too—survivors were trying to catch up with their families and trying to make them grow. Some reunions would be smooth, some anything but. Morrell put one arm around his wife, the other around his daughter. They walked off the platform that way. *So far, so good*, he thought.

XVIII

Clarence Potter took his place in the Yankee courtroom. The Yankee kangaroo courtroom, he feared it was. The judges had let his lawyer question witnesses and even bring in Irving Morrell, but how much difference would any of that make? He'd superbombed the town where they were trying him. Evidence? Who gave a damn about evidence? If they felt like convicting him, they bloody well would.

He nodded to Major Stachiewicz, who'd defended him. "You did what you could. I appreciate it."

"I didn't do it for you, exactly. I did it for duty," the damnyankee said.

"I understand that. I don't want to marry you, either. But you made an honest effort, and I want you to know I know it," Potter said.

"All rise!" said the warrant officer who doubled as bailiff and recording secretary.

Everyone in the courtroom got to his feet as the judges came in. As soon as the judges sat down, Brigadier General Stephens said, "Be seated." Potter sat. He didn't want to let the enemy know he was nervous. In the rows of seats in the spectators' gallery behind him, reporters poised pens above notebooks.

Verdict day today.

The chief judge fixed him with an unfriendly stare. "The defendant will please rise."

"Yes, Your honor." Potter stood at attention.

"Without a doubt, General Potter, you caused greater loss of life than any man before you in the history of the North American continent," General Stephens said. That was cleverly phrased. It ignored the hell the USA's German allies unleashed on Petrograd earlier, and it also ignored the hell the United States visited on Newport News and Charleston. All the same, it remained technically true.

"Also without a doubt," Stephens continued, "you were able to do what you did thanks to a ruse of war, one frowned on by the Geneva Convention. Carrying on the fight in the uniform of the foe skates close to the edge of the laws of war."

He looked as if his stomach pained him. "However . . ." He paused to pour himself a glass of water and sip from it, as if to wash the taste of the word from his mouth. Then he had to say it again: "However . . ." Another long pause. "It has also been demonstrated beyond a reasonable doubt that U.S. forces utilized the identical ruse of war. Executing a man on the other side for something we also did ourselves strikes the court as unjust, however much we might wish it did not. This being so, we find you not guilty of violating the laws of war in bringing your superbomb to Philadelphia."

Hubbub in the courtroom as reporters exclaimed. Some rushed out to file their stories. No one paid any attention to the chief judge's gavel. Through the chaos, Potter said, "May I tell you something, sir?"

"Go ahead." No, Brigadier General Stephens was not a happy man. And, over at the prosecutor's table, Lieutenant Colonel Altrock looked as if he'd just found half a worm in his apple.

"I want to thank the court for its integrity, General," Potter said. "I have to say, I didn't expect it." *Not from Yankees* was in his mind if not on his tongue.

Stephens had to know it was there, too. His mouth twisted. "Your enemies are men like you, General," he said. "That, I believe, is the principal meaning of this verdict."

Potter inclined his head. "The point is well taken, sir."

"Happy day," Stephens said bleakly. "Please understand: we don't approve of you even if we don't convict you. You will be under surveillance for the rest of your life. If you show even the slightest inclination toward trouble, it will be your last mistake. Do I make myself clear?"

"Abundantly." Clarence Potter might have complained that he was being singled out for discriminatory treatment. He might have—but he wasn't that kind of fool, anyhow.

"Very well. I gather the men who debriefed you have now finished?"

"Yes, sir," Potter said. "They have squeezed me flatter than a snake in a rolling mill." He'd told them everything about his trip up from Lexington to Philadelphia. Why not? Come what might, he wouldn't do that again. He'd told them a lot about Confederate intelligence operations, too, but not everything. They thought he'd told them more than he really had. If they wanted to ferret out C.S. operatives up here, though, he thought they'd need more than he'd given them.

The U.S. brigadier general didn't laugh, or even smile. "You may collect the balance of the pay owed you as an officer POW under the Geneva Convention. And then you may . . . go." He drank more water.

Go where? Potter wondered. Nothing left of Charleston, not any more. And not much left of Richmond, either. Not much left of the CSA, come to that. He was a man without a country. Turning him loose might have been the cruelest thing the USA could do. All the same, he preferred it to getting his neck stretched.

"May I ask a favor of the court, sir, before I return to civilian life?" he said.

"What sort of favor?" If you needed a dictionary illustration for *suspicious*, General Stephens' face would have filled the bill.

"May I beg for a civilian suit of clothes? This uniform"—Potter touched a butternut sleeve with his other hand—"is less than popular in your country right now."

"There are good and cogent reasons why that should be so, too," the chief judge said. But he nodded a moment later; he was at bottom a fair-minded man. "I admit your request is reasonable. You will have one. If, however, you had asked for a U.S. uniform in place of your own, I would have refused you. You've already done too much damage in our clothing."

"My country is no longer at war with yours, General." *My country no longer exists.* "While our countries were at peace, I lived peacefully"—*enough*—"in mine. I intend to do the same again."

The suit they gave him didn't fit especially well. The wide-brimmed fedora that went with it might have looked good on a twenty-five-year-old . . . pimp. The kindest thing he could say about the gaudy tie was that he never would have bought it himself. He knotted it without a murmur now. The less he looked like his usual self, the better he judged his chances of getting out of Philadelphia in one piece.

Green banknotes—no, they were bills up here—filled his leatherette wallet. He wondered what the economy was like down in the ruins of the CSA. Would inflation run mad, the way it had after the Great War? Or were the Yankees ramming their currency down the Confederacy's throat this time? Either way, a wallet stuffed with greenbacks looked like good insurance.

They even gave him a train ticket to Richmond. That settled where he would go, at least for the time being. If he didn't have to pay for the ticket, he could hang on to some more of his POW pay.

That seemed a good thing, because he had no idea how to make more money. All his adult life, he'd been either a soldier—and the bottom had been blown out of the market for Confederate soldiers—or a private investigator—and he was, at the moment, one of the least private men on the continent.

His chuckle was sour, but not sour enough to suit one of the U.S. MPs keeping an eye on him. "What's so damn funny?" the Yankee asked.

"I may be reduced to writing my memoirs," Potter answered, "and that's the kind of thing you do after you don't expect to do anything else."

The MP's glance was anything but sympathetic. "You want to know what I think, Mac, you already did too goddamn much."

"That only shows I was doing my job."

"Yeah, well, if I was doing my job . . ." The U.S. sergeant swung his submachine gun toward Potter, but only for a moment. Discipline held. *A good thing, too*, Potter thought.

They hustled him out of the courthouse through a back door. A crowd of reporters gathered at the front of the building. None of them paid any attention to the aging man in tasteless clothes who went by in the back seat of a Ford.

U.S. train stations didn't work exactly the same way as their C.S. equivalents did, but they were pretty close. Potter found the right platform at the Broad Street station and waited for the train to come in.

Some of the men on it turned out to be released Confederate POWs. Some looked like Yankee hotshots on their way down to the CSA to see what they could make by picking the corpse's bones. Some just looked like . . . people. Potter wondered what they thought of him. In his present getup, he thought he looked pretty shady.

He got to Richmond late in the afternoon. A U.S. first lieutenant stood on the platform holding a sign with his name on it. He thought of walking by, but why give the United States excuses to land him in trouble? "I'm Clarence Potter," he said.

"My name is Constantine Palaiologos," the U.S. officer said. "Call me Costa—everybody does." His rueful smile probably told of lots of childhood teasing. "Since I got word you'd be coming here, I found an apartment for you."

"How . . . efficient," Potter murmured.

Lieutenant Palaiologos didn't even try to misunderstand him. "We do intend to keep an eye on you," he said. "The building wasn't badly damaged during the war, and it's been repaired since. It's better than a lot of people here are living."

"Thanks . . . I suppose," Potter said.

He smelled death in the air as the lieutenant drove him through the battered streets. He'd smelled it in Philadelphia, too; it was part of the aftermath of war. It was stronger here, not surprisingly. People looked shabbier than they did in the USA. They walked with slumped shoulders and downcast eyes—they knew they were beaten, all right. For the first time since the early days of the Lincoln administration, the Stars and Stripes flew all over the city, not just above the U.S. embassy.

The apartment building didn't look too bad. Some of its neighbors still showed bomb damage, but it even had glass in the windows again. Freshly painted spots of plaster probably repaired bullet holes, but there weren't a whole lot of buildings in Richmond that a bullet or two hadn't hit.

"So—is this where you keep all the old sweats?" Potter asked.

"No, General," Palaiologos answered seriously. "We try to separate you people as much as we can. The further apart you are, the less you'll sit around plotting and making trouble."

In the USA's shoes, Potter probably would have arranged things the same way. He let the young lieutenant show him his new digs. It was . . . a furnished apartment. He could stand living here. Once he got a wireless and a phonograph and some books, it might not even be too bad.

"Did I see a stationery store around the corner?" he asked.

"I think so," Lieutenant Palaiologos said.

"As long as you've got a motorcar, will you take me over there and run me back?"

"All right." Palaiologos spoke without enthusiasm, but he didn't say no.

Potter bought a secondhand typewriter, a spare ribbon, and two reams of paper not much better than foolscap. He got the U.S. officer to lug the typewriter up to the flat, which was on the second floor.

"I said I might write my memoirs," Potter told him after he put it on the kitchen table. "I may as well. Maybe the book'll make me enough money to live on." Palaiologos' grunt was nothing if not skeptical (and weary—the typewriter weighed a ton). Potter didn't care. He ran a sheet of paper into the machine. HOW I BLEW UP PHILADELPHIA, he typed in all caps. By Clarence Potter, Brigadier General, CSA (retired). He took out the title page and put in another sheet. I first met Jake Featherston late in 1915. . . .

One more Election Day in New York City. One more trip to Socialist Party headquarters over the butcher's shop. One more tray of cold cuts from the Democrat downstairs.

Flora Blackford put corned beef and pickles on a bagel. "One more term, Flora," Maria Tresca said.

"*Alevai.*" Flora knocked wood. One reason she kept getting re-elected was that she never took anything for granted. She wasn't too worried this time around, not for herself. She hadn't been worried about the national ticket, either, not till the past couple of weeks. Now . . . "I hope Charlie La Follette does what he ought to."

On paper, the President of the USA had the world on a string. The war was over. He'd been at the helm when his country won it. The United States bestrode North America like a colossus: the Stars and Stripes flew from Baffin Island to below the Rio Grande. Surely people would be grateful for that . . . wouldn't they?

Not if they listened to the Democrats, they wouldn't. Tom Dewey and his running mate were saying the war was all the Socialists' fault in the first place. If Al Smith hadn't given Jake Featherston his plebiscite, the Confederate States wouldn't have got Kentucky and the state of Houston back. How could they have gone to war without Kentucky?

Nobody now seemed to remember there'd been guerrilla war in Kentucky and Houston and Sequoyah before the plebiscite. Flora agreed that Al Smith might have chosen better. But what he did choose wasn't halfway between idiocy and treason, no matter how the Democrats made it sound.

They were saying they could have fought the war better, too. And they were saying the United States went into it unprepared because the Socialists spent years gutting War Department budgets. Those budgets hadn't been exactly luxurious when Democrat Herbert Hoover ran things, either. Because of the economic collapse, nobody'd had much money to spend on guns . . . nobody but Jake Featherston.

The Democrats blamed the collapse on the Socialists, too. More to the point, they blamed it on Hosea Blackford. That made Flora see red. Yes, her husband was President when it happened. That didn't make it his fault. Except, in too many people's minds, it did. Hosea was a one-term President.

Herman Bruck looked at his watch. Every two years, he seemed a little plumper, a little grayer. *Oh, and I haven't changed at all*, Flora thought. That would have been nice if only it were true.

"Seven o'clock," Herman said ceremoniously. "The polls are closed." He turned on a wireless set.

None of the results from the East Coast would mean anything for a while. That wouldn't stop the broadcasters from reporting them and pontificating over them. It wouldn't stop inexperienced people from flabbling over them if they were bad or from celebrating too soon if they were good.

"Dewey jumps out to an early lead in Vermont!" a reporter said breathlessly. Flora had to fight the giggles. Of *course* Dewey led in Vermont. The sky would have to fall for him to do anything else. Vermont had been a rock-ribbed Democratic stronghold for years.

"Do you think we can hold New York?" Maria asked. That was a more important question. New York had a ton of electoral votes. It went Socialist more often than not, but Dewey the Democrat was a popular governor. How many people would vote for him for President because of that? Enough to swing the state?

"I hope so," Flora said. She didn't know what she *could* say past that. Polls called the race close, but she didn't have much faith in them. Pollsters had proved spectacularly wrong before.

Maine held its elections early, and had already gone for Dewey. A moment later, New Hampshire also fell into his column. Again, none of that was too surprising; only in landslide years did upper New England fall out of the Democratic camp.

But when early returns showed Dewey with a substantial lead in Massachusetts and Connecticut, Flora began to worry. Both states were in play in most elections. Herman Bruck said, "All depends on where the returns are coming from," which put the best possible face on things. He wasn't wrong, but they shouldn't have needed to fret so soon.

New Jersey seemed to be going Socialist, and by a solid majority. That made Flora breathe a little easier, anyhow. Any year the Socialists lost New Jersey would probably not be a year where they held on to the Presidency.

To drive her crazy, returns from Pennsylvania started coming in before any from New York. Those showed the race there neck and neck. How many people in western Pennsylvania were blaming the Socialists for the Confederate invasion two years earlier? Flora thought that would have happened regardless of who was running the country at the time, but she could see how others might see things a different way.

"Here is some of the early tally from New York," the newsman said. Everybody yelled for everybody else to hush. "These results show Governor Dewey with 147,461 votes to President La Follette's 128,889. In the race for Senator—"

"Where are they coming from?" This time, Bruck wasn't the only one to ask the question. Several people shouted it at the same time. The newscaster? He went blithely on to results from West Virginia.

"I'll find out," Herman Bruck said, and got on the telephone with the canvassing headquarters downtown. When he hung up, he might have been a balloon that had sprung a slow leak.

"What's the matter?" Flora asked, seeing his face.

"Those are city returns, not upstate," he answered. The news felt like a blow in the belly to Flora. New York political battles centered on whether Socialist New York City could outvote the Democratic hinterland. If New York City leaned Democratic . . .

If New York City leaned that way, it was liable to be a long, unhappy night.

And it was. The air in Socialist district headquarters went blue with tobacco smoke, and bluer with profanity. State after state fell to the Democrats. The Republican candidate, the energetic young Governor of Minnesota, stole his home state and Wisconsin from the Socialists in three-cornered races, and also took traditional Republican strongholds like Indiana and Kansas.

Flora held her own seat. Her margin was down from the last election, but she still won upwards of fifty-five percent of the vote. All the same . . . "I don't think we're going to do it," she said somewhere around one in the morning.

"How could they be so ungrateful?" Herman Bruck said. "We won the war for them. What more could they want?"

A country too strong for the Confederates even to think of attacking, that's what. Flora looked around in the gloomy, smoky headquarters. No, the ghost of Robert Taft wasn't sitting right behind her. But it might as well have been. The old Democratic stalwart had an answer for the Socialist *cri de coeur*.

After another hour, the newsman said, "Governor Dewey and Senator Truman are going to claim victory."

The Vice President–elect spoke first. His high, twangy voice full of good humor, he said, "I'm holding in my hands a copy of the *Chicago Tribune*. The headline reads, LA FOLLETTE BEATS DEWEY! I don't know where they got that headline from, but tonight Tom Dewey and the Democratic Party are winners!" Cheers interrupted him. He went on, "And tonight the American people are winners, too!" More cheers. "It is now my privilege to introduce the new President of the United States, Tom Dewey!"

"Thank you, Harry," the President-elect said. "I am humbled and honored to be chosen to lead the United States in these tense and trying times. I call on all people—Democrats, Socialists, and Republicans—to unite behind me to bind up the wounds of war and help guide the country into an era of peace and one of renewed prosperity and hope."

Applause almost drowned him out. He said all the right things. Charlie La Follette could have used his speech without changing more than a couple of words. Flora would rather have heard it from La Follette than Dewey.

La Follette had gone back to Wisconsin to vote. He didn't even carry his home state. A few minutes after the Democrats, he came on the wireless. "The people have spoken," he said. "I congratulate Governor Dewey—President-elect Dewey, as he is now—and wish him the best of luck in the next four years. I did not expect to be President of the United States during the most profound crisis of the twentieth century. Under Jake Featherston, the Confederate States aimed not merely at beating us but at crushing us and subjecting us so we could never rise again. Instead, we triumphed in the hardest war ever fought on this blood-soaked continent.

"Perhaps we did not do everything as well as we might have. That is easier to see in hindsight than it was through foresight. But the people have called us to account for it, as is their right. May the new President fare well in ruling the territories we have gained, and in the complex field of international relations. With superbombs, everyone is suddenly everyone else's nearest neighbor. I will serve President Dewey in whatever capacity he may find useful, or in none if that be his pleasure. Serving the people of the United States has been the greatest privilege of my life. Thank you, God bless you, and good night."

"That was Charles La Follette, the outgoing President of the United States," the announcer said unnecessarily.

"A good good-bye," Herman Bruck said as the wireless started catching up on races that remained close.

"I wanted a good victory speech, dammit," Flora said. All through the crowded Socialist headquarters, heads bobbed up and down.

"Changeover time," Maria Tresca remarked, and it would be. It looked as if the Democrats would also capture the House, though the Senate would stay in Socialist hands. But an earthquake would hit the executive branch. Since 1920, only Herbert Hoover's single term had broken the Socialists' hold on the Presidency. Lots of new and untested officials would try out lots of new and untested policies.

Flora might have been in line to chair the House Judiciary Committee. Not now. Back to the minority. That hadn't happened very often since the end of the Great War. If the Democrats proposed foolish laws now that they ruled the roost, she would do her best to keep them from passing.

"Why are the people so ungrateful?" Bruck wondered out loud.

"There's a story," Maria said. "Back in the days when Athens held ostracisms to get rid of politicians they didn't like, an illiterate citizen who didn't recognize Aristides the Just came up to him and asked him to write 'Aristides' on a potsherd. He did, but he asked why. The man answered, 'I'm tired of hearing him called "the Just." ' And that's what happened to us, or something like it."

Flora found herself nodding. She said, "Still, it's a shame to run on a platform where the main plank is 'Throw the rascals *in*.' "

She got a laugh. If it was tinged with bitterness—well, why wouldn't it be? She thought the Socialists deserved better than they'd got from the people, too. No matter what she thought, though, she couldn't do anything about it. Every so often, the government turned over. The world wouldn't end. The country wouldn't go down the drain—even if the party in power always tried to make the voters think it would if the opposition won.

She'd lost a brother-in-law to war. Her own brother had lost a leg. Her son lost only a finger. Other than that, Joshua was fine, and it wouldn't much affect the rest of his life. Next to important things like that, how much did elections really matter?

All the arguing was over. Jonathan Moss had done everything he could. He'd tried his damnedest to convince the U.S. military court that Jefferson Pinkard had followed his own superiors' legal orders when he ran his extermination camps in Louisiana and Texas. He'd done his best to persuade them that the USA had no jurisdiction over what the Confederates did to their own people.

Now the military judges were deliberating. Pinkard sat in the courtroom, large and blocky and stolid. Only the way his jaw worked on some chewing gum showed he might be nervous.

"You gave it everything you had," he told Moss. "I thought that Jew who got hurt was hot stuff, but you're good, too. Don't reckon he could've pulled any rabbits out of the hat that you didn't."

"Thanks," Moss said. If he'd satisfied his client, his own conscience could stay reasonably clear. That was just as well, because he had no doubt in his own mind that Pinkard was guilty. If they didn't hang him, would they—could they—hang anybody?

"All rise!" the warrant officer who transcribed the proceedings intoned as the panel of judges entered the courtroom.

Moss stood and came to attention. Jeff Pinkard stood but didn't. He'd loudly denied that the court had any jurisdiction over him. That wouldn't endear him to the men who judged him. Everyone sat down again.

"We have reached a verdict in *United States vs. Jefferson Davis Pinkard*," the chief judge said.

Beside Moss, Pinkard stiffened. His jaw set. He might claim he was ready for the Army to convict him, but he wasn't, not down deep. Who could be? No one was ever ready to face his own death.

"The defendant will please rise," the chief judge said.

Pinkard did. This time, without being asked, he did come to attention. Maybe the solemnity of the moment pressed on him in spite of himself. He'd fought in the Great War. Nobody said he'd been anything but brave. Nobody said that about Jake Featherston, either. Bravery wasn't enough, not by itself. The cause for which you showed courage counted, too.

"Jefferson Davis Pinkard, we find you guilty of crimes against humanity," the chief judge said. Pinkard's shoulders sagged. The breath hissed out of him, as if he'd been punched in the gut. The officer pronouncing his fate continued, "We sentence you to be hanged by the neck until you are dead, at a date to be set by competent military authority. May God have mercy on your soul."

Jonathan Moss jumped to his feet. "Your Honor, I appeal this conviction and the sentence you've imposed."

"You have that privilege," the chief judge said. "Appeals will be heard by the Secretary of War and, no doubt, by the President of the United States. I do not believe the upcoming change in administrations will affect the process."

He was bound to be right. The outgoing Socialists wouldn't show mercy to someone like Jeff Pinkard. They were the ones who'd brought him to justice in the first place. And the Democrats had campaigned by saying, *If we were running things, we would have been even tougher.* Still, you had to go do everything you could.

"Do you have any statement for the record, Mr. Pinkard?" the chief judge asked.

"Damn right I do," Pinkard said—he had no quit in him. "You can hang me. You won, and you caught me, so you can. But that don't make it right. I was doing a job of work in my own country, following orders from the Attorney General of the CSA—"

"Ferdinand Koenig has also been sentenced to death, among other things for giving those orders," the chief judge broke in.

Jeff Pinkard shook his head. He was furious, not bewildered. "It's none of your goddamn business what we did. It wasn't your country, and they weren't your people."

"We made it our business," the chief judge replied. "We want people everywhere to get the message: doing things like this is wrong, and you will be punished for it. And besides, Mr. Pinkard, you know as well as I do—if you'd won the war, you would have started in on us next."

Pinkard didn't even waste time denying it. He just said, "Yeah, and you'd've had it coming, too. Fuck you all, assholes."

"Take him away," the chief judge said, and several burly soldiers did just that. With a weary sigh, the chief judge used the gavel. "This court is now adjourned."

Major Goodman came over to Moss. "You did everything you could, Colonel. You had a losing case and a losing client. He's a cold-blooded, hard-nosed son of a bitch, and he deserves everything he's going to get."

"Yeah, I know," Moss said. "You still have to try. He's got courage. I was just thinking that a minute ago."

"Courage is overrated. How many brave butternut bastards did we just have to kill?" the military prosecutor said. "You have to understand what you're fighting for. Otherwise, you're an animal—a brave animal, maybe, but an animal all the same."

"I won't argue with you. I feel the same way," Moss said.

"He can't complain he wasn't well represented," the chief judge said. "You did a fine job, Colonel. You did everything we let you do, and you would have done more if we'd left more in the rules."

"Not letting me do more will be part of the appeal," Moss said. "The question of jurisdiction still troubles me."

"You saw the evidence," the chief judge said. "Did you go to Camp Humble and see the crematoria and the barracks and the barbed wire? Did you go out to Snyder and take a look at the mass graves?"

"No, sir. I didn't want to prejudice myself against him any worse than I was already," Moss said.

"All right. I can understand that. It speaks well of you, as a matter of fact. But what are we supposed to do with him? Tell him not to be naughty again and turn him loose? I'd break every mirror in the house if we did."

"Well, so would I, when you put it that way," Moss said. "One of the reasons I don't feel worse about defending him is that I knew he wouldn't get off no matter what I did. Still, technically . . ."

The chief judge made a slashing motion with his right hand. "The law is about technicalities a lot of the time. Not here. We aren't about to let quibbles keep us from making Pinkard and Koenig and the rest pay for what they can. I hear we were going to shoot Featherston without trial if we caught him, but that got taken care of."

"Didn't it just?" Moss said. "That colored kid's got it made. He'll be a hero the rest of his life. Too damn bad all the other blacks had to pay such a price." He suspected one reason the United States were making so much of Cassius was to keep from noticing their own guilty conscience.

"What about you, Colonel?" the chief judge asked. "You're going through the motions with the appeal, and we both know it. What are you really going to do once this case winds down?"

"Looks like private practice," Moss answered without enthusiasm. "In wartime, the Army didn't mind using pilots with gray hair. I even got to fly a turbo in combat, and that was something, no two ways about it. But they don't want to keep me in that slot now, and I can't even say I blame 'em. Fighter pilot is really a young man's game."

"I was impressed with the way you handled yourself here," the judge said. "Are you interested in joining the Judge Advocate's staff full time? This is one of those places where you can count on skill to beat reflexes. Look at me, for instance." His hair was grayer than Moss'.

"Huh," Moss said: an exclamation of thoughtful surprise. "Hadn't even thought of that, sir. Don't know why not. Probably because I got this assignment taking over from the poor guy in the motorcar crash. It always felt temporary to me."

The chief judge nodded. "I take your point. And if you've had enough of living on an officer's salary, I can see that, too. You'll eat steak more often if you go civilian."

Moss started to laugh. "I'll tell you another reason you took me by surprise: I spent my whole career between the wars, trying to kick military justice in the teeth up in Canada."

"I know. I checked up on you," the chief judge said calmly. "If you wanted to, you could do the same thing here. Lord knows you'd have plenty of business."

"That crossed my mind, sir," Moss said. "Can't say it thrills me, though. Far as I can see, the Canucks got a raw deal. I think I'd say the same thing if I didn't fall in love with a Canadian girl. But the white Confederates? I was on the ground in Georgia for a couple of years, remember. Those people deserve everything they're getting, and another dollar's worth besides."

"Think about switching sides, then," the chief judge said. "Plenty more trials coming up. Not all of them will be as cut-and-dried as Jefferson Pinkard's, either. We do need people who can conduct a good defense, and you've shown you can do that and then some. But we need prosecutors, too."

He was bound to be right about the upcoming trials. How many people had helped shove Negroes into cattle cars? How many had run up barbed wire and put brick walls around colored districts in the CSA? How many had done, or might have done, all the things the Confederacy needed so it could turn massacre from a campaign promise to reality?

And what would they say now? *I was at the front* or *I was working in a factory* or *I never liked the Freedom Party anyway*. Some would be telling the truth. Some would be telling some of the truth. Some would be lying through their teeth. Sorting out who was who and giving the ones who deserved something what they deserved would take years. God only knew it would take plenty of lawyers, too.

"I don't think I'd want to defend Vern Green, say, any time soon," Moss said. The guard chief at the Texas camps Pinkard had run was on trial here, too, and it was a sure thing his neck would stretch along with his boss'. "One of these is about as much as I can stomach, at least from this side. Somebody where there really was some doubt about what he did . . . That might be a different story."

"Nobody wants to do many of these," the chief judge said. "I don't think you *can* do many of these, not if you're going to stay sane. We try not to drive our staff members loopy . . . on purpose. Think about it. You don't have to make up your mind right away. In fact, if you want to think about it over a drink down in the officers' club . . . God knows I need one, and I bet you do, too."

"Sir, that is the best idea I've heard in a long time," Moss said.

Whiskey probably didn't do much for the thought process. It worked wonders on Moss' attitude, though. And attitude mattered here at least as much as actual thought. Was this what he wanted to do with the rest of his working life?

Halfway down the second drink, he asked, "Will the Judge Advocate's staff handle claims by Negroes against whites in the CSA?"

"I don't know." The chief judge looked startled. "There'll sure be some, won't there?"

"Only way there'd be more was if more Negroes lived," Moss answered. "But if you're involved in that, count me in. And if you're not, you ought to be ashamed of yourselves. I can't think of anything down here that needs doing more."

"Now that you mention it, neither can I," the chief judge said.

He'd sentenced Jefferson Pinkard to hang. That was his—and the

USA's—obligation to the dead. That the USA might also have an obligation to the living didn't seem to have crossed his mind till now. Moss wondered how many other important people's minds it also hadn't crossed. Too many—he was sure of that. People in the USA kept doing their best not to think about Negroes or have anything to do with them, the same as they had ever since the CSA seceded.

Moss finished that second drink and waved for another one. He was also sure of something else. He was sure he'd found himself a new cause.

What happened to your legs?" By the way the girl at Miss Lucy's eyed Michael Pound, he might have come down with a horrible social disease.

He shrugged. "I got caught in a burning barrel."

"Oh." She was about twenty-five, cute enough even if she wasn't gorgeous, and plainly not long on brains. "That must not have been much fun."

"Sweetheart, you said a mouthful. And speaking of which . . ." Pound gestured. With a small sigh, the girl dropped to her knees.

He liked officers' brothels a hell of a lot better than the ones enlisted men had to use. The girls were prettier. Nobody hurried you here, either. That was best of all. He could take his time and enjoy it. He could, and he did.

Afterwards, he left the girl—her name was Betty—a couple of dollars for herself. "You don't need to say anything to Miss Lucy about 'em."

"Well, I'll try. But when it comes to cash, that old bitch has a Y-ranging set like you wouldn't believe." Betty spoke with more resignation than rancor.

Pound got back into his uniform. "See you again, maybe," he said. She nodded. If she was enthusiastic, she hid it very well. She didn't mind his money, but she sure wasn't thrilled about him.

Well, he was old enough to be her father. And he was a damnyankee. And she was a whore and he was a trick. That left it fourth down and time to punt.

Miss Lucy's had a bar, too—one more amenity enlisted men's brothels didn't enjoy. Maybe the assumption was that officers wouldn't get plastered and smash whiskey bottles over each other's heads. From everything Pound had seen, whoever made that assumption was an optimist.

Things seemed peaceable enough in there now. Pound stepped in and asked for a whiskey over ice. "Comin' up," said the woman behind the bar. She was one of the working girls; maybe she had her monthlies or something.

"Thanks," he said when she gave it to him. "Did this place have a regular bartender back before the war?"

"Sure did. But Hadrian, he, uh, don't work here no more."

"Right." Pound knocked back the drink. The booze wasn't bad, but it tasted foul in his mouth. With a name like Hadrian, the ex-bartender had probably been colored. And the odds that he was dead now were pretty damn good. Pound set the glass on the bar. "Let me have another one."

"Sure will." The woman poured whiskey into a fresh glass and added a couple of ice cubes. "Boy, you drank that last one in a hurry."

"Yeah," Pound said. She didn't know what was eating him. She didn't have the faintest idea, as a matter of fact. That she didn't was a measure of the CSA's damnation.

Two good knocks of whiskey made Pound a little less graceful on his burned legs than he would have been without them. He walked back to BOQ through deepening twilight. There was a nip in the air. Tallahassee lay in the northern part of Florida; it got cool in the wintertime, unlike places farther south.

But the weather wasn't the biggest thing on his mind. His head kept going back and forth. He wished he had an eye that would let him see to the rear. This was the time of day when U.S. soldiers got knocked over the head. By the time anyone found them, the bushwhackers were long gone. That didn't keep hostages from being taken and shot, but killing innocent people also made the guerrillas have an easier time recruiting.

He got back to BOQ without any trouble. Most people did, most of the time. Anything that could happen, though, could happen to you. Anybody who didn't understand that never went to war. Being careless—being stupid—made living to a ripe old age less likely. Pound aspired to getting shot by an outraged husband at the age of 103.

When he went to breakfast the next morning, he realized something was up. He didn't know what; Colonel Einsiedel wasn't letting on. Something was cooking, though. A few people in the know were all excited about it, whatever it was. Pound and the others who noticed that tried to get it out of them. The rest of the officers shoveled in bacon and eggs, oblivious to the drama around them.

The double-chinned major sitting next to Pound was one of those. "Dammit, they should have had hash browns," he complained. "I don't like grits." He might not have liked them, but he'd put away a good-sized helping.

Pound didn't like them, either. He also hadn't taken any. He'd doubled up on toast instead. To him, that was simple common sense. It seemed beyond the major.

Dear God! How did we win the war? he thought. That answer seemed only too obvious. There were just as many thumb-fingered, blundering idiots on this side of the former border as on the other one. No matter where you went, you couldn't escape the dullards. Life would have been easier and happier if you could.

That afternoon, the other shoe dropped. Harry Truman was coming to Tallahassee to talk to the troops and to any locals who wanted to listen to him. An officer who was with Pound when the news got out knew exactly what he thought of that: "They better frisk these bastards before they let 'em within rifle range of the guy."

"Amen!" Pound said, and then, a beat later, "Dibs on the girls." He held out his hands as if he were cupping breasts. The other officer laughed.

Truman arrived by airplane two days later. That was judged safer than traveling by train. Sabotaging railroad tracks was easy, but Confederate diehards didn't have much in the way of antiaircraft guns. Pound's barrel was one of the machines guarding the airport as the Vice President–elect's airliner touched down on the runway.

Pound stood up in the cupola and peered at Truman through binoculars. The Senator from Missouri wasn't young, but he walked with crisp stride and straight back: an almost military bearing. Fair enough— he'd been an artillery officer in the Great War. Not many healthy men in the USA had missed military service in one war or the other. Even fewer in what had been the CSA.

The Vice President–elect spoke in front of the state Capitol. They set up a podium and lectern for him by a palm tree on the lawn in front of the Italian Renaissance building. Sure enough, military policemen and female auxiliaries searched people in civilian clothes before letting them past rope lines half a mile from the podium. They also searched uniformed personnel. The war had shown that people had no trouble getting their hands on uniforms that didn't belong to them and doing unpleasant things in the other side's plumage.

What sort of Floridians would listen to the Vice President–elect of the USA? Michael Pound eyed them curiously. Some he recognized— collaborators. They figured they knew which side their bread was buttered on. There'd been some of that flexible breed north of the Ohio a couple of years earlier. They caught hell when they turned out to have guessed wrong. These plump fellows and their sleek women were less likely to be mistaken.

Others—more ordinary folks—seemed honestly curious. That gave Pound at least a little hope. If they could get used to the idea of being part of the USA . . . *It'd take a miracle, and when was the last one you saw?* the cynical part of his mind jeered. The rest of him had no good answer.

Colonel Einsiedel stepped up to the mike mounted on the lectern. "Ladies and gentlemen, it is my pleasure and my privilege to present the Honorable Harry S Truman of Missouri, Vice President–elect of the United States of America."

Along with the other soldiers, Pound clapped till his palms stung. Applause from the local civilians seemed much more measured. Well, that was no surprise. Metal-framed eyeglasses gleaming in the sun, Truman looked out over the crowd. "If anybody would have told me ten years ago that I would come to Florida to speak to my country's soldiers here, I would have said he was crazy." To Pound's ear, shaped in the northern Midwest, Truman's Missouri twang had more than a little in common with the local drawl.

"Didn't Jake Featherston say, 'Give me five years, and you won't recognize the Confederate States'?" the Vice President–elect went on. His jaunty grin invited soldiers and locals alike to see the bitter joke. "Well, the man was right, but not quite the way he expected to be.

"And now the United States have to pick up the pieces. The buck stops with us. If we do this wrong, our grandchildren will be down here fighting guerrillas. If we do it right, maybe we can all remember that we started out as one country. We have a lot of things to put behind us before we're one country again, but we can try."

His voice toughened. "That doesn't mean the USA will be soft down here. You people who spent your lives as Confederates have no reason to love us, not yet. And we have to be careful about trusting you, too. You stained yourself with the darkest crime a people can commit, and too many of you aren't sorry enough. So things won't happen in a hurry, if they happen at all.

"But, for the past eighty-odd years, people in the USA and people in the CSA have all called themselves Americans. Maybe, if we work together, one day that will mean what it did before the War of Secession. Maybe it will mean we really are all part of the same country once again. I hope so, anyhow. That's what President Dewey and I will work for. We'll be as firm as we need to be. But we won't be any firmer than that. If people down here work with us, maybe we'll get where we ought to go. God grant we do."

He stepped away from the lectern. This time, the applause from the soldiers was less enthusiastic, that from the civilians more so. Pound didn't think it was a bad speech. Truman was setting out what he hoped would happen, not necessarily what he expected to happen. If the survivors in the CSA got rambunctious, the Army could always smash them.

The Vice President–elect didn't just go away. He plunged into the crowd, shaking hands and talking with soldiers and locals alike. Reading the ribbons on Michael Pound's chest, he said, "You had yourself a time, Lieutenant."

"Well, sir, that's one way to put it," Pound said.

"I just want you to know that what you're doing here is worthwhile," Truman said. "We have to hold this country down while we reshape it. It won't be easy. It won't be quick. It won't be cheap. But we've got to do it."

"What if we can't?" Pound asked.

"If we can't, some time around the turn of the century the new Vice President–elect will come down here to tell your grandson what an important job he's doing. And they'll still search the locals before they let them listen."

Pound had no children he knew about. The Army had been his life. But he understood what Truman was talking about. "What do you think of our chances?" he asked.

"I don't know." Truman didn't seem to have much patience with beating around the bush. "We've got to try, though. What other choice do we have?"

"Treating these people the way they treated their Negroes." Michael

Pound sounded perfectly serious. He was. He faced the possibility of massacring twenty-odd million people as a problem of ways and means, not an enormity. The Army had been shooting hostages since it entered the CSA. Now the whole Confederacy was a hostage.

But Truman shook his head. "No. Not even these people will ever turn me into Jake Featherston. I'd sooner blow out my own brains." He passed on to another officer.

Had Pound worried about his career, he would have wondered if he'd just blighted it. He didn't. He could go on doing his job right where he was. Even if they busted him down to private for opening his big mouth, he could still help the country. And they wouldn't do that. He knew it. He had his niche. He fit it well. He aimed to stay in it as long as he could.

Winter in Rivière-du-Loup started early and stayed late. After close to three years in warmer climes, Leonard O'Doull had to get used to the weather in the Republic of Quebec again. He tried not to grumble too loud. People here would just laugh at him. They took month after month of snow in stride. They'd never known anything else.

O'Doull had to get used to a new office, too. He hadn't sublet the other one when he rejoined the Army; he'd just let it go. He reached for things in places where they had been, only to find they were somewhere else. Little by little, he made such mistakes less often.

And he had to get used to a practice that wasn't nearly so frantic as what he had been doing. A sty on the eye or a boil on the butt hardly seemed exciting, not after all the quick and desperate surgery he'd performed. In a way, that was heartening. In another way . . . He felt like a man who'd gone from ten cups of coffee a day to none, all at once. Some of the energy had leaked out of his life.

His wife was convinced that was a good thing. "You're home. You can relax," she told him—and told him, and told him. After a while, he got better at pretending to believe her.

One freezing morning in early December, his receptionist said, "A *Monsieur* Quigley is here to see you." She made a hash of the name, as any Francophone would have. O'Doull had had to get used to speaking French again, too. That came back fast. These days, he sometimes switched languages without noticing he was doing it.

"Send him in," he said at once.

Jedediah Quigley had to be well up into his seventies now. The retired U.S. officer was a little stooped, but still seemed spry. "Your country owes you a debt of gratitude, Dr. O'Doull," he said in elegant Parisian French. The back-country patois spoken here had never touched his accent, the way it had O'Doull's.

"That's nice," O'Doull replied in English. He waved to the chair in front of his desk, then pulled out a couple of Habanas. "Cigar?"

"Don't mind if I do," Quigley said. "Where'd you come by these?"

"Friend of mine—a sergeant named Granny McDougald—is a medic in the force occupying Cuba. He sent me a present," O'Doull answered. They both lit up and filled the air with fragrant smoke.

Quigley eyed the cigar with respect. "Smooth! That was mighty kind of him."

"I'll say." Leonard O'Doull nodded. "The box got here a few days ago. Granny and I worked together for a long time, till he took a bullet in the leg. He remembered the name of my home town, and so . . . *Damn* kind of him." O'Doull smiled. McDougald didn't have to do anything like that. If he did it, it was because he wanted to, because he thought the doc he'd worked with was a pretty good guy. Knowing somebody you thought well of figured you were a pretty good guy would make anybody feel good.

"I'm glad you came through in one piece," Quigley said. "I would have felt guilty if you stopped something."

O'Doull didn't laugh in his face, but he came close. "Tell me another one," he said. "You've got the conscience of a snappy turtle."

"Why, Doctor, you say the sweetest things." Damned if Jedediah Quigley didn't bat his eyes. It was as ridiculous as watching Michelangelo's David giggle and simper.

This time, O'Doull did laugh. "Well, what can I do for you, you old fraud?" he said. "Or what are you trying to do to me?"

"Do to you? If I hadn't taken Lucien Galtier's land for that hospital, you never would have met your wife. Is this the thanks I get?" Quigley said.

"*Merci beaucoup.* There. And you sent me off to war, and I almost got ventilated more times than I can count. I'd call that a push, or close enough," O'Doull returned. "And you never come around for no reason. What's your game this time?"

"Game?" Quigley was the picture of offended innocence. "I don't know what you're talking about."

"And then you wake up. Now tell me another one—one I'll believe." O'Doull blew a smoke ring.

"I never could do that," Jedediah Quigley complained. He tried, and blew out a shapeless cloud of smoke. He puffed again, and again managed only a smoke blob. O'Doull sat and waited, smoking his own Habana. Sooner or later, the retired colonel would come to the point. If he wanted to go slow, he could go slow. Maybe a patient would come in. That would give O'Doull an excuse to throw him out.

Time stretched. Quigley smoked his cigar down small. He eyed the glowing coal. O'Doull kept on waiting. Here in Rivière-du-Loup, nothing was likely to happen in a hurry. Relearning that had taken O'Doull a while.

"If you were going to improve U.S. Army medical care, how would you go about it?" Quigley asked at last.

"Simple," O'Doull replied. "I wouldn't get in a war."

"You're not as funny as you think you are," the older man told him.

"Who's joking?" O'Doull said. "It's the God's truth. And I'm a citizen of the Republic. You can't do anything horrible to me unless I'm dumb enough to decide I'll let you."

"The way you were when you put on the uniform again?"

"*Oui. Certainement.* Just like that," O'Doull said. "And I damn well *was* dumb, too. *Calisse!* Was I ever!"

"How many lives did you save?" Quigley asked.

"A good many. But any other doc could have done the same. Hell, Granny McDougald could have saved most of them. An experienced medic gets to where he's just about as good as an M.D. He makes up in experience what he's missing in education."

"That's something we'd want to know. Can you write it down, along with anything else you can think of?"

"Why are you picking me? Why are you picking *on* me?" O'Doull asked. "You've got lots of doctors down in the USA and CSA who still belong to the Army. Let them crank out the recommendations."

"Some of them will." If anything fazed Quigley, he didn't let on. "But we want you, too, exactly because you're an outsider. You don't have a military career to care about. You don't need to worry about stepping on toes."

"Who's 'we'?" O'Doull inquired. "You and your tapeworm? We've got some new medicines for that, too."

He couldn't get a rise out of his not especially welcome guest. "Come on, Doctor. don't be silly. You know I still have connections."

"Sure you do. You're the guy the USA uses to tell the Republic which way to jump," O'Doull said. "But I'm not the Republic, and you're not in Quebec City. So you can play nice or you can get lost."

"I am playing nice," Quigley said. "I could be much less pleasant than I am. But if I browbeat you, you wouldn't do a good job. You really would be helping here, if you'd take the time to do it."

How nasty could Jedediah Quigley be if he set his mind to it? O'Doull wasn't sure he wanted to find out. The thought reshaped itself. He was sure he didn't want to find out. Yes, that was a lot more accurate.

"You talked me into it," he said. Quigley didn't even look smug. He knew he was a power in the land, all right. Grumpily, O'Doull went on, "You know, you'll be making me remember some things I'd rather forget."

People here didn't understand what this war was like. They didn't understand how lucky they were to be ignorant, either. O'Doull would have been happy to let his memories slide down into oblivion, too. But Quigley, damn him, was going to make sure that didn't happen. Once you started putting things down on paper, they were yours forevermore.

All Quigley said was, "This is for your country's good."

O'Doull wasn't having that. "Guys get their balls blown off for their country's good. You think that makes them feel any better about it?"

"No, of course not," Quigley said. "I doubt this will hurt quite so much, though."

He was right, dammit. Sighing, O'Doull asked, "When do you want this report?"

"Two weeks?"

With another sigh, the doctor nodded. "You'll have it." *And stay out of my hair after that.*

"Thank you kindly." By the way Quigley said it, O'Doull was taking care of something he wanted to do, not something he'd been browbeaten into taking on. The older man rose, nodded, and went on his way.

Outside, snow would lie at least ankle deep. This was Rivière-du-Loup, all right. O'Doull had grown up in Massachusetts. He was used to rugged weather. Rivière-du-Loup outdid everything he'd ever known back in the States. It wasn't even close.

Half an hour later, he had a patient. "Hello, Doctor," said Martin Lacroix, a plump, prosperous baker whose shop lay down the street from O'Doull's new office.

"*Bonjour*," O'Doull replied. "What seems to be your trouble, *Monsieur*?"

"Well, I have this rash." Lacroix pulled up his shirt sleeve to display his left biceps. "I've tried home remedies on it, but they don't do much good."

"I'm not surprised—that's ringworm," O'Doull said. "You should keep it covered as much as you can, because it can spread. I'll give you a prescription to take to the pharmacy. Put it on twice a day, and it should clear things up in a month or so."

"A month?" the baker said in dismay. "Why not sooner? If you give me a shot or some pills, can't I get rid of it in a few days?"

People knew there were new medicines that could cure some ailments quickly and easily. Naturally, people thought the new medicines could cure any ailment quickly and easily. But things didn't work that way. O'Doull spent a while explaining the difference between microbes and fungi. He wasn't sure Lacroix got it. The baker left carrying the prescription but shaking his head.

After a case like that, writing about the work O'Doull had done during the war didn't seem so bad. That, at least, had mattered. This? While he was sewing and splinting and cutting, he'd looked forward to this with a fierce and simple longing. Now that he had it again, he discovered the danger of getting exactly what you thought you wanted. It could prove as unfortunate in real life as in fairy tales.

He was home with Nicole. That was as good as it always had been. But his practice . . . After you'd spent time as a battlefield surgeon, prescribing ringworm salve didn't seem the same.

Another patient came in. Françoise Boulanger had arthritis. And well she might—she was seventy-seven, and she'd worked hard all her life. She hurt, and she had trouble moving. O'Doull didn't have much to offer her: aspirin to take the edge from pain and inflammation, heating pads and warm baths to soothe a little. He would have given her the same advice before the Great War. If he'd been practicing before the War of Secession, he would have substituted laudanum for aspirin. Françoise might have got hooked on the opiated brandy, but it would have done as much for her pain as the little white pills did, maybe more.

Leaning on her cane, she shuffled out of the office. *Is this what I've got to look forward to for the rest of my professional life? God!* If he could have brought Nicole with him, he would have run for Alabama and a military hospital.

A little boy with strep throat made him feel happier. Penicillin would take care of that, and would make sure the kid didn't come down with rheumatic fever or endocarditis. O'Doull felt he'd earned his fee there and done some real good. All the same, he wasn't used to taking it easy any more. He wondered if he ever would be.

A corporal waited on the platform when Abner Dowling got off the train at the Broad Street station. Saluting, the noncom said, "I'll take you to the War Department, sir."

"Obliged," Dowling said. The corporal grabbed his suitcase, too. It wasn't heavy, but Dowling didn't complain. Ten years earlier, he knew he would have. He still wasn't as old as George Custer had been when the Great War broke out, but he needed only another six years.

Philadelphia looked better than it had the last time he was there. More craters were filled in. More ruined buildings were torn down. Of course, the superbomb hadn't gone off right here.

"How are things on the other side of the river?" he asked.

"Sir, they're still pretty, uh, fouled up." The corporal would have said something strong talking with one of his buddies. As he braked for a red light, he added, "That's such a big mess, God knows when they'll set it to rights."

"I suppose," Dowling said.

"Believe it, sir. It's the truth." The corporal sounded missionary in his zeal to convince.

Dowling already believed. He'd spent too much time talking with Henderson V. FitzBelmont to do anything else. FitzBelmont wasn't the most exciting man ever born—an understatement. But he'd put a superbomb together while the United States was doing their goddamnedest to blow Lexington off the map. Dowling didn't like him, but did respect his professional competence. So did the U.S. physicists who'd interrogated him. They were impressed he'd done as much as he had under the conditions in which he had to work.

The War Department looked a lot better than it had when the Confederates tried their best to knock it flat. Now repairmen could do their job without fighting constant new damage. The concrete barriers around the massive structure remained in place. No C.S. diehards or Mormon fanatics or stubborn Canucks—rebellion still flared north of the border—could grab an easy chance to auto-bomb the place.

Dowling walked from the barricades up to the entrance. He wheezed climbing the stairs. His heart pounded. He was carrying a lot of weight around, and he'd just reminded himself how young he wasn't. *I made it through the war, though. That's all that—well, most of what—really counts.*

Despite the stars on his shoulder straps, he got frisked before he could go inside. The soldiers who patted him down didn't take anything for granted. When Dowling asked about that, one of them said, "Sir, the way things are, we'll be doing this forever. Too many assholes running around loose—uh, pardon my French."

"I've met the word," Dowling remarked. The enlisted men grinned.

A corporal in a uniform with creases sharp enough to shave with took Dowling down into the bowels of the earth to John Abell's office. These days, the more deeply you were buried, the bigger the wheel you were. And Abell *was* a bigger wheel—he now sported two stars on his shoulder straps.

"Congratulations, Major General," Dowling said, and stuck out his hand.

"Thanks." The General Staff officer's grip was stronger than his slender build and pallid face would have made you think. He'd been fair almost to the point of ghostliness even before he started impersonating a mole. But he had to be really good at what he did to rise as high as he had without a field command. Well, that was nothing Dowling hadn't already known.

"What's the latest?" Dowling asked.

"We finally have a handle on the rising in Saskatoon," Abell answered. "They surrendered on a promise that we'd treat them as POWs—and that we wouldn't superbomb the place."

"Good God!" Dowling said. "Were we thinking of it?"

"No—but the Canucks don't need to know that," the younger man replied.

"Well, well. A use for superbombs I hadn't thought of," Dowling said. "Just knowing we've got 'em on inventory is worth something."

"Indeed," Abell said. "Speaking of which, how is Professor Fitz-Belmont?"

Before answering, Dowling asked, "Am I allowed to talk about that with you?"

Abell's smile was cold, but his smiles usually were. "Oh, yes. That's one of the reasons you were ordered back here."

"He's a more than capable physicist, and he had some good engineers working under him," Dowling said. "That's the opinion of people who ought to know. What with as much of this town as he blew up, I'd say they're right."

"What do we do with him?" Abell asked.

"He's kind of like a bomb himself, isn't he? All that stuff he knows . . . Damn good thing Featherston didn't want to listen to him at first. *Damn* good thing. If the Japs or the Russians kidnapped him, I'd flabble," Dowling said. "And he'd sing. He'd sing like a nightingale. He'd probably think it was . . . interesting."

"Our German allies don't want the Russians getting a super-bomb," Abell said. "Nobody wants the Japanese getting one."

"Except them," Dowling said.

"Yes. Except them." John Abell jotted something in a notebook. Even upside down, his script looked clear and precise. "Probably about time for him to have an unfortunate accident, don't you think? Then we won't have to worry about what he's up to and where he might go—or, as you say, might be taken."

What had he just written down? *Kill Henderson FitzBelmont*, the way someone else might have written *eggs, salami, ½ pound butter?* Dowling didn't know, but that was what he would have bet. And Abell wanted his opinion of the idea, too. What was he supposed to say? What came out of his mouth was, "Well, I think we've learned about as much from him as we're going to."

Abell nodded. "That was my next question."

"If we're going to do this, it really does have to look like an accident," Dowling said. "We give the diehards a martyr if we screw up."

"Don't worry about it. The people we use are reliable," Abell said. "Very sad, but if the professor tried to cross the street in front of a command car . . ."

"I see." Dowling wondered if he saw anything but the tip of the iceberg. "How many Confederates have already had, uh, unfortunate accidents?"

"I can't talk about that with you," the General Staff officer answered. "Some people we can't convict for crimes against humanity still don't deserve to live, though. Or will you tell me I'm wrong?"

Dowling thought about that. He thought about everything that had happened in the CSA since Jake Featherston took over. Slowly, he shook his head. "Nope. I won't say boo."

"Good. I didn't expect you would." Abell gave another of his chilly smiles. "Tell me, General, have you given any thought to your retirement?"

The question might have been a knife in Abner Dowling's guts. *So this is the other reason they called me to Philadelphia*, he thought dully. He didn't know why he was surprised. Not many men his age were still serving. But he thought he'd done as well as a man could reasonably do. Of course, when you got old enough, that didn't mean anything any more. They'd kick you out regardless. If it had happened to George Custer—and it had—it could happen to anybody.

With that in mind, Dowling answered, "Custer got over sixty years in the Army. I've had more than forty myself. That doesn't match him, but it's not a bad run. I'm not ready to go, but I will if the War Department thinks it's time."

"I'm afraid the War Department does," Abell said. "This implies no disrespect: only the desire to move younger men forward. Your career has been distinguished in all respects, and no one would say otherwise."

"If I'd held Ohio . . ." But Dowling shook his head. Even that probably wouldn't have mattered much. The only way you could keep from getting old was by dying before you made it. The past three years, far too many people had done that.

"It's *not* personal or political," Abell said. "I understand that you feel General Custer's retirement was both."

"Oh, it was," Dowling said. "I was there when the Socialists stuck it to him. There was blood on the floor by the time N. Matoon Thomas got done."

"I shouldn't wonder. Custer was a, ah, vivid figure." Abell wasn't lying. And the sun was warm, and the ocean was moist. The General Staff officer went on, "I repeat, though, none of those factors applies in your case."

"Bully," Dowling said—slang even more antiquated than he was. "I get put out to pasture any which way."

"If you'd been asked to retire during the war, it might have shown dissatisfaction with your performance. We needed your experience then. Now we have the chance to train younger men," Abell said.

He was putting the best face he could on it. He wasn't a hundred percent convincing, but he didn't miss by much. Even so . . . "How long before they put *you* out to pasture?" Dowling asked brutally.

"I may have a few more years. Or they may ask me to step down tomorrow," Abell answered with every appearance of sangfroid. "I hope I'll know when it's time to say good-bye. I don't know that I will, but I hope so."

"Time to say good-bye," Dowling echoed. "When I started, no one was sure what the machine gun was worth. Now FitzBelmont talks about blowing up Rhode Island with one bomb."

"Best thing that could happen to it," Abell observed.

"Heh," Dowling said. "Maybe it is time for me to go."

"Believe me, the Army appreciates everything you did," Abell said. "Your success in west Texas changed the whole moral character of the war."

Dowling knew what that meant. Not even U.S. citizens who didn't like Negroes could stomach killing them in carload lots. That was why Jefferson Pinkard would swing. Dowling's Eleventh Army had shown that the massacres weren't just propaganda. The Confederates really were doing those things—and a lot of them were proud of it.

"Well . . . thank you," Dowling said. It wasn't exactly what he'd hoped to be remembered for when he graduated from West Point, but it was better than not being remembered at all. As Custer's longtime adjutant, he'd been only a footnote. The one time he'd been important was when he lied to the War Department about what Custer and Morrell planned to do with barrels. That, he hoped, *wouldn't* go down in history. In this war, he'd carved out a niche for himself. It wasn't a Custer-sized niche. If anybody had that one this time around, it was Irving Morrell. But a niche it was.

"You might do worse than think about publishing your memoirs in timely fashion," Abell said. "A lot of high-ranking officers will be doing that. If you get yours out there before most of the others, it can only work to your advantage."

If I do that, Dowling thought, *I will* have to talk about lying to the War Department. A good many people would read a memoir of his precisely because he'd worked with Custer for so long. But work with

Custer wasn't all he'd done—not even close. Didn't the world deserve to know as much?

"I'll think about it," he said.

"All right." Abell nodded briskly. He'd solved a problem. Dowling wouldn't be difficult, not the way Custer had. The General Staff officer went on, "Do you want to head over to the press office to help them draft a release about your retirement?"

"Do I *want* to?" Dowling shrugged. "Not especially. I will, though." What did Proverbs say? *One generation passeth away, and another generation cometh: but the earth abideth forever.* He hadn't passed away yet, but he was passing. The United States, like the earth, would abide, and he'd helped make that so.

XIX

Hi, hon," Sally Dover said when Jerry came back to the house. "You got a telephone call maybe half an hour ago."

"Oh, yeah?" Dover gave his wife the kind of absentminded kiss people who've been married a long time often share. "Good thing we didn't take it out yet, then." That was coming soon, he feared. You could pretend to stay middle-class for a while when you were out of work, but only for a while. After that, you started saving every cent you could, every way you could. The Dovers weren't eating meat very often these days, and most of the meat they did eat was sowbelly.

"Here's the number." She gave him a scrap of paper.

He'd hoped it would be the Huntsman's Lodge. It wasn't. He knew that number by heart, of course. He knew the numbers for just about all the restaurants in Augusta by heart. This wasn't any of them. If it was anything that had to do with work, whether in a restaurant or not, he would leap at it now.

He dialed the operator and gave her the number. She put the call through. It rang twice before someone on the other end picked it up. "This is Mr. Broxton's residence." The voice was unfamiliar. The accent wasn't—if the man hadn't been born in Mexico, Jerry Dover was an Eskimo.

Hope was also unfamiliar. Charlemagne Broxton—and wasn't that a name to remember?—was the principal owner of the Huntsman's Lodge. Heart thuttering, Dover gave his name. "I'm returning Mr. Broxton's call," he said.

"Oh, yes, sir. One moment, please," the—butler?—said. Back before the war, Charlemagne Broxton had had colored servants. Who among the wealthy in Augusta hadn't? Where were they now? Nobody who'd lived through the war wanted to think about things like that. Nobody on the Confederate side, anyway—the damnyankees were much too fond of asking such inconvenient and embarrassing questions.

"Broxton here." This voice was deep and gruff and familiar. "That you, Dover?"

No. My name's Reilly, and I sell lampshades. The mad, idiot quip flickered through Dover's mind and, fortunately, went out. "Yeah, it's me, Mr. Broxton. What can I do for you, sir?"

"Well, I hear you're looking for work," Broxton said. "How would you like your old job back?"

"I'd like that fine, Mr. Broxton. But what happened to Willard Sloan?" Jerry Dover asked.

Shut up! Are you out of your mind? Sally mouthed at him. He ignored her. No matter how tight things were, he didn't want to put a cripple on the street. That could have happened to him if a bullet or a shell fragment changed course by a few inches.

"Well, we had to let him go," Broxton answered.

"How come?" Dover persisted. "Not for my sake, I hope. He could do the job." Sally looked daggers at him. He went right on pretending not to see.

"Didn't have anything to do with that," Broxton said. Jerry Dover waited. The restaurant owner coughed. "Can you keep this quiet? I don't want to hurt his chances somewhere else."

"C'mon, Mr. Broxton. How many years have you known me? Do I blab?" Dover said.

"Well, no." Charlemagne Broxton coughed again. "We caught him taking rakeoffs from suppliers. Big rakeoffs. And so . . ."

If some food disappeared from the restaurant, well, that was part of the overhead. The manager and the cooks and the waiters and the busboys all stole a little. Skimming cash was something else again. If you got caught, you got canned. The one might not cost more than the other, but it went over the line. Dover wondered why Sloan needed to do it. Was he a gambler? Was he paying somebody else off? (Dover knew too much about that.) Or did he just get greedy? If he did, he was pretty dumb. And so? People *were* dumb, all the goddamn time.

"If you need me back, you know I'll be there," Dover said.

"Good. I hoped you'd say that." Charlemagne Broxton coughed one more time. "Ah . . . There is the question of your pay." He named a figure just over half of what Dover had been making before he went into uniform.

"You can do better than that, Mr. Broxton," Dover said. "I happen to know you were paying Willard Sloan more than that." Sally gave him a Freedom Party salute. He scowled at her; that was dangerous even in private. And if you did it in private you might slip and do it in public. His wife stuck out her tongue at him.

Broxton sighed. "Business isn't what it used to be. But all right. I'll give you what I was giving Sloan." He named another figure, which did indeed just about match what Jerry Dover had heard. Then he said, "Don't try fooling around to bump it up, the way Sloan did."

"If you think I will, you better not hire me," Dover replied.

"If I thought you would, I wouldn't have called," Broxton said. "But I didn't think Sloan would, either, dammit."

"When do you want me to start?" Dover asked.

"Fast as you can get over to the restaurant," the owner answered. "I've got Luis tending to it now, and I want him to go back to boss cook fast as he can. A greaser in that spot'd steal me blind faster'n Sloan did."

From what Jerry Dover had seen, honesty and its flip side had little to do with color. He didn't argue with Charlemagne Broxton, though. "Be there in half an hour," he promised, and hung up.

Sally flew into his arms and kissed him. "They want you back!" she said. He nodded. Her smile was bright as the sun. She'd worked in a munitions plant during the war, but times had been lean since. Money coming in was a good thing.

After Dover detached himself from her, he put on a tie and a jacket and hustled off to the Huntsman's Lodge. He didn't want to be late, even by a minute. As he hurried along Augusta's battered streets, he contemplated ways and means. He didn't want the head cook pissed off at him. That was trouble with a capital T. He'd have to find a way to keep Luis sweet, or else get him out of the restaurant.

To his relief, the Mexican didn't seem angry. "I'd rather cook," he said. "The suppliers, all they do is try to screw you. You want to take it, *Señor* Dover, you welcome to it."

Dover's grin was pure predator. "I don't take it, man. I give it." Luis blinked. Then he grinned, too.

Before Dover could give it, he had to find out what was there. He checked the refrigerators and the produce bins. The menu had changed a little since he went into the Army. Part of that was because some things were unavailable. Part of it was because the damnyankees who made up such a big part of the clientele these days had different tastes from the regulars who'd filled the place before the war.

A glance at the list of telephone numbers in the manager's office said a good many suppliers had changed, too. Some of the old bunch were probably dead. Some were more likely out of business. And some of the new ones had been giving Sloan kickbacks.

"Damned if you don't sound like Jerry Dover," said a butcher Jerry'd known for a long time.

"Yeah, it's me all right, Phil," Dover agreed. "So your days of fucking the Huntsman's Lodge are over, through, finished. Got it?"

"I wouldn't do that!" Phil the butcher sounded painfully pure of heart.

He gave Dover a pain, all right. "Yeah, and then you wake up," he said sweetly.

He also enjoyed introducing himself to the new suppliers. If they gave him what they said they would and gave him decent prices, he didn't expect to have any trouble with them. If they tried to palm crap off on him . . . He chuckled in anticipation. They'd find out. Boy, would they ever!

For tonight, the place would run on what Luis had laid in. From what Dover had seen, the boss cook hadn't done badly. If he didn't want the job—well, that made things easier all the way around.

Most of the time, Jerry stayed behind the scenes. He would only come out and show himself to the customers if somebody wasn't happy and the waiters couldn't set things right by themselves. Tonight, though, he felt not just an urge but an obligation to look around and make sure things ran smoothly. He didn't want Charlemagne Broxton to regret hiring him back.

Everything seemed all right. The Mexican waiters and busboys sounded different from the Negroes who'd been here before, but they knew what to do. He'd started hiring Mexicans during the war. He'd already seen that they weren't allergic to work.

The customers seemed happy. Some of them were locals. One or two even recognized him, which left him surprised and pleased. More were U.S. officers. They didn't know him from a hole in the wall, which suited him fine. If the local women with them did know him, they didn't let on.

Then, around ten o'clock, a woman waved to him. She wasn't local, which didn't mean he didn't know her. He wished he'd stayed in his office. Melanie Leigh waved again, imperiously this time. He didn't want to go over to the table she shared with a U.S. colonel, but he feared he had no choice.

"Hello, Jerry," she said, as brightly as if she hadn't been his blackmailing mistress and a likely Yankee spy. "Don, this is Lieutenant-Colonel Jerry Dover. We've been friends a long time. Jerry, this is Don Gutteridge."

"I'm very retired, Colonel Gutteridge," Dover said, hesitantly offering his hand.

Gutteridge shook it. He was about fifty, in good hard shape for his age. "You were in the Quartermaster Corps, isn't that right?" he said.

Dover nodded. "Uh-huh. How did you know?" He looked at Melanie. Her blue eyes might have been innocence itself . . . or they might not have. Knowing her, they probably weren't.

"Let me buy you a drink, Dover, and I'll tell you about it," Gutteridge said. "War's over. We can talk about some things now that we couldn't before."

At his wave, a waiter appeared. He ordered whiskey all around, asking Dover with his eyebrows if that was all right. Dover nodded. The waiter went away. Before the drinks came back, Dover asked, "Were you Melanie's . . . handler? Isn't that what the spies call it?"

"Yeah, I was, and yeah, that's what we call it," Gutteridge answered easily. "You almost got her caught, you know."

Jerry Dover shrugged, as impassively as he could. "I gave it my best shot. I could afford the money—and I got value received for it, too," he said. Melanie turned red; she was fair enough to make that obvious, even in the low light inside the Huntsman's Lodge. Dover went on, "I could afford that, yeah, but I didn't want to pass on any secrets. And so I talked to some of our own Intelligence boys, and. . . ."

"I didn't even wait for the answer to the letter I sent you," Melanie said. "Something didn't feel right, so I took a powder."

The drinks arrived. Dover needed his. "How'd you land on me, anyway?" he said.

"In the trade, it's called a honey trap," Gutteridge answered for his former lover. "We ran 'em all over the CSA, with people we might be able to squeeze if push ever came to shove again. It wasn't like your people didn't run 'em in the USA, either."

"A honey trap. Oh, boy," Jerry Dover said in a hollow voice. He looked at Melanie. "I thought you meant it."

"With you . . . I came a lot closer than I did with some others," Melanie said.

"Great. Terrific." He finished the drink in a gulp. What did they say? *A fool and his money are soon parted.* He'd parted with money, and he'd been a fool. He'd needed a while to realize how big a fool he'd been, but here it was in all its glory. He got to his feet. " 'Scuse me. I have to go back to work." Well, he wouldn't be that kind of fool again—he hoped. He hurried away from the table.

You know what Mobile is?" Sam Carsten said.

"Tell me," Lon Menefee urged him.

"Mobile is what New Orleans would've been if it was settled by people without a sense of humor," Sam said. New Orleans was supposed to be a town where you could go out and have yourself some fun. People in Mobile looked as if they didn't enjoy anything.

"Boy, you've got something there," the exec said, laughing. "Even the good-time girls don't act like they're having a good time."

"Yeah, I know." Sam had seen that for himself. He didn't like it. "Pretty crazy—that's all I've got to tell you. This was a Navy town, too. If a bunch of horny, drunk sailors won't liven you up, what will?"

"Beats me," Menefee said.

Sam pointed. "Crap, that's their Naval Academy, right over there." It and the whole town lay under the *Josephus Daniels*' guns. Several C.S. Navy ships and submersibles lay at the docks. U.S. caretaker crews were aboard them. Sam didn't know what would happen to them. People were still arguing about it. Some wanted to take the captured vessels into the U.S. Navy. Others figured the spares problem would be impossible, and wanted to scrap them instead.

"Academy's out of business," Menefee said. Sam nodded. All the cadets had been sent home. They weren't happy about it. Some wanted to join the U.S. Navy instead. Some wanted to shoot every damnyankee ever born. They weren't quite old enough to have had their chance at that. The exec waved toward the Confederate warships. "What do you think we ought to do with those, sir?"

"Razor blades," Sam said solemnly. "Millions and millions of god-damn razor blades."

Menefee grinned. Anything large, metallic, and useless was only good for razor blades—if you listened to sailors, anyhow.

Here on the Gulf coast, winter was soft. Sam had wintered in the Sandwich Islands, so he'd known softer, but this wasn't bad. Things stayed pretty green. It hadn't snowed at all—not yet, anyhow. "A couple of more days and it's 1945," he said. "Another year down."

"A big one," Lon Menefee said. "Never been a bigger one."

He wasn't old enough to remember much about 1917. Maybe that had seemed bigger in the USA. Nobody then had known how awful a war could be. A lot of people were inoculated against that ignorance now. And 1917 had shown the USA *could* beat the Confederate States and their allies. Up till then, the United States never had. Now . . . Maybe now the USA wouldn't have to go and do this all over again. Sam could hope so, anyhow.

He didn't feel like arguing with the younger man, nor was he sure he should. "What with the superbomb and everything, I'd have a devil of a time saying you're wrong."

"We've got it," the exec said. "Germany's got it. The Confederates had it, but they're out. The limeys had it, but—"

"Maybe they're out," Sam put in. "You never can tell about England."

"Yeah," Menefee said. "Japan and Russia and France all have the hots for it."

"I would, too, if somebody else had it and I didn't," Sam said. "I remember how rotten I felt when Featherston got Philly. If he'd had a dozen more ready to roll, he might have whipped us in spite of everything."

"Good thing he didn't," the exec said. "But how are you supposed to fight a war if everybody's got bombs that can blow up a city or a flotilla all at once?"

"Nobody knows," Sam answered. "I mean nobody. The board that talked to me when we came in for refit right after the war ended asked if *I* had any bright ideas. Me!" He snorted at how strange that was. "I mean, if they're looking for help from a mustang with hairy ears, they're really up the creek."

"Maybe the Kaiser will be able to keep England from building any more and France from getting started. Japan and Russia, though? Good luck stopping 'em!" Menefee said.

"Uh-huh. That occurred to me, too. I don't like it any better than you do," Carsten said.

"It's going to be trouble, any which way," Menefee predicted.

"No kidding," Sam said. "Of course, you can say that any day of the year and be right about nine times out of ten. But just the same . . . Hell, if Germany and the USA were the only countries that could make superbombs, how could we stay friends? It'd be like we mopped the floor with everybody else, and we had to see who'd end up last man standing."

"Hard to get a superbomb across the ocean," Menefee said. "We don't have a bomber that can lift one off an airplane carrier, and the Kaiser doesn't have any carriers at all."

"We don't have a bomber that can do it now. Five years from now? It'll be different," Sam said. "They'll shrink the bombs and build better airplanes. Turbos, I guess. That's how those things always work. I remember the wood and wire and fabric two-decker we flew off the *Dakota* in 1914. We thought we were *so* modern!" He laughed at his younger self.

Lon Menefee nodded. "Yeah, you're probably right, skipper. But the Germans still don't have carriers."

"Maybe they'll build 'em. Maybe they'll decide they don't need 'em. Maybe they'll make extra-long-range bombers instead. If I were fighting the Russians, I'd sure want some of those. Or maybe they'll make rockets, the way the damn Confederates did. I bet we try that, too. How's anybody going to stop a rocket with a superbomb in its nose?"

The exec gave him a peculiar look. "You know what, skipper? I can see why the board asked you for ideas. You just naturally come up with things."

"Well, if I do, the pharmacist's mates have always been able to treat 'em," Sam answered. Praise—especially praise from a bright Annapolis grad—never failed to make him nervous.

He got a grin from Menefee, but the younger man persisted: "If you'd gone to college, you'd be an admiral now."

Sam had heard that before. He didn't believe it for a minute. "I didn't even finish high school. Didn't want to, either. All I wanted to do was get the hell off my old man's farm, and by God I did that. And if I was the kind of guy who went to college, chances are I wouldn't've been the kind of guy who wanted to join the Navy. Nope, I'm stuck with the school of hard knocks."

"Maybe. But it's still a shame," the exec said.

"Don't flabble about me, Lon. You're the one who'll make flag rank. I like where I'm at just fine." Sam wasn't kidding. Two and a half stripes! Lieutenant commander! Not bad for a man up through the hawse hole, not even a little bit. And his superiors still wanted him around. Maybe he *could* dream of making commander, at least when they finally retired him. He sure hadn't wasted any time sewing the thin gold stripe between the two thicker ones on each cuff.

He'd flustered Menefee in turn. "Flag rank? Talk about counting your chickens! I just want to see what I can do with a ship of my own."

"I understand that." Sam had waited a long, long time for the *Josephus Daniels*. But doors opened to young Annapolis grads that stayed closed for graying mustangs.

Menefee pointed across the water. "Supply boat's coming up."

Before Sam could say anything, the bosun's whistle shrilled. "Away boarding parties!" Sailors armed with tommy guns went down into a whaleboat at the archaic command. Others manned the destroyer escort's twin 40mms. After that bumboat attacked the *Oregon*, nobody took chances.

If the boat didn't stop as ordered, the guns would stop it. But it did. The boarding party checked every inch of the hull before letting it approach. Sam hadn't had to say a word. He smiled to himself. This was the way things worked when you had a good crew.

Sooner or later, conscripts would replace a lot of his veteran sailors. By now, he knew what he needed to know about whipping new men into shape. He didn't look forward to the job, but he could do it.

Meat and fresh vegetables started coming aboard the destroyer escort. The chow was better than it had been when she spent weeks at a time at sea. Sam had never been one to cling to routine for its own sake. If he never tasted another bean as long as he lived, he wouldn't be sorry.

"I'm going to my cabin for a spell, Lon," he said. "The paperwork gets worse and worse—and if something disappears now, we can't just write it off as lost in battle, the way we could before. Damn shame, if you ask me."

"Sure did make the ship's accounts easier," Menefee agreed. "Have fun, skipper."

"Fat chance," Sam said. "But it's got to be done."

Dealing with the complicated paperwork of command might have been the toughest job for a mustang who'd never been trained to do it. You could end up in hock for tens of thousands of dollars if you didn't keep track of what was what, or if you absentmindedly signed the wrong form. Because he'd had to start from scratch, Sam was extra scrupulous about double-checking everything before his name went on it.

He absently scratched the back of his left hand, which itched. Then he went back to making sure of his spare-parts inventory. Some of that stuff—the part that petty officers found useful—had a way of walking with Jesus.

A few minutes later, he noticed his hand was bleeding. He swore and grabbed for a tissue. He must have knocked off a scab or something. When he looked, he didn't see one. The blood seemed to be coming from a mole instead. After a while, it stopped. Sam went back to work.

Things on the *Josephus Daniels* were just about the way they were supposed to be. If he had to turn the ship over to a new CO tomorrow, he could without batting an eye. His accounts were up to date, and they were accurate—or, where they weren't, nobody could prove they weren't. People said there was a right way, a wrong way, and a Navy way. He'd used the Navy way to solve his problems about missing things.

Sam grinned. Of course he'd used the Navy way. What other way did he know? He'd given the Navy his whole life. He hadn't known he would do that when he signed up, but he wasn't disappointed. He'd sure done more and seen more of the world that he would have if he'd stayed on the farm.

The only way he'd leave now was if they threw him out or if he dropped dead on duty. He'd been scared they would turn him loose when the war ended, but what did they go and do? They promoted him instead.

"Nope, only way I'm going out now is feet first," he murmured. "And even then, the bastards'll have to drag me."

A U.S. warship under his command anchored in Mobile Bay? He'd never dreamt of that when he signed on the dotted line. He hadn't imagined he could become an officer, not then. And he hadn't imagined the USA would ever take the CSA right off the map. The way it looked to him then—the way it looked to everybody—both countries, and their rivalry, would stick around forever.

Well, nothing lasted forever. He'd found that out. You went on and did as well as you could for as long as you could. When you got right down to it, what else was there?

Miguel Rodriguez said . . . something. "What was that?" Jorge asked.

His brother tried again. "Water," he managed at last.

"I'll get you some." Jorge hurried to the sink and turned the tap. When he was a little boy, he would have had to go to the well. This was so much easier.

Bringing the water back to Miguel, seeing his brother again, was so much harder. Now he understood why the Yankees had kept Miguel so long. Miguel sat in a U.S.-issue military wheelchair. He would never walk again. So said the letter that came with him, and Jorge believed it. His body was twisted and ruined. So was his face. U.S. plastic surgeons had done what they could, but they couldn't work miracles.

The shell that didn't quite kill him damaged his thinking, too—or maybe he was trapped inside his own mind, and his wounds wouldn't let him come out. The U.S. doctors had kept him alive, but Jorge wasn't even slightly convinced they'd done him any favors.

He gave Miguel the cup. His brother needed to take it in both hands; he couldn't manage with one. Even then, Jorge kept one of his hands under the cup, in case Miguel dropped it. He didn't, not this time, but he did dribble water down what was left of his chin. Jorge wiped it dry with a little towel.

How long could Miguel go on like this? Ten years? Twenty? Thirty? Fifty? Would you want to go on like this for fifty years? If somebody took care of you, though, what else would you do?

Pedro came in and looked at Miguel, then quickly looked away. What had happened to his brother tore at him even worse than it did at Jorge. And what it did to their mother . . . Jorge tried not to think about that, but he couldn't help it. She'd be taking care of and mourning a cripple for as long as she or Miguel lived.

"Those bastards," Pedro said savagely. "Damnyankee bastards!"

"I think they did the best they could for him," Jorge said. "If they didn't, he'd be dead right now."

Pedro looked at him as if he were an idiot. "Who do you think blew him up in the first place? Damnyankee *pendejos*, that's who."

He was probably right—probably, but not certainly. Jorge had seen men wounded and killed by short rounds from their own side. He didn't try to tell his brother about that—Pedro was in no mood to listen. He just shrugged. "It's the war. We all took chances like that. What can you do about it now? What can anyone do?"

"Pay them back," Pedro insisted. "*Señor* Quinn says we can do it if we don't give up. I think he's right."

"I think you're *loco*," Jorge said. "What happens if you shoot somebody? They take hostages, and then they kill them. They take lots of hostages. They've already done it here once. You think they won't do it again?"

"So what?" Pedro said. "It will only make the rest of the people hate them."

"Suppose they take Susana or her kids? Suppose they take Lupe Flores?" Jorge said, and had the dubious satisfaction of watching his brother turn green. Yes, Pedro was sweet on Lupe, all right. Jorge pressed his advantage: "Suppose they take *Mamacita*? Will you go on yelling, 'Freedom!' then? It's over, Pedro. Can't you see that?"

Pedro swore at him and stormed out of the farmhouse again. Jorge noticed his own hands had folded into fists. He made them unclench. He didn't want to fight Pedro. He didn't want his brother doing anything stupid and useless, either. The Army had taught him one thing, anyhow: you didn't always get what you wanted.

Miguel had listened to everything. How much he'd understood . . . How much Miguel understood was always a question. It probably always would be. He struggled with his damaged flesh and damaged spirit, trying to bring out words. "Not good," he managed. "Not good."

"No, it isn't good," Jorge agreed. Just how his injured brother meant that . . . who could say? But Miguel wasn't wrong any which way. If Pedro went and did something stupid, people for miles around could end up paying for it.

Miguel tried saying something else, but it wouldn't come out, whatever it was. Sometimes Jorge thought Miguel knew everything that was going on around him but was trapped inside his own head by his wounds. Other times, he was sure Miguel's wits were damaged, too. Which was worse? He had no idea. Both were mighty bad.

If Pedro really was planning on doing something idiotic . . . Whatever Jorge did, he would never betray his own flesh and blood to the occupiers. If you did something like that, you might as well be dead, because you *were* dead to all human feeling. But that didn't mean he couldn't do anything at all.

The next time he went into Baroyeca, he did it. Then he went into *La Culebra Verde* and drank much more beer than he was in the habit of putting down. He didn't walk back to the farmhouse—he staggered. If the electric poles hadn't marched along by the side of the road to guide him back, he might have wandered off and got lost.

His mother looked at him with imperfect delight when he came in. "Your father didn't do this very often," she said severely. "I wouldn't stand for it from him. I won't stand for it from you, either."

"Shorry—uh, sorry—*Mamacita*," Jorge said.

"And don't think you can sweet-talk me, either," his mother went on. "You can call me *Mamacita* from now till forever, and I'll still know you've come home like a worthless, drunken stumblebum. I told you once, and I'll tell you again—I won't put up with it."

Jorge didn't try to argue. He went to bed instead. He woke up with his head feeling as if it were in the middle of an artillery barrage. Aspirins and coffee helped . . . some. Pedro eyed him with amused contempt that was almost half admiration. "You tied a good one on there," he remarked.

"*Sí.*" Jorge didn't want to talk—or to listen, for that matter. He poured the coffee cup full again.

"How come?" Pedro asked him. "You don't usually do that." Miguel sat in the wheelchair watching both of them, or maybe just lost in his own world.

"Everything," Jorge said. "Sometimes it gets to you, that's all." He wasn't even lying, or not very much.

Pedro nodded vigorously. "It does. It really does! But I don't want to get drunk on account of it. I want to do something about it."

You want to do something stupid about it, Jorge thought. He kept that to himself. If you got into an argument when you were hung over, you were much too likely to get into a brawl. He didn't want to punch Pedro—most of the time, anyhow.

The Bible said a soft answer turned away wrath. No answer seemed to work just as well. When Jorge didn't rise to the bait, Pedro left him alone. He wondered whether he ought to remember that lesson for later. A shrug was all he could give the question. Maybe he would, maybe he wouldn't.

He went on about his business. Even in winter, the farm needed work. He tended the garden and the livestock. He went into Baroyeca once more, and came back sober. Magdalena Rodriguez nodded to him in somber approval.

Then Pedro went into town a few days later. When he came home, he was wild with rage. "The Yankees! They've taken *Señor* Quinn!"

"I was afraid of that," Jorge said.

"But how could they know what he stands for?" Pedro demanded.

"He talks too much," Jorge answered, which was true. "And too many people know he was the Freedom Party man here. Someone in town must have blabbed to the *soldados* from *los Estados Unidos*." Most of that was true, but not all.

"What can we do?" his brother cried.

"I don't know. I don't think we can do anything. The Yankees have machine guns and automatic rifles. I don't want to go up against them. If you do, you have to be out of your mind."

Pedro frowned; that wasn't what he wanted to hear. "I hope nobody decides to inform on me," he said. "All we've got here are a couple of .22s, and you can't fight anybody with those."

"Of course not. That's why the Yankees let us keep them," Jorge said. Then his brother brightened. "Maybe we could get some dynamite from the mines, and we could—"

"Could what?" Jorge broke in. "You can't fight with dynamite, either. What are you going to do, throw sticks of it?"

"Well, no. But if we made an auto bomb—"

"Out of what? We don't have an auto," Jorge reminded him. "Besides, do you know how many the Yankees shoot for every auto bomb that goes off?"

"We've got to do something for *Señor* Quinn," Pedro said.

"*Bueno*. What do you want to do? What can you do that will set him free and won't get us into trouble?"

Pedro thought about it. The longer he thought, the more unhappy he looked. "I don't know," he said at last.

"Well, when you answer that, then maybe you can do something. Now we have to worry about keeping ourselves safe, and keeping *Mamacita* safe, and keeping Miguel safe," Jorge said.

Miguel sat in the wheelchair. Was he listening to his brothers argue, or not paying any attention at all? Jorge was never sure how much Miguel understood. Sometimes he even thought it varied from day to day. Now, though, Miguel's eyes came alive for a moment. "Stay safe!" he said clearly. "Get down!" Was that the last thing he said or the last thing he heard before the shell crashed down and ruined his life? Jorge wouldn't have been surprised.

Pedro gnawed on the inside of his lower lip. "You can put up with things easier than I can, Jorge."

"Sometimes, maybe," Jorge said.

"But it gets to you, doesn't it? It gets to you, too." His brother pointed an accusing forefinger at him. "Otherwise, why did you need to go to the cantina and get drunk?"

Jorge spread his hands. "Well, you've got me there."

"I thought so." Pedro sounded smug. Not many things anyone liked better than being sure he knew what someone else was thinking.

"Careful," Miguel said, maybe at random, maybe not. Was he still thinking about getting shelled? Or was he warning Pedro not to think he was so smart? How could anyone outside the wreckage of his body and mind and spirit guess?

With a sigh, Pedro said, "I *will* be careful. I won't do anything that gets us into trouble or gets us hurt."

"That's the idea." Jorge hoped his brother would keep the promise. "Maybe things will get better. We just have to wait and see—what else can we do that's safe?"

"*Señor* Quinn didn't talk that way." Pedro wasn't ready to give up, not quite.

"No, he didn't," Jorge agreed. "And look what happened to him. If he'd just tried to fit in, the Yankees would have let him alone, I bet. But he started running his mouth, and—"

"Some dirty *puto* ratted on him," Pedro said savagely.

"*Sí*. It only goes to show, it can happen to anybody who isn't careful," Jorge said.

He knew what he was talking about. He knew more than he would ever talk about. He'd written the anonymous letter that betrayed Robert Quinn to the U.S. authorities. He hadn't been happy about it, not then. That was why he came home drunk that evening. But he wasn't sorry now that he'd done it. He'd kept Pedro safe—safer, anyhow. He'd done the same thing for the whole family. They could go on. After you lost a war, that would do.

* * *

George Enos and Wally Fodor and most of the other guys at the twin-40mm mount had their shirts off. They basked in the warm sunshine like geckos on a rock. "January," George said to the gun chief. "Fuckin' January. I tell you, man, Florida's been wasted on the Confederates too goddamn long."

"You got that straight," Fodor agreed.

It was somewhere close to eighty. Up in Boston, the snow lay thick on the ground. George had just got a letter from Connie talking about the latest blizzard. He missed his wife. He missed his kids. He sure as hell didn't miss Massachusetts weather.

"When I get old and gray, I'll retire down here," he said.

"Good luck, buddy. The Confederates'll blow your old gray ass from here to Habana," Wally Fodor said. "Do you really think these guys'll be glad to see us even by the time we get old?"

"Probably be glad to take our money," George said.

The gun chief laughed. "Like that's the same thing. A whore's glad to take your money, but that doesn't mean she's in love with you." Fodor laughed again. "Hell with me if you ain't blushing."

"Hell with you anyway, Wally." George smiled when he said it, but he knew how uneasy the smile was. He always felt bad about going to brothels. That didn't stop him, but it made him flabble afterwards.

All the joking stopped when a supply boat approached the *Oregon*. The 40mm crews and even the men on the battlewagon's five-inch guns covered the vessel while sailors searched it. That was, of course, locking the door with the horse long gone, but what else could you do? The diehards might hurt other warships, but they wouldn't get the *Oregon* again.

Everybody hoped like hell they wouldn't, anyhow.

This particular boat proved harmless. So the searchers said. If they were wrong, if the locals had outfoxed them . . . George did his best not to think about that. He breathed a sigh of relief when hams and flitches of bacon and sides of beef came aboard. Nothing explosive there.

He wasn't the only one who relaxed after seeing everything was on the up and up. "We keep eating awhile longer," Wally Fodor said.

"Yeah." George nodded. "We keep breathing awhile longer, too. Ain't it a pisser that we aren't getting combat pay any more?"

"Hey, we're at peace now, right?" Fodor said, and the whole gun crew laughed sarcastically. He went on, " 'Sides, all the bookkeepers in the Navy Department are a bunch of damn Jews, and they make like it's their own personal money they're saving, for Chrissake. You ask me, we're fuckin' lucky we still get hazardous-duty pay."

"What would you call it when the bumboat blows us halfway to hell?" George said. "Hazardous enough for me, by God."

"Amen, brother," the gun chief said, as if George were a colored preacher heating up his flock.

The gun crews also covered the supply boat as it pulled away from the *Oregon*. If its crew were going to try anything, logic said they'd do it while they lay right alongside the battleship. But logic said people down here shouldn't try anything at all along those lines. They were well and truly licked. Didn't they understand as much? By the evidence, no.

A few minutes after the boat drew too far away to be dangerous, the *Oregon*'s PA system crackled to life. "George Enos, report to the executive officer's quarters! George Enos, report to the executive officer's quarters on the double!"

As George hurried away from the gun, Wally Fodor called after him: "Jesus, Enos! What the fuck did you do?"

"I don't know." George fought to keep panic from his voice. If the exec wanted you, it was like getting called to the principal's office in high school. Here, George figured he'd be lucky to come away with only a paddling. But he wasn't lying to Fodor, either—he had no idea why he was getting summoned like this. Did they think he'd done something he hadn't? God forbid, had something happened to his family? He found the rosary in his trouser pocket and started working the beads.

Going up into officers' country gave him the willies on general principles. He had to ask a j.g. younger than he was for help finding the exec's quarters. The baby lieutenant told him what he needed to know, and sent him a pitying look as he went on his way. By now, the whole ship would be wondering what he'd done. And he was wondering himself—he had no idea.

He knocked on the open metal door. "Enos reporting, sir."

"Come in, Enos." Commander Hank Walsh was about forty, with hard gray eyes and what looked like a Prussian dueling scar seaming his left cheek. "Do you know a Boston politico named Joe Kennedy?"

"Name rings a bell." George had to think for a couple of seconds. "Yeah—uh, yes, sir. He used to get my mother to do work for the Democrats sometimes." What he really remembered was his mother's disdain for Kennedy. Piecing together some stuff he hadn't understood when he was a kid, he suspected Kennedy had made a pass, or maybe several passes, at her.

"Family connection, is there?" Walsh said. George only shrugged; he hadn't thought so. The exec eyed him. "Well, whatever there is, he's pulled some strings. You can have your discharge if you want it, go back home and pick up your life again. I've got the papers right here."

"You mean it, sir?" George could hardly believe his ears.

"I mean it." Commander Walsh didn't sound delighted, but he nodded. "It's irregular, but it's legal. No hard feelings here. I know you're not a regular Navy man. I know you have a family back in Boston. You've served well aboard the *Oregon*, and your previous skippers gave you outstanding fitness reports. If you want to leave, you've paid your dues."

George didn't hesitate for a moment. Walsh might change his mind. "Where's the dotted line, sir? I'll sign."

The exec shoved papers across the desk at him and handed him a pen. "This is the Navy, Enos. You can't get away with signing just once."

So George signed and signed and signed. He would have signed till he got writer's cramp, but it wasn't so bad as that. When he got to the bottom of the stack of papers, he said, "There you go, sir."

"Some of these are for you, for your records and to show the shore patrol and the military police to prove you're not AWOL." Walsh handed him the ones he needed to keep. "Show them to your superiors, too. We're sending a boat ashore at 1400. Can you be ready by then?"

By the clock on the wall behind the exec, he had a little more than an hour to let people know and throw stuff into a duffel. "I sure can. Thank you, sir!"

"Don't thank me. Thank Joe Kennedy." Walsh raised an eyebrow. "I wouldn't be surprised if you get the chance to do just that once you're home. If Kennedy's like most of that breed, he'll expect favors from you now that he's done you one. Nothing's free, not for those people."

From what George knew of Joe Kennedy, he figured the exec had hit that one dead center. "I'll worry about it when it happens, sir. . . . Oh! Could you have somebody wire my wife and let her know I'm coming home?"

Commander Walsh nodded. "We'll take care of it. Get moving. You don't have a lot of time."

"Aye aye, sir." George jumped to his feet and saluted. "Thanks again, sir!"

When he showed Wally Fodor his discharge papers, the gun chief made as if to tear them up. George squawked. Grinning, Fodor handed back the precious papers. "Here you go. Good luck, you lucky stiff!"

A sailor in the waiting boat grabbed George's duffel at 1400 on the dot. George climbed down into the boat. The sailor steadied him. The boat's outboard motor chugged. It pulled away from the *Oregon*. George didn't look back once.

When he came ashore, he got a ride to the train station in an Army halftrack. "Nice to know they love us down here," he remarked to the soldier sitting across from him.

"Yeah, well, fuck 'em," the guy in green-gray said, which only proved the Army and the Navy had the same attitude about the Confederates.

The station was a young fortress, with concrete barricades keeping motorcars at a distance. There were barrels near the entrance, and machine guns on the roof. George showed his papers at the ticket counter and got a voucher for the trip up to Boston. When the train came in, it had machine guns atop several cars. All the same, bullet holes pocked the metalwork.

Most of the men aboard were soldiers going home on leave. When they found out George didn't have to come back, they turned greener than their uniforms. *You lucky stiff* was the least of what he heard from them. George just smiled and didn't let them provoke him. He didn't intend to end up in the brig instead of in Connie's arms.

Nobody fired at the train while it worked its way through the wreckage of the Confederacy. As George had when he traveled through the USA during the war, he eyed the damage with amazement—and with relief that he hadn't had to fight on land. He'd seen plenty of danger, but it might have been nothing next to this. Connie'd got mad at him for joining the Navy, but he figured he was more likely never to have come home if he'd waited for the Army to conscript him. Of course, his old man had made the same calculation. . . .

What now? he wondered. Now he would go out to T Wharf, hope his boat didn't hit a mine loose from its moorings, and come home to watch the kids grow up and to watch Connie get old. It wasn't the most exciting way to pass the next thirty or forty years he could think of. But he'd had enough excitement to last him the rest of his days. Fishing was honest work. What more could you want, really?

The stretch from the border up past Philadelphia was as battered as anything down in the CSA. He didn't see any of the damage from the superbomb in Philly—or miss it. The towns closer to New York City hadn't been hit so hard. From New York City north, he saw only occasional damage. The main exception was Providence. The Confederates had plastered the Navy training center as hard as they could.

And then he got into Boston. On other leaves, he'd seen the pounding his home town had taken. Now he had other things on his mind, and hardly noticed. He slung his duffel over his shoulder and pushed out of the train car. Lots of people—sailors, soldiers, civilians—were getting off here.

"George!" Connie yelled, at the same time as the boys were squealing, "Daddy!"

He hugged his wife and squeezed his kids and kissed everybody. "Jesus, it's good to be home!" he said. "You know that Kennedy guy pulled wires for me?"

"I hoped he would," Connie said. "I wrote him about how you'd been in long enough and who your folks were and everything, and it worked!" She beamed.

He kissed her again. "Except on a fishing boat, I'm never leaving this town again," he said. Connie cheered. The boys clapped. They tried to carry the duffel bag. Between them, they managed. That let him put one arm around them and the other arm around Connie. It was an awkward way to leave the platform, but nobody cared a bit.

Rain drummed down out of a leaden sky. Chester Martin's breath smoked whenever he went outside. It was nasty and chilly and muddy. He only laughed. He'd lived here long enough to know this was nothing out of the ordinary. "January in Los Angeles," he said.

Rita laughed, too. "The Chamber of Commerce tries not to tell people about this time of year."

"Yeah, well, if I were them, I wouldn't admit it, either," Chester said. "They do better with photos of orange trees and pretty girls on the beach."

"I've never seen a photo of an orange tree on the beach," Carl said. While Chester was off being a top kick, his son had acquired a quirky sense of humor. Chester sometimes wondered where the kid had got it. Knowing Carl, he'd probably won it in a poker game.

"You might as well hang around the house today," Rita said. "There won't be any work."

"Boy, you got that right," Chester agreed. Rain in L.A. left construction crews sitting on their hands. "In the Army, they just went ahead and built stuff, and the heck with the lousy weather."

"Yeah, but you're not in the Army any more. Good thing, too, if anybody wants to know what I think." By the way Rita said it, he'd better want to know what she thought.

"Hey, you get no arguments from me. It wasn't a whole lot of fun." Chester still didn't want to think about what he'd done in that little South Carolina town. Oh, he wasn't the only one. He could blame Lieutenant Lavochkin for most of it. He could—and he did. But he was there, too. He pulled the trigger lots more than once. That was one thing he never intended to talk about with anybody.

Carl asked, "If it wasn't any fun, why did you do it?"

"Good question," Rita said. "Maybe you can get a decent answer out of him. I never could." She gave Chester a dirty look. She still resented his putting the uniform back on. Chances were she always would.

He shrugged. "If Jake Featherston beat us this time around, I was just wasting my time in the last war. I didn't want that to happen, so I tried to stop it."

"Oh, yeah. You were going to whip Jake Featherston all by yourself. And then you wake up," Rita said.

"Not all by myself. That colored kid did, though." Chester shook his head. "Boy, am I jealous of him. Me and all the other guys who put on the uniform. But everybody who fought set things up so he could do it." He looked at his son. "Is that a good enough answer for you?"

"No," Rita said before Carl could open his mouth. "All it did was get you shot again. You're just lucky you didn't get your head blown off."

"I'm fine." Chester had to speak carefully. Rita's first husband *had* bought a plot during the Great War. "Wound I picked up doesn't bother me at all, except in weather like this. Then it aches a little. That's it, though."

"Luck. Nothing but luck," Rita said stubbornly, and Chester couldn't even tell her she was wrong.

"How many people did you shoot, Dad?" Carl asked.

That made Chester think of the massacre again. It also made him think of firing-squad duty. Neither of those was what his son had in mind, which didn't mean they hadn't happened. "Some," Chester answered after a perceptible pause. "I don't always like to remember that stuff."

"I should hope not!" Rita made a face.

"Why don't you?" Carl asked. "You joined the Army to kill people, right?"

Rita made a different face this time, a see-what-you-got-into face. Chester sighed. "Yeah, that's why I joined," he said, as steadily as he could. "But it's not so simple. You look at a guy who got wounded, and you listen to him, and it doesn't matter which uniform he's wearing. He looks the same, and he sounds the same—like a guy who's been in a horrible traffic accident. You ever see one of those?"

Carl nodded. "Yeah. It was pretty bad. Blood all over the place."

"All right, then. You've got half an idea of what I'm talking about, anyway. Well, imagine you just ran over somebody. That's kind of the way you feel when you've been through a firefight."

"But when you're in a wreck, the other guy isn't trying to hit you," Carl objected.

"I know. Knowing he's trying to get you, too . . . I think that's why you can do it at all. It's a fair fight, like they say. That means you can do it—or most people can do it most of the time. It doesn't mean it's a game, or you think it's fun," Chester said. *Unless you're Boris Lavochkin*, he added, but only to himself. Maybe that was what made the lieutenant so alarming: killing didn't bother him the way it did most people.

Carl was full of questions this morning: "What about guys who can't do it any more? Is that what they call combat fatigue?"

"This time around, yeah. Last war, they called it shellshock. Same critter, different names." Chester hesitated. "Sometimes . . . a guy sees more horrible stuff than he can take, that's all. If you can, you get him out of the line, let him rest up awhile. He's usually all right after that. War's like anything else, I guess. It's easier for some people than it is for others. And some guys go through more nasty stuff than others, too. So it all depends."

"You sound like you feel sorry for soldiers like that. I thought you'd be mad at them," his son said.

"Not me." Chester shook his head. "I went through enough crap myself so I know how hard it is. A few guys would fake combat fatigue so they could try and get out of the line. I am mad at people who'd do something like that, because they make it harder for everybody else."

"Did you run into anybody like that?" Rita asked.

"Not in my outfit," Chester answered. "It happened, though. You'd hear about it too often for all of it to be made up. Over on the Confederate side, they say General Patton got in trouble for slapping around a guy with combat fatigue."

"What do you think of that?" Rita and Carl said the same thing at the same time.

"If the guy really was shellshocked, Patton should have left him alone. You can't help something like that," Chester said. All the same, he was sure Lieutenant Lavochkin would have done the same thing. Having no nerves himself, Lavochkin didn't see why anybody else should, either.

Before Chester's wife and son could come up with any more interesting questions, the telephone rang. He stood closest to it, so he got it. "Hello?"

"Hello, Mr. Martin. Harry T. Casson here."

"What can I do for you, Mr. Casson?" Chester heard the wariness and the respect in his own voice. Rita's eyes widened. Harry T. Casson was the biggest building contractor in the Los Angeles area. Before the war, he'd wrangled again and again with the construction union Chester helped start. They didn't settle things till well after the fighting started. Now . . . Who could guess what was on Casson's plate now? If he wanted to try to break the union—well, he could try, but Chester didn't think he'd get away with it.

He started off in a friendly enough way: "Glad you're back safe. I heard you were wounded—happy it wasn't too serious."

"Yeah." The only wound that wasn't serious was the one that happened to the other guy. Chester asked, "Did you ever put the uniform on again yourself?"

"A few weeks after you did," Casson answered. "I was bossing construction projects, mostly up in the Northwest. I'm embarrassed to say I didn't come anywhere close to the sound of guns. Well, once, but that was just a nuisance raid. Nothing aimed my way."

"You paid those dues last time around." Chester knew the building magnate had commanded a line company—and, briefly, a line regiment—in the Great War.

"Generous of you to say so," Casson replied.

"So what's up?" Chester asked. "Latest contract still has a year to run."

"I know. All the more reason to start talking about the new one now," Casson said easily. "That way, we don't get crammed up against a deadline. Everything works better."

He was smooth, all right—smooth enough to make Chester suspicious. "You're gonna try and screw me, and you won't respect me in the morning, either."

Harry T. Casson laughed. "I don't know what you're talking about, Chester."

"Now tell me another one," Chester answered. "C'mon, man. We both know what the game's about. Why make like we don't?"

"All right. You want it straight? I'll give it to you straight. During the war, you got a better contract than you really deserved," Casson said. "Not a lot of labor available, and there was a war on. We didn't want strikes throwing a monkey wrench into things. But it's different now. Lots of guys coming out of the Army and going into the building trades—look at you, for instance. And it's not unpatriotic to care a little more about profit these days, either."

"So how hard are you going to try to hit us?" Chester asked. When Harry T. Casson told him, he grunted as if he'd been hit for real. "We'll fight you if you do that," he promised. "We'll fight you every way we know how."

"I think you'll lose," the building magnate said.

"Don't bet on it, Mr. Casson. You know how big our strike fund is?" Chester said. Casson named a figure. Chester laughed harshly. "Make it three times that size."

"You're lying," Casson said at once.

"In a pig's . . . ear," Chester replied. "We've been socking it away since 1942. We figured you'd try to give us the shaft first chance you got. We'll fight, all right, and we'll make your scabs sorry they were born. We whipped Pinkertons before. With all the vets back, like you say, sure as the devil we can do it again. Piece of cake, the flyboys call it."

"Siccing the Pinkertons on you was a mistake. I said so at the time, but my colleagues didn't want to listen," Harry T. Casson said slowly. "Do you swear you're telling the truth about your strike fund?"

"Swear to God." Martin made his voice as solemn as he could.

"Damnation," Casson muttered. "That could be difficult. Not just a hard strike, but bad publicity when we don't need it . . . Will you agree to extend the present contract unchanged for another two years, then? Come 1948, both sides can take a long look at where they are and where they want to go."

"You can get your friends to go along with that?" Chester asked.

"Yes, if you're sure the rank and file will ratify it."

"They will," Chester said. "Some of them might want a raise, but they're doing all right. Staying where we're at's a good enough deal."

"A good enough deal," Harry T. Casson echoed. "I'm not thrilled with it, but I think you're right. It will do. Good talking with you, Chester. So long." He hung up.

So did Chester. He also started laughing like a maniac. "What was that all about?" Rita asked.

"New contract. Two years. Same terms as the wartime one," Chester got out between guffaws.

"But what's so funny?" Rita demanded.

Chester didn't tell her. One more thing he never intended to tell anybody. The real strike fund was smaller than Harry T. Casson thought, not three times as big. He'd raised Casson with a busted flush, and he'd made the magnate fold. Rain? So what? If this wasn't a good day's work, for him and for everybody else in the union, he'd never done one. *The sooner we sign the papers, the better*, he thought. But they would. After the war, a contract was . . . a piece of cake.

Elizabeth clucked at Cincinnatus. "Aren't you ready yet?"

"I been ready for twenty minutes. So has my pa," he answered. "You're the one keeps checkin' her makeup an' makin' sure her hat's sittin' just the right way."

"I'm doin' no such thing," his wife said, and Cincinnatus prayed God would forgive the lie. Elizabeth added, "Not every day you marry off your onliest daughter."

"Well, that's a fact," Cincinnatus allowed. "That sure enough is a fact."

Amanda was at the beauty parlor, or maybe at the church by now. Cincinnatus reached up and fiddled with his tie. He'd never worn a tuxedo before. The suit was rented, but the clothier assured him plenty of white men rented tuxes, too. Seneca Driver wore Cincinnatus' ordinary suit. It was a little big on him, but he didn't have one of his own;

he'd got away from Covington with no more than the clothes on his back, and money'd been tight since.

"You look mighty handsome," Elizabeth said.

"Glad you think so. What I reckon I look like is one o' them fancy servants rich folks had down in the CSA," Cincinnatus said. "They're the only ones I ever seen with fancy duds like this here."

His wife shook her head. "Their jackets always had brass buttons, to show they was servants." She snorted. "Like them bein' colored wouldn't tell you. But anyways, they did. Your buttons is jus' black, like they would be if you wore them clothes all the time on account of you wanted to."

Cincinnatus couldn't imagine anybody wanting to. The tux fit well, yes. But it was uncomfortable. On a hot summer day, it would be stifling, with the high wing collar and the tight cravat. He didn't even want to think about that. "I ain't sorry Amanda didn't want to wait till June," he said.

"Do Jesus, me neither!" his wife exclaimed. "She try an' do that, maybe she have herself a baby six, seven months after they do the ceremony. People laugh at you an' talk behind your back when somethin' like that happens."

"They do," Cincinnatus agreed. There was something he hadn't worried about. Well, his wife had taken care of it for him. He sent her a sidelong look and lowered his voice so his father wouldn't hear: "Only fool luck we didn't have that happen our ownselves."

"You stop it, you and your filthy talk," Elizabeth said, also quietly. He only laughed, which annoyed her more. It wasn't as if he wasn't telling the truth. Plenty of courting couples didn't wait till the preacher said the words over them before they started doing what they would have done afterwards.

For that matter, Cincinnatus had no way of knowing whether Amanda had a bun in the oven right now. He almost pointed that out to his wife, too, but held his tongue at the last minute. Maybe Elizabeth was already worrying about that, too. If she wasn't, he didn't want to give her anything new to flabble about.

Someone knocked on the door. "Ready or not, you're ready now," Cincinnatus told Elizabeth. "There's the Changs."

When Elizabeth opened the door, she might have been ready to meet President-elect Dewey and his wife. "Come in!" she said warmly. "Oh, isn't that a pretty dress!"

"Thank you," Mrs. Chang said. She didn't know a whole lot of English—less than her husband—but she understood enough to nod and smile and say the right thing here.

Joey Chang had on an ordinary suit, not a tux—he wasn't father of the bride, only father of the bride's sister-in-law. "I bring beer to reception, right?" he said.

"Right!" Cincinnatus said. Mr. Chang was also one of the best homebrew makers in Des Moines. Since Iowa remained legally dry, that was an important talent. The authorities didn't seem to be enforcing the law the way they had before the war, but you couldn't just go round to the corner package store and pick up a couple of cases of Blatz.

"I do it, then," Chang said. "You have colored people at your wedding, right?"

"Well, I think so," Cincinnatus said dryly.

"You have Chinese people, too." Chang nodded and pointed to himself and his wife. Their and Cincinnatus' grandchildren could have gone into either category. Chang went on, "You have white people, too?"

"Yeah, we will," Cincinnatus replied. "Some of the guys from the butcher shop where Calvin works. Little bit of everything."

"Maybe not so bad," Joey Chang said. Considering how hard he and his wife had resisted Grace's marriage to Achilles, that was a lot from him. He insisted they would have liked it just as little had Grace married a white guy. Cincinnatus . . . almost believed him. Grandchildren had softened the Changs, as grandchildren have a way of doing.

"We should go," Elizabeth said. "Don't want to be late." The church was a block and a half away, so there was very little risk of that. But Elizabeth *would* flabble. It was a wedding, after all.

"Long as Amanda and Calvin are there—and the minister—don't hardly matter if we show up or not," Cincinnatus said. He made his wife sputter and fume, which was what he'd had in mind. Joey Chang tipped him a wink. Cincinnatus grinned back.

The Changs made much of Seneca Driver as they walked to church. They took old people seriously. "Mighty nice great-grandchillun," Seneca said. "*Mighty* nice. I don't care none if they's half Chinese, neither. I wouldn't care if they was red, white, an' blue. *Mighty* nice."

Cincinnatus wished he could move along with his back straight and without a stick in his right hand. His leg still hurt. So did his shoulder. The steel plate in his skull made mine detectors go off—an amused Army engineer had proved that one day.

Beat up or not, though, he was still alive and kicking—as long as he didn't have to kick too hard. With a little luck, he'd see more grandchildren before long. Compared to most of the surviving Negroes in the conquered Confederacy, he had the world by the tail.

Calvin's father and mother were already at the church. They were pleasant people, a few years younger than Cincinnatus. Abraham Washington ran a secondhand-clothes store. It wasn't a fancy way to make a living, but he'd done all right. Calvin had a brother, Luther, a year younger than he was. Luther wore a green-gray uniform and had a PFC's chevron on his sleeve. He looked tough and strong—and proud of himself, too.

"I didn't see any combat, sir," he said to Cincinnatus. "Heard stories about what you truck drivers went through, though. What was it like?"

"Son, you didn't miss a thing," Cincinnatus answered. "That's the honest to God truth. Getting shot at when they miss is bad. If they hit you, it's worse."

"I told him that," Abraham Washington said. "I told him, but he didn't want to listen. He went and volunteered anyway."

"He got the chance to show he was as good as a white man, and he went and took it," Cincinnatus said. "How you gonna blame him for that?"

Luther Washington grinned from ear to ear. "*Somebody* understands why I did what I did!"

His father only sniffed. By the way Abraham Washington sounded, his people had lived in Des Moines for generations. He was used to being thought as good as a white man—or nearly as good, anyhow. Having grown up in the CSA, Cincinnatus could see why Luther was willing to lay his life on the line to get rid of the *nearly*. During the Great War, plenty of Negroes joined the Confederate Army to win citizenship for themselves. Plenty more would have this time around, if only Jake Featherston had let them. That urge to prove himself—that feeling you *had* to keep proving yourself—stayed strong in Negroes on both sides of the old border.

Cincinnatus didn't want to think about Jake Featherston, not at his daughter's wedding. He looked around the church. The Changs had gone over with Achilles and Grace and their grandchildren—who, in Cincinnatus' considered and unbiased (of course!) opinion, were the brightest and most beautiful grandbabies in the whole world.

And there were a few whites, as he'd told Joey Chang there would be. They were doing their best—some doing better than others—to be friendly with the colored people sitting around them. Cincinnatus smiled to himself. The whites were a small minority here. They were getting a tiny taste of what Negroes in the USA went through all the time.

But it was better here than it ever had been down in the Confederacy. Not good, necessarily, but better. Cincinnatus had experience with both places. He knew when he was better off. He'd voted here. His children had graduated from high school. Maybe his grandchildren would go to college. Down in the CSA, back before the Great War, he'd been unusual—and an occasional object of suspicion—because he could read and write.

A burly young man whose shoulders strained the fabric of his tuxedo jacket came up. His name was Amos Something-or-other. He was one of Calvin's friends, and the best man. "Wedding procession's forming up," he said.

"That's us," Elizabeth said. Cincinnatus couldn't very well tell her she was wrong.

Amanda seemed ready to burst with glee. That was how the bride was supposed to act on her wedding day. Calvin didn't look ready to run for his life. For a groom on his wedding day, that would do.

The organist struck up the wedding march. Down the aisle everybody went. A photographer fired off one flashbulb after another. Yellow-purple spots danced in front of Cincinnatus' eyes.

Up at the front of the church, he and the rest of Amanda's supporters went to the right, those of Calvin Washington to the left. The minister did what ministers do. After a while, he got to, "Who giveth this woman?"

"I do," Cincinnatus said proudly.

Amanda and Calvin got to say their "I do"s a couple of minutes later. Amanda's ring had a tiny diamond on it. Tiny or not, it sparkled under the electric lights. It shone no brighter than Amanda's smile, though. The kiss the new husband and wife exchanged was decorous, but not chaste.

Down the street three doors to the reception, Joey Chang's good beer was highly unofficial, but also highly appreciated. The minister drank several glasses and got very lively. Cincinnatus hadn't expected that. Preachers were supposed to be a straitlaced lot, weren't they? But if this one wanted to let his processed hair down, why not?

One of the white men congratulated Cincinnatus. "Your daughter's a pretty girl, and she seems mighty nice," he said.

"Thank you kindly." Cincinnatus was ready to approve of anybody who approved of Amanda.

"This is a good bash, too," the white man said. "People get together and have a good time, they're all pretty much the same, you know?"

He seemed to think he'd come out with something brilliant. "I won't quarrel with you," Cincinnatus said.

"And you've got to tell me who makes your beer," the white man added.

"That fella right over there." Cincinnatus pointed to Joey Chang, who held a glass of his own product. "His daughter's married to my son."

"Well, how about that?" the white man said, which was safe enough under almost any circumstances. "Stir everything around, huh?"

"Why not?" Cincinnatus waited to see if the ofay would go any further.

But he didn't. He just said, "How about that?" again.

Good, Cincinnatus thought. He wanted no trouble, not today. He never wanted trouble, but he'd landed in some. He wouldn't worry about that, either. This was Amanda's day, and it should be a good one. He smiled. He wanted her night to be better yet.

You! Pinkard!" After Jeff Pinkard got convicted in the Yankees' military court—kangaroo court, he thought of it still—U.S. personnel replaced all the Texans at the Houston jail. He hated those sharp, harsh, quick accents.

"Yeah?" he said. "What is it?"

"Get up," the guard told him. "You got visitors."

It was only a week till they hanged him. "Yeah?" he said again, heaving his bulk off the cot. "Visitors?" That roused his curiosity. The only person he'd seen lately was Jonathan Moss, here to tell him another appeal had failed. He had none left—the President of the USA and the U.S. Supreme Court had declined to spare him. "Who?"

"You'll find out when you get there, won't you?" The guard unlocked his cell. Other men in green-gray stood by with submachine guns at the ready. If Jeff got cute, he'd die a week early, that was all. *And nobody'll miss me, either*, he thought miserably. When you were going to hang in a week, self-pity came easy.

He went down the hall in front of the guards. Was getting shot a quicker, cleaner way to go than the rope? He didn't want to go at all, dammit. As far as he was concerned, he hadn't done anything to deserve killing.

When he got to the visiting room, he stopped in his tracks. There on the other side of the wire were Edith and Willie and Frank, and little Raymond in his wife's arms. All of them except Raymond started to cry when they saw him.

"Aww," Jeff said, and then, "You shouldn't have come."

"We would've done it more, Papa Jeff," Willie said, "only the damnyankees wouldn't let us for a long time."

"We're here now," Edith said. "We love you, Jeff."

"Yeah, well, I love y'all, too," Jeff said. "And a whole fat lot of good it's gonna do anybody."

He went up to the mesh that separated him from his family. He pressed his hands against it as hard as he could. They did the same thing on the other side. Try as he would, he couldn't quite touch them.

"It's not right, Papa Jeff," Frank said. "They got no business messin' with you. It was only niggers, for heaven's sake."

"Well, you know that, and I know that, and everybody down here knows that, too," Jeff answered. "Only trouble is, the Yankees don't know it, and they're the ones who count."

"Can't anybody do anything?" Edith asked.

"Doesn't look like it. Oh, people *could* do something, but nobody wants to. What do you expect? They're Yankees."

His wife started crying harder. "It's not fair. It's not right. Just on account of they won the damn war . . . What am I gonna do without you, Jeff?"

"You'll do fine," Jeff said. "You know you will." *What am I gonna do without me?* he wondered. That, unfortunately, had no good answer. He was going to die, was what he was going to do. "And don't you worry none about me. I'll be up in heaven with God and the angels and stuff."

He didn't really believe in heaven, not with halos and harps and white robes. Playing the harp all day got old fast, anyway. But Edith was more religious than he was. If he could make her feel better, he would.

She went on crying, though, which made Willie and Frank snuffle more, too. "I don't want to lose you!"

"I don't want it to happen, either, but I don't have a whole lot to say about it," he replied.

"You've got a baby. You've got me. You've got my boys, who you raised like you were their daddy," Edith said.

All of that was true. It cut no ice with anybody up in Yankeeland. The Yankees went on and on about all the Negroes he'd killed. As if they'd cared about those Negroes alive! They sure hadn't wanted them going up to the USA. From what he heard, they still didn't want Negroes from the CSA going up to the USA.

They were going to hang him anyhow. They could, and they would.

A guard came in on the other side, the free side. "Time's up," he said.

"We love you, Jeff!" Edith said through her tears. She carried Raymond out. The boys were still crying, too.

"Come on, Pinkard," said a guard on Jeff's side of the visiting room. "Back to the cell you go."

Back he went. The cell was familiar. Nothing bad would happen to him while he was in it. Pretty soon, though, they'd take him out one last time. He wouldn't be going back after that. Well, what else did *one last time* mean?

Two days later, he had another visitor: Jonathan Moss again. "Thought you gave up on me," he said through the damned unyielding mesh.

"I don't know what else I can do for you," Moss said. "I wish I did. I haven't got a hacksaw blade on me or anything. Even if I did, they would have found it when they searched me."

"Yeah," Pinkard said. "So—no reprieve from the governor. Hell, no governor. Son of a bitch thinks he's President of Texas now. No reprieve from the President of the USA. No reprieve from the assholes on the Yankee Supreme Court. So what else is there?"

"Well, you're not the only one they're coming down on, if that makes you feel any better," Jonathan Moss replied.

"You mean, like misery loves company?" Jeff shrugged. "I'd love it if I didn't have the misery. But yeah, go ahead—tell me about the others. I don't have a wireless set, and they don't give me papers, so I don't know jack shit about what's going on out there."

"They hanged Ferdinand Koenig and Saul Goldman yesterday."

"Goddamn shame," Pinkard said. "They were good men, both of 'em. Confederate patriots. Why else would you Yankees hang people?"

"For murdering millions? For telling lies about it in papers and magazines and on the wireless?" Moss suggested.

"We didn't get rid of anybody who didn't have it coming," Jeff said stubbornly. "And like your side didn't tell any lies to your people during the war. Yeah, sure."

The military attorney sighed. "We didn't tell lies about things like that. We didn't do things like that—not to Negroes, not to Jews, not to anybody."

He undercut what Jeff would have said next: that the USA didn't have many Negroes to get rid of. The United States were crawling with Jews. Everybody knew that. Instead, he said, "What other kind of good news have you got for me?"

"If it makes you feel any better, you aren't the only camp commandant and guard chief to get condemned," Moss told him. "Vern Green goes right with you here. And . . . you knew Mercer Scott back in Louisiana, right?"

"Yeah." Pinkard scowled at him. "You know what? It doesn't make me feel one goddamn bit better."

"I'm sorry. If there were anything else I could try, I'd try it. If you have any ideas, sing out."

Jeff shook his head. "What's the use? Nobody in the USA cares. Nobody in the USA understands. We did what we had to do, that's all."

" 'It looked like a good idea at the time.' " Moss sounded like somebody quoting something. Then he sighed. "That isn't enough to do you any good, either."

"Didn't reckon it would be," Jeff said. "Go on, then. You tried. I said that before, I expect. Won't be long now."

In some ways the days till the hanging crawled past. In others, they flew. The last days of his life, and he was stuck in a cell by himself. Not the way he would have wanted things to turn out, but what did that have to do with anything? He asked the guards for a copy of *Over Open Sights*.

"Wouldn't you rather have a Bible?" one of them said.

"If I wanted a Bible, don't you reckon I would've told you so?" Jeff snapped.

A little to his surprise, they brought him Jake Featherston's book. He paged through it. Everything in there made such good sense. A damn shame it hadn't worked out for real. But the Negroes in the CSA were gone, or most of them were, and the damnyankees couldn't change that even if they did win the war.

The night before they were going to hang him, the guards asked what he wanted for supper. "Fried chicken and fried potatoes and a bottle of beer," he answered. They gave it to him, except the beer

came in a tin cup. He ate with good appetite. He slept . . . some, anyhow.

They asked him what he wanted once more at breakfast time.
"Bacon and eggs and grits," he told them, and he got that, too. He
cleaned his plate again, and poured down the coffee that came with
the food.

"Want a preacher?" a guard asked.

Pinkard shook his head. "Nah. What for? I've got a clean conscience. If you don't, you need a preacher worse'n I do."

They cuffed his hands behind him and led him out to the prison
yard. They'd run up a gallows there; he'd listened to the carpentry in
his cell. Now he saw it was a gallows built for two. Another party of
U.S. guards led Vern Green out from a different part of the jail.

Vern looked like hell. His nerve must have failed him at last. He
gave Jeff a forlorn nod. "How come you ain't about to piss yourself
like me?"

"What's the use?" Jeff answered. "I'd beg if I thought it'd do any
good, but it won't. So I'll go out the best way I know how. Why give
these assholes the satisfaction of watching me blubber?"

Reporters watched from a distance. Guards made sure they stayed
back. Otherwise, they would have got up to the condemned men and
yelled questions in their faces. Jeff figured Yankee reporters had to be
even worse than their Confederate counterparts, and the Confederates
were pretty bad.

A guard had to help Vern Green up the stairs to the platform. Jeff
made it under his own power. His knees were knocking, but he didn't
let it show. Pride was the last thing he had left. *And much good it does
me, too*, he thought.

Along with more guards and the hangman, a minister waited up
there. "Will you pray with me?" he asked Jeff.

"No." Jeff shook his head. "I made it this far on my own. I'll go
out the same way."

Vern talked with the preacher. They went through the Twenty-
third Psalm together. When they finished, Vern said, "I'm still scared."

"No one can blame you for that," the minister said.

A guard held out a pack of cigarettes to Jeff. "Thanks," he said.
"You'll have to take it out for me."

"I will," the guard said. The smoke was a Raleigh, so it tasted
good. Vern also smoked one. The guards let them finish, then walked

them onto the traps. The hangman came over and set the rope around Jeff's neck. Then he put a burlap bag over Jeff's head.

"Make it quick if you can," Jeff said. The bag was white, not black. He could still see light and shadow through it. His heart pounded now—every beat might be the last.

"I'm doing my best," the hangman answered. His footsteps moved away, but not far. *They've got no right, damn them*, Jeff thought. *They've—* A lever clacked.

The trap dropped.

Stuck in fucking Alabama," Armstrong Grimes grumbled. "What could be worse than this?"

Squidface was cleaning his captured automatic Tredegar. He looked up from the work. "Well, you could be in hell," he said.

"Who says I'm not?" Armstrong said. "It's a godforsaken miserable place, and I can't get out of it. If that's not hell, what do you call it?"

"Pittsburgh," Squidface answered, which jerked a laugh out of Armstrong. After guiding an oily rag through the Tredegar's barrel with a cleaning rod, Squidface went on, "If you're gonna get screwed any which way, lay back and enjoy it, you know?"

"Tell me another one," Armstrong said. "Army chow. The people fucking hate us. We're not careful, we get scragged. Even the broads are scared of us now. If they get friendly, they end up dead. And we don't take hostages for that, so there's nothing to hold the locals back."

"Army chow's not so bad," Squidface said. "There's always enough of it nowadays, anyhow. Back before I went in, I couldn't always count on three squares." He was skinny enough to make that easy to believe.

But Armstrong was in the mood to bitch, and he wasn't about to let anybody stop him. "You're just saying that 'cause you're turning into a lifer."

"Yeah? So? You oughta do the same," Squidface answered. "God knows how long you're gonna stay stuck here. You make a pretty good soldier, even if you are a big target. Why not leave the uniform on? You go back to Civvy Street, you'll end up bored outa your skull all the god-damn time."

"I'd sooner be bored than bore-sighted," Armstrong said.

Squidface ignored the joke. That pissed Armstrong off, because he thought it was better than most of the ones he made. But, as if he hadn't spoken, the PFC continued, "Besides, you can't tell me you aren't getting any down here. Up in the USA, the girls'll slap your face if you try and cop a feel. You want to fuck, you gotta get married."

"There's still whorehouses in the USA," Armstrong said.

"Yeah? So?" Squidface said again.

He left it right there. Armstrong grunted. With a whore, it was nothing but a business deal. Some of the gals down here were looking for love. They wanted to think they mattered to you, so you mattered to them. They weren't just going through the motions. That did make it better.

All the same . . . "You figure because you want to stay in, everybody ought to want to stay in."

"My ass," Squidface retorted. "Plenty of the cocksuckers in this company, I wish they'd get the fuck out. Raw recruits who don't know their nuts from Wednesday'd be better. But you're all right. You could do it. You might even end up an officer."

"Christ! What're you smoking?" Armstrong laughed out loud. "Whatever it is, I want some."

"I'm serious, man," Squidface said. "Me, I'm a noncom. It's what I'm made for. You've got more of the 'Yes, sir!' they like when they promote people."

"Oh, man, give me a fucking break," Armstrong said.

"You do," Squidface insisted. "Shit, you're Armstrong. You never got a gross nickname hung on you or nothin'."

"That's 'cause I've got a gross name instead," Armstrong said. "Hot damn."

"All the same." Squidface wasn't about to let up. "I can see the newspaper story now. It's fucking 1975, and Colonel Armstrong Grimes gets a Medal of Honor for leading the regiment that takes Paris away from the Germans."

"If the Germans want the place, they're welcome to it, far as I'm concerned," Armstrong said. "It's full of Frenchmen—or it was till they blew it up."

"So don't listen to me."

"Like I ever did." As long as they were zinging each other, Armstrong was happy enough. But they'd come much too close to getting serious there, and getting serious made him nervous.

He wasn't the only U.S. soldier who got nervous in Alabama. Somebody well up the chain of command had the bright idea that a football game between occupiers and locals might show people that men from the USA weren't so different from anybody else—no horns, no tails, no pitchforks.

The company CO asked Armstrong, "Didn't you play football in high school?"

"Some," he answered. "I was second string. I wasn't that great or anything."

"You want a chance to knock Confederates on their ass without getting gigged for it?"

"Where do I sign up?"

Squidface wanted nothing to do with that. "I'm glad I'm a little guy," he said. "Those assholes on the other side, they're gonna be lookin' for a chance to rack you up. This ain't gonna be no friendly game."

"Yeah, well, we'll work out on them, too," Armstrong said.

"They better have plenty of ambulances ready," Squidface said darkly.

They got uniforms. Whoever was in charge of what they were calling the Peace Bowl had clout. U.S. soldiers wore blue suits, their Confederate counterparts red. They got cleats to take the place of their boots. They got helmets. Armstrong wondered if he wouldn't do better with his regular steel pot than with this leather contraption.

The athletes on the U.S. team were in much better shape than the high-school guys had been. Armstrong felt he'd earned something when he got named a starting tackle. They had a quarterback who could really throw and a couple of ends who could catch. The ends weren't the swiftest in the world, but they'd do.

They played the Peace Bowl at a high-school stadium. U.S. soldiers filled half the stands, locals the other half. To make sure the bowl stayed peaceful, the locals got frisked before they could go inside.

Armstrong got his first look at the red team then. He didn't like what he saw. They were slimmer and rangier than the U.S. players. They looked fast. That wasn't what worried him, though. One glance told him these guys were going to play as if they were fighting to hold the U.S. Army out of Chattanooga. Squidface had it straight. Peace Bowl, nothing. This wouldn't be football. This would be war.

The red team—they seemed to call themselves the Wolves—won

the toss. When the U.S. kicker booted the ball, Armstrong thundered down the field. The first collision was always welcome. He slammed into a guy in red. "Yankee cocksuckin' motherfucker," the man said, and tried to lift a knee into his family jewels.

"Kiss my ass, Charlie." Armstrong twisted and took the knee on his hip pad. "You want to play like that? We'll play like that."

"Bring it on," the other guy said.

And they did. Both sides did, the whole game long. Armstrong got punched and elbowed and gouged and kicked. Every tackle was a piling-on penalty. It was trench warfare, only without trenches. The Confederates *were* faster. The U.S. team was a touch stronger.

One Confederate broke his leg. As far as Armstrong could tell, that was an accident—the tackle looked clean. One U.S. player had his shoulder dislocated. On the next play, the Wolf who dislocated it got racked up. Armstrong couldn't see just what happened to him; somebody was trying to step on his face. Whatever it was, the guy in red got carried off on a stretcher.

With four minutes to go, the Confederates punted to the U.S. team. The blues were on their own thirty, down 28–24. "This is it," the quarterback said in the huddle. "We get a touchdown, we win. We fuck up, we look like chumps in front of these shitheads and in front of our own guys. We gonna let that happen?"

"No!" they chorused.

"All right. Short pass into the left flat on three. Let's go get 'em."

"You shot my brother, asshole," said the guy across the line from Armstrong.

"Don't worry, cuntlips," Armstrong said sweetly. "You're next."

And he was right, but not the way he meant it. The first mortar bomb hissed in then, and burst right on the midfield stripe. But the red team shielded the blue from most of the fragments. As soon as Armstrong heard the bang, he flattened out. So did the Alabaman who didn't like him, but the guy in red was bleeding from his back and his leg.

"Fuck," he said hoarsely.

Another Confederate player was down with a ghastly head wound. It proved again what Kaiser Bill's army had found out the hard way in the Great War—leather helmets didn't do one damn thing to stop shell fragments. A couple of U.S. soldiers clutched at themselves and groaned, too. Their uniforms showed the blood more than their opponents'.

Armstrong crawled over to the closer one. He didn't want to rise up, in case more mortar rounds landed on or near the football field. And they did—one near the far end zone, and another, gruesomely, in the side of the stands filled with people cheering for the red team. Screams and shrieks and wails rose high and shrill.

"Son of a bitch!" Armstrong said, not entirely displeased. "We may not even have to take hostages this time. They're doing it to themselves."

The wounded U.S. player expressed an opinion that would have assigned every white person in the former Confederacy to an even warmer if less humid clime. Then he said, "I wish I could bandage myself. This cloth doesn't tear for shit."

"Hang on." Armstrong extracted a small clasp knife from his right sock. "I'll fix you up."

"What are you doing with that?" the other soldier asked.

"Never can tell when it'll come in handy," Armstrong said, slicing at the fellow's shirt. "If I could've got my hands on a derringer, I would've packed one of those, too." He cut at the soldier's tight trousers so he could see the wound. "Not too bad. Looks like you're sliced up some, but I don't think there's any iron in there."

"Oh, boy," the injured player said. Armstrong knew it was easier to be optimistic if you weren't the guy who'd stopped one.

Another round burst on the far side of the field, and then another one in the Confederate side of the stands. The bastards with the mortar could have done much worse to the people they were trying to harm. Instead, they unleashed horror on the men and women who would have applauded had damnyankees been sliced to cat's meat.

"I think the game's over," somebody not far away said.

"Boy, I bet he had to go to college to be smart like that," Armstrong said.

"Heh," said the wounded football player lying beside him. "I hope they drop on that fucking mortar crew pretty damn quick."

"Good luck," Armstrong said. Mortars didn't make a great big bang when they went off. If you drew a mile-and-a-half circle around the football field, the crew was . . . somewhere in there. If they wanted to throw their weapon in a Birmingham, go somewhere else, and set up again, they could do that, too. And most of the soldiers who could be chasing them were here at the game instead.

The guys in green-gray were emptying from the stands as fast as they could without panic. Medics came out to get the injured off the field. They'd been there for the football injuries, but they knew how to deal with battlefield wounds, too. They'd had plenty of practice. Armstrong stayed right where he was. He wished he could have stashed an entrenching tool in his sock. Like every U.S. soldier in the CSA, he felt pinned down.

Everything faded. Cassius found that out the hard way. He could remember the fierce, incredulous joy he'd known when he shot Jake Featherston, but he couldn't feel it any more. All he had now was the memory, and it wasn't the same thing.

Fame faded, too. It wasn't that people didn't recall what he'd done, here more than half a year later. He got greeted with smiles and nods wherever he went. But he wasn't fresh news any more. Too much had happened since. The United States was about to get a new President. That was why he'd been invited down to Washington, D.C.: to see Tom Dewey inaugurated.

He wondered if his would be the only black face at the inauguration. He feared it might. Down in the CSA, he'd always been among his own kind. But Negroes in the United States were thin on the ground. He had to get used to dealing with white people.

A lot of them didn't know how to deal with him, either. The ones who treated him like an eight-year-old who wasn't very bright were easy to avoid. Even the ones who plainly meant well, though, often acted as if they couldn't expect much from him. In some ways, they bothered him more than the other kind, because they were harder to shake off.

"Such neat handwriting!" gushed the desk clerk at Willard's Hotel when Cassius checked in the evening of January 31. He looked at his signature. *Cassius Madison*, it said in his ordinary script, which was not too bad and not too good. Everybody in the USA needed a surname. He'd taken his from the town outside of which he shot Jake Featherston. Only later did he learn it also belonged to a U.S. President from before the War of Secession. Were Cassius white, the clerk never would have remarked on how he wrote. The man had to be surprised he could write at all.

Once he'd checked in, Cassius knew what to do at a hotel. He tipped the man who carried his bags up to his room. Watching a white man do what would have been nigger work in the CSA was a kick.

"Thanks," the fellow said, pocketing the half-dollar. "You want a girl, buddy, you talk to me. I'll get you a lulu, I will. Fifteen bucks, and you'll be a happy guy—I guarantee it."

"Not right now," Cassius answered. Right after he came to the USA, he couldn't keep women away from him, not that he tried very hard. But they didn't throw themselves at him like that any more— another sign his fame was wearing thin, and one he really regretted.

The bellhop shrugged. "You change your mind, you can find me. My name's Pete. See you around." He strode out of the room.

Cassius shrugged. He didn't like paying for it. He did like doing it, though, so maybe he'd hunt up Pete and maybe he wouldn't. In the meantime, he looked at the room-service menu. He ordered a steak and a salad and fried potatoes. Experience had taught him that those were hard for even a kitchen asleep at the switch to screw up too badly.

Another white man, this one with a foreign accent, brought the dinner into his room on a cart. Cassius tipped him, too. With a nod that was almost a bow, the waiter left. Cassius attacked the steak. They'd got medium-rare right, and the meat was pretty tender. He'd had plenty worse.

He went to bed without looking for Pete. He felt more tired than virtuous. He didn't know why sitting on a train for the trip down from Boston should have worn him out—he hadn't done anything *but* sit. But he'd seen several times that traveling long distances could be as wearing as a march with Gracchus' guerrillas.

After the alarm clock woke him, he showered and shaved and dressed in a sober suit set off by a bright red tie. Then he went downstairs for breakfast.

Willard's, at the corner of Fourteenth and Pennsylvania Avenue, was only a couple of blocks from the White House, on whose battered grounds the inauguration ceremony would take place. It was even closer to the security perimeter, which featured barbed wire, machine-gun nests, and search points.

Even though Cassius had one of the most recognizable faces in the USA and an official invitation, he got frisked. "I shot the President of the CSA," he complained. "You reckon I'm gonna shoot the President of the USA?"

"Not our job to take chances," answered the soldier patting him down. "But I'll tell you something—Congresswoman Blackford came through this checkpoint a few minutes ago. She was married to a guy who was President. One of our gals searched her anyway." He paused. "You're clean. Go on through."

"Thanks," Cassius said. If they were searching members of Congress, they hadn't singled him out because he was a Negro. He'd wondered.

He showed his invitation to an usher who might have been a soldier dressed up for the occasion. "Oh, yes, sir," the man said—he couldn't have been more than a year or two older than Cassius. "Come with me. We've got you a place right near the podium."

Cassius went past bleachers filling up with dignitaries and their wives. A woman waved to him. That *was* Congresswoman Blackford— the soldier hadn't been lying to him. He waved back.

There was a special grandstand right behind the podium where the new President would be sworn in. Newsreel cameras in front of the podium would capture the moment so people all over the country could see it. They were sure to capture Cassius. He didn't mind. Till he learned some skill to help him get through the rest of his life, all he had to trade on was the one moment when his rifle spoke for him.

Some of the people sitting around him were generals and admirals. Others had to be important Democratic dignitaries. Their party had been out of office for eight years. Now they got to run things again. They were friendly to him. They shook his hand and congratulated him. Then they went back to chatting with one another, talking about all the things they would do now that they could do them.

The seats on the podium started to fill up: there were the incoming Vice President and his wife. There was the Chief Justice of the U.S. Supreme Court. There were outgoing President La Follette and his wife. And there, at last, were incoming President Dewey and *his* wife— and a flock of hard-eyed bodyguards around them.

Vice President Truman was sworn in first. He gave no speech and had no counterpart to shake his hand. President La Follette had been Vice President before the Confederate bomb killed his predecessor, and the office stayed empty after he left it.

When Truman sat down, Dewey stood up. So did La Follette, who took his place beside the Chief Justice. The new President took the oath: "I do solemnly swear that I will faithfully execute the Office of

President of the United States, and will to the best of my Ability, preserve, protect and defend the Constitution of the United States."

As soon as Dewey finished the oath, President—no, ex-President—La Follette took a step forward and shook his hand. Then he sat down on the podium. The Chief Justice also shook hands with President Dewey. He too sat down.

Dewey stood behind the lectern and its undergrowth of microphones. All the wireless webs would be sending his words live across the country. "It is a privilege to be here," Dewey said. "You have entrusted me with the great responsibility of winning the peace. I would like to congratulate my distinguished predecessor, President La Follette, for winning the desperate war Jake Featherston started."

Cassius clapped along with everybody else. Now that Dewey had won, he could afford to be gracious to the man who'd gone before him.

The new President looked out at the crowd. He was young and smartly dressed. He looked eager to get on with things. He sounded the same way: "Now that peace has come, we will be prosperous. And we will stay strong. Some in what were the Confederate States may think they can drive us out. I stand before the people of the United States—I stand before the people of the reunited States—to tell them they are wrong."

More applause rose. Cassius clapped harder this time than he had before. He wanted the Confederates to get everything that was coming to them and then some. People around him clapped again, too. He didn't think most of them clapped as loud as they had before. He did think that was too bad.

"And I stand before the foreign powers of the world to remind them that the United States are strong, and to remind them that we shall protect ourselves come what may, and with whatever means seem necessary," Dewey went on. "The superbomb is an awful, terrifying weapon. We shall not use it unless provoked. But those who might provoke us had better know they do so at their peril."

This time, the hand he got was loud and long. Was he telling Japan to watch out? Or was he warning the Kaiser? Cassius had found out more about foreign countries since coming to the United States than he ever knew down in Georgia. The only foreign lands he'd ever thought of there were the USA—which wasn't foreign any more—and the Empire of Mexico, because Mexicans had come to work in Augusta and

Mexican soldiers had tried to kill him. The world seemed a wider, more complicated place than it had in the days before he shot Jake Featherston.

"My administration will seek to prevent nations that do not now possess the superbomb from acquiring it," Dewey said. "We have seen at first hand the devastation it inflicts. The German Empire walks side by side with us in this effort. Both Germany and the United States recognize the danger to world peace if irresponsible governments gain the ability to split the atom."

Japan, then—not the Kaiser after all, Cassius thought. He also wondered how President Dewey knew the United States and Germany would be responsible. Cassius decided he probably didn't. But they already had the superbomb, and they didn't aim to let anyone else join their club.

Wasn't Dewey whistling in the dark about his chances of succeeding? The thought had hardly crossed Cassius' mind before the President said, "I know preventing others from building superbombs will be neither easy nor cheap. We do intend to try, however. The safety of the world is at stake."

Behind Cassius, a general leaned over to his wife and murmured, "When it doesn't work, he can say we gave it our best shot." Cassius was sure he wasn't supposed to hear that. He was also sure it made more sense than he wished it did.

Dewey continued, "We will cleanse the old Confederate States of the evil influence of the Freedom Party. We will ensure that the Negroes surviving there gain full rights as citizens, and that the atrocities of the past can never come again."

As Cassius applauded that, a newsreel camera swung toward him. He was here not least as Dewey's object lesson. He didn't mind, or not very much. If the new President kept his pledge or even came close, the Negroes who remained south of the Mason-Dixon Line would be better off than they ever had before.

Dewey made more promises about all the wonderful things he would do within the United States. Cassius didn't know whether they would be wonderful or not. He hoped so. What could you do but hope?

After the speech ended, Dewey turned to the crowd. People came up to congratulate him. He and Truman shook hands and smiled while photographers flashed away. Cassius went down with the rest of the people in his special grandstand.

"Good luck, suh," he said when he worked his way up to Dewey.

"Thank you." The new President gave his hand a quick, professional pump. "Thank you for everything. You've made my job much easier."

"I was mighty glad to do it, suh," Cassius replied. No, nobody would ever think of him without thinking of his one moment. He didn't mind that very much, either. It was one moment more than most of his luckless people ever got.

Atlanta again. Irving Morrell would rather have stayed home with his family, but even leave was welcome. The Atlantic Military District hadn't come to pieces while he went back to the USA. (Well, he supposed that, technically, Atlanta was part of the USA again, too. The locals didn't believe it for a minute. Morrell had trouble believing it himself.)

Things could have been worse. None of the morale officers—there were such things—in *his* command had had the brilliant idea of a soldiers-against-locals football game, the way that maniac in Alabama had. Why not issue any Confederates with a grudge an engraved invitation? *Plenty of damnyankees to shoot at right here!* The only lucky thing was that the mortar crew hurt their own people worse than the U.S. soldiers they were aiming at.

Morrell didn't know what the CO of the Gulf Coast Military District had done with his intrepid football-planning officer. He knew what he would have done himself. If it were up to him, that major or whatever he was would be running the coast defenses of Colorado right now.

He had his own problems. Railroad sabotage just wouldn't stop. There were too many miles of track, and not enough soldiers to keep an eye on all of them. The War Department didn't think that kind of offense justified executing hostages, which was the only thing that might have ended it. Morrell supposed the military bureaucrats in Philadelphia had a point. If the U.S. Army murdered Confederates for any little thing, how did it differ from Jake Featherston's regime except in choice of victims?

But not killing Confederates for any little thing sure made Morrell's life harder.

Then there were the two dozen command cars in and around Rocky Mount, North Carolina, that somehow got sugar in their gas tanks: as good a way of wrecking an engine as any ever found. The local CO had dealt with that one on his own and sent Atlanta a report later. Morrell approved of officers with initiative. This one had commandeered motorcars from the locals to make up the lack and fined the whole town.

Even fines got tricky, though. Confederate silver and gold were still legal tender; weight for weight, those coins matched their U.S. counterparts. Confederate paper wasn't, not for dealings with the occupying authorities. Brown banknotes stayed in circulation among the locals; there weren't enough green bills to go around yet.

Pretty soon, all Confederate paper would be illegal. Then squeezing the occupied states would get easier, anyhow. Right now, the situation with money was the same as it was most ways. Wherever the U.S. authorities reached, they ruled. Where they didn't, or where they turned their backs even for a moment, the old ways went on.

"Here's an ugly one, sir." A light colonel from the judge-advocate's office set a manila folder on Morrell's desk. "From Greenville, South Carolina. They strung up a Negro for coughing at a white woman."

"Coughing?" Morrell said.

"That's what they do a lot of the time down here instead of whistling like we would," the younger officer explained.

"Do we know who did it?" Morrell asked. "Sounds like those people need stringing up themselves."

"Yes, sir." But the lieutenant colonel sounded unhappy.

"Want to tell me more, or do I need to go through all this stuff?" Morrell set a hand on the folder.

"Well, I can give you the short version," the military attorney said.

"Good!" Morrell was drowning in paperwork. "Do that, then."

"Right. For one thing, we know who did it, but we can't prove anything. Everybody denies it. Everybody who was there swears he wasn't and nobody else was, either. As far as they're concerned, that colored guy hanged himself."

"No U.S. witnesses?"

"No, sir."

"All right. You said, 'For one thing.' That means there's something else, doesn't it?"

"Yes, sir. That town will go off like a bomb if we arrest these people. Greenville does not want to put up with the idea that a Negro can get fresh with a white woman, no matter what. I don't know if the dead guy really did or he didn't. But the whites may have surrendered to us. They sure haven't given up on the way things were before they did."

"No, huh?" Morrell had heard that song too many times before. It made up his mind for him. "Send orders to the officer in charge there. Tell him to get his heavy weapons ready and make sure he has air support ready to fly. Then tell him to arrest those people and get them out of there. If Greenville rises, we'll level the place."

"Are you sure, sir?" the lieutenant colonel asked.

"If I had a superbomb handy, I'd drop it on those bastards. That's how sure I am. Now let's get cooking."

"Uh, yes, sir." The military attorney saluted and left his office in a hurry.

U.S. soldiers arrested seventeen men and two women in Greenville. The town didn't rise. Morrell hadn't thought it would. Diehards here bushwhacked and raided and made godawful nuisances of themselves. They showed no signs of being ready or able to fight pitched battles against U.S. troops.

He called in a couple of writers from *Stars and Stripes*, the Army newspaper. "I want you to draft a pamphlet for me," he told them. "Aim it at whites in the former CSA. We can call it *Equality*. Tell these bastards they don't have to like Negroes, but they can't go pissing on them the way they did before the war."

"Yes, sir," the men chorused. One of them added, "When do you want it, sir?"

"Say, a week," Morrell answered. "Then I'll get War Department approval for it, and then I'll issue it. I'll issue it by the millions, by God. From now on, nobody's going to be able to say, 'Well, I didn't know what the rules were.' We'll tell 'em just what the rules are. If they break 'em after that, it's their own damn fault."

He got the first draft six days later. He didn't think it was strong enough, and suggested changes. When it came back, he sent the text to Philadelphia. He wondered how long things would take there. With the new administration coming in, the bureaucracy was even bumpier than usual.

But he not only got approval four days later, he also got a message saying that the powers that be had sent his text to the U.S. commandants in the Gulf Coast Military District, the Mid-South Military District, and the Republic of Texas. They had orders to print and distribute *Equality*, too. What the written word could do, it would.

As soon as the pamphlet hit the streets, complaints hit his desk. He might have known they would. Hell, he had known they would. The former mayor of Atlanta was in prison for aiding and abetting the removal of Negroes from the town. The new town commissioner was a fortyish lawyer named Clark Butler. He would have been handsome if his ears hadn't stuck out.

He'd always cooperated with U.S. authorities before. He was hopping mad now. "You mean we have to put up with it if a, uh, colored fellow"—he'd learned it wasn't a good idea to say *nigger* around Morrell—"makes advances to a white woman?"

"As long as he's peaceable about it, yes," Morrell asked. "Do you mean to tell me white men never make advances to colored women?"

Butler turned red. "That's different."

"How?"

"It just is."

Morrell shook his head. "Sorry, no. I'm not going to budge on this one. Maybe it was different before the war, or you thought it was because you were on top and the Negroes were on the bottom. Things aren't like that any more."

Butler scratched the edge of his thin mustache. "Some of the states in the USA have miscegenation laws. Why are you tougher on us than you would be on them?"

"Because you abused things worse," Morrell answered bluntly. "And I don't think they'll keep those laws much longer. You gave them such a horrible example, they'll be too embarrassed to leave 'em on the books."

"You're going to cause a lot of trouble," Butler predicted in doleful tones.

"I'll take the chance." Morrell, by contrast, sounded cheerful. "If people here start trouble, I promise we'll finish it."

"It's not fair," Butler said. "We're only doing what we always did."

"Yes, and look where that got you," Morrell retorted. "Let's take you in particular, for instance. I know you didn't have anything to do with shipping Negroes to camps—we've checked. You wouldn't be sitting there if you did. You'd be in jail with the old mayor. But you knew they were disappearing, didn't you?"

"Well . . ." Butler looked as if he wished he could disappear. "Yes."

"Good! Well done!" Morrell made clapping motions that were

only slightly sardonic. "See? You can own up to things if you try. I would've thrown you out of my office if you said anything different."

"But treating . . . colored folks like white people? *Equality?*" The city commissioner pronounced the name of the pamphlet with great distaste. "People—white people—won't like that, not even a little bit."

"Frankly, Butler, I don't give a damn." Morrell was getting sick of the whole sorry business. "Those are the rules you've got now. You're going to play by them, and that's flat. If you try to make some poor Negro sorry, we will make you sorrier. If you don't think we can do it— or if you don't think we will do it—go ahead and find out. You won't like what happens next. I promise you that. Wake the town and tell the people. We mean it."

"Colored folks in the same church? Colored kids in the same school?" Plainly, Butler was picking the most hideous examples he could think of.

And Morrell nodded as if his head were on springs. "That's right. Negroes working the same jobs as white people, too, and getting the same pay. Oh, I don't expect colored lawyers right away—you didn't let them get the education for that. But they'll get it from here on out."

"I don't reckon we'll put up with it," Butler said. "I truly don't. Segregation now, segregation tomorrow, and segregation forever!"

"Are you saying that in your official capacity, Mr. Butler?" Morrell asked. "If you are, you just resigned."

Clark Butler reconsidered. He had a well-paying, responsible job at a time and in a place where jobs of any kind were hard to come by. "Well, no. I wasn't speaking officially," he said after a brief pause. "I was just expressing the feelings of a lot of people in this part of the continent—and you know that's so, General."

Morrell knew, all right, much too well. After a pause of his own, he replied, "I don't care what people feel. I can't do anything about that. But I damn well can do something about how people behave. If you want to hate Negroes in your heart, go ahead. While you're hating them, though, I will make you sorry if you treat them any different from whites. Have you got that?"

"Equality enforced at the point of a bayonet?" Butler jeered.

"Sounds pretty silly, doesn't it?" Morrell said with a smile. The city commissioner nodded. But Morrell wasn't finished: "Still, when you get right down to it, it beats the hell out of camps and ovens and mass graves."

"I wasn't involved with that," Butler said quickly.

"You wouldn't be talking with me now if you were," Morrell replied. "But you think you're serious about what you're going to do? So are we. You can find out the easy way or the hard way. Up to you."

Butler left in a hurry after that. Morrell wasn't sorry to see him go, and resolved to keep a closer watch on him from here on out. He wondered whether the United States *could* enforce anything like equality on the old CSA. He still wasn't sure—but he aimed to try.

The only way Clarence Potter could have avoided seeing the pamphlet called *Equality* was to stay in his apartment and never come out. The Yankees plastered the damn thing all over Richmond. During the war, that common a propaganda leaflet would have meant the Quartermaster Corps didn't need to issue toilet paper for a while.

When he first read the pamphlet, he thought it was an A-number-one asswipe, nothing else but. After he looked at it again, he still thought it was an asswipe. But it was a clever asswipe, and a determined one. The damnyankees weren't out to change hearts or minds in the dead CSA. They were out to change behavior. If they rammed different behavior down people's throats from Richmond to Guaymas, they figured hearts and minds would eventually follow.

What worried Potter most was, they had a fighting chance of being right.

He'd watched the same thing happen when the Freedom Party took over the CSA. Even people who didn't like Jake Featherston and the Party started greeting one another with "Freedom!" It was safer. You couldn't get into trouble if you did it. And, after a while, you didn't even feel self-conscious about it. You took it for granted. Pretty soon, you took the truth of everything the Party said for granted. And you, and the Confederate States of America with you, followed Jake Featherston into the abyss.

Now the Yankees wanted to push what was left of the Confederacy into . . . *Equality.* They didn't ask whites to love Negroes. They just said, *Treat them the way you'd treat yourselves, or we'll make you regret it.*

Was there ever a more perverted application of the Golden Rule?

Potter was sure lots of people hated the idea of Negro equality even more than he did. He'd spent sixty-odd years in the CSA; he knew what was what here. But he also knew he was being watched. The damnyankees didn't waste subtlety showing him that—which didn't mean there weren't also subtle spies, ones he didn't notice right away. He assumed his telephone was tapped and his mail read.

And so he sat tight and worked on his memoirs. A generation earlier, he'd done what he could to free the CSA from the onerous terms of the armistice after the Great War. But the Confederacy wasn't crushed then. It wasn't occupied, either. The USA had learned a bar fighter's lesson since: once you knocked a guy down, you needed to kick him in the head so he couldn't jump up and come after you with a broken bottle.

One day in early March, when spring was just starting to be in the air, he went over to Capitol Square to look around. Woodrow Wilson had declared war on the USA there in 1914. Potter himself and Nathan Bedford Forrest III had halfheartedly plotted against Jake Featherston there, too.

Forrest was dead now, because you needed to be a better plotter than he ever was to go up against the wily President of the CSA. Featherston never found out Potter was involved in that scheme. If he had, Potter knew he would have died himself.

Capitol Square had been battered when the two generals sat on a park bench and talked about where the Confederacy was going. Down the drain, though neither of them knew it at the time.

The square looked even worse now than it had then, which wasn't easy. The grass was still mangy and leprous from winter's freezes. No one had mowed it for a long time. It softened the outlines of bomb and shell craters without hiding them. Signs with big red letters shouted blunt warnings: WATCH WHERE YOU STEP! and MINES & LIVE AMMO!

Thus cautioned, Potter didn't walk across the square to the remains of the Capitol. A neoclassical building, it had been bombed into looking like an ancient ruin. From the pictures he'd seen, the Colosseum and the Parthenon were both in a hell of a lot better shape than this place.

Workmen were hauling away the wreckage of Albert Sidney Johnston's heroic statue. Like the Confederacy, it was good for nothing but scrap metal these days. George Washington's statue, now out from under its protective pyramid of sandbags, had come through better. Even the Yankees still respected Washington . . . some, anyhow.

Two blue jays screeched in a tree. A robin hopped on the ground, eye cocked for bugs. A skinny red tabby eyed the robin from behind a low mound of earth. "Go get it," Potter murmured. The cat had to eat, too. But the robin flew off. The cat eyed Potter as if it were his fault. It was a cat—it wouldn't blame itself. Potter sketched a salute. "You're a loser, too," he said fondly. The cat yawned, showing off needle teeth. It ambled away.

He'd been looking for the bench where Forrest first broached getting rid of Featherston and getting out of the war. Once he sold his memoirs, that bench would become a historical monument of sorts. Or rather, it would have, because he saw no sign of it. One more casualty of war.

He found another bench, deeper into Capitol Square. Despite the signs, he didn't blow up getting to it. He sat down. Getting out of the apartment felt good. So did the sun on his face, though he'd grown used to being pasty during the war. A man in a filthy Confederate uniform was sleeping or passed out drunk in the tall grass not far away. Some newspapers did duty for a blanket.

Potter didn't think the derelict was watching him, though you never could tell. Somebody was, somewhere. He was sure of that. He looked around to see if he could spot the spy. Not this time. That proved exactly nothing, of course.

After the end of the last war, Jake Featherston had spent some time in Capitol Square as a drifter, one more piece of flotsam washed up by the armistice. Then he ran into the Freedom Party—and it ran into him. Before he joined, it was a tiny, hopeless outfit that could keep its membership rolls and accounts in a cigar box. Afterwards . . .

Now it was more than twenty-five years afterwards. Potter could see that everybody would have ended up better off if Jake Featherston went down some other street and never met the hopeless chucklehead who founded the Freedom Party. Once upon a time, he'd known that chucklehead's name. He couldn't remember it now to save his life. Well, it sure didn't matter any more.

He closed his eyes. He wished he could close his nose. The stench of death still lingered in Richmond. It would only get worse as the weather warmed up, too. How many years would it need to go away for good?

"Hey, friend, you got any change you can spare?"

Clarence Potter opened his eyes. The sleeping soldier—he still had a sergeant's chevrons on his sleeve—had come to life. He was filthy, and badly needed a shave. God only knew when he'd bathed last. But Potter didn't smell whiskey along with the—what did that Yankee soap ad call it?—B.O.

"Here." He dug in his pocket and found a half-dollar. "Buy yourself something to eat." He tossed it to the man.

"Much obliged, sir." The vet caught it out of the air. He eyed Potter. "You went through it, I reckon."

"Twice," Potter agreed. "Not always at the front, but yeah—twice."

"You've got the look, all right." The demobilized soldier stuck the fat silver coin in a trouser pocket. "You reckon we'll ever get back on our feet again?"

"Sooner or later? I'm sure of it. When?" Potter shrugged. "It may be later. I don't know if I'll live to see it. I hope you do."

The younger man eyed him. "You talk kinda like a Yankee." *He* probably came from Alabama or Mississippi.

With another shrug, Potter answered, "I went to college up there."

"Yeah? You like the Yankees, then? If you do, I'll give you your money back, on account of I don't want it."

"Keep it, son. It's no secret that I don't care for the United States. We can't fight them now—we're licked. I don't know if we'll ever be able to fight them again. But I won't like them if I live to be a hundred, and my bones tell me I won't."

"Huh," the vet said gravely, and then, "We oughta fight 'em. We oughta kick the snot out of 'em for what they done to us."

Was he another Jake Featherston, still unburst from his chrysalis of obscurity? It was possible. Hell, anything was possible. But long odds, long odds. How many tens of thousands had there been after the last war? Potter had no idea. He did know only one rose to the top.

He also knew this grimy fellow might be a provocateur, not an embryo Featherston. The Yankees wouldn't be sorry to have an excuse to stand him against a wall with a blindfold and a last cigarette. No, not even a little bit.

"I have fought the USA as much as I intend to," he said. "Keeping it up when it's hopeless only makes things worse for us."

"Who says it's hopeless?" the young vet demanded.

"I just did. Weren't you listening? Even if we rise, even if we take

Richmond, what will the damnyankees do? Pull their people out of the city and drop a superbomb on it? How do you aim to fight that?"

"They wouldn't." But the man's voice suddenly held no conviction.

"Sure they would. And if we'd won, we'd've done the same thing to Chicago if it rebelled and we couldn't squash it with soldiers. What else are the damn bombs for?"

The man in the shabby, filthy butternut uniform looked up into the sky, as if he heard the drone of a U.S. heavy bomber. One would be all it took. The cities of the conquered CSA lay naked before airplanes. No antiaircraft guns any more. No Hound Dogs waiting to scramble, either. The only reason the damnyankees hadn't done it yet was that nobody'd provoked them enough.

"Teddy Roosevelt used to talk about the big stick," Potter said quietly. "They've got the biggest stick in the world right now, and they'll clobber us with it if we get out of line. We lost. I wish like hell we didn't. I did everything I knew how to do to keep it from happening. We can't get too far out of line now, though. It costs too goddamn much."

"What am I supposed to do with myself, then?" the veteran asked. Tears filled his voice and glistened in his eyes. "I been living on hate ever since we gave up. Don't hardly got nothin' else to live on."

"Clean up. Find a job. Go to work. Find a girl. Plenty of 'em out there, and not so many men. Help build a place where your kids would want to live." Potter shrugged. "Where we are now, what else is there?"

"A place where kids'd want to live? Under the Stars and Stripes? Likely tell!" the young man said scornfully.

"Right now, it's the only game in town. Maybe things will change later on. I don't know. You'll see more of that than I do." Potter's hair was nearer white than gray these days. "But if you go on feeling sorry for yourself and sleeping in the square, maybe get drunk so you don't have to think about things, who wins? You? Or the USA?"

"I need to think about that," the vet said slowly.

Potter rose from the bench. "You've got time. Don't take too long, though. It's out there. Grab with both hands." He never would have had to say that to Jake Featherston. Jake always grabbed.

And look what it got him. Look what it got all of us. Clarence Potter walked back toward the street the way he'd come, trying to step just where he had before. Again, nothing blew up under him. But how much difference did that make now? Jake Featherston had blown up his whole country.

Flora Blackford loved the smell of a kosher deli: the meaty odors of salami and corned beef harmonizing with the brine and vinegar of the pickle barrel and contrasting with the aromas of bagels and fresh-baked bread. Philadelphia had some decent delis, but you needed to go back to New York City for the real thing.

Her brother waved from a table in the back. David Hamburger had a double chin these days. His brown hair was thinning and going gray. Flora was graying, too. She thought the thirty years just past would have grayed anybody, even if they'd somehow happened in the blink of an eye.

"Don't get up," she called as she hurried over to David.

"I wasn't going to. It's too much like work," he said. The artificial leg he'd worn since 1917 stuck out in front of him, unnaturally straight. "Good to see you. You still talk to me even though we won for a change?"

"Maybe," Flora said. They both smiled. David had been a Democrat, and a conservative one, ever since he got hurt. Violence had done its worst to him, so he seemed to think it would solve anything. After this round of war, that seemed less foolish to Flora than it had before. Sometimes nothing else would do.

She sat down. A waiter came up. "*Nu?*" he said. She ordered corned beef on rye and a bottle of beer. David chose lox and bagels with his beer. The waiter scribbled, scratched his thick gray mustache, and went away.

"How are you?" Flora asked. "How's your family?"

"Everybody's fine. Me, I'm not too bad," her brother answered. "How's Joshua doing?"

She told him what Joshua had said about not being able to give anyone the finger with his left hand. David laughed an old soldier's laugh. Flora went on, "He's lucky, I know, but I still wish it never happened."

"Well, I understand that," her brother said. "I've had a pretty good life, taking it all in all, but I sure wish I didn't stop that one bullet."

David sighed. "I'm lucky, too. Look at poor Yossel—the first Yossel, I mean. He never got to see his son at all."

"I know," Flora said. "I was thinking about that every minute after Joshua got conscripted. But he wanted to join. What can you do?"

"Nothing," David answered. "Part of watching them grow up is figuring out when to let go. When Joshua got old enough for conscription, he got too old for you to stop him."

"He told me the same thing," Flora said ruefully. "He wasn't wrong, but what did it get him? A stretch in the hospital."

"And an idea of what the country's worth," David said. The waiter brought the food and the beer. David piled his bagel high with smoked salmon and Bermuda onion and ignored the cream cheese that came with them. Flora thought that was perverse, but no accounting for taste. David Hamburger proved as much, continuing, "Now that he's bled for it, he won't want to let it get soft."

Flora had seen reactionary signs in Joshua since he got wounded, and didn't like them. Tartly, she answered, "You don't have to get wounded to love the United States or be a patriot."

Her brother was busy chewing an enormous mouthful. He washed it down with a swallow of beer. "I didn't say you did," he replied at last. "But you sure don't see things the same way after you catch one."

Now Flora was eating, and had to wait before she could say anything. "Putting on the uniform doesn't turn everybody into a Democrat. Plenty of Socialist veterans—quite a few of them in Congress, in fact."

"I know, I know," David said. "Still, if they'd sat on that Featherston *mamzer* before he got too big to sit on—"

"Who was President when Featherston took over?" Flora asked indignantly, and answered her own question: "Hoover was, that's who. The last time I looked, Hoover was a Democrat."

"Yeah, yeah." David did his best to brush that aside. "Who gave away Kentucky and Houston? Al Smith was no Democrat, and he handed the Confederates the platform they needed to damn near ruin us."

"That was a mistake," Flora admitted. "The trouble was, nobody here really believed Featherston wanted a war. The Great War was so awful for both sides. Why would anybody want to do that again?"

"He didn't. He wanted to win this time. And he almost did," her brother said. "He wanted to get rid of his *shvartzers*, too. Who would have believed *that*? You were ahead of everybody there, Flora. I give you credit for it."

"Sometimes you don't want to be right. It costs too much," Flora said. "Nobody in the USA wanted to let C.S. Negroes in when he started persecuting them. The Democrats were worse about it than the Socialists, though."

"All right, so we didn't have things straight all the time, either," David answered. "Dewey'll do a better job of holding down the CSA than La Follette would have."

"That's the plank he ran on. We'll see if he means it," Flora said.

David laughed. "Was there ever a politician you wouldn't say that about?"

"I can think of three," Flora replied. "Debs, Teddy Roosevelt, and Robert Taft. When they said they'd do something, they meant it. It didn't always help them. Sometimes it just left them with a bull's-eye on their back."

After a moment's thought, David nodded. "And two more," he said: "you and Hosea."

"Thank you," Flora said softly. "I try. So did Hosea—and he never got the credit for it he deserved." He never would, either, and she knew it, not when the economic collapse happened while he was President. After a pull at her beer, she went on, "I'll give you another one: Myron Zuckerman."

"He was an honest man," her brother agreed.

Flora nodded. "He was. And if he didn't trip on the stairs and break his neck, I never would have run for Congress. My whole life would have looked different. I would have stayed an organizer or worked in the clothing business like the rest of the family."

"Zuckerman's bad luck. The country's good luck."

"You say that, with your politics? You'll make me blush. It's only because I'm your sister." Flora tried not to show how pleased she was.

"Hey, I disagree with you sometimes—well, a lot of the time. So what? You *are* my sister, and I'm proud of you," David answered. "Besides, I know I can always borrow money from you if I need it."

He never had, not a penny. Flora had always shared with her parents and sister and younger brother, but David stubbornly made his own way. *I'm doing all right*, he would say. It seemed to be true, for which Flora was glad.

He grinned at her. "So what does it mean, what we've been through since the Great War started? You're the politician. Tie it up for me."

"You don't ask for much!" Flora exclaimed. Her brother laughed. He picked up his beer bottle, discovered it was empty, and waved for another one. Flora drank from hers. If she was going to try to answer a question like that, she needed fortifying. "Well, for starters, we've got the whole United States back, if we can ever stop the people in the South from hating us like rat poison."

"Since when do they like us that much?" David said: a painfully true joke. He went on, "We can hold them down if we have to, them and the Canadians."

"A Negro who got out of the CSA before the Great War said that if you hold a man down in the gutter, you have to get into the gutter yourself," Flora said. "Do we want to do that?"

"Do we want the Confederate States back in business? Do we want them building superbombs again?" David asked, adding, "The one they used almost got you."

"I know," Flora said. "Don't remind me."

"Well, then." By the way David said it, he thought he'd proved his point.

But Flora answered, "Do we want our boys down there for the next fifty years, bleeding a little every day? It would be like a sore that won't heal."

"Better that than worrying about them blowing us off the map," David said. "And they would, too. We've fought them four times in the past eighty years. You think they don't want to try to get even because we won the last two?"

"No, I don't think so, not for a minute." Flora knew some Socialists had thought such things after the Great War. It was unfortunate, but it was true. Nobody thought that way any more, though. Once bitten, twice shy. Twice bitten . . . "Still, if we can't turn them into people who belong in the United States, what are we going to do with them?"

"Do we want people like that in our country? People who murdered eight or ten million Negroes? Even when the Tsar turns loose a pogrom, it's not as bad as that."

"A *choleriyeh* on the Tsar." Flora hated the idea of Russia with a superbomb, too. Germany would have to deal with Russia, though; the USA just didn't have the reach. She got back to the business at hand: "They didn't kill *all* the Negroes."

"No, but they didn't try to stop the Freedom Party goons, either. They cheered them on, for crying out loud," David said. "And you know what scares me?"

"*Nu?*" Flora asked.

"If it happened down there, it could happen here. It could happen to Negroes here, or, God forbid, it could happen to Jews. If you get enough people hot and bothered, anything can happen. Anything at all."

"God forbid is right," Flora said. "I like to think we wouldn't do anything like that . . ."

"Yeah. Me, too. And how many *shvartzers* thought their white neighbors wouldn't do anything like that? How many of them are left to think anything now?" Her brother answered his own question: "Not many."

"Maybe seeing what the Confederates did will vaccinate us against it," Flora said. "We can hope so, anyway."

"*Alevai,*" David said.

"*Alevai omayn.*" Flora nodded. "But can you imagine a politician saying, 'I want to do the same thing Jake Featherston did. Look how well it worked down there'?"

"Mm, maybe not—not for a while, anyway." David smiled crookedly. "Let's hear it for bad examples. I always aimed to be one for my children, but massacring people goes a little too far."

"A little. Sure." Flora reached out and set her hand on his. He looked astonished. She realized she hadn't done that in—oh, much too long. "And some bad example you are."

"Hey, I'm a Democrat. How can I be anything but a bad example?"

"You'll have to work harder than that." Flora hoped he wouldn't get angry. He *had* worked hard, all his life.

He didn't. "Here. I'll give it my best shot." He pulled out a pack of cigarettes and lit one. "How am I doing?"

"I think you need to try something else." Flora fought not to laugh.

"Don't know what. I already drink. Don't want to chase women— I'm happy with the one I caught. And you're the family politician."

"Well! I like that!"

David's smile got crookeder yet. "You know what? Me, too."

Flora pointed to the pack. "Give me one of those."

"You don't smoke."

"So what? Right now I do."

He handed her a cigarette, then leaned close to light it from his. She thought it tasted terrible, but she didn't care, not just then. They blew out smoke together.

Read on for a preview of Harry Turtledove's
thrilling saga,
THE MAN WITH THE IRON HEART

PROLOGUE: BEFORE

29 May 1942—outskirts of Prague

The big green Mercedes convertible bore a number plate of stark simplicity: SS3. The Reichsprotektor of Bohemia and Moravia sped from
his country estate toward the Castle of Prague. German soldiers in
field-gray and Czech guards in tobacco-brown would salute him when
he arrived. Czech president Hacha also had his offices in the castle, but
his will was as nothing when set against the Reichsprotektor's. Everyone knew it—including Hacha.

Reinhard Heydrich glanced at his watch. "Step on it, Klein," he
said irritably. "We're running late."

"Right, sir," Oberscharführer Johannes Klein answered with a
silent sigh. If they were late, the senior noncom knew it wasn't by more
than thirty seconds. Heydrich didn't tolerate tardiness . . . or much of
anything else.

Klein checked his own wrist. Not even half past ten yet. Like a lot
of big wheels, Heydrich bitched for the sake of bitching. He might look
like the perfect Aryan—tall and lean, blond and handsome. He might
be a first-class fencer and pilot and violinist. But he had some little old
lady in him all the same.

They came to a corner a minute later. "Slow down," Heydrich said.
"The trolley's pulling up."

"I see it, Herr Reichsprotektor." Klein sighed out loud this time.

You couldn't win. "I see those worthless layabouts who've been hanging around the stop the past couple of days, too. Bums." To him, all Czechs were bums till proved otherwise.

"They look like men with jobs," Heydrich said. "That's a new overcoat one of them has on."

"What's he doing with it?" Klein asked. The Czech fumbled with something in an inside pocket.

He got hold of it and pulled it out: a submachine gun, an ugly, brutally effective British Sten. He aimed it at Heydrich's chest and pulled the trigger.

However effective Stens usually were, this particular tin tommy gun jammed. The Czech looked horrified. He jerked at the cocking handle and yelled something inflammatory in his own language.

"Jesus Christ!" Heydrich yelled, and then, "Halt!" He stood up in the passenger side of the car and drew the pistol he wore on his belt. The hammer clicked uselessly—the Luger wasn't loaded. Heydrich said something that had to be worse than what came out of the Czech's mouth.

Oberscharführer Klein had to fight not to piss himself—and not to giggle like a schoolgirl. Nobody's weapon wanted to work! Was this a fight to the death or a low farce?

Then, perhaps with the instincts he'd picked up flying a 109 on the Eastern Front, Heydrich thought to check six. When he looked behind him, he saw the other Czech who'd been hanging around this corner snaking up on the car. "Gun it, Hans!" Heydrich shouted.

Klein's big-booted foot mashed down on the accelerator. The Mercedes was heavy, but it leaped ahead as if somebody'd goosed it. The second Czech threw something. A bomb of some sort—it had to be.

It burst a few meters behind the hurtling auto. Heydrich yelped and swore and jerked his left hand. Blood ran down his palm and dripped from his fingers to the Mercedes's rubber floor mat. He tried to make a fist, then yelped again and thought better of it. Only after Klein flung the car around a couple of corners did the Reichsprotektor think to ask, "Are you all right?"

The driver reached up to touch his left ear. His gloved hand came away red. "Just a scratch." He paused a few seconds. "I think we've got away from the stinking bastards."

"Ja . . . if more of them aren't lying in wait for us." Again, Heydrich needed a moment to add, "You did well."

"Uh, thanks." Klein sounded a little shaky. Heydrich supposed he did, too. Anybody who suddenly got dropped into combat was liable to. The driver went on, "How's your hand? Shall I get you to a hospital?"

Heydrich was already wrapping a handkerchief around the wound. "No, don't bother. I'll live," he said. "Take me on to the Castle. A doctor'll be on duty there, or we can send for one. And then—" He stopped in grim anticipation.

"Then what, sir?" Klein asked.

"Then we peel this pesthole of a town—this pesthole of a country—to catch the assassins," Heydrich answered. "We don't overlook wrongs from Czechs—never, any more than we let Jews get away with anything inside the Reich."

"We don't let anybody get away with anything," Klein said—a good enough rule for the way Germany ruled.

Heydrich nodded. He tried to close his hand again. No luck. It hurt too much. Blood was soaking through the handkerchief. "No. We don't," he agreed. "And when somebody tries, we make him pay."

5 February 1943—Berlin

The Reich was in mourning after the fall of Stalingrad. Taverns, theaters, movie houses—all closed, at the Führer's order. Funereal music played on every radio station. Reinhard Heydrich thought he'd kick in a receiver if he heard "Ich Hatt' Ein Kamerad" one more time.

Oberscharführer Klein pulled up in front of SS headquarters. "Here you go, sir," he said.

"Right." Heydrich got out of the Mercedes convertible. Not a trace of the damage from the assassination attempt remained visible on the car. The Czech repairmen who'd worked on the Mercedes would have answered with their necks if any had.

Guards stiffened to attention as Heydrich approached. In his SS Obergruppenführer's uniform, with the SD patch on his lower left sleeve, his slim, athletic figure was one to conjure with. "State your name and business, sir." The young officer who made the demand knew damn well who—and what—Heydrich was. His voice wouldn't have wobbled if he hadn't.

After naming himself, Heydrich paused a moment for effect before continuing, "I am here for an appointment with the Reichsführer-SS."

"Yes, sir," the youngster said, and his voice wobbled again. If he'd had an appointment with Heinrich Himmler, he would have been in more trouble than he could imagine. A parish priest was an honorable part of the Catholic Church, but that didn't mean he expected to get an audience with the pope. Gathering himself, the officer told off two of his men to escort Heydrich to Himmler's office.

Somebody inside headquarters was listening to a radio. Sure as hell, it was playing "Ich Hatt' Ein Kamerad." Heydrich fumed. He couldn't do anything more, not when one of the black-uniformed men walking with him said, "Terrible thing, what happened in the east."

"Yes," Heydrich said. "Terrible." And it was. The whole Sixth Army . . . gone. Germany was in plenty of trouble in the rest of southern Russia, too. Heydrich was still sick of that goddamn song.

Hastily, the trooper added, "But we'll lick 'em anyway, won't we, sir?" You could get in trouble for showing defeatism. In these nervous times, you could get in trouble for almost anything.

More guards stood in front of the door to the Reichsführer's sanctum. Heydrich's escorts handed him off to them, then went back toward the entrance with every sign of relief. "You're right on time, Herr Obergruppenführer," one of Himmler's guards said.

"I should hope so." Heydrich was affronted. If he was ever late, he made whoever caused the lateness sorry. That he might be late through no fault of anyone else's never crossed his mind.

The guards brought him into Himmler's office. At a nod from their chief, they disappeared. "Good day, Reinhard," Himmler said. "How are you?" He used the familiar pronoun.

"Well enough, sir, thanks. And you?" Heydrich used the formal pronoun. He always had with Himmler, even if they'd worked hand in glove for years. He expected he always would.

It was a funny business. Heydrich knew he could tear Himmler to pieces if he wanted to. Himmler was on the pudgy side. He'd never been very hard physically. The round, almost chinless face behind the pince-nez could have belonged to a chicken farmer or a schoolmaster. To the man who led the outfit that vied with Beria's NKVD for deadliness? It seemed unlikely.

But it was true. And therein lay the rub. Himmler might not look like anything much. When he spoke, though, people listened. Having listened, they obeyed. If they didn't, they quickly departed the land of the living. Himmler, the mild-mannered bureaucrat, had even bureaucratized death. And, because he had, he could intimidate an outwardly tougher man like Heydrich.

And Himmler had another hold on the Reichsprotektor. There were rumors of Jews in Heydrich's family tree. Heydrich's father's mother's second husband had been named Süss. He'd even looked Jewish, though he hadn't been. A private genealogist had confirmed that, and the SS had accepted it. Further back, though, there was an unexplained Birnbaum. If Himmler decided that what had been accepted should be rejected . . .

A bead of sweat trickled down Heydrich's back. It seemed to burn like acid. He deliberately slowed his breathing. To his relief, his heart stopped fluttering. He couldn't let Himmler intimidate him, not today. His mission was too important, not for himself but for the Reich.

The Reich. Think of the Reich, not of yourself. As long as that was his lodestone, he'd be all right. He hoped.

Himmler steepled his fingers. "Well, Reinhard, what brings you up from Prague today?" His voice was fussy and precise, like a school-master's.

One more deep breath. Forcing his voice to steadiness, Heydrich asked, "Herr Reichsführer, what do you think of Germany's war prospects in the light of recent developments?"

Himmler's right eyebrow twitched—only a couple of millimeters, but enough to notice. Whatever he might have expected, that wasn't it. He usually chose his words with care. He seemed especially careful now, answering, "In view of our, ah, misfortune at Stalingrad, this may not be the best time to ask."

"It isn't just Stalingrad, Herr Reichsführer," Heydrich said. Himmler's eyebrow twitched again. He also hadn't expected Himmler to persist. But the Reichsprotektor of Bohemia and Moravia did: "The Russians are taking big bites out of our positions in the east."

"That will stop. The Führer has personally assured me of it," Himmler said.

"Yes, sir." Heydrich's agreement was more devastating than any argument could have been. After letting it hang in the air, he continued, "Our allies aren't worth the paper they're printed on. Hungary? Romania? Italy?" He snapped his fingers in vast contempt. "The Finns can fight, but there aren't enough of them."

"What are you driving at, Reinhard?" Himmler's tone went silky with danger. "Are you saying the war is lost? Do you dare say that?"

"Yes, sir," Heydrich repeated. This time, Himmler's eyebrow didn't just twitch. It leaped. Heydrich had put his life—not only his career, but his life—in the Reichsführer's hands. Having done so, he explained why: "The east is coming undone. Maybe we can patch it up, but I don't think so. And even if we can . . . the English and Americans are going to drive us out of Africa. We can't supply our troops there—that's been plain for a long time. And after they do, Sicily's one short hop away. Italy is one more. Can you tell me I'm wrong?"

"Is the castle in Prague haunted? You talk like a man who's seen a ghost," Himmler said.

"I wish it were, Herr Reichsführer. I wish I had," Heydrich said. "Instead, I've spent too damned much time looking at maps." He paused, then added, "The bombing's betting worse, too, isn't it?"

"And how do you know that?" Himmler asked quietly.

"Because now we have to talk about it in the papers and on the radio," Heydrich answered. "We can't pretend it isn't happening any more. Everybody knows it is. We'd only look like idiots if we ignored it."

"Dr. Goebbels is many things. An idiot he is not." Himmler spoke with a certain regret. The great lords of Party and State were rivals as well as colleagues.

Heydrich nodded. "I know. And so, Herr Reichsführer, I ask you again: what do you think of our war prospects?"

The leader of the SS didn't answer directly. Instead, he said, "We can't lose this war. We mustn't. If we do, it will make what we went through in 1918 look like a kiss on the cheek. Bolshevik hordes storming into Germany . . ." He shuddered at the idea. "And I don't imagine we could get terms before the enemy crossed our western border, either, the way we did last time."

"No, sir. I wouldn't think so," Heydrich agreed. "And if we are invaded, if we are occupied . . . what do we do then?"

"I think I'd rather take poison than live to see the day," Himmler said.

Heydrich looked at—looked through—him. He seldom held a moral advantage over the Reichsführer-SS, but he did now. "Sir, wouldn't it be better to fight? To keep on fighting, I mean? Even if the armed forces get ground down—"

"I don't believe it. I won't believe it," Himmler broke in.

"Devil of a lot of Ivans. Devil of a lot of Americans, too," Heydrich said. "And the Amis can bomb us, and we can't bomb them. Too damned many Englishmen with them. And all the Jews in Washington and Moscow and London will want revenge on the Reich and the Führer. You know what was decided at Wannsee a year ago."

No one at that conference had come right out and said Germany aimed to get rid of all the Jews in the territory she held. Nobody had needed to. The high functionaries had understood what was what. So did Himmler, of course.

"Can you imagine the circus they'd have if they took the Führer alive?" Heydrich asked softly.

That turned out to be a keen shot, keener than he'd expected. Imagining, Himmler looked almost physically ill. "It must not happen!" he choked out. Maybe he was also imagining the circus the Allies would have if they took him alive. And maybe—no, certainly—he had reason to. Heydrich had had imaginings like that more often than he liked since the Czechs almost assassinated him.

"I hope it doesn't. I pray it doesn't," he said now. "But this is war—war to the finish, war to the knife. Shouldn't we be ready for anything, even the possibility of the worst?"

"What exactly do you have in mind?" the Reichsführer asked. Himmler's voice was almost back to normal. Almost, but not quite.

"You'll know, sir, probably better than I do, how much trouble the Russian partisans have given the Wehrmacht," Heydrich said.

"And the Waffen-SS," Himmler put in. "Several of our formations are in action behind the lines against those devils."

"Yes, sir. And the Waffen-SS," Heydrich agreed. "And the Soviets improvised those bands on the spur of the moment after the war broke out against them a year and a half ago. How much grief could we give enemy occupiers if we started preparing now, this instant, setting aside weapons and training men to fight as partisans if the worst comes? The more we did in advance, the more ready we'd be if, God forbid, they had to do what we'd trained them for."

Himmler didn't answer for some little while. He plucked at his lower lip with thumb and forefinger. That lip was oddly full, oddly sensuous, for the hard-boiled leader of an even more hard-boiled outfit. At last, he said, "This is not a plan I can deliver to the Führer. He remains unshakably convinced we shall emerge victorious in spite of everything."

"I hope he's right." Heydrich knew he couldn't very well say anything else.

"So do I. Of course." By the way Himmler said it, he wasn't optimistic no matter what he hoped.

"But don't you think it's something that needs doing?" Heydrich persisted. "It might not be something we could manage to scrape together at the last minute, with everything going to the devil around us.

If we'd taken Moscow the first autumn and hanged Stalin in front of the Kremlin, what would the Soviet partisan movement be worth now?"

Himmler plucked at his red lower lip again. He let it spring back into place with a soft, liquid plop. After another pause, he said, "If we were to go forward with these preparations, it would be an SS undertaking."

"Aber natürlich, Herr Reichsführer!" Heydrich exclaimed. "This is the SS's proper business. The Wehrmacht fights ordinary battles in ordinary ways. We need to be able to do that, too, but we also need to be able to do whatever else the State may require of us."

"Jaaaa." Himmler let the word stretch. Seen through the pince-nez, his stare didn't seem too dangerous—if you didn't know him. Unfortunately, Heydrich did. The Reichsführer-SS said, "Since you propose this project, do you expect to head it?"

"Yes, sir," Heydrich answered without the least hesitation. "I've been thinking about it for some time—since things, ah, first went wrong last fall at Stalingrad and in North Africa. Even if worse comes to worst, it would give us the chance to do the enemy a great deal of harm. In the end, it might save the Reich despite what would ordinarily be reckoned a defeat."

"Do you think so?" Himmler looked and sounded unconvinced.

But Heydrich nodded. "I do. Especially in the west, the enemy is basically soft. How much stomach will he have for occupying a country where his soldiers aren't safe outside their barracks—or inside them, either, if we can smuggle in a bomb with a time fuse?"

"Hmm," Himmler murmured. He plucked once more. Plop—the lip snapped back. Heydrich thought the mannerism disgusting, but couldn't very well say so. Pluck. Plop. Finally, the Reichsführer said, "Well, you've given me a good deal to think about. I can hardly deny that. We'll see what comes of it."

"The longer we wait, the more trouble we'll have doing it properly," Heydrich warned.

"I understand that," Himmler said testily. "I have to make sure I can get it moving without . . . undue difficulties, though."

"As you say, sir!" Heydrich was all obedience, all subordination. Why not? Himmler played the cards close to his chest, but Heydrich was pretty sure he'd won.

AFTER

I

Lichtenau was a little town, not much more than a village, a few miles south and west of Nuremberg. Charlie Pytlak walked down what was left of the main street, a BAR cradled in his arms. He had the safety off and a round chambered. He knew the Nazis had surrendered the day before, but some damnfool diehards might not have got the word—or might not care. The only thing worse than getting it during the war was getting it afterwards.

He admired the shattered shops and houses and what had probably been a church. The bright spring sun cast his shadow ahead of him. "Wow," he said with profound unoriginality, "we liberated the living shit out of this place, didn't we?"

"Bet your ass, Sarge," said Dom Lombardo. He'd liberated a German submachine gun—a machine pistol, the krauts called it. He kicked a broken brick out of the way. "Got any butts on you?"

"Sure thing." Pytlak gave him a Chesterfield, then stuck another one in his own mouth. He flicked a flame from his Zippo to light both cigarettes; his unshaven cheeks hollowed as he sucked in smoke. He blew it out in a long stream. "Dunno why they make me feel good, but they do."

"Yeah, me, too," Lombardo agreed. "Couldn't hardly fight a war without cigarettes and coffee."

"I sure wouldn't want to try," Pytlak said. "I—"

He broke off. Half a dozen German soldiers came around a corner. A couple of them wore helmets instead of Jerry field caps—a sign they'd likely fought to the end. One of the bastards in ragged, tattered field-gray still carried a rifle. Maybe he just hadn't thought to drop it. Or maybe . . .

"Hold it right there, assholes!" Pytlak barked. His automatic rifle and Dom's Schmeisser swung to cover the enemy soldiers.

The Germans froze. Most of them raised their hands. The guy with the Mauser slowly and carefully set it down in the rubble-strewn street. He straightened and reached for the sky, too. May 1945 was way too late to die.

One of the krauts jerked his chin toward the Chesterfields Charlie and Dom were smoking. He wasn't dumb enough to lower a hand to point. "Zigarette, bitte?" he asked plaintively. His buddies nodded, their eyes lighting up. The past couple of years, they must have been smoking hay and horseshit, except for what they could take from POWs.

"I can't give 'em any, Sarge," Lombardo said. "I had to bum this one offa you."

"Fuck. I don't wanna waste my smokes on these shitheads. A week ago, they'd've tried to waste me." Pytlak looked the Germans over. They were pretty pathetic. A couple of them couldn't have been more than seventeen; a couple of the others were nearer fifty than forty. The last two . . . The last two had been through the mill and then some. One of them wore an Iron Cross First Class on his left breast pocket. But they were whipped, too. You could see it in their eyes.

Charlie flicked the BAR's safety on. He leaned the weapon against a wall and dug in his pocket for more cigarettes. As he started toward the Germans, Dom said, "I'll cover you."

"You goddamn well better, Ace."

But there was no trouble. The German soldiers seemed pathetically grateful as Pytlak passed around the Zippo. And well they might have. The way things were in the ruins of the Reich these days, he could have got blown for half a dozen Chesterfields. He really was wasting them on these guys.

He scooped up the rifle the one guy had carried. Its safety was off, too. He took care of that. Then he tapped the other kraut's Iron Cross. "Where?" he asked. The guy just looked at him. "Uh, wo?" Like most GIs, he'd picked up a few words of German.

"Ah." The Jerry got it. "Kharkov." He pointed east. "Russland."

"Right," Charlie said tightly. If you listened to the Germans, all of them had done all their fighting on the Eastern Front. Trouble with that was, Uncle Joe's boys fought back a hell of a lot harder than the Nazis figured they would. As the war wound down, all the Germans wanted to do was get away from the Red Army so they could hand themselves over to Americans or Englishmen.

Well, these guys had made it. Charlie carried the rifle back to Dom and handed it to him. "Here. You can handle this and your grease gun. I've gotta lug the BAR around."

"Thanks a bunch," Dom said, slinging the Mauser. But Charlie knew he was right. The Schmeisser didn't weigh even half as much as a Browning Automatic Rifle. And he was a sergeant, and Dom nothing but a PFC. What good was rank if you couldn't use it?

They marched the Germans out of Lichtenau. There was a camp of sorts a couple of miles outside of town: a big barbed-wire cage in a field, now rapidly filling up with Jerries. If the surrendered soldiers had to sleep out in the open and eat U.S. Army rations for a while, well, too goddamn bad.

A truck's carcass lay by the side of the road. It wasn't a big, snorting GMC model from the States, but some shitty little German machine. It must have been machine-gunned from the air and then burned like a son of a bitch. Later, a tank or a bulldozer shoved it to one side so it wouldn't block traffic.

A German in civvies was fiddling around in the wreckage. "Wonder what he's up to," Charlie said.

"Scrap metal—waddaya wanna bet?" Dom returned. "Fucking scavengers are gonna be everywhere for months. Years, probably."

"Yeah, I guess." Charlie laughed. "We turned this whole stinking country into scrap metal and garbage. Just what the assholes deserved, too."

"I ain't arguing," Dom said.

The POW camp looked to be getting more organized by the minute. Charlie had to sign a paper saying he'd brought in six krauts. The corporal who manned a typewriter actually gave him a receipt for them. "The fuck'm I supposed to do with this?" Pytlak asked. "I feel like I just got into the slave-trading business."

"Hang on to it," the typist said. "We need to ask you anything about these guys, now we can."

"Hot damn," Charlie said, and then, "Jesus! I gotta figure out how many points I have. Sooner I get out of the Army, happier I'll be."

You earned discharge points for time in the service, for time overseas, for medals, for campaign stars on theater ribbons, and for kids under eighteen back home. Eighty-five would get you home. Till now, Pytlak hadn't worried about them much. But the war was over. That still took getting used to; damned if it didn't. And damned if I wanna hang around on occupation duty, either, he thought.

"Don't get hot and bothered, man," the typist advised him. "They're gonna ship all our asses to the Pacific so we can punch Hirohito's ticket for him, too."

Charlie's reply was detailed and profane. Dom also chimed in with some relevant opinions. The corporal just grinned. He'd got under their skins, so he won the round. The really evil thing was, on top of that he was liable to be right.

Finally, in disgust, Pytlak said, "I'm gone. Next to this crap, Lichtenau looks goddamn good. You with me, Dom?"

"Oh, hell, yes," Lombardo said.

They were both shaking their heads as they trudged back toward the town. "Fight the fuckin' Japs," Charlie muttered. "That's just what I fuckin' need. Time they ship my butt home, I'll have a long white beard."

Dom was more than ready to help him bitch. Dom was always ready to help a guy bitch. He'd been pretty handy with that Schmeisser when they really needed it, too. Before long, it'd be nothing but a souvenir—that or more scrap metal. Charlie had heard they weren't letting GIs ship weapons home. One more chickenshit regulation, almost as bad as getting a receipt for POWs.

He and Dom came up to the corpse of the German truck. The scrounger who'd been messing around there was gone. "Who's that asshole gonna sell his scrap to?" Charlie said. "Us—you wait and see. We're dumb enough to pay good money to put these mothers back on their feet now that we stomped 'em."

"Yeah, that's like us, all right," Dom agreed. "We—"

The truck blew up. Next thing Charlie knew, he was sprawled on the ground a surprisingly long way from the road. Dom—no, a piece of Dom—lay not far away. Charlie tried to reach out. His arm didn't want to work. When he looked down at what was left of himself, he understood why. It didn't hurt. Then, all at once, it did.

His shriek bubbled through the blood filling his mouth. Mercifully, blackness enfolded him.

Lieutenant Lou Weissberg looked at the crater by the side of the road. "Son of a bitch," he said. "Looks like a five-hundred-pound bomb went off here."

That won him the first respectful glance he'd got from the ordnance sergeant already on the scene. "Damn near, sir," Toby Benton agreed, his slow Texas or Oklahoma drawl halfway to being a different language from Lou's clotted New Jersey. "Reckon some Jerries snuck one of their two-hundred-and-fifty-kilo jobs into the truck an' then touched the mother off. Blew two of our guys to hell and gone." He pointed over to the corpses.

They'd left the GIs where they lay, so Weissberg could look them over and use his brilliance to pull a Sherlock Holmes and tell everybody what was what. To ordinary soldiers, the Counter-Intelligence Corps did stuff like that. Lou belonged to the CIC. He wished like hell he could do stuff like that. Unfortunately, unlike ordinary soldiers, he knew better.

He went over anyway and trained a camera on the bodies. "I hate taking pictures of these poor guys, you know?" he said, snapping away anyhow. "But I gotta have something to bring back to Nuremberg so the big shots there can see what happened."

"You better be careful, sir," Sergeant Benton said.

"How come? Is the ground mined?" Lou stood stock-still, as if he intended to take root right where he was. And if Benton nodded or said yes, that would be about the safest thing he could do.

But the noncom shook his head. "Nah, didn't mean that. You keep talkin' the way you are, though, people're liable to reckon you're a human being or somethin'."

"Oh." Lieutenant Weissberg wondered how to take that. To ordinary grunts, CIC officers probably weren't human beings, if by human beings you meant those who lived the same way they did. Lou had fired his carbine exactly once during the war, when his outfit almost got overrun during the Battle of the Bulge. He'd slept warm and eaten well, unlike most mudfaces. Therefore . . . this was likely a genuine compliment. He treated it as one, answering, "Thank you, Sergeant."

"You're welcome, sir," Benton said seriously. "I figured you'd be one o' them behind-the-lines assholes . . . uh, no offense. But you don't want to be doing this shit, neither."

"You better believe it," Lou said. "Somebody has to, though. German army surrendered. Un-fucking-conditionally surrendered. If they think they can get away with crap like this . . ."

"What do we do about it?" Benton asked. "Take hostages and shoot 'em if the mothers who did this don't turn themselves in? That's what the Jerries woulda done, and you can take that to the bank."

"I know." Lou's voice was troubled. "All kinds of things the Jerries would've done that I don't want anything to do with."

Toby Benton eyed the CIC man in a way he'd seen before: as someone who knew the straight skinny and might be tempted into talking about it. "That stuff they say about those camps—Dachau an' Belsen an' them all—they really that bad?"

"No," Lou said tightly. Just when Benton started to breathe a sigh of relief, he went on, "They're worse. They're a thousand times worse, maybe a million. Far as I'm concerned, we should hang all the mamzrim who ran 'em. And you know what else? I think we're going to."

"If that shit is true—Jesus!—we ought to." Sergeant Benton paused. "The what? Mom-something?"

"Oh." Weissberg realized what he'd said. "It's Yiddish. Means bastards. And they are."

"I ain't arguin'." Benton eyed him again, this time not as a source but in another way he'd seen before. "Yiddish, huh? You're, uh, a Jewish fella?"

"Guilty," Lou said. How many Jews had the sergeant seen before? If he came off an Oklahoma farm, maybe not many. And was he a Regular Army guy or a draftee? Lou thought he might be career military, and not many Jews were.

"You really don't like the krauts then, right?"

"You might say so, Sergeant. Yeah, you just might. If they were all in hell screaming for water, I'd pull up with a gasoline truck."

"Heh." Benton let out only a syllable's worth of laughter, but his eyes sparked. "I like that—damned if I don't."

"Glad you do." Lou came back over to the crater. "Me, I don't like this. If the Germans think they can fuck around with us while we're occupying their country . . ." His voice trailed away. What exactly could—would—the United States do about it?

"Awful lot of guys just want to head on home an' pick up their lives where they left off," Sergeant Benton remarked. "Hell, I sure do." He was a draftee, then.

"I know. So do I," Lou said. He'd been teaching high school English in Jersey City when the Japs bombed Pearl Harbor. Nothing would make him happier than to go back to diagramming sentences. But he was not the master of his fate or the captain of his soul. The master of his fate was back in Nuremberg, waiting to hear what he had to say about this. He sighed. What could he say that wasn't obvious?

Benton's eyes slid to what was left of the two GIs' bodies. Those would either get buried in a military cemetery here or go back to the States in sealed coffins, probably with sandbags to keep them company and make them weigh what they should. Lou hoped the Graves Registration people would plant them here. The less these guys' relatives knew about what had happened to them, the better.

He walked over to the jeep that had brought him out from Nuremberg. Benton had his own jeep. A bored-looking private sat in Lou's machine, checking out a magazine full of girls in pinup poses. Reluctantly, the driver set down the literature. "Take you back now, sir?" he asked. Violation of the surrender terms? A honking big crater and two mangled bodies? He probably didn't care much about anything, but he cared more about the leg art than this business.

And maybe he had the right attitude, too.

"Yeah, let's go," Lou said.

The driver started the engine. Jeeps were almost as reliable as Zippos. They fired up first time every time. Not much traffic on the road. What there was was nearly all U.S. military: olive-drab vehicles marked with a white star, usually inside a white circle.

Lou didn't get his ass in an uproar about trucks and jeeps and half-tracks that ran. He didn't worry about the Germans he saw, either, even though a lot of them still wore Feldgrau and some hadn't handed in their weapons yet. But he flinched whenever he rolled by crumpled metal wreckage—and there was plenty of it. If those Nazi schmucks had booby-trapped one dead truck, who could say they hadn't done it to more than one?

Nuremberg looked as if God had jumped on it with both feet and then spent a while kicking it, like a kid throwing a tantrum. The town where the Nazis threw their big wingdings, the town where Leni What's-her-name filmed *Triumph of the Will,* was the biggest rubble field in the world.

Or maybe not. Lou hadn't seen Berlin yet. The Russians played for keeps. And well they might. Hitler's team had come that close—that close—to doing unto them instead, and they had to know it. It never occurred to most Americans that they might have lost the war. The Atlantic and Pacific didn't shield the USSR from nasty neighbors. Fighting their way west across their own smashed and shattered country, Red Army soldiers could see what a narrow escape they'd had.

Lou suddenly snickered, which made the driver look at him as if he'd started picking his nose. He didn't care. Suppose that truck had been sabotaged by organized diehards who weren't ready to quit. Maybe they thought Americans were too soft to give them what they deserved. Maybe they were even right.

But he would have bet dollars to doughnuts that the surviving Nazis had too much sense to piss off the Russians. He laughed again, louder this time. If the krauts didn't have that kind of sense, the Reds would be happy—fucking delighted—to pound it into them.

Marshal Ivan Stepanovich Koniev was about as unhappy as a jubilant man could be. His First Ukrainian Front had done everything an army group could do to smash the last German defenses in the east. It had broken into Berlin, and paid its share in blood to take Hitler's capital away from him and throw the Third Reich into the coffin it deserved.

So far, so good. But Stalin's orders gave the most important targets in Berlin to Marshal Zhukov's First Byelorussian Front. "Yob tvoyu mat', Georgi Konstantinovich," Koniev muttered.

No matter what he said about Zhukov's mother, Koniev hadn't really expected anything else. Hoped, yes; expected, no. Zhukov was Stalin's fair-haired boy, and that was that. Stalin trusted Zhukov not to try to overthrow him: the kind of trust a dictator didn't give lightly—or, sometimes, at all. Having given it, Stalin could afford to be extravagant in giving Zhukov anything he fancied.

That Zhukov was a damned good general had nothing to do with anything, not so far as Koniev was concerned. Without false modesty, the commander of the First Ukrainian Front knew he was a damned good general himself. So did Zhukov. And so did Stalin.

All the same, Stalin had only one favorite. Koniev knew he wasn't it. Zhukov was. So Zhukov's men got the Chancellery and the Führer's bunker. It seemed unfair. It certainly did to Koniev, whose men broke into Berlin ahead of the other marshal's.

"Nichevo," Koniev said. And it couldn't be helped, not unless he felt like quarreling with Stalin. He might be—he was—irked, but he wasn't suicidal.

Scrawny Germans, many still in threadbare uniforms, trudged gloomily through Berlin's wreckage-strewn streets. They got out of the way in a hurry when Red Army soldiers came by. If they didn't, they'd pay for it. The stench of death hung in the air. Corpses still lay in the gutters, and sometimes in the middle of the street. Quite a few of them had got there after the surrender. No surviving Germans wanted to give the conquerors an excuse to add more.

Off in the distance, a woman shrieked. A Russian a few meters from Marshal Koniev chuckled. "One more cunt getting what she deserves," he said. His buddies laughed out loud.

Koniev didn't. The Red Army had avenged Nazi atrocities inside the USSR ever since it crossed the Reich's borders. Berlin was no exception. Who'd wanted to say the Russian and Asiatic soldiers couldn't have their fun after the war's last battle? They owed the Germans plenty. But discipline was supposed to be returning. That scream—and others like it Koniev had heard in the ten days since the surrender— argued it still wasn't all the way back.

Which went a long way toward explaining why almost all the Germans Koniev could see were men. German women feared Red Army soldiers would drag them off and gang-rape them if they showed themselves. They might have been right, too. They'd be safe enough in a few weeks. But not yet.

A driver came up to Koniev and saluted. "Comrade Marshal, your car is ready," the man said.

"Good," Koniev said. "Very good. I won't be sorry to get out of this place for a while. It stinks."

"Sure does." The driver didn't seem to care. "If you'll come with me, sir . . ."

The car was a captured Kubelwagen—the German equivalent of a U.S. jeep—with red stars painted all over it to keep trigger-happy Russians from shooting it up. The driver carried a PPSh41 submachine gun to fight off not only stupid friends but stubborn enemies. Little dying spatters of resistance went on. Massive reprisals killed plenty of Germans, and would eventually snuff out the resistance, too—Koniev was confident of that.

Even a couple of kilometers outside of Berlin, the air improved. And then, abruptly, it got worse again: the Kubelwagen rattled past the bloated carcasses of a dozen cows in a cratered meadow. Koniev scowled at the stink, and also at the waste. "Our men should have butchered those animals," he said.

"Sorry, Comrade Marshal." The driver sounded afraid Koniev would think it was his fault. He added, "I never saw the beasts till this minute."

"All right, Corporal." While the fighting was still going on, Koniev might have looked to blame . . . somebody, anyhow. With the war over, he could afford to be more easygoing.

Artillery had chewed up the woods outside of Berlin, too. Some trees still stood straight. Others leaned at every angle under the sun. They'd been down long enough that their leaves were going from green to brown. Some of them would have fallen on the road from Berlin to Zossen—the former Wehrmacht headquarters, now taken over by the Red Army. Koniev wondered whether Red Army engineers or German POWs had cleared it. He would have bet his countrymen put the Germans to work.

Three or four men in field-gray scrambled off to the side of the road when they heard the Kubelwagen coming. "Those fuckers better move," the driver said. "They stand there knocking pears out of the trees with their dicks, I'll damn well run 'em over."

"Right." Marshal Koniev had to fight to swallow laughter. Russian profanity—mat—was almost a language in itself. The driver might have said "If they stand there goofing off" . . . Or he might not have. Even generals sometimes felt like using mat.

The road bent sharply. The driver slowed down. Something stirred among the dead trees near the asphalt.

Alarm stirred in Koniev. "Step on it!" he said urgently. If he turned out to have a case of the vapors, the driver could tell everybody he didn't have any balls. Koniev wouldn't mind, not one bit.

As the driver's foot came down on the gas, somebody—a man in a gray greatcoat—stood up. He aimed a sheet-metal tube at the Kubelwagen. "Panzerfaust!" the driver yelped. He grabbed his submachine gun at the same time as Koniev reached for the pistol on his belt.

Too late. Trailing fire, the bazooka-style rocket roared toward the car. Marshal Koniev ducked. That did him exactly no good. The Panzerfaust was made to smash tanks. A soft-skinned vehicle like the Kubelwagen was nothing but fire and scrap metal—and torn, charred flesh—an instant after the rocket struck home.

HARRY TURTLEDOVE is an award-winning author of science fiction and fantasy. His alternate-history works have included several short novels such as *The Guns of the South; How Few Remain* (winner of the Sidewise Award for Best Novel); the Worldwar saga: *In the Balance, Tilting the Balance, Upsetting the Balance,* and *Striking the Balance;* the Colonization books: *Second Contact, Down to Earth,* and *Aftershocks;* the Great War epics: *American Front, Walk in Hell,* and *Breakthroughs;* the American Empire novels: *Blood & Iron, The Center Cannot Hold,* and *Victorious Opposition;* and the Settling Accounts series: *Return Engagement, Drive to the East, The Grapple,* and *In at the Death.* He is married to fellow novelist Laura Frankos. They have three daughters: Alison, Rachel, and Rebecca.